CONCEIVED WITHOUT SIN

From the Author of the Spectacular
Nationwide Bestseller *Pierced by a Sword*.

"I liked this book very much because it is about real people. I *loved* the humor. It explores the hidden battles in the war that is waged over every soul. It's a great read, and I believe it will change the lives of many, many readers."

Michael O'Brien, Father & Author

"This book grabbed me and held me faster and more powerfully than the author's first book. The characters are fascinating and funny, yet gritty and real. I can't recommend this book more! A great story!"

Patricia Noble, Mother & Homemaker

"I really liked Donna. She was genuine. She reminded me of a few girls I know—or would like to get to know. And the ending was a big surprise."

Marie Ames, College Student

"The scene where the Kemps and Mark Johnson deal with their marriage problems was an eye-opener. It changed my outlook on marriage, my wife, and fatherhood. It helped me a lot."

Bill McNeil, Businessman & Father

"*These* are characters I can relate to! I simply couldn't put this book down. You'll laugh, too—really laugh. This story will stay with you for a long, long time."

Vin David, Computer Analyst & Father

"Movies! Basketball! Marriage! Friendship—all weaved together like nothing I've ever read before. This book is unique!"

Eileen Burns, UPS Driver

Characters who jump off the page.
A story that will grab you and surprise you.
Hilarious dialogue and thoughtful discussion.
A novel about the true meaning
of friendship in modern America.
A book about your life.

CONCEIVED WITHOUT SIN

For Sam Fisk, the quiet, driven owner of a computer company, the day began like any other day—until a big, sleepy-eyed man slams into him on the basketball court...

...Donna Beck found herself drifting after college, watching videos, living at home, wondering if she would ever find any excitement or meaning in her boring suburb of Rocky River, Ohio...

...Mark Johnson was a tough guy, used to getting his way, but now his marriage is on the rocks, his wife has kicked him out of his house, and is threatening to call her lawyer...

...Ellie James is beautiful, blond, and rich—in total control of her life. She is accustomed to attracting *any* man she desires. Now she falls in love with a man who might not want her...

From the raging summer waters of the New Jersey shore to the peaceful solitude of cold winter nights on Lake Erie, CONCEIVED WITHOUT SIN *plunges you deep into the hearts and lives of people so real you'll swear you know them.*

IF YOU REALLY
LIKE THIS BOOK

Consider Giving it Away.

Saint Jude Media, the nonprofit publisher of this
novel, invites you to send for copies to distribute
to your family, friends, and associates. We are
making it available in quantities for a nominal
donation. We will even send a free copy to individuals who write to us directly. There is no catch.
It's a new concept in book distribution that makes
it easier for everyone to read great books!

See the back pages of this book for more details,
or write to us for more information:

Saint Jude Media
Box 26120
Fairview Park, OH 44126

www.catholicity.com

Discover a New World.
Change Your Life Forever.

Published by Saint Jude Media
Box 26120, Fairview Park, OH 44126
www.catholicity.com

ISBN 0-9646316-1-X
Library of Congress Catalog Card Number: 97-91810

PRINTING HISTORY:
June 1997 (50,000)
August 1997 (50,000)

Cover Design by Ron Wiggins
Typesetting by Joe Vantaggi on a Power Macintosh 8500
Printing by Offset Paperback Manufacturers, Dallas, PA

Printed in the United States of America

To my bride, Bai.
I love you, I love you, I love you, and I always will.
I just wish I did a better job of it.

ALSO BY BUD MACFARLANE JR.

PIERCED BY A SWORD

CONCEIVED WITHOUT SIN

BUD MACFARLANE JR.

SAINT JUDE MEDIA
CLEVELAND, OHIO

Foreword

"Am I my brother's keeper?"

This snotty comeback to God, somewhere in the Old Testament, runs down the centuries to nullify human relationships from start to finish. The modern equivalent is "Live and let live."

You will not find in this story of a small group of friends any honoring of that trite adage. Here are characters cajoling, interfering, philosophizing, yapping like a bunch of Russians on a train in a novel by Dostoyevsky. They are strong just when you expect them to be weak, or suddenly freak out when you expect them to be rocks of stability. Sam the computer nerd, Donna the tomboy, Buzz the iron man; each one will fool you in the end. One strange and wonderful thing about Bud Macfarlane Jr.'s storytelling is that his people are so loved by the author that they grab and hold you and make you say, "No, Sam—don't say that—" or "Come on, get up and—" You turn the page and say, "Yes! Thank God for Ellie's kindness (insight, sensitivity...)" Few authors writing today can command that depth of emotional commitment from the reader.

It is all done with dialogue and a bit of interior monologue, and some dreams, and some action. Macfarlane's first novel, *Pierced by a Sword,* was filled with extraordinary events: apocalypse, supernatural warnings, war and rebellion. It is set in the near future. This novel, on the contrary, is plainly a story of love and marriage and friendship and conversion. Supernatural forces weave in and out, as they must do in real stories of the faith.

But there is no world-consuming, world-redeeming, world-wide stage action. It is all in the here and the now, all in the relationships young adults begin to have and then build on, and then consummate with one another and with God. Its heroism and its tragedy are on the small side of things. What happens can happen to you and me, without even the first bong of the End of the World Clock. But the story grabs hold and grips you as it plunges you into the characters and personalities, the changing, deepening, accepting or unaccepting faith of Buzz, Mark, Ellie, Donna, Sam, Maggie, Maxine...

It explores faith in its most personal manifestations, in the grace that comes to people, how it comes, how it moves the pieces on the chessboard. It explores the meaning of the virgin birth in a way that has never been explored before. It describes the depths of falling away doubt and the anguish of redemptive suffering. It describes the crucifixion of Jesus Christ as if you were there, looking at it, cringing with horror. It shows, in the finale, how God will use the deliberately irreligious despair of a self-hating man to bring glory to the people he tried to love.

All of this, which should take hundreds of pages of stale theology, is done with the emotional talk, the pain, and the crabby wants of ordinary people. People who won't leave well enough alone.

I am a convert to the faith. It hasn't been easy sailing. Often it has seemed to me that I have to carry the faith around in my head. There is no cultural tapestry to make me feel at home. There are no crucifixes on the barroom walls. No one hails me on the street with a hearty "Praise be Jesus and Mary!" In communist Bosnia, which I visited some years ago, they did. In a novel by Bud Macfarlane Jr., I am able to live in a Catholic culture for a time. Though that culture is carried by only a few characters, those characters make up the whole of this novel, so the world is suddenly Catholic, for as long as I live in the novel. And for that experience, I wish to thank Mr. Macfarlane. He's even got me wearing the Miraculous Medal sometimes.

THOMAS W. CASE
6 JUNE 1997
FEAST OF THE SACRED HEART OF JESUS

Acknowledgments

I want to thank all the people who read my first novel, and especially those who were kind enough to pass it along to another reader. This second book would not exist without you. I want to thank my mother and father for their encouragement, and my lovely bride, Bai, for all her sacrifices during the writing of this book.

My editors, Michael O'Brien and his son John, Tom Case, Rosanne and Andrew Hawley, Dave Baugh, Bill Merimee, Dave van Hecke, Amy Koopman, Jamie Hickey, Dan Davidson, Matt Minarik—they all played a tremendous role in bringing this book to you. Joe Vantaggi did his usual spectacular job on typesetting, and Ron Wiggins created another beautiful cover. Thanks, guys.

Thanks also to Father Tony Anderson, S.O.L.T., my spiritual director and fellow Knight of Immaculata, for grace merited, and advice given. A special thanks to Mr. and Mrs. John Merrill. I want to thank the Perpetual Adoration Corps of the Mary Foundation: the hundreds of priests, nuns, deacons, and brothers who prayed for me; and all the benefactors of the Mary Foundation who support Saint Jude Media, and all those who prayed for me as I wrote this book, especially the workers at Saint Jude Media. Thanks, Bill Whitmore: this book is part of the long shadow of your work. Special thanks to a Hoosier friend who is too humble to want his name printed here. Thanks to Scott Helm, for prayers.

To all my fellow CatholiCity Chat Room addicts: thanks for the constant support and prayers! ::::) spider smiles on the World Wide Web!

Finally, thank you to all those who have written to me with your comments and reactions to my first novel. It humbles me to hear that God's grace has changed your lives through a gift He has given me. I never tire of hearing from you. Pray for me; I pray for you.

Preface

There are two kinds of people in this wacky world: those who read prefaces, and those who don't. I'm a preface reader myself. But if you're not, imagine yellow police tape around this section with a police officer waving at you, saying, "Move along, move along, nothing to read here. Move along…"

All others, follow me.

If someone had told me three years ago that I would be a novelist, and, that I would be the most widely read Catholic novelist in the United States during the last two years, I would have laughed hard. Ten years from now, I'm going to read this, and I will tell myself what I tell myself whenever I read something I wrote ten years ago: *What a jerk.*

There is a poet and singer named Jim Carroll. I saw him on the old Tom Snyder show. Snyder asked Carroll why he named his first album "Catholic Boy."

Carroll replied that he was a Catholic.

"A Catholic?" Snyder was shocked, as if being a Catholic was like being a leper or something. You could practically see him making a mental note *to fire the guy who asked Carroll to be on his show.*

Carroll went on to explain that Catholicism is the only religion that finds any value in suffering. Carroll had recently stayed by the bedside of a friend who had suffered tremendously from leukemia for months before passing away.

He explained by saying something like, "All the other religions promise you happiness and contentment. But that's not what life is like. That's not what it was like for me watching my best friend waste away; I felt totally helpless. That's not what is was like for Mary to watch her Son get nailed to a cross. Catholicism isn't afraid of blood and suffering, or death. It's real."

The next day, I went right out and bought the album. Carroll, who wrote *The Basketball Diaries,* turned out to be a better poet than singer. He did have one song that was almost a hit which is both hilarious and eerily sad, *All the People Who Died*.

This book is not as long as my first novel. If you put off housework to read books, you'll put off less for this book. Just think, less guilt, Mom.

But moms and dads should beware. I wrote what I see in the world we live in, not some made-up fiction world. This story has a lot do with marriage, and, because sex is a part of marriage, it has to do with sex. Read it first before you give it to your kids.

I have a few more comments for you diehard preface readers who are still with me. I'm always surprised by one or two things when people write to me with their reactions. First, *the narrator is not the author.* Neither are the characters. If the narrator or a character tells you how cool smoking is, or how great the Beatles are, or how selfish Generation X is, it doesn't mean *I* agree with him. One reader of my last book was all over me (like a cheap suit) for writing about Maker's Mark, a fine bourbon. "You must have gotten paid off by that company, or you're an alcoholic!" Hey, I don't even *drink* bourbon. About twice a year, I do have a nip of Scotch (the fine, twelve-year-old kind; single malt, and please, no ice!). Day-in, day-out, I'm a Pepsi guy. By the way, and this *is* the preface after all, a few other readers, including my holy and wise spiritual director, actually sent me bottles of Makers. I thought that was *way cool.*

I wrote what I like to read. If you don't like something, it's probably something my editors begged me to take out. So blame me. Pray for me, too. I'm still learning.

Here's an answer to a question I'm often asked, and an answer that is never in a preface. All told, it took me roughly ten weeks of writing to complete this book. Like my first novel, most of it was written between midnight and six in the morning. On a Mac. Quiet. No phones. Music in the background put me in the zone. Prayed to the Holy Spirit, my Guardian Angel, Saint Anthony, Saint "Uncle Max" Kolbe, Blessed Monsignor Escrivá, and, of course, to Immaculate

Mary, my queen, before I started typing. I got to see the sun rise. (A friend joked that we should have called it 'Conceived Without Sun.')

One last note of interest: in Chapter Eight a story is told about an astronaut and a piece of wood. This is a true story, just so you know. The astronaut has a niece who is the godmother of one of my sons. I changed the names around, of course, 'cause that's the law. Also, the story Buzz tells in Chapter Five regarding the Saint Anthony statue really happened. In some instances I have refrained from depicting certain details of the events, truth being (as the cliché goes) far, far stranger than fiction. I won't tell you whether or not the big scene at the end really happened to somebody in real life. Maybe it did. Maybe it didn't. *Maybe it did*.

Also, if you like movies, you might want to jot down the ones mentioned in this story as you read. That way you can rent the videos and kind of 'watch along' with the characters. Kinda cool, huh? Interactive! Yikes!

Finally, there is no need to strap on your seat belt this time around. Instead, put on your walking shoes and pour some coffee in the ol' Thermos. Pack a lunch. Grab your favorite jacket—the old, well-worn one that you keep, yes, over there, on the hook by your back door. Let's go for a stroll, together, with some friends I would like you to meet. *Oremus*.

BUD MACFARLANE JR.
13 MAY 1997
FEAST OF OUR LADY OF FATIMA

Prologue

It would come to him. Things always did.

Sam Fisk finished tying his shoe, and looked up from the marble floor of a gallery in the Art Institute of Chicago. He saw the El Greco for the first time, and according to his curious, methodical habit, made a point of looking at the title and artist before giving the painting a close look. This work was part of a traveling exhibit from Spain.

The Savior of the World by Domenikos Theotokpulos, "El Greco," meaning "the Greek," Sam mouthed the words as he read them. He already knew about El Greco. His father had taught him. But he had never seen this particular work before.

He stared gently at the painting, a depiction of Christ from the waist up with his left hand on a globe the size of a basketball and his right hand floating, arm raised, his fingers making a sign of blessing that looked like an anachronistic peace sign. Sam almost turned away from the painting after a cursory twenty seconds, but the eyes in this Christ penetrated him. Held him. His father had taught him never to rush inside a museum, so he quite unconsciously allowed the enjoyment of a great piece of art to hold him.

Sam looked for a minute. Then two minutes. A matronly lady courteously made a small sound in her throat, waiting, but he did not hear her. She frowned a gray frown and moved on. He kept staring, thoughtless, held by the eyes of Christ.

Who are you?

He often skipped class at the University of Chicago to come here. It gave the sophomore a sense of peace. *A museum is the only authentic cathedral for the man who loves humanity,* his father had said.

It was as if Edward Fisk lived inside his son's head. His father, a devout atheist, worshipped often and reverently in museums, and tried valiantly to pass on his love for art, literature, and history to his boy in a thousand different ways. Sam could have been a better student of humanity. His father's love for the achievements of mankind seemed sufficient for the two of them. If the atheist father was devout, then the agnostic son, while still believing as the father did, had lapsed, not into Christian faith, but into the practice of the "lower arts," as his father would have called them.

Edward taught philosophy; his specialty was the Enlightenment. Sam was studying business and computers, to the great disappointment of his father. The son wanted to experience the joys of triumphing over the world—a world which his father only studied. Sam pondered at the biggest blank space in his father's life.

Why did I choose business over art?

He squinted at Jesus.

Sports, he told himself, pleased with his choice.

Triumph, defeat, endurance, will. The real world is my world—not the world of thoughts and books and lectures. He wanted to be a player, not a reporter.

He remembered his first solid hit on the football field, in fourth grade. Sam's impact had broken the other boy's chin strap, and the other kid had almost passed out. His teammates clapped Sam on the back, his coaches nodded approvingly. Edward, who was still alive and talked with Sam on the phone practically every evening, had lost his son to football, basketball, and baseball on that fall day. Instead of leisurely reading books on the back porch with his father, Sam was out playing ball games and starting little companies to mow lawns, walk dogs, sell papers, and paint fences.

Please, who are you? Sam requested of the Christ staring at him from the El Greco.

No answer came.

Or maybe I can't hear you. Probably because you're not there. Just paint and light from the mind of a saint in the cathedral of humanity.

Still, the tall business student stared. There was no bitterness in his question and answer. Just relief and a certain smugness; a legacy from his father.

"Hey, good looking," a sharp, female voice came from behind him, "you gonna stare at that El Greco forever?"

Sam turned and saw an absolutely striking blond woman, a stranger standing a few feet behind him, with her arms folded. She was not quite a woman yet—a girl, really—probably no older than seventeen. She had a Mona Lisa smile and seemed to enjoy his awkwardness as he turned. He looked at his watch. He had been standing motionless in front of the El Greco for over ten minutes!

"Um, I was just daydreaming, that's all, I uh—"

He started to blush.

"Don't be embarrassed. It's my father's favorite painting, or was. He's been dead for a long time—" the girl said.

There was something about her that reminded him of the painting. He was a bit surprised, and he shuffled his feet and looked down. He was always uncomfortable around women.

"I'm sorry—" he began.

"No need to be. I got over it. It's just that my class is over at the Sunday Afternoon in the Park with Harry exhibit, and I'm playing hooky to see Daddy's favorite painting. You remind me of him—my father, that is." There was a sparkle in the blond beauty's eye, betraying mirth and confidence.

She's just a high school chick, he thought.

"It's George," he corrected.

"What's George?"

"The painting your class is studying. Sunday Afternoon in the Park with George, or was that the name of the musical?" he asked himself as much as the pretty girl.

She squinted her eyes and shook her head. She had no idea what he was talking about.

"Whatever," she replied. "Look, I'm sorry I interrupted you. I've got to get back, and I just wanted to see Daddy's painting, but it's no big deal." She sounded sincere, her voice lower, a bit nervous.

It's the eyes, he thought. *Their eyes are the same. Beautiful, haunting. What am I saying?*

"I'm playing hooky, too. I attend the University of Chicago…" he offered awkwardly. *God, I sound so stupid!*

His words hung in the air. The blonde looked down the hall, toward the wing where her class was.

"Look, I've got to go now. Nice meeting you."

She smiled a perfect smile and started to walk away.

"Don't go, I don't even know your name…"

But she was already walking away with a somewhat boyish gait, leaving him.

"It's Becky," she called over her shoulder as she turned the corner, smiling, somehow relating to him that she was just fine.

"But I don't know your last name…" he called softly to himself, knowing she couldn't hear him. He looked back quickly to the El Greco. Surrounded by beauty.

What? he asked, feeling foolish.

He had just seen the most beautiful girl in Chicago and let her walk away. It was time for the self-castigation.

Good job, Romeo. She's gone forever. You can't even get a date with a high school girl.

Now for the rationalizations.

Who cares? Besides, she had to be kidding, calling me good-looking.

Sam was not handsome. Sure, he was tall and had the lankiness and easy grace of an athlete, but his skin was full of pockmarks, and tight against the stern bones of his face. The residue of a horrendous war, now peacefully settled, that his face had lost to acne in high school. His teeth seemed too big for his mouth, marring his smile.

No, Sam Fisk was not handsome. And girls had never found him attractive. Until Becky Macadam this very day.

But he could never be certain if she had truly found him attractive, because he would never meet her again. She was meant for another man in the great plan of life.

But her beauty had inspired him, and something his father had made him memorize swam up from the pools of his memory about a faint heart. His memory grasped it.

Yeah. 'The faint heart never captured the fair maiden.' Was Dad preparing me for something? Usually, it's more like 'The good-looking guy gets the hot babe.' Hey, Dad, hearts pump blood. They don't faint or wake up even. But thanks for the tip.

Next time, he told himself for the hundredth time, *I'll be more confident. I'll ask her, whoever she may be, to go out. This one was way too young, anyway. If I ever meet a girl as pretty as Becky again...*

He looked down, and away from the El Greco.

Yeah, right.

PART ONE

Three Friends

And it's something quite peculiar. Something shimmering and
white; it leads you here, despite your destination,
under the Milky Way tonight.
The Church

Man cannot be forced to accept the truth.
*Pope John Paul II, **Crossing the Threshold of Hope***

We should strike our enemy where and when
we can hurt him the most.
*General A. M. Gray, USMC, **Warfighting***

The virtue of man ought to be measured,
not by his extraordinary exertions,
but by his everyday conduct.
Blaise Pascal

If you can't talk your wife into it,
it ain't worth putting your foot down over it.
Anonymous

Happy, and I'm smiling,
walking miles to drink your water.
You know I love to love you, and above you,
there's no other.
Jethro Tull

Chapter One

1

A few years later, Sam had begun to win the world. It all seemed to come to him.

After college, he stayed in Chicago and got a job with IBM, which was then at the peak of its dominance. The personnel director in his department had recommended that IBM *not* hire him—his psychological profile showed too much independent thinking. But Sam's boss had pushed to hire him anyway because of the young man's intensity and excellent grades. He was also well-spoken for his age. So IBM hired him and sent him down to Texas for the famous training session there. He returned to Chicago, and over the next two years he did quite well selling mainframes to big companies as part of a four-person sales team.

Despite his success and frequent raises, the stuffy-white-shirt corporate culture suffocated the entrepreneur in him. IBM, despite its dominance, was beginning a tailspin that would last for a decade. Its first hiring freeze—ever—had just been implemented. Sam sent memos to upper management, diplomatically pointing out that local area networks tied into ever more powerful personal computer "servers" were the wave of the future. Memos came back, agreeing with Sam, promising action, but nothing ever happened.

One brisk, sunny spring day, while sitting in traffic on the Kennedy with his team member, Sam opened the passenger door and got out of the car. He heard the gravel crunch beneath his feet.

"Where you goin', Slim?" John Traverse asked him, leaning across the seat.

"I don't know," Sam replied, pulling his tie out of its knot and looking toward the Sears Tower less than a mile away. "I just can't wear the monkey suit anymore. Tell that to the old windbag you guys worship as our boss. Tell him that Sam Fisk can't wear the monkey suit anymore."

"Get back in the car, Sam. What's come over you?"

"That's just it. Nothing's come over me. It's time to cut the cord on Big Blue—" a car horn cut off his speech. Traffic had started to move.

"You're throwing away a good career. You'll lose your severance…" John warned, glancing ahead at the growing gap between his car and the one in front of him. Sam laughed, his big teeth shining like chicklets in the sun.

"Go sell your mainframes while you can, Johnny Boy. You'll be late for the appointment with First Chicago. I got to get this white shirt off. Suits just make me look uglier than I am."

Johnny, who had always liked the softly articulate, hard-driving Sam, finally cracked a smile. Several horns were honking by now. Johnny Traverse pulled over to the cramped shoulder, inches away from the concrete barrier.

"Networks?" Johnny asked seriously as he got out and walked over to Sam.

Sam nodded, and looked down to his shoes. That said it all. This nervous habit of looking down confirmed to Johnny that Sam was serious.

"Then good luck, my friend. Give me a call when you need a good salesman."

"I will, John. Get going or you'll miss your appointment. Make up some excuse for me."

The two men shook hands and parted. Sam picked his way across the highway, jogged up the ramp, and left his tie behind on the macadam. He hailed a cab and went back to his apartment, fired up his Compaq, and broke out his advanced Novell manual.

Two weeks later, he broke his lease and moved back to his hometown, Rocky River, Ohio, rented a small office on Detroit

Avenue, and using his modest savings, started his own computer consulting firm.

Five months later, he hired Johnny Traverse. Sam named his company after his father: Edwards & Associates. He almost went out of business that first year, exhausted his savings, and fell behind two months on his rent. Sam spent all his money on computers, Novell training, and chicken pot pies. But he and Johnny made decent money in their second year, and big money this past year. There were ten technician-salesmen on the payroll now. Six of the "salesmen" were women, picked for their looks and brains—engineers out of Notre Dame, Northwestern, Case Western Reserve, and the University of Chicago.

Sam never wore white shirts and checked IBM's steadily falling stock every day on a strange, relatively unknown new network called the Internet. For the past two and a half years, he worked an average of eighty hours a week —more in the first year when he quit to start Edwards & Associates. He had virtually no social life except for his daily visit to the courts in Rocky River to play pick-up basketball during the summer. He never missed his hoops.

That's where he met Buzz, and really, where our story begins…

2

It was a typical day running the courts in Rocky River; the sun rushed past the few clouds to bombard the asphalt. The sky was so blue and clear that Sam felt he could wave to the passengers in the jets overhead.

He relished this game, and the peculiar unwritten rules of pick-up basketball—called "running" by the blacks and whites alike. This was a melting pot court which seemed to attract more serious players, black, white, or any other color you could think of. Some were good high school players in their day. A few others, good college players. Others were simply out for the exercise. Sam was a respected regular, considered a good but not great player. As with his work, he was quiet, intense, focused on unselfish play and winning above all else. He was tall—six-foot-six—strong, could jump, and had a nice, easy stroke on his shot. A lack of speed and quickness kept him off the upper tier of players.

An old guy everyone called "the Man" kept a chart by the side of the court. The Man wore the same outfit every day— blue shorts and a Notre Dame jersey. Both would start the summer new and fade and tear by the end of the season. The Man ruled the court with a mixture of powerful tools: a deep voice, tradition, and a profound sense of fairness. In his late forties, skinny as a marathon runner, he was always the first on the court and the last to leave after the sun went down. And the Man, who happened to be black, could play. He didn't hang with any of the other players after the games ended.

It seemed like he had made up his rules for these two courts before time was recorded, and the regulars liked the rules so much that newcomers had no prayer at getting them changed. There were two courts: the winners court and the losers court. The winners of the games on the winners court kept playing until they lost. The winner on the losers court had the honor of challenging the winner of the winners court. New players would sign the Man's chart as they arrived, and wait their turn on the losers court. In a Darwinian way, only the best got to play the most, but even the losers would get some time in, unlike most pick-up courts around the country.

The Man had the authority to expel players for violence and cheating, but this rarely happened. His fairness was unquestioned. The Man's real name, which nobody knew, was Hal Smith. He was a concierge at the Stouffer's Plaza Hotel in downtown Cleveland, and a graduate of the University of Notre Dame (where he had not played basketball, but football, as a defensive back during the 1960s). Hal's father had been a district judge.

This evening, Sam's team was embroiled in a close game on the winners court. Sam was feeling good. His stroke was on, and music seemed to be playing in his head as he shot swish after swish. He knew he was going to win this game for his team now that they had the ball for game point. He could take the slow stockbroker trying to guard him. He just knew it—and so did his teammates, who had been feeding him the ball and setting picks for him.

The score was tied at eight. The Man didn't like "win by two," and the next point would win it all. Sam had been saving a move to get open for the winning shot. He ran under the basket and then back and forth along the baseline, just fast enough to wind the stockbroker, and just slow enough to lull him into thinking he could cover Sam just this once. Sam's eyes met Tommy Clemens's, the dribbler, who then looked at Big Tim Yaztremski, who clenched his fists together down by his waist. *I'm setting the pick,* Tim was telegraphing to Sam and Tommy. All three had played against and with each other on these courts for almost two years. It was in the bag.

Sam made a quick move through the crowded paint, and faded quickly beyond the foul line as Tommy drove to his left. The startled stockbroker fought through the crowd and ran right into Big Tim. Tommy reversed his step, and threw a quick lob back toward Sam. The ball was practically in Sam's hands as he prepared to loft his fluid jump shot. Sam could almost anticipate the sound of the ball swishing into the net...

Just before he began to stroke the ball, a dull thud blew all the air out of Sam's lungs. He released a wild shot as he looked down at a brush of brown, sweaty hair and realized that someone's shoulder had rammed into his stomach. An almost-silent *oomph* escaped his mouth, and he was not able to call the foul (the fouled player calls the foul on the Man's courts...).

Sam slammed down onto his rear end and the fireplug-shaped opponent—a new guy—rolled over him, knocking Sam's head on the asphalt. Pain followed. Sam ignored it and looked down the court. *Didn't anybody see the foul?!*

The rebound had gone to the opponents, and a fast break started the other way, leading to an easy lay-up and a loss for Sam's team. Rage filled his mind as he looked at the thick, overweight tree-stump who had tackled him. Actually, the guy was quite tall—he was just *shaped* more like a linebacker than a hoop player. And he was laughing at Sam!

From all fours, Sam lunged at the newcomer, incensed. For the first time ever on a basketball court, he threw a punch at another man. The other man *appeared* sluggish, with his ample paunch and lazy, half-closed eyelids.

But the other man surprised Sam by jumping quickly to his feet and slipping the punch with ease. Sam fell flat on his face. This enraged Sam even more, who was not accustomed to losing his temper. The other man laughed harder, actually bringing a finger to one eye to wipe away a tear.

Now Sam scrambled up to his feet, and the other players were coming up the court to watch the developing fight. Sam yelled out as he lowered his shoulder to tackle the big slob, but found only air as the guy niftily—almost magically—moved sideways just before Sam reached him. Sam fell to the grass next to the court. Now other players joined the heavyset man in laughter.

"We're laughing at you, Fisk, not with you!" one joker teased between gasping guffaws.

What's so freakin' funny?

Still on the ground, red-faced, grass in his mouth, Sam turned and looked at the crowd. He looked at his nemesis, who now had his arm around the Man's shoulder. The Man had been playing on the other court during Sam's game.

What? The Man knows this jackass?

"Take it easy, Fisk," the Man's deep voice cut through the laughter.

"Sorry man, I was hustling to run by you, and I slipped," the heavyset man said, trying to add a serious line to his smile. "That cute little surprised sound you made when I rammed into you," the guy laughed again. "It just killed me, man. It was so pathetic. I shoulda called a foul for you."

Sam's tormentor stuck out his hand. A gesture of peace.

The anger had already drained out of Sam. He looked at the Man, but didn't take the overweight fireplug's hand.

"Who the heck is this guy?" Sam asked the Man.

"An old-timer, Sam. He used to come here during his college days. Haven't seen him in years, though. He can run."

This last comment got a few nods from the other players. If the Man said a guy could run, then the guy could play basketball quite well, and more importantly, the guy was welcome on the Man's courts.

Sam looked around, feeling slightly foolish. He grabbed the hand, which was still extended toward him. The grip was amazingly strong, even for a court filled with strong men. The other man lifted Sam up to his feet effortlessly, a faint smile in his eyes.

"My name is Buzz," he said with understated joy. "Buzz Woodward. Let's go get a drink or something." His smile was winning.

The Man snorted at both of them, shook his head, and turned to walk away. Most of the other players drifted off. In the peculiar way of pick-up games, everyone knew the running was over.

Sam looked at Buzz intensely, knowing in a far off kind of way that some kind of bridge was being crossed. He couldn't stay mad at this guy any more than he could land a punch on him.

"Sure. Sure, no problem. Where to, Buzz?"

✛ ✛ ✛

They ended up at Applebees. During the fifteen minute walk over, Sam discovered that Buzz was a UPS driver who had just transferred to Cleveland from New Jersey. They hadn't talked much during the walk—small talk. What they did for a living, where they lived. Sam made the mistake of thinking that Buzz didn't like to talk.

"Can I buy you a beer?" Sam asked as they sat down at their table.

"No. I'm an alcoholic," Buzz answered nonchalantly, looking Sam right in the eye. Sam immediately looked down at his fork and knife wrapped in a napkin. "I'll have a Pepsi. Nothing else is a Pepsi."

"Sorry," Sam mumbled.

"About what? Are you a Coca-Cola guy?" Buzz asked seriously.

"No. I mean, I don't drink cola. I mean, about the, you know…" he barely mumbled the words, trailing off.

"Oh yeah. Look, I was teasing. I've been a drunk since I was in college. It's just that I haven't had a drink in years. You know, AA and all that. No big deal."

Sam squinted at the heavyset man seated across the table, confused, and beginning to become mildly annoyed. *Who does this guy think he is?*

Buzz picked up on his irritation.

"Hey, Sammy Boy, don't be so serious. I have a bad habit of coming on strong. My shrink told me that it's my way of sizing people up, that is, until I dumped the shrink. What a way to make a living. 'Your dad was a jerk, that'll be a hundred bucks—see you next week.' What a waste of time. Anyway, I've decided that you're going to be my best friend in Cleveland, so I figured that I'd get the alcoholism thing out of the way, right up front."

"Best friends?" Sam stifled a laugh. *This guy is a nutcase.* He began to get up to leave.

"Where you goin'?"

"Home," Sam said.

"See you on the courts tomorrow?" Buzz said, a trace of humor in his voice.

"I might not go. I don't *care* if the Man likes you. Geeze, you're a piece of work." Sam finished, exasperated, satisfied that he had gotten out the words.

"You make snap judgments," Buzz replied, looking up, unperturbed. He looked past Sam toward the waitress stand. No luck. "Look, sorry. I am what I am. Obviously, you're not Catholic—"

"What do you mean by that? What does that have to do with anything? You're the one who ran into me on the court, pal…" Sam rolled his eyes. "Why am I even talking to you?"

"Because we're going to be friends."

"Hmmn. In case you haven't noticed, I'm getting up to leave."

"In that case, okay, you win. I'll buy the drinks *and* the burgers. Sit down." Buzz was smiling.

Something kept Sam from turning and walking away. Maybe it was the obvious mirth in this jerk's eyes. *What's so funny?*

"Just tell me one thing before I go, Buzz. How come you think we're going to be friends?"

Buzz gestured to Sam's seat. Sam found himself sitting down lightly, just as the waitress came. Buzz ordered a Pepsi and two bacon cheeseburgers. Sam ordered a Bud Light to be polite, but was still planning to leave as soon as he heard Buzz's answer.

After the waitress left, Buzz seemed to take a long time to take his knife and fork out of the napkin. He pulled out a pack of smokes, and lit up, taking a long drag. Sam held back an urge to leave the table again.

"Thanks for waiting. Look, to answer your question, I just know. I have one other friend in the world, and he lives in New Jersey, and because he can't stop drinking, I don't get to hang out with him very much. I just know. I knew it the minute you tried to hit me. I just know a lot of things. Like I know you went to college in the Midwest."

"So what? The Man told you."

"He didn't tell me. Let me prove it to you. I'll guess several things about you right now."

Sam said nothing. Buzz took it as a signal to start guessing. He was enjoying himself.

"First, I know you're probably an only child, or at least don't come from a big family. You grew up around here. I know you played hoops in high school but not in college. I know you don't like to have fun—probably you're a workaholic." Buzz noticed that this last guess caused something to happen behind Sam's eyes. He plowed on. "I know you don't hang out with many girls. I know, even if all my other guesses are wrong, that you're not Catholic and that you're one lonely sonufabitch. You reek loneliness. Sorry, you asked me to guess."

Sam looked down. He felt strange, almost like crying. He was a grown man, so tears were out of the question.

"How do you know all these things?" he asked in a melancholy tone. "Are you a mentalist or something?"

"No. Just lucky guesses. I may be a UPS driver now, but mostly I'm a drifter. I watch people. My father said I have a gift, that I should be a writer or something, but I don't know. It's not psychic, though, just guesses. I just watch people and find them fascinating and study human nature. I could do the same thing with our waitress. I'll tell you how I do it."

Sam wasn't buying any of this, but he was curious, and there was something about this guy that he liked. He no longer wanted to leave. *Amazing*.

"Tell me."

"Your accent gave away where you grew up. You talk like a college grad, it's in your vocabulary, your sentence structure. How many people know the word 'mentalist,' for cripes sake? The hoop thing was obvious—I got a chance to watch you play today. You're too smart and have too good a vocabulary to have wasted your time playing in college. You don't play like you were coached all that much, but like you taught yourself to be as good as you are. For example, you don't set good picks or come off them closely—self-taught all the way. It's obvious that you're shy, and since you fall into the great ninety-percent of us in the world who are either a little bald, a little fat, a little ugly or whatever, I guessed that you're not a lady's man. Most guys aren't. As for the loneliness stuff, well, I've sung my own version of Old Man River a few times, and to tell you the truth, I can just feel it. Not Catholic? Pure guess. My odds were four to one, given the population of the U.S., a bit lower in this part of the country." Buzz finished with a big breath, propping his eyebrows up while keeping his mouth in a bit of a frown.

The waitress came with the beer and Pepsi. Buzz drank half his down in one big gulp and took another toke on his cigarette, looking at Sam. That self-satisfied expression was still on Buzz's face.

"I am Catholic," Sam lied, testing this strange companion.

"Then say the Hail Mary."

"Right. Hail Mary…full of grace…" Sam started to falter. "Okay, I was testing you."

"So, did I guess right? It's a gift. But it's really just guesses. Anyone could do it if they paid attention."

"Sure. I suppose you're a Catholic."

"My day rises and sets on it. Hey! Let's skip religion and move right on into politics…"

"You're dodging me. How come you start something like saying 'My day rises and sets on' being Catholic and then stop right there? You can't start the conversation by telling me I'm not a Catholic and just drop it."

Sam took his first swig of beer. He closed his eyes. *Nothing like a beer after a workout.* His father's words echoed on his mind's speaker system: *Beer was invented before civilization…*

"Good question, and you're right," Buzz replied. "Maybe it's because I'm a conversational bully, used to getting my way. Arrogant. Either way, you've already got a keen insight into my personality. I would say you're getting to know me pretty well."

"That doesn't mean we'll be best friends, or even friends," Sam replied, a bit exasperated. "You're strange."

"Does that disqualify friendship? And who isn't strange?"

Sam chewed on this for several seconds, and said nothing.

"You want to know why Catholicism has to be true compared to Protestantism?" Buzz asked, as if they had known each other all their lives, and that all the previous conversation had gone in some other direction—as if they had been discussing philosophy and religion for a couple of hours.

"Let me guess. Because *you're* a Catholic," Sam answered sarcastically.

"Hmmn. Interesting answer, but no." Buzz smiled, excitement growing in his voice, his eyes quickly checking to see if the food was coming. No luck. "Because the answers that devout Catholic pro quarterbacks give during post-game interviews conform to reality more than the answers devout Protestants give."

Buzz paused, waiting for Sam to take the bait.

"Huh?"

"Look, last year, that guy on the Colts," Buzz looked up as he spoke, trying to remember the name, "the one who everybody likes, led his team to victory in the playoffs. He's a very serious Christian, a non-Catholic. After the game, he says something along the lines of, 'I want to thank Jesus Christ, my personal Lord and Savior, for helping me win this game.'"

"Yeah," Sam interrupted, "like God had somehow helped the other team lose the game. I hate when they say things like that."

Sam was surprised to find himself sucked into the topic. A few minutes earlier, he had been ready to leave. It was as if Buzz had forgotten that already.

Buzz, already absorbed by a favorite topic, had indeed forgotten.

"Good, you follow it so far. Now here's the key. When the quarterback for the Steelers, Tommy O'Connor—"

"The Notre Dame grad," Sam interjected.

"Yeah, he was in my class; that's how I know he is a devout Catholic, even though I wasn't at the time. Well, when Tommy helps the Steelers win a game, he talks about the game, not God."

"But so would an atheist, or an agnostic."

"Let me finish?" Buzz asked, not unkindly. After a pause, he continued. "First of all, you're right. But Tommy always thanks his linemen—and you can tell he's sincere, not just saying what's expected of him by the press—and even goes into the actual inner-workings of the game. You know, stuff like what the linebackers were doing and the defensive schemes and stuff. All very oriented toward direct reality."

"What do you mean by 'direct reality?'" Sam interjected quickly.

"Just what the words mean. Reality. I threw in the word *direct* to add emphasis. I'm not a philosophy major or anything. But I'm assuming that Catholicism is true, for the sake of conversation, and therefore conforms to reality, stuff that truly is, as it is. Linemen, game plans, and defensive schemes are real things—"

"And God is not real, so the Protestant is not in tune with reality," Sam finished.

"Hmmn," Buzz seemed to process Sam's interruption quickly. "Interesting, but not really. You see, even though God does exist—this conversation assumes He does in order to discuss the topic, although you might not believe in God, which is fine for now—the Protestant's answer jumps *over* all the reality between the game and God, Who, as the creator of much of that reality, was in the reality."

"You're losing me, Buzz. In the reality? Sounds like nonsense," Sam said honestly.

"That's because I got caught up in describing it. You see, if the reporter asks the Catholic quarterback more detailed questions, the Catholic still won't give the 'Personal Lord and Savior' answer, which we'll call the PSL answer, or, it should be PLS," Buzz looked up at the ceiling while he sorted out the first letters of the phrase. "Yeah that's right. Now, where was I?"

"The Catholic gives different answers…"

"Right. O'Connor, and I've heard him say stuff like this, would answer along the lines of, 'That's how we practiced it. That's how the coaches taught me since high school. That's how my dad taught me to play.' In short, reality-based answers. If the reporter were to ask him something about God in the game, I'm sure O'Connor or any reflective Catholic would be confused.

"You can hear it now. Reporter asks, 'Tommy, how did God affect your game today?'

"Tommy gives the reporter a funny look, then answers, in this hypothetical world of VSPN, Vatican Sports Network, 'Well, I prayed for the Blessed Mother to watch over me before the game, to keep me from getting injured, stuff like that.' But the reporter presses him, 'Give me the deeper answer, Tommy; you can speak freely; nuns and high level Vatican officials are watching.'"

Sam laughed. "I still have no idea what you're talking about, but I don't think that will stop you."

"Thank you," Buzz said happily before continuing. "Suppose Tommy thought deeply and then gave the real Catholic answer, along the lines of, 'Well, God created me through the sacramental love of my mom and dad, who sacrificed for twenty-five years to raise me. Recognizing and supporting my gift of athletic ability, they made sure I had every opportunity to play and learn the game from good coaches. By choosing Notre Dame and working hard, I increased my chances of being drafted in the third round by the Steelers, who continued to teach me until I could play with the skills I demonstrated today. In terms of morals, which relate to my belief in being a good sport and trying my best to win within the rules using such virtues as prudence, courage, and humility, I would like to thank the Pope for being Christ's visible guide on earth, who in an apostolic line that extends in history back to Jesus, ensured that the Church would not err in teaching me faith and morals. I would like to thank God the Father, by the way, for being the source of Being Itself, and preventing the universe from ceasing to exist during the game today.'"

Buzz almost seemed out of breath at the end of his monologue. "But of course, that answer is too long and too preachy, and too philosophical and theological, and so the Catholic quarterback doesn't say it. Besides, he's just a football player, not a lecturer. He skipped half his classes while majoring in phys-ed. He just talks about reality, which assumes all these things. Call it the NFL Proof of the Superiority of Catholicism."

"But then how come most professional athletes are black, and are therefore probably not Catholic?"

"I never said that you had to be a Catholic to be a pro ballplayer, just that Catholics give better answers than Protestants. How come most pros are blacks? I don't know. Probably cultural reasons. Even so, the Catholic's answer is just as true for all the other players in terms of their parent's love, good coaches, etcetera. God doesn't make pro quarterbacks. Pro quarterbacks develop because of experience and talent—and luck, or fortune—and are the result of a civilization that began with the Catholic Church."

"It's funny, Buzz, but my dad, who is a very strong atheist, would agree with you on that," Sam said somewhat pensively.

"With what?" Buzz smiled as the burgers were set on the table.

"That western civilization comes largely from the Christian culture. Schools, hospitals, social norms. Those kinds of things. He doesn't like the Catholic Church, but loves what it gave civilization. He always talks about it, but he doesn't put it that way. He also thinks the Catholic Church gave us a bunch of superstitions and rules that were pure horse manure, and is glad that it doesn't run the show any more, civilization-wise."

"Civilization-wise?" Buzz raised his eyebrow.

"Sorry, bad diction. I can't talk as glibly as you about these things. I don't think I've ever talked about these things, at least not over beers with guys I play hoops with."

"You're right, nobody has as far as I know," Buzz concurred. "I thought of the NFL Proof today while I was driving back to the UPS center. Just thought I'd try out a funky idea. What about you? What do you think of the Catholic Church? Do you agree with your dad?" His tone was light.

"Buzz, sorry to shatter your world, but I rarely even think about religion. I guess my dad is right, but I'm more interested in computers, my business, and getting on with my life."

"You just gave a very Catholic answer."

Sam gave Buzz a confused look.

"It was based on direct reality—computers, business, your life."

Sam bit into his cheeseburger.

"I don't know about your concept of reality. What you're saying is just words to me. Words aren't reality. If you're so into reality, how come you talk so much?"

"How come you asked that word-filled question?"

"You can't answer a question with a question, Buzz."

"I just did. That's real." Buzz laughed.

Sam didn't get the joke; when Buzz noticed this, he said, "Look, I've never met anybody who's gotten more than half the things that make me laugh, except for my ex-wife. Don't feel bad. I won't even explain why I found what I just said to be humorous. If you can live with that, it will help our friendship."

"There you go again with that best-friend stuff. Are you gay or something, or trying to convert me?"

"I'm not a homosexual. It's sad that your question is a reasonable one. No, I'm not that way. And I try to convert everybody, so I'm not treating you exceptionally in that sense, any more than I believe that God helps one quarterback win and his opponents lose. I just like to talk about weird stuff. The fact that you follow even some of it qualifies you to be my friend. You don't have to be."

"Thank you, Buzz, for the permission to reject you as a friend," Sam said with mock solemnity.

"You're certainly welcome. Live and let live. Your reality is as valid as mine. What is truth—is it unchanging law? And what of truth—is mine the same as yours?"

"Where's that from?" Sam asked. "Sounds familiar."

"Jesus Christ Superstar, a decidedly un-Catholic musical, despite the subject matter."

"Should I start calling you Pope Buzz? After all, you seem to be the judge of what's Catholic and what isn't."

"Don't bother. I doubt the College of Cardinals would ever elect a divorced, alcoholic, cigarette-smoking, pompous jerk like me."

"Now you're talking reality," Sam laughed.

"You're going to make a great Catholic, someday, reality-*wise,* I mean," Buzz replied, not laughing so much as expressing his mirth with a smirk and a shake of his head.

"There you go again. Look, I don't want to be converted. I like being an agnostic. No church on Sundays. No moral codes. So on and so forth."

"You haven't got a moral code? Do you steal?" Buzz asked, suddenly serious.

"I don't steal. Bad for business. Stealing comes back and haunts you. I couldn't stay in business if I made a habit of ripping people off—"

"So your personal moral code, for whatever reason you have it, precludes you from stealing. Why?"

"Why? I don't know. Like I said, it's bad for business. And my father taught me not to steal," Sam replied somewhat sheepishly, wondering where this would go, a bit more aware that he was enjoying himself, the beer, the food—this strange guy. "What do you say to that, Pope Buzz?"

"Where did your father get his moral code?"

"From his parents..."

"And they got it from their parents, or from somewhere else, like the culture, which your dad already said was based on Judeo-Christianity. You might be an agnostic—let's shorten that to aggie—but I bet we share a common moral code, except for sex. That's too much to hope for. Everybody in our generation believes in having maximum amounts of sex."

"Actually, Buzz, I don't believe in sex until I get married, unless I really love the girl and plan to marry her—" Sam caught himself saying a very personal thing.

"Really?" Buzz looked down at his plate. Something in Sam's voice had conveyed a level of discomfort. A heavy silence ensued.

"Religion, sex—that only leaves politics, Sammy Boy. We'll run out of things to talk about before we're done with dinner."

"Yeah, right. But I bet you're more repressed than I am, being a personal pope and all."

"I detect a challenge in the area of sexual ethics. Let's go, Sammy. Wanna hear my NFL Proof that Premarital Sex is Wrong Theory?"

"I bet it's reality-based," Sam quipped.

"Right! Okay, let's start out with a little known fact—practically all of the most successful NFL coaches are devout Catholics. For example, both Don Shula and Chuck Noll are daily communicants—"

"Daily communicants?"

"Yeah, that's when you go to Mass every day and receive communion—hold on. Waitress?" Buzz called out. "May I have another Pepsi?"

"Coincidence," Sam said, implying that Shula and Noll's religion had nothing to do with their coaching records.

"At first glance, yes, it looks like a coincidence, but let's look at it from another angle…" Buzz continued, the understated excitement building. He had a high voice for a man his size.

It was an excitement Sam was having trouble resisting.

I was wrong, he thought of his initial impression that Buzz was a jerk, listening to Buzz's sometimes terrible, but always interesting logic. *I wonder how he got the name Buzz?*

And so the conversation went on for two more hours, with two additional beers and three more glasses of Pepsi, as Sam and Buzz became friends.

Chapter Two

1

"Still driving that old pick-up truck, Mr. Computer Magnate?" Buzz asked Sam a few days later after the hoops had ended.

"Yeah," Sam replied, wrapping a towel around his neck.

"Great, do me a favor—"

"What kind of favor?"

"An easy one. Look, I can't get any more days off from UPS, and I need someone to pick up a used refrigerator at this place that's only open during working hours. I figured you were your own boss, and that—"

"And that I would be super-willing to pick up your fridge because we're world record best friends. Hey, I've got work to do during the day, Buzz, and just because I own my company doesn't mean—"

"Forget it, then. I'll ask someone else." Buzz sounded disappointed.

"I didn't say I wouldn't do it," Sam added tentatively.

"Great!" Buzz lit up like a Christmas tree. "You're really easy to manipulate. Here's the directions." He shoved a folded piece of legal paper into Sam's hands. "I'll meet you after work at my apartment and we'll bring it up together. You look like a strong guy."

"Bring it up? How many flights?"

"I don't know. Three or four. Or seven." Buzz looked away, a slight smile on his lips. He lit a cigarette.

"Or seven, eh? I get the picture, now."

"Will you do it?" Buzz asked seriously.

"Sure. I can't wait," Sam said. "I'm looking forward to it already. In fact, I'm upset that I have to wait a whole day to get over there. You know, I'll be up all night, tingling with excitement—"

"Okay, okay. Sorry, man. I don't have anybody else to ask, and I've been living without a fridge since I moved here a month ago."

"Please stop; you're making me sad."

"You sure you weren't born in New Jersey?" Buzz asked. "You're pretty sarcastic when you want to be."

Sam just smiled.

2

It's funny how an entire life can change because of a chance meeting. But was it really chance? Because Buzz Woodward was a Catholic, he had asked Saint Anthony to help him round up an affordable refrigerator. Buzz also asked a few of the drivers at UPS. One driver sometimes made deliveries to a tiny appliance repair shop in Little Italy which often had a few used refrigerators for sale. Buzz called the place and arranged to buy an ancient fridge for fifty dollars, sight unseen. Then he asked Sam to pick it up…

It was not love at first sight.

But there was a kind of warmth at first sight when Donna Beck turned and first saw Sam walk into Nardi's TV & Appliance, the bell clanging on the door behind him. She turned back. She was not attracted to the tall man.

He stood behind her in line, looking down at the dirty tile floor.

It was late afternoon. There were two men in line in front of them. The proprietor of Nardi's was not the fastest man in the world. In fact, after a long argument in Italian with the man at the front of the line, he disappeared into the back with a huff. The sounds of banging promptly came from the back room.

Sam looked at his watch. "Is he fixing something in there?"

Donna, who was not facing Sam, shrugged her shoulders. "Maybe. He said something about it needing a new heating element in Italian before he went back there."

"You speak Italian?" Sam asked, looking down, wondering what the girl in front of him looked like, hoping she was as pretty as her voice, hoping she would turn around.

Donna Beck turned, smiling. Sam tried not to show his disappointment because she was not particularly pretty. She had dark, curly hair, a somewhat pudgy nose, a shiny forehead, and indistinct brown eyes.

"Yes, a little. Mostly from what my parents yell at me. I also took it in high school. And you?"

She did have a warm smile. Sam liked that, and maybe because she wasn't pretty, he didn't feel uncomfortable making small talk with this girl.

"Me? Italian? No. Foxpro. Fortran. Cobol. C+. Those are my languages."

"Computers, eh?"

"Yeah," Sam said, slightly excited. "Do you know computers?"

"Nah. Not for me. Too dull. Basketball is what I like to do more than anything else," somehow slipped from Donna's lips.

"You're kinda short for basketball."

"And you're kinda tall for stupidity. I'm a girl, in case you haven't noticed, and I only play against other girls, who are mostly short, and besides, I can make up for height with brains and speed," she finished with an air of confidence.

"Sorry," Sam said. "I didn't mean to offend you. I love basketball. As a matter of fact, I'm picking up a fridge for a buddy I play hoops with at the Rocky River courts."

"No problem." Her lack of concern was genuine.

She turned back to face the counter. A few minutes passed. She was bored.

"So, you live on the West Side," she guessed, half-turning her shoulders.

Rush Limbaugh's voice started to drift in from the back room. His voice was not familiar to them.

"Me? Yeah. Buzz, my friend, does, too. He lives in Rocky River. Near the lake. I live in Rocky River, too."

"So do I," she said. "With my parents. I still don't know why they insist on buying stuff in this dump."

There was an awkward silence.

"You men are lucky," she mused. "There's not much pick-up for women. I have to wait until the rec league opens the gym for us on Tuesday and Thursday nights. Even then, I play for five hours and feel like running for ten." Donna looked away, as if picturing the games in her head.

Sam took a closer look, and noticed the easy, athletic way she swung her arms when she talked, and that she wasn't so much overweight, but thick with womanly muscle in her shoulders and legs. *She's a fireplug like Buzz, only a lot shorter,* he thought.

They went to a dusty old couch and sat down, continuing to make small talk. They both liked the Cavs and loved the Indians—no surprise. She grew up in Little Italy and had one brother and two sisters, although her parents had moved to Rocky River a few years ago.

Sam's father, a widower, had moved to Ann Arbor to take a position at the University of Michigan a few years earlier. He told her about his computer company, but tried not to brag. It took more than twenty minutes for the repair to be finished on the first man's oven.

When the time came, it seemed only natural to offer to drive her home. Donna was picking up a small countertop refrigerator, and was planning to take the bus otherwise. He helped the proprietor load the two refrigerators onto the truck.

"How were you going to get that to your house?" Sam asked reasonably as she stood next to his rusty Ford F-150 on Murray Hill.

She hesitated, wondering if she could trust this stranger. She looked at him closely. *Yes, I can.*

"I asked Saint Anthony to help me find a way. If worse came to worst, I could manage to carry it to the bus stop. Saint Anthony sent you instead."

"Saint Anthony? You and Buzz are going to get along just great," Sam said softly, almost to himself.

"Are we meeting Buzz?" she asked, feeling the strangeness of the words, knowing that they assumed a bit too much, and were jumping the gun.

"Um," Sam paused. "Sure. If you want to. If you don't have any plans tonight. After we drop off your fridge, you can come with me to Buzz's place. That sucker back there has to go up seven flights. Maybe you could help."

He glanced at her stout legs. She noticed, and surprised him with a smile.

"Music to a tomboy's ear," she practically sang.

Sam chuckled.

Thus, two quickly became three. The agnostic, the believer, and the tomboy.

3

Donna looked down at her fingers as she sat in the spotless, spartan cab of Sam's pick-up. Her nails were clean and closely clipped, with no nail polish, unlike many of her acquaintances from the old neighborhood. She and Sam had already dropped off her refrigerator in her folks' garage.

This is a classy guy, she thought. Breeding was all over him: his walk, his casual preppy clothes, the way he pronounced his words. She was very sensitive to such things, having grown up in a working class neighborhood where few of her peers went to college. Oh, there were always the local community colleges, but these struck Donna as mere extensions of high school, places to kill time before getting dead end jobs in local factories or retail establishments.

She had related strongly to a movie that had come out recently, *Working Girl,* about a lower class Brooklyn girl who used cleverness and gumption to whittle her way into the professional world by posing as her high-class boss. It was not that Donna was ambitious for a professional career—she wasn't. She just wanted to improve herself, to marry and raise children in the suburbs somewhere, anywhere, where prosperity itself seemed to sprout like strong grass from excellently-watered lawns. She was a devout Catholic, and getting married and having children was her ideal.

After high school, Donna had briefly attended community college in pursuit of a teaching degree. Her father, a plumber, had not been able to help much with the expense, and she had been forced to cut back on classes and take a part-time job as a clerk at a small accounting firm on Madison Avenue in Lakewood. She was good with numbers, and conscientious, and was soon offered a full-time position, so she quit school altogether. Only five accountants worked at the firm, and the only one who showed any romantic interest in her was married. And he wasn't Catholic.

Donna was neither plain nor pretty. She had been asked out several times during her freshman and sophomore years of high school. After all, most guys were average-looking and there was something very approachable about Donna Beck. (*Beck* was an Americanized version of Becci, which had been shortened by a bureaucrat on Ellis Island in the late 1800s…) She almost always turned down the boys, unless she particularly liked them. The ones she did go out with only wanted to do what Donna called the Three Bad Things: Get Drunk, Have Sex, Do Drugs.

Soon she developed a reputation as a prude, and the boys left her alone. Because she played sports, a rumor began that she was a lesbian. But Donna had turned down the lesbians, too, so the rumor died. By the end of high school, her classes, athletics, and a handful of wholesome friends kept her comfortably insulated from the Three Bad Things. After high school and the move to Rocky River, she lost touch with her friends.

Were they really friends?

Why had she said *no* so many times to the Three Bad Things? At first, she wasn't quite sure—her refusals came like violent bolts from her gut. Then, as everyone discovers while growing up, she had to decide *why* she was saying no. She needed to adopt the Three Good Things and make them her own. She inwardly called them Sobriety, Chastity, and Clarity.

She had also consulted often with her older sisters, who were both married. Her sisters had experimented with the Bad Things during the Seventies, and they told Donna that these weren't worth the trouble they caused. Drugs got old and made you paranoid and apathetic—just look around at the 'heads' in your school, they told her. Sex before marriage was either a disappointing downer or a dangerous drug in its own right. Sex could make you *stunod*—stupid—about selfish men. Don't bother. One of her older sisters, Cindy, had been married briefly, outside of the Church, to an older divorced man, and *that* had been an ugly scene. The marriage had not been recognized by the Church. *"If I hadn't slept with him, I wouldn't have married him,"* Cindy had counseled Donna.

Then Donna answered the silent call. She wasn't aware it was a call at the time, but it was a real call nevertheless. It was the call of grace. A simple, lovely invitation from the Blessed Mother. Donna was walking home from school alone, and decided to take an alternate route, a route which took her by her parish church, Holy Rosary.

She found herself walking into the empty church on a sunny winter afternoon, the wind stopping as the thick door closed behind her, and grace flooded unknown into her heart. The Blessed Mother had been keenly following Donna's search for the truth, and had procured from her Son special graces for the stout little girl with nice hair and dark brown eyes.

While sitting in Sam's pick-up, Donna was suddenly back in the church, listening to her shoes tap the tile floor as she walked toward the front, which was filled with stained-glass-colored light reflecting off the marble and brass of the altar. She found herself kneeling before a particularly lifelike statue of Saint Anthony, but curiously found herself asking Our Lady for help. She had one question, which was her only prayer:

Why should I be good? Just because my parents are good?

Donna did not feel the grace that flooded her heart on that day, but a sluice door was opened that afternoon which was never closed again.

In her human perception, the grace came in the form of a prompting to pray the Rosary. Her family had prayed the Rosary every evening after dinner, but the prayer had become mere words to Donna over the last few years, even though she had loved the Rosary when she was a little girl. It was useless to try to get out of saying it because both her parents were so insistent.

Now, in this church, on this day, she felt an urge to say a *good* Rosary.

If I say this Rosary, I'll have the answer to my question, she thought, quite correctly.

She looked up at the statue of Saint Anthony, and then down to her right and saw a set of plastic rosary beads on the kneeler.

Strange, she thought.

She picked up the beads and began to *pray,* not *say,* the Rosary for the first time in years. She concentrated on the words, her eyes closed, and did not rush through the prayers. She asked sincerely during the last part of every Hail Mary, "Holy Mary, Mother of God, Pray for us sinners, now and at the hour of our death."

The words struck her as never before, especially the part about the hour of death.

The Rosary is a preparation for heaven, she thought.

Heaven.

Donna continued to pray, meditating on the Joyful Mysteries of the Rosary here and there between concentrating on the words of the prayers. She pictured Our Lady, a young girl herself, accepting the huge responsibility to conceive by the Holy Spirit and bear the Son of God. She pictured Mary visiting her cousin Elizabeth, with John jumping in the womb.

Why were you good, Mary?

In Donna's heart, Mary answered the simple question with a simple answer. To Donna, the answer came as a thought, and was not accompanied by lightning bolts or mystical phenomena.

Because God is Goodness Itself and she desired to please God.

The answer made sense to Donna. *God is Good. God is Good. I'm here on this earth to please God,* she repeated to herself. It was like the axioms she had learned in Geometry class; *the shortest distance between two points is a straight line. God is good; pleasing God is good; pleasing God requires that **I be good.***

There were a hundred different ways to put it.

Donna did not stay in the church for hours. In fact, she prayed for less than half an hour. Other than an unusual ability to concentrate on the mysteries and words of the Rosary without distraction, she did not feel one outward sign of the grace that flooded her heart on that day. But she was never the same. The ember of grace she received during the Sacrament of Confirmation four years earlier was inflamed that day. Now it was up to Donna to keep the fire burning, and she did. That weekend, she went to confession for the first time in over two years.

She got into the habit of visiting the Blessed Sacrament on her walk home from school at least a few times a week, even if only to say a quick *I love you* to her new friend, Jesus.

When the boys came at her over the next few years, rejecting the Three Bad Things was as easy as turning down a glass of poison. She found herself attending daily Mass with her parents before school, and even got her best friend, Gloria Santini, to go to Mass with her. Picking up a devotion to Saint Anthony seemed like the most natural thing in the world.

Besides, the guy's amazing. Ask Uncle Tony, and you get instant results, she now thought as she looked over at the silent stranger driving the truck.

She could tell that there was a goodness in Sam; he wasn't a barracuda. She just knew. Like most good women, she knew she could trust her instincts, now that the Three Bad Things weren't mucking up the works.

"You don't talk much, Sam, do you?"

He looked away from the road and gave her a quick, toothy smile. He confirmed her question with silence and a slow shake of his head.

A few minutes later, he said, "Don't worry, Donna. Buzz can talk enough for ten men."

4

Months earlier, in a suburb of New Jersey, a tall, well-built man slammed the door of his car just after climbing in.

From the rearview mirror, Mark Johnson saw the smile on his wife's face as she stood behind the screen door of their home. His daughter Angela was standing there, too, in front of his wife Maggie. Maggie said something to the girl, and closed the front door slowly, as if to mock Mark's anger.

He started the car, and pulled out of the driveway. His heart sank. *She's happy I'm leaving. Happy! She's relieved!*

She had kicked him out before, but had always let him return the next day. One time, two years earlier, she had been the one to leave him, taking the girls for a week to stay with her mother in Maryland. Not this time. Maggie was staying put. This time she had forced him to pack his clothes.

He had called her bluff, and she had won.

"If that's how you feel, Mag, why don't I just move out!" he had screamed an hour earlier, losing his temper, at the end of another long discussion-turned-shouting match.

They had stood in their newly remodelled kitchen. He had taken a night job for a security company to pay for it last summer. They were on opposite sides of the new island with the cook-top stove. Maggie had insisted on that stove.

The kitchen was so bright and cheerful. Angela was coloring in her Our Lady of Fatima coloring book at the kitchen table, listening with one ear. It remotely annoyed Mark that Angela rarely cried when the arguments came. She was used to them.

Maggie's pretty eyes had sparkled. "Okay," she had told him smugly, almost serenely. "But if you do leave, you're not coming back until I say so, and under my conditions."

She had the youngest, little Meg, in her arms. Meg was burying sobs into her mother's breast. Sarah, the oldest, was at soccer practice.

"Fine! I'll move out!" he yelled, calling her bluff.

"Good. You go pack," she closed the deal calmly. "I need to get dinner together. I'll pick up Sarah later."

She turned away from him and opened the refrigerator, and began pulling out ingredients for the meal.

He had never hit Maggie, and the urge he felt now as she ignored him, having outmaneuvered him, was sudden and fierce.

He took a step back, afraid for her, afraid for himself, not at all accustomed to the desire to strike her. He had just lost a battle. He hated to lose.

He was a warrior. A tough guy.

He retreated from the kitchen, and climbed the stairs to the master bedroom. He found his luggage, gathering dust, in the back of the fancy walk-in closet he had repainted two years earlier. He resisted an urge to run downstairs to renegotiate the treaty. She would no doubt make him beg, and mock his sincere apologies. She was tired of his apologies.

And he was too proud to beg. He had given his word to leave on her conditions. He was a man of his word.

What about the girls?

He put the girls out of his mind.

One hour later, he was driving away from his own home, not sure where he was going to stay for the night.

His late father had also been a tough guy—a cop. And Mark's older brothers were tough guys who had made sure their younger brother was nothing less than a tough guy. He was also an honorable man, and, despite his love for his wife and their three daughters, he was supremely frustrated because he did not know why his marriage was crumbling out of his hands, falling down through mental grates into dark sewers. Beyond his reach, irretrievable.

Mark was big, tall, muscular. He was an FBI agent. He had been an all-state football player and wrestler in high school, and received an appointment to the Naval Academy. He had towered over his fellow midshipmen, and earned second team All-American honors at tight end.

He was not a gentle giant, but there was a measured quality to his anger. He was calculatingly ferocious when he thought the situation merited it. This fierceness induced fear in others. The calculation brought success. His voice carried over land like a ship's horn over water. His voice alone could stop a bad guy in his tracks at times when other agents needed bullets.

He had more of everything. More charisma. More strength. More intelligence. More savvy. More, more, more. Men who weren't tough guys had a natural fear of him. The small fraternity who were also tough guys respected him, and saw him as a kind of modern king. Historians say Charlemagne was a foot taller than his peers, and his height alone commanded homage in an age so violent that war, not football, was a seasonal pursuit of the brave and wealthy.

But this king's marriage was crumbling. Mark Johnson was a Catholic. He loved his faith. But his faith wasn't helping him—not yet. His Rosaries weren't answered. His wife didn't respect him.

Maggie. Once you told me that you wanted to be by my side forever.

Maggie, he remembered, was truly a queen when they met. Queen of the high school prom the year before he met her, and Homecoming Queen of Hood College, the all-women school she was attending the weekend he met her at a formal.

She had not been able to keep her eyes off the king. As he drove away now, he remembered the tan color of her shoulders set off against a dress so white it made you squint. They had danced. Then he escorted her over to the ground-level balcony outside the reception hall. She was smiling. Looking at him.

"Let's get out of here," he had said.

"How?" she had asked, her blue eyes sparkling.

"This is how," he replied, lifting her up, making her feel like a small girl with his strength, as he carefully swung his leg over the stone banister, and took her across the lawn to his Jeep.

He drove her to Main Street in Annapolis, and they talked and walked, arm-in-arm, on the crowded sidewalk. Passersby stared at the king and queen. He was in the full dress whites of the Naval Academy. They made all that surrounded them seem a dull gray.

He could tell she wanted him. All the girls always did. Despite many opportunities to throw away his virginity, he had saved himself for *the one.* She had saved herself, too. Later, they would discover this secret about each other.

There was something different about Maggie that impressed him. She didn't fear him. She wasn't in awe.

Yeah, that's it. Maggie and Mom. My mom wasn't afraid of me either, the tough guy thought now.

Then, as they had walked along the street, he saw a friend sitting at a table in Riordan's Saloon.

"Wait here," he told her.

"Why?"

"There's a guy I used to wrestle with in there. I'll be back in a minute."

Before she could say a word, he darted off, leaving her alone. There were two other buddies in the bar, and Mark had few chances to drink at the Academy. One beer became two. But his queen was waiting, so he begged off on the third.

Twenty minutes after abandoning her, he returned.

"You're no gentleman," she seethed at him.

"What are you so upset about?"

"You left me here for almost half an hour! Take me back to the dance!"

He shook his head. "What?"

"Take me back."

She was really mad at me.

"Let's just walk a little bit more…" he suggested, offering his arm and a charming smile.

"Take me back," she insisted, looking him in the eye. Not backing off. Not a trace of fear.

Maybe that's when I fell in love with her.

He had smiled. He started talking. He changed the subject. He was not a dumb jock. He knew how to express his ideas. They talked as he walked her back to the car. He made her laugh in the car. He told heroic stories, in humble ways, of heroic battles he had fought. The Notre Dame game, when he had played with a busted up knee, got to her.

"My daddy played hurt," she told him. "He was an officer and a gentleman."

Later, when their first daughter had been born, Maggie hadn't uttered a word or let out a scream during the delivery. After Sarah came out, she told him, "See, I'm a tough guy, too."

She had loved him, then. He gripped the steering wheel tightly. His house in the pleasant suburb of Montclair was miles away now. *Where am I?*

Nowhere, man. Hey, didn't the Beatles sing that? I hate the Beatles.

He saw a Catholic church. He pulled into the driveway, parked, and went up to the large wooden doors. They were locked. He walked around the back, got down on his knees at the wall closest to the tabernacle, which he saw through the stained glass, and began to pray.

What's going on, Jesus? I'm a failure as a husband. I'm losing my little girls. What's going on? I gave everything to her. I worked hard. I never cheated. All I want is some respect.

He wasn't at the end of his line, however. He was nowhere near tears. Mark Johnson really was a tough guy.

He went to bed that night with swirling memories of arguments with Maggie banging around his head. He shouted at her. She snapped at him. Bang bang bang. Like gunshots.

And so it goes: another marriage on the ropes. One of millions. For all our love of work and cars and sports and magazines and minivans and computers and custom floor coverings and politics and sex and anything-but-anything-but-God, we still go to bed at night with love and lack thereof on our lips and hearts and minds.

5

"Is Buzz your real name?" Donna asked as she looked around Buzz's apartment.

"No. It's a nickname. But if people use it all the time, it is kind of real, isn't it?"

Donna squinted in confusion. "Huh?"

"It's not a fake name," Buzz explained.

"You see Donna," Sam cut in. "I told you Buzz would confuse you right off the bat."

"Are you trying to be funny?" she asked, noticing that everything in the kitchen had a car motif. There was a giant collage of classic Thunderbirds, cut from magazine ads, on the wall adjacent to the table.

"No, I'm serious. Buzz is my nickname, and it's my real name. My *baptized* name is Gwynne. Can you believe it?"

"Gwen?" Sam asked.

"Gwynne," he repeated, emphasizing the *i* sound of the *y*.

"Pretty cruddy name if you ask me. Buzz is much better," Donna offered.

"Sure is," Buzz agreed, wiping his hands on his apron. He was in the middle of cooking a huge omelette on a large cast-iron skillet.

"So how did you get nicknamed Buzz?" Donna asked after a moment, looking Buzz in the eye for the first time since walking into the apartment.

"It's a long story." Buzz smiled warmly.

"It's a great story. Tell her, Buzz," Sam said, adding, "It's a great story, Donna."

"Great, tell me this wonderful story," Donna said unenthusiastically.

"During dinner," Buzz conceded.

"Dinner?" Donna asked, turning to Sam. "I thought we were just gonna drop off Buzz's fridge."

"Oh yeah, thanks for picking up the fridge, Sam," Buzz interjected. "I'm cooking all these eggs for us because they were sitting out on the deck. They're going bad."

"Hmmn, appetizing," Donna said sarcastically, but it was a friendly sarcasm.

"We'll be perfect gentlemen, my fair lady. Sam can't lift heavy things on an empty stomach," Buzz reasoned weirdly.

"Why not, lifting heavy stuff is not swimming, you know," Donna rejoined, beginning to enjoy the strangeness of the conversation. It reminded her of the dinner table at her home. "And no one has ever described me as fair before. You sure are weird."

"Thank you," Buzz replied, pleased.

"It wasn't meant to be a compliment," Donna said dryly.

"But I took it as one. The world we live in is so messed up morally and culturally that being weird is the only normal way to be!"

"I told you he was a piece of work, didn't I?" Sam whispered into Donna's ear, bending over awkwardly to get close, purposely speaking loud enough for Buzz to hear him. He straightened up. "Hey, your omelette's burning, Buzzman."

"Hey, you're right." Buzz turned back to the stove. "Help yourself to Pepsi or juice in the cooler by the window. I don't have wine or beer to offer. I'm an alcoholic. Or did Sam already tell you I'm a drunk and in AA and all that, Donna?"

"No, I didn't tell her. I knew you would tell her right off the bat," Sam responded quickly.

Donna laughed.

"What's so funny?" Buzz asked.

"I think I finally found a couple of friends in Rocky River," she said quite seriously, the laughter curiously gone.

"Good, I knew we would be best friends the minute you walked through the door, Donna. I like you. You're a real snot," Buzz told her without turning from his giant omelette.

"Snottiness, the perfect basis for friendship?" Sam asked to no one in particular. "Can you turn that into a proof for the existence of God?"

"I'm sure I can, if you want," Buzz reassured his tall friend. "But after dinner, which is now ready. Paper plates are in the cupboard, Sam—over to your right.

"And pull out a chair for our new friend Donna. Remember, we're perfect gentlemen tonight," he added, looking at the woman.

"I feel as if I should curtsy or something," she observed sweetly.

"Be my guest," Buzz responded.

"I already am," she rejoined quickly.

"You always get the last word in, don't you?" Buzz got in.

"Always," she got back in.

"Then I guess you win," he shot back.

"So, you get to decide who wins, eh?" she asked with an arched eyebrow.

"I just did."

"When?" she asked.

"Just then," he explained.

Sam's head started to turn back and forth during the repartee.

"Okay," she confirmed.

"Okay," he asserted.

"Dokey," she zipped.

"Cut it out, you guys," Sam interrupted. "We'll be here all night."

"What's wrong with that?" Donna asked.

"Yeah, what's wrong with that?" Buzz asked with fake indignation.

Sam just shook his head, but didn't answer.

"Well then," Buzz said finally, winking at Donna. "Let's monge!"

A few minutes later, Donna started laughing when Buzz told the story of how he came to be called Buzz…

6

"I was probably eight or nine years old—I don't really remember. But I do know I was in third grade. Mom was long gone—I have no memories of her. Nobody called me anything but Buzz by fourth grade. It was a Saturday, and Dad got drunk as usual. Passed out on his Lazyboy.

"You have to understand where we lived at the time. It was the most boring place on the face of the earth: Waretown, New Jersey.

"Waretown is a stinky, sleepy little town in South Jersey, where nobody lives. Actually, a few people live there, but to give you some perspective, there are more people within five square miles of this apartment than in the whole southern half of New Jersey. Anyway, we only lived in Waretown for a couple of years before moving north. I think Dad lost his job or something—I wasn't filled in on the details and Dad was between steady girlfriends at the time of the episode.

"It was just me and Dad, our trailer, and about a hundred thousand pine trees on this side street off a side street. I think that Dad won the property in a poker game. He was a great poker player. And actually, Waretown is kinda nice, and people who have boats like to live there because of the inlets. There are summer cottages and such, but for me, a third grader, it was dull as doorjambs.

"Sometimes Dad wouldn't come home if he was on a trip, and a ladyfriend of his from the town would cook me dinner and look in on me. It was creepy sleeping alone in that creaky old trailer. Most days, the bus would drop me off after school, and I'd walk half a mile to the trailer. I was bored. I didn't read well or read much, and this was way before cable, so there usually was nothing on television except for reruns of Lost in Space.

"But this was a Saturday, during summer vacation, and the world seemed all right. I was feeling pretty good. My dad was a lush, but he was never violent or anything. He loved me a lot. Maybe I was the thing he loved most when he wasn't falling into a bottle. His passing out was pretty normal, just a part of my world.

"I headed out the front door.

"There was this brand spanking new thing on the front porch. It was in a big potato sack. Don't ask me why Dad put his new toy in a potato sack. Probably to hide it from me. It had a receipt on it. A big red sale tag.

"You know how good new things smell; all plastic and metal and motor oil. I could smell the gas. My dad must have made sure the salesman fired that baby up before buying it. It was almost as tall as me, it seemed, and half my weight.

"It was green and gray and calling me. 'Gwynne, pick me up.'

"Who was I to ignore it?

"I picked it up. Boy, was it heavy! But I was a strong kid, big for my age. Strong? Heck, I was a phenom. I could out-Indian wrestle anybody in my class or two classes above me.

And most of the kids older than that. Sam could tell ya. They called me the Bear on the playground.

"But mostly they called me Gwen, pronouncing *Gwynne* like the girl's name by accident. Hell, *nobody* called me Gwynne. A few guys called me Woody. After a while, I stopped trying to correct people and let them call me Gwen. It was pathetic. Even the principal of the school called me Gwen during an assembly in second grade, when I won an award for not being absent all year long. At least that's what everybody told me. I missed that day of school. I kid you not.

"Anyway, where was I? Oh yeah, I think it was the smell and the challenge of the thing that did it. I held it up in the air, the long business end of the thing shining in the sun, eye level, and I knew why God made me and why I was in the world: to level things. To cut things down, for good or for bad.

"I reached down, grabbed the rubber handle on the pull cord, and fired that chainsaw up on the first crank. It sounded great—big and loud and louder—and I just held it up in the air, revving that baby louder and louder, amazed that the old man wasn't up and out and after me.

"After a bit—I don't know how long—Dad wasn't coming out, and I had this buzzing saw in my hands, and I was getting used to the weight. And well, there was a wooden dock up the river with a bunch of little fishing boats, the rowboat kind with tiny little outboards on them. Thank God for those boats, because they rid me of the name Gwynne forever. I guess you figured out why they call me Buzz, but there are a few more twists. The boats are one twist.

"I cut up the landward end of the dock, and watched the boats drift away with it. It was mostly two by fours and some pilings. Lucky it was low tide, and the water was up to my ankles. It was nice practice to avoid the saw kicking back on me. I was surprised how easy it was. I guess I was too dumb to kill myself. Our few neighbors never saw me, though I suppose a few heard me and figured it was somebody cutting down trees. I guess if the saw had kicked back and cut off my right arm, they would've called me Lefty.

"Then I carved a name in the patch of trees. I didn't carve the words into the bark. Pine tree bark doesn't work that way anyway. No, I had to carve the name by cutting down trees in a pattern. Maybe it was the Gilligan's Island influence in my life. I don't know. Either way, if you were in a helicopter, you could've read the word Mary in tree stumps behind our trailer. Probably still can.

"Why Mary? Well, I did have a crush on a blond girl in my class named Mary Papchak. But I remember thinking I'd do something for Jesus to say thank you for letting me have such a great time, for the miracle of my dad staying passed out. It was like I figured that Jesus was up in heaven and could read His mother's name in my backyard. It was the least I could do. I didn't pray much back then, and Dad only went to Mass every month or so, but I liked Jesus, and I liked Mary. *Love* is too strong a word. *Like* is about right. I was happy when the nun at Sunday School told us Jesus was my brother. That made Mary my mother. I needed one. Still do need her, more than ever.

"So after about twenty minutes, and halfway through the letter *r* in Mary, I ran out of gas; so I filled the saw up using the metal gas can under the porch. Started right up on the first pull. Professional athletes call it being in the zone. I was in the zone. It was all so *adult*. It was so, well, interesting, after such a boring summer.

"So I finished off my first major piece of artwork for Our Lady, and started cutting anything in sight. I was truly amazed that Dad didn't wake up when I carved up the wooden porch.

"I tried to cut the trunklid of Dad's Impala, but it didn't cut, and the buzzsaw kicked like a mule. It made really cool sparks, though. My arms were getting tired. I knew I was going to get in trouble, but in a strangely adult way, I was willing to accept the consequences of my actions.

"That's a liberating thing. Accepting the responsibility.

"I woke Dad up when I started on the corner of the trailer near my bedroom. I was gonna cut myself a doorway. I guess I wanted him to wake up.

"I gotta hand it to him. He was kind of groggy, but what I had done was better than coffee. He was bald, and thin, and handsome in his own way. He almost fell when he went through the door without the porch, but kept his balance. He blew his nose on the bottom edge of his T-shirt. He didn't even yell at me. He just shook his head and chuckled.

"'You're just like your mother, Gwynny, dammit,' was all he said. Then he chuckled again. He even seemed touched when I told him that I spelled out Mary in the woods.

"He told me that what I had done was so astounding that he couldn't think of a proper punishment for it. It was like stumping God with a Jeopardy question—" Buzz began speaking in a game show host voice, "—Category! Bad Kids! Answer: A deed so awful that a hung-over dad can't think of a punishment for it.' Bing! 'What is cutting down a bunch of stuff with a chainsaw, Alex!'

"Anyway, he settled on public humiliation, and called the police after supper. He hadn't uttered a word to me all during the meal. The cops came by, and he must have told them to scare the hell out of me, because they did. They were all serious, and took out little notebooks and took notes and stuff. He must have convinced them to treat me as if I was a real criminal. They even threatened to take me to the station and fingerprint me, but my dad stopped them short of putting me in the squad car. I even saw one of them wink.

"Dad paid for all the damages, of course, and I didn't get an allowance ever again. He never held it over my head, though. I guess if you're a screw-up, you don't mind it as much in others, especially the ones you love.

"There was an article in the Asbury Park Press the next day. School started a couple of weeks later, and all the kids in school knew about it. The whole town must have been talking about it. The article had a lot of stuff about the dock and the boats. No mention was made of the Mary in the woods.

"Anyway, I was a hero. The other kids thought it was cool. Even the disapproving looks from the teachers had a kind of jealous 'I wish I could cut a bunch of things down' quality to them. Maybe I imagined that. I wasn't proud of myself, but I enjoyed the attention. You can guess the rest. Butch Hobbs called me Buzz that first day back to school and it stuck. Even Dad called me Buzz.

"So that's why they call me Buzz. I earned it. I cut things down. What do you think, Donna?"

"What do I think? I'm sorry," Donna replied. "I missed the part after you said you lived in Waretown. Could you start over?"

Sam laughed. Buzz laughed even harder. The omelettes were long gone. It was coffee time. Buzz got up to get it.

Donna spoke up. "Why don't we all tell a story about when we were kids? I remember hearing on the radio once that your first memories can tell you a lot about your personality."

Sam was quite uncomfortable with the suggestion.

Buzz brought the coffee to the table, and noticed Sam's discomfort. He decided to cut down that discomfort by putting him on the spot.

"Why don't you start, Sam?" Buzz suggested . . .

Chapter Three

1

Something about Buzz's kitchen felt old-fashioned. There was no microwave oven or electric can opener. Not one pot hanging on the metal hooks above the stove had a teflon coating. The building was old, and the kitchen had a vague smell, barely detectable, from decades of fried eggs and bacon.

It was a place for coffee and conversation, not a place for eating fast and rushing off.

They sat around an old formica table with a stainless steel trim edge. After some prodding, Sam began his story. Buzz lit a cigarette and was surprised when Donna asked to bum one. Buzz put cream in Sam's coffee. Sam took a sip and a deep breath. He wasn't sure what he was going to say, then the Red Memory came to him...

"...three years old or so. I was in the backyard with a friend. I was standing on the picnic table. We had a large yard in a development. I don't remember many details. My friend from next door, Timmy Goldblum, was making something with loose bricks next to the picnic table. I don't know where they came from. I remember that the grass was really green. It must have been sod and my parents had just had the house built. It was after dinner, but the sun was still out because it was summer.

"Timmy noticed me and told me not to jump off the picnic table. I remember that I wasn't planning on jumping off the table until he told me not to. Then, I just *had* to jump.

"So I jumped, and I was proud of jumping over Tim and the bricks until I landed, head first, into a brick which I hadn't

seen beyond Tim's pile. I cut my forehead up pretty bad, and
started to bleed. I've heard that head wounds bleed a lot. It
took twelve stitches, and you can still see a scar if you look
closely.

"'What a schmuck!' Timmy cried out, disgusted, and even
now, I can remember he was excited. Don't ask me to translate what *schmuck* means in Yiddish.

"I climbed to my feet, and looked up at the house. It was
red. The grass was purple. The Thunderbird in the driveway
wasn't beige anymore. It was a bright red!

"Timmy was trying to hold my hand, but I wouldn't let
him. I was crying for my mom, running faster and faster
toward the house. I knew I was in trouble, but I was afraid
that I was dying. I was confused, too. And happy about the
red. Of course, I was too young to realize that the blood
coming off my forehead had gotten into my eyes and tinted
everything.

"My memory blots out there for a while. I don't remember finding my mother. The next thing I remember is a memory
that I think of often when I drive my car.

"My mom got our other neighbor, Mrs. Epstein, and Mrs.
Epstein drove us in the Thunderbird to the hospital, though I
don't remember getting to the hospital. I was in my mother's
lap, the pain was gone. She was whispering nice things to
me, calming me. The red tint was gone. It was a warm summer night, and the convertible top was open, and I looked
past my mother to the sky. It must have been early evening,
because a full moon was rising above the trees. It wasn't quite
dark out yet.

"I remember how the moon was following us. You know
the optical illusion I'm describing. This was the first time I
ever noticed it. It delighted me. I was warm, in my mother's
arms, and curious about the moon. 'Mommy, how come the
moon is following us?'

"'Because it loves you,' she told me.

"That's where the memory ends.

"Mom must have died within a few months. It was a car accident, Donna. That's my last memory of her. I'm thankful that it's very happy and vivid." Sam finished.

"Thankful to whom?" Buzz asked.

"Beg your pardon?" Sam asked.

"You said you were thankful that your memory was warm and vivid. To whom are you thankful?"

Donna watched Sam's eyes drop to the table, and his hands, normally calm, nervously fumbled with a napkin.

"I know where you're going with that question, Buzz, and it won't work. It's just a figure of speech. A remnant of western civilization. I'm not thankful to God."

"That must really stink," Donna observed sympathetically.

"Not having a mom?" Sam asked.

"No. I'm sorry your mom died. Not having a mom is really awful, but what I meant was not having anyone to thank when something good happens to you."

"I can thank real people for things. I thank my father for things."

"So can I," Buzz offered kindly. "But I also thank God for things. I mean, who do we thank for getting better after we're sick?"

"Simple: nobody," Sam said.

"Nobody, huh?" Donna replied skeptically. "That still stinks. It's…it's so dry. I just met you, Sam, and I don't want to be critical of your beliefs, or should I say lack of belief, but they're so foreign to me."

"What Sam thinks is always interesting, Donna, because he *doesn't* believe. He's honest about it. That's what I like about you, Sam. You're honest, and about as thoughtful and kind a person as I've ever known. You never get defensive. You just reject any kind of proof of God and move on. You don't refute belief. You ignore it. Isn't that a fair assessment, Sam?"

"Pretty much. Christianity or Buddhism or Taoism simply don't interest me. Business interests me. Sports interest me, art interests me—"

"You like art?" Donna interrupted. "Who's your favorite artist?"

"El Greco, hands down."

"I like El Greco, too. But my favorite is van Gogh."

"He cut his ear off," Buzz said with a strange smile.

"Yeah, he did," Sam said.

"Do you ever wonder why when people bring up Vincent van Gogh they always tell you he cut his ear off?" Buzz asked. "I mean, they bring it up even though you already know it."

"No, Buzz," Sam replied. "I don't wonder about that."

"Well, I do. There's a whole grouping of information like that. For example, when you're getting ready to play any kind of sport, your coach always says, 'You should stretch out, Sam Fisk. Stretching out prevents injuries.' As if we hadn't heard that a million times before."

"Where are you going with this, Buzz?" Sam asked, slightly frustrated.

"The usual place, Sam—nowhere," Buzz responded. "I have more on my list."

"I just thought of a couple," Donna piped in.

Sam shook his head.

"Well?" Buzz asked Donna.

"Well, people always tell you that the original ingredient in Coca-Cola was cocaine," she began. "Then, they *always* say, for emphasis, 'That's where they got the name from.' As if they just let you in on some kind of secret." Donna's tone was almost miffed.

"That's it!" Buzz practically yelled. "You've got it, Donna! Coke. Excellent example. My favorite is the star one."

"All right, Buzz, I'll bite. What's the 'star one?'" Sam asked, finally hooked, and trying to think of his own example.

"Okay," Buzz started. "You're on a date. Summertime. Romantic. You're walking along the beach with your significant other, hand-in-hand. The sand is like gritty pillows under your toes. The engagement ring sits in a velveteen box in your pocket, waiting. The wind softly whispers off Lake Erie—"

"We get the picture." Sam rolled his eyes.

"Let him tell his story his own way," Donna corrected. "No matter how long-winded and dull it is."

"Ha ha, Donna," Buzz said, false hurt in his voice. He took a sip of coffee and a drag off his cigarette.

"Anyway, it's a romantic situation, you look up at the stars, and say, 'Look, my love, the stars in the sky are so beautiful,' and just as you're about to quote Shakespeare and pull the ring out, she says back, in a kind of know-it-all voice, 'We're not really seeing the stars—'"

Donna cut in to finish for Buzz, "We're seeing the light they're reflecting a million years later because they're light years away!"

They both laughed heartily, then looked at Sam, who wasn't laughing. He was lost in thought. Then his face brightened.

"I've got one!" Sam said excitedly.

"Go for it!" Donna encouraged.

"Okay," Sam began. "When you bring up the topic of computers, somebody always points out that they're getting faster and faster."

Sam's observation was met with unenthusiastic silence for a moment.

"Well, I guess that's true," was all Donna could say. She smiled warmly at Sam.

"Right," Buzz added.

"Okay, so it's not the funniest example," Sam protested. "But I've heard it a hundred times."

"Yeah, as if there's some computer company out there trying to make computers *slower* or something," Donna commented.

"I can just see the meeting in the boardroom," Buzz said. Then, in a lower, faux-businessman's voice, "'If we could just get the boys in R & D to put in that older, outdated chip, we can slow those babies down to a snail's pace!'"

"Okay, not bad, Sam. Not bad. You can't help it if you're not very funny. I love you anyway, man. In fact, your example was touching. Can we hug?"

Sam just rolled his eyes.

"My turn for a story," Donna said.

2

"...don't know how old I was. Three, maybe. It's not a long memory, and doesn't have any chainsaws or blood, but it's the first memory I have.

"I was in church. It must have been a daily Mass because there were only a few old women there, wearing black dresses and veils, 'cause that's the law in Little Italy. We had some Dominican sisters teaching in our parish—at least they were still there when I went to school a few years later.

"Anyway, six or seven nuns were in the second pew, and Mass had begun. Then, a young nun came in and practically ran down the side aisle to join the other sisters.

"I was fascinated by her habit. And her beauty. She was about the most beautiful woman I had ever seen. I still remember her face. She was light-skinned and blond. She looked a little like Princess Di, but more like that old-time actress who also became a princess. Uh, Grace Kelly.

"This was Little Italy. Even the nuns were Italian, with dark skin and dark hair. This beautiful woman looked like she came from another planet.

"She stopped short when she got to my pew, even though I was on the other side of the church. I'm not sure now, but as the memory goes, I was the only one looking at this nun at all. She stopped and looked at me, and smiled. Time kind of stopped. I remember waving back and saying 'Hi.' My mom turned and shushed me.

"The nun turned and went to her pew, more slowly now. She sat in the row behind the other nuns, alone. I stared at her for the rest of the Mass. I even remember that her habit was a different color from the nuns in front of her. They all had white habits. My nun had a blue habit.

"I never saw her again, and don't remember what happened after Mass—if she looked at me or not.

"Maybe she was a postulant, or just a visitor from out of the neighborhood. I guess I'll never know."

Donna was leaning back in her chair, almost slouching. She tapped her index finger on the table, waiting for the reaction. Sam looked down.

"Maybe she was Our Lady," Buzz said.

"Oh, get out of here!" Donna pursed her lips and waved Buzz away. Sam chuckled.

"But this is my apartment," Buzz rejoined.

"So what?" Donna asked.

"Hey," Sam said, looking at the clock over the stove. "It's almost ten. We still have to carry the fridge up seven flights of stairs."

"Carry it up?" Buzz asked, confused.

"Yeah, you said we had to carry it up. It was a real dog getting it on my pick-up."

Donna sat up and stretched out her arms.

"I never said we had to *carry* it up. There's a service elevator in this building. I just worded it so you would think it had to be carried up, so you would be relieved when you got here. You see, I'm very manipulative. But up front about it. Alcoholism. Codependency. Dysfunctional. All that happy stuff. I just need a hug, and I'll be okay."

"I don't think you'll ever be okay, *Gwynne,*" Sam observed.

Buzz frowned. Donna laughed lightly.

"Thank you. More good news: I got the landlord to lend me one of those heavy-duty handtrucks."

"Good news, indeed! Let's get it done," Sam said.

"I need to call my folks. They must be worried," Donna interrupted. "Can I use your phone, Buzz?"

"Be my guest."

"I already am your guest."

"Ha, ha," Sam said.

Donna called her folks. She was twenty-two, free, and a good girl about calling home.

Twenty minutes later, the fridge was in place in Buzz's kitchen.

"Time for a video!" Buzz exclaimed.

"Video?" Sam asked. "You've got to be kidding. I've got to go to work tomorrow."

"But it's Friday night, tomorrow's Saturday," Donna said, confused.

"Our friend Sam is a self-made man," Buzz explained. "A responsible captain of industry. A hard-driving entrepreneur creating much-needed high-tech jobs in a global economy, keeping America on the cutting edge. And he's a workaholic. Saturdays? Sam works on *Sundays*. Obsessive-compulsive. I've seen it before at my AA meetings, Donna. It's not pretty."

"It's late, Buzz. I'm going home," Sam said seriously.

"For your own good, Sam, I think you need to see this movie. It's an important film. It's cinema. A work of art. You need to see it to deal with your dysfunctional codependency workaholism. In fact, I rented this movie with you in mind. As therapy. Think of me as your support group."

Sam couldn't help but smile.

"Okay, Buzz, what movie is it? Is it one of those French flicks with subtitles and incomprehensible plots?"

"Even better. The Terminator—"

"I loved The Terminator!" Donna interrupted.

"Now you can love it all over again, this time on the small screen," Buzz told her.

"I've never seen The Terminator," Sam said. "I've heard it's good—and very gory."

"Actually, it's a love story," Donna said, quite seriously. "But it is violent, and Buzz will have to fast-forward through one racy scene for me. I'm in."

Buzz nodded.

"Okay, Buzz. I'm in. The Terminator," Sam said.

Sam found himself surprised he wanted to stay—because he knew it was more to spend time with Donna and Buzz than to see the movie. *I'll just drag myself out of bed early,* he told himself.

3

They were lounging on the couch. Two-thirds of the movie was over.

"This is the love story part," Donna whispered to Sam. "See, he came across time to rescue her. To be with her. He's suffering for her. Like a knight in shining armor."

"Yes," Sam whispered. "It is a love story."

Buzz didn't take his eyes off the screen. He didn't like it when others talked during movies.

4

In New Jersey, Mark Johnson wasn't watching a movie. He was asleep in the spare bedroom of a friend from the Bureau, dreaming of his wife…

…in the dream, she was holding on to him, her hands around his waist, as their Sea-Doo screamed across the glassy, calm water of Barnegat Bay. So much fun!

There was a small island up ahead. His wife's hold tightened as they came around it. There were buoys up ahead. They were fuzzy in his vision. He tried to focus.

"Don't hit them!" Maggie cried out, trying to outshout the high-pitched engine and the waves, which were now rough and white-capped. "Don't…"

But Mark couldn't make out what she was saying.

The first buoy came. But it wasn't a buoy. It was a little girl, flailing in the water, trying not to drown.

It was his middle daughter, Angela.

He was heading directly toward her. The controls on his Sea-Doo became sluggish, unmoving. He couldn't steer out of the way.

Most people would have woken up out of the dream just before the bow of the jet ski struck the child. But not Mark. He was a tough guy. And in that strange way of dreams, even though he was asleep, a part of Mark was aware of what was going on. He endured the battering as his own dream pummeled him again and again.

When he woke up the next day, he didn't remember the nightmare. He did feel an uneasiness, a sick feeling in the pit of his stomach. He did his push-ups and sit-ups, and lifted his weights. The exercise calmed him. He put on his shoes and his suit, and left for work.

Another day in law enforcement.

5

It was months later.

Buzz was late. Sam found himself seated at a small table in the side room of Mama Santas Pizzeria on Mayfield Road in Little Italy.

He stole a look at Donna as she searched for lip balm in her purse, which looked more like a backpack than a handbag.

No, he thought, *I'm not attracted to her. Too bad. Maybe not too bad, though. If I was attracted to her, maybe I wouldn't be able to hang out with her—I'd be too nervous.*

There wasn't any chemistry. He looked at her and felt no urge, no desire. Just a calm peace.

Better to have a friend than a lover. Why not both? I should ask Buzz when he gets here.

"Whatcha thinkin'?" she asked.

"Uh, nothing, really. Just daydreaming."

"Oh. Did you have a good day at work?"

"Yes," he replied, finally smiling. "Everything went wrong. That's good. That's how it works."

"I don't get it," she said.

"I know. I'm sorry. I'm starting to talk like Buzz. All riddles and mysteries."

"I like riddles and mysteries," she told him, looking up from her menu. "Now, why is everything going wrong at work a good thing?"

"Well, unless they go wrong, you can't fix them. So I fixed things, that was the day's challenge.

"One of our biggest customers called with a huge problem. His server had gone down, and he had been lax about doing his back-ups. He was trying to blame it on us."

"So what did you do?" Donna asked.

"I ignored his trying to blame it on us. That was just his emotions talking. He was bugging out because he was losing a lot of money and time. His information is the most valuable asset he has next to his experience. I tried to calm him down. I sent Johnny Traverse out with a technician, who diagnosed the problem. Johnny took the guy out and bought him a beer. That helped."

"Did you rebuild his computer?" she asked.

"Mostly. We'll have it fixed by tomorrow afternoon. The client is thrilled and relieved, and thinks we're the best supplier he's got. And he's right. We treated him right. We fixed his problem. He's happy to pay us."

"Buzz would call what you did acting charitably," she observed.

The waitress came to take their order. She recognized Donna immediately. They had attended the same grammar school. Sam and Donna ordered a Sam Adams.

"I call it good business practice. It was good for him, and good for me. We were both acting out of self-interest. How come you Catholics always read deeper meanings into ordinary things?"

"What do you mean?"

"Well," he explained. "You see a normal good business practice as somehow confirming the Catholic belief in the Golden Rule, Love thy neighbor as thy self. Why can't it just be what it is: good business practice. Also, you have your medals and those cloth things around your necks—"

"You mean my scapular?"

"Yeah, the scapular. Buzz told me about scapulars. They're supposed to get you into heaven faster or something. To me, they're just pieces of cloth. I'm sorry, I'm not ragging on your religion. As far as I can tell, you and Buzz are the first Catholics I've ever known who practice what you preach. Several of my workers are Catholics, but they don't act like you or Buzz."

"Thank you," was all she could say at first. Then, "We're just normal Catholics, you know, Sam. Just because most Catholics don't practice what they preach doesn't mean that those that do are somehow abnormal."

"Then exceptional is a better word," he responded.

"Fair enough. By the way, the scapular is just a piece of cloth to me, too. My Miraculous Medal is just a piece of metal. It's what they *stand for* that's so meaningful. They stand for Our Lady's love for us. That's real, but we can't see love, so God gives us ordinary things we *can* see to remind us of what we can't see."

"If you can't see it, then how do you know it's really there?" Sam asked sincerely.

"How do you know the wind is there? Have you ever seen wind?" she asked right back.

"Yes, I've seen—" he cut himself off. "Actually, I've never seen wind, just its effects…"

"Well, God's love is grace, and grace is God's wind. I can't see it, but I feel and see its effects."

"Then how come I can't feel grace? I can see the trees moving in the wind." His tone was calm. This was not an unusual conversation since meeting Buzz and Donna.

"I don't know. Maybe you need some leaves to catch the wind," she offered.

The beers came. They ordered a large pizza. Sam took a sip and smiled.

"All very poetic, Donna. But that doesn't apply to me. How am I going to get leaves? It's all so confusing."

"Well, I'm not confused. Maybe I was getting too poetic there. Maybe you need a sail. So you can move toward God. You're like a very efficient sailor doing all sorts of work on a ship lost at sea. Polishing brass. Cooking meals. Steering the rudder here and there, but the wind blows by you because your sails aren't up. You won't get anywhere.

"Buzz is wrong about you. Buzz thinks he can talk you into becoming a Catholic. I doubt he's ever talked anybody into Catholicism. He can talk us into watching videos with him; he can talk us into going where he wants us to go. Remember how he got us to agree to come here after work with just a phone call? He's a charming bully. But talking with you about the faith is like talking with that sailor on the ship lost at sea. Talk talk talk; but the ship goes nowhere. You've got to put up your sails for yourself."

"Nice. But what exactly *is* 'putting up your sails?'" he asked.

"Don't you know by now, Sam Fisk? Buzz is right, you are thick."

"Don't tease me. What is it?"

"It's praying, Sam. You have to pray. Praying is putting up your sails. God doesn't need to hear what you have to say. You need to listen." She rolled her eyes, but only a little.

"I've tried," he told her, "but I don't hear anything."

"I know," she said. She looked him in the eye. "Don't worry about it. Keep trying. It'll come."

"How can you be so sure? How do you know that's what I want or need? I haven't tried very hard. I sat in the easy chair in my apartment a couple of times, and during commercials I told the nothingness, 'Okay, I'm listening. Is anybody out there?' Then I heard nothing, except for really arrogant commercials for those new Infinities."

"Infinities? See the connection? God is infinite. Maybe that was a sign. You know, ordinary things stand for unseen realities."

"God speaking through a commercial on television? Does God come with leather interiors?"

"Yeah, it does sound kind of goofy, Sam."

"So where does that leave me?" he asked politely.

"I'm not sure. I do know that you are the real thing, a good guy, a friend, Sam. And that people always want what they don't have. My older sister told me that."

"What do I want that I don't have?" he asked.

She laughed. "Faith, Sam. Faith."

Sam spotted Buzz coming toward the table.

"To be continued," he said.

"Hey!" Buzz called out. He found his way through the maze of crowded tables and sat down. "Guess what I rented for tonight? A classic. An absolute classic!"

"More Arnold?"

"Even better. Crimes and Misdemeanors. Just out on video. Woody Allen. Normally, I hate the guy, but this one is a winner. And depressing as all get out. True to reality. A wealthy doctor has his mistress killed and falls apart. Guilt. Flashbacks to his long-forgotten Jewish religious upbringing. Sam will love it. Super depressing ending, too. We might want to do a Jonestown afterward. Kamikaze Kool-Aid Coolers."

"I have no idea what you're talking about," Sam informed Buzz.

"And I'm not following you, either, which means that you've finally gone over the edge. This is wonderful. Maybe we'll get some peace and quiet for once," Donna added.

"No way. If I go insane, I'll be the kind of guy who talks and shouts all day long. The kind of guy who drives Nurse

Ratchet right up the wall. That's me, I'll cut her down with my buzzsaw. I'll yack her to death."

"Enough already, Buzz. We ordered for you. You're tardy. No popcorn with your movie tonight," Donna chided.

"I'll be good. I'll shut up. I won't dominate the conversation," Buzz promised happily.

"Yes, of course, Buzz," Sam patronized.

After the not-very-surprising discovery that Mama Santas did not serve Kool-Aid, Buzz ordered a Pepsi. "I'm part of the New Generation," he told the waitress. "I'm not the Real Thing."

Both Donna and the waitress rolled their eyes.

Toward the end of dinner, the waitress came up to Sam, put a Sam Adams on the table, and leaned over to whisper. "Do you see the blonde on the other side of the room? Look, there. See her?"

Sam nodded. Donna spotted the girl next. Her heart sank. The blonde was striking.

"Yes, I see her."

"She says she recognized you from an article about your company in Craines Cleveland Business. Wants to buy you this. Okay?"

Sam blushed. He smiled quickly at the blonde, who was smiling back at him. The image of El Greco's *The Savior of the World* came into his head, then disappeared. *The faint heart never captured the fair maiden,* he thought.

Sam looked down at his shoes, clenched his fists under the table, and forced himself to look up. She was stunning. A Grace Kelly in the middle of Little Italy. *Don't get carried away, Sam.*

"Pretty woman, walking down the street," Buzz sang, quite loudly, in a bad impersonation of Roy Orbison.

The moment broke. Sam turned back to his friends.

"What does she want?" Donna asked tersely.

"Oh, I don't know. I guess she saw that front cover article about me in Craines."

"What article? Front cover?" Buzz asked. "You didn't tell me about any article. I've invested months in being your friend, and you still hide things from me. I'm hurt. Stunned. I need a hug. Can we hug, Sammy?"

"Oh shut up, Buzz," Donna said. "I'm sick of your repetitive sense of humor."

"What's gotten into you, Donna?" Buzz asked. "Sorry."

"Too late," she told him. "Oh, crap. Okay, you're forgiven. I'm just having a bad day. Now shut up."

In fact, Donna was in the middle of her time. Everything was dark. Everything seemed to be rolling toward the edge of a cliff. Just one more thing to make a lousy night lousier.

"Okay." Buzz was truly chastened.

The dinner was oddly silent. Sam actually tried to make small talk to get things going. He couldn't help but steal glances at the blonde. She didn't look back at him. His heart sank with a familiar thud. *Nothing. It was nothing. Just a friendly gesture.*

"So tell me, Buzz," Sam asked. "How was work?"

"I got into a big brown truck, which is called a package car at UPS, and delivered packages all day in the suburban splendor of Parma and select parts of North Royalton. Then, I picked up some packages at prearranged times and places. Then I drove back to the center. I changed my clothes and came here. Would you like to know more?"

"No. But I'm glad I asked. Now I know," Sam observed.

Donna said nothing, and picked at her single slice of pizza.

It was Donna who first saw the blonde walking toward their table, her eyes on Sam Fisk.

6

"I'm Ellen James," she said, holding out her hand. "I read about you in Craines."

She was wearing an elegant black cotton dress. Simple. Timeless. A tasteful gold Miraculous Medal hung around her neck.

Sam sat motionless for a second. Buzz kicked him under the table.

"Uh, I'm Sam Fisk," he finally said, taking her hand in the manner of a gentleman—the way his father had taught him, grasping her four fingers in his upturned palm. He managed a nervous smile. *She's beautiful,* was all he could think.

"And…" she prompted, looking at Buzz and Donna.

"And this is Donna Beck and Buzz Woodward."

"Pleased to meet ya," Buzz offered, taking Ellen's hand in the same manner as Sam.

"Hello," Donna said evenly.

"Hi Donna," Ellen said with a pleasant smile.

A small pause ensued.

"Would you like to join us?" Buzz offered.

"Well," Ellen paused. Donna kicked Buzz under the table. Ellen saw the slight squint in Donna's eyes. "I really couldn't. I'm with my father." She looked back to her table. Sam hadn't noticed the older man at Ellen's table. "He enjoyed reading about your company, too. He wants to meet you."

"Really? How nice," Sam said. *I sound like a doofus. How nice?*

"Yes. His company specializes in insuring high-tech start-ups like yours. But he doesn't want to meet you for business. He's also an entrepreneur."

"I'd like to meet him," Sam found himself saying. He turned to his friends. "Just one drink."

"And the video?" Donna asked.

"The video?" Sam asked.

A confused look came to Ellen's face.

"Crimes and Misdemeanors," Buzz reminded him.

"I'll just be a minute," Sam said.

"Wonderful!" Ellen exclaimed.

Sam looked at his hands, then rose from his seat.

Donna and Buzz both tried, but failed, to avoid noticing that Ellen had a nice, if slim, figure, as she glided back to her table with Sam. Even though Ellen was quite tall—almost six foot—he towered over her by six inches.

"Beachwood," Buzz guessed.

"Naw," Donna opined. "Shaker Heights all the way."

"Too nouveau rich," he countered.

"Betcha a video they live in Shaker," Donna offered.

"You're on." Buzz lifted his Pepsi.

"What just happened?" Donna asked.

"Dunno."

"Yes you do. You know all about her. You're doing that guessing thing in your head right now. Tell me about Ellen James."

"Smart as a whip," Buzz began after a thoughtful pause. "Humanities degree from a college like Saint Marys across the street from Notre Dame. American Studies. Drives a Jap car with all the options—Nissan. The kind of car that looks like a sports car but really isn't. Knows what money means and what money does. Goes to Mass every Sunday with her folks. Lives at home because it's so wonderful, even though she can afford an apartment. Works for a company owned by one of her daddy's best buds. Can't guess her occupation. And despite what you think, she's a nice girl. See that Miraculous Medal? Her mom prays. Gave it to her, I bet."

"It's just a piece of jewelry."

"That's not like you, Donna. Look, I know you like Sam more than as a friend."

"Do not." She spoke unconvincingly. She grabbed Buzz's pack of Marlboro Lights and took one out, but didn't light up. Buzz fumbled for his Zippo and lit it for her. "And so what if I do?"

"Keep praying. You waited too long. I should have told you to pounce weeks ago."

"How can you possibly know any of this?" she asked, sounding genuinely saddened.

"I just know," he put a big arm around her. "You know what sucks most, Donna?"

"What sucks the most?"

"It's gonna take a lot of my energy to keep Sam around if Ellen really likes him. I hate girlfriends when they're girlfriends to one of my friends. Did I ever tell you about how my marriage broke up?"

"No, you never talk about it. But I don't want to hear it right now," she snapped, out of character. "I know what you're doing. You're trying to distract me. I can see right through you. Thanks, but no thanks."

She took a long drag while squinting at *their* table.

"Look at him. He's relaxing. It took him two months to relax with me. You'd think that a guy like Sam would be wigging out before so much beauty and wonderfulness. She actually said *wonderful* in front of us! What nerve."

"You forget that Sam comes from academia. He breathes fondue and wine and cheese and the America's Cup. He just never talks about stuff like that with peasants like us." Bitterness had crept into Buzz's voice, too. But he stopped himself. "And maybe he's relaxing because of grace…"

"Look! They're laughing," Donna said.

"Why don't we go to my place now; watch the video. I'll be a perfect gentleman."

"Grace?" Donna asked, ignoring the video offer. "What do you mean, grace?"

"Maybe they're meant for each other, Donna. Maybe she's his ticket to the sacraments. Sam's just the kind of guy to convert for the sake of a woman. He's so thoughtful."

"Yeah, I know he is. He's a prince. It's just that…" She tried to casually wipe the bit of tear from her eye.

"Donna, don't think about Sam. There's somebody out there for you. Maybe my guesses are all wrong. Maybe he'll never see Ellen James after tonight and we'll get our friend back. Listen to me; I'm talking about him like he's dead. Nothing's happened yet. By the way, did you know that I pray for you to find somebody every night."

"You do?"

"Every night, little girl," he said tenderly.

"I'm not a little girl. I'm a fireplug. A brick you-know-what."

"You're my little one," he insisted.

"Have it your way, Buzz. Maybe *we* should date. Get married. Have kids that are wider than they are tall."

"Us? Date? I never thought of it."

"You're a lousy liar," she informed him ruthlessly. "You did consider it. That time in the park. You rejected me in a heartbeat."

"You wouldn't have gone out with me, admit it," he told her. "Besides, we can't date. It would ruin a good friendship—"

"That's beside the point. You're right—I wouldn't go out with you. But you wouldn't go out with me even if I would date you. Why not?"

Buzz, who was usually quite direct, looked away from his friend. "It's not you, Donna. I'm messed up. You know that. It took me two years to fill out my annulment papers. I only heard last year—it went through; I'm free to marry. But right now, romance would bring up a lot of crud from the bottom of the cesspool."

"Nice image," she said.

"Apropos. I joke about being a drunk, but I'm not ready for women. Maybe never. My daughter doesn't even talk to me anymore. I only see her twice a year since her mother moved to Florida."

"Sandi still sends your letters back?"

"Every time. Every time. It's not right," a dark line came onto his forehead as he spoke. "Let's change the subject."

"And talk about Sam—oh, here he comes," she said as she fussed with the shoulders on her shirt.

I'm acting like a schoolgirl.

"Hey guys," Sam said.

"No video?" Buzz guessed, looking past Sam. Mr. James and Miss James were watching. Mr. James smiled and nodded. Buzz resisted an urge to wink.

"Sorry—"

"No need to be sorry—" Donna spoke quickly.

"It's just that Mr. James and I really hit it off. It's like we're brothers. Strange, huh. Anyway, he's invited me for a drink with Ellen…"

"Knock yourself out, Sam," Buzz said royally. "I'll drive Donna home. Have fun."

"I'll try." He looked at Donna. "Mind?" he asked, referring to missing the video.

"Mind what? *Her?* She seems wonderful," she answered, squinting with a small smile. "Buzz and I are fine. Like the man says, knock yourself out. If James is buying, get expensive drinks. Have one for me."

"And have a Pepsi for me, buddy," Buzz added.

"Sure thing." Sam turned.

"Sam! Wait!" Donna called.

"What is it?"

"Beachwood or Shaker Heights?" she asked, leaning back in her seat, looking over to Buzz.

"Huh?"

"Where does she live," Buzz explained. "Which town?"

"Oh," he said, looking down at his shoes. "Beachwood. Why?"

"Nothing," Donna said. *Rats.*

"Good-bye then," Sam said, turning finally, and walking back to the James's table.

"Bye," Donna said softly, but Sam didn't hear her.

PART TWO

The Small Cross

Bed's too big without you.
The Police

Are you strong enough to be my man?
Sheryl Crow

Come with me if you want to live.
*Kyle to Sarah in **The Terminator***

He won't let the pain blot out the humor.
No more'n he'll let the humor blot out the pain.
*Ken Kesey, **One Flew Over the Cuckoo's Nest***

Now is not the time for talk.
Now is the time for action.
Nathan Payne

Well I hate TV; I want to find somebody other than me,
who's ready to ride off immediately, I'm looking for a cynical girl.
Marshall Crenshaw

You see George, you really had a wonderful life.
*Clarence to George Bailey in **It's a Wonderful Life***

And would you cry if I told you that I lied,
and would you say good-bye,
or would you let it ride?
Bachman-Turner Overdrive

Chapter Four

1

That evening, as they drove home without Sam in Buzz's Festiva, Donna remembered the brief romantic interlude she had shared with Buzz two weeks earlier in the park. A freezing Friday night.

Sam was out of town on business with his biggest customer. Most of Sam's clients were in Northeast Ohio, but he had picked up a large bank in River Forest, Illinois. A company he knew from his IBM days.

Buzz and Donna had gone to Mass at Our Lady of the Angels, gone dutch on dinner at Joe's Deli on Hilliard (the best corned beef in Cleveland), and rented a video from Blockbuster. It was an established pattern of spending time together, and a comfortable one for cold weather.

They watched a classic: *To Catch a Thief,* with Cary Grant and Grace Kelly. It was one of Donna's favorites—she had seen it several times. It was new for Buzz. Afterwards, they decided to take a walk in Clague Park. So they bundled up and drove over. It was past midnight, and the park was empty and dark. The moon managed to send some light through the perpetual clouds of Cleveland.

"Let's run!" Buzz shouted, then took off. Donna shook her head at the big man running full speed across the large field. She followed him. It felt good to run. She missed the sports she played in high school, and was soon huffing and puffing as she caught up to him. He had fallen onto his back, looking up at the sky.

She joined him. There was cold, old snow beneath them.

"See those clouds," Buzz began. "We're not really seeing them. We're seeing the light they're reflecting several seconds after the light leaves them. They're what, four thousand feet away?"

Donna laughed an easy laugh.

"Why are you laughing? That's really far away."

"Cut it out," she told him, continuing to laugh.

"Cut what out?"

A few moments passed.

"Was that the most romantic movie kiss ever or what?" Buzz began.

"You mean when Grace Kelly pulled Cary Grant to her at the door of the hotel room?" she asked.

"You got it. Best movie kiss ever."

"Tied with the kiss Dustin Hoffman gave Katherine Ross in The Graduate. Great movie kiss," she opined.

"What scene was that?"

"When he took her out to all the awful places to please his folks against Anne Bancroft's wishes. Ross got all sad, and he kissed her in the street to say he was sorry," she explained expertly.

"Oh yeah, great movie kiss. But I like Grace and Cary's better. More realistic."

"Nothing about the movies is realistic," Donna complained.

"Rocky was realistic," Buzz joked dryly.

"And don't forget Bambi," she added.

They laughed in their heads. It was way too cold.

Buzz turned on his side, and propped himself up on an elbow. The snow was too frozen to be wet. Their faces were only a foot apart.

"Donna?"

"Yeah?"

"Nothing," he said softly.

"You never have nothing to say, Buzz Woodward."

"Well, I was just thinking about something I heard in the readings today."

Her look told him to continue.

"Usually, Saint Paul goes right over my head. I don't know why. He's always giving advice, I guess, and I'm pigheaded. But today it was like he was talking directly to me through the reading. The phrase 'putting on Christ' struck me. What does that mean?"

"I guess it means," she started, taking a stab, "doing God's will and not your own."

"I guess you're right. But what I mean is, what does God's will mean? Do people see Jesus when they see me? I don't think so. They see Buzz Woodward."

"I see Christ in you, Buzz. I hear His voice every time you come up with one of your Buzz Woodward Original Proofs of God's Existence for Sam. That's your way."

Buzz didn't say anything for a while.

"But Donna, I don't really pray. I go to Mass. I say morning prayers and night prayers, and a Rosary, but mostly I'm distracted."

"Who isn't?"

"Saints. Saints are *communicating*," he explained awkwardly, looking closely at her. "Like we're doing right now. What would it be like to be this close to Jesus or Mary, or for that matter, Saint Paul, and really be talking with them? Really communicating. That never happens when I pray."

"I feel close to God when I pray," she said with muted excitement. "Especially in front of the Blessed Sacrament. But it's not like this. Not like this with you and me. It's in my heart. It's a warmth. Like the furnace in the basement. Touch it and you get burned, but it's nice and warm in the living room."

"I never feel warmth," Buzz replied sadly. "I believe in my head. I really do believe. I *belong* to the Catholic Church, lock, stock, and barrel. But my heart must be dead. I must have killed it. Cut it down like I cut everything down in my life. My wife. My daughter."

He began to cry. He wasn't a tough guy tonight. He turned his head.

She was confused. Her heart went out to him. She put her gloved hand on his cheek.

"Oh, Buzz," was all she could say.

Then she found herself bringing her lips to his, not thinking about it, really. Her boldness surprised her.

He kissed back warmly for a second, then another. Then he stopped, and fell back to facing the clouds.

"Well," he said.

"I know, I screwed up, Buzz. Sorry. I don't know what came over me."

She really didn't know what had come over her.

"Don't be sorry, Donna. I like you. But not that way."

You're lying, she thought. Donna always trusted her instincts. She knew Buzz was lying. In that odd way, in the middle of that heavenly friction that exists between men and women, and not between women and women, or men and men, she forgave and forgot his lie. *Buzz must have good reasons.*

It was grace. Grace came.

"Amazing grace," Buzz sang softly, in a very deep voice, crying again, his voice cracking. "How sweet the sound, that saved a wretch like me—"

"—I once was lost, but now I'm found—" she sang. She had a lovely voice.

"—was blind, but now I see," they finished together, lingering on the last word.

Buzz took off his gloves and fished a smoke out of his softpack, then lit up.

"I can't believe you're smoking after our movie kiss," she said. The romance of the moment was gone.

"Strictly a nic fit," he explained. "I'm not even enjoying it. My fingers are already numb."

"Why don't you just quit?"

"It's not so easy. My AA meetings are so smoky you can cut it with a knife. Besides, I don't want to live forever. Earth sucks. Heaven is great. Plus, emphysema is great reparation at the end of a sinful but saved life."

"Buzz, Buzz, Buzz. You're so full of it."

"You have an occasional smoke yourself," he replied.

"Very weak comeback. I've had seven cigarettes this year."

"I hate smoking conversations."

"Me too. Let's drop it."

They got up and walked back to his car, snow crunching under their boots. Donna prayed a prayer from the Divine Mercy Chaplet to herself: *For the sake of His sorrowful passion, have mercy on us and on the whole world.* She didn't know why she was praying. Grace knew, but she didn't.

Instead of saying good-bye, he said, "Someday, Donna, let's go to Fatima and Lourdes. We'll get Sam to go."

"Sure, I'd love that. How we gonna pay for it?"

"Pray to Saint Anthony. He'll find us the money. Besides, we'll get Sam to spring for it. He's loaded already."

"You're a piece of work, Buzz," she said with a certain admiration, shaking her head.

"That I am."

It was their last moment together without Sam until Ellen James showed up.

✝ ✝ ✝

Buzz dropped Donna off after watching the Woody Allen movie. He briefly wondered how Sam was getting along with Ellen. He had an intuition that they would be engaged within the year. Buzz had a gift for knowing such things.

Good for Sam, he thought.

He wasn't tired, and it wasn't even midnight. He rarely watched television, except for ESPN. There were no novels to read. His shelf was filled with over a hundred, but he had read all of them.

He tried to read *The Conservative Chronicle,* but apart from Joseph Sobran's columns, he became bored.

He tried praying, but was distracted.

He sat down to write a letter, but the page remained blank. No one to write to.

Donna's kiss from two weeks earlier came to his mind, but he drove it from his imagination.

Don't go there, cowboy. Only trouble there. Think of something else. He knew that lingering on the kiss might lead to other images which would endanger his soul.

He paced, looking around his small living room. He barely noticed his Salvation Army couch. There were no knick-knacks, besides a few model cars he had glued together in high school, sloppily painted. And three bookshelves, full, but with no order to the titles. There was only one signal that he had gone to Notre Dame: leather coasters he found at a garage sale during college stamped with the school's logo, stacked on a small butcher block bench that served as an end table.

He sat in his cherished green leather chair, looking at the image of Our Lady, an old print from Saint Anthony's Guild he found in the trash during one of his UPS stops. It was the only image that came close to his high standards for religious art.

He closed his eyes and tried to picture Mary in his mind's eye. He couldn't. A fuzzy cloud. He saw her feet. Not her feet, really, but the bottom of her gown. There was a snake there.

It frustrated him.

He tried to picture Jesus' face, but couldn't.

For the ten thousandth time since going on the wagon, he resisted an urge to have a drink.

Death through that door, he thought, terrified.

He stood and paced again.

Donna.

No!

He put on his only Gregorian Chant CD and sat back down in his chair.

He grabbed the Bible, said a prayer to the Holy Spirit and opened it.

The words of Jesus: *"No one who puts his hand to the plow and looks back is fit for service in the kingdom of God."*

Yeah, he thought.

How can I serve you, Jesus? Where's my plow? Give me one and I'll put my hand to it.

He closed the Bible.

He went to his fridge and got a Pepsi. *This will help you sleep,* he thought sardonically. He took one sip, and threw the can away.

He went to his bedroom, undressed, and climbed into bed.

Using an old trick, he kept his eyes open, staring at the ceiling, and tried to sleep. Distracted, he looked at the clock.

Now it's Saturday.

He thought of Donna again, but in a generic way, not the image of her face inches away.

Dear Jesus, help her find a husband. Why did you put this new girl between her and Sam?

The Lourdes Shrine in Euclid popped into his head. He decided to go in the morning. He decided to make sure Sam and Donna went.

Sam's not home yet. Betcha dollars to donuts.

He carefully reached for the phone, but knocked into the old cup of water on the night stand, spilling it. It didn't phase him. *It's only water.*

He speed-dialed Sam's number, got the answering machine, and told Sam that he would stop by at ten to "take you to a great place. A classic place," purposely not mentioning the Lourdes Shrine. He didn't worry about calling Donna. He knew she would go.

Grace had finally cut its way through Buzz for the day.

He set the handset down, flipped onto his stomach, turned his head on the pillow, and thought of the Blessed Mother.

For the first time in months, he saw her face in his mind's eye. She smiled.

Well done, he imagined her telling him. *I know it's hard for you, but you must be patient.*

2

"Here's to success!" Bucky James raised his Whiskey Sour to Sam and Ellen.

"Cheers," Sam said, feeling a bit of a buzz.

They sat at a table at the posh Garden Club in Beachwood.

"Sam, would you like to see our home?" Bucky asked directly.

"It's getting late, Daddy," Ellen said, smiling. "Sam might have to get going."

She casually took hold of his arm.

"I'd love to see your home. I've got no plans for tomorrow," Sam volunteered.

Actually, he was mentally dreading dragging himself out of bed. *Seven years,* he told himself. He had promised himself that he would work Saturdays for seven years to build his business.

"Then let's go," Bucky said. "You can follow along in your car, Sam." Bucky reached for his wallet.

"This round is on me, Mr. James," Sam offered.

"Call me Bucky, Sam."

Sam placed a twenty on the table.

"Why don't I ride along with Sam, Daddy? That way he doesn't have to follow you."

Sam could hardly take his mind off Ellen's hand on his arm. It was all so dreamlike. *This is not happening.*

She had to let go of his arm when he helped her put her coat on. She put on her scarf, and took his arm again, and held it all the way out to the car.

✦ ✦ ✦

"Nice car," she said, reclining in the leather seats of Sam's Accord. He had special-ordered the leather. She noticed that he kept it perfectly clean. There were no empty cans or papers on the floor. Just like Bucky's car.

"Thanks, I just got it six months ago," was all he could say. His nervousness was back—big time.

She waved as her father drove by. Sam started the car and let the engine idle. The parking lot was now empty. A light shone on the other side of the lot, near the club entrance.

"You know, when I asked you to our table, it was only to please my father. He really wanted to meet you," she told him. Sam's heart sank. "But I have a feeling about you, Sam."

Before he could ask her what she was talking about, she put a warm hand behind his neck, and pulled him to herself, and gave him a lingering kiss on the lips. She stopped, and let out a breath which he could see; the heater had not warmed the car up yet.

He was shaking with excitement and nerves.

"Ellen, I—"

"Don't say anything," she said, and kissed him again, for about the same duration. The air around them was crisp, cold; her lips were pliant, warm.

"Why, you're shaking," she said after she stopped, alarmed, looking directly into his eyes. "Are you cold?"

"No, not cold," he told her honestly. "I've never kissed a girl like you before. Never like that. I'm nervous."

I can tell, she thought, charmed by his innocence. *What have I found here?*

The concept of marriage came to her mind now.

Is he the one?

She was surprised, and a bit afraid. This evening had begun with a heavy ordinariness; it had taken an unexpected turn.

Don't scare him away. When was the last time you liked a guy who was taller than you?

He wasn't handsome. But he reminded her of Bucky. Yes, he *felt* like Bucky, but with a twist—there was a quality in Sam that her father lacked.

Selflessness? She had had enough of selfish men. Sam was different from the prep boys and college sharpshooters and the go-go lawyers at the nightclubs down in the Flats. Or so she thought.

"Drive me home, Sam. I really do wish to show you where I live. I hope I wasn't too forward. I never kiss on the first date. Or the second or third, for that matter. You're the first."

She must be a serious Catholic, he thought.

It keeps me in the driver's seat, she thought.

"As my friend Buzz might say, Ellen, neither do I," he replied, surprising himself with his glibness.

"You can call me Ellie," she told him.

Later, she showed Sam her father's beautiful, expansive home on one of the long boulevards of Beachwood. Buzz had guessed correctly about her living at home, but for the wrong reasons. Bucky was all Ellie had, and Ellie held on tight. She had no mother. Divorced and gone.

After a quick nightcap with Bucky, Sam and Ellie paused on the front porch. She kissed him again, this time on the cheek.

On the drive home, Sam was driving too fast. He didn't care. He lucked out, and avoided the speed traps. He remembered the kiss on his cheek, and rubbed his fingers over the spot, smiling to himself. He tuned the radio to an alternative rock station, and turned the volume up. It was a haunting tune, *Under the Milky Way,* by a group called The Church.

He replayed the events of the evening over and over in his mind. It was a dream. Beautiful woman, chance meeting. Great dad.

The only sour note came when the words of Donna Beck swam into his dreaminess. *Who do you thank, Sam?*

3

Donna cried herself to sleep that night.

4

"Sure, Buzz, I'll wind up early today. I'm dragging after last night," Sam told his surprised friend over the phone. He looked at the neat but large stack of work in the in-box and shook his head. The list of action steps on his computer screen was even bigger. "I want to tell you about Ellie. She's something."

"Great," Buzz said. "I want to hear all about her."

"Where are we going, anyway? Why won't you tell me?"

"Because you might not go otherwise. Remember, I'm a highly manipulative person, Sam. But I'm up front about it. A Machiavelli you can hug."

"I appreciate that. But there's another way. You could trust me. Or treat me like an adult."

"That's a novel concept. I'll give it some consideration. Did you read that in a self-help book?"

"Yeah," Sam replied. "It's a book called Hug Me, by Dr. Gwynne Woodward."

"I'll have to read it. Pick you up in a half hour."

5

Sam pulled open the door to Buzz's car and asked, "Where's Donna?"

"She had to go to some family-thing. She's taking the bus later," Buzz replied. He saw Sam make a face.

"That girl needs a car."

"You know, Sam, not everybody can afford one. Besides, Donna's from a non-car culture—the big city."

Sam frowned. *She still needs a car.*

Buzz pulled out of the parking lot of the building where Sam's office was located and lit a cigarette. Sam rolled his window down.

"So, where are we going, Buzz—or should I put a blindfold on?"

"You'll see when we get there. Tell me what happened with you and Ellen."

Out of the corner of his eye, Buzz noted a rare smile come to Sam's face. *Too bad for Donna,* Buzz thought.

"She's great, man," Sam started.

"Very descriptive."

"She likes me," he continued.

"Better…"

"Mostly, I talked with her dad. They're members at the Garden Club…"

"Very nice." Buzz whistled in admiration as he took the entrance onto I-90.

"What should I do next? Do you have any experience with women?"

"Mostly bad experiences, Sammy. But experience? Yes. The best advice I can give you for women is to assume that they won't feel or react or think like a man does."

"Huh?"

"Look Sam, I read this article in Reader's Digest once, and it made a lot of sense. I was in high school, and was going on my fifth girlfriend. The article confirmed everything I ever knew about women. It's like playing pick-up basketball—there's all sorts of unwritten rules, and if you follow them, you get to play the game.

"Anyway, the article was by this love doctor, and it was about how long it takes men and women to fall in love. Did you know that women fall in love after an average of fourteen meetings and men fall in love after an average of four?"

"No. Makes sense, though."

"Sure does," Buzz continued. "Women have different internal clocks and thermostats, that's what I think. They think it's cold when we think it's warm. My wife used to turn the temperature up all the time on me; drove me crazy. Their clocks are even more off kilter—"

"Clocks?" Sam asked. Talking about women was like discussing creatures from another planet. "What clocks?"

"Women have their own internal clocks, and the hands are set on emotions, not thoughts. Pay attention to the emotional time, and you get to play the game."

"Is this leading to another proof of God's existence?" Sam asked, curious and kidding.

"No. Listen to me, do you like Ellen? Do you want to see her again? Have you given any thought to when you're going to call her up—"

"One question at a time, Buzz...but, yes, I like her. Yes, I want to see her again—though we didn't make any plans; and no, I haven't thought about when I'm going to call her up. I just got up and went to work. I was walking on air, until you started talking."

"You're going to mess up, then, Sam."

"I am?"

"Look, if Ellen's a normal woman, she's sitting at home and enjoying *how she feels* right now. She's treasuring last night 'in her heart,' like Mary did when she found Jesus in the temple as a boy. She's looking forward to your phone call. If you call her too quickly, you'll ruin her enjoyment, and ruin her anticipation of hearing from you again. If you wait too long, her good feelings will turn bad, to anger. She'll start resenting that you haven't called her. Calling her late will confirm her resentment. Mark my words."

"I'm completely baffled. So when *should* I call her?"

"In about two or three days." Buzz squinted, looking up as if there was a chart on the sun shade of his Festiva. "Monday or Tuesday. Wednesday or Thursday is too late. Today and tomorrow is definitely too early."

"It sounds so mechanical, Buzz. Isn't this the eighties? Don't women call men up?"

"Have you been reading Cosmo again? All that 'eighties woman' stuff is a bunch of crapola. Pure manure. Emotional clock stuff is genetic. Goes back before recorded history, and getting the right to vote and equal pay for equal work has nothing to do with it. It's the way they're wired. Men and women are like two different operating systems in computers. Women are Macs, men are DOS."

"Not very complimentary to men, even if most of my work involves IBM clones..."

"But it fits," Buzz said. "Think women, think emotions. Think men, think heartless jerks. And send flowers."

"I like flowers."

"Sure you do, Sam. You're a sensitive guy. But when somebody gives you a rose, you chop the bottom off and stick it in a vase. When a woman gets a rose, she smells it, and looks at it, and feels a bunch of emotions that we can only describe, as men, in a theoretical way."

Sam pondered Buzz's words.

"How do you know all this stuff?" he finally asked Buzz.

"Because I pay attention. I watch people. I study human nature. Maybe it's the way God made me. More likely, it's a coping mechanism. I study people so I can control them. So nobody can hurt me. Being a drunk son of a drunk and all that pyschobabble stuff.

"And because I love women. Name something more beautiful than a beautiful woman? Compare Ellen to the finest piece of art you know. Which is more beautiful?"

Sam paused. "Ellic."

"No mountain landscape is more beautiful than a beautiful woman. You can't say that about men. Oh. Here's your proof of God's existence! Ready?"

"Lay it on me," Sam said affably. He was getting used to Buzz after all these months.

"Did a slimy bunch of amino acids *evolve* into an Ellen James, or was she *designed* by someone, namely, God?"

"Slime."

"You've got to be kidding me."

"I am. I don't know where Ellie came from, except from Bucky and his ex-wife."

"So it's *Bucky,* now, is it?" Buzz asked. "And he's divorced?"

"Yes, and yes."

"And no comment, Sam?"

"What's there to say? Lots of people are divorced. You're divorced." There wasn't any accusation in Sam's voice. He was only stating a fact.

"It will mean a lot if you ever get serious with Ellie. Divorced children fear commitment," Buzz said with a remote sadness in his voice.

"Now you're the one who sounds like he was reading Cosmo," Sam joked.

"Just take her slowly, my friend. Show her she can rely on you, and don't assume she trusts you. She may think she does, but trust is more emotional than logical."

"How do I do that? How do I build trust?"

"Wait," Buzz said quickly, "one second. Look over there. That's where they're going to build the new baseball stadium for the Indians."

"I heard about that on the Internet," Sam added.

"The Internet?"

"Yeah, the Internet. It's a computer network that's been around since the sixties. It's going to be a big deal in a few years. I got an electronic message from one of my clients who's involved with an engineering company that's working on the new stadium."

Buzz slowed as he negotiated Dead Man's Curve, then suddenly remembered Sam's question.

"You can build trust by being yourself, Sam. You always do what you say you're going to do. You're always honest."

Sam had nothing to say to that. *How am I going to put off calling Ellie for two whole days?*

"You're thinking about how you're going to survive without calling Ellen James, aren't you?"

"Are you a mind reader?" Sam asked.

"Just a student of human nature. Besides, I can read your face like a book. Think of hunters, Sam. Hunters sitting in the woods, waiting for the right moment. Hunters play by the rules of the prey. They wait. They picture what they're going to do when the prey shows up."

"Listen to you, Buzz. When do I shoot Ellie?"

Buzz chuckled, then shook his head.

"Me Sam. Big wampum hunter," Sam said with a deep voice. "Me grab Ellie by hair. Take to teepee. Buck-ee give Sam many cattles. Sam not like golf with Buck-ee."

"You know, Sam, your sense of humor is getting better."

"It's a coping mechanism for hanging out with you," Sam replied.

"See, that proves it. Soon, you'll actually *be* funny, as opposed to *almost* being funny."

"How come you always get in the last word, Buzz?"

"It's the way the world is. Accept it, Grasshopper, and you will be truly at peace."

Sam gave up and gave in.

"So what should I say when I call her up?" he asked Buzz after a minute.

"Not much. The shorter the better. Keep it simple. Ask her out for coffee, or a drink. Get a commitment. Then the whole thing starts over again, as she emotionally looks forward to whatever it is. After the date is set, start firing flower salvos. Again: keep it simple. A rose. A simple arrangement. Send it to where she works so she can talk with the other chicks in the office about you."

"Wow."

"Yes, wow. Think wow, Sam. Women are wow. Drop the *w* and wow becomes woe."

"Huh?"

"Forget it. It's a bad pun, or word play, or whatever. Ah, here's our exit. We'll be at the Lourdes Shrine in a few minutes."

"Huh?"

"Hey, McFly? I'm talking to you. You need to expand your vocabulary. 'Huh' is limiting. It alienates me. I don't feel like hugging you. Expand your grunts, Tarzan. Use more than one word per sentence—"

"Why so nasty, Buzz?"

"I'm nervous, that's all. The Lourdes Shrine is just that: a religious shrine. It's not big, but it's beautiful and peaceful."

"So why would you think I wouldn't want to go there?"

"Dunno. Maybe because you don't believe in God. Just guessing…"

"You're right. I would have stayed at work if you told me. But now that we're here…besides, your advice for Ellie seems pretty sound. Thanks. I really like her."

"Maybe you could pray for her here," Buzz suggested, purposely testing and pushing, as was his nature.

"You know I don't pray. But I'll look around. You can pray for me, if you want."

Buzz just nodded at his friend. *I sure will, Sammy. Better luck next time.*

Buzz parked. They walked into the little shrine. Sam was impressed by the grounds, which were simply immaculate. There was a reproduction of the grotto at Lourdes, France, where Mary appeared to Saint Bernadette in 1858. Buzz knelt and began to pray. Sam sat on a bench behind him.

Dear Jesus, Buzz prayed. *Grant my friend the gift of faith. And give me a plow to put my hand to.*

Then he got up, sat next to Sam, and pulled out his rosary beads. They were simple; made out of wood. Buzz prayed silently. He didn't want to make Sam nervous, or appear to pressure him to pray along.

Ten minutes later, Donna walked up and knelt at the grotto in front of them for several minutes. She turned and smiled at her friends, then sat down next to them. There was a bead of sweat on her forehead—Sam guessed it was from the walk up the hill from the bus stop.

It was sunny and cold, but not windy. There were only a few other pilgrims at the shrine, and they were at the stations of the cross. Sam and his friends were alone at the grotto.

Sam, responding to grace he did not believe in or feel, found himself fumbling for his keys. He worked the key for his old pick-up truck off the ring. *I don't need two cars,* he thought.

He took Donna's hand, and placed the key into her palm, and closed his hands around her hand.

"What's this?" she whispered.

"Keys to my pick-up," he informed her in a hushed voice. "I'm giving it to you."

She let out a breath, shook her head, and smiled. "I can't take it."

"You need wheels. I have my Accord."

Buzz, who had been praying with his eyes closed, opened them and whispered to Donna, "Take the keys. And why are we whispering? There's nobody here."

Donna closed her eyes. She had been praying for a sign regarding Sam minutes before. Now he was giving her his pick-up truck! *What does this sign mean?* she asked Mary.

There was no answer.

She thought of his pick-up. It was old and rusty, but mechanically sound. She decided she wanted it.

If I can't have him, at least I could have his truck. It had a certain—feminine—kind of logic.

"Thanks, Sam." She gave him an awkward hug.

"You're welcome. No more busses."

"No more busses," she repeated, looking at the statue of Mary in the grotto.

"No more busses!" Buzz shouted.

"You're weird, Buzz," Donna said.

"Thank you," he whispered, completing the doxology. "Now shush!"

Afterwards, Buzz and Donna made a visit to the Blessed Sacrament in the church next to the grotto. Sam waited in the back of the church.

Donna leaned over to Buzz, and said, "Well?"

"They had a great time last night. Sorry, Donna."

She closed her eyes and began to pray, stifling tears. When she opened them, she saw a beautiful young nun at the altar, preparing it for Mass. The nun smiled.

They rose to their feet and walked to the back of the church. Buzz told Sam they wanted to stay for Mass. Sam agreed to sit in.

Yeah! Buzz thought. *I got him to Mass!*

Mass was nicely paced—daily Mass usually is—and over in less than twenty-five minutes. Sam rose and sat and knelt following the examples of his friends. He was silent for the responses and opening and closing songs. Buzz and Donna consciously tried to avoid looking at him. Sam fidgeted with his fingers and the buttons on his winter coat.

All three went to the cafeteria for lunch.

"So?" Buzz asked, lifting a tuna sandwich.

"How was Mass, you mean?" Sam asked.

Buzz nodded.

"It was moving. I've decided to become a Catholic."

Donna gasped.

"You're kidding, right?" Buzz asked.

"Yes," Sam replied, smiling.

Donna hit him on the arm. "Don't joke about stuff like that!"

She got up and left the table. Sam was open-mouthed.

"What's got into her?" Sam asked Buzz.

"You don't want to know."

✝ ✝ ✝

Donna walked to the gift shop behind the church. When she walked in, she saw the pretty nun again, who noticed the dark frown on her face.

"Having a bad day?" Sister Elizabeth asked.

"Dismal." Donna was looking at her boots.

"Oh. Shopping helps. I used to shop when I was having a bad day in my former life. Can I interest you in something? We're not the Eastgate Mall, but we have a fine selection of rosary beads."

Donna looked up, stifling a smile. Sister Elizabeth was young. In her thirties. *Everywhere I look, pretty girls.*

But there was kindness in Sister's eyes.

"Unfortunately, shopping only made me feel better for a few hours. I'm Sister Elizabeth. I live here and run the shop."

She held out her hand.

"I'm Donna. I live on the West Side."

There was an awkward silence. Unknown to each other, they both prayed a silent Hail Mary.

Sister Elizabeth took a deep breath. "Look, Donna, it's really slow today. I'm going to close up for a bit. Do you want to come to the back room and have a cup of tea with me?"

Donna nodded.

✝ ✝ ✝

Sam had Buzz drop him off at Edwards & Associates after the visit to the Lourdes Shrine. He worked until midnight. Seven years.

6

The next day, Ellen James opened the front door and saw a delivery man holding one white rose.

"Dear Ellie, Thanks for the wonderful evening. Yours, Sam."

Words did not come to her mind. The emotions from her first night with him swelled gently in her heart. She remembered their kiss, and wondered if she had been too bold.

Then she held the rose up and smelled it. Nature's perfume was her answer. *No, not too bold.*

Just bold enough.

Sam's game had reached the second inning.

7

Sam never told her that the color of the rose had been Buzz's idea.

"Mystery," Buzz had advised over the phone while Sam was still at the office, "is as important to romance as it is to religion. It's what makes it exciting."

"Mystery, eh?" Sam had asked, curious.

"In the Garden of Eden, the serpent offered Adam and Eve the fruit from the Tree of Knowledge, knowing that it would kill the mystery. Take the joy out of it. Science is interesting, and necessary, but it's not joyful."

"Isn't that anti-intellectual?" Sam countered.

"Not at all. I'm not against knowing things, Sam. I'm against the idea that you can know everything. Send a white rose. She'll wonder what it means, and enjoy the wondering. A red rose is too bold. It means love. Too early. She needs thirteen more 'contacts' with you. A contact can be a phone call, a date, a letter."

"You go from mystery to counting contacts…"

Buzz had no response to that. He was remembering his first date with Sandi, his ex-wife.

Chapter Five

1

Buzz's first flower to his ex-wife had also been a rose—a red rose.

A tattoo.

Seven years earlier, he had met Sandi at a bar in the Flats. He had been working as a salesman at the time—selling pre-fabricated chimneys to building contractors during the early eighties building boom, fresh out of Notre Dame. It had been months since he had a steady girlfriend; his father had been in the final stages of cirrhosis of the liver, and that had thrown Buzz into a funk. He had long since abandoned the already spotty practice of his faith.

He had been with a few other salesmen from work, and she had been with some of her Cleveland friends. They had all gotten together, drank like fish, and danced to the pound-ing New Wave music of the Talking Heads, the Eurythmics, and the Cars. The dancing had convinced Buzz that Sandi Hackett was special. She had a manic energy, and a serious way of looking into his eyes as she whirled and juked. She made out with him right on the dance floor. They slept to-gether that night. He moved in with her two months later. He had been with women before her, but the sex had fooled them both. Many people who find compatibility on the dance floor find chemistry in bed. In former centuries, it was the waltz.

And chemistry was a big part of their time in bed to-gether. Both metaphorically, and in terms of actual practice. Sandi knew all the tricks: spermicides, IUDs, the pill. Condoms came last on the list—they got in the way.

Sandi and Buzz worked and partied and played like two kids in a giant suburban sandbox, piling up debt on their credit cards, reading nothing more stimulating than *People* and *Sports Illustrated,* shopping at the malls, and generally having the time of their lives. They were the energetic power couple of their social set, the model for their friends with their indefatigable zest for life. It seemed to Buzz as if they were living inside a Wrigley's Spearmint Gum commercial.

He surprised her on her birthday when he rolled up his sleeve and showed her the rose with *Sandi* underneath it.

And, in their own way, they loved each other. After the athletic playtime in bed, they talked each other to sleep, building lifetime castles in their skies. The plan was set. Enjoy a year of fun. Get engaged and married. Then two years to get to know and enjoy each other and save for a house (Sandi was into selling office copiers using a spectacular combination of excellent presentation of product benefits and not-quite-mini skirts). Then, finally, two children; hopefully, a boy and a girl—sometime.

When the pastor at Saint Christines turned them down after they frankly told him they didn't plan on coming back to church until their first child's baptism—after all, the kids will need *some* religion—they found a pastor who *would* marry them on the West Side. That pastor was much less rigorous about marriage preparation.

Buzz and Sandi did not have big dreams, but they shared the same dreams. Just having a mother- and father-in-law who paid attention to him attracted Buzz to Sandi. A bonus! That, and her energy in bed. He pictured an entire life of it.

Sandi's parents looked at Buzz's new Datsun 280Z and his nice suits (off the rack from Syms) and steady job, combined with his sense of humor and devotion to their only daughter, and approved. They even approved of their living together. She had picked a winner.

"She could do worse," her parents said to each other. "He's a good boy. He went to Notre Dame!" (They didn't quite put

it this way, but Buzz did keep six or seven of the ten commandments…)

One day in a bar, Buzz was buzzed when he asked Sandi
to marry him. He looked into her brown eyes and up at her
sandy hair and said, "Our chances are fifty-fifty one of us
will die married to each other. I'm willing to take the chance.
Either way, we'll have a few good years together now, while
we're young."

I can do better than fifty-fifty, she thought.

"I'm yours, forever," she told him, looking him in the eye,
raising her glass, meaning every word. At least meaning it
when she said it.

They left the bar, drove to J. B. Robinson Jewelers at Great
Northern Mall, and bought a thousand dollar, pear-cut ring
with very reasonable monthly payments, starting five months
after the original purchase. That night, they invited both Jack
Daniels and Bud Light to the intimate party at their apartment. Sandi was a light drinker, but did enjoy a steady toke
off a marijuana cigarette. They slow danced in front of Johnny
Carson interviewing Dolly Parton, as the stereo played Frank
Sinatra's "Fly Me to the Moon."

Human life has an uncanny way of popping through the
tightest cracks in the cold white sidewalk plans of life. Four
months after the wedding, Sandi got pregnant. *Somebody must
have screwed up at the G. D. Searle factory,* Buzz had thought
at the time.

The Fifth Commandment was one that Buzz was partial
to keeping, but Sandi didn't think that abortion was killing.
It just couldn't be. Sure, it was ugly. She didn't *want* an abortion. But she didn't *want* a baby right now, either. After a few
days of intense discussions, she decided to go along with
Buzz and keep the baby, to exercise her right to choose. Maybe
the house would have to wait (day care would put a dent in
their house savings).

She was the first of her group of friends to have a baby,
and aside from horror stories from her mom and aunt about

the pain of giving birth, she had no realistic idea about the time and effort required to care for a baby.

They worked and played and never once prayed until practically the day Jennifer was born.

2

Mark Johnson hung up the phone in the FBI office. Maggie had not lost her temper this time. Just a steady, strangely sad "no" each time he asked to come see the girls.

"No," she said. "I need more time. I'm just getting my feet on the ground. Maybe later."

So now they were officially separated. With each "no" he feared that she would be able to live without him, and that she would be able to call the lawyer, and ratchet up the separation to divorce.

The fear turned to anger by the end of the conversation. After all, by Mark's accounting, he had been a good husband and a good father. She said he didn't listen to her, but he had listened. She just didn't like what he said back after she said her piece. She didn't like that he wasn't "there emotionally" for her—whatever that meant—but he had given her all the emotions he had. She had told him that he wasn't reliable, that he had abandoned her during her times of need on the whim of the moment—that time he had gone hunting the week after their second daughter was born, leaving her alone. But he had already made the plans for the trip, and a man's got to have his freedom, and wasn't Maggie just being a control freak, and didn't he "pay" for that trip with her angry words and stares for two weeks after he returned?

"You married *me,* not somebody else, Maggie," he had explained to her then. "You knew what I was like when you married me. I was here for the baby. So I took a week off a week later? What's the big deal?"

Then she really made him angry by calling up her mother and her sisters and her friends and complaining and comparing. Complaining about him, never mentioning the way he provided for the family, or his way with the girls (when he found the time). Comparing him to other husbands.

Being compared angered him almost as much as her taking his business all over the country using the phone lines. After all, what single man can compare with the good traits of ten other guys? It piqued his sense of justice.

"I have to talk to somebody about our relationship," she pleaded, not understanding that she was taking a knife and sticking it into his heart with every phone call. "Talking to you is like talking to the wall!"

"Good," he replied calmly. "That means I'm the kind of guy who sticks to his principles. Why don't you tell that to your sisters when you're on the phone?"

He had walked out of the house after that long-ago argument. The needle kept skipping over the same groove.

He went to a bar and had a beer that time. He never had more than one or two beers. He was a tough guy, after all, and he could control his liquor. He could control himself.

But I can't control Maggie, he thought, looking at the phone, wondering what to do next.

3

Sam and Ellie held gloved hands as they walked along the wide, empty beach at Mentor Headlands. He stopped walking, and turned to kiss her on the lips, still amazed that she kissed back. It was not a long kiss.

"I want you to meet my father," he told her.

"Yes, I would like that," she replied. "Funny how we both have only our dads."

He nodded. It seemed to Ellie that everything about her and Sam ran parallel like this lake and its shoreline.

"I'll call him," Sam said. "He's going to be in Cleveland for a lecture series next month. We'll go to dinner."

Love. Or so it seemed. Sam had surprised and pleased her when he told her that he wanted to wait a while—maybe even until the wedding, though no firm date was set and no ring was bought—before sleeping with her.

She found herself falling in love with aspects of him she hadn't imagined on their first, charged night together…

…the way he kissed her, as if that was the only thing in the world to him, not merely a prelude to sophomoric grop-ing or intense coupling. He was not boyish in this…

…the way he seemed to anticipate when she needed the salt shaker at dinner, handing it to her just as she was about to ask him to pass it…

…the way he reached over to tuck her coat neatly under the seat belt before starting the engine…

…the way he opened doors in such an unassuming way, and at every opportunity was a gentleman. She knew that he had been raised this way, that manners were a part of him, and that they wouldn't fade or lose intensity over time. That was just it: he was not intense in the nuts and bolts move-ments and motions of spending time with her. It gave all the more impact to his deeds…

…the way he held her hand with a firmness and a soft-ness all at once. He communicated to her through this simple, gentle way, responding to what she said, to looks she gave him, with his hands. She was perfectly sound in her reason-ing that this would portend well as to how he would treat her after they were married, in bed…

…the intensity of his eyes when he sat before a computer or talked to a client at his business (once, she had taken a vacation day just to watch him work)…

…his immunity to style. He dressed in Brooks Brothers pants, button down shirts (although never white ones), and laced up Johnston and Murphy shoes—and would forever-more. He exuded steadfastness…

…the almost bizarre way he became more physically attractive the longer she knew him. She didn't see the pockmarks on his skin anymore—only the depth in his eyes. He was thin, but she saw through his thinness to the wiry strength he possessed. And she had been wordlessly thrilled by the gracefulness of his movements on the basketball court during the one time she had gone with Buzz and Sam to watch them play at the YMCA Winter League…

…he called at just the right times. (He had caught on quickly after Buzz's discussion of womanly emotional time clocks, and still relied heavily on Buzz for advice. Ellen was not aware of this). He did not bring up the topics of commitment or marriage, but he didn't shy away from discussion when she brought them up. There was a manliness to his lack of fear…

…there was the wedding of the daughter of one of Bucky's clients at the Garden Club last week. He wasn't a great dancer, but it was a welcome change to look up to a man as they waltzed!

But it was the jealous looks of the sharply dressed, handsome men—married and single—when they saw Sam dancing with her that gave her a certain paradoxical satisfaction. She knew that she had been given beauty (and she worked diligently at the health club to preserve it…). She knew that many of the men in the room—married and single—would gladly, madly date her. She knew that Sam was attracted to her beauty, also. There would be something wrong with him if that was not the case. But she felt that he liked *her*, not just her looks. Distinguishing between the two had always been a difficulty for Ellie with other men. And while it never quite came to the consciousness, the part of her that feared divorce took solace in Sam's plain looks. All the better to keep other women away from him.

In short, being with Sam was like participating in a low intensity, steady, constant waltz. Strength and gracefulness will capture the heart of a woman over looks and money every time—for the woman who is open to those qualities.

Too often, women mistake worldly success for strength. And style for grace.

Ellie was mistaken that Sam's lack of handsomeness would protect him from other women. After all, for the same reasons, Donna Beck was in love with him too.

4

"You know what we all have in common?" Donna asked one unseasonably warm spring day, sitting by the pool at Buzz's apartment complex.

"You mean me and you?" Buzz asked.

"And Sam."

"Oh yeah, Sam, that guy who shows up and socializes with us when he's not working or with Ellie?"

There was a bitter note in Buzz's voice. He missed Sam. They saw him once a week—usually during a weekday—and practically never on weekends. The Wednesday night video was still sacrosanct. Buzz suspected that even Wednesday night would fall by the wayside when Ellie's classes on Wednesday evenings ended come summer. She was getting her MBA.

"Give Sam a break," Donna said curtly.

"Boy, you've changed your tune, Donna," Buzz replied, but the bitterness was no longer in his voice.

"Time heals all wounds—and a little dab of Sister Elizabeth helps. I'm over him. Mostly."

Buzz dipped a strip of celery into a bowl of sour cream. He was fighting another diet war—and winning this time. Mostly.

"So what do we all have in common?" he asked.

"We never watch television. Except for videos and you for sports. But none of us watch network television. It bores me. Sam says he's too busy. And you say it's a window box with a first class view of hell."

"Maybe that's why Sam has good morals…" Buzz trailed off, uncertain.

"Oh, I don't know. I think he has good morals because of fear and momentum."

"Fear and momentum? You sound like me, Donna."

"I know I do. Sounding like you really scares me."

She allowed herself a chuckle. Buzz smiled wanly.

"Back to Sam," Donna said. "He's afraid of screwing up his life, because he has nothing else. If you don't believe in God, all you have is your life. The momentum thing is something different. You've got me reading Degenerate Moderns, and it got me to thinking about Sam the other day."

She was referring to a book that chronicled the sordid personal lives of the intellectual heroes of the last two centuries.

"Sam's not modern," she continued. "He's not like these post-Enlightenment guys. It must come from his father. Sam acts like, well, a gentleman. You could even say he acts like a, well, like a good Catholic—except he doesn't go to Mass or do Catholic things. He keeps all the Commandments except the First and Third."

Buzz couldn't help but note that Donna was becoming more of a thinker after hanging out with him over the months. She was reading more and more. And learning how to express her thoughts. *It's not you,* he told himself. *It's the books. I should give her more books.*

"I see what you mean about Sam," Buzz agreed. "About his not being modern. He's one noble agnostic. A virtuous man who doesn't rely on grace for his virtue. But what does that have to do with momentum?"

"I suspect," she explained, "that Sam comes from a family that practiced virtue for generations. I bet you that his dad is quite an honorable man—"

"—who keeps every commandment but two?"

"Yeah," she agreed, smiling pleasantly. "Something like that. That's Sam, too. And Sam's grandfather, who was an engineer from Scotland; I bet he was probably a virtuous man. I wonder if he believed in God?"

"We should ask Sam," Buzz mused. "Somewhere in his past—maybe in Scotland, before the Reformation—he's got Catholic relatives. Just about every Protestant or agnostic has them. Maybe they're in heaven now, interceding for their descendants."

"Something has to explain Sam."

"Well, and it's weird hearing myself say this, Donna, but virtue—being good, not just being nice—is its own reward. It's hard not taking a drink. But I get a satisfaction from being sober—a low grade satisfaction, for sure, not filled with excitement—but it beats the quick, high octane thrill of getting drunk hands down. Maybe Sam gets satisfaction from being virtuous."

She got up and stretched. Buzz avoided looking at her figure. Like Ellie's growing attraction toward Sam, Buzz found himself admiring Donna in a way that just had not been there in past months. She dove into the pool with an awkward strength. She swam back and pulled her elbows up onto the side of the pool.

"You know, Buzz, when I was a little kid, my brothers and sisters and I used to run into my parents' room on Saturday mornings and jump onto the bed. Sometimes we'd romp around. Sometimes we'd stay sleepy and lay on the bed, listening to Mom and Dad talk about the day. Every once in a while, Daddy would say to my mom, 'You know, Regina, this ain't the Riviera, but it doesn't get any better than this.'

"What he meant was, the best things in life are simple, and don't cost a lot of money, and are always caught up in family."

A dark look came to Buzz's face.

"I'm sorry," Donna said, tenderly. "I didn't mean to remind you of your daughter."

"Don't be sorry, kiddo. You didn't mean it. Before my marriage went to hell, Jennifer used to climb into bed with me and Sandi. Half the time I was hung over."

Donna looked away, embarrassed. Then she looked back.

"Come on in. The water's freezing!" she called out.

"Naw. Not in the mood," he replied.

"Don't be such a lug. It's good for you."

"Nah. Not me. I can't swim."

"Liar," she said amiably.

"You know me so well, Donna."

"And I know you want to go swimming. Rather, that you'll have fun once you get in."

Buzz placed his glass of club soda on the table, and quickly leaped with two long strides into the pool, forming a cannon-ball, causing a huge splash.

"Arghh! It's freezing!" he cried after he surfaced. "How come you're not shivering?"

"I'm cold. I'm just not a wimp like you. Race you to the end!" Used to Buzz's cheating New Jersey ways, she took off ahead of him without hesitating.

He followed and expertly overtook her, beating her to the other side of the large pool by two body lengths.

"Liar," she said when she reached him. He was whistling.

"I used to be a life guard. I won all the swim meets."

She shook her head.

"How many jobs have you had, anyway?" she asked.

"About fifteen, since high school."

"Wow. Lou Gehrig you're not."

"I might have to quit UPS when we go to Fatima," he said casually.

"Why?"

"They won't let me take the time off."

"So you're going to quit your job? What will you do for money?"

"Oh, yeah. Money. I guess I can't quit. Dunno about the money. Maybe I'll drive a cab nights. Work for Sam. I've been playing around with computers lately, after hours, at Edwards," he replied. "I haven't really decided to go or not. I have to watch my bank account; making money is one of the only ways I get to be a dad—besides prayer."

"Okay," she said. Then, "Beat ya," and took off even more quickly for the other end.

This time, Buzz bore down and beat her by three body lengths. He was breathing normally by the time she caught up.

"Liar," she said between huffs and puffs.

5

Sam and Buzz and Ellie and Donna had lives outside of their conversations at pools and at restaurants...

Sam walked into the office and Johnny Traverse greeted him with a smile and a frown. The executive meeting scheduled for nine was about to begin. Sam sat down and listened carefully to the verbal reports from his three managers: Traverse for sales and marketing, Sheila Burkett from Technical Support, Ro Mack from Operations and Accounting.

Mack's report was disturbing as usual. The fast growth of the company was causing a cash flow crunch. The office was too small to support the growing staff, the cost of finding and training new workers (Edwards & Associates needed four more to keep up with the new accounts Traverse and company were bringing in). Sam had never considered the headaches involved with managing so many workers.

He listened carefully, spoke rarely, and took the advice of his most talented and experienced executives. He agreed to meet with Edwards & Associates' banker to try to secure a line of credit to make it through the next several months. The meeting ended. Everyone filed out except for Johnny.

Johnny had a suggestion about their beautiful (but not as beautiful as Ellen James) young saleswoman named Amy Winters. Winters, a recent graduate from Case Western Reserve University, had a degree in Computer Science. Sam had interviewed her for an hour two weeks earlier, and found her charming, confident, and hungry for a chance to prove herself.

"I'm loaded with appointments until the weekend, Sam. Why don't you take Amy with you to meet the folks at Western Graphics," Johnny suggested. Western Graphics was one of their biggest and most loyal customers.

So Sam took Amy to an early lunch, and then to Western Graphics. He was pleasantly surprised when two suggestions Amy made during their meeting with the information systems manager there were accepted.

He was more impressed when Amy asked him how she had done after the visit.

"Not bad. Listen more and talk less. You paid for one-tenth of your salary in your first day if Western goes for the options you gave them."

✝ ✝ ✝

Buzz started his day by dragging himself out of bed on the alarm's third ring. He showed up late for Mass, and punched the time card at UPS with a minute to spare. Buzz didn't like today's delivery route. He was a split driver. That meant he had to fill in for vacationing drivers by taking parts of their routes, or parts of overloaded routes. Most drivers had one regular route. Buzz had to know the ins and outs of twenty-six routes to do his job.

He had a good memory. There were literally thousands of streets, house numbers, names of shipping dock workers, traffic patterns, and timings of traffic lights stored in the hard drive of his head.

UPS drivers work hard all day long. His truck had been overloaded today. He rushed to make his appointments, and despite the union rules, skipped his lunch to get to his pickups. It seemed like every dock had twenty to thirty packages near the weight limit. He had a strong back. His hands, forearms, and fingers were so strong from lifting and carrying boxes that he had to consciously pull back his grip when shaking hands after hours.

He enjoyed working alone, with his thoughts to himself between stops. He prayed on and off to Our Lady, carrying on a casual conversation that ofttimes slipped into daydreaming.

Finally, toward the end of the day, knowing that he was not only caught up but ahead of his work, he pulled his truck into the parking lot of the Poor Clares on Rocky River Drive. He parked his package car facing the chapel, toward where he knew the tabernacle would be. He prayed the Divine Mercy Chaplet for seven minutes, then drove back to the center, punched out, changed his clothes, walked to his Festiva, picked up a video and a sub on the way home, then collapsed onto the couch. He read parts of five magazines; *Fidelity, Inc., Conservative Chronicle, Sports Illustrated,* and *Crisis;* until Sam and Donna arrived to watch the video.

✛ ✛ ✛

Donna rolled out of bed on the second buzzing of her alarm, and knelt to pray her morning offering. She showered quickly, spent five endless minutes on her make-up, leaning over the sink to get closer to the mirror, and dressed quickly. Then she gave her hair a quick brushing while sitting in the front seat of the car as it warmed up.

Work was a boring, dull grind.

After work she arrived a minute late for five-thirty Mass at Saint Chris, then home by six-fifteen. She helped make the salad for her mother before dinner, and barely noticed how much she enjoyed the preparations. There was only her mom and dad, her brother Vinny, and her older sister Cindy at home now.

Tony Beck got home just in time to sit down for spaghetti, plus leftover lasagna from last night. Her mother sat down to pray, then got up to prepare more food, according to a timeless Italian tradition. Vinny talked about his planned canoe trip with the Eagle Scouts, Cindy about her newest boyfriend's legal problems with his landlord, and Donna about nothing. In large families, there was always a role to play, and Donna played the silent daughter.

They took turns leading the decades during the family Rosary. Donna found it hard to keep her mind on the mysteries, but was able to remain recollected during the fifth mystery, the Finding of the Child Jesus in the Temple. *May I find you at the end of every Rosary, dear Jesus,* she prayed.

She watched *Jeopardy!* with her amazing dad, who got most of the questions right—more than most of the contestants on most nights. Tony Beck was the best-read plumber in Rocky River and had a quick mind.

During the television show, God's grace prompted her to notice, several times, the book that Sister Elizabeth from the Lourdes Shrine had given her a few weeks ago. It was on the shelf above the television. Donna's eyes kept returning to the book. She hadn't read it yet.

It was *But I Have Called You Friends* by Mother Mary Frances, a Poor Clare.

At eight Donna kissed her father.

"Where you goin', Donna?"

"Buzz's. We're watching a video with Sam."

"Again." It was a statement.

"Yup."

"How come you never bring these boys home? I'm not sure they really exist," Tony said without reproach. He was curious.

"They're not boys, Papa. And I don't know. I just never asked them over," she said, avoiding a lie.

Sure, it was true she never asked them to visit. It was also true that she was afraid that Sam wouldn't be comfortable in their cramped house. Of course, Buzz would like her folks.

Would they like Buzz? Donna didn't know.

God's grace had prompted Tony to ask the question. Grace prompted Donna to reconsider.

"You know, Papa, I'll ask them over. Maybe this week-end."

"I'd like that," Tony said, opening his copy of George Gilder's *Men and Marriage*.

On the table next to his ancient, well-worn chair, lay a copy of *Forbes*. George Gilder was on the cover. There was a sticker from the Rocky River Library over Gilder's kneecap.

✝ ✝ ✝

It took Ellen forty-five minutes to shower, apply her make-up, and fix her hair (not that it was all that broken). She sat at a tasteful cherry vanity that Bucky had somehow kept from her mother during the bitter divorce (Ellen had been six at the time). Ellen enjoyed getting ready for the day, and thought of what she would do at work. Her bedroom was almost as big as Buzz's apartment and larger than the living room and dining room in Donna's house.

She was an efficient worker. She didn't have Bucky's "spark," but as Bucky's only child, she was as close as he would come to having a son. He had taken her on business trips since she was a child during her summer breaks, explaining to her the tricks of his trade.

After she graduated from Saint Marys in South Bend (Buzz was right on the money about that guess) with a degree in Business Management, Bucky refused to take her into his company. "I'm done being your teacher," he told her with love in his voice. "Go make it on your own. You'll enjoy it more."

She got a job with a small management consulting company in downtown Cleveland after college, and switched after three years (last summer) to a higher paying firm on the West Side. She didn't like driving across town, but she liked the work and higher pay. She bought herself a black Accord as a reward. The same car as Sam had (but hers didn't have leather seats). That night when she met him, it had seemed like a sign that they both owned the same model and color car. Like stars lining up in the sky to form a pointing arrow.

She immersed herself in her duties (mostly research today) in a quiet cubicle. At eleven, she called Edwards & Associates and was disappointed that Sam had already left for lunch. Lately, she had been meeting him for lunch at least three times a week.

After work, she went home, cooked stir fry for Bucky, and took a short nap. Reading was out of the question after a day straining over spreadsheets and reports. She wasn't a reader, anyway, unless it was practical. Like Sam and Buzz, she also read *Inc.* on occasion. She was hoping to start her own company, like Sam, one day. She went upstairs to prepare for night school.

✟ ✟ ✟

Mark Johnson sat in a car on a stake-out for the entire day. He ate a lunch of cold bagels. He was fasting for his marriage.

6

"That's got to be one of the best movies I've ever seen," Buzz said as the credits began to role.

"Shush," Donna said from the rocking chair next to the couch. "I want to see who played the girl who loved Jimmy Stewart."

They had watched *The Philadelphia Story*. Donna was turning both men on to the classics.

"Put me in your pocket," Sam mused, quoting Katherine Hepburn. All the actresses seemed to remind him of Ellie lately.

"Definitely on my all-time top ten list," Donna added to no one in particular. "I've seen it a dozen times. There's a remake in color with Bing Crosby and Grace Kelly. A musical that doesn't quite cut it. What did you think, Sam?"

"I haven't seen the musical," Sam explained.

"Not the musical," she said. "This one. The original."

"I liked it a lot. Makes my top fifty."

"Top fifty? That's an insult to this movie."

"There's no accounting for taste," Buzz offered.

"I wish I lived in the movies," Donna said, a tinge of sadness in her voice. "I wish Cary Grant was in love with me."

"In that one statement, you've summarized the appeal of movies," Buzz observed. "We put ourselves in them. When we're watching them, we're in them. I forgot I was on this couch for the last two hours. I was in Philadelphia."

"Maybe our era is the era of movies because people don't like living their lives during the day," Sam said.

That got them all thinking.

"I don't know about that," Buzz finally said. "It's just a diversion. An art form."

"They're more than that," Donna said. "I think Sam has a point."

"Think about it, Buzz," Sam continued. "Where else can everything turn out right except in a movie like *The Philadelphia Story?* Everyone is beautiful and witty. Even the little girl."

"I don't know," Buzz said. "I heard a story the other day from Sister Elizabeth that was so wild you would think she made it up. If it was in a movie, it wouldn't seem real—unless it was a stupid French flick."

"So what was the story?" Donna asked.

"It's about Saint Anthony of Padua. By now, Sam, you realize that we pray to him a lot. He finds lost stuff. But he's a powerful all-purpose intercessor, too. Next to Saint Joseph and Saint Jude, he's the top dog, the WD-40 of saints."

"I'm sure he's thrilled with your comparison. So what's the story?" Sam asked.

"Sister Elizabeth told me it happened to her aunt, so it's a real story, not an urban myth. It even got written up in *Catholic*

Digest in the 1960s. Seems her aunt wasn't all that pretty, and got into her late thirties without so much as a date. An old maid. And she had prayed to Saint Anthony since she was a teenager to find a husband.

"Year after year she prayed. She found herself looking in the mirror one day, counting gray hairs, when her statue of Saint Anthony caught her eye. She became filled with rage.

"Fat lot of good asking you for help has done! she yelled, holding the statue. She became so incensed that she threw the statue out the window!

"Turns out the statue hits this guy walking outside on the head—"

"I can just guess what happens—" Donna interrupted.

"You got it. The guy goes to the door to find out who owns the statue and meets Sister Elizabeth's aunt. They start talking. He comes back to visit. They get married."

Sam shook his head in disbelief.

"You know one thing for sure: Saint Anthony has a sense of humor," Donna observed.

"Sounds like a sadist to me," Sam said. "If he's such hot stuff, why did he make her wait so long to find the guy?"

Buzz had no answer.

"Maybe the guy was late for everything, and Saint Anthony got him to show up early..." Donna offered.

"How does Saint Anthony get the guy to do something in the first place?" Sam asked reasonably.

"Grace," Buzz said.

"That's no answer. What is grace?" Sam asked.

"Grace is God's free gift," Donna quoted from her catechism.

"That means nothing to me. How does it work? Where is it? What's the reality?" Sam practically fired the questions.

"The reality is, Sam, Sister Elizabeth's aunt has a husband," Buzz tried to say patiently.

"Coincidence," Sam rejoined.

"Then how come when I ask him to help me find something, I always find it?" Donna asked. "It's happened a hundred times if it happened once. He even helped me find you. Remember the fridge?"

Sam smiled. "Yeah, I remember it. But I didn't see Saint Anthony that day. I saw you.

"Tell me, Donna. Have you asked him to find you a husband?"

Donna looked down at her hands.

"Yes," she said quietly.

Sam saw that he had touched upon a sore spot. He didn't think that winning an argument was worth hurting his friend.

"Sorry," he said.

"Don't be sorry, Sam."

"Maybe you should throw a statue out the window," Sam found himself suggesting to her.

Buzz got up, and walked purposefully to the mantle of his faux fireplace. There was a statue of Saint Joseph there. He quickly carried it to the window, opened it—

"Oh Buzz, don't—" Donna cried. "It's seven stories!"

—and threw it out the window, flipping it behind his back. He smacked his hands up and down. A moment later, they heard the sound of crashing plaster, then a loud, "Hey!" from down below.

"Oops," Buzz said. "Uh oh."

"Didn't you look to see if anybody was down there!" Donna yelled.

"With my luck, I just hit a lawyer," Buzz quipped.

"Did you hit somebody?" Sam asked.

"Naw," Buzz said, looking out the window. A cold breeze was taking over the room. "Landed at her feet."

"Her?" Donna asked. For a second there, she had hoped that it might be a guy. *Like Sister Elizabeth's aunt…gee, you're getting desperate.*

"Yeah, a girl. It's hard to make her out in the dark."

"Are you okay!" Buzz shouted. "Are you hurt?"

"No! Are you Buzz Woodward?"

Buzz looked back at his friends in the room with a puzzled look and a shrug of his shoulders.

"Do you know her?" Sam asked, finally finding his feet and coming to the window.

"Not really, but I think you do."

7

Mark Johnson pulled into the driveway of Bill White's house. He had been on the road for eight hours. Bill lived in Rocky River, a suburb of Cleveland, and had cheerfully agreed to spend the weekend with Mark. Both men had gone to Our Lady of the Valley High School together, where they were the stars of the football team. Bill had been a small, quick— and tough—wide receiver. He attended college at the University of Delaware, but didn't play football. Studies were too important.

Bill and Mark had kept up with each other by talking on the phone every few months (it was usually Bill who called). Bill owned one of the largest advertising firms in Cleveland, and was the prototypical bachelor. He had been best man at Mark's wedding. Once a year, they went deer hunting together in central Pennsylvania.

They also shared something that cemented their friendship, and that cement worked because it was stronger than friendship; they shared the faith.

Mark had no one else to turn to. If he went to his older brothers, they would inevitably take his side *against* Maggie. It was only natural in a family that prized loyalty. Because they were tough guys like himself, he doubted they would be any better at finding solutions to his problems than he was. Besides, admitting (and worse, *dissecting*) failure was beyond humiliating. It was emasculating. Had they not taught him to solve his own problems? Isn't *that* what a real man does?

The parish priest in New Jersey had offered him a few bromides about "communication" being the key to a happy marriage, and suggested counseling. He heard Mark's confession with little enthusiasm.

Mark was not dumb. He was quite intelligent, an able engineer from his Naval Academy education, and a savvy FBI agent. His smarts told him that Bill had a *different kind* of intelligence. Bill White would be objective. Bill would try to help Mark save his marriage. He would not blow smoke up Mark's petard. Bill might be disappointed with Mark, but would never show his disappointment, and better yet, would show no sympathy. Bill would get down to the business at hand. Helping his friend.

Chapter Six

1

Buzz opened the door and saw Ellen James standing there with a pleasant smile on her face.

Ellie? What are you doing here? Sam thought, surprised and curious.

"Hi Ellen," Buzz said. "Sorry about the statue."

"Oh that? Everybody knows you're a character, Buzz. Don't even think about apologizing."

"How did you know where I live?" Buzz asked directly.

"Sam told me. I wrote it in my Day Timer."

Sam came to her and gave her a kiss. "Ellie, you remember Donna from Mama Santas. She's the one I'm always talking about."

Donna managed a neutral smile. "You look cold. Can I make you a cup of tea?"

Be nice, Donna thought. *There's nothing you can do about her. Remember what Sister Elizabeth told you: offer it up. Besides, you're over Sam.*

Despite her silent pep talk, Donna felt a surge of sadness and helplessness. It surprised her that she felt these emotions for her own sake, and they left no room for contempt towards Ellie.

"That would be great. Thanks, Donna."

Donna beat a path to the kitchen, relieved. *What time is it? Midnight. And she came all the way over here? Ellen must really like him.*

Like him? Maybe she loves him, a small voice inside whispered to her. Donna tried to put that from her mind. To concentrate on making tea. Watching water boil.

"You missed the movie," Buzz said. "A classic: *The Philadelphia Story.*"

"It's one of my favorites." It was a polite white lie. She had seen it ages ago, and barely remembered it.

"So, what brings you to the West Side?" Sam asked. "Didn't you have classes tonight?"

Ellen blushed. "I just wanted to see you, that's all."

She ended the sentence in a whisper, looking at Sam, avoiding Buzz's eyes.

Buzz's smile grew. *I'm gonna be sick. They really **are** in love. Was I ever this sappy?*

He looked at the window. It was still open. He ran through his lost loves in his mind. *No. Never. Well, there was the girl I fell for at Notre Dame.*

Then, after he closed the window, he turned and saw Sam slip his hand into Ellie's as they went to the couch to sit down. *Too bad for me,* Buzz thought. *It would be nice to fall in love. What's wrong with that?*

Donna stuck her head out the kitchen doorway and called: "Cream or sugar?"

"Just a little honey, thank you."

"You missed an interesting post-movie conversation, Ellie," Buzz said presently. "Uh, do you mind if I call you Ellie? That's what Sam calls you when he tells me about you."

"Not at all," Ellen said, her smile a bit more strained. She couldn't help herself. She turned to Sam. "What have you been telling Buzz about me?"

Sam looked down at his shoes, and came close to blushing. "Uh, not much. You know, guy talk. When to call you up and stuff."

Buzz winced. *Better rescue him. You don't have to be that honest, Sammy Boy.*

"What Sam means to say, Ellie, is that I'm kind of like a father figure to him. I'm like that old Japanese guy who taught Ralph Macchio to wax on and wax off. In fact, I convinced Sam to go into computers years ago—"

"You did no such thing," Sam interrupted.

Donna, who was listening from the kitchen, stifled a laugh. Ellen laughed.

"You're okay, Buzz. And Sam, don't be so serious."

How can you not like this girl? Buzz thought, trying not to stare at her.

"So tell me, Buzz, what conversation did I miss?" Ellie asked with a gentle tone.

Buzz retold the story of the Saint Anthony statue and Sister Elizabeth's aunt. "I didn't have a Saint Anthony statue, so I tossed my Saint Joseph. I figured Saint Joseph is a big leaguer too."

"I can believe that," Ellen said. *Well, almost. It's a nice story, though.*

Donna came in with the tea.

"How's your job coming along, Donna?" Ellen asked after the tea was served. She took a sip. "This tea is wonderful."

"Thank you. My job is going just fine. Kind of boring," Donna said with a clipped tone. *Wonderful?*

A long pause ensued.

"What kind of things do you do?" Ellie persisted.

Donna listed a few office manager-type duties.

This isn't working, Ellie thought. *Switch tacks.*

"Sam tells me you're a movie buff. Who is your favorite director?" Ellie saw Donna's eyes widen.

"Uh, James Cameron," Donna answered, despite herself. "Aliens. The Terminator. I don't like all his stuff. But I like how he combines humor, love, terror, and normal characters in unusual situations."

Bingo, Ellie thought.

"I liked Aliens," Ellie commented. The truth.

"And who's your favorite director?" Donna asked, feeling bold, tired of answering all the questions.

"Me? Let me think," she said, taking her hand from Sam's and putting a finger on her chin.

"Oliver Stone." He was the first director who came to her mind. *What movies did he make?*

"I don't like him," Donna blurted. She saw a look of disapproval in Sam's eyes—or did she imagine it? "What I mean is, he's a talented director, but I don't like how he twists the facts to fit into his liberal version of history."

"Is that so?" Ellie said. "I won't kid you. Sam was right when he said you really know your movies. I didn't know Stone did things like that. I liked Platoon. Didn't he make Platoon?"

She's either real humble or real charming or real smooth, Buzz thought, watching Ellie bring Donna out of herself.

"Yeah, he did. It's a perfect example of what I'm talking about. For instance…"

And so the conversation went, gradually losing tension. Ellie struggled to keep up with Donna, not quite holding her own. She learned a lot about movies over the next hour. Buzz started to join in the conversation, too.

Ellie was not really all that humble, but what she was doing took a certain kind of humility. She wasn't afraid of Donna. Ellie's almost feline sense of staking out her territory told her that she had to win Sam's friends over to win Sam. She was taking no chances, and turning on the charm, and using the most devastating business tool Bucky had ever taught her: *Find out what your client likes and start asking questions. Find what they love, then sit back and listen and learn.*

Ellie was not being insincere. She was learning about movies, of which she knew little. That was good, because Sam apparently liked movies. She discovered that Donna was more than she appeared to be on the surface. She had a quick mind and an earthy articulateness. With a proper education and a few breaks, Donna could have been a professional.

That's life, Ellie thought.

As the conversation wore on, Ellie decided that Donna simply wasn't Sam's type, and relaxed a bit. *Better safe than sorry.*

Ellie wasn't fooling Buzz, and she knew it. But she wasn't trying to fool Buzz. Buzz was not as talkative as usual, and Ellie knew from Sam that Buzz loved to talk.

He must be sizing me up, Ellie surmised. And she was right. *I have nothing to hide.*

But deep down, on the feminine-threat meter, Ellie was picking Buzz up loud and clear: *Don't hurt my friend. Love him and I'll help you, Ellen. But don't hurt him.*

Ellie respected this. In fact, it made her proud of Sam. He knew how to pick strong friends.

Ellie was not a manipulative person. Sure, she had come here to surprise them, hoping to catch them off guard (Buckyism: *Always do business when the other side is tired, or not expecting it...*). But her goal was not sinister; she was crossing her *t's* and dotting her *i's* in the relationship with Sam. Sam had kept his friends hidden from her all these months. Probably because he was shy; maybe he was afraid she might reject them. Ellen James had to show him that she could and would like them.

Ellie was relieved. Overall, as she calculated in that most female way (using intuition; with no calculation at all), she knew that Buzz and Donna were good people. Easy to like.

Donna's a little rough around the edges. Insecure. From the wrong side of the subdivision, for sure, but honest and nice. And Buzz! She knew he was unique. Different. *Just like Sam.*

At two, good-byes were made. Donna drove home in her "new" pick-up truck.

Before getting into her own Accord, Ellie slipped into Sam's car and gave him a long, lingering good-night kiss.

"Thanks for being such a sport about me crashing your party. I like your friends."

*But they're probably not going to be **my** friends. Especially if you end up on the East Side.*

"And I missed you. I missed you all day long." There was no exaggeration in her last statement.

Sam, who was quite tired, and quite thrilled about all the night's events, answered with a bold kiss.

She found something inside herself responding to his kiss—something natural, something good. *Is it love? Is it his tenderness?* She wasn't certain. Either way, it was new to her.

Even Ellie barely realized that she was fertile. The egg about to drop into her womb was still a part of her; as much a part of her as her past. It needed something more to no longer be a mere part, but a whole of its own. The half-life needed a man. Nothing would happen between Gentleman Sam and Lady Ellen on this evening, of course. It was a foregone conclusion that they would be engaged soon. Why not wait until the wedding?

But a woman's reproductive system is never far from her heart. Most married men could tell you the same, if they pay the least attention to their wives' shifting moods and physical cycles. Grace had planned it this way. When a baby is close to being conceived, a woman can be swept along in the strongest current; the undertow in the ocean of human life.

C.S. Lewis once wrote that God gave mankind a strong sexual drive because He knew that we would sit on our duffs otherwise, barren and distracted by dry, dead things like cars and diplomas and MTV.

Sex means life. Life needs love. Dead things don't need either. Ellie didn't think of it in these terms. Which one of us does?

Love and life. Life and love.

Conversations and touches.

And grace from above.

2

"I want you to meet some friends of mine," Bill told Mark after an hour of listening. "There's not much I can tell you. But you can see with your own eyes what you need to see."

"Who are they?"

"Friends," was all Bill would say.

Mark placed his half-finished courtesy beer into Bill's sink. "Then let's go."

"Tomorrow," Bill replied.

3

Two weeks later, Ellen was out of town at a training seminar. Donna still hadn't invited Sam or Buzz to her home.

Buzz convinced Sam and Donna to take a long weekend—including Monday and Tuesday off—for a road trip. He managed to keep the destination from them. "Bring a hundred and fifty bucks and pack for three nights and four days," was all he would tell them.

4

The next day, Bill White and Mark Johnson stood on the front porch of the home of Mary and Joe Kemp. Bill rang the doorbell.

"Come in, come in!" Mary Kemp said as she opened the door.

The Kemps lived in a modest ranch in North Royalton. It had a large backyard.

"Remember," Bill had told Mark earlier, "don't talk about your family. Just have a good time. Just watch them."

Joe came into the foyer from the living room and shook the visitors' hands. Introductions were made.

Lunch was prepared. Cold cuts, cheese, bread, lettuce. Mark turned down a beer. Joe opened a beer for himself and one for Bill. Mary had a Diet Coke.

The Kemps had seven children. Mary breastfed the youngest right at the table.

Two of the older children were at practice for sports. Two other children played peacefully in the living room—Legos. Another, a girl, Helen, who was twelve, was reading on the couch. *Treasure Island.*

There was another girl, Annie, eight, who sat on her father's lap, listening to the adult conversation. After a few minutes, she stood next to "Uncle Bill," her arm on his shoulder. Soon, she was sitting on his lap.

Mary served coffee after lunch.

The conversation hung around the topic of the state of the Catholic Church. The Kemps considered themselves fortunate to live in a town that had a parish with a pastor loyal to Rome, and one of the two or three Catholic grammar schools in the diocese which didn't water down the faith or have a humanistic sex-ed program.

"If Father Dial dies," Mary said. "We'll have to consider home schooling."

"Home schooling?" Mark asked.

"Yes," Bill explained. "A few Catholic families are already doing it—pulling their kids out of school. Teaching them at home. The evangelicals have been doing it more and more for the last few years, more than Catholics."

"Sending your kids to public school is like rolling dice with their souls. Catholic schools are almost as bad," Joe added.

Mark nodded. His oldest two girls, Sarah and Angela, were in third grade and kindergarten. A gradual and subtle change had taken place in them since starting school—Catholic, in this case. Their center of gravity had shifted; from mom and dad to their friends and classmates. Maybe that was natural, but Mark didn't like the morals and mouths of his daughters' friends.

There was a peacefulness and calmness about the Kemps. Joe and Mary seemed normal, typical, average. Good Catholics. Concerned parents. But the children were different. The children were the ones radiating the peace.

They were gentle. Not fighting or bickering. The young ones weren't crying or whining. When was the last time Mark had seen his girls like this?

There was a shine in Annie's eyes. Yes, Annie's eyes had something. *Bill told me to watch and listen.*

What did the Kemps have that Mark had missed along the way with Maggie?

"Are your children always this way?" he asked Joe.

"What way?" Mary asked.

"Like this. So calm. So well-behaved."

"They have their moments…" Joe trailed off.

"But is today a typical Saturday?" Mark pressed.

Joe and Mary looked at each other.

"Yeah," he answered for both of them.

Bill gave Mark a sober look.

Annie seemed to sense the tension in the huge man across the table, and smiled at him. Mark was embarrassed.

Embarrassed by what? he asked himself.

Embarrassed that you don't have a clue why this family is so different, he answered.

This family has what I want, Mark thought. *Now how do I get it?*

"Uh, sorry to leave so soon," Bill told his hosts. "Mark and I have an appointment. Thanks for letting us stop by."

"Are you leaving, Uncle Bill?" Annie asked sweetly, but with a tinge of sadness.

"I'm afraid so, Annie."

She gave him a hug and a little kiss. Bill whispered, "Pray for my friend," into her ear. She pulled away and nodded.

As the door closed behind them, Bill turned to Mark and said, "Let's talk."

Mark nodded. They went back to Bill's house.

Bill offered Mark a beer. He turned it down.

"So?" Bill asked.

"Tell me what I just saw," Mark said.

"A happy family. A holy family."

"I know that," Mark replied. "Tell me why they're that way."

"I'm not sure I can. I just know the Kemps are the best family I've ever known. I was showing you what to shoot for. That can be you and Maggie."

"I don't see how."

Mark's voice did not portray the despair he felt. These were not tough guy words. These were quitter's words.

"Are you man enough to ask the Kemps?" Bill asked, knowing that he was challenging his friend on the most intimate and deeply held foundations.

Mark tried to hold Bill's gaze, but looked down. Mark hadn't looked down since—well, since he could remember.

"I'm not sure," Mark said. "I've tried everything."

"Everything you could think of…" Bill eased up.

"And…"

"Maybe there's more."

5

"We're going down the shore!" Buzz shouted. "Long Beach Island!"

"Why are you shouting?" Donna asked from the back seat. "And why are we going *down* to the shore? Are we going to Florida?"

"No, *down the shore* is a New Jersey expression. In New Jersey, you go *down the shore,* and once you're there, you go *to the beach.* New Jersey has a couple hundred miles of the most beautiful white sandy beaches in the world."

"But it isn't summer yet. What's there to do besides go to the beach? Come on, Jersey?" Sam asked. He pronounced it *Joisey,* without the *r* sound.

"Going to the beach is a great thing in and of itself. And nobody in New Jersey says *Joisey,*" Buzz corrected proudly. "We pronounce the *r* hard and slur the *new* right into New

Jersey. New**jer**sey, like that. Only people from Brooklyn say Joisey. Except for people who live in Jersey City. They say Joisey, but they're referring to their own city, not to the state."

"Welcome to the Geography Channel," Donna intoned. "Your host is Buzz Woodward. Today's topic is New Jersey."

Buzz laughed. "At least you pronounced it right."

"So what do you do at the beach?" Sam asked. "I've never gone to the ocean."

"You don't do much of anything at the beach. That's the whole idea. Read. Listen to tunes. Talk. Play in the sand. If the Gulf currents running north drift in toward the surf, you can swim—body surfing for the initiate—even in May. By the end of June, the water's warm all the time.

"It's good for the soul. One of God's many earthly chapels. And the beaches won't be crowded. Too early in the season."

"Where are we staying?" Donna asked.

"My uncle has a duplex. He's not there, but he sent me the keys. You've got your own two bedroom place, right above me and Sam. All on the up and up."

"Good, you guys are real gentlemen. It'll sound better to my folks—"

"You told them, didn't you?" Buzz asked.

"I'm in the process…"

Buzz rolled his eyes.

"Look, they're old-fashioned," Donna said, her voice rising. "And that's not a bad way to be. It doesn't look good for a girl to travel with two single men. You know that, Buzz."

"Single girls, single men, travel rules," Sam observed. "It's not like we're going to have an orgy or anything. Sometimes you guys drive me crazy with your unwritten Catholic rules. Don't your parents trust you?"

Buzz lit up a smoke, and cracked his window open.

"It's not a matter of trust, Sam," Donna said. "Sure, my parents trust me. But they don't trust original sin, and neither do I. For you, it's not a big deal. But if the chances are one in a thousand of falling out of the state of grace, it's not worth risking. It's like playing poker with the devil. My soul's at stake."

"Can't you just go to confession if you fall?" Sam asked. He was catching on to Catholic ways.

"I could see how you might think that, Sam," Buzz cut in. "But that's the sin of presumption. You can't presume upon God's grace—"

"Sin of presumption? Another sin? Didn't you tell me once that God's, what did you call it, his divine mercy, was infinite, endless? There's no sin that can't be forgiven and all that. Very beautiful. Now you're saying you can't count on it?"

Buzz found himself temporarily confused.

"It's not like that," Donna came to the rescue. "It's not a math equation: commit a sin, go to confession, go to heaven. It's a matter of love. You don't hurt people you love. It's just common sense that if we took off all our clothes and hung out in bed all weekend, we're upping our chances of doing something God doesn't want us to do."

She took a deep breath. "What if I did something bad to you, presuming you would just forgive me? Is that loving you? I wouldn't even consider putting myself in a situation where I would come close to hurting you, Sam."

Buzz sighed relief inwardly. Donna really came out with some profound stuff every once in a while. And she had said something very close to saying that she loved Sam. *Good for her.*

"That makes sense," Sam said, rubbing his chin. "You know, I don't always agree with you guys. You know that. But most of your Catholic stuff has its own internal logic. It's a beautiful way to live. It's a beautiful vision. If only it were true."

"You're not patronizing us?" Buzz asked, pushing again. Always pushing, cutting, probing.

Sam just shook his head in mild disgust.

"Turn on the stereo, Buzz," Donna said. "You're such a jerk."

"What?" Buzz asked, feigning innocence.

"Just turn on the radio," she persisted.

Come On Eileen was playing on a light rock station.

"Great road tune!" Buzz shouted.

He started singing along. After a minute, they were all singing. Buzz turned the volume up louder, then louder. They sang louder.

They sang together the way only friends who aren't married and aren't hooked on classics and grew up in the Seventies can sing together: all out, for fun, abandoning themselves not to some lofty Woodstockian demon or, as would come later, a depressing, small-world nihilistic Grunge devil.

They were part of the lost generation. A *generation-nothing* between a leviathan of Baby Boomers and an ugly toad of X-ers.

No one made movies about them. No one sang songs to them. No one wrote novels about them. Forced to watch re-runs of *Gilligan's Island* and listen to classic rock stations since Pampers, they had no place in American culture. No articles in the purple section of *USA Today*. They weren't spoiled. They didn't make money for its own sake, or start companies for status. They had normal dreams, which made them even more invisible. Generation Nothing.

Their parents had almost crushed most of them under the goose-stepping boots of free love (divorce) and drugs (insanity). Some of their generation didn't exist at all on this world because of abortion (death), which the Boomers had legalized, then embraced. But some Catholics and their friends were emerging from the lost generation; singing, hopeful, bearing burdens, becoming a bridge to those who came before and after them, ready to storm endless beaches while being careful to stay boy-girl-boy-girl in separate accommodations to please their sweet Jesus.

Buzz and Sam and Donna sang their hearts out as Buzz's little 7-Up can of a car zipped through the badlands of Pennsylvania.

"Come on, Eileen!" they sang.

Buzz's Festiva had a pretty good, four-speaker factory sound system.

Shout by Tears for Fears came on next, and they nearly lost their voices.

When the commercials came on, Buzz turned the radio off. Miles stretched before and behind them. They all looked out different windows, sipping cokes and coffees.

Sam felt like shouting for joy. *I've got great friends. I'm going to marry a beautiful woman. Who* **do** *I thank?*

Buzz felt like shouting and crying. *I've got great friends.* He knew who to thank.

Donna took a peek at Sam from the back seat and felt intense longing and emptiness.

I still love him. I can't keep hanging out with him or I'll go crazy. She felt like hitting Buzz for bringing her along.

Who needs to go to the beach, anyway?

Oh, pardon me, she thought, *down the shore.*

A few hours later, when they rolled down the windows in the Pine Barrens on Route 72, and smelled the salt and the sand, no one regretted the trip.

6

It was lovely but cool on the first afternoon when they arrived. They went to the Acme to stock up on supplies: tea for Donna, Bud Light for Sam, and Pepsi for Buzz. And some food. They rented a video for the evening. Buzz cooked omelettes for dinner.

"Can't you cook anything other than omelettes? Not that they're bad. You make great omelettes," Sam said.

"Cheese dreams. I can cook cheese dreams. My dad made them up. Thomas' English muffins, a slice of tomato, two slices of mozzarella, and bacon, lightly toasted."

"Mmnn," Donna commented. "Sounds good. I can cook, too, you know. So good it would make you cry."

That night they watched *Back to the Future*. It reminded Buzz of a modern *It's a Wonderful Life*.

It was windy and rainy the next morning.

"Great weather," Donna said, when she came down for breakfast, shaking the raindrops from her hair.

"We can play cards," Buzz suggested.

Sam and Donna, who both hated to play cards, gave Buzz a look.

"Oh," Buzz said.

"God's natural cathedral, eh?" Sam teased.

"Let's go for a jog, Sam," Donna suggested.

"Sure."

Buzz loved to sleep. After breakfast he went back to bed and napped while his friends jogged on the windy beach. He fell asleep praying his usual prayer, the Rosary, for his friend Sam to find the true faith, and for his friend Donna to find a husband. He was set on praying for both those intentions until they were answered, or until he stopped breathing.

Donna was huffing and puffing by the second jetty. So was Sam. Their jog became a walk. The beach was deserted.

The ocean. It's huge. Makes Lake Erie look like a puddle, Sam thought. *Makes me feel small.*

He suddenly remembered standing before the El Greco in the Art Institute. The young girl he had seen back then had looked a bit like Ellie. That had been so many years ago; he was surprised by the clarity of the memory.

Feeling small is good for the soul.

It was so windy and rainy that they needed to shout to be heard, so they didn't talk much.

Have they gotten me to believe in the soul? he asked himself.

Donna wished that Sam would take her hand. She tried to take her mind off him. It was not easy.

Sam didn't mind the silence.

Their sweats and windbreakers became soaked. They were still walking away from the beach house with the wind at their backs. The breakers were loud—louder than the wind.

"Tell yourself you're warm, Sam!" Donna shouted over the wind and waves. "It works."

She took off her windbreaker.

"See, it's not so bad."

The rain had flattened her hair. Drops of rain came down her forehead and cheeks. She smiled.

It really wasn't all that cold. Just wet and windy.

He took off his jacket. *She's right.*

Buzz was right, there's something about getting to the ocean. It's cleansing.

The sand was thick under their feet. It was wearing them out. Only when they turned back did they realize that walking against the wind was quite a chore.

7

Buzz was still asleep. The drive the day before had worn him out. Donna and Sam had two hours alone together after their walk. After drying off and changing clothes, Sam called Ellie's hotel (her seminar was in Boston) and left a message.

Donna made more tea for them both. It was quiet except for the whistling of wind on the windows, and the sound of the ocean, which was less than forty yards away. The bottom apartment of the duplex was brightly decorated, but the clouds and the curtains made the lighting pleasantly grey. In that way of the shore, it seemed as if all the universe outside the apartment was an illusion, and that all that existed was the table and tea, and the bamboo chairs and stained glass chandelier over the kitchen table at which they sat.

Perfect atmosphere for a conversation.

"So tell me about the secret life of men," Donna began.

"What do you mean?"

"Well, I get the feeling that whenever I'm around you and Buzz, some kind of forcefield goes up, and just because I'm a woman, you act differently, and say different things."

"I still don't follow you," Sam replied. "Can you give me an example."

Donna took a sip of tea, thinking.

"My sister Cindy and I have heart-to-heart talks all the time. We share stuff. Girl stuff. I could see a guy sitting in on that, and Cindy and me talking the same way. But if you and Buzz went on a hunting trip, and I went along, it would be a whole different thing than if I wasn't there."

"I get it. The secret life of men. Yeah, we clam up when women are around. But it's not like we share our deepest and darkest secrets when we're alone. We talk in code. If we talk at all."

"What kind of code?"

"Action code. Take Ellie; I don't tell Buzz what I really feel about her. I'm not sure I could put what I feel about Ellie into words. This might sound weird, but I'm not sure I feel anything about her. She's just there, a word or an image in my heart. It's like when I'm in the zone on the court. I can't miss. Every shot is a swish. I don't put words to how I'm feeling while I'm shooting. I'm just in the zone."

"I know about the zone," Donna offered.

"Do you? Or do you have a girl version of it? When I'm in the zone, I'm in another world. Except for Ellie, I can't say I've ever felt anything like being in the zone in any other sphere of my life. Not even at my company."

There was a long pause in the conversation. Sam looked at his tea.

"Maybe guys don't talk about things like love and the zone because they don't have words for it," Donna finally observed.

"Yeah. Yeah, the words inside are in another language. That's why guys go away to be together. If it's not a bar, or a hunting lodge, or a boat, they go away by watching television. We don't really talk when we're 'away' like that. We do stuff. That's the best way to translate the words in our hearts into the world outside.

"Buzz is a regular guy, despite being so different. Notice how he's always taking us places, going away. You know, maybe because you're a tomboy—"

Donna smiled at his frank statement.

"—Buzz and I have let you see behind the curtain of the secret life of men. But there's not much to show you. The key is that we don't really talk to each other. Buzz and I talk a lot for men, I guess. And to tell you the truth, Buzz has gotten me to talk more in the last few months than I've ever talked in my life. I mean, talking about real things. God, if he exists. Women. Me talking to you now because he brought us here.

"He cuts through the crap of life, the pre-programmed conversations we have every day at work and at bars with strangers. You know what I mean?"

"I think so," she said, straining to follow. She was a smart girl; she was letting him roll.

"Buzz has a way of cutting through to the real stuff. He was right about the ocean doing stuff to you. I can't put into words how that walk with you did something to me. It knocked me off my usual thought patterns. I actually was thinking that there might be such a thing as a soul."

Donna's heart leaped when Sam said this.

"In here," he continued soberly, looking up to her from his tea. "I know there's no soul. But out there, today, with you, with the rain on your face, the soul didn't seem like such a preposterous idea."

"Buzz…" Donna said, not knowing why.

"I'm used to being certain about my atheism. Or agnosticism. Maybe the difference is that an atheist cares more about the subject. It was weird having a doubt. If there is a soul, then my whole world crumbles. Is a soul immortal? What happens after the body dies? How is it related to the body? The whole world would become a swirling cyclone of doubt. I might even be tempted to adopt a philosophy that supplies ready answers, like…" he hesitated.

"Like Catholicism. Like our philosophy?"

He didn't answer.

"It's not a philosophy, you know," she said. It was not a rebuke so much as a reaction. "But I know what you mean. It doesn't have all the answers. Maybe all Catholicism has is the right assumptions."

"Huh?"

"Oh Sam. Think about it. Geometry has axioms. You can't prove them. You know—the shortest distance between two points is a straight line—but if you don't accept axioms at face value, you can't *get* any answers. You don't believe because you accept different axioms. Like the soul. The Catholic axiom isn't complicated: There *is* a soul. It's immortal. God made it. It either goes to heaven or hell after the body dies—with a stop in Purgatory maybe before heaven. Simple."

"Simple?"

"You understood it, didn't you?"

"Yes," he said, after a moment's reflection. His tone was low, soft.

I love your honesty, Donna thought. She caught herself. *Careful how you use that **love** word when Sam's involved.*

"Well, *your* axiom," she continued, "is that there isn't a soul, all for the reason you can't see it or feel it or touch it."

"Well," he rejoined, but lacking his usual certainty, "what is there that exists that you can't see or feel or touch?"

Donna smiled. *Got ya.*

"Love, silly. Love exists, Sam."

Sam immediately thought of Ellie, and the ocean, and the soul. And how all those things wouldn't be in his life if Buzz hadn't rammed into him during a pick-up game.

For the first time since Donna knew him, he didn't have a strong, ready reply. He stood up and stretched. He yawned.

Wow, Donna thought. *He's stalling.*

She let him stall. She never thought this moment would ever come. A chink in the agnostic armor of Sam Fisk.

Don't get too excited, she thought. *He'll come back with something.*

But he didn't. Not on that odd, generation-nothing day down the shore.

He excused himself, like a gentleman should before a lady, and went into the bathroom. He threw cold water onto his face. He looked into his own eyes. He didn't see a soul there.

Good, he thought.

But without conviction.

Chapter Seven

1

"I just don't get it," Sam said, putting his Stephen King novel down. *The Stand.* Buzz had recommended it to Sam. It was captivating. His beach chair was between Buzz and Donna's. The ocean was at low tide, and although the water was not warm enough to swim in, the sun was out, and the sky was clear.

The rain had passed, but the wind was steady. They hadn't bothered with bathing suits. There were only a few others on the beach, spread far apart.

Sam was too distracted by Buzz's last statement to Donna to keep reading. "What do you mean, the Father sees the Son in you?" he asked.

"Don't feel bad that you don't get it," Donna said. "I barely get it myself. Tell us again, Buzz."

"Well, just make believe you're a believer, Sam, a Catholic. Catholics believe that they are temples of the Holy Spirit; that the Holy Spirit lives in our hearts.

"They also believe that Jesus physically comes into our bodies when we receive Communion. But not just Jesus, but Jesus in His full divinity. He Who lives in us is not just the historical Jew who lived in Palestine, Who died and rose from the dead, but the very creator of the universe. In fact, the one Who keeps the universe in existence—"

"I don't believe that—" Sam interrupted.

"I know, I know. No sweat. I'm just asking you to follow the logic."

"Okay," Sam replied. "I forgot. Keep going."

Donna adjusted the blanket over her legs. She kept them covered. Partly because she was cold, partly because she was modest, and partly because she thought her legs were chunky and was embarrassed.

"So," Buzz continued, "God the Father is in heaven, ruling this universe, and He looks down at a Catholic. Let's say He looks down at Donna. Sure, it's more complicated than that, because we also believe that God is everywhere. Much of trinitarian theology is beyond our ability to comprehend, but for the sake of conversation, the Father is looking at Donna right now. Assuming that Donna is in a state of grace, then the Son is dwelling in her. The Father sees not only Donna, and loves her, but also sees the Son. And the more Donna does the will of the Son, she is the Son to the Father.

"The morning prayer of Saint Patrick got me thinking about all this. 'Christ above me, Christ below me, Christ on my left, Christ on my right, Christ before me, Christ behind me'—it goes on and on like that—then 'Christ in the eyes of those who see me, Christ in the ears of those who hear me speak' and so on. Or something like that. I don't have it memorized. If people can see Christ in us, then so can the Father.

"If Donna wants to really be a Christian, she should let Christ be Christ through her. That will connect her to the Christ in others, who are part of His Mystical Body. It connects her to the Father in heaven. It connects her to the universe itself. Well, maybe not the universe. Sometimes I get carried away with my high-minded ideas. Maybe it connects her, in the fullness of time, to the past."

"That last part sounds like time-travelling," she observed. "And maybe you are getting carried away, Buzz."

"Weird, and as I said before, kind of beautiful," Sam added.

"Yeah," Buzz said. "Beautiful."

Buzz took a sip of his Pepsi. Sam got up and stretched. From their low-slung beach chairs, he looked like a very skinny Gulliver.

"Your whole religion is weird. I hope you're not offended by my saying that. I never knew there was so much to it.

Before I met you guys, I thought Catholics were all holy candles and rosary beads and superstitions."

"Scott Hahn said that Fulton Sheen said that millions despise what they *think* is the Catholic Church, but less than one hundred hate what it really is," Buzz added.

"Who's Scott Hahn?" Donna asked.

"He's a really cool guy," he answered. "He's a Presbyterian minister who became a Catholic. I just heard a tape by him from the Kolbe Foundation, an apostolate from Indiana. The whole story of how he converted. Great speaker. Some of his Protestant friends are converting in a trickle. I think it's going to turn into a river."

"Do you have it here?" Donna asked.

Buzz shook his head. "Too bad, we could have listened on the way home."

"So you're saying," Sam said, returning to the subject, "that most people don't understand what the Catholic Church is?"

"Even most Catholics; it's sad." Buzz started digging a hole in the sand next to his chair. Always moving. Always doing something.

"It sounds like you need to be a college professor to be a Catholic," Sam observed.

"You don't have to be a scholar to be a Catholic," Buzz replied. "You have to be a mystic. For example, we believe that Jesus is in heaven right now, in His body, probably standing on something. He's wearing something. But He lived and died and rose almost two thousand years ago.

"At the same time, we believe that He is also present in every tabernacle in the world: body, blood, soul and divinity. Forget about religion for a minute, and name one thing in all of the world that even remotely comes close to that for sheer funkiness."

Sam and Donna could think of nothing.

Buzz was on a roll, and kept rolling, the excitement rising in his voice. "That's why I don't mind your agnosticism, Sam. In a real way, it makes sense. We're not trying to get you to believe in something that is ordinary or natural like a combustion engine, but rather, something that's far out, something supernatural. That's what *super*-natural means—beyond natural. You've got to believe a lot of funky stuff to be a Catholic."

Sam couldn't help but laugh quietly. Here was Buzz, the ultimate believer, the rock of faith, telling him that being an agnostic was reasonable—and using it to somehow show that belief was authentic.

"I've got an example," Donna offered. "An example of how funky the Catholic faith is. It's one of my favorite things about the faith."

"Shoot," Buzz said. Sam looked at her.

"First, look up in the air, and keep looking up," she commanded. "Sit down for a sec, Sam."

"Huh?" both men echoed.

She pursed her lips. "Just do it."

Sam sat back down. They dutifully looked up. It just happened that a seagull was circling over their heads, high up.

"Right now," she said, looking up with them, "I believe that three Guardian Angels are above us. They've been trying to get us to do and not do stuff all day. I've never seen them, or heard them, or had any physical proof they exist, but I believe they're there."

"I don't," Sam said, enjoying the sky, and the freedom to let them know he didn't believe without losing their friendship. *I love these guys. I believe that.*

"I do," Buzz said. He laughed loudly. "Hey, Angel. If you're there, show me a sign."

"Careful, Buzz," Donna said, quite seriously. "It's dangerous to ask for signs."

"Yeah," Sam said. "That seagull might *drop* a sign."

"It's good luck to get pooped on by a bird if you're Italian," Donna said, still serious.

"That's why I'm glad I'm not Italian. For dumb Irishmen like me," Buzz said, "it's good luck to win the lottery and stuff like that."

"Is that really true about Italians?" Sam asked.

"Yup," Donna said. "My gramma said that all the time."

"Do Italians have other good luck signs, like getting cancer or getting hit by a bus?" Buzz asked. "And can we look down from the sky now. My neck hurts."

They all brought their gazes down. They looked at each other.

They burst out laughing.

After the laughter died down, Buzz jumped up suddenly and sprinted toward the ocean, stormed into the water up to his hips, then smacked into a breaker, his arms and legs askew. His jeans and polo shirt getting soaked.

"He's a nut," Sam said.

Buzz screamed in faux pain. "It's freezing!" he yelled.

"Then why do you hang out with him?" she asked.

"I could ask you the same thing."

2

The analogy queen sat on claustrophobic hill, holding court, a cigarette dying a certain death between her fingers. The queen's legs where folded Indian-style on a ratty, if not typical, couch in a rundown house she shared on Oak Grove Avenue on the hill across from Franciscan University of Steubenville. She had crashed their party.

Judy Pierce, the analogy queen, *hated* Franciscan University of Steubenville, and was telling a group of innocent, devout Catholic students who went there with her why.

"You're nuts," her friend Silvio told her, his Spanish accent thicker because of the beers in his belly. He sat next to Judy, his arm scandalously around her shoulders.

"I'm perfectly sane," she replied. "For a normal person like me, Steubenville is like going to prison, but worse, because in prison everybody else there is a criminal like you.

Here, I'm an outcast. At Rutgers or Ohio State I would be considered run-of-the-mill for my beliefs, if not a bit prudish.

"But here I'm an outcast who everybody treats with pity and kindness, all because I don't go to Mass every day and wave my hands in the air when I pray. It's just like this dream I had the other day, that I was ironing something in my room, when I looked down, I saw it was my term paper, not my skirt, and it started to burn."

"What does that have to do with not liking it here?" Michelle, a freshman, asked. Silvio rolled his eyes. *Dumb freshman. Never ask the analogy queen a question.*

"Michelle, it's like something I read in my philosophy class the other day," Judy began.

Silvio Morales tuned her out. He didn't much like Steubenville, either. But his dislike was not as passionate as Judy's. He was in love with her.

Judy was a fox.

She pulled another cigarette out of her pack. She gently placed her hand on Silvio's wrist as he popped his lighter for her. She barely skipped a beat during her explanation to Michelle why Steubenville was Being *and* Nothingness, or at least *like* Being and Nothingness.

All sorts of rumors were going around about Silvio and Judy.

That they got drunk every weekend.

*Buzzed maybe. Drunk, occasionally. But not **every** weekend,* he thought.

That they slept together. *Sure, we sleep together,* he thought, *but we actually sleep together, as in snoozing, catching z's.*

They did stuff with each other and to each other, but had not done what Donna Beck would have called one of the Three Bad Things. Judy wasn't ready. He wasn't sure he was, either. One of these days, though, that rumor might be upgraded into a true story.

Silvio was surprised that his small network of friends hadn't reported to him a rumor that Judy and he were cutting off chicken heads in their spare time.

Never underestimate the power of rumor at Steubenville.

It was a small school, with a fairly modern campus atop a small mountain overlooking the Ohio River and the City of Steubenville. The little rust-belt town's claim to fame was that Dean Martin had been born and raised there.

And he never came back, Silvio thought.

But for most parents and students and supporters, Franciscan University of Steubenville was heaven on earth. For kids like Silvio and Judy, it was purgatorial punishment for being a wild high school kid.

An oasis of orthodox Catholicism for some.

A claustrophobic hill for Judy, Silvio, and their few friends.

Living off-campus in the tenements off Wellesley helped relieve some of the dullness and (to Silvio) hypocrisy, but not by much.

Judy came from a huge family that lived in California. She was the black sheep of a devout group of twelve children. Her father had money, and had bribed her with a new Subaru wagon to return after a disastrous freshman year, when she came within an inch of failing out.

Silvio's dad was a (now rare) steel worker from nearby Pittsburgh who got all caught up in the Charismatic Prayer Movement in the seventies. Eduardo Morales had moved to Steubenville to join the charismatic community that had formed around the university. His father had traded steel-working for carpentry, then dragged his equally fervent wife, Silvio, and two daughters along.

Absolutely no choice was given to Silvio as to where he would attend college. Just being able to move out of his folks' house to live near his friends had been a war of attrition.

But despite himself, and the dirty looks from Judy, Silvio had started going to Mass on Sunday.

Why? he asked himself.

Because there's something about this place. And the homilies were great—interesting.

Some of the priests really spoke to him during their homilies. And he had gotten caught up in the singing a few times. There was another reason.

Grace.

Is that why you haven't slept with Judy, Silvy? a small voice asked him as his girlfriend surfed into another analogy.

He inhaled deeply on his cigarette.

First Mass. Next, you'll be going to confession.

The voice was starting to really annoy him.

Confession? What? Give up all the fun in life? Become like these weenies? No way.

In his heart, grace was begging to differ.

3

Donna was disappointed when Sam politely declined to join her and Buzz for Sunday Mass.

"I'm going to my own services on the beach. I want to think," he told her, softening the blow.

He didn't miss much, she thought afterwards. The Mass was twisted and bizarre compared to what she was used to in Ohio. No kneelers. Kids surrounding the altar steps for the homily.

And the homily! Donna felt like gagging when the priest changed all the words of the Eucharistic Prayer around to suit his tastes.

*No mention of the Virgin Mary. Why don't I get to change around my responses? 'The Lord be with you.' 'Yeah, Father, and **maybe** with you.' I'm glad he didn't mess with the words of the consecration.*

Buzz refused to complain after Mass about the blatant abuses. And not because he didn't mind them.

"I don't want to get distracted," he told her. "I go to worship the Father and receive the Son. Period. Besides, the friars are almost—but not totally—hopeless, here. Keep telling yourself they mean well. I'm not sure if they do, but it helps keep me calm."

His advice didn't sound all that profound when he gave it to her, but his response ate at her all the way back to his uncle's duplex, and during the curiously silent breakfast. It was as if Buzz knew she was chewing on his words, not his omelette.

He's right, she finally concluded.

Ellie called while Sam was walking on the beach. There was no answering machine at the duplex, so they missed each other completely.

4

There is nothing—nothing—like a day at the beach down the New Jersey shore on Long Beach Island followed by a long, hot shower. Sand and salt fall away, and there's a dryer quality to the dryness once one has towelled off. The clothes one dons are cleaner. The music playing on the boom box is clearer. The Pepsi more refreshing.

As Buzz poured himself a Pepsi on the front deck, he thought about the special dryness. It reminded him of sobriety. *I love the shore!*

He smelled the ocean. He looked at the ocean. He listened to the ocean. Even his cigarette tasted better, crisper—almost, but not quite, healthy.

I'm a rich man.

He stifled an urge to shout. He gave in to another urge to sing, and burst out in a deep tenor:

"Tantum ergo sacramentum, veneremur cernui…"

"Watcha singing?" Donna asked, finished with her own shower, coming down the outdoor steps from the apartment above.

Buzz stopped singing; the moment was broken. He was chagrined but not embarrassed. It was nearly impossible for Buzz to become embarrassed.

"A love song to the Eucharist by Saint Thomas Aquinas," he told her.

She sat down on the deck chair. She held a Gin and Tonic that she had mixed upstairs. She noticed how simple the deck was; it was a large rectangle with two deck chairs, a picnic table and benches. The faded lengthwise planks were worn smooth by years of weather and children.

He continued without singing, translating some of the lyrics into English: "Humbly let us bow before thee, for so great a sacrament. What the senses fail to fathom, let us grasp with faith's assent."

"Sounds like what we were talking about on the beach," Sam commented through the screen window of the kitchen, a few feet away from his friends.

"Exactly," Buzz said, nonplussed.

"Precisely," Donna concurred. "What our senses fail to fathom…"

Sam came out and joined them, Bud Light in hand.

"I needed a vacation. Thanks, Buzz," he said.

"You're welcome."

"Yeah, thanks, Buzz," Donna added. "I'm glad I came."

After a bit, Sam asked, "So what are we renting tonight?"

"How about Risky Business?" Buzz suggested.

"Too much graphic sex," Donna said.

"Yeah, sorry; I forgot. Then what? Any classics?"

"They had Sergeant York at the rental place. I saw it on the classics rack," Donna told them.

"I haven't seen it. How about you, Buzz?" Sam asked.

Buzz had evolved into the final movie-rental arbiter. This was partly because he possessed a domineering personality;

partly because with three of them, it was practical; partly because he was always fair, and willing to rewatch movies he had already seen for the sake of the other two.

Donna loved seeing movies over and over again. She got a special satisfaction in rewatching a movie while turning the others onto it for the first time.

"Sure. I've never seen it. Not even on television. Isn't it a true story?" Buzz finally said.

"Yup," Donna said, stifling a smug smile. She allowed herself a glance at Sam, then turned to look at the ocean.

Sergeant York is a very Christian movie.

The mid-movie climax involved York's conversion after being struck by lightning, while literally getting knocked off a horse. *Maybe Sam will get knocked off his horse, too.*

Unexpected goose bumps rose on her arms. She took a big gulp. *What's going on here?*

The goose bumps went away as quickly as they came.

Buzz left them to begin making cheese dreams.

Joe Jackson Band wafted gently in from the living room. A not-so-oldie: "Don't You Know It's Different for Girls."

"Hey, I thought of another funky Catholic thing," Buzz called in from the kitchen. "I'll tell you at dinner. It has to do with genetics and the Immaculate Conception."

"Sounds pretty weird," Donna called toward the window, sharing a wink with Sam.

"Exactly," Buzz called back.

Later, the cheese dreams were served on the deck.

"You could make a fortune opening a chain of stores to sell these," Sam said, working on his seventh one. "I can't stop eating them. The bacon. The tomato. The cheese in all the nooks and crannies."

"The world wouldn't appreciate cheese dreams," Buzz said, patting his stomach. "They rejected van Gogh. They rejected Sony Betamax. They rejected Edgar Allan Poe. They rejected Boston's second album."

"Boston's second album sucked," Donna reminded the big man across the table.

"Ya got a point there," Buzz said, rubbing his chin. "Oh well."

"Nonsense, these would sell. I could start a company—" Sam said.

"In all your spare time?" Donna asked.

"You're right," Sam said finally. "I've got my hands full."

He was thinking not only of Edwards & Associates, but of getting engaged to Ellie. *I've got to call her.*

"So, do you want to hear my funky genetic thing?" Buzz asked.

"Absolutely not," Donna said, raising her head high.

"No. Let's talk about farming," Sam said with a straight face.

"Very funny," Buzz commented, false hurt in his voice.

Donna laughed first.

"Okay, okay," Buzz began after a while. "I think I've thought of something nobody else has ever thought about regarding genetics and the Immaculate Conception."

"Isn't the Immaculate Conception when the angel appeared to Mary and Jesus was conceived, or so the story goes?" Sam asked.

"No, but that's a common mistake—an immaculate mis-conception," Buzz punned.

"Don't joke about Our Lady," Donna said.

"Sorry, Donna. Anyway, Sam, the Immaculate Conception refers to the Catholic dogma that Mary was conceived free from original sin in the womb of her mother, Saint Ann."

"This is all new to me," Sam said apologetically.

"Believe me, Sam, you now know more about the faith than most Catholics I know. Even ones who go to Mass every Sunday," Donna consoled.

"Anyway," Buzz continued, "think about this: nowadays we know stuff about genetics that wasn't even scientific speculation just a few decades ago. DNA theory. Gene mapping. Double helixes. Genetic engineering."

"I've invested in a few genetic engineering firms," Sam said. "Gentech, others. High flyers. They're talking about curing cancer and birth defects while babies are still in the womb within two decades.

"There are literally billions of lines of 'code' on one gene. It boggles the mind. It makes our computers look like caveman stuff."

"Right. It's a whole new scientific frontier. That's why I don't think anybody's ever thought about what I'm going to talk about. At least nobody's ever written about it.

"Just for a minute, Sam, just for the sake of conversation—" Buzz repeated a familiar mantra.

"—I know, I know," Sam interrupted. "For the sake of conversation, accept some Catholic position."

"Right," Buzz said, warming up, oblivious to Sam's discomfort. He was, after all, Buzz. "Let's assume that the Catholic story of Jesus' conception—not Mary's Immaculate Conception, but Jesus' conception—is true. Picture a young girl, probably no older than fourteen or fifteen. Her fiancé's from a poor family with a royal bloodline that is pretty much forgotten—the House of David. She's a nobody. Mary of Nazareth. She had consecrated herself to God as a little girl— her own presentation, as it is called.

"She's sleeping one night, peaceful, when she sees a light and an angel appears to her. This is where I love the Bible and think it's so true to life. And you have to forget that you've heard this story so many times—even you, Sam. Everybody's heard it so many times they don't see it for the unique event it was. Just having an angel show up in your room is wild."

"I'm getting off track," Buzz interrupted himself, taking a deep breath, and a hit off his cigarette.

"The first thing the angel says, in effect, is 'Mary, you're going to have a baby, and he's going to be the Messiah.' Fair enough. She's a good Jewish girl. She knows the Messiah's coming. She even knows he's coming from her line, from the House of David. But you have to remember that nobody knew, not even the Jews, that the Messiah would also be God. They thought he was going to be a big king, a super version of

David. Super enough to kick the Romans back to hell. But a king who was a man. Not a God.

"So Mary says a very reasonable thing. And, if you think about it, a very levelheaded thing, considering she had just been told that she would have *the Messiah,* for heaven's sake. I mean, there's a shining angel, Gabriel, floating in the air next to the oil lamp by the bed or the window or whatever. So Mary says, 'How can this be? For I have not been with a man.'

"She doesn't shout for joy, or faint, or fall to her knees and worship or do any girl stuff. 'How can this be? I haven't been with a man.' That seems very real to me. Like it wasn't made up, so much as recounted, by Saint Luke, who asked Saint John what happened, or asked Mary himself. I'm not a Bible scholar.

"Now it really gets wild. The angel tells Mary, basically, that this son she is going to have, this Messiah, is going to be God himself. Yahweh, the God whose name is so sacred you're not allowed to say it. The God whose name means I Am Who Am."

Buzz jumped up and ran inside to a bookshelf in the living room. He came out a moment later with a Bible in his hands. They were shaking.

Boy, he's really getting worked up. And I have heard this story, somewhere. In art appreciation class? On television? Sure, Sam thought. *But Buzz makes it real.*

Buzz found the page in Luke. Chapter One.

"Everything I'm about to read is Jewish scripture code for saying, 'This child you are about to conceive will be God Himself.'

"Here it is; Gabriel says, 'you are to give him the name Jesus. He will be great and will be called *the Son of the Most High.'*"

Buzz emphasized the last phrase. His voice was rising.

"'The Lord God will give him the throne of his father, David. And he will reign over the house of Jacob *forever;* his kingdom *will never end.'*

"Again, remember that Mary asked, uh, here it is exactly: 'How will this be; since I am a virgin?'

"The angel answers, 'The Holy Spirit *will come upon you,* and the power of the Most High will overshadow you. So the holy one to be born will be called *the Son of God.'* And then the angel says that Elizabeth, who is barren, will have John the Baptist."

Buzz closed the Bible. He saw the excitement in Donna's eyes. Sam was listening carefully.

"So it's pretty clear that the Bible and Catholics believe that the Father of Jesus is God Himself. Mary then gives what is called her fiat, 'I am the handmaiden of the Lord. Let it be done unto me according to thy word.'

"Then, and it's not recounted by Luke, *it* happens."

Buzz paused for effect. Sam took the bait.

"What happens?"

"Mary," Buzz replied with utter sobriety and conviction, *"conceives* by the Holy Spirit. To put it directly, and without being graphic, for the first and last time in all of recorded history, God enters the womb of a woman. Her womb. God mixes *His* life with *her* life. Do I have to spell it out graphically? When I talk about the Blessed Mother, it's too serious to use even the biological terms."

Her egg was fertilized, Sam thought, fascinated. *And Buzz's love for Mary is so, so…extraordinary.* It was the reverence in Buzz's voice.

Both Donna and Sam shook their heads. They didn't have to hear the biology. They understood.

There was a lump in Buzz's throat. He cleared it.

"This means that God mixed with the billions of lines of Mary's genetic code. That the Jesus who walked on the earth, and was a man of flesh like you and me, got at least half his genetic code from *a mere woman. A woman He and His Father created.* He was conceived in a sinless woman by a sinless Spirit. Conceived without sin. Jesus' flesh was *her* flesh. There was no earthly father, either. It's clear that Saint Joseph was a foster father. Unlike every single person who has ever lived or died on this rock we call earth, Jesus had only one human earth-parent. We all have two.

"His eyes—their color came part from Mary, and part from well, that's what is not so clear to me. God the Father doesn't have genetic code, per se. He's immutable, spirit. Maybe all the genetic code came from Mary? How can we know for sure? I like to think that the male part of the code came from nothing, like Adam did. Either way, God *designed* the male part. So Jesus' hair was like Mary's hair just as Donna's hair comes at least halfway from her mother. Jesus was a perfect genetic mix between Mary and God. His fingers, his legs, his forearms. A mix so close it can't be torn apart. They ripped the life out of Jesus on the cross, but they couldn't rip Mary out of Him.

"In a billion ways, in a way that the greatest scientists of that time couldn't even comprehend or imagine, and inside a space—the double helix of a DNA strand—so incredibly tiny that the scientists of our time can't even watch or photograph, God joined Himself to mankind through Mary. It's awesome; truly awe-inspiring.

"Jesus' genes are as much Mary's as God's. And you wonder why Catholics love her so much. And you really have to wonder why Protestants make like she's just a random chick who was in the right place at the right time.

"The Immaculate Conception makes a lot more sense if you think about it. Would God mix His genetic code with code that decays and dies? Remember, in Genesis, death is one of the punishments for Original Sin. Would He mix with sinful flesh if He had another option? He made Mary, and He created her sinless. That's what the Franciscans always argued.

"Now some theologians I've been reading say she died after a fashion, or fell asleep, and then was assumed into heaven. I read somewhere that the Eastern Orthodox call it her Dormition. The details have not been revealed. But I don't think she died the way we died, if she died at all. I don't think her body decayed. I think Jesus woke her up and took her up to heaven wide awake. That's just my opinion."

Buzz saw he was losing Sam. He caught himself, and decided he was done.

"Look, Mary was given the option to nix the whole thing right then and there. She could've said 'no.' Thank God she didn't. Thank her when you pray. Two thousand years later, it's still the most interesting thing to talk about in the world.

"Now that is funky stuff, Sam. And Donna and I believe it. Or at least the part that's not speculation."

Buzz leaned back in his chair and slouched a bit. He was worn out, but in a good way.

"You know," Donna said after a pause. "When we receive Communion. When we consume Him, we consume Him *body, blood,* soul and divinity. We must also be consuming Mary's flesh. Well, maybe not her flesh—" Donna was thinking on her feet "—but her genetic code. Far out."

But she wasn't quite sure if everything Buzz had said was true. It was interesting, though. She would have to think about it. Maybe ask Sister Elizabeth about it.

Sam took a long, hard look at the ocean. There was a word in his heart, but he couldn't hear it. Even if he did, he doubted he could translate it into English.

"That's pretty wild," he said softly. "Thanks, Buzz. I'm not sure what to say. Your…your religion, it's…intimate. Flesh. Eating. Flashes of light from Angels. I don't believe it. It's just not in me. But I want to believe it. It's not cardboard gods hurling flameballs at each other from Mount Olympus, or a cold, old man on a big throne with a giant tablet listing your sins. It's…"

Sam had come to the point where he was able to describe what the faith wasn't. He couldn't say what it was. It was beyond him. Beyond the ocean's slashing waves a stones throw away from him.

"It, our religion," Buzz finished for him, searching for words that wouldn't hurt his friend, but still pushing, challenging—still relentlessly loving—Sam, "is something most people don't want to hear about because it's so jolting, so wild, so interesting and beautiful that you have to come to terms with it."

"No, Buzz," Donna said. "You're wrong. Well, you're right and you're wrong. Sorry. You don't come to terms with *it,* you come to terms with *a man.* You come to terms with Him.

"Either Jesus was a mere man or He was what the angel implied He was, true God and true man. You've got to come to terms with Him. Who is He? Was the angel lying? If He wasn't a mix of Mary and the Father, then who was the human father?"

"You don't have to come to terms with him," Sam disagreed, still looking at the ocean, a distant look in his eyes and a far away sound in his voice. "You can *ignore* him. Even though his footprints are all over our civilization. At least that's what my father used to say. Jesus is everywhere. I've lived my whole life without ever really thinking about him except in an academic way. Now, I'm becoming uncomfortable.

"No," he continued, "there was one time."

He turned back to his friends.

"One time, in a museum. I wondered about him. A long time ago."

"Tell us about it," Donna asked.

Buzz knew that she had pushed too much. He didn't know how he knew. Maybe it was the look in Sam's eyes. *I've pushed him pretty hard myself.*

"Sorry," Sam said, standing up. "My brain is fried."

A very awkward silence ensued.

Buzz spilled his Pepsi, on purpose, on Donna. He practically aimed it at her.

"Buzz!" she yelled, genuinely angry, rising up. Her wrap skirt was soaked and already sticky.

"Sorry," Buzz said, not sorry.

"Is this your way of breaking the tension?" Sam demanded, sounding a bit unbalanced.

"Yes," Buzz said, smiling. "Donna, why don't you empty your Gin and Tonic on me?"

Her eyes narrowed to slits.

"Don't mind if I do," she said in a huff, and flicked the contents of her glass into Buzz's face as if she had been practicing for years. Then she took the beer out of Sam's hand, walked around the table and poured it on Buzz, who sat as calm as a kid in a barber's chair.

"You guys are weirder than your religion," Sam finally said.

"Thank you," Buzz said.

Donna made a frustrated noise. "I'm going for a walk. Let's go, Sam."

Sam looked back from Donna to Buzz and back again.

"Go ahead, Sam. See you in while. I'll go rent the video. Sergeant York?" He looked to Donna.

She had already started toward the beach.

"Whatever," she said without turning back. "Come on. Let's go, Sam. Race you to the water!"

She began to jog.

Sam paused, then jumped over the rail of the deck and started walking after her.

"That went well," Buzz told himself aloud.

He pulled the keys out of his pocket. Then he put them back in. He went inside to change his shirt and dry off his hair. He hadn't smelled of beer like this in a long time.

✝ ✝ ✝

Sergeant Alvin C. York got under Sam's skin, too.

6

That night, before Donna could fall off to sleep, the enemies of Grace arrived. She did not see them. They began with an effort to push creepy images to the edge of Donna's consciousness, hoping her mind would grasp them.

Horrible images from two movies she had seen seemed to pop uncalled into her mind.

Donna had never slept alone in an empty house, not once, not even during college, before this weekend. The dark room, the unfamiliar bed, the unusual sounds of the wind on the window, combined with her aloneness, managed to give her a chill.

A fright. The willies.

She found it hard to keep her eyes closed. She imagined a shadow near the closet.

Come on, she told herself, *you're acting like a child.*

The wind kicked up. The wind *was kicked* up. A window somewhere else in the house rattled. She turned her head quickly. Now, she was frightened.

Is someone in the house?

Her ears perked up. She heard more sounds.

This is crazy.

The enemies of grace were not used to taking shots at Donna Beck, who was normally well-protected.

Suddenly, she remembered to pray. Then she remembered that she had left her rosary beads in Rocky River. With great effort, she began to move her lips silently and began the Rosary, keeping count on her fingers.

She offered her fear up for Sam.

The enemies of grace saw her lips moving and became incensed. They were allowed more leeway…

…Donna felt hot breath on her face. She stifled a scream.

Jesus! she cried out in her head.

Then she prayed the Name out loud.

"Jesus."

That worked. She was not a veteran of spiritual warfare. But she had good instincts.

She prayed the Saint Michael prayer.

"Saint Michael the Archangel, defend us in battle. Be our safeguard against the wickedness and snares of the devil. May God rebuke him, we humbly pray, and do thou, O Prince of the Heavenly Host, by the power of God cast into hell satan and all the evil spirits who prowl about the world seeking the ruin of souls. Amen."

But she still had the creeps. She kept praying her Rosary. She rejected the idea of going downstairs.

She was a tough guy.

Grace had taken a chance with her, and she was responding. Grace knew that Sam couldn't bear the attacks alone, and allowed the attacks to fall upon one who loved him.

Donna managed to fall asleep by the third decade.

She dreamed that she was in a hospital. She had hurt her knee in a basketball game. She was in a large ward, with rows of beds, and hundreds of patients. Most were convicted killers.

They've brought me to the wrong hospital! I'm in the prison ward!

She tried to get up, but her busted knee made the effort fruitless.

A nurse with one of her eyelids pierced by a safety pin ran up and floated near the end of her bed. Donna saw a snake's tongue come out of her mouth as she spoke: "Treatment time!"

There was evil good cheer in the nurse's voice.

"You're here for life! Hard time!"

The nurse laughed a sickly laugh.

"No!" Donna cried out.

She saw three human frogs in orderly's uniforms coming up the hallway (now her room was a single—no other patients in the room now). Two were carrying rusty axes. The other was carrying a medieval club and flail.

"For life!" the nurse screamed. Her face had turned into a webbing of crumpled metal screening, like an insane fencer.

"Or death!"

The frog men were all around her. Donna couldn't move…they raised their axes and saws and chains and spikes and giant scalpels…and began to chop at her leg…

…Donna awoke from the nightmare, clawing at her knees, screaming. Beads of sweat were on her forehead. Her hair and nightshirt were soaked.

Screw this.

She tightly clasped one end of her scapular in her hand.

She gathered her blanket around her with her free hand and fumbled the light on once she got to the door. She remembered that she kept a Saint Benedict medal in her travel kit. Her father had given it to her before she went on a trip with the Girl Scouts.

What? Ten years ago? The trip to Washington.

She went to the bathroom, pulled the kit open, and found the tricolored medal quickly. She let go of the scapular and grasped the medal. She adjusted the blanket around herself, and walked purposefully to the door, then out and downstairs.

When Sam opened the door, in answer to her loud knocking, he was rubbing sleep from his eyes.

"Donna? What's the matter?" he yawned.

"Heebee jeebees," she said, anger in her voice. She was embarrassed. Like a little kid.

That woke Sam up. "Yeah, all alone. Buzz is a jerk for making you stay up there all alone. I'd get the creepy crawlers up there all alone."

She wasn't going to argue with him. She was shivering. Quite innocently, he gave her a hug to warm her.

He was Sam. And still a bit sleepy.

She allowed herself an extra moment of solace in his arms.

This is where I belong. She pulled away. *But not right now. And not this way. Not out of pity.*

She was disoriented herself.

"Why don't you take my bed, Donna," he suggested. "I'll sleep on the couch. I'll be right outside your door if you get spooked again."

"You don't have to," she said, then added, "I'll take the couch. You won't fit on it."

"I'll put the cushions on the floor. No more discussion. I'm waking up." He yawned.

He turned and walked to the couch, then quickly arranged the cushions on the floor. He practically collapsed onto them.

"My bed is still…warm… for …you." And then he fell asleep.

She got a blanket from the hall closet, and lovingly placed it over his long body, resisting an urge to stroke his face with her hand.

The willies were gone by the time she slipped into Sam's bed. She was still mildly disappointed with herself for not being man enough to stick it out upstairs. Even so, there was a peaceful countenance on her face as she drifted off to sleep; she was pleased that she managed to finish her Rosary.

Grace, however, was not disappointed. His stout little soldier had fought well. For Him. For herself.

And for Sam.

Chapter Eight

1

Sam Fisk dialed the number he dialed most often.

"Hello. This is the Fisk residence," Edward Fisk said.

"Hello Father," Sam said, stealing a furtive glance toward the surf, where Buzz and Donna were standing, beyond the tall dune grass, with their feet up to their ankles in the water.

"Hello son. How are you enjoying your first visit to the ocean?" Edward asked.

✝ ✝ ✝

"You know something, Buzz?" Donna said, looking out at the water. There were clouds in the sky, but the temperature was pleasant.

"What?"

"You don't know everything," she said. Her tone was not unkind, but there was a faint hint of accusation.

"Never said I did. What's bothering you?" Buzz replied, turning to look at her. She didn't look back.

"I think you're pushing Sam too hard," she replied. "With all that genetic stuff and connecting to the past because the Father sees Jesus in you—things like that."

"What's the harm? I'm just throwing out ideas, trying to get him excited. I'm not a theologian."

✝ ✝ ✝

"I love the ocean," Sam said, hesitating. He wanted to say more, but somehow he couldn't. *The secret life of men,* he heard Donna's voice in his head.

"And how are your friends?" Edward continued.

"Just fine. Characters, really. I want you to meet them when you come to Cleveland for your lecture."

"I would enjoy that. It's good to see you're not spending all your time on your business. All work and no play…"

"Makes Sam a dull boy. I understand, Father. So how is your new book coming along?"

"Oh that. I've been procrastinating. But it's going to come out just fine. I'm excited about it. Maybe ten other professors will read it."

"Don't say that," Sam said. "You know it will be well received."

✝ ✝ ✝

"Besides, he's my friend, too. I'm only trying to help him," Buzz defended himself, trying to keep the hurt out of his voice. He wasn't normally this sensitive to criticism.

"But you have to take into consideration that Sam is just starting to open up to new ideas. Some of your speculation could lead him right out of agnosticism into—"

"Pantheism or Protestantism?"

"What's pantheism?" she asked.

"The belief that God and nature aren't separated. That God is nature, or nature is God. Me, you, those seashells, the medical waste floating out there—it's all God."

"Kinda like taking God as the source of all Being and remaking Him into the stuff He keeps in existence," Donna observed.

"Yeah, you got it. Most religious falsehoods are based on a truth.

"Look, I want to think about what you said about misleading Sam. I wouldn't want to be responsible for leading him out of the darkness right back into heresy. He's an honest agnostic. There's something noble about that. Can you imagine him spouting Bible verses outside Tower City Center, calling the Church the Whore of Babylon?"

"No, not Sam," she said, a kind of dreaminess in her voice. "He'd be a kind and considerate Protestant. The kind that's really hard to change."

✝ ✝ ✝

"Father…may I ask you something?" There was hesitation in Sam's voice.

"Of course," Edward said.

"Do you…do you ever think about death?"

"Yes. It's part of my next book. Sartre says that death and knowledge are—"

"No, not that way," Sam cut him off nervously. "Do you ever think about your own death?"

"I don't know what you mean." Edward's tone changed. It was not cold—but it was less warm.

"I mean, do you ever think of what will happen *to you* when you die?"

There was a pause that seemed to last as long as the tides took to change.

"No. There is nothing for me after. Nothing after death."

Edward's tone had risen to a slight level of agitation. Sam could not remember the last time his father, whom he talked to every other day, had used such a tone.

He's telling me the subject is closed.

"But Father—"

"It's the only rational position," Edward's voice softened. "Please forgive me for snapping at you."

Another long pause.

"Yes, of course. You're right. It must be the ocean."

"Yes, the ocean. The ocean is not rational."

That's not a rational statement either, Father, Sam thought, shaken. Shaken worse than by anything Buzz or Donna had told him in the last two days.

"Samuel? Are you still on the line?"

"Sorry, Father. I was just thinking."

"Thinking? About what?"

"Uh, nothing. Nothing at all, sir," Sam lied. "I was day-dreaming. My friends are expecting me down at the surf. Can you hear it?"

"Yes, and I understand. You wish to join them. I have a bit of reading to do. I love you, Sam."

"I love you, Father."

✝ ✝ ✝

"So where *do* you get all your theological ideas?" she asked.

"You're not going to like the real answer," he said, confusing her.

"So give me the phony answer first," she said after a moment.

She's quick, Buzz noted. *Here goes.*

"Phony answer: I read a lot. Well, that's even true. I read four or five hours a day. Sometimes six or seven hours if I don't see you or Sam. When I was married, I read almost as much. Anything, fiction, science, sports, anything. I'm great at Jeopardy."

"So's my dad," Donna said. "What does that have to do with anything? No—wait—I get it. You read a lot of theology now. And that doesn't sound phony. That sounds normal. Which leads me to another question. How did you ever end up at Notre Dame? Isn't that a hard school to get into?"

"One question at a time, Grasshopper. And yeah, I do read a lot of spiritual books. Even about other religions—it's good to know the competition. I've read like a crazy man ever since I came back to the faith after my divorce. One time I read a quote by the founder of Opus Dei, Monsignor Josemaría Escrivá. 'For the modern apostle, an hour of study is an hour of prayer.' But—"

Buzz stopped to throw a clam shell sideways into the ocean. Its trajectory went on a curve upward before falling to the water.

"Cool," Donna said, referring to the shell's flight. "How do you do that?"

He fished another half-shell from the sand below the water at their feet. It was about three inches across.

"You hold it like this. See? Then you just throw it side-arm, but straight. It'll rise on its own."

He threw his shell, and it took the same surprising trajectory.

She found a shell. He helped her find the right grip. She threw it, and it climbed like Buzz's, but not nearly as far or high, and with a wobble.

"You got it," he said.

"Cool."

She began to search for another shell. They were both enjoying the leisure of the ocean, knowing there was plenty of time for talk.

After a few more tosses, she asked, "So what's the real answer? Do you call the pope every night?"

"No, but you're close. You're close."

He threw another shell. Sam came out the door of the house behind them. They heard it bang. Donna saw him and waved.

"Quit stalling," she told him plainly, before turning back to the ocean. *If he doesn't want to tell me, then he doesn't want to tell Sam, either.* She could just tell.

"I have a gift," he began. "I just know what the Church teaches and what it doesn't. I'm not infallible or anything, but whenever I read or hear something the Church teaches, it's like it was already inside my heart and mind. It's weird. It's like I'm learning something I already know. The only problem is, I can't always express it in words. It comes out weird. Sometimes it comes out wrong, but when I hear what the Church really teaches, I accept it without reservation. Maybe that's why I like to talk about things with you and Sam. It helps me figure out how to say what I already know. Or think I know."

He finished, a slightly helpless look on his face. *She's going to tell me I'm full of it.*

"Oh, Buzz. Maybe all you're describing is the gift of faith, and the way God works through you," she said, turning to him.

"You think so?"

"Yes."

"You mean you believe me?" he said. He wasn't really asking, so much as looking for confirmation.

"Of course, Silly. Why would you make it up? I'm just wondering why you kept something like that to yourself."

"Because I'm not sure what it is. One time I was praying and asking God about it and…"

"And what?" She was genuinely curious.

"And I could have sworn I heard a voice say that it pleased God."

"What pleased God? And what voice?" the young woman pressed. She was the one pushing now.

"It pleased Him that I knew what the Church teaches. That He made me that way. And the voice? I don't know. It wasn't inside or outside of my mind. It was just there."

Donna remembered the first time she had prayed the Rosary well at her parish.

"Hmmn. You are a strange one, Buzz. But not as strange as you think."

"Thank you," he said, without his usual smugness.

*Why **did** you hide that from us?* she thought. *Maybe you're insecure.*

She shook her head at him, and smiled. She resisted an urge to hug Buzz. Sam was only a few yards away now and it would look wrong—it would look, well, like she was excluding a friend.

Why haven't you brought either one home to your family? a little voice asked her. *Who's the insecure one?*

Oh shut up, she told herself.

"Hey Sam! How's your dad? Did you get through?" Buzz called out. She turned.

"He's doing well. He's looking forward to meeting you both."

Sam reached for a clam shell. "Show me how you throw it?"

Buzz taught Sam the same method he taught Donna.

Sam's toss, slung from his long thin arm, put Buzz's earlier throws to shame.

"Show off," Donna kidded.

"Luck," Buzz weighed in.

"Skill," Sam rejoined casually.

It was nice to be back with his friends. *What does that say about your father?* an inner voice asked him.

Warm friends and cold feet in the ocean, at the beach, down the shore.

Sam chose to ignore the voice.

Why spoil things?

✛ ✛ ✛

Later, they watched *Heaven Can Wait.*

"Her lips are really big," Buzz said seriously after the credits.

"Julie Christie's?" Sam asked.

"So are Warren Beatty's," Donna added.

"They should have called it *Big Lips Can Wait,*" Buzz said.

"Is that a joke, or a serious cinematic critique?" Sam asked.

Donna giggled, and the bowl of popcorn slipped off her belly. Buzz caught it.

"Did you know," Buzz asked, changing the subject, "that Siskel and Ebert have changed their names? Officially, on their driver's licenses and everything."

"Seriously?" Donna asked.

"Seriously, to help their show."

"What did they change them to?" Sam asked.

"The Fat Guy and the Other One," Buzz deadpanned.

"I don't get it," Sam said. "Why would they do that?"

"Very funny, Buzz," Donna said. "Sam, nobody can remember which one is which, so they always say, 'the fat guy gave it thumbs up and the other guy didn't.'"

"Oh."

"I'm going for a walk," Donna said, rising, too sensitive to let Sam know she was going for a walk to pray a Rosary for him.

"Is it safe?" Sam asked.

"Sure," Buzz said. "Seriously. This island is safe. But stay within shouting distance, and bring my gun with you, Donna."

"You have a gun?" Donna asked skeptically, tilting her head.

"No," Buzz said, smiling. "But you'll be safe. There are beach patrols. Sam and I will stay out on the deck. It's low tide, and we'll hear you if you yell for us. Stay close."

"You guys are great. Don't stop being so overprotective. It makes me feel like a princess."

"That's what you are," Buzz said, touchingly sincere. Sam nodded.

She blushed sweetly, then turned to walk to the door. She pulled her Indian's sweatshirt on, then walked out, grasping Buzz's rosary beads in her pocket. She had borrowed them earlier. Sister Elizabeth's words echoed in her mind: *Do you pray, Donna? I mean, **really** pray, putting your whole self into it the way you put yourself into sports?*

"No," Donna told herself now, feeling the cold sand beneath her feet, looking back at the lights on the deck. Sam and Buzz were coming out. The moon was out, and they waved. She waved back.

But tonight will be different. And tomorrow. She had something to pray for. *Someone to pray for.*

2

Most resolutions are like sandcastles, quickly washed away with the first worldly wave. But Donna's resolution was a real one. She would keep it. She would *really* pray. She was inspired by a friend who read books as his prayer; another friend who couldn't pray for himself; a nun who suggested she put normal human effort into prayer; and by the soulful sounds of calm breakers in God's natural cathedral. She took a giant step toward sanctity. Her first step toward her own destiny, which was still a mystery to her. Grace had called. She answered. And neither would break the connection—until forever. Now and forever.

3

Sam was leaning on the weathered rail of the deck. Buzz was sitting at the circular picnic table, a glass of water before him.

"You wanna call Ellie? I'll stay here and keep an eye out for Donna," Buzz offered.

"No, it's still early," Sam replied. "I'll call her later. She's probably out on a business dinner. Besides, I want to ask you about her."

Buzz took a sip of water. He lit a cigarette. He waited. Sam remained silent. Time to push.

"Let me guess," Buzz said, a prelude.

"Go ahead."

"You're gonna marry her."

Sam smiled sheepishly, but managed not to look down at his shoes.

"And," Buzz continued, "you want to know about timing."

Sam nodded. "And sex."

Buzz raised his eyebrows. "Hmmn."

"Yeah," Sam agreed.

"Timing first," Sam said finally.

"Timing. You mean like when to ask her?"

"Yeah. Is it too soon? I haven't known her for very long. She's brought it up. Sometimes hints. Sometimes outright. It's like she's just assumed it since we started dating."

"Let's see," Buzz continued, rubbing his chin. *I need more information. Dear Saint Anthony, help me find the right advice.* "Tell me something, first."

"Like what?"

"Like if you love her. Like why you want to get married. Like what you think marriage is."

"That's a lot," Sam said.

"I've got all night."

"Well, yeah, I guess I love her."

"You *guess* you love her?"

"Look, am I on trial?"

"Hey, Sam, relax. I'm not going to give you advice without doing some background research."

Sam paused. "Sorry, man."

"Forget it. I was being too pushy. Of course you love her. I've seen too many movies. I feel like the dad in every marriage discussion scene in every movie ever made. 'Do you love her, son? Do you *really* love my Muffy?' Then you say, 'Yes, sir. I love her more than anything in the world, sir.' Then the dad says, 'Just don't hurt her, boy, or I'll kill you.' 'Sir, yes sir, sir!'"

Sam snorted softly, and took a sip of beer.

"Look, Sam, I'm no expert on marriage. I'm an expert on bad marriages…"

"I know you, Buzz. You're dying to give me the Catholic perspective on things. I'm willing to listen. I'm open. Not to believe. But I know you won't shovel manure on my plate."

"Long version or short version?"

"Short version," Sam replied, businesslike.

"You've got to agree on three things first: kids, money, religion. Religion first. You've got to pray together every day."

Buzz saw Sam's eyebrows rise.

"Relax, Sam. I know you're going to have trouble praying together, because you don't pray. But not praying hurts your odds. Couples who pray together daily have a one-in-one thousand chance of breaking up."

"You're kidding," Sam said.

"I kid you not. I read it in Reader's Digest. Then I saw it on Mother Angelica—she's a Catholic Billy Graham with her own cable television network. Doesn't matter what religion, either. Jew, Catholic, Muslim. There was a big study. And get this: couples who didn't pray together every day but still attend weekly services—their odds for divorce are only one-in-ten. Wild, eh? Beats fifty-fifty."

Sam thought for a minute.

"Ellie goes to Mass just about every Sunday," Sam said, practically musing out loud. "She says her faith is very important to her. But she's never pushed me to convert or anything. She has dropped hints that she wants a church wedding."

"I think, if you get permission, you can get married in a Catholic church, and you don't have to become a Catholic. Her pastor can fill you in. After the wedding, maybe you could go to Sunday Mass with her. Keep her company. There's no law against it."

Sam grunted, thinking.

Boy, he's open tonight, Buzz thought. *Is Donna praying?*

"What else did you say? Religion, kids—"

"And money," Buzz finished. "Wanna talk about money first?"

"Well, we're okay in the money department. My business is going great, and computers are going to be around for a long time. Ellie has a good job. No debt. Her dad is wealthy."

"That's not what I mean," Buzz said. "Sure, you don't have any money problems, but rich people get divorced, too."

Buzz was keeping his advice religion-neutral as much as possible. Trying to sound factual, practical.

"What I mean is, you've got to agree on what money is all about, and, on what you want to do with it together. If she thinks money can make a person happy and you don't, you're in for rocky roads."

"Yeah, I get you."

"Before I go on, I can confirm all this by telling you that Sandi and I screwed up every single one of these. We thought we had them down, but we really didn't. It caused huge battles."

"You make it sound like war," Sam said.

"My marriage was. And our daughter was a casualty."

A dark cloud came over Buzz's eyes. He looked away.

"Anyway, you and Ellie have a lot more going for you. I was a drunk. Immature. Sandi had her own problems."

"Do you mind telling me about her?"

"I'd rather not. I'm trying to encourage you, not discourage you."

"Didn't mean to pry."

"Forget it, Sammy. I brought it up."

Silence came, a welcome respite.

"I guess we agree on money." Sam picked up the thread as if there had been no pause. "We've never talked about it. But it seems like our backgrounds are the same. We take money for granted. Neither one of us has ever wanted for anything a day in our lives. I suspect we never will. It's just not a big deal to either one of us. Even when I struggled during the start-up of Edwards & Associates, it didn't bother me. Money is just a means to an end."

"Good. You don't strike me as a materialist. Funny, when it comes to spiritual truth, you are. But day-to-day, I've never seen anything about you that showed you were preoccupied with money. But that's getting off the subject. I think you should talk to Ellie about it."

"I will."

"Good. That leaves…let's see…"

"Kids," Sam filled in.

"Which brings us back to sex. You can guess what I think. No, that's not fair. Maybe you can't."

"Whatever it is, it's Catholic," Sam said, but there was no teasing in his voice. It was—almost—a compliment.

"Yeah," Buzz said, standing up. He stretched. He walked over to Sam, who was still leaning against the deck rail, and put an arm around his neck, bearishly.

"Sex," Buzz began, pausing slightly for effect, "equals kids. We've come full circle. You said you wanted to talk about sex. But maybe you had something different in mind. In my opinion, Sam, and I tell you this as a friend who loves you—"

Buzz cut himself off. He stifled a violent urge to get emotional. That would lead to tears. That was not in the playbook. He took his arm away and continued, gesturing with his hands.

"—that the religion and the money are tied to the kids and to the sex. I'm not just saying that. That's the key to understanding marriage. It's not a war. No, it's not a war.

"But it's the most important thing people do: they get married. And I'm telling you right now that marriage boils down to kids. Everything else is just window-dressing and Bing Crosby singing White Christmas."

Sam thought suddenly of his mother, holding him, riding in the convertible, the moon following them.

"I'm still listening, Buzz. Just because I don't believe in God doesn't mean I don't think kids are important. I've never told you this, but…"

Now it was his turn to bang his emotions down, hard and fast, before they even considered showing up in this conversation.

"But I've always wanted kids. Not a lot. No numbers. My dad is my best friend. He's all I have. I—I want more of that. I don't know how to say it."

"I know," Buzz said, thinking of his own father. He had truly loved the old lush, and still mourned him.

"You don't have to say it. I ache for my daughter. I…" he trailed off. They both shook their heads, then turned to look at the ocean.

After a while, Buzz said, "Can you see Donna?"

"Yeah, she's there on the jetty. She's staying close by."

"Good," Buzz said. *Dear God, if she's praying, give us some of the grace. I know Sam responds to it, even if he's not aware of it.*

✝ ✝ ✝

The jetty was made of stone. Huge black boulders formed a wide spine that stretched out into the ocean. It was the width of two men, and its tail reached back into the beach until it disappeared beneath the sand. At low tide it was like a huge armored whale sunning itself. At high tide, it became like a submarine perpetually diving into the big waves that surrounded it.

The boulders nearest the surf had rough craggy surfaces pitted with barnacles or ancient seaweed. Donna stood upon one, her feet set firmly, the water lapping in the crevices around her as the waves broke and receded. It was louder here, and the breezes seemed to shift from warm to cold in a flash.

She was having a particularly difficult time concentrating on the fourth sorrowful mystery, the Carrying of the Cross.

God was aware of this. He had not pulled away from His daughter, so much as hidden Himself from her for her greater good.

Donna was disturbed. Her concentration had been excellent up to that point. She called time out.

What would I do if I was having trouble on the court? she asked herself. *Hustle. Try harder. Win.*

Grace rejoiced!

She looked up at the stars.

They're not light coming to me across light years. They're angels. They're weeping.

She bore down. She forced herself to imagine what it was like for Christ; bruised, His flesh in tatters on His back from the scourging, His blood dripping on the rocks, His mother softly sobbing nearby, the shouts and taunts from the crowd distracting Him, and much worse to come on the top of the hill…

If He could gut it out, so can I, she thought.

She began praying again.

*Hail Mary, full of grace, the Lord is with thee, blessed art thou among women, and blessed is the fruit of thy womb, Jesus. Holy Mary, Mother of God, pray for us sinners, **now** and at the hour of our death.*

She didn't know why she emphasized the word *now*. She allowed herself a pause. *Because now is here. Now is where I am, on this jetty. Jesus is hearing me now.*

His mother prayed *now*. Donna fought on beside her, climbing Calvary with her and her Son.

✜ ✜ ✜

After a while—a whole cigarette on Buzz's part, the conversation began again. Buzz had looked up at the stars, and was inspired.

"Wanna hear a story? A true story. In a roundabout way, it's about marriage and kids, my friend." Buzz's tone, usually straightforward, was almost tender.

Sam nodded, watching Donna on the jetty.

"I know this guy. His name is Bill White. He runs a big advertising company in Cleveland. The biggest. He's a bachelor. I don't see him much. I ran into him in a deli during lunch while driving my truck a few months back. He noticed my scapular hanging out the front of my shirt. Anyway, he's a good Catholic, and I've had lunch with him now and again. I even asked him to pray for you and Ellie."

He watched for Sam's reaction. None. Sam kept looking at the shadow on the jetty. Buzz took it as a good sign. *He's used to me,* Buzz thought. *And he's still my friend?*

"So at lunch about two weeks ago he told me this story. I just thought of it as I was looking at the stars, at the Milky Way. It's amazing how many stars you can see when you're down the shore.

"Bill has a cousin, Whitey Michaels. Whitey told him this story. Nobody really knows about it, and I'll explain why at the end. Turns out that Whitey's mom is one of the founders of the Breastfeeding League, which has its headquarters in

Chicago, but that's not part of the story. His uncle was an astronaut."

"Really?" Sam asked. He had always been fascinated by astronauts and space travel.

"Really. That reminds me, we should rent *The Right Stuff*. I didn't see it when it came out—"

"Yeah, yeah, tell me the story," Sam interrupted.

"Sorry. So Bill's cousin Whitey's mom's brother is an astronaut, and he got to go up on Skylab. He donned the white monkey suit and surfed the stars, man, for like four months. Well, I don't know how long, but it was a long time.

"Now, they let astronauts take a tiny box of stuff up with them. You know, knickknacks and things, so they can bring them back and give stuff that's been in space to their kids. But every extra ounce costs a billion dollars in fuel, or something like that, so they don't let them bring much up there.

"Well, Bill told me that his mother gave her brother a special something to bring up with him."

Buzz stopped talking. He lit a cigarette. He went back to the table and got his water, and slowly took a sip.

"Okay, Buzz. Tell me, what did the guy bring up to Skylab with him."

"Thought you'd never ask," Buzz said calmly. He paused again, and took another drag on his smoke, smiling all the while.

"He took a piece of the True Cross," Buzz finally said.

"The what?"

"The True Cross. The cross Jesus Christ was crucified on," Buzz whispered.

✟ ✟ ✟

Donna carried herself—supported by Grace—up the fifth sorrowful mystery. Jesus is Crucified on the Cross. Tears flowed freely from her eyes now, their salt mixing with the salt in the ocean at her feet.

✝ ✝ ✝

Buzz looked up at the stars again. *It's up there. Right now.*

"When Emperor Constantine converted and became a Catholic, it was because he had a dream of his legions winning a battle with a cross on their shields. Your father must have told you. You know the story," Buzz began.

"Yes," Sam said, "I know the story."

"But did you know about Helen?"

"You mean Helen of Troy?"

"No, Saint Helen, Constantine's mother."

"Okay." Sam's tone told Buzz to continue.

"Well, Saint Helen also converted. As the story goes—"

"You mean, as the legend *goes*," Sam said. His tone, for the first time, was hard to decipher.

"Whatever. Story for me, legend for you. How's that?"

"Fair enough," Sam answered equably. "Just keeping you honest."

Buzz stifled an urge to sigh relief. *Go! Go!* he told himself. *Hit the hole.*

"So Saint Helen, according to *legend*," Buzz began again, diplomatically. A small act of charity. *It can't hurt.*

Sam smiled. His hunter-at-the-opening-of-deer-season smile.

Bingo, Buzz thought, knowing, in the way of grace, that a lot was riding on this story. He looked to Donna on the jetty. *She* **is** *praying for us.*

"According to legend," Buzz repeated, "Saint Helen became devoted to the cross that changed civilization, both by Jesus, and by Constantine. She set out for the Holy Land, and went to the hill where they crucified Him. They dug nearby, and found a cistern. Inside, she found three wooden crosses.

"They didn't know which cross was the one Jesus died on. Two other guys got crucified with Him, after all, so they laid a sick guy—I think it was a leper—on two crosses, and nothing happened—"

"And when they put the leper on the third cross, he was healed," Sam guessed.

Buzz nodded gravely. *I wonder if he's writing the whole story off at this point.* Sam's face gave no clue.

"Ever since, Catholics have believed that the cross she found was *the* cross. The True Cross. Over the years, it was sawed and cut into thousands of bits and pieces, relics we call them, and distributed around the world. Mostly, they're venerated in churches. But many pieces are in the possession of laymen. I say 'in the possession' because you can't own a relic. You can't sell them, either."

"Didn't they sell them in the Dark Ages?" Sam asked, vaguely remembering something from a history class.

"Yeah, there were many abuses," Buzz conceded. "But it got cleaned up. I'm sure a lot of phony true cross pieces were hawked. Chaucer, who was a devout Catholic, ripped the guy who sold phony relics in The Canterbury Tales."

The information seemed to flow into Buzz's mind uncalled, like the answers that came to him while watching *Jeopardy.*

"So you're saying that this guy's astronaut uncle took a piece of wood up into space," Sam said, then stopped himself. "Sorry, the *true* cross. I know you believe. It must mean a lot to you. To you it's more than wood."

"I appreciate that, Sam. I always appreciate how you let me be myself, let me be Catholic, and don't demand that I always talk like it's not important to me," Buzz said sincerely.

"I feel the same way about you," Sam said. "About letting me be myself."

"Gosh, we sound like a couple of guys at an AA meeting," Buzz joked, playing the man. No mushy stuff. Not in the playbook.

"Anyway," Buzz continued. "Here's the cool part. You see, Whitey's uncle didn't go up there just to bring it up and take it down. It never came down. The True Cross, that is."

"What do you mean? You mean he left it on Skylab?"

"No," Buzz said, lowering his voice. "He snuck it out with him when he was in his monkey suit, floating on the tether, and launched it into space."

"Ya don't say," Sam said, looking up to the stars for the first time.

"I do say. Pretty wild, huh?"

"Did it float away? No, I guess it couldn't have. It must be orbiting."

"That's what Bill told me. It's orbiting."

"Good story, even if it's not the cross of Jesus. The astronaut—there's a man who got something done. He did a unique thing. I like that. If it is the True Cross—" Sam stopped to think for a moment. "—then it's even funkier. It's right there, right now, either way." Sam was still looking up. So was Buzz.

He did it! Buzz thought, elated. *He made the connection for me!* Grace told him to wait. Without realizing it, Buzz obeyed.

After what seemed like a long time, Sam cleared his throat.

"Buzz, aren't you forgetting something?"

"Forgetting what?" Buzz asked. *Don't get too cute.*

"What does the cross floating in space have to do with anything?" Sam asked reasonably.

"You said it yourself. It's up there right now, whether you believe it's the True Cross or just a piece of wood. It's the same wood that Helen dug up, most likely, in the fourth century, and as far as we're both concerned, it might even be the same piece of wood Jesus died on. That Mary's tears dried on.

"Let's suppose it is. This next part is going to be hard to follow, because I just thought of it, but bear with me."

"I'll try, Buzz. Don't worry. I never fully understand you. I don't know if you understand what you say yourself, but it's always interesting. Maybe that's because I'm *not* a believer."

Buzz prepared to plow on. *Let grace tell him. I've never said one thing that convinced Sam of anything,* Buzz prayed in response to grace. A small act of humility.

"Okay. Where was I?" Buzz asked.

"Bear with me," Sam helped out.

"Oh. Yeah. Bear with me. Let's just suppose that it *is* the cross Jesus was on. Whether or not Jesus was God, let's set that aside. Don't we both agree that Jesus was a real person?"

"It's hard to deny he walked on the earth. The historical record and a couple billion Christians can't be that wrong," Sam said, with a rare affirmation. "Even my father believes in the historicity of Jesus."

That explains a lot, Buzz thought.

"Well, then. Here we are. That piece of wood above our heads is like a real, solid, material time machine. That piece of wood stretches across history. No matter what minute, no matter what hour, no matter what day, no matter what month, no matter what year, that piece of cross is always in its own *now*—you know, the present. It's always circling the world. It's in *our* now. It's in the now of every human being on earth. It will be in the now of every person who ever walks the earth, just as it was in *Jesus'* now two thousand years ago."

"I'm sort of following you," Sam said politely, straining.

Buzz was straining too, trying to think, trying to form the right words. Trying to carry the cross. A small act of perseverance.

"I know. Hang with me. Hang with me. Let me think."

Both men noticed that Donna was no longer on the jetty. She was walking back.

Don't come back, Buzz thought disjointedly, deeply alarmed. *Keep praying. Please, Mary, have her keep praying.*

Donna stopped in her tracks.

Overtime? she thought.

She felt worn out.

But wasn't Jesus worn out?

The prayer had been difficult, but it had also been almost, almost—fun. Either way, it had been exhilarating.

Okay, she told Grace. *Overtime.*

She turned around.

Overtime. Now. *For Buzz.*

Not for Sam? No.

For Buzz, Grace replied.

✛ ✛ ✛

The emotion in Buzz's heart when he saw Donna turn and begin trudging back to the jetty was overwhelming. Exhilarating. Her shoulders were drooping. But she was going back. Puzzle pieces, like thousands of tiny pieces of wood, came together in his mind. And formed a cross.

Now. Go for it.

"Back to the now, Sam. I'm ready."

"I'm ready, too. Shoot. The now."

"The greatest illusion in the world," Buzz began again, "is that there is a yesterday and a tomorrow. Sure, we talk about yesterday and tomorrow like they're real, but we never live in them. We can only live in the now. Right here. You and me, we're here, in God's cathedral, that's where we are. We're here, now. That's reality."

"I follow that completely. It's completely rational."

"Right. I knew you would. I knew you would," Buzz allowed excitement to enter his voice. "And that's the key to understanding life in general, and kids in particular. Sam, my marriage died because of me. Not because of Sandi. I was an alcoholic, and the reason was because I didn't want to be in the now. I got wasted so I didn't have to face the now.

"The now scares me, it scares the daylights out of me, even today, sober. I wouldn't let Sandi have a kid. My reasons sounded so innocuous at the time, but they were deadly. Deadly. I kept telling her, 'Someday we'll have a baby, sweetheart. But not now. Someday. When we're ready.'

"Don't you see it, Sam?" Sadness had crept into Buzz's voice. In addition to trying to convince Sam, he was also trying to convince himself. This conversation had taken a turn Buzz wasn't expecting. He pushed forward, ignoring the sadness creeping up on him.

"No, Buzz. I'm not trying to be a jerk, but I don't see it. I wish I did." It was the truth. Sam loved the truth.

Please, God! Buzz prayed.

I'm so tired, Donna prayed.

"You see, someday never came, Sam. It was all in the illusion of tomorrow. Tomorrow would come, and I would be in the now again, and I would shovel that kid into the next tomorrow. When Sandi got pregnant by accident, and my daughter came into the now…well, I just freaked out."

Buzz's words had started to pour out. He was looking down at the sand, remembering images, seeing faces, and hearing screams he hadn't faced in a long time.

"All my plans for tomorrow," he went on, his voice beginning to waver, "which were illusions anyway; they fell apart, and I was too selfish to give them up. I resented my own daughter. Everything I did after that, every decision I made, every shot glass I brought to my lips, every time I screamed at my wife, and, and…every time I hit her. I hit Sandi a lot. I put her in the hospital once…"

Buzz's voice cracked. Sam turned to look at him.

"Yes, I beat my wife. She was a beautiful, slender little thing. How could I?"

Buzz was no longer talking to Sam.

"Every time I hit her—it was all because I wasn't man enough to carry the cross in the now. I ran from responsibility. Sandi wasn't so bad. I can't blame her for dumping me. I wasn't a father. I wasn't even as good as my own father. He never ignored me. He never…he…oh God. I'm just rambling."

Buzz fell into a dark silence. He refused tears. He forced himself to finish.

"I cheated on her, too," he confessed, his bitter words coming from far away. "Four or five times. Cheating is too nice a word. I had sex with other women. I broke my vows, my word. I even flaunted it before Sandi, one time, to hurt her. Sure, I've gone to confession, but I can't undo what I've done. The images come back—from the, you know—the other women; they haunt me. Show me what I really am. I'm…I'm *lost."*

Buzz was finished; he put his hands into his hair. He started to shake. A wind blew.

"It's so frustrating," he croaked, unable to stop talking. "Knowing what I mean to say, but not being able to say it!"

His anguish was right with him now. His emotions were on the surface, battering him like the huge breakers.

"The secret life of men," Sam whispered, a distant melancholy in his voice.

"What's that?" Buzz asked, looking up. Sam seemed so tall, so dignified. Above him.

Buzz felt weak, inconsolable, small.

"Something Donna said to me once," Sam continued, surprising Buzz with his calmness. "We were talking about how hard it is for us, for men, to say what is inside our hearts. To translate the word inside into a word outside. Until I met you guys, I never even tried. I just floated through life, ignoring the words inside. As you might say, I wasn't living in the now."

"I think I get it," Buzz said, falling silent.

Why hasn't he said anything about me hitting my wife? Cheating on her? About me failing as a father? He must think I'm a piece of trash.

He lit a cigarette, but it tasted stale, useless, unsatisfying. He threw it into the sand.

Donna came off the jetty for the second time. Buzz's heart sank.

It's over. He could feel it. His shoulders sagged and his body shuddered. A giant, silent sob welled up from his belly.

I'm lost.

But Buzz was wrong. Men are often wrong about their emotions. Donna was still praying, saying a word of the Hail Mary with every step, struggling to keep her eyelids from closing.

I just want to go to sleep, she thought between words of prayer in her heart. She was spent. Running on empty.

Buzz felt like a sandcastle in the wind and waves, being worn away, on the verge of collapse. He leaned forward, tottering, his eyes unfocused, his head spinning, when he felt Sam's graceful hand on his shoulder.

It seemed to Buzz as if his friend's one hand was keeping him from falling into an abyss. Buzz looked up.

Please, help me.

"What you mean to say," Sam said serenely, "is that Ellie and I shouldn't put off having kids. For you, as a Catholic, having kids is why you get married. You're saying that if I'm not ready to bear the burden of having kids right now, like your Jesus carried the cross, because that's how you describe bearing burdens—carrying the cross—if I'm not ready for that now, then I'll always put it off, because someday never comes. And Ellie and I should be clear on that before we get married. Somehow, the cross in the sky above us reminded you of that. I don't follow all that stuff about the piece of wood up there being in the now. I don't think it matters. I don't think—Buzz?"

"Yeah," Buzz said, crushing sadness in his voice. He was looking down again. His mouth was as dry as cotton.

"Look at me," Sam commanded. There was power in his voice.

Buzz looked up again. His eyes were watery, salty.

"You did it, man," Sam said enthusiastically, bringing his other hand up to Buzz's other shoulder. "You convinced me. You're saying I should be a man. Have the kids. Be happy with Ellie. I know that. My father is a good father. When you see me, you see my father. It's not a mystery to me. You should cut yourself some slack. I know you loved your dad. I can hear it in your voice. But the guy was an alcoholic. He let you down. You got lost. He didn't show you the way. Your faith did. Your faith is beautiful, man. It saved you. You're not lost anymore. Even if I don't believe in it, I can see that it saved you. And I love you for it. I love how it makes you bend over backwards to try to save me too."

These words reached into Buzz and held him. Buzz had no reply. Emotion washed over him, and he began to cry like a boy. He couldn't help it.

Neither could Sam. The two men hugged each other hard, sucking in sobs, already working at shutting off the faucet.

When they looked up, they saw Donna. She was crying too, but not trying to hold it in…

"Come here, Donna," Sam said. She joined their embrace. The men stopped crying. Not in front of the girl.

The believer, the agnostic, and the tomboy.

They didn't hold each other long. For one thing, they didn't fit. Short, tall, big. Awkwardly, they collapsed onto the benches around the table.

"This is too weird, and I'm too tired," Donna said finally, yawning. "I'm going to bed."

"Thank you," Buzz said, a little late completing the doxology.

"You're welcome," Donna yawned.

She got up and shuffled into the apartment. Without thinking, she collapsed onto Sam's bed, her clothes on, and fell directly to sleep.

"What's up for tomorrow?" Sam asked.

"I guess we come out of the closet and tell Donna we're gay."

Sam shook his head and stood up. He was suddenly dog tired. Spent.

"That's a very, very bad joke. I'm going to bed, too. Donna's the only one with any sense around here."

"No argument here on all three points," Buzz said, getting up. "Good night."

"And Sam?"

"Yeah," Sam said, stopping at the screen door.

"Nothing."

Chapter Nine

1

Donna opened her eyes and was momentarily disoriented.

Where am I? Then it came to her.

Down the shore.

How did I get to Sam's bed again?

Then, she remembered coming off the beach. *Oh.*

She pulled herself up, leaned her back against the headboard, and began her morning offering. She began it halfheartedly, repeating the words without thinking about them. Then, she came to a halt, realizing that she had fallen into the old habit, and remembered her resolution.

She started over—and prayed it *with normal human effort*.

She walked into the living room and passed the gangly Sam sprawled over cushions on the floor. He was wearing nerdy, paisley pajamas that made her smile. Then she went upstairs to shower and change.

It was a warm, beautiful, knock-your-socks-off day.

When she came down, feeling refreshed and chipper, she found Buzz wide awake, wearing worn-out clothes, arranging buckets, scrub brushes, rags, and cleaning fluid on the picnic table.

"What's that for?" she asked, blinking.

"This?" He held up a bucket.

"Yeah, *that*," she said.

Sam came to the door, rubbing his eyes with one fist, and holding a glass of orange juice.

"This is cleaning equipment," Buzz said, putting the bucket down.

"Oh," Donna said. "For a minute there, I thought it was your CD collection."

"Huh?" Sam asked, still groggy.

"Out with it, Buzz. What do we have to clean?" Donna asked.

"Nothing. You and Sam enjoy the beach. My uncle needs the windows cleaned. That was the deal," Buzz explained, hesitating. "We're not very close, my uncle and me."

"I get it now," Sam said. "Do you want us to help you?"

"Yup. Great!" Buzz said, heading for the door. "Let's have breakfast first!"

"Uh, Buzz," Donna said, smiling. "I think you're supposed to insist on doing it by yourself a couple more times."

"Why bother? I knew you guys would help. It'll be fun, and we'll do a quick job and we'll get some beach time this afternoon."

"Buzz," Sam said, looking at his watch, "it *is* the afternoon."

"Details, details," Buzz said, already pouring himself a big glass of Tropicana Pure Premium.

✝ ✝ ✝

Cleaning the windows was alternately dull and fun. Buzz started the fun by spraying his friends with the hose when they climbed the ladders.

Donna poured a bucket of diluted Top Job on his head.

Sam remained silent, grooving to the job at hand.

The Knack cranked out the boom box. *My Sharona*.

Lunch consisted of micro-dogs and Pepsi. They tasted great. There seemed to be an unspoken, casual agreement to lay off the philosophical talk for a day.

✝ ✝ ✝

After the windows were cleaned, Buzz drove off alone and went to confession. He knocked on the rectory door and asked for a priest. The priest tried to get him into a counseling session, and to convince him that his sins weren't so bad. The priest even quoted Martin Luther.

Buzz played it straight, didn't get sucked into a gabfest, and received a halfhearted absolution. He believed in the sacrament, and the priest's lack of faith in the teachings of his own Church simply proved to Buzz the need for penance.

✝ ✝ ✝

The afternoon turned windy, and they didn't stay long at the oceanside. That evening, they went to dinner at Kubels, and topped the night off by watching *Tin Men*. They laughed heartily. It felt like Sunday all day, even though it was Monday.

Buzz and Donna prayed a Rosary together on the deck while Sam read parts of a book he found on a bookshelf in his bedroom, *Alive,* by Piers Paul Reed. Sam had seen the television movie years before. It was the true story of a plane crash in the Andes that left a team of young rugby players from Uruguay stranded for weeks. They were forced to eat the flesh of their dead to survive.

Sam was struck by the role the survivors' Catholic faith played in their ordeal, and tried to imagine himself in the place of several of the characters. Which one was he? Which was Buzz? Was Donna like the last woman to die?

✝ ✝ ✝

After Donna went upstairs, Sam and Buzz found themselves on the deck. They looked at the ocean.

"About last night," Buzz began. "I'm sorry for losing it."

"Forget it," Sam said. "No need to be sorry."

Buzz nodded. "Thanks."

Sam kept his gaze on the ocean; a silent *you're welcome.*

2

New Jersey faded into the east with every mile as they chased the sun to the west. Ohio was hours and hours away. They were in the long, dull, concrete badlands of Pennsylvania.

"You never did tell me how you ended up going to Notre Dame. You never talk about it," Donna told Buzz. "You don't even wear Notre Dame sweatshirts."

Buzz hesitated. *There's not much to tell.*

"Come on, Buzz," Sam prodded. "Were you a good student? Did you play sports in high school? Why N.D.?"

"It's a long drive. Plenty of time to kill," Donna added.

"There's not much to tell. But I'll tell you, anyway," Buzz finally said, taking a sip of coffee. After the night of the cross in the sky, Buzz felt released inside. Now that they knew the worst—at least Sam did—what could it hurt to talk about his past?

Sam leaned back in the front seat. Donna leaned forward, and rested her elbows on the tops of the front seats, with her hands clasped under her chin...

"I wasn't much of a student in grammar school. I was one of the zillions of kids in the middle eightieth percentile. Then Dad's company transferred him to Cleveland during the summer after eighth grade. It was one of the few jobs he kept for more than a couple of years. He told me once it was because the owner was an alcoholic, too. He used to fly in from New Jersey and go drinking with Dad every once in a while. Mr. Pat McSorley of the McSorley Automotive Company. They made parts for machines that made engines or electric motors or something.

"I don't remember much about freshman year, just how lonely it was on the first day of school, standing in the cafeteria holding my lunch tray, not knowing where to sit, not knowing anybody, ashamed of my thrift store duds. Isn't it funny how our recollections are tied to what grade we were in, not to years?

"Anyway, we lived in Lakewood, and I went to Lakewood Public High School. It's a big school, and I kind of got lost there, too. I got mostly Cs and Bs, and made the football team. I got cut from basketball; I wasn't very good at the time. I hung out with the guys on the football team, and did the usual stuff with girls and parties. Stuff I'm ashamed of now. But even then, I didn't stand out. I wasn't the impulsive person you know me as. I was shy.

"Don't laugh; I really was a shy kid. Introverted. It's funny, but I never really made friends. I had lots of kids I hung out with, but I never connected. I never found that best friend it seemed like everybody else had. I was the new kid from New Jersey, too, and not used to Ohio. I never brought friends home. You can guess why not.

"When I was a sophomore, I had this really cool English teacher. We had this assignment at the beginning of school to describe something that happened during summer vacation. I don't know what got into me, but I didn't write about my summer, which had been pretty boring. Lots of television. So for the essay, I made believe that I was a cinder block in the school wall and described empty classrooms. I was just filling out words on the page. Weird, huh?

"Well my English teacher, Mr. Snodgrass, really liked it. I can't believe his name was Snodgrass, but it was. Other kids called him Snotgrass, of course.

"But I thought he was a really cool teacher. He wasn't nerdy, and he wasn't the kind who tried to buddy up to you, either. You could tell he liked teaching. He was creative. He taught us how to write poetry, haikus and sonnets, and how to write speeches, and even how to write lyrics by using our favorite rock songs as examples. I remember he flipped over my rewrite of Pink Floyd's "Wish You Were Here." He wrote that my version was better than the original.

"I started looking forward to his class. He even taught me how to write fiction by picturing everything in my mind's eye and writing it down. He was always giving me A-pluses. I was his favorite.

"It was all very subtle, though. He didn't talk to me after class and give me heart-to-hearts. He didn't single me out in front of the class. It was like we were having a conversation on paper. He was talking with his red pen in the margins, and I was telling him things with what I was writing. He changed my life with the language.

"I started to notice things outside of the classroom. For example, I was watching television one night, and I looked over to the outlet on the wall, and noticed that the third hole for the grounding prong looked like a sad, tiny mouth and the top slits in the socket looked like two eyes with a big wide nose. Look at an outlet sometime. You'll see a face. I wrote about the face on the electrical outlet in class, and Mr. Snodgrass liked it.

"Then, I started to listen to people talk. To their accents, how they formed their sentences. What they *meant* as opposed to what they *said*. Nobody knew this was going on. I barely realized it myself. I looked at what people were wearing. I liked cars, and I tried to guess what kind of cars their parents drove, right down to the year and color, just from what people wore and talked about.

"This might sound strange, but I fell in love with the world. I remember when my daughter Jenny first started talking. It was like that. She looked at everything for the first time, and was filled with wonder. One time I showed her the engine of my Volkswagen bug, and she flipped out. It was her first engine. Something that bores us to death was a whole new world for her. I can picture the excitement in her eyes now.

"So I was discovering the *wonder* of the world, like a little kid. I had found my calling: to wonder about the world. Except for becoming a Catholic, of course.

"I think Mr. Snodgrass is responsible. He helped me pay attention. I started to try to put words to things that don't have any words.

"If we want to get really deep, maybe I was relating to those things I was discovering. You know, I was unseen and un-noticed, too, like the guy in the electric socket. Do you ever feel that way, like you're there, but nobody sees you? Lots of things are like that. I like those things. I've never wanted to be anything; I probably never will want to be anything. I just want to really see the world.

"So Mr. Snodgrass changed my life. I can see now that he had an agenda for me: to open my mind. Maybe he saw the things that don't have words, too. I don't know. In red pen in the margins, he suggested I read a few books. Novels, mostly. Not profound stuff like Moby Dick, but stuff you couldn't stop reading, like Stephen King and Watership Down. Did you ever read Watership Down?

"No? It's about rabbits. It's great. There's a rabbit called Bigwig in that book that reminded me of myself. Stupid and strong, and loyal.

"I started reading more and more. I couldn't afford books, so I went to the library. I started picking out my own books. I read slowly, and methodically, night after night, after school. Sometimes I even read during classes. Compulsively. Winds of War and War and Remembrance blew me away. I got into Robert Heinlein but got sick of him after a while. Lucifer's Hammer, about an asteroid hitting the world. All my favorites come back to me.

"I know what was going on then because it's still going on. I was escaping the *now*. I was escaping the world, even as I was falling in love with it. Maybe it kept me out of trouble. Slowly but surely, in my own, quiet way, going to parties and listening to the trite conversations and making out with ditsy girls, and—well, I won't get into that—all that stuff became pretty dull compared to travelling the world with heroes like Natty Bumpo, or Stu Redman and Nick Andros from The Stand. I read that book over and over, every few months. It was my favorite. Good good guys, bad bad guys. I swear I might have married Sandi because she reminded me of Frannie Goldsmith, a character in that book.

"Am I boring you guys?

"No? You want me to keep going?

"Okay, here's what happened. My grades started to go up in other classes. By the end of sophomore year, I even got a couple of As. Somehow, I got straight As in the first semester of junior year. It was like the stars were lining up when that happened. Easy classes, along with the discipline of playing football, and Dad having a good year—all helped me catch my stride. Even algebra, usually my toughest class, just seemed easier.

"I wasn't thinking about going to college, or even *applying* myself to my studies, as the counselors were always prodding me to do. Getting good grades came with the same amount of effort. I think Mr. Snodgrass was talking me up in the teacher's room, because teachers started looking at me funny, and giving me the benefit of the doubt with grades.

"Before senior year, guidance counselors started trying to get me to take honors classes. I avoided tough classes in math and science, but did take honors English. I gave it a little more effort, but not much. I hope this doesn't sound arrogant, but it was easy, especially with teachers pulling for you. Lakewood High wasn't a great school. I kind of resented the special treatment from the teachers, but I took the good grades. I didn't want to *study;* I wanted to *read*.

"When they sent my report card to my dad, he gave me twenty bucks. That was a fortune for me. It was one of the happiest days of my life. I spent it on Oh Henry chocolate bars and a hard cover of The Stand. I still have it. But I ate the Oh Henrys." Buzz snorted.

"Then I saw Mary on top of the Golden Dome at Notre Dame, and I knew I had to go there. No, it wasn't for religious reasons. I was long since out of the faith. Dad half-heartedly tried to get me to go to Mass when he went—which wasn't very often, but I had rejected the Church. It seemed to be all guilt and rules. Or all sappy love stuff.

"I saw the Golden Dome while watching a Notre Dame game on television. I wasn't a fan. But I played football, and something about that dome called me. I saw it during that corny plug they always give at half time. You know, 'Penn State has the world's largest facility for researching mountain lion leukemia and over eight hundred thousand students—blah-blah-blah,' with an aerial shot of the campus.

"During the Notre Dame plug that day, I saw Mary in the aerial. Maybe it was the snake. I know this sounds awful, but I noticed the snake under her foot when they zoomed in on her statue. You know, I told you I was into details. I really wanted to see that snake in person. Somehow, this equated with getting in there as a student. I had done pretty well on my PSATs—not spectacular, but okay in math and very high in English. I was all-conference on the football team at nose tackle.

"Maybe I'm exaggerating about the dome attracting me. Who knows how we pick a college? Now, I look back, and I think that maybe it was as simple as God wanted me to go there, and He used a television program to pique my interest.

"I told the guidance counselor, and he pooh-poohed the idea. He tried to get me to go to Slippery Rock State College. *Slippery Rock,* can you believe it? I still don't know where it is. Could be in Montana or the next exit for all I care.

"Then I did a bad thing. I lied like hell on my application. I made up that I was part of a bunch of student activities like being the president of the chess club, and that I made all-state in football. Big, bold, bald-faced lies. There were two essays, and they really were hilarious looking back on it.

"Now, today, I'm not proud of lying on that Notre Dame application. When I filled out my UPS application, I was perfectly truthful. But Notre Dame was different. Well, okay, it was lying. But it wasn't serious lying. I was laughing the whole time. I looked at that empty application form, and pictured all the preppy students from the west side of Lakewood and Shaker Heights and Bay Village, and how they were going to write perfect, boring essays and have their parents type it up, or even have their parents write the essay for them. I knew that my first two years would weigh against me, along with the weak courses. I was ranked 75th in my class.

"I threw caution to the wind, and decided to roll the dice on being different. I knew I was different on the inside by this time, so I embellished my high school career to reflect that.

"Except for Mr. Snodgrass, I even wrote my own teacher recommendations on stationery I pilfered when the lady behind the desk wasn't looking. Stuff like 'young Gwynne is destined for greatness' and so on.

"For the big essay, I wrote about my family. Brothers and sisters I didn't have, basing them on fictional characters. Not too fantastic. The part about my mom dying in a car accident and dad having cancer that would take his life right around the time I would graduate from college was good, solid fiction writing. I called a hospital to find a cancer that takes five years to kill its victim. I forget what it was—some Latin name. I even wrote that I would be the first person from my family to go to college; this was not true, either. Dad went to Glassboro State.

"For the other essay, I wrote about dedicating myself to being a quarterback in football, *despite not having two fingers on my throwing hand*. I wrote about lifting weights every morning, and then walking to school while tossing footballs in the air. I wasn't a quarterback, of course, and as you can see, I'm not missing any fingers; maybe a few marbles. I got the school photo of the best-looking guy in school—he just gave it to me when I asked for it, and he didn't even know me. His name was Jim Lynn. I stapled the photo to the application and signed it without a scruple. I scrounged up the application fee.

"I sent it in, and forgot about it. I was sure they would catch the lies, or simply reject me anyway. I didn't apply to other colleges. It was N.D. and the snake under Mary's feet or nothing. I got on the waiting list, and got in just before summer ended. I believe the guy in the admissions office told me that I was the second to last student accepted.

"I was poor. Even when Dad kept jobs, he didn't make much, and a lot of money went into the pocket of Old Grand Dad, if you get my drift. I got through with loans, a couple of small 'poor kid' scholarships, and working two jobs during school and three during the summer and lived like a pauper. It was touch and go every semester. I was still in thrift store clothes, but they came into style, so that wasn't so bad.

"Today, between child support and alimony and student loans, I barely make it through the month. I don't have any savings. My extra money still goes to books. I've never had money.

"That's it."

✜ ✜ ✜

Donna felt sorry for Buzz. She had no idea that he had been so lonely his whole life.

"There's got to be more," she said softly, with tenderness. "What happened at school?"

"Nothing, really. It was the most dull college experience in history."

"Tell us anyway," Sam said, clearing his throat. "After this rest stop. I have to be excused."

Buzz saw the sign for the rest stop exit. He put his blinker on. They pulled up to the ugly, bureaucrat-designed building. Buzz got himself a Pepsi and a pack of smokes. After they were back on the highway, and with a bit of prodding, he took up the story again...

"I'll never forget the first night I went to bed in my dorm room. I didn't have a roommate. I had a single. I knew that my four years at Notre Dame wouldn't be normal. I stared at the ceiling and was both excited and disappointed.

"I had high standards. Everybody was so plastic. In my quest for things with no words, I was becoming arrogant and insufferable. But there was something repulsive about the materialism of the place. They had a god at Notre Dame, and it wasn't Jesus. I think their god was getting good reviews. Having people speak well of them, think well of them, and donate well to them was the god. Taking a couple of thousand students as freshmen and turning them into corporate ants by senior year, all sugarcoated with condom-covered Catholicism, was the result.

"Do you know what it's like going to a school where everyone loves it except for you? I didn't tell anybody this, of course. I moved off-campus, lived alone, worked my jobs, and tried to enjoy my English classes, where most of the teachers couldn't hold a candle to Mr. Snodgrass. I didn't care. I got poor grades. I'm not sure why I didn't just quit school. Everyone else had a mom and a dad to write to, or to come visit, or so it seemed. I didn't go to one football game. I couldn't afford the tickets anyway.

"I knew what it was like to be poor. I had always been poor, but compared to the spoiled, upper middle class kids at Notre Dame, I stuck out. I never had enough money for food. One time, I saw this guy rummaging through a dumpster behind the ALDIs on Eddy Road, and jumped in with him. I found a huge box of Oreo cookies, a mother lode. I stuffed them into my mouth. Dad never could afford cookies, much less the kind with the soft sugary stuff in the middle, and I felt like I won the lottery. Man, stores throw away lots of food. Campbell's soup, cans of salmon, stale bread in the bags, Pepsi, you name it.

"People don't believe this, but one semester I spent less than thirty bucks on food. Thirty bucks! Mostly for milk and eggs and stuff. Putting up with some stink and getting ultra-ripe bananas on your sneakers makes you feel like you earned it. I found other stuff at the mall dumpsters. Books, clock radios. One time, I found seven pairs of leather Converse All-Stars in my size, and ten pairs in other sizes. I sold the other ones, and I'm still working on the seven pairs. I've got three left!

"Anyway, I don't feel poor now. I don't ever think I'll ever feel poor again. Not after living like that. Not after watching those Notre Dame students spending more on pizza and beer in one night than I spent on food in a semester. It doesn't sound dignified to pick food out of a dumpster, but I didn't look at it that way. It wasn't degrading. I was being resourceful. I was proud that I found a way to get by. It was a secret thrill. Now, I know I can live on whatever amount of money I make. This is America, dumpster heaven.

"Then, in junior year, I met Kelly Pauling, fell in love, and my world fell apart."

✝ ✝ ✝

"Time out," Sam said. "That's quite an introduction. Have you ever told us about Kelly before?"

"Never," Buzz said.

"But you'll tell us about her now?" Donna asked. "You don't have to if you don't want to."

"But I want to," Buzz said, his voice barely audible above the noise of the engine.

Sam and Donna were silent. Their silence asked him why he wanted to tell them about Kelly Pauling.

"Because you're my friends," Buzz added.

"...I met her in a bar on Eddy Street. It was called the Black Horse Cafe or something like that. It was winter, late January. It wasn't a loud bar, but there was dark, jazzy music in the background, and it wasn't the kind of place students hung out at. I saw Kelly Pauling sitting in a booth in the back, alone. For some reason, after walking in and spotting her, and getting myself a Screwdriver, I went to sit down with her.

"She didn't say hello when I sat down; she just asked me for a light. She acted like I had always known her the way she asked. She smoked and smoked—all the time. Marlboro Reds.

"I remember what she was wearing. Worn-out jeans, very tight, and a plain blouse. Compared to the preppy clothes most Notre Dame girls wore, she was a breath of dirty air. In the following weeks, it seemed like she wore the same outfit every day. She was really skinny. For some reason I've always been attracted to thin women. Her clothes made her seem thinner, almost starved. Her hair was long, thin, brown, and completely unstyled, parted in the middle, falling just below her shoulders. Her skin was about average, but her blue eyes, while not striking, had a joyless, far away quality. She had the fine, long features of an aristocrat, and an air of world-weariness that was as thick as a wool blanket. I liked that. Just like I told Sam that we would be best friends, I knew I would have a history with this woman.

"We didn't talk about much that first night. She talked more than me, and mostly it was complaints. Complaints about Notre Dame and complaints about the plane flight back from Paris before school started. Nothing pleased her. She wore her dissatisfaction with all things on her sleeve, but delivered her complaints in a way that made it seem like she didn't really care.

"I guess I connected to her. After all, I didn't like Notre Dame either, but never found a way to express it. She seemed to make hating life cool. She was a sophomore, and her daddy was a rich N.D. grad who had practically forced her to go there. Compared to the perky coeds at Notre Dame who ignored me, she was different and exotic and exciting.

"I got my courage up and asked her to dance. We danced slow, and close, and were the only ones on the floor. The music put a field around us, and to me at least, it was like we were the only two people in the world. I remember the mix of wine and beer on her breath when I kissed her.

"I took her home that night, and we made love. It was all so decadent, with her feigning complete detachment in the middle of her, uh, pleasure.

"Remembering it now doesn't excite me; it's distasteful. I wish I could wipe the images from my memory, like how Sam cleans off a hard drive.

"Without getting too much into it, it was like we were there but we weren't there. We used contraceptives, of course, which added to the detached effect. She even compared me out loud to other men with a disdain for the others that made me feel proud and at the same time, like a trained seal or something.

"I fell hopelessly in love with her. It was like selling my soul to something. To the devil? I wouldn't go that far, but there was an evil, a modern evil, that was on the altar she worshipped at. The music we listened to, the dark humor we shared, the contempt for Notre Dame; being above the crass materialism it stood for, or at least *we* thought it stood for.

"We shared all that. It was like sharing the darkness in your heart. We never laughed, or smiled, except when tearing something down. Not that we talked much. Talk was cheap. We sang, though. We sang with our bodies, and the songs we sang were hopeless, bluesy, low, and mean. We sang and danced with death.

"I started skipping classes to be with her. She was failing out. I quit one of my night jobs to have time for her. I spent all my money on her and booze and drugs, though mostly we drank. In fact, I think that's when I became an alcoholic, even though I stopped drinking by degrees after it was over. A month later, after she got bored with me, and found another guy, she dumped me. She left me a note. 'It was great while it lasted. I'll always remember you, Buzz.' I didn't try to get her back. I knew her.

"Just like that, Kelly Pauling was gone from my life. I lost track of her and I think she dropped out before the year was over. I sometimes, but not often, wonder what became of her.

"You know, we think of sex and sin as something that men corrupt women with, but it was the opposite with me. She corrupted me, but I was a willing participant, enchanted by her corruption. I became depressed, and almost failed out that semester. It seemed like I went for months without talking to other students. I could see it in other students when they looked at me. I was different, a pariah. An outsider. Maybe I imagined that.

"I got another job loading boxes for UPS, to kill time, and to distract myself. I needed the money. I'd strap myself up in the giant web of conveyer belts in the shipping center, sorting thousands of boxes by zip code. You should see it. You can't think when you do work like that. I couldn't face going home a failure. Not that Dad would have cared. He would have told me 'Nice try, son. Nice try.' That would have been that.

"One time, I wandered into the Crypt, a chapel in the basement of Sacred Heart, and prayed for help. I even cried. Nothing happened. I guess I felt better for crying—sorry, I cry easily. I cried during the national anthem when I played sports in high school. I didn't get any lightning bolts from God. I guess I wasn't expecting any.

"Now I look back and wonder what would have happened to me if I died in the middle of all that darkness. Would I have gone to hell? Was I in a state of grace? My conscience was dead, and I didn't think about life—or death, in those terms. It gives me chills.

"But Kelly changed me. I looked at the world differently after that. Before her, I was a child. My evil was a child's evil, the kind that comes from the outside; from doing things because the crowd does it. But I had chosen the evil with Kelly. It was adult evil. Sam, you think you're an agnostic because you can't see any evidence for God's existence. I respect that, as much as I disagree with you. But with Kelly, whether or not God existed was beside the point. He wasn't even in the equation. It was just me and her and the darkness of the world.

"If God was up in heaven, and was leaving us alone, then screw Him for making the world that way. *I Don't Care* was her religion, and I made it mine.

"Of course, I'm painting everything with a dark brush now, but I'm describing a mood that permeated my life at the time. Eventually, I pulled out of the depression, but lost a big part of that sense of wonder about the world that Mr. Snodgrass inflamed in me.

"I came home to Ohio at the end of junior year, and compared to Kelly, my father was a saint of optimism. All I did was work that summer. When I got back to school for my senior year, I joined the off-campus intramural football team, full pads and everything, and did pretty well. Hell, I was a force. I made some fleeting, normal friends on the team, who were, by degree, less dark than Kelly. My nutty side came out then, or started to come out. Nothing seemed to matter. I could say or do anything. Along those same lines, I once took a psyche exam for an insurance company job, and I tested, quote, 'three degrees above the norm,' unquote, for sociopathic behavior.

"I started playing a lot of basketball, too. Did you know that Notre Dame has more courts per student than any college in the country? I played every day I could. I made myself a good player. The playing gave me something to look forward to, and I think more than anything else this helped me keep my sanity after Kelly. I never talked to the other players. I just played and played. It was my drug.

"My friends and I got drunk and fooled around, but I didn't really go out with anybody again until Sandi, the year after I graduated.

"I squeaked by in my classes. I got my degree in English, of course, but I didn't even interview for jobs my senior year. Dad came out for the first time to see me graduate. We skipped all the pep rallies and fancy—expensive—dinners, and drove home together. I was kind of happy during that drive. My dad and I didn't talk much, but I know he was proud of me. I could tell by the way he didn't get drunk during the graduation, which was his odd kind of present for me. I knew that took a lot out of him.

"By that time, he had been transferred back to New Jersey. We left nothing in Lakewood. Nothing. And I had the feeling that we drunken Woodwards from New Jersey had conquered Notre Dame together, on our own terms. Getting a job with IBM or some Big Eight accounting firm seemed a waste of time at that point.

"A lot of people think of Notre Dame as this great Catholic school, but I got nothing there—absolutely nothing—in terms of the faith I love so much today. My two theology courses were a joke, and there was a dark thread—similar to the black blood that flowed through Kelly's veins—that wound its way through most of my English courses. Implicitly, Sartre and Sex and Nietzsche rule there. There are no absolutes, only treadmill illustrations of meaninglessness.

"It's like what Chesterton wrote about jazz; its only novelty is novelty. It's a treadmill. Rock is the same way—sex, drugs, and a pounding beat. It never really changes. The underlying philosophy in most of my classes at Notre Dame had the same quality.

"Maybe I'm exaggerating. Everything I remember is seen through a depressed, darkened lens.

"After I graduated, Dad got me a lead on a job selling prefab chimneys, so I moved back to Cleveland. I met Sandi at the end of that summer. In a lot of ways, that summer was the last happy summer of my life until Dad died—until I met you guys. He went pretty fast. Me and McSorley and a few others at the funeral. He received last rites and went to confession the day he died."

Buzz's voice had begun to crack. He took a moment and a drag on his cigarette.

"But I'm getting off track...Notre Dame, Notre Dame. I never framed my diploma. I don't get a happy feeling when I put Notre Dame down on job applications. Even though I see I was self-absorbed, I'm glad I rejected their phony, glittery brand of Catholicism.

"So I don't root for the football team; I don't wear their sweatshirts. It was like they let that snake under Mary's feet loose, and it got to me under the covers with Kelly and poisoned me. I wonder how many other students get lost there? I mean, isn't it a parent's job to protect their children, and isn't a university like a parent?

"Oh, I don't know. I've got to stop talking. I can feel the darkness coming back. You guys must think I'm nuts."

"No we don't," Donna said. "No we don't."

She put an arm over the seat and gave Buzz an awkward hug. "And you're a good storyteller. You should be a writer."

"Donna's right," Sam said.

"You think so?" Buzz asked, surprised at their reaction, wondering when the rejection would come, then knowing it never would.

So this is friendship, he thought, realizing that he had never truly had a real friend before in his whole life.

Now he had two.

PART THREE

Waltzing With Dragons

One, two, princes kneel before you.
Princes, princes who adore you.
One has diamonds in his pockets.
This one, he wants to buy you rockets.
Aw, marry him or marry me;
I'm the one who loves you baby, can't you see.
Spin Doctors, **Two Princes**

Be careful, or your hearts will be weighed down with dissipation,
drunkenness and the anxieties of life, and that day will close on
you unexpectedly like a trap.
Jesus, on the End of the Age, Luke 21: 34

I read in a book that a man called Christ went about doing good.
It is very disconcerting to me that I am so easily satisfied
with just going about.
Toyohiko Kagawa

Friendship is a miracle which requires constant proofs. It is an
exercise of the purest imagination and of the rarest truth.
Henry David Thoreau

Yours is only a small love if you are not zealous for the salvation
of all souls. Yours is only a poor love if you are not eager to
inflame other apostles with your madness.
Blessed Josemaría Escrivá, **The Way**

Chapter Ten

1

Mark Johnson was about to live with the Kemps for an entire Saturday, breakfast to bedtime. Bill White had filled in Joe and Mary on the purpose of the visit. They were eager to open their home to the two men. They agreed to treat Mark as a casual friend. He was a likeable man, so that was not a problem. There was one ground rule: if Mark had a question, they would try to answer it for him, but otherwise they were to simply let him observe their family for a day.

It seemed like an awkward arrangement at first, but like a film crew, Mark faded quickly into the background. The presence of Uncle Bill legitimized Mark's presence for the children.

Despite his efforts to stay in the shadows, the Kemp's two preschool children sought him out for play. Once they got used to his size and strength, they played like all children play: with their whole selves, quick to laugh if thrilled, quick to cry if injured. They tumbled and rumbled on the carpet in the living room, using the couch cushions for wrestling mats.

Mark feigned happiness, but every laugh caused a pithy anguish to rise in his heart. He was thinking of his three girls, and how he could no longer play with them. This, more than anything, strengthened his resolve to learn what he could on this day. Suddenly, the mere thought of the possibility of life without daily contact with his daughters caused him to become angry…and, to become something else. What was it? What was it he felt besides anger?

Fear. Yes, fear. The tough guy was finally *afraid* of something. Life without his daughters. Being kicked out by Maggie had not been a fearful thing in itself. He could live without her. Frankly, she had not been easy to live with during the last few years. No, he was not afraid of her. Angry with her, yes. Confused by her, yes. But he was not afraid of her. Mark feared no man, much less a woman.

But he was afraid of not being with his daughters. He knew that the world was a hard place on girls, filled with traps; traps only a father could guide daughters around. He knew they needed him. He knew they would become twisted and deformed without him.

Presently, he asked the children to let him rest, and insisted despite their protests. He put the cushions back and sat on the not-very-fancy couch, then pulled out his wallet. There was a photograph of Sarah, Angela, and Meg.

His little tough guys. His girls.

Right now, Maggie was not threatening divorce. She wanted time, undetermined, to get her head together, to adjust. "Call me once a week," she had told him. She also told him that she would let him come visit the girls after she "adjusted."

In the meantime, if he tried to push her, or charm her, or rush her, she would call the lawyer. She had the law on her side if she took that route. *How many separations survive those barracudas?*

Not any that I know, he answered himself, looking at the photo. *When was the last time a divorce lawyer saved a marriage?*

His prayers for Maggie to change her mind had not been answered. His attendance at daily Mass since he got kicked out had not helped change her either, despite his requests after communion for help. Or so he thought.

His prayers were dry, but he kept praying. Bill had prayed the Rosary with him after Mass this morning. More dryness, more silence from heaven. He would not admit it to himself, but the idea of going to the Kemps was humiliating, and didn't make sense. What would he possibly see?

He was trusting Bill on this one. Bill was a smart guy, a good guy, and in his own way, a tough guy.

Mark slipped the photo back into the wallet. He closed his eyes.

*For the girls. You **will** do **whatever** it takes to win Maggie back for their sakes!*

He opened his eyes, his resolution clear in his mind.

Are you willing to do anything? a little voice taunted him. *Swallow your pride? Hold your temper? Suffer humiliation? Lose an argument? Beg to go back? Quit your job?*

Swallow. Hold. Suffer. Lose. Beg. Quit.

Unfamiliar words to Mark. Words that his father and brothers had taught him were anathema.

Shut up, he told the voice, thinking of the three little girls in the photo.

He stood up. *Anything.*

He was ready.

2

Eighty miles east of the Ohio border, Buzz's Festiva scooted over a hill, and its small, right front tire rolled over a block of wood with a rusty nail sticking out of it.

"What was that?!" Donna cried out, alarmed by the blunt blowout sound.

Sam was silent as he felt the little car's weight become unbalanced, and he was instantly terrified by its trajectory toward the shoulder, and beyond that, the flimsy metal guardrail. Beyond the guardrail loomed a rocky cliff, and below it, perhaps one hundred yards down, stood a patch of low pine trees in a crazy-crag gully.

"Hail Mary!" Buzz called calmly, desperately attempting to angle the car parallel to the rail, fearful of braking too hard and losing complete control.

Donna screamed.

"Full of grace," Buzz continued, in a loud whisper. His tongue came out now, covering his lower lip in concentration. Sam gracefully reached back and pressed his long forearm and hand onto Donna's chest, preparing to cushion the certain blow and tumble.

None were wearing seat belts.

The car's front right bumper hit the rail first, at a thirty degree angle, slowing to forty miles an hour, sparks flying, metal screaming. The back fender smacked the rail, a wacky Hot Wheels toy along a Pennsylvania track. Donna held in a second scream when she saw the distance to the gully below them, distantly aware of Sam's silent strength on her chest.

Buzz gingerly tapped the brakes and the car came to a herky halt.

The only sound was the hum of the Festiva's tiny engine.

Buzz looked at his passengers. "The Lord is with thee."

Donna's eyes widened; she shook her head slowly.

"Are you okay?" Sam asked her. She nodded.

"And you?" Buzz asked Sam, knowing the answer.

"I'm fine," Sam replied, finally taking his arm off Donna. "And too calm."

"Yeah," Buzz said, opening his door. Sam quickly rolled his window down as he watched Buzz amble around to the front of the car to inspect the damage.

There was no one on the road. No one had seen them crash.

"How's it look?" Sam asked.

Buzz didn't answer. He got back in the car, and carefully inched it away from the rail. Then both he and Sam got out; they inspected the long, ugly dents and scratches on the right side of the car. Buzz spit over the side of the cliff, and waited, as if there would be a noise from a landing.

He motioned for Sam to come close. Buzz pulled out a smoke, and facing away from the car, lit up.

"I think the car is okay," Buzz began. "We'll need to change the tire. It's not insured for bodywork, I think. Who cares? It's only a Festiva. I picked it up at a police auction in Newark."

"Change the tire?" Sam asked, not really following Buzz.

"Yeah, get the jack. Turn the lug nuts. I'll do it. Donna looks pretty shaken up," he said, looking back briefly. "Best thing to do is get the tire fixed, and get back on the road."

"Shouldn't we wait for the cops?" Sam asked.

"What for?" Buzz asked back in a friendly tone.

Sam didn't answer.

"There's nothing to report," Buzz said plaintively, holding his hands out. "Look, as soon as I heard the blowout, I knew we would be okay."

"You did?"

"Didn't you?"

Something in Sam's eyes told Buzz that the answer to his question was affirmative.

"I wasn't afraid after I put my hand on Donna."

Sam looked down at his feet. Behind them, they heard the creaky sound of the dented door as Donna climbed out from the back seat. She walked to them, her arms folded, her hands on her shoulders, despite the warm temperature.

"Our Lady saved us," Buzz said, looking down the cliff.

Sam decided to let that slide. Maybe Buzz was in shock. He didn't look like it, though.

How would I know? Sam thought.

Buzz was right. Despite Donna's scream, Sam had felt a peaceful calm in the car as it hit the rail.

A premonition? Buzz asked himself.

He tossed his cigarette over the cliff, and crossed himself. He walked to the back of the Festiva, and pulled open the hatch. He pulled the luggage out, lifted the fiberboard cover, and began to unscrew the little jack and tiny spare. He thanked God when the spare bounced as he dropped it to the stones on the shoulder. It had pressure.

Sam and Donna watched in silence as he adjusted the jack, and began to crack the lug nuts loose by stepping up on the lug wrench with all his weight. He seemed expert at it, as if this was his fourth or fifth tire change of the day. He whistled as he worked, the theme to the *Odd Couple*.

"He told me that he knew we wouldn't get hurt, even as we were crashing," Sam told her, shaking his head, looking at the crouching worker.

"I thought we were going to die," she said, squinting. "All I could think of was: now I get to find out."

"Find out what?" Sam asked.

"If all that I believe is really true," she said.

Sam turned away.

They really believe. It's all they care about. God. What was I thinking as we were crashing?

He wasn't thinking about anything, he realized. He was just *observing*. He knew, during the crash part of the crash, that they would be just as fine as fiddles in Finland.

"This might sound weird, Donna," he told her, still facing away. "But I knew we were going to be okay, too."

"What do you mean?"

"I just knew. Just like Buzz said. After I put my hand on you, I just knew. And here we are. Having a conversation, all sundry bones unbroken."

Why am I talking so lyrically? Maybe I'm the one in shock.

"Sam?" she asked. He turned.

"I—" she began. But something held her back. She didn't know what it was. *I love you,* she finished in her head.

"I believe you," she said finally, firmly.

A few minutes later, Buzz was finished with the tire. He began to repack their luggage.

"Let's go," he said, smacking the grime off his hands. "Let's find a rest stop. I'm thirsty."

"Just like that?" Donna asked incredulously.

"Yeah, just like that. Let's just drive away. It's not like we're taking an exam on how to have an accident. We're not being graded."

"You changed that tire pretty quickly," Sam observed.

"Yeah," Buzz said. "I worked at a few fill-up stations when I was at Notre Dame. Look, it's getting dark. This tire will hold 'til Cleveland. Do you want me to tell you the rest of the story of my life? I'll tell you about Sandi. Maybe Our Lady saved us so you could hear it. And now you know why I call this part of Pennsylvania the Badlands."

"Are you sure you want to tell us," Donna said, remembering the gloom that had crept into Buzz's voice earlier.

"Sure," Buzz said. "Our brush with death somehow makes me feel pretty good."

Buzz held a cupped hand over his eyes, looking at the brilliant orange sun diving toward the tree line to the west.

They all slowly got into the car. They all put on their seat belts without a word. A truck whizzed by.

Buzz carefully pulled onto the road, and eased his way up to fifty-five. *Feels fine,* he thought, referring to the Festiva. *Feels the same. The spare is pulling me to the right, but not badly.*

After ten miles, he muttered "Screw it" under his breath, unlatched his seat belt to an unseen horrified look from Donna behind him, and sped up to sixty-four, his normal speed.

Buzz noticed their looks.

"What?" he asked his passengers.

"You're so, so—" Donna fumbled for the words.

"So weird, yeah, thanks," he finished for her. "Look, what are the chances of getting into two accidents in one day? I'm not going to change my driving habits because of a chance blowout. It's probably even safer to drive normally than to be overcautious. Seat belts make me feel claustrophobic. They distract me."

Neither passenger could follow his logic, if that was what Buzz was using.

Ten minutes later, without any prompting, Buzz finished his story, as if there had been no interruption from the accident…

"There's not much to say about my marriage with Sandi. After Jennifer came, my drinking got worse. It started with staying out late with the guys after work. One of them, Harry Thomason, was an alcoholic too, I guess. Of course, like most drunks, we could never admit it to ourselves. For me, that came after the divorce.

"I don't want to go into the details. It hurts too much. Filling out my annulment form was hard enough, and I guess that was good for me. Let's just say I did it all: adultery, abuse, the whole nine yards. I never laid a hand on Jennifer, but I might as well have, considering how I treated her mother in front of her. Sandi was faithful, I guess. I became paranoid, and accused her of a bunch of things. I went to a shrink for a couple months after the divorce, but that didn't help much.

"Sandi was doing pretty well at her job, which helped in her decision to dump me. Her friends, who knew me maybe better than I knew myself, encouraged her. Her parents must have supported her, too. I had no allies. My drinking buddies weren't really friends—they were doing the same thing I was to their own wives or girlfriends, differing only by degree. They weren't about to set me on the straight and narrow. My friends and I were holding hands as we jumped off the cliff.

"I came home one day after a long weekend with one of my, uh, girlfriends, and the apartment was empty except for a few of my things. Sandi had moved in with her parents. They had been watching Jennifer while Sandi was at work since she was born. I sobered up for a few hours, and went to see Sandi there, and we all sat at their kitchen table.

"Her mom stared at me like I was the devil while Sandi's dad did the talking. The whole thing was surreal, and reminded me of getting cut off by a customer. He even said, 'It just didn't work out. You didn't deliver,' like I was some kind of machine. They told me I needed help. I stalled, promised to get better, go to AA, but Sandi kept shaking her head. I remember the needlepoint on the wall above her head better than the expression on her face. It was Home Sweet Home, with flowers around it.

"Inside, I knew that they were right. I never made a home with Sandi. She was at home with her folks. I even rationalized that Jennifer was better off with them, not me, the Screw Up.

"She had already called the lawyer. It was a done deal. We had been married almost three years. I went to AA in a desperate, last ditch attempt to get them back, but I wasn't ready for it, yet. I stopped going after the first couple meetings. I actually convinced myself that the people there were plastic, weak, and that I wasn't that bad.

"Sandi wasn't taking any chances, and moved to Florida two months after the divorce went through. Her lawyer, a woman who was divorced herself, took me to the cleaners. Things happened so fast. I felt sorry for myself, and in typical alcoholic fashion, went on a bender when she moved to Florida.

"I showed up at work late, or drunk, and missed whole days with blackouts. I lost the job. I lost the apartment, which I couldn't afford without Sandi's income. I hit rock bottom. Deep depression. That's when I saw the shrink. He put me on drugs, which didn't work for me, even though they help others. They just made me go up and down. I couldn't afford them, either.

"I went back to AA. It worked. That's all I can say. My conversion, or reversion, back to my faith happened because of AA. My conversion was nothing so spectacular, really. When it got to the part about the necessity of a Supreme Being to overcome the disease, I simply went to the first parish I drove by after the meeting, and prayed before the Blessed Sacrament.

"Peace came. I didn't cry or anything. I just, well, gave it up. Gave everything up. I lost hope in myself, and found hope in God. I read this little book once, after all this happened, just a bunch of sayings by Saint John Vianney, and one of them was something like, 'God's reserves begin when our reserves are empty.' When I read it, I thought of my first day back into the faith. That's what it was like. I was out of my own gas, and God filled the tank with His gas.

"I often wonder how many people's lives would change if they just let go like that. 'Offer it up,' the saints advise us. I offered up my life to God, figuring it was worthless, and to my surprise, He took it. Is God crazy?

"Oh, I almost forgot—one thing did happen that was out of the ordinary. Just as I was finished praying, and this happened at Saint Angelas, the pastor wandered in. He came right up to me, even though he had never seen me before, and told me that he had forgotten to lock the doors, and that he had to close the church. I said okay, and started to get up. He started to walk away, then turned back, and asked if I wanted to go to confession. I said yes.

"It took an hour. I cried some. He absolved me and encouraged me to keep going to AA, and to try to not lose touch with Jennifer.

"That's it. I started going to daily Mass the next day. It gave me peace, and enough grace to stay off the bottle. I moved back to New Jersey when my Uncle Charlie called me out of the blue and told me that one of his centers needed drivers for Christmas. He's the personnel director there. He wasn't doing me a favor; he was doing himself a favor. He didn't know I was a drunk or out of work or divorced or anything.

"Like I said, we're not close. He must have figured that a Notre Dame grad could work his way into management and be a feather in his cap. Looking back, I think it was the Holy Spirit. I never liked Ohio. Sorry, Donna and Sam, but Ohio just isn't home. I needed a new start in an old place. New Jersey is as close to home as I'll ever have. People are more gritty there, more real. I'm not saying they're better.

"And I was alone, and needed the money. I didn't think I could handle moving to Florida. New Jersey was halfway there in my twisted logic.

"Here's where the Holy Spirit comes in. There were three guys in my UPS section who were in AA. What are the chances of that? We met for lunch every other day, depending on our routes. I put psychology down a lot, but these guys were like an encounter group. They were all Catholics, and one, Jimmy Huckelby, was very devout, and off the bottle for almost fifteen

years. I had already been reading like a madman since I started
with AA the second time around. Jimmy helped me fill out
my annulment papers; said it was an open and shut case and
he was right. Alcoholism. Adultery. Abuse. The triple As. No
real marriage preparation. Not open to children. I wasn't
capable of making a lifetime vow the day I got married. I'm
a classic. He also gave me some good Catholic books to read.
The Story of a Soul by the Little Flower, stuff like that.

"The Little Flower? That's a nickname for Saint Thérèse
of Lisieux.

"It was Jimmy who convinced me to put in for a transfer
to Ohio. Uncle Charlie wasn't thrilled, but I don't want to be
a manager. Our managers treat drivers like boxes, and I can't
do that.

"Anyway, now Sandi doesn't talk to me on the phone.
Geeze, she can be cold. I get Jennifer for four weeks a year,
but I have to pay for the airfare and she ends up staying with
her grandparents every time. I won't get into it, but basically,
she hates me. She acts up, and never warms up to me. She's
coming next month. You'll see. Maybe when she gets older
she'll understand. She's only six. Anyway, when I was in New
Jersey, Sandi's folks told me that Sandi doesn't like Florida,
and might move back up to Ohio soon.

"I don't have any hope that she'll take me back. No hope
at all. I just want to have another chance with Jennifer, that's
all. I pray for them both, every night and every day. I'm still
Jenny's dad, and Sandi hasn't remarried, though her folks told
me that she lived with someone briefly in Florida.

"So I moved here, hoping that Sandi will come back. That's
how I got here. Buzz Woodward, this is your life. I'm still
working through things. You know, one day at a time. I guess
I can tell you, but I still battle depression. Just getting up and
going to work is a struggle sometimes. Exercise is the best
drug I know. The ocean helps, too. I'm toughing it out.

"Thanks for letting me get this off my chest. I guess I feel
better. But it's not how I feel that counts. It's what I do that
matters. It's what I do. When I was drinking, I was always

trying to feel good, or feel better, or feel something. One of the most amazing things—to me at least—when I started reading Catholic books, especially The Imitation of Christ by Thomas à Kempis, and Introduction to the Devout Life by Saint Francis de Sales, was how deceptive emotions can be. They come and go like the weather. We can't ignore them, of course, but we can't let them run our life, either.

"Look, we're coming out of Pennsylvania. Two miles to Ohio. We're almost home."

3

Bill and Mark had gone to Sunday Mass before visiting the Kemps. Two hours before dinner, Bill excused himself, and left. He didn't tell Mark where he was going. Bill went to Our Lady of the Angels, which had a perpetual adoration chapel with the Eucharist exposed in a monstrance. He prayed for his friend. Toward the end of Bill's first full Rosary, Mark had a small, but pivotal, revelation about the Kemps.

Mark was sitting in the living room. Annie Kemp had come and sat on his lap, reading a book about horses. Mary Kemp was in the kitchen with the older daughter, frying chicken breasts for parmigiana. Joe was outside with his two oldest sons, fixing the deck, and preparing it for a coat of water sealant.

"Do you like horses?" Annie asked, turning to look into his eyes. Her gaze was utterly direct.

"I suppose. I've never had experience with them."

"Do your daughters like horses?"

"I... I don't know. I guess so."

"Oh," Annie said, disappointment in her voice.

Why don't I know if my girls like horses? Mark asked. *Should I?*

Because he was an FBI agent, he was trained in the practice of reading little things. A memory from an interrogation he had one time with a small-time mobster came back to him. The interrogation had yielded no useful information. It was early in his career, and afterwards, his supervisor had critiqued him, standing outside the glass window of the empty interrogation room in the FBI offices.

"Johnson, you failed to get squat out of that lowlife because you don't realize that these guys don't think like cops. You asked him questions like he was a frat buddy from the Academy. You've got to get into their heads."

"Get into their heads?" Mark had asked.

"Look at most families nowadays, Johnson. Do the parents think like the kids think? No. The parents like Gershwin, and the kids like Billy Idol. Do they read the same books? No. Parents read Harold Robbins and the kids read—if they read at all—they read Stephen King. They live together, but they don't think together.

"It's the same way with us and the bad guys. I'm not telling you to forget what they taught you at the Academy—FBI or Naval. But you've got to read and think the same way these thugs think, or you'll never be a good agent. Get into their heads. It's not so hard. You'll meet enough of them. You'll follow them. Some of the older agents can tell you things. Just pay attention. It takes time and effort. You can't just pick it up by osmosis, unless you're a natural, and frankly, Johnson, after what I just saw in there, you're not a natural. You can't intimidate these guys, no matter how tough you are."

Now, all these years later, Mark put two and two together. *Get into Maggie's head. Get into your daughters' heads.*

"Why do you like horses?" he asked Annie now.

"I don't know. I saw National Velvet, and I started reading about horses. They're beautiful. Dad took me to a stable last summer."

"He did? Did he see National Velvet, too?"

"He rented it for me," she replied.

"For you? Or for the whole family?"

"Just for me."

She turned back to her book. She adjusted her head on his arm.

Get into her head, he thought again, not sure what he was surfing up to.

Later, Bill returned from prayer. Dinner began.

Mark started to get excited during the meal. There was no major revelation. There was nothing unusual about the dinner conversation, except that the Kemp children seemed more articulate than most kids. Mark was watching with agent's eyes now.

When the oldest boy, Steven, who was in high school, had a discussion with his father about *The Catcher in the Rye,* it clicked.

Joe's in Steve's head!

The Kemps thought *together.* They talked about these things, too. About ideas, not just sports.

In Mark's home, the old rule, that children don't speak unless spoken to, was always in effect. His mother and dad talked, mostly about his father bringing down bad guys or the politics in the department, but never, ever, about ideas.

Mark finished his meal quickly, and excused himself from the table. He went outside. The backyard was well kept. Not in any way unusual. Mark threw himself into thought, concentrating.

Finally, he prayed. *Dear Lord, help me.*

What else was different about his dinner table as a boy compared to the dinner table in the house behind him?

The ideas were different.

The Johnsons had ideas for sure. Those ideas underscored every conversation, every facial expression, every gesture. But the Johnson ideas were limited to a few simple, easily understood areas. Mark simply couldn't imagine having a discussion about a book with his father, who had not gone to college, at the dinner table. His father didn't read much besides the occasional detective novel.

Our ideas weren't bad, Mark thought now. *They were always the same. How to be tough. How to be a man. How to crush other men. It was never so obvious as all that, but that's what it always boiled down to. We never talked about women, or the faith* (even though both his parents were rock-ribbed Catholics in practice), *or philosophy. It was like our house was a barracks.*

Somehow, talking about anything beyond the restricted area of, to put it roughly, what men do, was considered, well, unmanly. Is this true?

My dad was in my head, but only part of it. The guy part.

And somehow, ideas outside 'guy ideas' were considered too effeminate for a real man to entertain. Art. Literature. Even political ideas were restricted; the rules were set—Vote Democratic. Period. Back when Mark was a child, before the abortion issue came up, the Democrats were for the little guy, and in New Jersey, they supported the cops. His father's short, terse dinnertime speeches, which brooked no discussion, came back to Mark now. They were in his head.

Indeed, Mr. Johnson was always in Mark's head, silent, watching his every move. *Is that true?*

But I love my dad.

Of course Mark did.

But did he teach you how to relate to your wife? a little voice, but a strong voice, asked.

The answer was obvious.

No. I mean, yes. I treated Maggie like he treated Mom. He didn't treat Mom badly. Mom didn't have a problem with it. She never gave him any lip. She followed the rules.

She did? What did she really think of the rules? What was in your mother's head? the voice asked.

It was time to be honest. He thought for a moment, watching clouds slip behind a neighbor's roof.

I don't know, Mark thought. *I have no idea what was going on in Mom's mind.*

What's in Maggie's head? the inner interrogator persisted. Mark felt weak.

I...I'm not sure. She hates me.

Does she? his conscience continued.

You don't have a clue, do you, Mark?

Shut up, he told himself.

What's the matter, can't you take it? Big Mr. Tough Guy. Admit it. You don't know your wife's mind, or heart or soul while we're at it. You know the criminals you track down better. You don't even know if your Sarah likes horses. When was the last time—

Mark broke the dialogue with himself.

He looked at the neighbor's yard. A man and his teenage son were playing catch with a football. There was a shiny new shed near their house. The kind of shed where folks keep rakes, shovels, and maybe a lawn mower. A strikingly lucid memory came quickly to Mark's mind.

The Ulster brothers, he thought bitterly...

The scene was one of several little league baseball fields in his hometown of Cedar Grove, New Jersey. Fifth grade. Football practice for Saint Katherine's Pop Warner team had ended. The team practiced daily in the outfield. The coaches were long gone. It was a chilly fall day, and the sun was a few paces from stepping behind the trees on the horizon.

A few of the players had stayed to throw the ball, kidding around. Then the Ulster brothers and a few of their friends had walked by the field. They stopped. Mark and five or six of his teammates had already taken off their shoulder pads. He didn't remember exactly how, all these years later, but a game had started up.

It was supposed to be a touch game, not tackle.

The Ulster brothers, Henry and Marshall, were from the public school. They had just finished their own practice for the public school team. Mark, who had yet to hit his growth spurt, had not been much bigger than any of the other boys. He didn't know who the Ulsters were. After all, they were from the public school, which might as well have been Mars.

The game started off friendly. Then, Henry Ulster, younger and scrawnier than his older brother Marshall, tackled somebody on Mark's team.

Everyone laughed. The game had changed. It was tackle football now. Twelve sets of shoulder pads and helmets watched the game from the rickety wooden stands outside the third baseline.

The grass at their feet was worn and torn from weeks of practice. There were stones in the grassless patches. Fall leaves, carried by a fluttery wind, drifted past the ball as it sifted through the air.

The game was close.

Mark was rising to the occasion, making most of the tackles for his team, and effectively doing most of the blocking on the offense.

Then, on one crucial play, he turned his head while blocking Marshall, and felt a blow at the base of his neck. He collapsed on the ground, writhing in pain as the play went on. Marshall rushed past him to the quarterback.

Mark looked up and saw scrawny Henry laughing at him. Enraged, he climbed to his feet and tried to punch the dirty little player.

Henry sidestepped his punch, and counterpunched Mark in the stomach. The little squirt packed a wallop. Mark doubled over. Suddenly, he felt more sharp blows on his back.

Marshall! The older brother, who was bigger than Mark, was now pounding him on the back.

Mark looked up just as Henry threw dirt into his eyes. Blinded, he never saw Marshall's sucker punch. He fell to the grass.

His teammate, Johnny O'Hara, the quarterback, saw what was happening, and took a step forward.

Mark heard Marshall shout: "Stay outta this, Johnny, this is between me and this faggot."

Johnny hesitated.

Then Marshall had shouted at Mark, who was still disoriented, still in pain, on the ground. "Teach you to pick on my brother, you scumbag!"

Both brothers had started kicking him in the thighs and ribs. Henry spit on him, and got on his knees to punch Mark in the face several times. Blood mixed with spittle.

Mark didn't remember much else from the fight. Johnny had eventually jumped in, and a melee ensued between the two teams. Mark was too beat up to be of much help. He had been sandbagged by the Ulster brothers.

The bitterest part of the memory was not the humiliation of losing a fight—the first such loss of his young life. The real humiliation had been after the limp home. When he slumped into the kitchen, his older brothers Tim and Shawn were at the table with his mom and dad. He saw the shock in their faces when they saw the bruises on his face and neck and forearms.

Then their shock turned to complete disappointment. The young boy could see it in their eyes. Mark broke down, then, and cried.

"What happened!" Mrs. Johnson had called out, leaving her seat to comfort him, but Mr. Johnson had clamped a thick-fingered hand around her wrist.

"There's no part in this for you, mother," Mr. Johnson had said coldly, tightening the grip on her forearm, pulling her away. Then his father had nodded to Tim and Shawn, who were three and two years older than Mark, respectively.

"But Paddy!" Mrs. Johnson had protested.

"I *said,* this is no business of yours, Sheila," Mr. Johnson whispered loudly, boring in on her with his eyes.

"It is my business, Paddy. He's my son," she rasped back.

Mark's father continued to stare at her through icy blue eyes. The time for discussion was over. Mark remembered being frightened by his father's eyes then. Mr. Johnson was a statue, a rock, bigger than any building, stronger than any steel—and no longer in the room with his family, really, but atop some far off Spartan mountain, up high, beyond them all.

Sheila Johnson finally broke her husband's gaze, and violently yanked her wrist out of his grasp. She felt her bones creak as she returned to her seat—to her place. Her jaw was set in furor. Her eyes could light a match. But she had not said another word. She had lost the battle for her son on this day, but the war was not over. She didn't say a kind word to her husband for weeks afterwards.

Tim and Shawn had taken him outside, behind the old shed where the lawn mower was kept. They told him to quit bawling. Mark couldn't help himself.

Then Tim, the oldest, had slapped him.

"I'll beat the crap out of you if you keep bawling, Marky; make you think you just came back from a dance with Raquel Welch. I swear I'll do it."

Mark tried to stop. But he couldn't keep the sniffles in.

Tim and Shawn exchanged looks. Little Mark had always been the softest. He hadn't gotten into many fights. Everybody liked him. That had to change.

"Not on the face," Tim whispered to Shawn, looking at his slumped-over little brother, still heaving with painful, silent sobs.

So they beat him, too. Several punches to his already sore ribs and stomach, until he stopped crying.

Even now, in the Kemp's backyard, Mark winced. Even now, the humiliation of not living up to his brothers' standards hurt more than the punches themselves. The pain from the punches was long gone, but the other pain wasn't.

A week later, Tim and Mark waited outside the fence of the public school practice field, staring at the Ulsters. Everyone in town, Catholic or public, knew about Tim Johnson, the cop's son. The toughest kid in Cedar Grove. When the idiot Ulster boys picked a fight with Mark, they hadn't known his last name. Now they were afraid.

Boy's Justice waited outside the fence.

After practice, the Ulsters tried to escape through the woods behind the field, jogging in the opposite direction, trying to look nonchalant, but Shawn, who was hiding behind a clump of bushes, jumped the two brothers, letting out a whistle. Tim and Mark ran around the fence to the woods. Shawn had held his own for less than a minute.

That was all Tim and Mark needed.

Toward the end of the now one-sided brawl, Tim and Shawn knocked Marshall out cold. Henry, whose face was already bloody—some of the blood from his broken nose, some from the gashes in Mark's fists where they had torn on Henry's teeth—tried to run.

But Tim caught him.

Tim held him up, while Mark worked the body. None of the Johnson boys had made a sound during the fight. That had been agreed upon beforehand. Partly, it was a family tradition for brawling that Mr. Johnson said went back all the way to the wars against Oliver Cromwell on the Old Sod, and partly it was to keep anyone from hearing the ruckus. No need for police during this serious business, no sir.

Mark remembered now how he had not enjoyed the revenge. He had even felt sorry for Henry a bit towards the end of the brawl. But he knew now and he knew then that there was no room for pity when dealing with trash like the Ulsters.

Marshall's parents eventually took their son to the hospital with two broken ribs, and Henry's nose stayed broken for the rest of his life. Neither boy ratted on the Johnsons, despite their parent's entreaties. Henry and Marshall knew the rules.

And neither Ulster boy desired another visit from the Johnson brothers. Tim and Shawn weren't known for *starting* fights or being bullies. But the Johnson boys were known for *ending* fights. They rarely got into trouble at school. They would have to answer to the head tough guy, Mr. Johnson, for any unwarranted shenanigans. Yes sir, indeed.

It was Mark's last serious fight, except for a few tiffs during football practice over the years. But that was different. Coaches didn't mind their players mixing it up every once in a while. It showed that their heads were in the game. It was part of football. No, those fights didn't count. The fight with the Ulsters had counted. And in the end Mark had won.

Mark had never cried again.

What did you win? he asked himself now.

He went back inside. He took a deep breath, and looked into Bill's eyes. Then he looked into Joe Kemp's eyes. Joe was doing the dishes.

If I wasn't here, Joe, looking for your help, would I have thought you were a wimp for talking about some stupid book with your son? Mark asked himself.

"Coffee?" Mary asked, breaking the tension.

"Yes, thank you, ma'am," Mark said, sitting down. The table had been cleared.

"Do you always do the dishes?" Mark asked.

"Not usually," Joe said. "Just to give Mary a spell every once in a while. Why?"

"Uh, no reason."

Bill, sensing Mark's discomfort, changed the subject, and began talking about television commercials.

"Let me tell you about this campaign we put together for Kenny King's Chicken which caused all sorts of publicity to come our way…"

Mark looked into his coffee. He wasn't listening to Bill. His being was disjointed. The wooden chair seemed too small.

What is my world? he asked himself. *Is my world the real world?*

What does it mean to be a man?

He had never asked this question.

Annie came in from the living room, and casually walked up next to Mark. She was such a pretty little girl. So innocent. She put an arm on his shoulder.

Mark tried not to think. He tried to ignore her. She had been affectionate like this with Bill yesterday. It was obvious she was taking a liking to him.

After a moment, she climbed onto his leg, and leaned back into his chest. She listened to Uncle Bill.

Mark ached for his daughters.

She half-turned her head up, and sideways, to look at him. "Your eyes look angry," she said.

"I'm not angry."

"I was just praying for you," she said, her gaze steady into his. "My prayers are always answered."

"They are, are they?"

She nodded vigorously, smiling. She looked back to the table.

"Keep praying, then," Mark whispered into her ear.

4

They were in Bucky's huge den. Her father had gone to bed earlier. They were quite satisfied sitting close on the couch, kissing occasionally, chatting, holding hands—all without the pressure to do much more. Ellie had gradually become excited about the idea of waiting until the wedding.

Would I have slept with him if he had pressured me? she asked herself now, aware of his firm grip on her hand. He had surgeon's hands.

Probably, maybe—I don't know.

Because he hadn't pressured her, she really didn't know. She hadn't been forced to decide whether or not to cross a river that most of the others had, sooner or later, asked her to cross.

Maybe that's why I love you so much. If you had pressured me, you wouldn't be Sam. You would be like the others. And I wouldn't be here now, with you.

And with the others, with a few exceptions, she had decided not to cross the river, to stay on the banks. Now, with Sam, the river had turned into an ocean. Rather than swim the river alone, she now saw herself sailing across a calm sea, holding Sam's hand, standing at the mast of a white, pristine sloop, gazing toward an unknown horizon.

With the others, sex had been a power game. A game she had played well, like the great game of business. She was too smart and had too much self-respect (and perhaps too many alternative choices for lovers) to play *that* trump card capriciously.

But what Sam had done, or rather, had not done, had made her feel precious and unique. Like a woman. Ironically, she felt that he had kept the power over her heart by letting her keep the power over *when* to give her body to him. It was no longer a game.

With the others, the power of sex had been a raw power, a matter of control, a matter of who was going to control the chains. She had always been careful to be the one with the key to the chains. With Sam, it was a different kind of power, a power that was not about chains but about freedom.

She no longer needed to be careful with Sam. She no longer needed to worry about who was in control. She was free to love him, and free to feel like a woman, free to decide on her own, without the worries that came with the pills and condoms of her past.

She also enjoyed the anticipation of making the wedding night special, singular. A first time together.

I could wait forever. Her conclusion surprised her. *True love is full of surprises.*

What had started as a novelty—chastity—was forming into a habit. Sam's self control also surprised and impressed her. She knew his body was telling him to *do more;* she could tell by the way he kissed her, and by other signs. But Sam Fisk was not a slave to his body. He exercised authority over himself.

"Ellie?"

"Yes, Sam."

"I want to talk to you about marriage. About serious things."

Her heart jumped. He had never initiated a conversation about marriage. It was uncanny, considering her conclusions moments before.

She kissed him on the cheek. He flushed.

Okay, she told him with a look.

"I want to talk about three things," he began after clearing his throat. "Money, religion, and children."

"Okay. Why do you sound so nervous?"

"Because I've been doing a lot of thinking lately. I think we should agree on those things."

"Don't we agree already?" she asked, leaning away a bit to look him in the eye.

"Do we?"

"Let's make sure, then," she said matter-of-factly. "Where do you want to start?"

She let go of his hand. He felt her tense up. She looked toward the faux fire, fueled by natural gas, in front of them. It looked so real.

"Money?" he suggested.

She nodded.

"I've been talking to Buzz," he continued. "During the trip to the ocean. Maybe that's why I sound so wooden. We talked about these three things."

"I know he's your friend, but isn't that kind of personal?" There was hurt in her voice.

"Yes. Very personal. But I didn't talk about you and me, per se, just the whole idea that any couple thinking about getting married should be straight on these things. You know Buzz is divorced. He got hurt. His daughter doesn't love him. He was just trying to help me avoid mistakes. He was trying to help us."

She thought about that for a moment. She took his hand again.

"I don't think we're going to have problems with money," she said finally.

That's what I said to Buzz at first, he thought, resisting the urge to bring his name up again.

"I agree. I mean, money doesn't mean that much to me."

"That's easy to say when you have a lot of it," she observed keenly.

"Hmmn," was all he could say.

"Bucky and I had some lean years, Sam. Especially after my mother left us. I don't want to live like that again. Money is important. It's not the most important thing, but it is important."

"That's why we should talk about it. It is important. But not to me. Success is important to me. Doing well at Edwards. The money will come with doing well at my job, which I love.

"Being with you, by comparison, is not just more important, but in another whole category to me. I would..." he stopped himself.

He wasn't used to talking with Ellie about serious things. It was hard to read the look on her face. It was not the same as talking with Buzz and Donna, and for the first time, he was aware of the difference, although he had a hard time putting his finger on what exactly was different.

"You would what?" she asked kindly.

"I would rather have you than have money, or even success in business. I don't think I would have felt that way before meeting you."

She hugged him, touched.

"You can have all three, you know," she said, the side of her face on his chest.

I guess I will, he thought, surprised that the surprise of her giving herself to him never ceased.

A long silence ensued.

"I want children," she began, riding the ebb and flow of her thoughts. "Not many; two would be nice. And not right away. I want to spend some time with you after we get married. I want to start my own business, too. Get settled."

"Sounds reasonable," he found himself saying.

"You don't sound too excited, Sam," she said directly. It was true.

"Oh, sorry. Yeah, I want children too. I want to spend some time with you, too, after we, uh, get married." He paused for a long time. "Are we getting married?"

"Is that a proposal?" she asked, her voice lower, pulling herself close to him.

The topic of the conversation, so clear a minute earlier, was fading, pulling away like a boat from a dock. She put her lips close to his, looking into his eyes.

I love your eyes, she told him. *I love you.*

You're the most beautiful woman I've ever known, he thought, wanting only her.

"Yes," he said simply, thinking of shooting basketballs. *Swish.* Sam had always been the last to lose his nerve on the court. "But I want to ask you formally; to do it right—later, in a restaurant with candles, on my knees. So you can't forget, ever. I don't want to ask you now."

She kissed him. He kissed her.

"Then I accept," she whispered into his ear. "And I'll never forget this time. We can get a ring—as a matter of fact, I want to help you pick it out—and you can surprise me again."

"I would like that," was all he could think to say. She put her head back onto his chest. He felt so good, so right. *Beware of feelings,* Buzz's voice came to his mind.

He let her enjoy the moment.

"Shouldn't we finish the conversation?" he asked after a while.

"Conversation? Oh. Yes. Children and money and religion."

"Yeah," he said, stroking her hair, looking at the fire. "You know I don't believe in God. Does that bother you?"

"No," she said.

"Really?" he asked.

"Faith is too personal to try to force it on other people. You're a good man, Sam. The best man I've ever met. That's enough for me. I've dropped hints about having a church wedding, but I don't expect you to become a Catholic or anything. Has that Buzz got you thinking about becoming a Catholic?"

Was that slight agitation back in her voice?

"Not in the least. He tries in his own way. But it doesn't do much good. I just don't believe. I do appreciate your religion more, so you shouldn't be irritated by him—"

"I'm not irritated by Buzz," she said plainly.

"Did I say you were?" he asked.

"You just did."

"Sorry. Look, let's not talk about Buzz. All I'm saying is that I respect your religion. You respect mine, which is no religion at all. Be we have the same values, don't we?"

"I guess we do. That's what really matters."

The tension slipped away, up the chimney above the false fire.

"Ellie?"

"Sam?"

"Buzz did make one suggestion that I want to try. Would you mind if I came to Mass with you and Bucky? To keep you company. If we have kids someday—" the word *someday* jumped out at him, but he didn't stop talking "—it would show them that I respect your faith."

She turned back to look at him. She kissed him again, putting a hand behind his neck as she had done on the first night in his Accord.

"That's why I love you, Sam," she whispered into his ear. *You make me feel treasured.* "You always put me first, and you make me want to do the same."

Chapter Eleven

1

"Wow," Buzz said. "That's the best movie I've ever seen. Ever!"

He jumped from his chair.

"Ever!" He thrust a fist into the air, then whooped. His apartment echoed with it.

"I've never heard a New Jersey boy whoop before," Donna said dryly. "But it's my favorite movie ever, too."

"Is he always like this?" Ellie whispered impishly into Sam's ear.

Sam laughed, and nodded.

"Look, it's midnight," Buzz said breathlessly, after settling down, looking at his watch. "It's times like this when I—" he stopped. *Wish I had the freedom to take a drink.*

"High Noon," Donna said, not knowing why Buzz cut himself off, still tingling over her tenth viewing of Gary Cooper's classic. "The best movie ever made. I agree with Buzz."

"I liked it a lot," Ellie said. "But to be honest, I don't know why you think it's so spectacular."

Donna almost rolled her eyes, but caught herself. She looked at the perfect emerald-cut diamond on Ellie's hand.

Sam's happy. If I'm his friend, I'm happy, too. Ellie's not so bad.

It wasn't that Donna didn't like Ellie. She just didn't like her with Sam. She tried to ignore her jealousy, to tell herself it was petty, but it kept creeping back up from under a rock in her soul.

I need to see her as a person, not as a competitor. I've already lost the competition, anyway. How can I be so shallow?

"I bet I can tell you why Buzz and Donna think it's the best movie ever made," Sam said mellowly, reaching for his glass of grapefruit juice.

"Please, Sam, tell us all," Ellie asked.

"This should be interesting," Donna said.

"Yeah," Buzz said.

They all looked at him. Buzz standing in front of him, Ellie sitting next to him on the couch. Donna in Buzz's favorite leather chair.

Sam had not meant for his little boast to cause such a dramatic pause. He took a deep breath.

"Because it showed the power of love. Grace Kelly loved her husband more than her Quaker beliefs. Gary Cooper loved duty and the law over his own life. The bad guys loved nothing, as usual, except revenge and money and booze. Everybody else in the town, well, they couldn't find anything to love that was more important than their own lives. They were willing to live as slaves rather than help the one good man in town. For a morality play, that movie was very, very realistic, at least as far as the townsfolk were portrayed. Why don't they make movies like that anymore?"

"I feel like clapping," Donna said. "You should be a movie critic."

Ellie was deep in thought.

"Why didn't he leave?" Sam's fiancée asked finally. "You say it's love, Sam. I think it was just so they could have a movie. Everybody seemed to have a good reason to abandon him. In real life, Cooper would have been outta there."

"Movies aren't real life, Ellie," Buzz said, but without a patronizing tone. "And I know what you mean. I think you just answered Sam's question as to why they don't make movies like that anymore. Because Cooper's kind of love isn't realistic to the modern mind. Back when they made that film, moviegoers wanted to think they would be like Gary Cooper or Grace Kelly in a tough spot. Now, people wonder why he stuck around, and think he just got lucky in the end. I don't think people would like a modern version of High Noon, because it cuts too close to the bone. They would relate to the townsfolk, and feel, deep down, like cowards."

"Would you have gotten off the train if you were in Grace Kelly's place?" Sam asked innocently, not realizing that he was putting Ellie on the spot.

You dummy, Sam! Donna thought. She saw that his question had given Ellie pause. *Bad sign.*

"Of course she would have, Sam," Donna chided, trying not to sound melodramatic. "She even looks like Grace Kelly, you moron!"

Ellie blushed. *Yeah, I guess I would have gotten off that train—for Sam,* she thought, smiling at Donna.

You would have too, wouldn't you, Donna. For Sam or Buzz. That's why you like that movie so much.

Ellie realized, maybe for the first time, that Sam's misfit friends were extraordinary. They didn't fit into the 1980s. They fit into *High Noon.*

Buzz, who realized exactly how charitable Donna had just been to Ellie, laughed loudly, straining successfully not to sound strained. *That's my girl!*

Sam, realizing his mistake, grabbed Ellie's hand, and whispered in her ear. "Thanks, but would you shoot a bad guy for me?"

"What was that, Sam?" Buzz asked.

"He wants me to start shooting people, too," Ellie deadpanned.

That made them all laugh.

Ellie's not so bad, Donna thought hopefully, realizing that Ellie was more than just Sam's fiancée. *I might like you even more if it was just you and me.*

"Can I make the tea tonight?" Ellie asked. "Or are we calling it quits early?"

Buzz cleared his throat. "If I were Sam, and I were engaged, I would call it quits early."

"Just one cup?" Ellie asked.

She was having a nice time. It was only her second Wednesday night video since the engagement. Last Wednesday they had watched *Woman of the Year* with Spencer Tracy and Katherine Hepburn. "In your honor," Buzz had said then, smiling deviously.

"I've got to work tomorrow," Sam said, frowning.

"And like we don't work, too, Mr. Computer Magnate?" Buzz kidded, walking into the kitchen, where he put a kettle on the old gas stove.

"I swear I haven't had a productive Thursday in months," Sam said, smiling, trying to poke fun at himself.

"Me neither," Ellie said. "Or Mondays, Tuesdays, Wednesdays, or Fridays. You always keep me up late."

"My job is so dull, it doesn't matter if I'm tired on Thursdays. It puts me to sleep either way," Donna offered.

Buzz started singing a very bad rendition of the theme song of *High Noon* in the kitchen. "Do not forsake me, O my darlin'..."

"Someday," Sam said. "Buzz is going to be famous. But not for singing."

"Be nice," Ellie said, slapping him gently on the thigh.

Sam got a sheepish look on his face.

I've never seen him try so hard to be funny before, Donna thought. *He really is in love.*

A dull sadness came to Donna, but she was used to it by now.

"It still hurts, though," she muttered under her breath, looking away from them.

"What was that?" Sam asked.

Donna turned back and smiled. "Oh nothing."

In the kitchen, Buzz was pondering the surprise twist.

Ellie's not so bad, he echoed Donna's thoughts. *And she's enjoying our company. I just hope that Donna hangs in there.*

But he knew she couldn't. Not indefinitely.

✛ ✛ ✛

After Sam and Ellie left, arm-in-arm, Donna sat down with Buzz in the kitchen, waiting for a second pot of water to boil.

"After they get married, they won't come over every week," she said.

"I know," he told her. "Is that so bad?"

"No, not really. She makes him happy. She's a nice girl. Very smart. Very, well, sophisticated. Very beautiful. Perfect. But I still—" she stopped herself.

"Still what?" Buzz asked.

"I still don't think she got High Noon. That worries me."

"You can't expect everybody to be like us," he said, taking her hand across the table. "Not that we're that great. We're nobodies in this culture."

"Sister Elizabeth wouldn't stand for you saying such a thing, Buzz Woodward."

There was more than a touch of anger in her voice.

"Don't ever speak that way about me or you again. We're perfectly normal, even if the world is messed up." She took her hand away.

"I've never felt normal," Buzz said, sadness almost creeping into his voice. Donna saw it in his eyes.

"Sorry, Buzz, but you hit a nerve. My mother would never let me speak that way either. We've all got a role to play in God's plan, that's what she would say. You should read up on the Mystical Body of Christ. We all help Jesus bring His grace into the world, not just Our Lady and the saints. We all count."

Buzz didn't answer. He took a sip of tea.

"Sorry, Donna," he said finally. "You know me, Mr. Happy."

"You've been down again, lately, haven't you?"

He looked away. Now she took his hand back.

"I'm praying for you," was all she could think to say. She wasn't much for trite advice.

"I know. Don't stop. I need it. I'll pull out of it. I always do."

The tea kettle started to whistle again.

"You're my Gary Cooper, you know," she said kindly when she caught his eye again.

"You're the best, Donna Beck."

He got up slowly to get the kettle.

She didn't blush. She let go of his hand, saddened that the wall was still up between them, frustrated that the two men she loved were both unavailable, but still thankful that she had them both for friends.

Maybe men and women are just not meant to be such close friends, she thought. *I'm going to talk to Sister Elizabeth about that.*

2

When Mark Johnson finally understood what he needed to know and what he needed to do in order to save his marriage, it seemed so simple, yet still a mystery.

The children and adults gathered in the living room, and prayed a simple family Rosary, led by Joe Kemp. Mark noted the understated fervor with which Mary Kemp prayed, her eyes closed, kneeling before a crucifix on the wall above the mantelpiece. She did not concern herself with keeping an eye on her children; her example set the tone. The two older boys also prayed with calm concentration. The other children prayed with various states of distraction, except for Annie. The youngest child beside the baby, Eileen, who was only two years old, and just learning to talk, played quietly with a plastic statue of Saint Joseph at her mother's side. Joe held the baby for his wife, as he sat on the couch.

Annie prayed wide-eyed, her eyes on the cross, a smile on her moving lips. She seemed to be speaking directly to Jesus. Her composure moved Mark, but he did not know why. He wished that his daughters could exhibit such recollection during prayer.

After the Rosary, Joe Kemp played with his younger children on the floor of the living room, chasing and wrestling, tumbling and laughing. After the fun, the two older boys and the older girls helped Mary prepare the children for bed. Joe and Mary prayed simple, brief night prayers with their children in their rooms while Mark and Bill waited in the living room.

Annie snuck out of her bedroom, which she shared with her older sister, Sarah, to give Uncle Bill a good night kiss and hug. She gave Mark a hug, but no kiss, and padded back to her room.

It was a bit past nine-thirty by the time the younger ones fell asleep. The older children were allowed to stay up reading in their rooms; the oldest, the boys, were also allowed to do homework—in their rooms, where they had two old desks next to a bunk bed.

The Kemps did not have a family room; the children shared the three upstairs bedrooms, and the basement had been converted into a large bedroom, which had a modest bathroom, for Joe and Mary. The baby slept in their bed, and would do so well into her second year. Mary had also explained earlier that the two-year-old, Eileen, would leave her bed most nights to climb into her parent's bed. Joe had installed a special railing just for her, and at the expense of three weekends of work with his older sons, widened and lengthened the basement stairway to make it safer.

"We couldn't afford a larger home, so we did the best we could to maximize space. I'm not sure the zoning laws allow a bedroom downstairs, but so what? It's more private for, well, you know," he had explained after Mark's query earlier in the day regarding the unusual sleeping arrangement.

The living room, which was quite large, had been the center of family life during this day. It was lined with bookcases. There were also bookcases in the basement bedroom. The Kemps had an impressive home library. The television had not been turned on all day.

Joe came out of the boys' room, then fetched four wine glasses from the kitchen, along with a bottle of Sutter Home White Zinfandel.

Mary came in from Annie and Sarah's room, and collapsed onto the couch with a huge sigh. Joe handed her a glass of wine, and sat down next to her, facing Mark and Bill, who sat in two solid, upholstered chairs.

"So that's your day?" Mark asked.

Mary exchanged a look with Joe. She took his hand, and they both smiled.

"My day is finally getting started," she said quite seriously. "It's couch time."

"Couch time?" Bill asked, knowing that Mary and Joe were being a bit too melodramatic.

"Couch time," Joe confirmed.

"Okay," Mark said. "I'll bite. What is couch time?"

"Mark, Bill told me why you're here, of course. I wish I had a magic answer for all your problems. It might look like Mary and I have a perfect marriage, but it wasn't always so. We had some pretty rough times in the first five years, when the kids were coming, and money was very tight—it's always been tight, but it was worse then. We got into debt. We started worrying. Life was hectic. We had a few bitter arguments, and—"

He paused, looking back to Mary, who nodded. "Everything suffered," he continued. "Our children. Our spiritual life, too. Mary almost had a nervous breakdown. We never considered separation or divorce, but we were at wit's end.

"Bill asked us to not mention our problems during the day. But we were eager to let you into our home because we understand the difficulties you must be going through right now.

"Throughout the whole time, we prayed together and went to Mass every morning, but something was missing. Our spiritual director played a big part in helping us sort things out. We're not in Opus Dei, but he's an Opus Dei priest, Father Rocky Hanson, who I met on a retreat I went on just as we were at the end of our rope.

"Our little slang term 'couch time' represents to us what saved our marriage and our family, but it's not so easy to explain. We're willing to try, though, if you want us to. It took us months to change, but we did it."

"I want you to tell me everything you know," Mark heard himself say. For the first time all day, he pulled his cop's notepad out of his pocket, and twisted open his golden Cross pen.

I'm taking notes.

3

Donna drove downtown to go to Mass and confession on a Saturday afternoon, and found herself heading east afterwards. Soon, without any planning, she watched herself take the exit for the Lourdes Shrine.

I guess I want to talk to Sister Elizabeth.

She found the nun locking the doors to the gift shop. Sister Elizabeth was only a bit taller than Donna, and the smile she gave the girl from Rocky River was on the level.

"Hi Donna. I'm just closing up. Do you want to take a walk? I have about twenty minutes before dinner begins."

"I guess so," Donna said unenthusiastically, shoving her hands into her pockets.

"I see. Guy trouble?"

"I wish. That's just the problem. There is no trouble. It's hopeless," Donna said.

They began to walk. They crossed behind the benches at the grotto and climbed the path up a hill where there was a station of the cross every fifty feet.

"Jesus falls," Sister Elizabeth said wistfully.

"I don't know what to say. My job is dull. The guy I like just got engaged. And he isn't even a Catholic. The other guy, Buzz, is not interested. I'm not interested in him, either. It's just..." she trailed off.

"Just what?"

"It's just that I feel like there's no meaning to my life. I love my parents, but living at home is like, well, like being a kid. I fall into the old patterns. Dinner. Rosary. Watch television or read. Go to bed. Go to work. There's no, well, no *weight* in my life. Sometimes I think I'll never get married. Is there something wrong with not being happy or unhappy, but just being in between? My parents, they have weight; their kids; things to worry about. People to worry about…"

Donna looked away. She was frustrated.

They stopped briefly before the next station. Jesus falls for the second time.

"I know what you mean," Sister said after a moment.

You do? Donna asked her with a look.

"I used to feel that way—before the convent. I'm almost ten years older than you. There's something about being single that lacks, as you say, weight. I'm not going to go into details, but in my old life, I tried to fill the hole with men and material things. That never worked. Sometimes I think that people think they're pursuing happiness with all the worldly things, but what they're really after is meaning. Weight, as you say."

Donna bent over to pick up a twig. "I don't want to sound so, well, like some girl complaining about how bad her life is on Oprah." Donna pursed her lips. "I'm not a crybaby. I guess my life could be much worse. So, how did *you* solve *your* 'weight' problem?"

The phrase struck Sister as funny. Donna smiled when she got it herself.

"It wasn't complicated, Donna. I answered the call. I'm here. I'm married now. This life has weight. The common life with the other nuns has meaning. We pray for the world. We're helping my spouse save the world. That has weight."

The two women walked in silence for a moment. A spring breeze kicked last fall's leaves across their path.

"So what did make you decide to become a nun?" Donna finally asked. This was her fifth conversation with Sister since they first met. Donna had been avoiding the question. She did not want to sound like she was doing research.

"I had a great advantage over most Catholics nowadays, even though I was living a typically worldly life by the time I was in high school, and throughout college. I, uh, did all the usual bad things.

"But my great advantage was that my parents and most of my brothers and sisters were the real thing. Good Catholics. When I fell away, I knew what I was falling away from. So I knew the way back. I suspect you have never fallen away like I did, and you have the same kind of parents.

"You know, during my novitiate, I was told that most vocations come from large families with more than five or six kids. The religious life is like a big family. I'm rambling now. But my point is, I knew the way back. I don't think one in ten Catholics knows the way back. They fell away from nothing. You live in their world, a world without meaning, and you want more meaning.

"Maybe you can find it with me. Here."

There, Sister Elizabeth thought. *I said it. And not very well, either.*

The younger woman didn't say a word. She looked Sister Elizabeth in the eye.

"No way," Donna said finally. "I don't have a vocation. I've never felt the call. I wouldn't know what it was if I did have a call. I mean, do you hear something inside?"

"Not exactly. It's less like a calling from a voice, and more like a surgical implant. It's just in there, in your heart. You can ignore it, but you can't get rid of it."

"Oh," was all Donna could say.

"Look, Donna, I didn't mean to push you," Sister Elizabeth said apologetically.

"Don't worry about it. I was expecting it. My mother told me I was going to be a nun since I was a baby. 'That's easy for you to say,' I used to tell her in grade school, before she quit bugging me. 'You're already married.'"

"I always wanted to get married," Sister Elizabeth said. "It still gets to me when I see little children with their parents when they come here. It aches."

"It does?" Donna asked, genuinely surprised.

Sister Elizabeth laughed. "I forgot. There are so many misconceptions about the religious life. Well, maybe ache is too strong a word. I've never regretted my vows. It's more like being a young man in college who had a choice between going pre-med or pre-law, and chose to become a doctor. He can still love being a doctor, still be perfectly happy with his choice. I'm more than happy with my choice. I'm thrilled. Now I can be a mother to all, rather than just a few. People who haven't lived the religious life just don't understand.

"You don't know how many times I've gotten funny looks from people when they see my face, and they think or even say—"

"What is a pretty girl like you doing wasting your life in a convent?" Donna finished for her. "I get the reverse. I can practically hear Mom thinking, 'You're plain, Donna. The convent's a good place to hide out till you die.'"

"You don't really think that about your mom, do you?" Sister asked.

"I'm afraid so. Look, I love my mom. I just made her sound mean, but she isn't. She and I have always been close; always had a special relationship. I can tell her just about anything. But lately, living at home, I feel like, well, it's hard to describe…"

"You feel like she relates to you as a daughter, not as an adult?" Sister guessed.

"How did you know?" Donna asked.

"It's pretty common. I felt the same way. A hundred years ago, most kids were out of the house by age seventeen. Now it's thirty-two. That's just not normal. Or better, it's more normal to get out, to get on your own.

"That's what I mean about misconceptions about religious life. It's natural, perfectly normal, to want to get married. It's normal for me to have, let's say, motherly instincts, when I see little kids. Motherhood is in a woman's bones—if she's a normal woman.

"The religious life is supernatural. It's beyond the normal, and doesn't negate the normal. My spiritual director told me some time ago that if there wasn't Original Sin, and therefore wasn't a need for Jesus to die and rise, then there wouldn't be any religious orders."

That gave Donna pause for thought.

"Religious life," Sister Elizabeth continued, speaking as much to herself as to Donna, "is not for broken people or misfits. It's for the strong. It's not for people who want to run away. That's why I asked you if you've ever considered it. You're strong, Donna. But being strong is also an asset for getting married."

"I know. Strength also repels men," Donna replied quickly.

"Maybe strength in a woman repels a *weak* man. Maybe you just haven't met your match, Donna."

Donna stopped walking. Sister didn't notice her stop, and walked a few paces before realizing this, and turned back. She saw Donna behind her, looking up at a station.

The Crucifixion.

"What is it?" the nun asked her friend.

"Oh, nothing," Donna said, lying. She quickly caught up to Sister Elizabeth.

But it is something, Donna's little voice insisted.

Because as Sister Elizabeth had made her last remark about Donna not yet meeting her match, Donna had looked up to the cross, and the Man on it.

He's strong, Donna had thought, shaken. *He's my match.*

4

Mark wrote "couch time" down on his notepad. He looked at the Kemp's couch itself. It had a dark-brown, light-brown, checkerboard pattern, and a few tears here and there. On the cushion to Mary Kemp's right, there was a large, five-inch-diameter stain from what Mark guessed to be grape juice.

Maybe it's wine…

"Listen, Mark," Joe Kemp said, following Mark's gaze, glancing to the stain. "There's a lot of marriage-counseling talk about communication, and how important communication is for marriages. Heck, they don't even use the word *marriage.* They usually talk about *relationships."*

All three men made a slightly disgusted face. *Relationship* was a euphemism for *shacking up.*

"I don't think that communication is the key," Joe continued. "It's just one of many key things. That's not what Couch Time means to me. Mary and I communicated all the time when we were having our problems. I won't speak for Mary. But here is what Couch Time means to me: Mary has an emotional tank. It gets filled mostly by what I put into it. What I say to her can fill the tank—or empty it."

He saw the confused look on both Mark and Bill's faces.

"Maybe I can explain," Mary suggested. Her husband nodded. "I heard this radio program once, about four years ago; there was this so-called 'love expert' lady on it, and she was saying that most people fall into three categories for communication. She said that communication is like trying to get a message to the other side of a fence. The fence is around the person's heart.

"She went on to say that you could slip a note through the slats, or tie it to a rock and throw it over the fence, or even dig a hole and pass the message under the fence. Okay?"

All three men nodded. Bill took a sip of wine.

"Now with people, this lady's theory was that there are three ways to get messages across to other people. One was with words, another way was with touches, and the last way is with actions. She called it verbal, tactile, and visual. She said most people are wired to prefer one way over the others.

"Some people respond to what is said to them. That's not me. When Joe tells me he loves me, well, I hear it, but it's like the message was slipped through the crack in the fence, and I need to have him throw a rock over the fence. I need to feel it. If he gives me a hug—" she turned to look at her husband as he took her hand, "—and tells me he loves me by whispering in my ear, the message goes into my heart. I 'hear' it if it's physical.

"Now Joe is different. Talk is cheap with him. And, while he can be very affectionate, what matters to him is order. I can tell him I love him by making his bed, or keeping the house tidy, or putting his tools from the garage back in their proper place after I borrow them. He's a general contractor, after all, and the way things look, the way they're put together is how his mind works.

"Are you following me?" she asked.

"I wonder what I am?" Bill mused.

"Definitely verbal," Mark said. "Just look at how you make your living; you talk to people all day long and you design ad campaigns around words and their meanings."

"Very true," Bill agreed. "But ad campaigns also require a lot of visual input. There's an old saw that the best radio commercials are the ones that paint a mental picture.

"Maybe that's why advertising has so many mediums; there are billboards, television commercials, radio, print, etcetera. I've always told clients that people respond to different mediums depending on the person."

"Right," Joe Kemp said, leaning forward. "Couch Time is a medium—a place where different kinds of messages can go through the fence. I might be talking to my wife verbally, and I'm picking up verbal messages, but what's really filling *her* tank is the physical—uh, tactile—message of my holding her hand, or putting my arm around her shoulder."

"Sometimes," Mary added, "it's not what Joe says to me. It's just the fact that he's listening to me, that he's not talking to me while he's in the middle of something else. I don't like to talk to him while he's working on a project. Sure, he listens to me then, but I feel like I'm playing second fiddle to a piece of wood."

"I don't think you're second fiddle to wood," Joe said, feigning hurt. "But it was Couch Time where I figured out that it doesn't necessarily matter what I think. What matters is the message that is being received on her end."

"This must sound confusing to you, Mark," Mary said sympathetically.

The wheels in Mark's head were turning furiously. He was confused. He was trying to process what he was being told and compare it to his communication with Maggie at the same time.

"Keep talking, don't worry about me," he said softly. "I'm listening. I do have a question."

There was a long pause.

"How do you avoid arguing on the couch?" Mark asked, embarrassed, but not knowing why he was embarrassed.

Every couple argues, he told himself. *You're separated, for heaven's sake! They know you've argued with Maggie.*

"And how do you keep from losing your temper?" the big man added.

Mary and Joe exchanged looks. Mary nodded this time.

"Listen, Mark," Joe said. "I don't know you that well; what I'm going to say might sound, well, kinda strange, to a guy like you. I'm sure you're a great guy, from what Bill's told me—"

"Just give it to me straight," Mark commanded, edginess in his voice.

Joe Kemp took a deep breath.

"Men have always used their tempers to control women. I see it with my workers all the time. The Rolling Stones had a song called Under My Thumb. I hate that song now. The true test of most married men is not how they communicate with their wives, or how much money they make, or what kind of grades their kids get in school. The true test of a man is how he controls his temper, his will, his very self.

"At our lowest point, it seemed like every time Mary and I sat down to talk, I would lose my temper, or in the least, talk to her in such a way as to show her who the boss was. Tone of voice was the real clue, as well as if I interrupted her, cut her off, didn't let her make her point, or belittled her side of things.

I was more interested in winning the argument, as if I was playing one-on-one with her, than really, truly, trying to see her side of things.

"Here was the pattern, and I'm sure this same pattern could be found all over the United States, in just about every home. Mary would call me on the job and ask when I was coming home. I would tell her six. Well, you know how it is, six o'clock rolls around and something happens at the site. I might come home at six-fifteen, or six-thirty. Meanwhile, Mary has been battling the kids all day, and getting dinner ready. She's holding off for me, waiting. Getting disappointed.

"I get home and the first thing I do is say 'Hi honey,' and I can tell by the look on her face that she's not happy. Instead of saying I'm sorry, or even if I do say I'm sorry, the first thing I go to do is check the mail. I do that every day when I get home. From my point of view, this is totally justified, but it aggravates Mary. She wants me to sit right down and start dinner. The kids feel the tension, even if they can't put it into words.

"Mary is stuck. If she asks me to skip the mail, I say, hey, I do this every day. I'll be just a minute. But I take five minutes, or ten. Now I've been late for two things. If she ignores my opening the mail, she has to wait anyway. Maybe she's not steaming mad at me, yet, but she's irritated.

"Finally, I sit down to eat. We say prayers. We talk about the day with the kids. Dinner at our house is Couch Time for the kids. Maybe after dinner, if I don't turn on the television, and start helping her clear the table, Mary complains about this and that regarding the kids' behavior. You know, Annie was acting spoiled with her dolls, Steve talked back to her after school— that kind of thing. I think, hey, I don't complain about *my* job. She's the one who wanted the kids. You see, I don't see it as her getting it off her chest, I see it as her being a whiner. Note the two different perceptions. I think she's a whiner; she thinks she's trying to share a problem.

"After dinner, I play with the kids. We usually prayed the family Rosary, but we were losing discipline at the time.

Sometimes we skipped it if it was late and there was a lot of work piling up. Maybe do a few chores. Before you know it, it's after ten, and the kids are late to bed—again—late. It's not my fault, I tell myself. That's Mary's job. I'm a little miffed, because she's asking me for help, but doesn't realize that I'm worn out from work, and need to let my mind and body take a rest. I turn on the television, and zone out while she does all the work. There's something on ESPN. I get into it. Mary's thinking that she'd love to have time to zonk out watching television, and maybe she could if I would just give her a hand. She asks for help again. I say, yeah, yeah, at halftime. But the halftime show has an interview with a running back I like, so I put her off. Eleven o'clock rolls around.

"It's been a week since we've, uh, been together as man and wife—"

"Just say *made love,* darling. There are no kids around," Mary suggested kindly, looking furtively at Bill and Mark.

"Yeah. We haven't made love in a week," Joe continued. "We've both been too busy. You know, there's a lot of talk about women and PMS and their emotional and physical cycles nowadays, but there's no talk about the male cycle. It's not as pronounced, but it's there. Men have cycles. Every married guy I know would agree with me. Our cycle is three or four days, especially when we're in our twenties, thirties, and forties. I don't know about fifty-year-olds. Anyway, about three or four days after your average man has made love, he starts to feel the urge again. I believe God made us that way.

"On this hypothetical night, I've got the urge. After prayers with the kids, I give Mary the signal. Either I tell her, or look at her just so. Every couple probably has their own signals after a few years.

"Well, I don't realize it, but Mary is dreading the signal. She's not in the mood. I've been draining her tank since the phone call at work. Making love when she's not in the mood would drain it further. I can't speak for you, Mark, and Bill, you're not married, but I can say that Mary is a good Catholic wife. She took a vow. She'll keep that vow, and part of it was that she would give herself to me.

"So let's say *she does* give herself to me," Joe paused. He was on a roll. He looked at his wife. There was an old hurt in her eyes.

"Keep talking, Joseph," she said, playing nervously with his hand. She looked up to Mark.

Mark didn't say a word. He and Maggie had not been good with each other in bed for the last two years, except for a few scattered occasions. That had led to arguments. Mark wanted Joe to continue, despite all their discomfort.

Joe took the silence as consent.

"So Mary does what I want. But she doesn't enjoy a second of it. Maybe she tells me, maybe she doesn't. Either way, her tank might be completely empty when it's over. We both fall off to sleep unfulfilled, knowing, compared to the way it used to be, when we were first married, that what we have just done together was nothing to be proud of. After a while, I guess, we throw ourselves into our kids, or our jobs, or our season tickets to the Browns, and that part of our marriage dries up. If we're good Catholics, we console ourselves by saying that we're open to having kids. We even have a strong desire for more kids. At least I do.

"If we're not good Catholics, the child that may result is a source of fear. You all know what I'm talking about. How many people have more than one or two kids these days? You go to the playground and the first thing other parents tell you about is their vasectomies and tubals.

"Either way, month after month of days more or less like that turn into year after year. By our third child, and our sixth year, there was a pattern. There were good times in between, of course. We were still friends. We might have even described ourselves as happily married. At least our friends thought we were.

"Maybe I am speaking out of place. Mary knew all was not right. She tried to tell me. But I took it personally, like it was an attack on me. Maybe it was, maybe it wasn't. But I didn't want to admit to myself that I was failing at something. I loved Mary. I really did. She was and is my best friend in the whole world…"

Joe's voice started to crack. He cleared his throat. He took a sip of wine, then another.

"But our marriage was in trouble. I had a couple of bad years with my contracting company. I got sued over an easement—I won't get into the details—and lost the suit. We almost lost the business and the house. We had to take out a second and third mortgage. We drove beat-up cars and ate macaroni and cheese for dinner for two years. I had to lay off some good men, good carpenters. I got behind on my bills at work and at home. That didn't help. Our credit cards started carrying bigger and bigger balances.

"I read somewhere once that when they poll women and men about how well they are relating to each other, almost twice as many women than men say that something is wrong with the relationship. That tells you something about men. At least half the husbands think their marriages are healthy while their wives think their marriages aren't.

"It's just my opinion, but I believe that men are either out of touch with their wives' outlooks, or, they are unwilling to admit to themselves that they're not doing a good job at being a husband. When I was in that boat, I thought that just being a good provider and a good father was enough—but that's not why God gave Mary to me.

"God gave Mary to me so I could be the best *husband* I could possibly be, and to help her get through this life with as much peace, and joy, and happiness as possible. That's how I should judge my life: how well am I fulfilling my responsibility to my wife *as a wife,* as a woman.

"I was doing a bad job at that, six years into our marriage, and I didn't see any way out. We would talk about it; we would argue; I would lose my temper; I would apologize, promise to be better, because I was a good guy with a conscience; but it just kept getting worse, or staying on the same dismal plane.

"I've never told anybody this before, but I started to have this fantasy about getting in my truck in the morning, and driving away, never coming back. Going to California and starting over. This scared the living crap out of me.

"In desperation, I went on a retreat for men, with Father Rocky, and I figured it all out. I saw a flyer in the bulletin at church. The retreat wasn't about how to save your marriage. The retreat was pretty standard stuff. The real key was that I forced myself to tell Father Rocky about my problems. I talked to him a lot, after hours. He helped me see the real problem."

Joe stopped to take a sip of wine. Bill was amazed at how well-spoken Joe was. Bill had always taken the contractor to be a man of few words. In reality, Joe was well read. His father had been a professor. Most of Joe's brothers were professionals. Joe had received a degree in English, with honors, from Ohio State.

"What *was* the real problem?" Mark asked.

"Before I get to that, and I'm not trying to be melodramatic, I have to say something that's been on my mind for years. It used to be that all this marriage stuff was automatic. You did what your parents did and things worked out."

Mark instantly thought of his own parents. If they had any marriage problems, he sure didn't know about them.

"But our society hates fatherhood. Just look at the divorce laws. Just look at the welfare system, which pays teenage girls to have children just as long *as they aren't married.* Look at the way corporations treat fathers. If you have a big family, and show an interest in putting your children before your career, you're taken off the fast track. Most companies reward not just the hardest workers, but the guys who put in the longest hours. Who gets the raises? The guys who are willing to travel the most. The guys who are willing to uproot their families and move away from friends and relatives. How many friends do you have who work sixty, seventy, eighty, even one hundred hours a week? My brothers took that route, and they're practically slaves to the law firms and companies they work for. That's why I went into my own business, so I wouldn't have to put up with that.

"Plus, men have to compete with women in most jobs nowadays. I won't get into women's rights or anything like that, but it's got to keep salaries down, especially when it counts, in those first crucial years when most guys are just married, and trying to get on their feet.

"Even the income tax system punishes marriage. There's another contractor in town who got divorced and lives with his former wife to save a few thousand bucks a year on his 1040!

"Culturally, the family is being attacked from all sides. From values clarification courses hidden in 'health classes' in public schools, to social workers who can have a father taken out of his home without any due process, on hearsay from an irate neighbor. We don't know what kind of sick pornography might be in the video case at the neighbor's house down the street where our kids want to go for a slumber party. And children are having sex in fifth grade now. There was a big scandal about that last year in one of the Cleveland suburbs. It was all over the Plain Dealer.

"Then there are drugs, satanic rock music, occult messages in movies, and a world filled with kids whose values are completely without religion because that's the way their parents are. These are the kids who might make friends with your kids.

"Fathers are the point men, leading their families through a minefield. It's scary.

"And if we want to bail out, there are plenty of unhappy, screwed-up women willing to jump into the sack with us at just about every bar down in the Flats.

"If we really wanted to get into that truck and drive to California, well, that's no problem, because legally, the marriage contract is the only legal contract that can be broken by either party for no reason at all. No fault divorce. It's not a contract at all. The warranty on your kid's bicycle has more binding force.

"Right now, my wife could get pregnant with our child, my child, and decide to snuff out its life at the local abortion mill, and there's nothing I can do to stop her.

"That's what we got in exchange for the sexual revolution."

Joe closed his eyes.

"Geeze, Joe, what's gotten into you?" Mary asked.

"I guess I'm wound up, that's all. I was just trying to tell Mark that being a good husband and father is perhaps the greatest challenge in any man's life, and the deck is stacked against him. There's no shame in screwing it all up. I always thought that I was a tough guy, and coming this close to losing everything almost overwhelmed me."

Bill cleared his throat. "Joe, you were going to tell us what Father Rocky told you that changed everything. What was it?"

"Oh, I forgot," Joe said with a sheepish grin. "I'm sorry. It's so simple, but not obvious. I don't know why. I was in confession with Father Rocky, pouring out my tale of woe, telling him what a rat husband I was, confessing to losing my temper for what seemed like the hundredth time, when he told me these words, which changed my life forever—"

"Okay, Joe," Mary interrupted. "You've built it all up."

Joe took another deep breath. "Father Rocky said to me: 'Joe, the only person who can make you lose your temper is you. Period.'

"What do you mean by that? I asked him. He answered: If you think you're so strong, if you think you're so in control, then explain to me how one little complaint from your wife— which is probably perfectly justified if you look at it from her perspective—explain to me how just a few words from her mouth can make you blow up?

"I'll tell you why this is, Joe, Father said, not waiting for me to answer. You blow up because you're weak. Because you don't have control of yourself. Because you're more concerned about winning an argument with your own wife than you are with finding out what's really bothering her.

"When was the last time you asked her what was really bothering her? Go home and ask her what's really bothering her, and then listen to her when she tells you what it is, *and then* ask her what she wants you to do about it, *and then do it*.

"If you're a real man, you will do just that when you get home on Sunday night. And you'll find that most of your problems will just melt away in a few weeks.

"But she'll wrap me around her little finger—that's what you want to tell me, isn't it? Father went on. And I bet you have a million reasons and objections to what she would ask from you, he told me.

"But I'm telling you, Joe Kemp, none of that matters. I'm not asking you to obey your wife; I'm just asking you to please her.

"Somebody has got to be the first to lay down his life. That's what marriage is, Joe, laying down your life. You do that by getting control of yourself. Never let something your wife says get the best of you. You probably bite your tongue at work ten times a day, yet you probably haven't bitten your tongue at home for years.

"I swear that the most invisible word in the world for husbands is *meekness*. Do you know what that word means, Joe? Do you know that Saint Joseph was meek and that's what made him a saint? Did you know that it takes strength to be meek!?

"Father was really worked up. I think he had heard the same crybaby stuff in the confessional so many times that he was just sick of it. I'm glad he was.

"He saved my marriage.

"He kept going. Father told me to do whatever it was that Mary wanted of me, and that I would be surprised how she would be willing to do whatever I wanted in return. He told me to treat her like she was Grace Kelly herself, to imagine what I would be willing to do if Grace Kelly showed up in my house and had my wedding ring around her finger.

"Would I let myself get into an argument with Grace Kelly? Wouldn't I wait on her hand-and-foot? What would my tone of voice be like? Would I snap at her? Would I help Grace Kelly put the kids to bed?

"He was a clever priest. I don't know how he knew Grace Kelly was my favorite movie star. Maybe he just guessed. I don't know.

"But I wasn't treating Mary like Grace Kelly. In fact, even though I claimed to love her, I was treating Mary worse than I would treat my mother, my dad, my kids, my subcontractors, or even my dog.

"Ironic, isn't it?

"The only person who can make you lose your temper is you, Joe. Period. That's what Father Rocky said. When he put it that way, it was like a lightbulb went on in my head. Instead of me wanting Mary to change, or Mary to do this, or Mary to do that, it was up to me to change, to get true control over myself.

"I think most guys could understand that. We've got to stop looking at our wives as the opponent we have to beat in some verbal game. The way we win contests in the male world is the way we play sports or succeed in business: we go for the throat, we try to destroy the other guy. That doesn't work with women. You can win an argument with your wife, sure, but you might have to cut her up to do it. It makes us feel good to win, but it makes her feel lousy. That's not much of an aphrodisiac, by the way.

"Father turned the tables. He told me that the real opponent I had to beat was myself. That if I wanted to really look at myself as a virtuous man, and a worthy husband, I would have to win the contest in here first—" Joe pointed to his chest. "—in my heart, in my will. If I could control myself, then I could have a decent discussion with Mary, and I would also have the ability to follow through with what she wanted of me.

"The devil is so clever. He gets men to think they're men by having them beat up on their wives. God gets men to be men by having them master themselves. Nobody can make me do anything but me. Period. I believe that now. The Catholic teaching on virtue, the sacraments, and the grace that comes from prayer gives me the strength to master myself. In the end, we don't even own our own bodies. The only thing we own is our will.

"I'm going on and on again, but I guess I made my point."

There was a long, heavy silence in the room. Mary leaned over and kissed her husband.

Mark had a question. "So what happened when you got home from the retreat?"

"It was like he changed completely," Mary said.

"I don't think I changed," Joe said, but not in a unfriendly way. "I think I just started trying to be a good husband and good father *in another direction.* I never stopped trying to be a good husband, not through all our difficulties. It felt like I was simply switching tactics. It was like solving an engineering problem at work. What was a mystery, a frustrating problem with no solution, always seems so simple once you solve it.

"More specifically, I went home determined to treat Mary like she was Grace Kelly. When I asked her what she wanted from me, she seemed very skeptical. I'll never forget what she first asked me to do for her." He turned to her.

"I asked him to sit on the couch with me," Mary explained, smiling, a loving look in her eyes as she gazed upon her husband's face. "I told him that I missed him, that I missed the Joe who dated me and fell in love with me, and that I missed how we used to sit on the couch before we got married in my folks' basement and just hang out."

Her face was like a newlywed bride's.

"When she asked me that, everything fell into place," Joe picked up from Mary seamlessly. "I thought, first, that if Grace Kelly asked me to sit on the couch with her, I would do it without hesitating. Then I thought, Gee, that doesn't sound so difficult.

"So we sat on the couch after we got the kids down that night. It was pretty late, close to midnight. We talked small talk, we talked about our marriage. I wish I could say that all the talk went well, but it didn't. Not at first. We fell into old patterns of complaining. But I was looking out for those patterns. It was like a game. I gave myself a point for every time I held my tongue. I kept saying to myself, Mary can't make me lose my temper. Only I can make me lose my temper.

"If I said a sharp word, I asked her to forgive me, just like I would ask Grace Kelly."

"I could tell he was trying something new," Mary added. "He was giving me hope. I was still skeptical. But how could I not forgive him when he apologized in such a nice way? I didn't know at the time about the whole Grace Kelly thing, but I was seeing some of the old Joe, the Joe I fell in love with before we got married, coming out. His nobility was back. He was like a king. I was starting to feel like a queen.

"It's funny, but I'm still miffed a bit about Grace Kelly. If I had known that he was making believe I was a beautiful actress, I would have been deeply offended. I'm not Grace Kelly. I'm not a beautiful actress, I'm me. I want Joe to love me. Even now, when he calls it a tactic, it sounds strange, wrong. And maybe Grace Kelly illustrates the whole problem: men and women don't see the world in the same way."

Joe looked down at his hands.

"Look, I knew Mary is not Grace Kelly," he said a touch defensively. "And I guess Father knew that too. But it helped me get started. I was desperate, and willing to try anything to save my marriage.

"Every time I lost my composure that night, I was *aware* of it. That was the big difference. It had nothing to do with Grace Kelly. And it wasn't so hard. It wasn't as hard as going to work each day. Especially with Mary cooperating. I could see that holding my tongue and avoiding the old arguments at all costs was getting to her."

"Before I knew it, we were holding hands. It seemed like we hadn't done that in ages," Mary took over. "I starting telling him all my complaints, expecting him to go into his usual rationalizations. Instead, when he replied by saying things like, 'It must be hard living with a guy who is so chronically late that you can't plan a simple meal,' or, 'Honey, I can imagine how you might feel that way about it, even if I don't agree completely with the way you're saying it'—well, it was like talking with a whole new Joe. Or the old Joe from before we got married. *Better* than the old Joe." Mary finished, still smiling.

"And I found a sense of, well, power," her husband continued. "By controlling myself, and not trying to control Mary, suddenly I was in the driver's seat. The goal was no longer to get her to do something by convincing her how wrong she was or how right I was. The object was to get myself to do something.

"It sounds weird, but by getting control of yourself, and by being willing to do whatever *your wife* decides will make her happy, you get control. It's a paradox. I guess the reason is because a good and loving wife like Mary will usually just ask you to sit on the couch with her, to spend more time with the kids, to give up a few meaningless hobbies for the sake of the family. She's not the enemy, you know."

Mary smiled broadly when he said this. Joe chuckled.

"And so we had a great time that night," she continued. "By three in the morning, we were hanging all over each other like teenagers. We started to kiss…"

"And nine months later, Ginny showed up," Joe finished, smiling.

"We don't know that for sure!" Mary teased.

"Hey, who's telling this story, anyway?" Joe asked.

"We both are," Mary replied seriously.

"I guess you're right, Mary."

"So what happened next?" Bill White asked, genuinely curious, amazed by their story. He hadn't known that their marriage had ever been in such serious trouble.

"It took a few months to really get the schedule shifted around to accommodate, shall we say, the couch," Joe explained. "But we managed. We shoot for four or five days a week on the couch, starting at nine or nine-thirty. Sometimes we have a glass of wine. Light a candle. The kids know to stay in their rooms.

"There is absolutely no agenda, except that this is time we spend together. Sometimes we pray. Sometimes we talk about the kids. Sometimes about the company. Sometimes about Mary. A lot of times about Mary. My biggest challenge is to not dominate things, to let things flow.

"After all these years, it's not that big a challenge keeping my temper anymore. No television, no reading. Just me and Mary. It's our time to fall in love with each other. We did it before we got married, didn't we? Anybody who can fall in love with their spouse once, can do it again, I suspect. Heck, I know it. I fall in love with Mary every other week now."

"That's so sweet, darling," Mary said.

"It's true," Joe replied. "You don't have to spend time on the couch, of course. I'm sure other couples could do Couch Time in bed at night, or by taking a daily walk. That's kind of tough in Cleveland, with the cold winters. Sometimes we go out to the deck in the summers."

"We both feel it when we go more than a few days without Couch Time," Mary added. "With the kids and all."

"I find that I've had to cut a lot of things out of my life to make the time," Joe added. "Less time out with the guys. I quit my bowling league because it starts too late at night. I also spend less time being a workaholic, which I never enjoyed all that much anyway. Cutting back on the hours has definitely affected our income for the worse. We're still driving beaters. It's a sacrifice I don't mind making."

"And it's got to be better for the kids to have their parents in love again," Bill added.

"I can't tell you the difference it makes," Joe said enthusiastically.

Mark had remained so silent for the last ten minutes that Joe, Mary, and Bill almost forgot that he was there.

"The kids pick up on it. For better or worse, I think they treat each other the way Mary and I treat each other."

"Hmmn," Bill said, rubbing his chin. "Mark, did you get that?"

"Yes, I'm listening to every word. Don't mind me, just keep talking," Mark said quickly.

"There's not much more to say," Joe observed. "The more I strive to control my will, the more I strive to do the things Mary tells me she wants and needs, the more she strives to please me. We strive *together,* not *against* each other.

"I finally understand what Jesus meant when he said, 'My burden is light and my yoke is easy.' The burden, the yoke, the cross I carry is Mary's happiness, and I can tell you that this is God's will for me. That's what my marriage vows mean. Mary is light and easy to carry. I'm in love with her."

Chapter Twelve

1

On a warm, clear evening, Buzz and Sam found themselves walking along the boardwalk down on the Flats.

I don't like the endless winters here, Buzz thought wistfully, thinking of New Jersey. *But I wouldn't trade Cleveland summers for anything. It seems like every day is perfect for three months in a row. Warm. Sunny. Not humid at all. Even the summer showers are nice, a lovely break to help you appreciate the perfection. Just right. If only I felt like the weather.*

The Flats had been a dilapidated, ugly port-of-call on the Cuyahoga River next to the downtown section of Cleveland. To the everlasting embarrassment of residents of northeastern Ohio, it was the location where refuse and oil on the surface of the river caught fire a couple of decades earlier.

A partnership between the city and developers had transformed the area into a safe, exciting string of restaurants, night clubs, and family game rooms on both sides of the river. The only blemishes were a few 'men's clubs' on the fringes of the huge area.

The western side of the Flats had a long boardwalk, and on summer nights, cabin cruisers and cigarette boats came to dock there. Thousands of patrons, including whole families, came to enjoy the multicolored view shimmering off the river's surface, the sounds of live bands wafting across the water, the eclectic mix of food, and water taxis shuttling from one side of the river to the other.

Sam had invited Buzz to dinner at Shooters, one of the classier, and lower-key establishments. It was a treat for Buzz, who could not afford an expensive social life. The alcoholic in Buzz avoided places like the Flats anyway. Shooters happened to be the place where he had first met Sandi, his ex-wife. Sam had forgotten that.

They walked in and were taken to a reserved table with a view of the water. As they sat down, they heard the sounds of a freight train crossing the river to the north.

"I want you to be my best man," Sam said after his wine arrived, holding up his glass.

Buzz smiled broadly. "I thought you'd never ask!"

Sam was used to Buzz by now. That's why he was asking him to stand up for him in the wedding.

Buzz raised his Pepsi, a slice of lemon floating with the ice.

"Here's to you and Ellie," he said soberly, happily.

They drank.

"Why me?" Buzz asked.

"Because you're my best friend in the whole world, just like you predicted the day we met. I've never had a best friend. I've been a loner all my life. I don't even have a friend at work. I don't like getting close with people I might have to fire or lay off. Johnny's okay, but he has his own life. He's too wild for me.

"Listen to me! You've got me talking more and more since I met you. Anyway, you're the best man for the job, no pun intended. And I probably wouldn't have met Ellie without you, or been able to keep her without your advice."

"You underestimate yourself, Sam," was all Buzz could say.

Buzz felt mixed emotions. His daily battle with the blues had been wearing him down. This invitation from Sam should have perked him up. Instead, Buzz had the odd emotion of feeling *as if* he should be happy for Sam and himself, but not actually feeling happy at all.

I'm a good actor, though, he told himself. *Why spoil it for Sam? He's happy. What can I ask him to make him feel good?*

"So Sam, what do you want me to get you for a wedding gift?"

That gave Sam pause.

"Your presence is enough for me," Sam said sincerely.

"Oh, that's too bad. I had this lamp picked out," Buzz paused for a second. "It's got a shade with a Hawaiian girl on it, just like the one in Joe Versus the Volcano."

Sam laughed lightly. *Ellie would hate it.*

"Speaking of Ellie," Sam began.

"Were we speaking of Ellie?" Buzz asked innocently, lighting a cigarette. Sam had asked for the smoking section—a nice gesture. Buzz knew that Sam detested the smell, and the idea of smoking. From Buzz's point of view, it was one of Sam's few weaknesses.

A waitress arrived with a bowl of nachos. Buzz helped himself. *High salt. Low fat.*

They paused to order. Sam, throwing caution to the wind, requested the blackened catfish. Buzz asked for the biggest steak on the menu. *How often do I get to eat steak? Damn the torpedoes and the diet.*

"Where were we?" Sam asked, avoiding the nachos. Eating with his fingers still seemed gauche.

"Ellie," Buzz said, looking back from the water's edge. He quickly put his napkin on his lap, following Sam's example. Even as a salesman in the old days, he never quite felt comfortable while dining out. He felt like an interloper.

"Yes, Ellie. Buzz, I'm not sure how to go about asking you about a particular subject. I need advice."

"Hmmn. What kind of advice?" Buzz raised an eyebrow. *I bet I know what it is...*

"Well, uh. Advice for after the reception, let's say."

"Oh, that. That's easy."

"It is?"

"Yeah," Buzz said. "Use a limo."

"A limo!" Sam replied, surprised.

"Yeah, take a limo to the hotel. I suggest the Ritz-Carlton. It's the ritziest place in town. Ha ha!"

"You're teasing me, aren't you?" Sam said, grabbing a nervous nacho.

"Just trying to break the ice. To get you to relax a little bit. What you mean is that you want the lowdown on what to do after the limo arrives at the Ritz."

"Yes. That's about right. But it won't be the Ritz. Ellie wants a corner suite in Stouffer's Hotel. She says it's more old-fashioned."

"I wouldn't know about that. But I do know about the other thing. I have two caveats, though, before I start talking and say something I might regret. First, I want to remind you that you're asking advice from a divorced alcoholic. Second, are we talking about theology or, shall we say, technique?"

"Buzz, I know you pretty well; I think it's safe to say that you'll mix both of them in. But I'm, uh, not very experienced with women. I want our first night to be…" Sam fumbled for the right words. "…singularly memorable. I overheard one of the girls in the office say her first night was awful over an office divider the other day. It's been bothering me ever since."

"I see," Buzz said sagely. *Tell me more.*

"And," Sam continued, looking down at his hands, "Ellie is, without getting into details, experienced. I don't want to disappoint her."

"Why are we talking around this whole thing?" Buzz asked.

"Because I prefer it that way. Whenever I talk about this subject, I feel like my father is looking over my shoulder. I want to respect him. I don't mind respecting him. I don't think he's ever talked about the subject directly to me in his life.

"I used to feel like a total reject in high school and college. I had my books and my computers. I'm not a prude. But I'm glad that luck or whatever—" *being ugly,* he thought, "—saved me for Ellie. And maybe some of my father's strictness was justified. It filtered down to me. He thinks that premarital sex will destroy our civilization. Destroy the social compact."

"I see," Buzz said again, straight-faced, amazed by his friend. *What planet did you come from?* Buzz prayed a quick prayer to Saint Anthony.

There was a very long pause. Sam eyed his friend, who was deep in thought, looking down at his napkin. Buzz pulled a cheap pen out of his shirt pocket. He scrawled tiny markings on the napkin. Sam couldn't make them out.

"Then let's not talk about *that* subject," Buzz said finally. "Let's talk about violins."

"Violins?"

"Yeah, they're used in orchestras. Ever heard of 'em?"

"Yes," Sam replied, smiling. "I know what a violin is."

"Good, because," Buzz cleared his throat. "A tuba won't do for this conversation."

"A tuba?"

"You don't know what a tuba is? I thought you were a professor's son?" Buzz feigned surprise.

"Okay, okay. Forget tubas. Let's talk about violins."

"Yeah, let's. Think about a violin and a violin player. We'll call the violin player the violinist. Imagine that the violinist is a man, and he's playing a violin in a room in the Stouffer's Plaza Hotel, a corner suite, after arriving in a limousine."

Sam finally caught on. He gave Buzz a toothy smile. *The Magnificent Buzz!*

"Okay. I follow you now," Sam said, excited like a schoolboy, but in a good way.

"I've played a few violins in my day. Some of those musical experiences I'm not very proud of. But we'll set that aside. We're just talking about violins in a theoretical sense. Just a couple of music lovers, me and you, here in the Flats. But when we drove home from the shore, I told you about seeing the little man in the electrical socket. Well, that part of me, that gift I have to see things that don't have names, has given me insight into violins that maybe is not so common.

"My wife Sandi, when times were good, and there were some good times, used to tell me that I was quite a violin

player. The best ever. I'm not bragging. I've been told that by
many violins. That is, if violins could talk."

"I see," Sam said. "That's why I asked you. I've never
played the violin." Sam cleared his throat.

"I understand. That's a great advantage for you, Sam. As
your music teacher," Buzz cleared his throat again. *There's a
lot of throat-clearing going on,* he thought, enjoying himself.
"I would like to tell you that the enemy of good violin-play-
ing is having bad habits. As a true novice, you haven't developed any bad habits. That's good. That's very good."

"It is?" Sam asked.

"Yes. It is. I'm proud of you. That's the way God meant it
to be, violin-wise. Where was I?"

"Bad habits," Sam said. He was paying close attention.

"I'm not going to go into violin technical points, Sam.
Just theory. Let's start with the violin itself. What's the difference between a cheap violin and a Stradivarius?"

"Workmanship?"

"Right. Well, imagine a world where every violin is a
Stradivarius. This is the world of our violinist in the hotel.
The maker of his violin is better than a perfect master, better
than even the Stradmeister—"

"But I don't believe in God," Sam said, breaking from the
metaphor.

"Who said anything about God? Let's stick to violins. You
asked for my advice," Buzz said sternly.

"Okay, I'll use my imagination. Sorry. Go on."

"Okay. The way I look at it, Sam, every violin is a master-
piece. Every one. And like all masterpieces, every violin is
unique. Each one has different strong points. Sometimes the
differences are subtle. Very subtle. I know this from personal
violin experience. I'm sure a master violinist in any orchestra would tell you that there are even pronounced differences
between one Stradivarius and another Stradivarius. But only
a master could tell those differences. Your job is to become a
master of the violin you've been given."

Buzz paused for a nacho and a sip of Pepsi.

"For the master violinist," he continued, "it takes a lifetime to get to know his violin. He shouldn't expect to get to know everything in just one night or one month, or even one year, or even over a few years. Besides, violins, at least the ones we're talking about, can change over the years. From age. From the arrival of little baby violins. The master dedicates himself to knowing all the changes. He knows how the violin was made, its natural rhythms, how it feels in good weather or bad. You know what I mean?"

"I'm following you," Sam said. "I think."

The waitress came with the surf and turf. Neither man started to eat. Buzz did pause to pray a silent grace. He did not make a sign of the cross. *Why make Sam uncomfortable?*

"Good. Here is a key point, Sammy. A very key point. When the violin is being played, which one is more full of music, the violin or the violinist?"

"I don't know what you mean?"

"Then I'll just explain. The violinist is playing by using two main, er, characteristics. He's using his mind. He's using his hands, his eyes, his ears mostly. That's the way God designed it. Our violinist is a man, and men are separated from reality to a certain extent. They are not the violin. This is hard to say even without the metaphor.

"But the violin, its whole structure makes music. Let's call the violin a she. Her whole body is full of the music, resonating with it, when everything is going right. And if this violin could talk, she would say that it is very difficult to enjoy the music if her whole person is not involved. In fact, being played can be a very distasteful experience for the violin if it is not, shall we say, in tune.

"But if the violinist is a hack, he is still able to physically enjoy the experience of playing the violin even if the violin doesn't enjoy it. Oh, the music might not sound as good as playing a violin that's in tune, but he doesn't care. He can ruin a good violin that way, if he does that."

"He can?" Sam asked, mildly alarmed.

"Sure, he can. Even a Stradivarius like Ellen James."

"Oh."

"Yeah," Buzz said, taking a sip of Pepsi. "He can ruin it. Unless you learn to read the violin's every little quirk and preference. Unless you know how to tune the violin carefully before you start playing. Become a master. Don't play indifferently, or just to hack around, like having a quick beer after a game of hoops. Become a master.

"The biggest difference between a hack and a master, I think," Buzz continued, watching the words sink into Sam, "is charity. The violinist should put the, uh, pleasure, the violin feels before his own pleasure at all times. That's true charity. Seeking the good of the other over the good of the self. He should take his time, be patient. Stick around after he's done playing and make sure the violin is properly cared for, lovingly polished, and gently put back under the covers. The kind of violins we're talking about need time to cool off, even if the violinist cools off in a minute. But that kind of charity takes a kind of discipline that most guys are lacking."

"I've never heard charity being so closely associated with discipline," Sam observed. "Interesting. It's like the discipline required to be unselfish on the court, to hit the open man instead of hogging all the shots."

"Exactly," Buzz agreed. "You're catching on. I'm not proud of how I learned the truth about this next fact, but sometimes violins seek other violinists because, in part, the original violinist was selfish. Violins are not machines. They're works of art. And the music they make is a sublime art, too, that both violin and violinist enjoy in different ways.

"I'm stretching a metaphor, here, but let's just say that the violinist enjoys different aspects of the music. He enjoys *what he sees*. He enjoys *the reactions* of the violin to the manipulations of his hands."

Buzz paused to clear his throat yet again. "Tell me something, Sam. You're an artsy-fartsy type—"

"No I'm not," Sam protested.

"Your dad is, though," Buzz countered.

Sam looked up. "I guess you've got a point."

"Well it's not a put down. I shouldn't have said 'artsy fartsy.' I should have said that you and your dad appreciate high culture. Anyway, tell me why you can take two different violinists, one a master and the other a technically proficient player, and give them both a Stradivarius and the same sheet music, and it sounds different. Why does Itzhak Perlman fill concert halls downtown while some other guy with a normal name sits in the back row of the orchestra in Kalamazoo?"

"Talent?"

"Yeah, that's a good answer. But *what is* the talent the master has? I say it's creativity. It's putting life into it. Isn't badly played music often described as lifeless? Itzhak Perlman can make your mouth drop open because his music is vital—even the word *vital* means full of life. It's the difference between Babe Ruth and all the others. The Babe was creative, larger than life. He was the Sultan of Swing.

"I think that most guys think that this part of marriage comes naturally. They're wrong. It comes naturally to dogs, pigs, and monkeys. The difference is that man is rational. We're not animals, though we can act like them. Animals, on the other hand, can't act like men. Man applies his reason to his work, and to his art. Itzhak had to practice; he spent years perfecting technique before he could even let his creativity come through.

"To use a baseball example again, Ted Williams was not only the most talented hitter of all time, but he was also the hardest-working, hardest-practicing hitter of all time. He even wrote the best theoretical book on hitting ever printed, appropriately called Hitting."

"This is also where the analogy breaks down. The violin is also rational in our analogy. The violin has a mind, a heart, a soul. The needs of the heart must be met by the violinist, also."

Sam was sitting back now, sipping his wine, satisfied that he had asked Buzz for advice. Sure, the crazy logic—if that's what it was—was coming fast and furious. But it was fascinating. It was the best.

Why try to keep Buzz on track? Besides, some of the tangents were more interesting. Sam felt grateful for having a friend like Buzz—it was like owning a priceless piece of art.

Grateful to whom? a little voice asked.

"So your task, maestro," Buzz rolled on, "is to apply your mind and heart to the violin. Remember, it's different for the violin. Not that she doesn't apply her powers of reason, but it's different for girls, like Joe Jackson sings. The violin, when things are going just right, is getting caught up in powerful tides, in oceans of music that literally carry it away. I'm mixing metaphors. Sorry."

"No, keep mixing," Sam said happily. "I'm taking mental notes."

"Sure. Yeah. The violin," Buzz continued, looking Sam in the eye. "I feel strongly about the needs of the violin. That the master should concern himself with what makes the violin sound spectacular; another way of putting it is to say that the enjoyment of the violin comes from within, while the enjoyment of *the violinist* comes from seeing and hearing and feeling the music coming from the violin. His pleasure is basically on the outside. Outside things move his heart. Inside things move her heart. It's in the design of things. The violin can't play the violinist, really. Well, sort of. The metaphor isn't perfect. But I'm sure of what I'm saying."

"I see," Sam said. *I wonder how many men think of it this way?*

"And finally, if you concern yourself with making the violin happy, you'll find the violin very willing to make you happy in return. Curiosity does not kill the cat in this case. The violinist should be curious, seeking and exploring. He should know every inch of his violin as well as he knows himself. He can play a million different tunes on a few simple strings, if you follow me. That doesn't come naturally. That takes years. That takes patience. That takes charity.

"On a completely unrelated subject, I was reading census figures in the Almanac last week."

"You're kidding me. You actually read the Almanac?"

"I kid you not, Sam," Buzz replied with dignity. "There's a lot of interesting stuff in the Almanac. I'm serious. There's history. Lists of things. You just have to know how to sort through the dang thing—skip over the boring stuff. It helps for watching Jeopardy, too."

"Okay. Point well taken. Jeopardy is important," Sam apologized kiddingly.

"So I was reading about the, uh, habits of happily married violinists and violins in the census. Did you know that the ones who report the most satisfaction average a music session once or twice a week?"

"You amaze me with this stuff. Where do you get it?" Sam asked.

"I just told you; in the Almanac," Buzz answered.

"Hmmn," Sam answered.

"When you first start, uh, taking music lessons, you might practice every day for months. For a year. Then, and this might sound strange, the novelty wears off. The pressures and distractions of everyday life—the job, the kids, whatever—pull at you. Indeed, violin playing becomes one of those things that is just there every day, along with those other things. That's when the violinist is most susceptible to taking the violin for granted. Especially if he's let a few bad habits form.

"Look, that reminds me of one more thing. There's a sure and certain way to ruin the relationship between the violinist and the violin."

"Tell me."

"The violinist must never, ever, think about another violin while playing the one violin he has given himself to. Ever."

"Really?" Sam asked. "Why not?" *Where is this going?*

"Really. Take my word for it. It's wrong. It goes against good violin playing. Not that you would do such a thing. The violin might not know it. But over time, it will destroy the music."

"Why?"

"Because what you and I are really talking about, to me, is a sacrament. It's an avenue of grace. For me, it's a way of communicating with God. It has to do with the heart. You're going to make a vow with Ellie. You're going to give your whole self to her. That includes your mind, and your heart. Like I said before, you don't want to simply be a technically adept violin player. When violin playing loses the communication, the mystical aspect, it grows stale.

"Violins are not playthings. They are not for recreation, like basketballs. The violins we are really talking about are not *things*. We *play* with things. We don't *play* with people, or their hearts. The violinist is communicating with the violin, making music that drifts up through the clouds, into space, into eternity.

"You don't believe in God. I don't know why and I don't know why not. You're a mystery to me, Sam, as much as I love you, but we're talking about the way people come into existence. We're talking about a mystical union between a man and a woman, and a kind of communication that won't occur between you and any other person in the world.

"I believe that people are immortal. They live forever. They transcend time. Their souls are more definite and concrete than the earth itself. You can't take this part of your marriage lightly."

Buzz paused to look Sam directly in the eye. Sam nodded somberly.

Buzz lowered his voice to just above the level of the mild din in the restaurant. "The music you're going to play is singular, unique, and beautiful beyond belief if it's pure of heart. That's all I can say. Well, maybe I can say more. I can say that this kind of music simply cannot be played by one violinist with more than one violin and remain pure, graceful. I learned that the hard way. When I played other violins, the music was stale. I played the right notes, sure, but the music was hollow. It didn't ascend to heaven.

"I could go on and on, but I won't. I'm not sure if you want to really hear it..."

"Don't presume, best man. I asked you. I remember our talk on the beach that night. I take all of this very seriously. I really do."

"You are a serious person, Sam. Sorry," Buzz said.

"No need to be sorry."

There was a long pause. Buzz looked away from Sam's strong gaze. A heavy cloud of depression descended on Buzz after the brief respite during the conversation.

"Look," Buzz said. "Our food is cold."

"I know," Sam agreed. "Buzz, are you okay? Is something bothering you?"

"No, I'm fine. Let's eat," Buzz lied. *Why ruin his dinner?* Buzz managed a fake but convincing smile.

"So how's your business going?" Buzz asked.

"Still growing. Still spinning out of control. I had no idea how hard it was going to be."

"What do you mean?" Buzz asked, curious, looking to move out from beneath the cloud above him.

"I didn't realize how difficult success can be. It reminds me of the time I got straight As when I was a sophomore at the University of Chicago. The pressure to stay on top, to get more As was immense. To keep the standard up. Running a company is worse. When I got to Cleveland, we had few competitors. Our success and the success of a couple of other companies has brought in a dozen competitors. The new guys go to my customers with lower quotes. Signing up clients for long term contracts is practically impossible now. That makes it harder for me to plan for the future. I've borrowed a lot of money. But Johnny keeps bringing in business. Expand, or fall behind."

"I thought you were making a ton of money…"

"I pay myself well," Sam smiled. "And it's a good thing, too. You should see the house Ellie has picked out for us. We put an offer in two days ago."

"Let me guess—Beachwood?" Buzz asked.

"No. Shaker Heights."

Buzz whistled. *I should've known.*

"Can't you just tell her no, get a simpler house?"

"Saying no to Ellie is not easy. I don't mind. I like the house. She wants this particular house. And it's a good investment. But the taxes are unbelievable. We can afford it, though, I guess. I'm putting a lot of money down if the bid is accepted—I've got savings. And we will be able to afford the mortgage if Ellie ever quits her job. And it's right up the corridor from Bucky. She wants to be close to Bucky."

"You can't blame her. Do me a favor, Sam, if you get this house. Get one of those big screen televisions with a surround-sound system for Wednesday night videos."

Sam laughed. "Sure, Buzz. No problem."

"And get a popcorn maker. Not a cheap one. One that makes real movie popcorn. You know, the kind that uses that coconut oil which can give a marathon runner a heart attack."

"I'll look into it," Sam replied. He took a bite of his food. "This catfish is burnt."

"That's the new thing. Cajun cooking. Cajun is French for 'burned to a crisp,'" Buzz deadpanned.

"I see," Sam said, then laughed. He flagged the waitress, who came over. He ordered another glass of wine.

Violins, Sam thought, looking forward to his date with the music in the autumn.

2

Buzz was sitting at a computer in the offices of Edwards & Associates. He was trying but failing to teach himself how to use a Lotus spreadsheet. He was frustrated. He had gotten into the habit of keeping Sam company on Saturdays before they played basketball. Buzz had mastered the word processing programs quickly over the summer. Yet his mind simply did not conform to Lotus.

Sam came out of his private office, sat down next to Buzz, and began tightening the laces of his basketball sneakers.

"How'd it go today?" Buzz asked.

"Better than it went for you with Lotus, from the looks of your screen."

"I just don't get it," Buzz replied.

"You want me to show you next weekend?"

"Naw. It's a waste of time."

Sam laughed. "Probably is."

Buzz stood up and stretched. He was already wearing his basketball shorts and shirt. *Tabasco Sauce* was screened on the front of his shirt.

Sam spied the Miraculous Medal hanging off the side of the brown scapular around Buzz's neck.

"Buzz, can we have the Jesus conversation once and for all?"

"Huh?"

"You heard me," Sam said without a trace of nastiness.

"I'm sorry, but aren't you Sam Fisk, the died-in-the-wool agnostic? I must be losing my hearing. For a minute there, I thought I heard you ask me to talk about Jesus."

Buzz put a finger in his ear, and made a twisted pantomime of cleaning it.

"I did."

"Oh," Buzz said. Then he clapped his hands together. "Okay, where do you want to start?"

"Who was he? How do you know he's God? What proof do you have of God's existence? Even if God exists, how can you prove that Jesus was God's son?"

"Jesus said He was God. He wasn't lying," Buzz replied simply. "Was He lying, Sam?"

"How do we know he even said he was God? Can't someone say that the apostles were making that up?"

"So they could be crucified like Jesus? For a lie? Come on, now, Sam, nobody dies for a lie."

"So they believed he was God, but they were mistaken…" Sam said confidently.

"Why did they believe He was God? Jesus rose from the dead. Was Jesus a magician? Or did He really perform miracles all his life, then rise from the dead? Quite a trick."

Buzz sat down. Their faces were not far from each other.

"Before we go on, Sam, tell me why you're so interested all of the sudden?"

"I, uh, want to have it out, be done with it. I know I'm *not* going to believe you," Sam replied. Then he smiled. "And Ellie wants me to go to Mass with her. It was your suggestion. Then I suggested it to her. I want to be sure that I'm going to keep her company, not because I'm trying to talk myself into believing something I know isn't true. If I talk with you, I know you'll convince me I'm right, despite your best efforts to the contrary."

Buzz whistled. "And you accuse me of using twisted logic? Let me get this straight: you want to talk with me about Jesus so you can shoot my arguments down, and thereby be sure of your disbelief."

"Right," Sam said. "For Ellie's sake. I don't want to give her false hope. This might seem strange, but I do the same thing right here, at work. When I'm really sure of something, I ask my workers to shoot holes in it. If the idea survives the gauntlet, I know I'm right."

"I see," Buzz said, shaking his head. "I'm not sure I want to have this conversation. You see, I *want* you to believe."

"I know. Here's your chance. Make me believe," Sam said evenly.

Buzz looked up to the drop ceiling, his tongue on his lower lip.

Is he praying? Sam thought disjointedly.

"Wait a minute," Buzz said dropping to the floor at Sam's feet. He began to do push-ups.

"Buzz?"

"Shut up, Sam, would ya?" Buzz ordered, continuing his push-ups. Buzz did fifty push-ups every morning, so these were not taxing. He began praying one word, then another, over and over inside his head: *reparation... inspiration... reparation... inspiration...*

At push-up number thirty-eight, his prayer was answered. He did one more push-up for good measure, then popped to his feet.

"What was that?" Sam asked.

"I'd like to keep that to myself. I don't know if I could explain it even if I wanted to," Buzz said breathlessly. "But I'm ready now. Watch out, Sam. I might just surprise you today. I feel like such an underdog.

"But never mind that. Here are the ground rules: Let's start with God, and work our way over to Jesus," Buzz suggested. "I'll give you one proof of God's existence, then I'll talk about Jesus very, very briefly."

"That's all?" Sam asked, feeling distantly shortchanged.

"We'll miss our basketball game otherwise," Buzz observed.

"We can finish our discussion after the game—at Applebees, where it all started."

"I'm all for going to Applebees," Buzz said, an indecipherable gleam in his eyes, a game-player's grin on his mouth. "For old time's sake. But we'll be done here in ten minutes, maybe less."

One-two punch, Buzz thought. *One-two punch.* Those were the words that came to him at push-up number thirty-eight.

He had seen in his mind's eye an image of a fat, out-of-shape, poorly-trained boxer battling a larger, faster, highly-skilled champion. He couldn't see anything besides their legs at first. The ragged boxer was against the ropes. He was practically beaten. The champion was closing in for the kill. Then he saw the face of the champion; it was Sam Fisk's face. The words *one-two punch* popped into his mind. The whole image happened in a breath between the *push* and the *up.*

What must the underdog do in order to win?

"Then shoot," Sam said, feeling confident.

There was a coffee cup holding several pens and pencils on the desk. Buzz snatched a pencil from the cup. *World's Best Mom* was printed on the side of the cup.

Almost forgot, Buzz told himself. *Hail Mary, pray for us sinners.*

Not enough time for the whole prayer.

"Where did this pencil come from?" Buzz asked.

"Huh?"

"Just play along, Sam. Trust me," Buzz pressed. *Speed is a weapon,* a little voice told him.

"Sure," Sam said. "Sorry. I started this. Okay, the pencil came from the store."

"And how'd it get to the store?"

"Warehouse first. And it got to the warehouse from the pencil factory."

"Right. You see where I'm going. And before the factory, where did the wood in the pencil come from?"

"Sawmill. It got there from the lumber company. I know where this is going, Buzz," Sam said with a tinge of weariness. "I know this proof. You've used it before. You called it the Proof from First Causes."

"I know. But let's go all the way back, anyway. Okay? I'm making another point. It won't take long. Where did the tree that gave us the wood in the pencil come from?"

"From a seed," Sam said, almost impatiently. "And the seed came from another tree. And so on back to the very first tree—"

"And the first tree?" Buzz continued.

"From another kind of tree," Sam said.

"If you believe in Darwin's theory, yes. I'm not a big fan of Darwin. But let's not get into that. We'll go with your preference. Is it reasonable to say that the original tree came from some other kind of tree, and then that other kind of tree from a plant from another plant, all the way back to—"

"The ooze."

"Yes, the ooze, where all those amino acids and enzymes magically came together to make up the first life forms," Buzz filled in. "And the ooze, before the life—where did the ooze come from?"

"Well, let's not skip ahead of ourselves," Sam objected. "The first life on earth could have come from an asteroid carrying primitive organisms. The asteroid hits, dropping life into the ooze."

"That doesn't matter, really, does it? Doesn't the planet the asteroid came from need it's own ooze, if you trace everything back all the way?"

After a pause, Sam said, "Yes, you're right."

Buzz smiled. "Great. Let's talk about our earth with the lifeless ooze, zillions of years ago. Where did the earth come from?"

"The earth is a planet that came from gravitational pulls bringing it together in a cloud of matter," Sam explained, rushing. "It's been a while since I had this in high school. Either way, we're all the way back to the Big Bang. A big ball of compacted matter blew up, forming everything in the universe, including our planet, the sun, the solar system, and our galaxy. Scientists have proven that the universe is expanding, so it must have started in the, uh, middle, with a big ball of matter blowing up. We're done. We're back to the beginning."

"We are?"

"Yes, and now you ask me where the matter from the Big Bang came from. You'll say it was God."

"Yes, and what's wrong with that?"

"Well, I was watching PBS a couple of years ago, and a scientist was saying that the universe may be the result of several Big Bang-like cycles, expanding and retracting over time. Our universe will finish expanding, eventually contract, and then it will blow up again."

"Yes, I read about that *theory* in Scientific American. Even if that theory is true, I think the cyclical Big Bang idea begs the question. It basically says that the universe was always there. It still doesn't explain how the big ball of matter got there in the first cyclical bang. In that article, one guy said that before the big ball of matter, there was a bunch of mindless energy. He didn't explain where the energy came from, or the properties of the energy. The energy was just sitting there, waiting to form into the matter. For a bunch of scientists, it all sounded pretty sloppy and full of conjecture to me."

"Hmmn. I guess you're right. But everything you've said still doesn't prove that God exists," Sam replied.

"Not for you. Now you tell me something: how come everything in the universe has a cause, or at least a scientific theory of a cause, except for the universe itself? Science provides no answers to the crucial question: where did the original matter or energy that made up the universe come from? Isn't that true?"

Sam thought for a long time. A long time.

"So, okay, there is no scientific explanation of where the universe started," Sam conceded. "That doesn't prove that God started it. There are no records, no photographs, no evidence from back at the time it happened showing God opening his Jiffy Universe Kit and starting it all up."

"Really?" Buzz asked, the gleam still in his eye.

"Yes. It's a mystery."

"Good. I'm done with the God part of my proof," Buzz said, throwing his shoulders back.

"You are? But I'm not convinced," Sam said, wondering briefly why he felt disappointment. *Because you wanted to believe—for Ellie's sake.*

"I wasn't trying to convince you of God's existence, really," Buzz explained excitedly. "I'm just trying to show you how your whole scientific worldview, the view you put so much stock in, begins with a mystery. The universe's origin for you is a mystery. Period. You can't prove to me that the universe is anything other than mystery. You said it yourself; there's no proof of how it started. Just a bunch of theory."

"Where are you going with this?" Sam asked.

"Next time I tell you that the Incarnation of Christ, or the infallibility of the Pope, or the Holy Trinity is a mystery, don't be so smug. Your religion has mystery, too. You think your position is superior, but I want you to think about this: it's at least equal to mine. We both fall back on mystery when we get to the nub. In fact, I would go as far as to say that you have more faith than me about the origins of the universe. At least I can point to an omnipotent God creating it. That makes sense, at least to me. Your answer for the origin of the universe is, essentially, 'I don't know. It was just there.'"

Sam had no answer.

"I feel like Columbo," Buzz said suddenly, snapping his fingers.

"Why?"

"Because I just thought of another question for you about the First Cause. Look, I told you I would only talk about one thing…"

"Go ahead," Sam said, not surprised that Buzz's first proof had fallen flat. "I won't hold you to it. What's your question?"

"What's outside the universe?"

"You mean, after the universe ends, what's there? Nothing. There's nothing there."

"What is nothing?"

Sam shook his head and laughed. "What kind of question is that? Nothing is nothing!"

"Look, I'm not trying to get cute. It blows my mind. You just said it." Buzz spoke the next three words clearly: *"Nothing* is nothing. That means, literally, that *nothing* can't exist. So nothing *can't be* beyond the universe, because nothing is, by definition, *not there."*

"And…" Sam prompted, curious, straining.

"And, well, more mystery, eh?" Buzz tilted his head back, the gleam back in his eye.

"That one went over my head," Sam said.

"Mine too," Buzz replied honestly. "Let's just drop it. I think I've made my point. Your religion, agnosticism, is based on faith. You believe that the universe's origin can't be explained. You take it on faith that it is just here, of it's own accord."

"I guess so," Sam said. "I can live with that. I'm not an astrophysicist, or whatever they're called."

"Let's move on to Jesus. This one is easier."

"I hope so. That nothing stuff was hard," Sam said.

Buzz laughed. *Time for the two-punch.*

"You tell me if the following statements are true or false, okay?"

"Shoot," Sam said, his confidence back. So far, this conversation seemed to be like all Buzz's previous efforts; interesting, well-meaning pebbles thrown against a brick wall.

"You are not omnipotent; that is, you, Sam Fisk, do not have the power to do all possible things. You can't create universes, or even one hydrogen atom, from nothingnesses. True or false?"

"True," Sam said.

"And you can't read minds. You can't suspend the laws of nature. You can't feed five thousand people with a few loaves and fishes. You can't make the blind see or the lame walk. In short, you can't perform miracles."

"True."

"Right. This is easy, isn't it?" Buzz asked.

Sam nodded.

"Can we stop and get a Pepsi?"

"Sure," Sam answered. "I'll get it."

He rose and walked over to the small desktop fridge near the coffee stand.

It's like the fridge I helped Donna bring home the day I met her, he thought suddenly. Then he heard Buzz's voice from behind him as he reached for the can in the fridge.

"And if you died, you couldn't raise yourself from the dead," Buzz asserted.

Sam was slightly jolted.

"True," he replied, looking into the fridge, his voice lacking confidence. His father's words echoed in his mind: *After death, there is nothing.* He stood up.

He came to Buzz and held out the Pepsi.

"I'm almost done," Buzz said. "Thanks."

He took the can, popped the top, then sipped.

"What's next?" Sam asked.

"From all your true answers, it's reasonable to say that you are not God, and you are not Jesus. You can't create, and you can't rise from the dead. These are two of the defining traits of God and Jesus, if God exists, and if Jesus is God's Divine Son. True? Or False."

"True," Sam said. *Where is Buzz going?*

"Good, then you would also agree that you are fallible, finite, in one place, imperfect, and not the knower of everything knowable. These are also opposites of God, Who is infallible, infinite, everywhere, perfect, and omniscient. I don't have to walk you through it, right?"

"Right. I agree with all you've said so far."

"So, if God exists, and He's all powerful, it should be easy for Him to prove He exists. Furthermore, since you do not have His powers, the burden of proof should be on the all-powerful being, not the limited, mistake-prone being, which is what you are."

Sam rubbed his chin. "Explain again."

"If God exists, it should be easy for Him to prove it to you. After all, He's all-powerful. It should be a piece of cake. Why should you, or for that matter, me, since I'm also finite and fallible, have the burden of proof?"

"Buzz, that's a very good point. Why doesn't God just show me he exists? Like you said, it should be easy for him, especially if he's all-powerful. I'm just a man. Why do I have to ask you to prove it to me? God should be able to do it for himself."

"Precisely, Sam. So why don't you ask Him?"

Sam looked at his sneakers. "Ask him what?"

"Ask Him to show you that He exists. To prove it to you. Prove it beyond a shadow of your doubt. While you're at it, you can ask Him to show you that Jesus was His Divine Son. Why should I prove it? I'm a mess. Let's ask Him right now! Then we can go play hoops, and drop the question. Let Him do the work. Then you can marry Ellie with a clean conscience."

"How? How can I ask God to prove he exists when I don't believe he exists?"

"It's not so hard. We'll pray right now. If God doesn't exist, our prayers will be empty words. Nothing will happen. You're right; I'm wrong, and you'll remain an agnostic. If we ask Him to show us, and He does exist, He'll hear you whether you believe He exists or not. What do you have to lose?"

Sam felt like running out of the room. For his entire life faith had seemed so far away, a stranger on an island in an uncharted sea in another hemisphere. Now faith seemed so close, like a person in a sailboat, coming to a dock he was standing on. There it was, within his reach—the rope—just tempting him to grasp for it…

Don't touch it! Sam's instincts counseled wisely.

But Sam couldn't run away from the dock. Buzz's steady gaze, now very serious, was holding Sam; he felt weighted down. He had never seen such a look in Buzz's eyes, ever.

It was a *game face.*

Punch! Buzz thought wildly; enjoying the moment.

"Okay," Sam whispered, not looking down at his sneakers, as he might have done in the past.

"Then repeat after me," Buzz said, not taking his eyes off his friend. "And mean every word. It's worth it, Sam. Trust me. Ellie's worth it."

Sam's fear melted into nothingness. He felt nothing. *Okay, for Ellie.* He nodded at Buzz.

Buzz closed his eyes. Sam imitated him.

"Dear God," Buzz said softly, keeping his hands on his knees.

"Dear God," Sam repeated, a frown coming to his face.

"If You exist," Buzz continued.

"If… you exist," Sam repeated, a smile coming to his mouth. He shut his eyes tighter.

"…then show me…"

"…then show me…"

"…the Truth…"

"…the…truth."

Buzz purposely did not say Amen. He let out a deep breath.

Sam opened his eyes.

"We're done," Buzz said softly, rising. "Let's go run the courts."

He shut down the computer on the desk.

Sam remained silent. Eventually, he rose and retrieved his gym bag from his office.

Buzz took a sip of Pepsi. *Now he's yours, Jesus.*

Sam got out his keys, set the alarm, and the two friends walked out the front doors with Edwards & Associates etched into the glass. Fourteen computers stared blankly at them as Sam locked the door.

The sun slapped them like a warm, gloved hand when they stepped out of the building.

Later, during the walk up Wagar Road toward Hilliard Boulevard, Buzz spoke up, "Don't be surprised if God starts answering your request soon. Watch for signs."

"What kind of signs?"

"Signal graces, they're called. Not miracles or anything. Just things that don't normally happen. Or things that happen that have special meaning to you. My experience with God has shown me that He is very subtle. He doesn't overwhelm. I know that sounds like a bunch of malarkey, but it isn't."

"I'm still not following you, but I'm trying," Sam said.

"Signal graces are like those signs on the highway that come just after the exit. You know, it just says the name of the road and the direction—I-80 West or 271 South. They don't prove anything. They just confirm to you that you're on the right road, going in the right direction. Signal graces are God's way of telling you that you took the right exit."

"Give me an example," Sam requested.

"No. I won't. I don't want to get you looking for something, reading into things. Let's make it really hard for God. I don't want to spoil the experiment. I don't want you to have the excuse of saying I prompted you. Just keep your eyes open, that's all. *You'll* tell *me* if you get a signal grace."

"Fair enough," Sam said.

They were at the Rocky River Police Station. The courts, packed with players, were behind it, beyond a parking lot. The weather was almost perfect. A slight breeze would probably not affect their shooting.

✝ ✝ ✝

The game was close, just as it had been the day Buzz and Sam met over a year ago. For this game, however, Buzz and Sam were on the same team.

Buzz was frustrated. He had missed all his shots; he was off. He felt too strong. Only Sam's heroic rebounding and defense had kept them in the game. The other three players on Buzz and Sam's team, new guys from Lakewood, were giving Buzz dirty looks, and had stopped passing him the ball when he was open.

They were on defense now. If the opponents scored, it was over. The Man held the ball on the point for the enemy. The new guy covering him wasn't up to the task. The Man broke for the basket, blowing by Buzz's teammate.

"Help out!" Buzz shouted, unable to fill the lane. It was over. The Man was open, the ball on the way up for an easy lay-up…

Then Buzz saw Sam's long arm come from eons away and block the shot. Sam's long torso flew past the Man, just missing him. Sam fell past the basket, and crashed into the post; the Man followed.

A clean block! Buzz thought, as the ball zipped into his hands. Sam scrambled to his feet.

The new guy who had been on the Man streaked down the court—but Buzz didn't see him. Two tall opponents were swarming on him, knowing that Buzz was not the best ball-handler.

"Buzz, down court! Throw it!" Sam shouted.

Buzz tried to look. He saw the blur of the new guy sliding past half court, a bad guy in hot pursuit. A thousand arms surrounded Buzz.

"Jesus Christ! Throw it!" Sam shouted in frustration, at the top his lungs…as Buzz said, "Okay."

…and threw the ball in an arcing, lefty hook, leading his streaking teammate.

Too far, Buzz thought, then…something else…

He turned away from the ball, which was still in the air, and looked at Sam, who was following the ball's flight.

"Swish," Buzz predicted.

The ball thumped through the net.

Sam stood open-mouthed. A huge smile came to his whole face.

"Buzz! You did it! You made it! We win!"

The Man shook his head at Buzz, but didn't say anything. The new guy high-fived another new guy at the other end of the court.

Opponents cursed.

"Sam?" Buzz asked, ignoring the tumult around him. A wonderful light seemed hidden beyond his sleepy eyelids.

Sam stopped cold. *I yelled **Jesus Christ** before he threw it.*

"Signal grace," Sam croaked, looking away, toward the woods to their right. He could now see the trees from the forest.

Buzz didn't respond.

He didn't have to.

3

That night, someone came screaming after Sam like a wild, searing arrow shot from the heart of all that is good.

Sam forgot all about Buzz's incredible basketball shot by the time he got home from the game. He took off his sweaty

clothes, showered, and watched television in his skivvies,
distantly trying to distract himself. He didn't call Ellie, which
was as unusual as his watching television.

Like a drug that helps time pass without anything truly
meaningful happening, the television transformed eight
o'clock into eleven o'clock. Sam slowly lifted himself out of
his chair, walked to his fridge, poured and drank a small glass
of orange juice, then went to his bed.

His bedroom was like his office, all sparseness and effi-
ciency. The sheets on his bed were clean, white, J.C. Penny
all the way. The bed was simple, solid, not too modern, made
of wood. There was no rug on the wood floor. He used a
bookshelf for a dresser (it was easier to see and grab his
clothes, he reasoned).

He was on his back. The room was perfectly dark, except
for the slinky tinge of red from his electronic alarm clock.
He let his mind wander, lighting atop this image or that: a
scene from his job—that new girl, Amy, who was selling up
a storm; a moving picture of Ellie walking in front of him on
the beach at Mentor Headlands, her lithe hips swishing this
way and that way enveloped by clean, blue jeans. Without
trying too hard, he kept the image of the basketball, rotating
in flight toward the iron ring, out of his mind until…

…until he fell asleep. Then, he fell to deeper sleep, his
eyeballs rolling back and forth beneath their lids…

In his dream, Sam was tiny, a human gnat, clinging to a
basketball flying through the air, toward a hoop. It was the
Rocky River court. Buzz behind him, having tossed the ball
Sam was riding. The hoop came closer and closer. Sam closed
his gnat-eyes as he braced to thump through…

…then he was in the Chicago Art Institute, staring at a
painting, an El Greco. The Savior of the World. Jesus was
holding one hand on a basketball, his stare boring through
Sam.

Sam tried to look away, but could not. He heard an oddly
metallic sound behind him, and when he turned, he saw what
had to be a Roman soldier, also staring at the same painting…

...suddenly Sam was out of the museum, and in that way of dreams, no longer a man, but rather, he was now a photon, a screaming, speeding particle of energy capable of careening through matter itself. Sam was now smaller than microscopic. A smithereen was a giant world compared to this tiny Dream Sam, who found himself flying, jetting, darting out of his bed and out toward...

...toward what? There was a street below him now. There were no moving cars on it. It was dark. It was a main street in Rocky River, Detroit Road. Sam flew; he flew, smaller than all things, somehow able to see all things. He could see *the insides* of things. He could see their material structures.

Oh, the precision of the leaves on the trees to his right and left! He could see cell structures, mitochondria, and even perceived the workings of photosynthesis! Yes, photosynthesis happened at night, didn't it? Now, he could see beyond, inside the cells, to the subatomic structures. There was a vast universe in each existing thing!

In that way of dreams, he could see all the material things that had existence. After the leaves, he turned his gaze to the countless trillions of electrons that were streaming in torrents through the electrical lines on the poles next to the trees lining Detroit Road. He looked down, and marveled at the macadam; the many-faceted parts of things that were now to Sam as a daisy is to a child in a garden...

...But there was a being somewhere, a man, a priest, watching Sam. Sam could tell. But he could not see this other being. This man's name?

What is your name? Sam asked as he flew through the night...

"Thomas," the priest replied, his words coming from the ether. "I am a doctor, but not the kind of doctor you are familiar with..."

Sam felt that this being, this man-priest was a guide on this eerie dream ride through Rocky River.

"Where are you taking me?" Sam asked, somehow happy, somehow afraid. *Afraid of what?*

"Silence, blind man. This awakening in your sleep will not last long. See beyond the forms of things to behold the substance. Look, you have eyes now! Look!"

And the priestly-Thomas-being went away.

Samuel Fisk felt utterly alone. He longed for a companion. He could see all things, it seemed, but he was so alone. So lonely.

Buzz? Are you out there? Can you join me? he called out in the dark, intricately structured world around him. Suddenly, he felt guilt pile atop his loneliness.

Why didn't I call for my father?

Sam was still speeding through the ether of the night. He passed Rocky River High School, then Martin's Market, and an old folks home. He saw the form of them all. He saw the matter of them all, but he did not see the substance…

"Oh God whom I do not know or see, where is this substance of which Thomas spoke?" he cried out, anguished, not realizing that sometimes prayers within dreams are still prayers…

He saw the church bouldering toward him. It was Saint Christophers, where Donna often attended daily Mass.

Maybe Donna's inside!

It was a lovely church, with real stone masonry, and night-darkened stained glass windows, and giant wooden doors, with carved gargoyles and angels…

…the doors were very close to Sam—too close—he passed through them without them opening, watching in wonder as the basic molecules of wood blew by him. He came out the other side. There was a flickering red light beyond the altar. The color of a stop sign. The church was empty…

Donna's not here! He panicked. *Buzz? Father? Mother? Anybody!*

And now there were the pews, and the marble floor, and the steps before the altar, and now the altar, and Sam tried to close his eyes but could not, for beyond the altar was…was the tabernacle…and Sam passed through its brass doors, and saw the bread that was not bread, and beheld the Substance there…

…Sam awoke as if shot from the barrel of a Springfield. He sat upright. Sweat ran down his forehead, which he grasped in his long, lanky fingers. He tried to remember his dream; in the dark room, his short hair jutted from between his fingers like bluegrass from the cracks in a sidewalk.

Was it a nightmare? Was it…something else?

He simply could not remember any details from his dream. But he could feel the lingering emotion.

I met someone.

He fell back with a punctuated certainty. He stared at the ceiling, wide-eyed, wondering about…*what?*

El Grecos. Centurions. Impossible Hail Mary basketball shots.

Chapter Thirteen

1

Five weeks after Buzz's basket, Johnny Traverse came into Sam's office as his boss was just settling behind his Compaq.

"There's a guy from the FBI here to see you," Johnny reported furtively. "Serious-looking dude, too."

"Did he say about what?" Sam asked.

The Feds? He did a quick mental accounting. *Relax, we're clean as a whistle.*

"No," Johnny replied, a consternated look still on his face. "Except that he's with a special white collar something or other."

"Oh." Sam rubbed his chin. "We've got nothing to hide, have we, Johnny?"

Johnny laughed. "You see the spreadsheets and clear every dollar we spend and take in. You would know better than I would. Ro Mack files all the right papers with all the right agencies, as far as I can tell."

Sam chuckled sagely. "Yeah; it's probably nothing. Send him in."

Sam sat forward in his Herman Miller chair as Johnny walked out. The Herman Miller was his only luxury; it was difficult for a man of his height to sit in an ordinary office chair for hours on end. His desk, the bookcase filled with software manuals, and the filing cabinet were strictly functional, but solidly built—middle-of-the-road stuff out of the catalogs.

The FBI agent walked in alone. When Sam stood up, he was surprised to find that the agent was looking him directly in the eyes from the same level. The two men were the same height, but Sam could guess that the agent was at least fifty pounds heavier from the way he filled out the standard-issue blue suit. The G-man didn't have an ounce of fat on his frame. He had dark brown eyes. His face was all-American handsome, and his bristly brownish-red hair was the strongest clue that the agent was of Irish descent.

"Hello, Mr. Fisk," the agent said, holding out a large right hand. "I'm Mark Johnson, from the FBI Special White Collar Crime Unit here in Cleveland."

The two men clasped with strength. Sam strained to hide a grimace. *Wow,* he thought. *Agent Hercules.*

"It's my pleasure, or at least I hope it is," Sam replied smoothly, consciously trying not to look guilty, even though he wasn't. "Won't you have a seat?"

"Thank you," Mark said, taking a simple chair across from Sam's desk.

"There's no need to be alarmed, Mr. Fisk," Mark continued, accustomed to the anxiety his presence caused. "I'm not investigating your company. I'm doing a background check on one of your clients—"

"I'm not in the habit of discussing my clients with law enforcement officials without my client's prior consent," Sam said, a dark look coming to his brow. *Am I playing this right?* he asked himself.

"I understand," Mark said, his deep voice almost sweet, a wisp of a smile coming to his mouth, as if he had heard Sam's reply a thousand times before. "And if this, ah, discussion, goes well, you won't ever get into such a habit. In the big picture, I'm here for your benefit." Mark held up his hands.

Sam looked out the window. "I'm sorry. What did you say your name was?"

"My name is Mark Johnson," he replied evenly.

"I'm sorry, Mark. I overreacted. Of course I want to help you. I may not answer all your questions though, if they strike me as too intrusive. Okay?"

Sam turned to face the agent.

Mark gave a nod worthy of the Mona Lisa.

Did he just agree to something? Sam asked himself.

"I'm not here to harm your relationships with your clients, Mr. Fisk. Let's just get started. Answer what you will, but answer straight. I'm one of the good guys." The big man ended with a smile.

"Right, then," Sam sighed quickly. "Fire away."

"I understand that your company set up the computer systems for an international securities trading firm on West 9th Street, near the Flats, called Rutwielier Investment Partners."

"Yes," Sam replied, somehow relieved. "About two years ago. I worked closely on that account at the time. But I haven't had any direct contact in well over a year. I've delegated that account to associates."

"Did you have any contact with a man named Arlo Harpensburg, who worked there?"

"No," Sam replied in a clipped tone after a moment. "I didn't. I've never heard that name before."

"During your contact with Rutwielier, did you deal with the president, Herve Bittenvold?"

Sam paused. "No, I didn't. That was odd, because I usually deal with the top man of a firm that size. But no, I only dealt with their designated MIS man, Rick Carter, an American. He signed all the contracts and made all the phone calls. He walked me through the installation."

"I see," Mark replied, squinting, then nodding. "May I speak with your associates here who have had contact with Rutwielier?"

"Of course. John Traverse can show you to them. That would be, let's see, Heather Bach and Elm Pilsner," Sam replied, relieved. "That's all?"

"That's all, Mr. Fisk," Mark said, then rose from his seat.

Sam was accustomed to looking down to see another man's face.

"You watch too much television. Relax," Mark continued. "Most FBI interviews are quite mundane. That's what background means: perfunctory. I'll find Mr. Traverse. I know you must be busy. Thank you for your time. I may need to come back for more questioning over the next few months."

Sam rose. "Please call first if you can. You're welcome, though, Agent Johnson. That wasn't so bad. You probably run into nervous guys like me all the time. I'm not used to this kind of thing."

The two men shook hands. Sam, prepared this time, gripped hard from the get-go.

"I can tell. I run into that all the time, Mr. Fisk, especially in the White Collar Unit. Despite what they say on the television, most businessmen are quite honest. Thank you for your time," Mark repeated. He turned to leave Sam's office.

Sam felt something slip away. It was like letting go of a kite. He chased the string.

"You're new to Cleveland, aren't you, Mark?" Sam asked, aware that he had used the agent's first name without permission for the second time.

Mark stopped in mid-step and turned.

"I would rather not say," Mark replied, his eyes clouding slightly.

Sam smiled his toothiest smile. "I knew it! You're new here, aren't you?"

Mark looked slightly from right to left, as if Sam had not asked the question. He tried to hide the truth on his face.

"As a matter of fact," Mark replied, smiling a tad sheepishly. "I just moved here with my family three days ago. This is my first day on the job in Cleveland."

Sam nodded. Mark was not used to looking at another man at eye-level either.

I misjudged him, Mark thought. He filed that away. He wasn't used to dealing with executives.

They're bound to be sharp if they built their own company from scratch. A follow-up question arose in Mark's mind.

"How could you tell, Mr. Fisk?" Mark was genuinely curious.

"Call me Sam," Sam offered. "Lucky guess. That, and your accent gave you away. You sound just like my best friend. He's from New Jersey. Is that where you moved from?"

Mark laughed. The laugh told Sam that he had guessed correctly about New Jersey.

Buzz taught me how to guess about people...

"Good guess," Mark replied, not giving in to the temptation to use Sam's first name. "You should be in law enforcement."

Sam smiled broadly. He felt as if he had won a kind of competition against a superior foe.

Mark had an urge to leave the room. It wasn't professional to socialize on the job—even harmless conversation such as this.

But Mark found himself asking, "There had to be other clues besides my accent. I'm curious. For professional reasons."

Sam thought for a moment, looking up at the drop ceiling. *Yes.*

"There was one other clue. Everybody from Cleveland knows that West 9th Street is down by the Flats. You didn't have to point out the obvious. That was it. My friend from New Jersey taught me how to guess people's backgrounds."

"Well that explains it then. You can't put much over on us New Jersey boys."

Sam nodded. An awkward silence ensued. The string was leaving his hand again.

Mark half-turned, then stopped.

"Yes?" Sam asked.

"Well, this is off the record. Not FBI business. But you wouldn't happen to be a Catholic, would you?"

Sam was completely surprised.

"Not at all. I'm not a Catholic. Not even close."

"Really?"

Now Sam felt a brittle anger rising in his chest. *What kind of question is that? I just told him, didn't I?*

"Yes. Really. Why do you ask?"

Mark felt the ice in Sam's voice.

"I saw the Miraculous Medal on a shelf on your bookcase when I walked in, and I just thought…well. Forgive me. That's prying. I'm sorry…"

"The medal was a gift from a friend."

Donna had given Sam the silly thing months ago.

"No, tell me what's on your mind, Agent Johnson," Sam demanded, watching the big man reel back a bit on his heels.

"Nothing. It's a Catholic thing, that's all. I'm sorry for intruding. I was going to ask you where I could find a good Mass in the morning—that is, if you were a Catholic."

Sam quickly realized that Mark's question had been a reasonable one. *What's got into you today?*

"Sorry, Mr. Johnson." He found himself apologizing to Mark Johnson for a second time. "Good guess. My two best friends happen to be devout Catholics, including the one from New Jersey. He goes to Mass most mornings. He'll be able to tell you ten different Masses, and the theological views of all the priests who say them, if I know him. His name is Buzz Woodward. I'll give you his number. In fact, give me your office number and I'll have him call you."

"No, really. You've been too patient. I'll just find my own Mass—"

"I insist," Sam said, returning to his desk, pulling a yellow index card from a small file, and jotting down Buzz's number.

Mark looked at his watch. *Buzz, eh? The theological views of every priest?*

"Here," Sam said, holding out the card. "Take it."

Mark hesitated. It felt uncomfortable: hesitating. He walked back to Sam's desk and took the card.

"Thank you…Sam."

"You're welcome. I wish I could be of more help," Sam said with finality.

"Good-bye."

Mark Johnson left the room without another word.

Sam felt briefly that something monumental had just tran-
spired. Then he blew off the feeling. *I'll probably never see
Agent Mark Johnson again.*

2

After he left Sam Fisk's office, Mark Johnson finished his
two other interviews at Edwards & Associates, and took a
break for lunch at Joe's Deli on Hilliard. When he reached
into his pocket for a loose dollar for the tip at the end of his
meal, he pulled out the index card with Buzz Woodward's
phone number.

He really did want to find a decent Mass. The Mass he
attended this morning at the parish closest to his new house
in Rocky River had been unbearable. The priest had conjured
up his own version of a Eucharistic Prayer.

I should have asked Bill White for a morning Mass! he
chastised himself.

He threw down the tip and almost left the index card for
the busboy to throw away. But he didn't. When he saw the
pay phone near the men's room, he made a quick decision
and punched in the number. He left a message on Buzz
Woodward's answering machine, explaining briefly that Sam
Fisk had recommended that he call. Mark left his home number.

He returned to his government-issue Ford, and paused before inserting the key into the ignition.

It had been six short months since his fateful visit to the
Kemp's home with Bill White. At the time, he had lived in
New Jersey. Now he lived in Rocky River, near his friend
Bill, and the Holy Spirit had already lined up a contact to
help Mark find a good morning Mass.

In a few hours, after visiting another company for interviews about the nefarious Rutwielier Investment Partners,
he imagined pulling into the driveway of his new home. Maybe

one of his daughters would be playing in the front yard, would call out his name, then run up to him and give him a big hug.

Inside, Maggie would be finishing preparations for dinner. She would also give him a big hug and kiss. Later, after dinner, and after the kids were put to bed, he and Maggie would have Couch Time. After, they might try to make a son.

God gave it all back to me. He gave me my family back, my daughters, my life. Thank you, Lord!

Mark felt the emotion of gratitude well up within his heart. *Thank you!*

He wiped the ghost of a tear from his eye, and started the car. It had all happened so unexpectedly…

…months earlier, after leaving the Kemps, he and Bill had traded notes in Bill's kitchen the next day. His leave of absence was almost over.

But first, Bill insisted that Mark drive down to the University of Steubenville, on the Ohio River less than an hour west of Pittsburgh.

"There's a men's conference there this weekend. Today is the last day. We can go and pray together—like a pilgrimage. Maybe something will happen. I went to the men's conference last year. I learned a lot. But the best part was standing under a tent with five hundred other Catholic men who love their faith. I'll follow you down in my car, and we can say good-bye from there."

At Steubenville, the final piece of the puzzle fell into place for Mark Johnson. It had been a hazy, humid day. They arrived just after one in the afternoon, parked their cars and registered, receiving their conference badges at the student center, and walked to the big, red and white tent. They didn't need directions to the tent. All they had to do was follow the sound of the singing.

The singing blew Mark away. The voices of five hundred men raising their hearts to God was stunning. The only thing Mark could compare it to was singing during the Army-Navy games as a midshipman.

Neither Mark nor Bill were familiar with the songs, which were standards from the Charismatic movement. Finally, the music ministry played Faith of Our Fathers, and Mark found himself belting it out. He turned to Bill, who was also singing his lungs out, and put an arm around him.

Yes, Mark thought, *it was good to come here.*

The speaker, a Franciscan priest Mark had never heard of, talked about the duty of fathers to lead their families in the faith. His name was Father Mick Sconland. Mark listened with a skeptic's ear. The priest quoted from Old Testament passages that Mark had never read. Suddenly, all the good cheer from the singing ebbed right out of him.

Why am I here?

He felt itchy and sweaty. The plastic seat was tiny, sinking into the sloshy grass. He felt cramped. He didn't like standing with so many unfamiliar men behind him.

I don't belong here. These men have families.

He got up from his plastic chair, and walked out of the tent, leaving Bill's whispered protests behind.

He set off alone on the hilly campus, praying Hail Marys to himself over and over again, heading in no direction in particular. He walked by a construction site. The sign at the site read: *Future Home of the John Paul II Library.*

He found himself on a road that apparently wound around the whole campus. There was a bench next to a gravel parking lot, with a college kid sitting alone, reading a book.

Summer student? Mark asked himself. Bill had told him that all the students here are good Catholics…

"Hey kid," Mark asked, walking up to the bench.

"Yeah," Silvio Morales grunted without looking up from his book.

It was *The Watchers* by Dean Koontz. A horror story. Silvio was a Koontz fan. He was trying to distract himself while waiting for the next shift in the cafeteria. He hated the job, but needed the money to save for next year's tuition. All those devout Catholic conference pilgrims with their God Bless Yous and their Praise the Lords. It was driving him nuts.

To top it all off, he was losing the analogy queen, Judy Pierce. She hadn't returned his calls in days.

Silvio looked up.

Oh great, Silvio thought, looking at the towering hercules. *Another hypocrite Jesus freak looking for directions to the bookstore!*

"Whaddaya want?" Silvio asked Mark Johnson with a half-bored, half-petulant tone.

What a little snot, Mark thought.

"I thought you might be a student here—" Mark started.

"What if I am?" Silvio asked.

Mark looked over Silvio's head to the trees. Taking crap was not one of his favorite pastimes. He looked back fiercely into Silvio's eyes.

"Are you?" the FBI agent asked with a practiced interrogation tone. He saw some fear come into the kid's expression.

"Look, sorry mister. Yeah, I'm a student. Can I help you with something?"

That's better, Mark thought.

"I don't know. I've never been here before. I'm looking for... I'm looking for a place to be alone."

Silvio closed his book. There was something different about this big man before him. He seemed out of place.

"You here with the Men's Conference?" Silvio asked.

"Yes, but I just got here. I felt claustrophobic under the tent. I'm not sure what I'm doing here."

"I can relate to that," Silvio muttered, looking down.

"Huh?"

"I said, I can relate to that," Silvio said in a normal tone. He smiled wistfully. *Maybe I could help the guy out.* "Look, mister—"

"Call me Mark. I'm Mark Johnson," Mark said, extending a huge meat-hook of a hand.

Silvio hesitated, and took it quickly, then let go.

Kid's got a jello-grip, Mark thought.

Even though the sun was out, it seemed like the rays weren't cutting through the ozone.

"I'm Silvio. Look, I know a place. It's nearby. It's called the Port. It's a little church on campus. I'll take you there if you want." Silvio felt a weight lifting from his shoulders.

Mark hesitated, and turned to look back at the tent below, filled with all those happily married men. He could see several sets of chairs outside the tent. There, five or six priests were hearing confessions, right outside on the grass.

"Sure, kid. Take me there."

Silvio put his book into his ratty knapsack, shouldered it, and began walking down the road. "You can see it from here. It's a quiet place."

After a few minutes, they came to the large, wooden doors of the Portiuncula, a stone and mortar replica of the chapel where Jesus first asked Saint Francis of Assisi to rebuild the Church. The Port was nestled among the trees; it was quite small. It could barely seat fifteen people.

"Well, here it is," Silvio said, moving his feet back and forth as if he needed to be somewhere else.

"You coming in?" Mark asked.

"Naw," Silvio said distantly, not looking at Mark. "You'll find who you're lookin' for in there. Jesus is in there."

Mark took the young man's arm, but with a gentle grip. "Come on in, with me, Silvio. I need help. You're a student here, maybe your prayers could help."

"I…" Silvio hesitated. "I don't go in there."

"I see," Mark said, letting go. "Okay."

There was a sadness in Mark's voice. A sadness that Silvio related to. The sadness of being alone.

Mark reached for the door, and walked in.

"Bye," Silvio said after the door closed. He turned and walked away. He looked down at his Nikes as he walked, but he didn't see them. Instead, an image of Judy Pierce came to his mind. The night in his room. The night they were supposed to go all the way. Ten nights ago.

The night he said no to her.

She had not spoken a word to him since. He had lost his true love because he wouldn't sleep with her. He fought back tears. He was a tough guy, too, in his own way.

"Screw it," he muttered to himself, as he walked down the hill, toward the tent. *I hate this place!*

In the Port, Mark stood alone with his Savior. He forgot about Silvio Morales. The simple bronze monstrance seemed the only thing in the chapel. The off-white wafer hiding Him floated steadily above the altar.

"I have nothing to say." Mark spoke quietly, as much to himself as to the man in the monstrance, turning his eyes to the Eucharist.

He walked up close to the altar, and fell to his knees on the stone floor. There were only a few pews behind him.

I have nothing to say, he repeated, feeling unworthy to even kneel.

He dropped to the floor on his stomach, and spread his arms wide, feeling the coldness of the stone on his forehead.

I have nothing to pray, he prayed, filled with anguish, drained of inner reserves, drained of will. He tightened his clenched eyes, certain that he was wasting his time. How many of his prayers had gone unanswered since Maggie kicked him out? Thousands? All the advice of the Kemps seemed as straw now, here in this cold, stone chapel on a hill in eastern Ohio, far from home.

Mark's eyelids became heavy, filled with fatigue. He drifted, falling, falling to somewhere…to sleep.

Grace, moved with pity for this modern centurion, came from the Heart of the Eucharist, and manifested Himself in Mark's mind as a dream.

In Mark's dream, a lucid, clear picture of the True Cross appeared. On this cross, was Jesus. Mark stood before Him.

There were no surroundings, except for the bare, cold rock beneath Mark's feet. There was only the Cross and Jesus and Mark. No thundercloud sky above or wailing women below.

No sounds but the breathing of two men.

Jesus' breaths were strained, fluid-filled drags.

Mark saw Him not as portrayed on twentieth century crucifixes, but as He had really and truly been: bloody, his flesh hanging off his bones in shreds.

He was amazed that a human being could suffer so much torture and remain alive.

It was near the end. The lance had not yet been driven into His side…

Mark stared wide-eyed at Jesus' feet, the long metal spike just above the top curve of each foot, driven through them, a rough rope holding them together around the ankles. They were closer to the ground, perhaps ten or twelve inches, than portrayed in the antiseptic movies. Rocks had been jammed into a hole cut into the ground, holding the cross in place…

Mark realized that Jesus' death had been rated R.

Flies were crawling over and into the wounds on His feet. He saw the muscles and tendons strain as Jesus made the effort to lift himself up to take a deeper breath.

Slowly, slowly, Mark felt drawn to look upwards, away from the mangled feet, and even more slowly, he raised his eyes to the God-man on the Cross.

The crossbar was fastened by rope atop the thick, brown, sticky-blooded beam, forming a *T*.

Jesus looked at Mark but did not focus on him. Then he brought his eyes to the whitewashed, cloudless heavens and spoke.

"It is finished."

Lightning struck, and suddenly everything around the Cross was there. The two other crosses with their wretched prisoners were now on either side. The sky filled with clouds, and thunder roared! Cultivated fields suddenly appeared beyond the hills, illuminated by lightning, and if Mark were to turn back, he would have seen the gates of Jerusalem.

To Mark's side, unaware of Mark's presence, was a young man named John, who was holding a sobbing woman. She too was unaware of Mark Johnson.

Mary.

Mark did and did not want to remain where he was, fascinated and horrified at the same time.

Someone is no longer here, he realized.

Jesus was gone. His corpse hung in His place. The body of Christ, dead. The world empty. The world; dark and cold and windy.

From behind, just a few feet away, Mark heard a deep voice. He turned to see the voice…

"Truly this man was the Son of God."

…and Mark saw a Roman soldier, a centurion.

…and woke with a shiver from his dream. Mark had been asleep. He heard the sobs, soft, yet manly, of another person in the Port, coming from a pew behind him.

Mark pushed himself up from the floor, leaving a clear pool of—*tears!*—where his face had been.

The other person in the chapel was Silvio Morales. Mark stood up, feeling weary, still sleepy, and faced Silvio.

The young man gave Mark a plaintive look, as if to apologize, then croaked hoarsely, "I went to confession at the bottom of the hill. I didn't mean to go. I just felt drawn to sit down. I hadn't gone since, well, I don't remember. After I was done, the priest told me to come here for my penance. As I prayed, I saw—I can't say what I saw…"

Silvio looked down.

"I saw the crucifixion," Mark offered, coming to the boy, kneeling next to him, looking back to the monstrance. "I saw Jesus die. I don't know if it was a dream or what it was."

A look of genuine shock came to Silvio's face. His eyes bugged out. Mark thought briefly of ping-pong balls.

"I saw it too!" Silvio exclaimed in a high pitch of amazement. "Nobody knew I was there. I was alone at the Cross! Just Him and me. I had no idea…" A sob escaped.

"—I had no idea how tough He really was," Mark finished for him. "I had no idea. If He could stand that, then—"

"Then," Silvio finished, "then, we can stand anything. He did it for us, man. For everyone."

Both men looked at the toughest of tough guys. Tough enough to wait alone in thousands of churches for millions of nights.

"What's going on, mister?" Silvio asked. "What's happening to us?"

Silvio looked at the stranger. Mark matched his gaze.

"I don't know, Silvio. It is Silvio, isn't it?"

Silvio nodded.

"I don't know. I don't know." Mark couldn't find the words. *I still don't know what to say.*

But he did know the answer to getting Maggie back. The boy had said it: If Jesus could take that kind of punishment, then Mark could take anything.

"Let's say a Rosary," Silvio suggested.

Now Mark nodded.

The two men prayed for two more hours.

Later, Mark went to confession near the tent. The priest was young, with thick, bristly red hair. Mark read "Hello, I'm Father Chet" on his name tag. He was on a stop during a journey to Chicago. Mark was comforted by his New Jersey accent.

Silvio waited. Over dinner, he and Mark told Bill White what happened in the Port before Mark left to return to New Jersey.

✛ ✛ ✛

After several phone calls and then a visit from Bill White, Maggie Johnson agreed to let Mark move back home—on certain conditions, of course.

"The girls miss you," was all she said on the first day, when he walked up to the door with his suitcases. She refused to be pleasant to him. "They need their father. You can live here, but that's all. I don't want to have anything to do with you other than when the girls are involved. Even then, I make all the decisions. If not, I'll throw you out again. And don't lobby the girls to have me do otherwise. You're on probation indefinitely, Mark."

Mark swallowed a protest for a reply. "Okay," was all he said, trying not to look down. He thought of Jesus on the Cross.

Nothing is worse than that. Joe Kemp's words now had weight. "The battle isn't with your wife. It's with yourself. A real man is one who can control himself."

Maggie made him sleep in the attic bedroom. He wasn't allowed to have dinner with the family, and he left for work before the girls had breakfast in the morning. She did let him take the girls for walks and to the park, and to play with them in the living room after dinner, but Maggie never stayed in the same room with him. It was as if he didn't exist to her.

Over the next several weeks, Mark said the following words to himself a hundred times, whenever Maggie gave him a bitter, seething look, or mocked his attempts to begin a conversation: *The only one who can make me lose my temper is myself.*

"You're turning on the old Mark Johnson charm," Maggie accused. "Well, I won't go for it."

"I know what you're doing. You're trying to show me how you've turned over a new leaf. But if I fall for it, you'll be back to the old Mark within a month."

One time, inspired, he replied with boyish sincerity, "It must have been hard living with a tyrant like me all these years."

He had seen a connection, briefly, in her eyes when he said that. He saw how much he had hurt her.

Back in Cleveland, Bill White prayed like a madman, fasted on bread and water on Mondays, Wednesdays, and Fridays, and called a dozen priests to ask them to offer Masses for the Johnsons. He visited the Poor Clares and asked them to pray. It became Bill's personal mission to help save Mark's marriage through grace.

One evening, Maggie invited Mark to come to dinner. The girls shared happy looks, but the family ate in silence.

That night, when Mark was reading on his bed, Maggie knocked once and boldly walked in, closing the door behind her. She was wearing a nightgown.

They met each other halfway across the room, standing in bare feet on a woolen coil rug. Mark looked at the black and white photograph of Maggie's great grandparents on the back of the door, and wondered why the frames were always round and the faces humorless in olden times pictures.

She reached up, put her arms around his shoulders; she bent her head to the side, her eyes closed—Mark hesitated, then kissed her. He led her to the bed.

✝ ✝ ✝

"Come downstairs," she said when they were done.

Mark stifled a smile.

After they got under the covers, she told him coldly: "I don't know where you put him, but if the old Mark ever comes back, you're out forever. Do you understand?"

He nodded. *I understand.*

He put his arm under her pillow, so it rested beneath her neck as she turned on her side, facing away from him. She formed a little *c* within his capital *C,* like a teaspoon resting inside a tablespoon. It was an old, familiar position for them both.

He was amazed how much he missed this.

He waited for her to fall asleep, then turned to lie on his back. He put his hands behind his head, and chuckled softly.

"I'm back," he whispered.

The old Mark is not hiding somewhere. There is not a new Mark. The old Mark simply figured out how to fight this particular war and win it.

For a real man like Mark Johnson, it was a matter of tactics, not strategy. He had always tried his best to be a good husband and father. *And frankly, I was never that bad of a father.*

But he had been a lousy husband. He realized that now. He simply hadn't known how to be anything else. His father had taught him how to be a man, but not how to be a husband.

Go easy on the old man, an inner voice of wisdom cautioned. *He tried his best, too. He gave you life itself.*

It had taken Maggie almost as much discipline to avoid talking with him as it had taken Mark to avoid snapping at her. Maggie was a talker.

The next evening, she agreed to spend some couch time with him. He picked up strong vibes of skepticism as he explained some, but not all the lessons he had learned at the Kemps, and in the Port at Steubenville.

As Mary Kemp had been with Joe during their first few couch times, Maggie began to pour out her most serious complaints to her husband, amazed that he was listening to her without defending himself, not taking her to the mat on every point.

He was willing to concede that he had been a terrifically difficult person to live with. He agreed that he had been emotionally unavailable, but honestly did not know if he possessed emotions to share, even now. At least not the kind of emotions she was looking for. He promised to try his best and meant it.

One point he did not concede, however, was that an old Mark had ever existed.

"You don't have to worry about him coming back, Maggie. He doesn't exist. I'm just the old Mark living my life differently. I'll never sacrifice our marriage or the girls' well-being on the altar of my pride. You can't make me lose my temper. I control my temper. With God's help, I can master it."

He tried not to stare her down, but she held his gaze anyway, shaking her head.

Three days later, on the couch, she complained about his long hours on stake-outs. Unlike most cops' wives, she wasn't worried about him getting killed. She did detest not knowing when he was coming home. She was a person who, by nature, thrived on order, and her inability to plan around him drove her up the wall.

"You never complained about that before," he observed.

"I was afraid to bring it up, because I knew you would refuse to even discuss it," she replied, dead serious. "Now I don't care what you think. Well, I do care what you think. But I'm ignoring my fears."

"Oh," he said, but recovered quickly. "There's not much I can do to change my hours…"

"You can quit the Bureau," she suggested, still serious.

He caught himself, shocked. "But—" he said, stopping himself, realizing that she was testing him.

"You would ask me to quit the FBI? Is this a test of which I love more, you or the FBI?"

"Yes."

"Okay. I don't think it's a fair test, Mag. But okay, I'll quit the Bureau if you want me to. What should I do for a living instead?"

"You're not serious, are you?" she asked.

"I'm serious if you're serious," he told her evenly. "Are you serious?"

He saw the shock in her eyes. She caught her breath.

"You're so full of it! The old Mark would never quit the FBI. He wouldn't let his little wifey tell him what to do for a living."

"I am the old Mark. But I'm willing to really quit if we both agree that it's best for the family. I'm not sure if it's the best thing. After ten years of stake-outs, missing the kids' birthdays, well, I'm not a big fan of my working hours either. We should consider all the options. I'll talk to Howard. He might have a few ideas."

Howard Hall was Mark's immediate supervisor.

The next day, Mark talked to Hall about working more normal hours.

"The only guys who work normal hours besides desk jockeys are the white collar crime boys," Hall replied, a bit shocked by Mark's request. "But that's not your style, Mark. I thought you liked the action?"

"I do. But my wife hates it. White collar unit, eh? Sounds pretty stinking dull...but, what the hell. Have you heard about any openings in New Jersey?"

Hall was aware that Mark had just reconciled with his wife.

"Nothing. Budget cutbacks. There might be a few openings in that new computer fraud unit in New York. But you have to be a minority, a computer jockey, or an accountant to get those slots. Nothing can stop you from putting in. I'd hate to lose you, Mark. Another couple years, you'll be sitting in my seat."

"And I hate New York. Nothing's worse than the city," Mark mused.

Oh yes there is, a little voice told him, reminding him of his dream at Steubenville.

"But I could put in."

"I'll make a few calls, Johnson. But you'll regret leaving the streets. Guys like you waste away riding the desk."

"Thanks, Howie."

✝ ✝ ✝

Howard Hall didn't have to make a call. Four minutes after Mark left the room, an old buddy called from the Cleveland office. It was Phillip Breen. They had been in the same class at the Academy. Breen was heading up a new white collar unit in Cleveland.

"They keep sending me accountants, Howie. They can't catch a dead butterfly with a fly strip! I need a guy who's worn some leather off his shoes. Somebody good at getting into a bad guy's head. I'll pull whatever strings I need to pull to get around the quotas."

"You could lose your job talking like that," Hall suggested, smiling into the phone. "And good field agents don't like leaving the field."

"Come on, Howie, it's me, Phil. This white collar unit *is the field,* but with cushy hours, and smarter bad guys. It's not as easy as you might think. Have you got anybody for me? Come on, Howie. I'm dying out here. I need an East Coast guy, too. These mid-west agents are dumber than chicken snot on a bungee stick."

"You know, Phil, you're starting to sound like a perverse Dan Rather," Hall teased. "Cushy hours, you say?"

"Yeah. Sorry I wasted your time," Phil said dejectedly.

Just as he felt Phil was ready to hang up the phone, Howard said: "Don't be sorry. I'm riding you, Phil. I've got the perfect guy…"

✝ ✝ ✝

Weeks later, Mark found himself sitting in a nondescript Ford that was obviously a cop car, in Cleveland, Ohio. His house was a few blocks away from his best friend, Bill White. After a few more interviews, he would go home.

He pulled out of the lot at Joe's Deli.

Four hours later, after dinner, the phone rang.

"Is this Mark Johnson's residence?" a stranger asked.

"Yes," Maggie answered. "To whom am I speaking?"

A few moments later, she cupped the phone to her stomach and called into the living room, "Mark, there's someone on the phone for you saying something about finding you a daily Mass. Says his name is Buzz."

The next morning, in front of Saint Angela Merici, like one immortal chess piece lining up next to another, Mark Johnson shook hands with Buzz Woodward.

Buzz was wearing his brown UPS uniform. Mark was wearing his blue FBI uniform.

Mark was pleasantly surprised to find his strength matched almost perfectly with Buzz's during the handshake.

They were fifteen minutes early, and exchanged terse biographies.

At one point Buzz said, "Oh yeah, I'm an alcoholic. I always get that out of the way up front when I meet a friend."

Mark laughed, and resisted the urge to say, *"And for the last nine years, I've been a lousy husband."*

They were amazed to discover that they had lived less than ten miles apart during long stretches of Buzz's childhood.

They sat in the same pew, knelt with the same straight-backed strength, responded with the same New Jersey accent, and stayed a few minutes after the closing song to pray for help from the same Virgin Mary.

Outside after Mass, standing on the stone steps on the eastern side of Saint Angela Merici, in the light of the brightest sun in weeks, the two big guys agreed to meet for lunch.

"Oh, I forgot!" Buzz said, hitting his forehead with his palm.

"Forgot what?"

"I'm meeting a guy for lunch today. It's kind of a tradition. Do you mind him sitting in? We meet every two weeks for lunch at Joe's Deli. He's a great guy; you'll like him, he's an advertising executive. Maybe you could make a few contacts for your investigations."

"That's a coincidence. I called you from Joe's yesterday."

Buzz buried his top lip into his lower, raised his eyebrows and shrugged.

"I didn't catch your friend's name," Mark prodded, curious, his agent's instincts prompting him.

"Sorry. His name is Bill White. He grew—"

"—grew up in New Jersey. Yes I know."

"Wow, you FBI guys are really sharp. How'd you guess that?" Buzz wondered.

"I didn't guess. I know Bill White. He's my best friend. You could say he's one of the reasons why I moved to Cleveland."

For one of the few times in his life, Buzz was speechless. His sleepy eyelids opened wide. He shook his head. He inhaled deeply on his post-Mass cigarette.

"Mark, do you get the feeling the Big Guy is in on this?"

"This what?"

"This! Us getting together. The whole thing. Ya know what? Betcha Bill's a good athlete. Is he?"

"Yeah; all-state in football. Receiver. Starting guard for our basketball team three years," Mark shot in clipped New Jersey shorthand.

"I knew it!" Buzz cried out, causing Mark to wonder briefly if Buzz was slightly unbalanced. *The guy's spiked with energy,* Mark thought.

Mark waited for Buzz to continue.

"I don't know the whole picture yet, Mark. But I will. One thing I do know for sure. Our Lady's gonna have one hell of a basketball team in Rocky River! Wait 'til the Man sees you and Sam standing next to each other in the paint! We'll dominate! The Man will want to be our fifth man!"

Buzz was beside himself. The day had started out so drearily. It had been a chore to get out of bed.

"The man?" Mark asked.

"Oh. Sorry. You're gonna hafta get used to me, Mark. I speak in riddles. I'll explain all about the Man at lunch." Buzz glanced at his watch. "I can't be late again. I got a warning last week. I can't believe you know Bill White! Bye."

"Bye," Mark said, shaking his head as Buzz bounded off to his Festiva.

That guy is crazy, he thought.

But Mark Johnson had formed a positive impression of Buzz Woodward.

Tough guys usually like each other. It was an exclusive corps.

Chapter Fourteen

1

The next two months were the happiest of Buzz Woodward's life. The depression that had been creeping up on him seemed to sift out of his soul, day by day, as the summer inched along.

This was because of basketball. Just as Buzz predicted, the Man took to the massive Mark Johnson three days later, when he and Bill White showed up to play with Buzz and Sam. The Man joined the team on the first game of the day.

Buzz, reveling in the luxury of having two taller men on his team, moved to power forward. Bill, despite a sore back, had excellent range on his jumper and could shoot with a hand in his face. The Man was one of the best defensive guards around, and had a knack for driving through the paint for silky smooth lay-ups. Mark was not a polished player, but his strength, quickness, and agility made up for his lack of fundamental skills. He could dunk from a standing position and rebounded with an aggression that intimidated the few other tall players.

Sam was the icing on the cake: a shot blocker with an array of moves in close and the ability to pop jumpers from the perimeter.

Like the sun in the July sky, the Rocky River courts were reaching a peak. The regulars were now in shape, and their personal skills were honed by two months of constant play. The stands on the sidelines filled up with several teams waiting to get a chance on the losers court. Wives and girlfriends had begun to show up to watch. Competition became fierce because only the winners stayed on the court. Teams that lost on the losers court were forced to wait for up to an hour before playing another game.

The weather was basketball-perfect: warm, low humidity, and no wind. Donna and Ellie, who had come to watch Sam and Buzz, met Mark's wife Maggie for the first time before she took her daughters to the nearby mega-playground.

Buzz's team won the first game, 9 to 2. Then they won, on the winners court, 9 to 3. They won a third time, and a fourth time, dispatching the other teams with ease.

Ellie, wearing Jeans and an R.E.M. concert T-shirt, asked Donna if winning so easily and often was boring for the men.

"No way!" Donna told her. "If you think that, you don't understand men, or at least competitive ones like Buzz and this new guy, Mark. They'll whip you a thousand times, whipping you worse each time, and laugh. That's the name of the game: destroy the enemy."

"They do look serious, don't they," Ellie observed, watching the court to their right. The winners court.

"Notice how they don't start joking around until the game is put away, at say, five to nothing. Then they start having fun, toying with the bad guys."

"Yeah, you're right. Sam never jokes, though, does he?" Ellie asked, fascinated, and slightly jealous that Donna was a basketball player herself, and could understand the ins and outs of the game they were watching.

"That's because he concentrates so hard; he plays with his whole self. Watch him. Oh, I guess you already do…" Donna blushed a teensy bit.

Ellie turned and lowered her sunglasses to give Donna a friendly smile. "You got that right, sister."

Donna noticed the faint sparkles from her diamond on the lenses as Ellie adjusted the glasses back up.

After a moment, Ellie said: "I notice Buzz does a lot of talking. To his teammates, the other players. What's going on there? I know that Mark and what's his name—"

"—Bill White."

"Yes, Bill White. They're new. But is Buzz in charge?"

"Partly. I think the black guy, the one they call the Man, is the leader. He doesn't say much, but if you watch his eyes, you can see him telling the other players what to do, and with hand gestures. There! See, he just waved his fingers, and Buzz ran by the baseline—oh that must hurt—and slammed the guy guarding him into Mark's pick…"

Both women watched as Buzz squared up for a jump shot on the baseline after receiving a pass from the Man.

He missed.

Sam stuffed the rebound into the basket. The players turned and raced in the other direction. This latest team was putting up a good fight.

"I saw it!" Ellie cried out softly, taking Donna's arm. "There's more to this than I thought. I never played sports or watched them on television, except for Bucky's Super Bowl parties."

"There is a lot to it. For example, take Buzz's talking. He's not doing it to get laughs. I think he does it to rattle the opponent, or to set him up for something later. Buzz plays with his head, even though he's a good athlete, too. He's big and very, very quick for a man his size. Few teams have a player who can match up with him.

"Look, he's so happy! He's bounding around like a puppy. I can tell he's totally psyched to be on a team with such good players. Bill White's no slouch, El, either. I've seen him light up the basket. They're all good."

Eventually, Buzz's team won this game, too. During the brief intermission while the next set of victims warmed up, Buzz, Mark, and Bill trotted to the water fountain to cool off. The Man walked up to Sam, who was waiting with Ellie and Donna by the stands.

"What are those things around their necks?" he asked, referring to the scapulars which Buzz, Mark, and Bill were wearing. His team had been 'skins' during the last game, and the scapulars stuck out.

"Scapulars," Sam responded. "Some kind of Catholic thing."

"Oh yeah, I got one of those when I was a kid. First Communion or something. I thought they went out with Vatican II. Sheesh. Those guys can play. Where'd you find the big guy, Mark?"

"Buzz found him. He's an FBI agent. They go to daily Mass together. And Bill White's an old friend of Mark's, though Buzz knows him, too."

"Daily Mass, eh? Bill hasn't missed a shot. I missed a few lay-ups. Maybe I should go to Mass with 'em."

Sam laughed.

"You should call yourselves the Scaps," Ellie suggested wryly. "You can put a scapular on for the game, Sam. Like a uniform."

"After all," Donna added, "Buzz says the scapular used to be a shirt of some sort."

"What's going on?" Buzz asked, walking up, his face still dripping with sweat mixed with water from the fountain.

"The ladies are planning to call our little one-day dynasty the Scaps, short for those scapulars you guys are wearing," the Man explained.

"You're a Catholic," Buzz addressed the Man. "You can wear one too."

The Man raised an eyebrow, and shook his head. He wasn't going to be caught dead wearing a scapular. He hadn't been to Mass in years, and had fallen away from his faith during his playing days on the Notre Dame football team in the 1960s.

Bill and Mark walked up.

"You guys ready to run?" Bill asked pleasantly, still out of breath. He hadn't exercised all summer.

The others nodded. Buzz smiled broadly.

Maggie came to the stands with her three daughters fifteen minutes later. After the men won the final game of the night, Mark pulled her aside and politely asked if he could invite the team and their two groupies over for a beer and snacks.

"Normally, you would have asked me in front of the crowd, putting me on the spot, or simply brought them over," she told him with feigned anger. "And normally, I would have a hundred reasons for them to not come over, including that we've got unpacked boxes all over the house and it's going to take me longer to get the girls ready for bed."

She saw the disappointment, far away, in his eyes. But she knew her new Mark would abide by her wishes. She could see he really wanted to invite his new buddies over.

"But since you asked so sweetly, and because it will be months before we're unpacked, what the hey, let's have a party! We haven't entertained in ages!"·

Mark lifted her off the ground with a hug. *Joe Kemp was right. I should call and see if he can come over.*

It was eight-thirty, with more than an hour of sunlight left in the day.

Mark returned to the stands. "Party at my house!"

Everyone agreed to come except for the Man, who begged off politely, and walked to his car, a towel around his withered neck. He didn't want to set a precedent. He never socialized with the guys on the court.

Bill White called the Kemps from a nearby pay phone.

"Can the whole family come?" he called over to Mark.

Mark looked to Maggie, who rolled her eyes, but nodded. He gave Bill the thumbs up.

Bill hung up and announced, "They're coming. Everybody will be there."

"Who's coming?" Buzz asked for himself, echoing Donna, Ellie, and Sam's sentiments.

"Joe and Mary Kemp and their kids. I told you about them, Buzz, over lunch the other day." Bill looked at Maggie and Mark. "They've got a bunch of kids."

"Can Joe play basketball?" Ellie asked, surprising everyone with her question.

"I don't know," Bill said with a shrug. "We can ask him."

"You could use a sixth man," Donna said.

"What for?" Sam asked. "We only play five on these courts. To fill in if we're missing a guy?"

"No, silly," Donna said, a twinkle in her eye. "For the Revco Ten Thousand."

Buzz laughed hard at this. The Revco Ten Thousand was an annual charity tournament that featured hundreds of teams from all over the city. Rainbow Babies and Childrens Hospital got two hundred thousand dollars and the tournament champions got ten thousand. Revco got lots of publicity. A local cable station always broadcast the final game, which was played at Cleveland State's arena.

Buzz explained this to the group.

"Then we'll have to find out if Joe can run," Mark said, quite seriously. "Or find a ringer."

"You are a ringer," Buzz offered. *Like Spearchucker Jones in the original M.A.S.H.*

"Naw. I'm a hack. I mean a college guy. Somebody who can light it up."

"I might know somebody," Sam said hopefully, unlacing his shoes, looking up. "One of my biggest customers played for North Carolina-Charlotte when they made that run in the NCAAs. His name is Elmer Phipps. He looks like he's still in shape, but he lives in Euclid."

"That doesn't matter for the tournament," Buzz said. "But we'd have to talk the Man into playing. He was an all-American on Notre Dame's football team, and has one of those big gold rings with all the diamonds on it. He's another kind of ringer. He knows how to win. But the Man is kind of picky about who he hangs out with."

Mark and Bill nodded knowingly. *A ringer.*

"You fellas are sounding awfully serious after only one day on the court," Maggie said, holding her youngest. "And I know that look when I see it, Agent Johnson. You're like a shark smelling blood."

Ellie rolled her eyes.

Donna smiled. There was something special about the Scaps. *And I'm going to be their manager!*

✝ ✝ ✝

Grace triumphed with Bill White's simple announcement that "Everybody will be there."

The Father is a chess player, and the universe is His vast board. At the founding of America, deists worshiped at the altar of rugged individualism, assigning to God the role of clock maker; making Him into an indifferent god who cared little to intervene in the world He wound and left ticking.

The Father rarely needs plagues and earthquakes to bring His children together in groups designed not only for their happiness, but also for their salvation.

Could Ellie have foreseen that her cocktail with Sam at the behest of Bucky would have led her to Mark Johnson's backyard on this warm summer night, an engagement ring on her finger? Could Buzz have foreseen, even two minutes before he slammed into Sam during a basketball game, that Sam would become his best friend? Could Bill White have predicted that helping Mark Johnson's failing marriage would end up with them moving to Cleveland? Could Donna have foreseen that her decision to pick up a refrigerator on one day rather than the next would bring her a close friend in Buzz?

One half hour after the last game on the Rocky River courts during an evening in July, a group was becoming a web of grace, intertwined so thoroughly that the slightest pressure on one thread would affect every other thread.

In the Johnson's backyard, little Meg Johnson began a friendship with Eileen Kemp that would last a lifetime. Joe Kemp discussed computerizing his contracting business with Sam, and made an appointment to meet at Edwards & Associates. Maggie Johnson offered to help design and sew Ellie's wedding gown. Joe Kemp turned out to be a movie buff, and Buzz rented movies the following month because of suggestions from Joe. Bill gave Sam advice on how to advertise Edwards & Associates more effectively, and Sam would base decisions worth tens of thousands of dollars on Bill's expertise. Donna invited Maggie, the new girl in town, to visit the Lourdes Shrine, and almost convinced Ellie to come along.

Over beers, Pepsi, diet ice tea, and pretzels hastily dumped into Maggie's Tupperware bowls, conversations began that would never end.

Mark Johnson's deep laughter caused his new senior citizen neighbor to peek through the curtains of his window from his bed, awakened from his sleep.

Ellie found herself fighting against the temptation to become comfortable with these middle class westsiders, then gave in to the temptation, like a striking blue butterfly caught in a web. Without quite realizing it, she was reacting against the unarticulated certainty that there had to be a predator here, a spider waiting to inject her with suburban poison.

Mary and Maggie were different, just as Buzz and Donna were different—in a way she couldn't put her finger upon. These were the first mothers she had ever met who didn't seem concerned about the size of their families.

They even showed signs of wanting *more* kids. There just had to be something unhinged, something let loose, about *that*.

Ellie, like most people, didn't realize that all the universe is a web, from the web of grassy roots beneath her stylish leather Keds, to the web of planets and stars which Einstein proved were related to each other by forces unseen and unheard. Whirling angels sang above her, touching and canting, also unseen and unheard.

And Buzz Woodward was happy, his creeping depression fading away like a ball swishing through a hoop in slow motion. He had always been an intuitive person, even as a child. Perhaps because he had lost touch with himself in the past, he was more attuned to the web, because his fragile happiness depended more on things beyond himself. Or so it seemed.

He sat in a plastic Adirondack chair, unusually silent, sipping Pepsi, enjoying long drags on his cigarette, thinking about webs. He was aware that he had helped spin this web. He remembered slamming into Sam on the court more than a year earlier.

They're all here because of me. I was the first human cause, Buzz thought.

This awareness gave meaning to his life, and because it was true, it made him happy. As G.K. Chesterton wrote of the madman, he is the most rational of men, but his rationality is built on misperceptions of reality. During Buzz's frequent slides into mild depression, he grasped at webstrings that formed realistic-looking but irrational forms.

My daughter hates me was one of those false strings. So was: *It doesn't really matter if I get out of bed today.* Every morning for months had been a battle over this one false assumption. He was just sane enough to climb out of bed, deny the false assumption, hoping that *It doesn't really matter* was a fake thread.

In the Johnson's backyard, looking at Sam conversing comfortably with Joe Kemp (who, upon being asked, admitted to being a terrible basketball player), Buzz knew that it did matter. It did matter to get out of bed. There were webs to weave. Strings to grasp. Packages to deliver. Conversations to start. Thoughts to be expressed. Sams to slam into. Oceans to swim. And sad little men hiding in electrical sockets, waiting to be born of the human imagination. Every human being had dozens of strings to tie every day.

Maybe the socket guy isn't saying Nooooo! Maybe he's saying Yooooo!

"What are you smiling about?" Donna asked sweetly, coming to kneel next to her sleepy-eyed friend.

"Webs," Buzz said distantly, with a certain reigned-in excitement. "Weaving webs, getting out of bed, playing basketball on summer nights, little men in electrical sockets, and how much I love your friendship."

Donna smiled. "Talking in riddles again. Sounds poetic. What does it all mean?"

"I don't think I could say, Donna," Buzz told her honestly. "Just that it matters. It all matters, everything. Nothing is without purpose for God. Just look at this scene. How did we get here?"

"I don't know. It just happened."

"That's my point. I don't think anything *just* happens. It all matters. I know it does, because I'm happy. I haven't felt this good since springtime…"

"Oh, Buzz, that's wonderful! I've been praying for you. Every night."

He took her hand, and raised it to his lips, kissing her gently on the back of the hand.

"Keep praying. It's working," he whispered.

2

Late that evening, Buzz, Sam, Ellie, and Donna watched *Casablanca* in Buzz's apartment. Tonight they had another guest at their video showing: Bill White. Buzz had invited him to come over when the gathering at the Johnson's came to an end.

Sam and Ellie sat on Buzz's couch, one of Ellie's long legs casually draped over Sam's longer leg. Buzz sat on the floor, his back against the front of the couch, Donna sitting Indian-style behind him. Bill was given Buzz's comfortable green leather chair, a place of honor.

They watched in silence as the screen threw black and white lights upon them, mesmerized by the witty, often dark dialogue, the quick editing, and the superb acting. What a story: a classic love triangle, perhaps the best ever in movie history. By coincidence, it had been years since anyone had seen it. Sam had not seen it at all, not even on television.

At the misty climax of the movie, Donna's life was changed forever. As she listened to the dialogue, she was pierced by a certain inner knowledge of what she was called to do with the remainder of her life. It all became icy clear, after endless months of being drawn like a piece of iron between the two magnets of her hopeless desire for Sam and her ill-suited love for Buzz.

Rick's words to Ilse opened her heart to a greater possibility, and at the same time, a greater suffering. Tiny gray
images reflected in a single tear as it slipped down her cheek.
She quickly wiped it away, wondering if her love for movies
had been planted just for this moment, for this one singular
movie, from all eternity.

It all matters, Buzz's mysterious words earlier, under the
stars in the Johnson's backyard, vibrated in her mind now.

But it's just a movie, she countered.

No, it all matters. The little call would not let itself be
ignored. She could no longer unhear it.

After the movie, it was late and everyone was too worn
out for conversation. Sam and Ellie made their good-byes,
and Bill White left with a firm handshake. Donna meandered
behind, slowly cleaning up the empty glasses and bowls of
pot-cooked popcorn.

"You need to go, too," Buzz said wearily, slowly stretching, then rubbing the back of his crewcut. "I'll clean up."

She was in his little kitchen. She turned from the sink,
and found him standing behind her.

He looked down, then looked up. She raised her lips to
his, then tried to kiss him.

Why are you doing this? she asked herself. *This is not
good. This is a Bad Thing. Are you running away?*

Are you running away from a movie?

Buzz, who was fatigued yet thrilled by the long day, was
taken by surprise. Donna was opening a book that had been
finished months ago. He did not respond. He gently pulled
her arms down, but kept her hands in his. He saw a flash of
anger in her eyes that spread down to her mouth, forming a
line.

"Why?" he asked her.

She looked down at her feet, feeling intense shame. "I
don't know."

"I think you do know. Why did you just kiss me?"

"Because…"

She wanted to tell him, but she couldn't. "Please forgive me, Buzz."

She put her arms around his wide back. This was not like the kiss. This was chaste.

"I don't know what came over me."

It was a lie.

"Why do I need to forgive you?" His voice was gentle. He stroked her hair. "Tell me what's the matter, Donna. Is it Sam and Ellie?"

"No," she muttered sadly. "It's not that. It's something in the movie. I can't form it into words right now. Like you said in the backyard, some things you can't put into words. But it's the same thing you were talking about. Everything matters. Can I leave it at that? It all matters."

He let the string go. He held her for a few moments longer, then said, "I think you better go now, my little one."

His arm around her shoulder, he led her to the door. Wordless, she left him.

3

From the Diary of Ellen James

It's been two weeks since I started my company with the loan Sam gave me. He's also set up my one computer for this one-woman show. I'm so excited! I landed my first client today. I will pay him back, with interest, as soon as I can, though he hasn't mentioned the loan since I asked him for it. "It would be my pleasure," was all he said. If I thought he would hold it over my head, I wouldn't have asked. He's not the least bit competitive when it comes to my career. I keep waiting for his ego to show up. Then again, Sam is not like that. Sam is not even like Bucky when it comes to ego.

Am I really in love? How long does being in love last? Will I feel this way about Sam forever? Or will it wear off after a year or two of being married like it did for the bitter divorcées at my old firm? Will I catch the "fever," as Sam calls it, falling in love with my company, preferring the office to sitting with Sam in front of a cozy fire? Why can't I have both? Even as I made cold call after cold call over the last two weeks, desperate for those first crucial appointments, I felt restless without Sam near me. I look forward to going to work (I commute all the way to the downstairs den) and I look forward to being with Sam when the work is done. What's so wrong with that? Isn't that how he feels about me and work?

So many questions, Diary!

I'm looking at the ring on my left hand as I type this into my fancy new computer. Sam installed WordPerfect for me today, and this is my way of taking my computer out for a test drive. Sam also installed extra simms chips, or something like that.

I've never kept a diary before, so don't be surprised if I give it up tomorrow!

Only twenty-two days until the wedding! Each day seems like a month. Except for the choice of the band for the reception, Sam has taken little interest in planning the details with me. Even his interest in the band, Sam says, is to satisfy the tastes of Buzz. Seems that Buzz wants a band that will "rock the rafters." Well, the Garden Club doesn't have rafters, I said to Sam. Then we'll just have to have some rafters installed, he told me.

That, dearest Diary, is the extent of our disagreements over wedding plans. Our pre-Cana counselor at the parish told us that making wedding plans is a great opportunity to learn how to work with your future "mate" and to get to know each other better. It's supposed to be a chance to "bond" with my betrothed.

But Sam defies all the books; locking horns is simply not his style. And I've felt bonded to him since the first night we met. Frankly, Di, I'm glad Sam doesn't care about "sweating the details," as he calls it. And I'm having the time of my life planning the wedding. I just met a woman named Maggie Johnson who says she can make alterations to my gown better than the bridal shop. She's the wife of a friend of Sam's. (Do I have to explain every detail, or can I skip telling you more about Maggie? Are there rules for diaries?)

I just hope I'm not taking on too much between starting Northcoast Marketing Consultants and planning the wedding. The constant activity is helping pass the time until the Big Day. That, and my daily exercise program—aerobics and jogging. I'm going to make sure this old bod is perfect for the Big Night.

Last night, over a nightcap with Bucky, I asked him if he felt about my mother the way I feel about Sam. (News flash: we still haven't gotten her reply to the invitation. Bucky insisted on sending her one, but predicts she won't show. I really couldn't care less.) He said that he was more in love with *what* she was than with the woman herself, but that he is sure Sam and I are different. He says it's obvious that I'm in love with the man, not what he does. I'm not sure what Bucky meant by that. Maybe he was making a reference to mother being a blue blood. Oh, I don't know!

He rarely speaks about my mother. I've always been able to talk to Bucky about everything, though I can't recall talking to him about her until last night.

And Bucky also said that Sam is one in a million. Bucky says that Sam's not being nice to get something from you. Sam's being nice because that's the only way he can dream of being. I'm so glad that Bucky sees what I see in Sam. They're all I have in the world.

Unless you count Buzz Woodward! Yuck! Sam says Buzz will grow on me. Maybe he will. It's been almost a year and it still hasn't happened. Oh, it's not that I don't like Buzz. He can be sweet at times. It's just that he can be *so embarrassing* when he starts yelling at the top of his lungs in public places, thinking it's funny or something. Sam seems taken in by his riddles and philosophical babbling.

Maybe Buzz is like Tip Greyson, Bucky's gin rummy partner from yesteryear (died of a heart attack, I'm afraid to report, Diary. To Tip's relatives: if you're reading this, shame on you!). Tip was also a loud, overbearing, social bore. When I was still in knee socks and complained about old Tipper, Bucky told me he liked having Tip around because it made him (Bucky, I mean) feel like the calm, quiet one. Bucky, quiet? There's a laugher. But there's a certain logic to it. Sam's so quiet that maybe having a talker like Buzz around takes the pressure off Sam having to say anything at all. Sam's a doer, not a talker.

Still, I have to admit that Donna Beck has grown on me, and the people we met after Sam's basketball game the other night were very nice. And it looks like Sam is quite serious about this Revco Ten Thousand tournament. I'm actually looking forward to it myself. I don't know much about basketball, but this whole thing might be like going back to my cheerleading days at ole Beachwood High, dating the captain of the football team. I have truly enjoyed watching my Sam play. He's quite good, you know.

Well, well. I'm tired of typing. And I have a client to go see tomorrow: Built-to-Last Machine Tools, Inc. I'm going to straighten out their marketing strategy! Move over Edwards & Associates: Northcoast Marketing Consultants is off and running!

4

A week later, they were again gathered around a picnic table on the patio in Mark Johnson's backyard. Mark was a natural-born party thrower. Maggie and Mary had taken the children bike riding in the nearby Metroparks after dinner.

Mark held court with a regal bearing, a sweaty knee brace pulled down to his right ankle.

"To Boys Night Out, gentlemen!" he toasted, holding up his bottle of Michelob Light.

"Hear hear!" Bill White seconded.

Buzz raised his Pepsi with a lemon twist, while Sam and Joe Kemp raised their own beers.

"Bill tells me you were quite a wrestler in high school," Buzz said with a grin.

"I was okay," Mark responded modestly. "I miss it."

"I've never lost a wrestling match in my own career," Buzz bragged.

"Maybe that's because you never wrestled," Sam needled.

"That's perfectly true, Sam," Buzz agreed. "But I used to wrestle the guys for fun on the football team in high school. Nobody could get me to the ground. Greco-Roman style."

"I think our friend Buzz is drawing a line in the sand," Bill said to Mark.

"I think our friend Buzz is about to get his lunch handed to him," Sam observed, raising a beer in Buzz's direction.

"Hey, I was just making conversation," Buzz said, verbally backpedalling. "I don't want to wrestle Mark."

Mark eyed Buzz. *What's Boys Night Out for anyway?* he thought. "I wouldn't want to embarrass you, man. Don't let these boys goad you."

"Embarrass me? Embarrass me? How good can you be?" Buzz took the bait.

Mark didn't have a large backyard, but it was surrounded by a high, woodslat fence, and private. There was a large area of soft, uncut grass not ten feet off the patio.

Mark didn't answer. A fertile silence ensued.

"No offense, Buzz, but Mark is that good. I saw him in high school. You might get hurt," Bill added.

"Put your knee brace back on, big guy," Buzz said, putting down his Pepsi. "We'll see if you can hurt me."

"I won't hurt you, Buzz. We need you for the tournament."

This brought a laugh from Joe and Sam. Bill White wasn't laughing at all.

"I'll bet next week's Boys Night Out beers that Buzz will last for three minutes without getting pinned," Sam said.

Mark stood up, adjusted his knee brace, then tightened the velcro straps.

"Three minutes? Thanks for the vote of confidence," Buzz quipped.

"No problem."

"I'll take that bet," Bill said.

"So will I," Joe added.

Buzz gave them both a look. When he stood up, he realized how big Mark Johnson was. Mark was touching his toes now, stretching out.

How strong can he be? I'm strong. Maybe I can last for a long time. Certainly more than three minutes. Nobody's ever floored me.

"I'll time it on my watch," Sam said, pulling the Rolex off his wrist. "You can do it, Buzz. He's only a giant, former all-American football player and FBI agent trained in hand-to-hand combat. You, on the other hand, are Buzz Woodward, wild man from New Jersey."

Buzz was feeling as if he had been sucked into quicksand. *I shoulda kept my mouth shut.*

"Mark's from New Jersey, too," Buzz told Sam. "This is childish."

"Aw come on, Buzz," Mark called from the lawn. "You look like you can handle yourself. I've seen you on the courts. It'll be fun."

Buzz walked over to Mark. "Be gentle with me, Agent Johnson," he whispered, looking back at the patio, wishing his three minutes were over.

"Don't worry. Just for fun. Trust me. Let's go," Mark whispered back.

"Start the clock!" Buzz yelled, crouching down.

"Go!" Sam called back.

Mark pulled himself into a wrestlers crouch, his legs comfortably spread apart, but closer than his basketball crouch; his hands and arms were close to his chest—like a Tyrannosaurus Rex.

As soon as he saw Buzz's stance, Mark knew that Buzz was in big trouble. *He doesn't know how to wrestle.*

Mark reached for a grip behind Buzz's neck, but Buzz's neck suddenly wasn't there. *Not bad,* Mark thought, pursing his lips.

He reached again, caught Buzz's shoulder, but Buzz pulled down and away.

He's quick; that's good. Looks strong. This could be fun, Mark thought without the slightest trepidation.

Buzz smiled weakly.

They slowly circled each other.

"Fifteen seconds!" Sam called out.

Buzz tried to concentrate. *Ignore the time!* He carefully watched the big man before him. *If he can't get a grip on me, he can't get me down. Play defense!*

Mark reached for Buzz's right wrist, purposely a tad more slowly than he was capable. Buzz pulled his arm away with ease…

…then Mark's other hand shot out and locked on Buzz's left wrist.

"Thirty seconds!"

Buzz stopped circling, and tried to pull his wrist out of Mark's grip by yanking and twisting at the same time.

Mark's grip didn't unglue. Buzz yanked again, harder and more violently. His wrist remained in Mark's grip.

He looked into Mark's eyes. Mark chuckled sadistically.

"Uh oh," Buzz said weakly. "I guess now is the part where I get my butt kicked."

Bill White laughed behind them.

"That's right. Nothing personal, Buzz," Mark said as he pulled Buzz toward himself. Buzz resisted, but had the terrifying feeling of losing his balance. Buzz's entire sports philosophy was predicated on keeping his balance. He had, in fact, never been thrown to the ground in his life. *When in doubt, go on offense,* Buzz thought dejectedly.

"Aaayeeehhh!" Buzz cried out, dropping his butt backwards to the ground, swinging to lunge under Mark at the same time, trying to grab one of Mark's legs with his free hand.

Within a second, Mark, still standing in a crouch, had both arms in a lock under Buzz's armpits. Buzz, holding nothing in reserve, mightily resisted Mark's attempt to flip him on his back, and slithered out of Mark's hold, and found himself on his stomach on the ground.

Mark's full weight fell on top of him. Buzz felt an arm lock onto his thigh, and another slip effortlessly under his shoulder. Mark started to lift him.

"Time?!" Buzz called out desperately. *Why am I out of breath already?*

"Minute, five seconds," Sam called less loudly. *Buzz is like a toy in his hands. And Buzz is a naturally strong man. He could whip my butt in a heartbeat.*

Sam, who was much better than Mark on the courts from the viewpoint of refined skills, was just beginning to realize that Mark was a unique athlete.

Bill leaned over to Sam and said softly, "When you buy the beers next week, make mine a Bud Light."

"It's not over yet," Sam said with little hope. "Hang in there Buzz! You can hold out! Minute and a half!"

Mark pulled Buzz over and came extremely close to pinning him.

"You're a strong sonufabitch, aren't you?" he whispered in Buzz's ear, trying to soften the defeat before it came, knowing that the result of the contest was a foregone conclusion.

Buzz gurgled something incomprehensible.

"Two minutes!" Sam announced. "One more minute Buzz. Hang tough, Buddy Boy!"

Buzz, humiliated and claustrophobic beneath Mark's weight, struggled to find a way to slither from out beneath the experienced wrestler.

I'm a bear covered with grease, Buzz told himself. *Relax, then slip away…*

Buzz relaxed his muscles, hoping to lull Mark into letting up on his grip slightly, into thinking that he had given up.

There, Buzz thought, *he's loosening up.*

But a moment later, when Buzz tried to writhe, he realized that his strength had ebbed away. He was locked in, unable to move or leverage his weight. Mark expertly used Buzz's shift in weight against him, and flipped him like a pancake.

The contest ended with forty seconds left on the Rolex.

Buzz slowly rose to his feet, smiling at Mark, putting his hands on his knees, winded worse than after any of the basketball games earlier in the evening.

"Wow," Buzz rasped in awe between breaths.

"You're not so bad," Mark said genuinely. "You're strong, and you have good instincts."

"You're just sayin' that to make me feel good," Buzz replied. "But thanks for saying it anyway."

Bill came over with Buzz's Pepsi, and patted Buzz on the back. "You almost did it."

"Naw," Buzz said, straightening up. "He coulda pinned me in the first thirty seconds if he wanted to."

Mark knew Buzz was right. He was only slightly winded.

Then Buzz put a tired arm around Mark, and asked with the same impish smile that had started the whole contest in the first place: "Could you teach me to do better next time?"

Next time! Bill White thought. *The guy is nuts.*

"Sure," Mark said kindly. "I'll give you a few pointers. It's hard to find someone who's even willing to practice with me."

That soothed Buzz's ego even as it boosted it. *This is what Ali's sparring partners must have felt like.* Buzz realized that it was an accomplishment to last one minute against a guy like Mark Johnson.

I lasted over two minutes. Maybe I could last for three if Mark taught me a few moves.

Chapter Fifteen

1

It was Saturday, the morning of the semifinal game. Sam and Buzz were practicing the day before the championship game of the Revco Ten Thousand. If they won tonight, they would play in the final tomorrow afternoon. The Scaps had won their first six games of the tournament rather easily. There had been only one close game, the last one, but Bill White had caught fire, hitting three two-pointers to put the game away. (In the Revco Ten Thousand, as in pick-up games, a basket counted for one point. A shot made from beyond the "three point line" counted for two points).

Buzz had talked a security guard into letting them into the Cleveland State Arena. The guard was a big fan of the Revco Ten Thousand.

"Take some rebounds for me," Buzz said, having shot twenty times from just beyond the foul line to warm up. He backed up several steps, to ten feet beyond the three point line.

"That's out of your range," Sam said, stating the obvious.

"You never know when Bill is going to lose his touch. He's been carrying us on offense. I'm going to take a hundred shots from way out here, where nobody will think of guarding me. If we need a two pointer, I'm going to be ready."

"If you say so, Buzz." Sam flicked him the ball.

Buzz missed his first seven attempts from thirty feet. Then he swished one.

"Just getting warmed up. You watch. By the ninetieth shot, I'm going to be hitting half of these bombs."

By the fortieth shot, Buzz was hitting every third jumper. He had to really heave the ball to reach the basket; and concentrated on extending his follow-through completely.

"You see," Buzz explained, breathing heavily as Sam zipped another ball at him, "it's like Pavlov's dogs. If I repeat the stimulus, my arm and body do all the work, deciding for themselves how much force to use."

Buzz canned another shot. Three in a row. Then two misses. Then a swish. Then a miss.

"You're getting it down. Why don't you move to another spot?" Sam asked.

"That would screw things up. I've got to be in this spot, on this court, for my theory to work. I read somewhere that Larry Bird does the same thing, practicing the same shot, alone, hour after hour, day after day, until it's unconscious, until he can do it with his eyes closed."

"Interesting theory, Buzzman, but you don't have days and days to practice."

The semifinal game was tonight. Sam's 'ringer' had fallen through so the Scaps were playing with only five men. Great defense and Bill White's radar jumper had gotten them this far. He was the shortest man on the team, but could jump high and shoot with an opponent hanging in his jockstrap, especially coming off a pick from Mark Johnson.

"We have a few hours. We'll take turns. You practice the same hook shot from the same spot, and I'll keep practicing this long-range jumper. After we win the game tonight with either shot, we'll send the tape to the Birdman."

Buzz drained another jumper.

Sam really wanted to win the contest. The prize money mattered little to him. It was watching Ellie's growing excitement that spurred him on. In all his life, even in little league, he had never been on a championship team. This was the first Saturday in more than six months he had not gone into the office.

"You've already got us winning the whole thing, don't you, Buzz?"

"Oh, I wouldn't say that. I've already got my two grand spent, though. I'm going to Fatima, and I'm gonna take Donna along with me."

"Fatima, you mean where the Mother of God appeared to those two little kids? You're on shot number seventy-five, by the way."

"Three little kids. 1917. Has Donna told you about it? Oh crap!" Buzz shot an air ball.

"Just stroke, Buzz, just stroke. Don't think. And yes, Donna's told me about it. I don't get it, really."

Buzz hit the next four in a row.

"You should read a book about it. There were some bona fide miracles," Buzz paused to thump in his fifth in a row. "Now I've got the range."

"Like your signal graces?" Sam asked, half-convinced that Buzz's Pavlov-Bird theory had some merit. Buzz was hitting more than half his shots now.

"No, well, yes. Real miracles. Like, after the sun did its power dive, all the rain and mud and water around those seventy thousand witnesses was gone. Completely dry. There!" Buzz put an extra oomph on the last shot. It clanged off the back rim. "Speaking of signal graces, have you been getting any more of them yourself?"

"Not really, not since your Hail Mary shot. There was one thing, though…"

Buzz sank another basket while he waited for Sam to finish his thought.

"What was it?" Buzz stopped shooting when he realized that Sam was not planning to explain further.

"Don't stop," Sam ordered.

Buzz took a dribble and drained another basket. *I've got it down.*

"Nothing."

"Don't hold out on me, baby," Buzz teased.

"Forget it. Keep shooting. My turn in ten shots."

Sam didn't really remember the details of the dream where he entered the tabernacle. But the emotions from the dream had stayed with him. Until the sun went down the day he woke up, the world around him seemed…more real.

While he had been walking with Ellie that evening on Huntington Beach in Bay Village, after work, he had a sudden urge to stop. He turned to face her and put his hands on her shoulders, searching into her eyes. The sun was setting behind her, framing her blond hair, which was pulled back in a pony tail. She was so beautiful at that moment that Sam felt like melting, and wondered for the thousandth time why she loved him, and not a more handsome man.

"Sam, what is it?" she had said, concern in her voice.

"I can see your soul," he whispered, seeing something that did and did not seem to be there at the same time. There it was, behind her eyes…*life.*

Ellie laughed nervously. "The eyes are the windows to the soul," she heard herself saying.

She felt uncomfortable. *What does he see inside me?*

Sam had blinked and whatever it was he saw in her eyes was gone. They were only her blue eyes again.

"Sam? Sam?" Buzz called his friend. The ball was bouncing at Sam's feet.

Sam shook his head. "What?"

"Didn't you see? I made my last ten in row! I can't miss, man. I thought you were speechless because of my shooting."

Buzz trotted to the paint and picked up the bouncing ball.

"Yeah, oh yeah. Yes! Ten in a row. Great," Sam said with feigned enthusiasm. "I'm next. Where should I shoot from?"

"Pick a spot you don't normally shoot from. How about here, on the left post? You prefer the right post. I'll stand here with my arms up, to simulate a defender, but I won't move except to get the rebound."

Sam lined up with his back to Buzz. Buzz stood upright, with his arms straight up in the air. Sam shot and made it.

"There's one. Ninety-nine more to go," Buzz encouraged.

Fifteen minutes later, Sam finished with twelve straight swishes.

Buzz retrieved a bottle of Gatorade from a small cooler he had carried in.

"What do we do next?" Sam asked.

It felt good to practice. Donna had scouted the opponent, missing the Scaps last game. She reported that they were a balanced team that almost matched up to the Scaps, but were not as disciplined on defense. They had only one big man, a six-foot-eight monster and former college football player. He would probably cover Mark Johnson. That meant that Sam would be taller than the man guarding him. The mismatch.

"We do it all over again," Buzz said with a mischievous smile.

"Whatever you say, coach," Sam called after him as Buzz ran to pick up the ball, then dribbled over to his unlikely spot.

✝ ✝ ✝

That evening, the opponent proved worthy of the Scaps. The name of the other team was Maury's Boogies. Almost two thousand fans watched the game. The Boogies were led by a talented guard, a former Cleveland State player who had been a back-up on the cinderella team that went to the Sweet Sixteen. He matched Bill White jumper-for-jumper during the first blistering half of the game.

Then, as happens with all shooters, Bill went cold, for the first time in the tournament. He missed four straight jumpers. The Scaps found themselves trailing by two baskets, 17 to 15. The game would end at 21. Buzz called time out.

Unlike the earlier rounds, this game had referees, and Mark Johnson had gotten into foul trouble covering the other team's monster football player, who was clunky but effective. Mark was forced to lay off the physical game, and the monster dumped in four late baskets.

During the time out, Buzz yelled at his teammates, more out of desperation than anger. "Let's go to Sam! Buckle down on defense."

"You can do it, Sam," Donna said from the bench. Ellie clasped her hand. "You can take your man."

"Let's go to Sam," Bill agreed. "I'll only shoot if I'm open. Kick it out to me or Buzz if they double down on you."

Mark nodded, wiping his face with a towel.

"And tighten up on defense," the Man added. "Mark, you stay on the baseline, or flash up to the foul line. Let's make some room for Fisk."

As they walked onto the court, Buzz asked Bill to switch men. "I'm fresh. I can shut down your man. He's not quick. He's only a shooter. I'll shut him down, deny him. If he does get the ball, I'll force him to beat me with his dribble, and you can help out."

Bill looked at his sneakers. He did not have an ego. "Just watch out for the change of possessions. We don't want to give up any easy baskets if they don't switch up on defense like we will."

Buzz nodded grimly. There was no way to know if last-second decisions would work in this kind of game.

The whistle blew. Play started.

For the remainder of the game, the Man and Bill concentrated on dumping the ball into Sam Fisk, who hit five hooks in a row. Mark's Boogie monster continued to score, but missed two short jump-hooks.

Buzz played such intense denial defense that the shooter didn't touch the ball on offense for the rest of the game.

The Scaps were leading 20 to 19 when Bill White canned a jumper to win it.

Donna and Ellie ran out onto the court. Mark's girls came down from the stands and jumped up to him. He lifted the two youngest into his arms, then looked to Maggie, who had remained in the stands. She smiled knowingly. She expected nothing less than victory from her king. He gave her a wink.

The Scaps took a few moments to shake the hands of their opponents.

"We're going to the final!" Mark Johnson yelled, holding a fist in the air, then high-fiving the Man, who promptly walked to the stands, where he took off his brown jersey, replacing it with a fresh T-shirt.

Buzz ran up to the Man. "Where you going? We won!"

"We didn't win nothin' yet, Buzz. I'm going home to get some sleep. You should too."

The Man's demeanor had a sobering effect on Buzz.

"Gotcha."

Sam walked up to Buzz, Ellie under his arm, beaming. She had brown lipstick painted in streaks on her cheeks. Bucky had come down from the stands, and was happily chomping an unlit cigar behind her.

"How come you didn't shoot from your spot?" Sam asked Buzz.

"I'm saving it for the final, my man."

"Great game, Buzz. I'm glad you pushed to dump it into Sam down the stretch," Donna said, clipboard in hand.

"You scouted the mismatch," Buzz said with perfect seriousness.

"I'm staying to scout the next game, too," Donna said. Her demeanor was no different than the Man's.

"Can I tag along?" Ellie asked.

"Sure!" Donna replied, surprised. This tournament was turning out to be the best thing for her relationship with Ellie.

"Then Sam and I will go shower, then come out to sit with our crack scouting team," Buzz said happily. He turned to Mark. "Staying for the next game?"

"No can do, tough guy," Mark said, climbing up the stands to help Maggie gather her things. "Maggie and I have a date."

Couch time, they thought in unison. They shared a look, then kissed.

Bill bowed out from staying for the second game.

"Just tell me whether or not their guards can cover me, Donna. No wait, tell me they can't cover me either way. I'm going home to watch television commercials and pray myself to sleep. My back is killing me."

He winked at her. "You don't do massages, do you, coach?" He knew Donna loved to be called *coach.*

"Geeze, Bill. I'm just a lowly manager."

Ellie smiled, and said the kindest words that Donna had ever heard from her lips: "Don't say that. You're more than just a manager, Donna. Your scouting won the game for us. Isn't that right, Sam?"

Sam nodded, and smiled a toothy smile. "You're our ringer, Donna."

Then Sam turned to Buzz. "Let's sneak in again tomorrow morning and practice our Pavlov-Birds again."

"Sure thing, Kareem. I'll pick you up after I go to Mass."

"I'm going to Mass with Ellie tomorrow."

Buzz gave Ellie a look. *I see.*

"Okay, I'll pick you up after you go to Mass with Ellie. Saint Chris?"

"Yes," Ellie said. "I'm driving over from the East Side. Again."

2

That night, Buzz was so excited that he didn't fall asleep until four in the morning. To pass the time, he took mental shot after shot from his spot, praying a *Hail Mary* with each one.

✝ ✝ ✝

After couch time, Mark and Maggie Johnson conceived their first son.

✝ ✝ ✝

Donna Beck, having scouted their next and final opponent, Dantes Infernos, went to bed worried that she and Buzz might never get to see Fatima in person.

Infernos? I thought Dante only had one inferno. This Dante has four. There was only one weak player on the Infernos, who had demolished a very talented challenger.

The Infernos were a team with four polished players. They played stifling man-to-man and zone defense, and had been together as a team for five years. Their weakest player was almost as good as Buzz. Their best player, Dante Curry, had been on the Revco Ten Thousand championship team three years running.

He's as tall as Sam and as good a shooter as Bill. Who is going to cover him? He's too fast for Sam, and too tall for the Man. Can Buzz handle him? Contain him?

As much as she adored Buzz, she was a realist when it came to scouting. *Not likely.*

We'll need a miracle. We're gonna get smeared, Donna's practical side told her. She wasn't quite sure if it was kosher to pray for the Scaps to win a game. After all, did God really care who won a silly basketball game?

Maybe God doesn't care, a little voice told her. *But if the team is named after the brown scapular, maybe His mother does.*

She fell asleep praying an extra Rosary for the Scaps to win.

✝ ✝ ✝

Bill White went to bed in pain, a dull throb in his back. He took three Bayer aspirin.

Fifteen years earlier, he had been on the Bayer account team. He still used that brand out of sheer loyalty.

I'm getting too old to play this competitively, he told himself. *Then again, I haven't had this much fun in years.*

He decided to offer his pain to heaven for the Johnsons to conceive a child.

And while you're at it, Jesus, make it a boy.

He knew how much Mark wanted one.

He slept like a baby, barely giving a thought to the big game the next day before he fell off to sleep. After all, Bill White was a shooter, and shooters have ice (and sometimes, aspirin) in their veins.

✝ ✝ ✝

Sam and Ellie stayed up until one, sharing the love seat in Bucky's den, enjoying the natural gas fire. They talked about whatever came into their heads: their businesses, the Scaps, the wedding plans, their recent dinner with Bucky and Edward, who had driven down from Michigan.

She sat on one end of the love seat, her feet up on an ottoman. He was on his back, resting his head on her lap, his long legs hanging over the edge at his knees. She stroked his hair.

"You're starting to go bald up top," she remarked evenly, wondering how he would react.

"Sorry," he replied. "Do you mind?"

She shook her head with a slight smile. She couldn't care less.

"Our fathers don't have much in common," Ellie said wistfully. "It was weird listening to Bucky try to find common ground with Edward."

Sam laughed. "They're from two different worlds. You and I are about the only common ground they might ever have."

After a few minutes, Ellie sighed. "It's been a wonderful summer, Sam, a summer of dreams."

"I hope I never wake up. I don't remember what it used to be like."

"Used to be like?"

"Before you, I was alone. I thought that was okay. Now I can't imagine being alone. I thought I was going to live my whole life alone.

"Love is a surprise. I mean, who could ever plan on it? Our lives are an illusion of plans. We plan our educations, our careers, where we live, what kind of towels to put in the linen closet. Planning is dull compared to this. You and me. What a wonderful surprise."

She nodded. She stroked his forehead, gently touching his eyelids, closing them.

"I've had a plan for my life since I was a little girl. I always thought that I would get married later on, after I became established in my career. You were a surprise, sweetheart, but I don't normally like surprises. You're not what I expected. I didn't expect you to be…" she trailed off.

He opened his eyes, looking up at her. He liked looking up. He remembered briefly his own mother, stroking his hair like this, somewhere. *Yes, in the convertible, the Red Memory.*

"What did you expect?"

"I didn't expect my husband to be so kind."

She saw him blush, and leaned down to kiss him on the forehead.

"It's funny, but you don't hear much about kindness these days," she said. "Bucky has always been my measuring stick, and I love him dearly, but when I think of him, I think of strength and smarts, not kindness.

"In an odd, roundabout way, you've helped me finally figure out Donna, I think. She's like you. She's kind. She looks out for me at the games. Unlike the bitchy girls I called my friends at college, she's not competing with me, even though I can tell she likes you. I'm not used to that. I used to be one of the bitchy ones myself."

"Don't say that," Sam corrected quickly. She felt his back muscles tighten.

"Relax, Sam. It's true. I can be a real bitch. I don't blame myself. It's like it was part of my *training*. You told me that you saw my soul in my eyes. That stuck with me. It made me uncomfortable. I went home and looked at my eyes in the mirror, and wondered what you saw. I didn't like what I saw there."

"What are you saying, El?" Sam was shocked by the self-loathing in her voice. He had never heard anything like it from her.

Ellie's lower lip began to tremble. "Sam, I don't know what I'm saying. I was at the game yesterday, watching Donna, and despite myself, I found myself wishing I was like her. She's like you; she's dedicated to something outside of herself. She's so into the Scaps.

"You can see it in her eyes. I was watching her closely, watching how she put so much of herself into scouting a silly team like the whole world depended on it.

"I'm falling for her, Sam. Then I realized that I can't be like her, that I would have to go back and start over as a little girl to get to the point she's at. Suddenly I felt like a little bug."

Sam was listening very carefully, confused and concerned. It was like a whole different Ellie was in the room with him. He had never seen a crack in her perfect armor of confidence. He reached up, and put a hand on her check.

"Donna and Buzz do have a way of getting under your skin, Ellie."

Ellie sniffed. "I suppose so."

She looked away from him, toward the false fire. A tear escaped from her eye and she sniffed a second time.

"Who am I, Sam? Am I Bucky's daughter? Am I your wife? I don't see anything when I look in the mirror."

With a sweet agility, he swung his legs around, pulled himself up to her, and enveloped her in his arms.

"It's okay to be weak and confused, Ellie. If Buzz and Donna have taught me anything, it's that it's okay to not be in control. For Buzz, just going to work is a success. Donna has been drifting since high school. But they know who they are. They're still great people. They inspire me. Let them inspire you, too. Don't get down on yourself."

Her next question seemed to come out of nowhere.

"You won't leave me, will you? What if our marriage doesn't work out? What if we end up divorced like most of Bucky's friends?"

There are times when words are extra, like raindrops on drenched grass. There are times for holding. He held her. She shook in his arms. His hold was not enough to calm her.

This threw him off balance.

What should I do?

He had never seen this side of her, and wondered if he would see more of it after the wedding. It unnerved him. Her perfect control was one of the reasons he loved her.

If only Buzz's grace was real, I could ask his God for some of it to give to you. I wish I had more than words to offer.

Ellie's almost silent sobbing stopped. She raised her head, opening her eyes wide.

"I'm okay now."

The vulnerable Ellie had disappeared.

"You sure?"

"Yes. I'm fine. I don't know what got into me. Must be nerves," she said unconvincingly, with a small chill in her voice. "I'm thirsty, too. I need a glass of water. Want one?"

"Sure. But I've got to get going. We've got a big game tomorrow."

She got up and left the room.

What just happened? Sam thought. *Who am I marrying next week?*

He shook his head, and blew off a feeling of disorientation. He sat up straight and looked at his empty shoes on the rug.

This is no time for cold feet.

He slipped his shoes on and laced them slowly. Ellie returned with a glass of ice water.

After the long drive home to the West Side, he tossed and turned in bed. An image of Donna Beck, swimming in a pool, kept coming to his mind, half in a dream, half out.

Despite himself, he wanted to jump in.

Finally he fell asleep, not in the least aware that an attack had begun in earnest for his soul.

He dreamed he was in the Cleveland State Arena, making hook shot after hook shot into the basket, feeling pretty good about himself. Ellie was on the bench, holding a clipboard, cheering wildly each time his slender arm released the ball. Buzz was also on the bench, his leg in a cast, writhing in pain.

"It's up to you, Sam," he whispered. Sam heard the words in that strange way of dreams.

Sam was alone on his side of the court. The crowd roared with approval as he made each shot. He turned and looked at the bench and now Donna, not Ellie, was there with the clipboard. That seemed better. More practical.

Donna is a better scout, he thought sagely.

He sunk another shot. More cheers. This was too easy.

Why isn't anybody covering me? Why are they letting me shoot without covering me?

Suddenly, the Man was running toward Sam, waving his arms as Sam released the final shot. A buzzer rang, and the crowd became deathly silent.

The Man yelled: "Sam! You're shooting into the wrong basket!"

Swish.

3

"Hear that?" Buzz called to Sam the next day.

"Hear what?"

"That sound. That squeaking sound. That's the sound of basketball."

Sam stopped dribbling and looked up at the rafters of Cleveland State Arena, listening. He filtered out the sounds of the crowd of almost seven thousand people settling into their seats; he heard the crisp thrumps of basketballs being dribbled and the half-metallic sound of misfired shots clanging off the rims. That left the distinct sound of eleven players warming up for the Revco Ten Thousand championship game.

Squeak. Squeak squeak.

"I hear it," Sam said.

"It's a nice, unique sound. I'm always going to remember it. I've never played in a real basketball game before, on a court like this. I wanna remember something."

The Man was on the foul line, practicing foul shots. "You'll remember the win, Buzz," he said, not taking his eyes off the rim. "And you'll remember the loss."

"We're not gonna lose," Buzz said confidently, taking a shot from his spot. Air ball.

The Man had no reply. He looked back to Dantes Infernos, warming up on the other end. He recognized a few players. They were very, very good. Tall, fast, quick, good shooters.

"Sam! Mark!" the Man called out.

The two big men were practicing short baseline jumpers. They turned to their leader and trotted over.

"Yeah?" Mark asked.

"Let's put on a show. None of those guys have ever heard of us. Let's practice alley-oops, get this crowd going."

Sam and Mark lined up. Bill White came over with a ball. He tossed it toward the hoop, just off to the side.

Sam Fisk flew in, grabbed the ball in mid air, and slammed the ball down with ease.

Buzz stood in his spot beyond the three point line, and smiled, clapping. He heard a few claps from the crowd, and a cheer from Ellen: "Yeah Sam!"

The Man tossed the next ball. Mark Johnson left the ground from both feet, grabbed the ball and crammed it through the net with incredible force. The crowd cheered loudly. Mark held up a fist. More cheers.

Bill White, who was a six-footer, sliced down the lane for another, less impressive slam. The crowd, surprised by his ability, cheered again.

Sam and Mark followed with identical, backwards slams from the standing position. Some in the crowd started clapping.

Who are these guys? a few thousand of the fans asked themselves.

Out of the corner of his eye, the Man noticed a few Infernos stop their warm-ups to watch.

Buzz tossed a shot from twelve feet beyond the three point line. Swish. Sam snapped the ball back to him. Swish. Bill bounced him another. Swish.

One of the Infernos walked over to Dante Curry, who had not turned to watch the Scaps, and said something, looking upcourt as he spoke. Dante shook his head and laughed, refusing to look back.

Good, thought the Man.

✝ ✝ ✝

After the Star Spangled Banner was sung by local rock legend Michael Stanley, Donna handed Sam a scapular.

"For me?" she asked. "Just for the game."

He hesitated, then took it from her hand. He put in on. It felt vaguely itchy under his plain brown T-shirt. *Scaps* was silk-screened on the front, with *Edwards & Associates Supports Rainbow Babies* on the back. The plug on the back had been Ellie's idea.

The Man turned Donna's scapular offer down with a rare smile. "No offense, but I'm superstitious about not bein' superstitious."

Donna puzzled over his explanation for several seconds before giving up in bafflement.

✝ ✝ ✝

To make the game last longer for the paying crowd and the television audience, the point total to win was set at 42 for the final game. This was to the advantage of the Infernos, who had a sixth man.

✝ ✝ ✝

Ellie was nervous sitting on the bench next to Donna. She had decided not to paint her face. Buzz had mentioned the possibility of a television interview after the game. She wore a Scaps T-shirt, faded jeans, and diamond earrings worth sixteen thousand dollars.

As the Scaps took their positions on the court for the opening tip off, Donna paced up and down the sidelines.

Several workers from Bill White's agency, the Johnson family, Bucky, the Kemps, and Sam's father sat in the box seats directly behind the bench. Donna's parents and her sisters and brother had also come to watch. A few dozen of the regulars from the Rocky River courts were also in the stands.

Someone started chanting "Go Man go! Go Man go!"

Buzz closed his eyes, and prayed: *Dear Mary, help me play hard and play smart. Please, don't let me embarrass myself.*

Mark Johnson shouted "Let's go!"

Bill, Sam, and the Man remained silent. Buzz lined up next to Dante Curry. He was assigned to guard Dante, who was a full four inches taller, and a superior basketball player in every way except for one.

Dante didn't want to go to Fatima.

Donna nodded to the Man from the sidelines. Buzz covering Dante had been Donna's idea, but it had been the Man who made the final decision.

Take the bait, Dante. Donna urged with her thoughts. *Cover Buzz. Please, cover Buzz.*

She took a close look at the legend, Dante Curry, a handsome man with dark eyes, wavy black hair, and a deep tan. He walked with an easy grace and the air of a champion. He was thirty-one years old. She had seen him play before; as a little girl, Donna had watched him take Our Lady of the

Rosary High School all the way to the state finals—and win it. He was quiet and intense, and feared by those who knew how excellent basketball is played.

They called him, simply, the Italian.

A buzzer went off. One of the referees blew his whistle and walked to the center of the court.

4

Donna had formulated a simple game plan, and for the first third of the game, it worked like a charm on the surprised Infernos.

Dante took the bait and covered Buzz Woodward. This led to a good but lesser defensive player to taking up the job of covering Bill White, whose reputation as a shooter preceded him.

Using a triple-stack offense the Man had installed weeks earlier, Bill ran by pick after pick from Buzz, Sam, and finally, Mark, until he was open.

Bill lit up the Infernos by hitting a blistering ten of his first thirteen shots. Mark and Sam each crammed in an offensive rebound for points. Buzz and the Man popped short jumpers when their men sloughed off to help out on the amazing Bill White.

Buzz fared a little better on the other end of the court covering Dante, who hit more than half his shots. One time, when Dante blew past the slower Buzz to drive the lane, Mark knocked him to the wood with a hard foul.

Sam reached down and helped Dante to his feet.

The opposing captain was expressionless, but Donna and the Man could both see that the other Infernos, who had been expecting an easy game against a team of no-names, were rattled by the Scaps aggressive start.

When the Infernos called time-out, the score was 22 to 14 in favor of the Scaps. The Rocky River cheering section went nuts, and the crowd seemed to be leaning their way. A man from News Channel Five held a mini-cam over the Scaps huddle.

"Phase two!" Donna shouted. Everyone nodded. "Slow it down."

The Infernos came out in a zone defense. It was an attempt to slow down Bill White. And it failed. Bill burned the zone to extend the lead to 31 to 21.

We're gonna win! Buzz rejoiced wildly.

He didn't notice that Mark, the Man, and Bill were grabbing their shorts at their knees at every stop of play.

Dante had his own game plan: wear out the older, less well-conditioned opponents. The tall scorer held up two fingers after plunking through his third two-pointer; the Infernos switched back to man-to-man defense.

Dante was now covering Bill White. Donna's heart sank. He played denial defense, and Bill suddenly had trouble getting the ball. Bill finally ran past a pick, got the ball from Buzz, and leaped up to fire a shot. His legs were growing weary and he wasn't jumping as high as earlier in the game. Dante blocked the shot downcourt, and a teammate picked it up for an easy lay-up.

"Time out!" Donna called. The Man signaled for a time out. The Scaps trotted to the bench.

She said two words: "Power game."

Now Buzz was feeling his own fatigue. Chasing Dante was taking a steady toll on his stamina. None of the Scaps were accustomed to playing a regulation length court for such a long game.

"How the legs holding up?" the Man asked Bill.

"I'll hold out. Don't worry about me. I'll concentrate on defense, and rest on offense 'til the last few baskets."

The Man looked at Mark and Sam, who nodded. It was up to the big men now.

The next few exchanges were like lightning and thunder. Dante took over on offense for the Infernos, taking Buzz for jumpers several times. The Scaps countered by slowing down on offense, and pounding the ball in to Sam or Mark, whichever man was open. Sam and Mark hit half their inside shots. Sam was smoother than his cover man, and Mark was stronger. But neither could keep up with the fabulous Dante Curry, who more than matched them shot for shot.

Again and again, the Man drove the paint and dished off to the big men. The Infernos, terrified of Bill White's jumper, failed to collapse for help.

Dante called a time out with the Scaps leading 39 to 37. Three more points, and the Scaps were champions.

The crowd was getting into the game as it tightened up. Ellie had hugged Donna feverishly after every Scaps basket since 35. Their voices were hoarse from cheering.

"What do we do now?" Donna heard Sam ask the Man between breaths as he ran by the bench. The Man was in the best shape on the team and he was also wearing down.

"They're tired, too," the Man barked angrily, ignoring the stitch in his side. "Let's go to the well."

They all knew the well to which the Man was referring. Bill White was the well. But his face was coming more and more to resemble the color of his last name.

Bill's back pain had been a dull thud; now it was a screaming stab.

"I'm ready," Bill said through a wince as he lined up in front of Buzz before the set offense started. Buzz clapped him on the back. Bill darted quickly to the perimeter, received the ball from the Man, and fired a jumper over Dante.

The ball clanged off the rim. A miss.

An Inferno grabbed the rebound. Dante ran by a nifty pick and received the ball on the left top of the key, Buzz trailing behind him. Dante faked a jumper and Buzz leaped in the air; Dante took a long first step toward the hoop and flicked a running jumper. Mark Johnson tried desperately to block the shot, and landed on Dante's foot. The ball thumped through the hoop. Now the score was 39 to 38, Scaps leading.

Mark collapsed to the ground, grasping his bad knee. He mightily resisted the urge to curse. There were kids in the arena.

The sight of the proud Mark Johnson writhing on the wooden floor caused Buzz to despair. *We don't have a sixth man!*

What am I saying, Mark's hurt!

A ref blew his whistle. Injury time out.

"Hold on, Mark," Sam said, crouching down. "We'll get you a stretcher."

"Stretcher?! Forget the freakin' stretcher. Get Donna out here to tape me up."

Sam had a hand on Mark's forearm. Mark threw it off and struggled to his feet. He winked at Maggie in the stands, and gave the television camera a thumbs up. He hopped to the bench on his own power.

"Cut it for me!" Donna ordered Ellie, handing her a surgical scissors, while simultaneously wrapping athletic tape around Mark's knee, brace and all.

"Here!" Donna yelled.

Ellie cut the tape. Donna wrapped another piece around the knee. Cut. Wrap, cut. She wrapped hard. Mark set his jaw, his eyes unfocused on the crowd.

"Mark, you're crazy!" Bill White whispered loudly to his old friend. "This isn't high school. You've got to go to work tomorrow. We'll play short-handed."

Mark gave Bill a cold look.

"I'm playing."

Bill snorted and walked back onto the court.

"Are you sure you'll be okay?" Ellie asked.

"It's only pain, darling," Mark replied calmly.

The ref looked at his watch, and blew the whistle. The time out was over. The Man briefly considered taking their last time out to give Donna more time to wrap Mark's knee, but she ran out of tape.

There goes the game, the Man thought, watching Mark half-limp, half-hop to the top of the foul line on the Scap's side of the court. *He's a tough sonufabitch.*

When Dante Curry saw Mark's insanely taped knee, he trotted over and said, "Good luck, big guy."

Mark looked him in the eye. Neither man showed any emotion.

"Thank you."

All we need are three points, Buzz thought hopelessly, as a ref raised his arm and blew the whistle again.

Mark was hurt. Dante was shutting down Bill. Every Scap was dragging. The momentum had shifted.

Three points seemed like a hundred.

Even the crowd could feel the game slipping away to the Infernos.

Buzz looked over to Donna; she shook her head gravely.

Next to her, Ellie called out: "Forget about Mark! He's a tough guy. Win it for us, Buzz!"

Buzz took the ball from the referee, and inbounded it to the Man, who brought it up the court.

The Man spotted an opening and drove down the lane, drawing the defensive man who was supposed to be covering Sam. The Man bounced a pass toward Sam, but Mark's defender stepped away from his wounded opponent and flicked the pass away into the hands of an Inferno.

Turnover. The Infernos started a fast break. Dante finished with a jam. Mark had barely limped to half court by the time the play was over.

Now the game was tied, 39 to 39. That basket seemed to be the straw to break the camel's back. The crowd became quiet.

It was sad; it had been such a competitive game up to that point.

"Three points!" Buzz shouted. He saw fire in the Man's eyes. The Man drove the lane again, but kept the ball this time, and was fouled during his shot. The ball clanged off the rim. A miss. The Man would be given one foul shot.

He stepped up to the line, took a deep breath, and sunk his shot.

40 to 39, Scaps in the lead.

"Buckle down, help out on Dante!" Bill White yelled, watching a now-familiar play evolve designed to get Dante open. Buzz, tired but determined, fought through the picks, knowing that Dante would take the next shot.

For a split second, as Dante came off the last pick, Buzz felt as if he could hear only one sound: sneakers squeaking.

When Dante received the ball, Buzz was right on top of him. Dante took a hard step forward, feigning Buzz backwards. Then Dante pulled a new move; he dropped back two steps and fired from behind the three point line, fading away as Buzz tried hopelessly to recover and contest the shot.

The other four Scaps turned, hoping for a rebound, trying to box their men out.

Buzz didn't bother. For the first time since the game began, he had seen Dante smile as he released his shot. Buzz felt completely helpless; he was being taken to school by a far superior player.

Dante saved that move all day just for this moment.

Swish.

Two points.

Infernos 41, Scaps 40.

Game point for the Infernos. One more and it was over. They could even concede a one-point basket to the Scaps to get the ball back for Dante.

The Man called his team's final time out.

Maybe Sam should cover Dante next time, Buzz thought.

But that made little sense. Sam was shutting down another talented player, Robbie Dixon, a tall man who would simply take Buzz down low as easily as Dante was taking him up high.

"Give us a play," the Man told Donna in the huddle. "Let's go to Bill. Can you still set a good pick, Mark?"

Mark nodded, sweat dripping from every pore of his body. His brown shirt was almost black with moisture. He supported his injured knee by leaning on Sam's shoulder.

"No! Let's go to Sam! Inside, like last game!" Buzz urged.

The Man glared at Buzz. He bit back a rebuke. He realized that his teammate was desperate. "Settle down, Buzz," he said soothingly. "I need you to stay alert. We go with Bill, okay?" It wasn't really a question.

"Sure," Buzz said, distantly ashamed, looking down at his sneakers. He had written the letter *I* on the tip of his left shoe and an *M* on the tip of his right. *I.M. Immaculate Mary. I still think we should go to Sam.*

"Good, then Buzz will hang back after he inbounds the ball," the Man continued, addressing the others. "Just in case something goes wrong. No easy baskets on defense. Donna?"

She feverishly scratched the play on her clipboard. They were all familiar with it. Buzz would inbound. Bill would come off two picks and dart across the three point line at the top of the key. The Man would be the second option if Bill was covered, and Sam would be ready for a short jumper on the high post after setting the first pick. Mark would crash the boards and to hell with the bad knee.

"It may be our only chance," the Man finished, letting his words hang in the air, like droplets of water waiting to leave a thundercloud.

Bill would shoot for two points to put the game away.

The whistle blew.

✝ ✝ ✝

The crowd began to roar. This was basketball in its purest form. No clocks. No overtime. Just baskets. Every pick-up game, no matter how royal the surroundings, came down to sudden death.

Down to making the Big Shot.

And just as everyone watching the game—including the people at home watching on television—knew that Dante

Curry would take the final shot for the Infernos, everyone also knew that Bill White would fire the Big Shot for the Scaps.

On the bench, holding Ellie's hand, Donna prayed: *Hail Mary, full of grace...*

The referee handed Buzz the ball on the sideline and blew the whistle to signal the start of the play. Nine players on the court began a brutal ballet of bumping chests, poking elbows, and squeaking sneakers. As Buzz held the ball, waiting to inbound, watching the play develop, it seemed to set up perfectly for the Scaps.

Bill came around the low post, brushing his man off a grimacing Mark Johnson. Despite his fatigue, Bill continued quickly and cut sharply as he brushed off Sam's pick at the foul line, Sam leaned out and bumped the chasing Dante's hip in a rare lapse from perfection...

Buzz released the ball, then stepped onto the court, slightly dazed.

Bill White caught the ball as he squared up for the shot, just beyond the top of the key. Buzz's heart skipped as he realized that it was Dante's turn to labor to recover from Sam's pick.

Bill's feet were behind the line. He began to jump and release the ball with his patented quick-release, all in one fluid motion, his elbow in, his shoulders facing the basket—perfect form...

...He's going to make it, Sam thought...

...as Dante took a long step past Sam and left his feet, extending his long, tanned arm toward the ball as Bill released it, reminding Buzz of a ski jumper in the Olympics...

...Dante nicked the ball with one slender finger...

"Piece!" Bill hollered at the top of his lungs, letting Sam, the Man, and the helpless Mark know that Dante had gotten a "piece" of his shot, and that it would therefore miss badly.

Sam found himself blocked out. Buzz stood his ground, remembering his responsibility to stop the fast break, which was now likely. The Man was too far from the basket to hope for a rebound…

…and Mark Johnson awkwardly leapt from his one good leg with herculean strength, letting out a roar of pain heard in the highest seat in the house; he found a seam between two bodies and slipped through it. He batted the ball away from the Infernos defender…

…toward Buzz, who suddenly was completely aware that he was standing in his favorite spot…

…just as Dante Curry began rushing toward him from the left side…

"Practice," Buzz whispered to himself, focusing only at the impossibly far-away rim, as he cocked his one-hander and released it, willing himself not to think about the blur of Italian lightning streaking toward him…

…and Mark Johnson continued to scream as he landed on his bad knee, the pain echoing up his leg like a hot ice pick being driven into a tree trunk…

…Sam watched the ball…The crowd watched the ball…Donna, Bill, the Man, Ellie…Dante and his Infernos watched the ball—

—as it zipped through the hoop with a snap.

Buzz already had his hands up in the air. Two points.

Scaps 42. Infernos 41.

Chapter Sixteen

1

After the winning shot, Donna sprinted onto the court and jumped on Buzz, nearly knocking him over, reminding a few old-timers in the crowd of Yogi Berra jumping onto Don Larsen after the only perfect game in World Series history.

"We won! We won!" she cried.

"I know! We did it!" Buzz laughed, holding her up with one arm, her hands around his neck, holding his other hand in the air, as Dante's dejected Infernos, doused by defeat, strode by them.

Then Buzz saw Mark, still on the floor in pain, and he lowered his fist, and let Donna down to her feet.

"Donna, Mark's hurt real bad."

She turned to look, and along with Buzz, hurried over to crouch next to the warrior. Others gathered around.

Dante Curry was already examining Mark's injured knee, pressing it here and there, asking Mark questions.

"He's a doctor," someone said.

"I hope it was worth it," the Man said to no one in particular.

Mark heard the Man and smiled.

"It was worth it." Then he looked at Buzz. "Because you hit that shot, my friend. I just knew you would. Hoorah."

Having picked her way down the stands, Maggie rushed up to the scene. She pursed her lips and shook her head, her hands on her hips.

"I'm afraid you're going to need surgery, my friend," Dante whispered, but Maggie heard him.

"So the tough guy's going to the hospital, eh?" Maggie asked.

He grinned sheepishly. "We won, didn't we?"

"Yes you did. Nice play," she replied, trying to hide a smile. "You'll be getting plenty of couch time in over the next few days, I suspect."

The players who heard her couldn't translate the strange code between husband and wife—with the exception of Bill White.

Bill knew she was proud of her husband.

Mark struggled to his feet, and leaning on Dante and Sam, limped back to the bench.

"Well," Bill said to Buzz, watching Mark from the foul line. "Maybe right now you could beat him in a wrestling match."

"I wouldn't bet on it," Ellie said, echoing Buzz's thoughts exactly.

Mark called from the bench. "Party's still at my house! I'll come by after I go to the Emergency Room!"

Suddenly Buzz saw a sharply dressed News Five reporter walking toward him with a cameraman in tow.

"Is that camera rolling?" Buzz asked.

"In just a few seconds," the reporter, Wendy Swedenborg told him.

"Good, then ask me if I'm going to Disneyland like after the Super Bowl and all," Buzz directed her.

Wendy gave him a skeptical look.

"Go ahead, ask me," Buzz said with an angelic smile.

"Camera's rolling," the cameraman said. "Three, two, one…"

"I'm standing here with Buzz Woodward, hero of this year's Revco Ten Thousand championship team. So tell me, Mr. Woodward, do you have any travel plans for after the game? Disneyland?"

"Disneyland? Heck no, lady! I'm going to Fatima!" Buzz shouted, followed by a rebel yell. He turned and gave Donna a convincing but phony hug.

Wendy rolled her eyes. *That's not going on the news,* she thought. She hated these cheesy assignments. *They should have sent the sportscaster.*

She motioned for the cameraman to cut the tape.

Buzz read her thoughts. "Look, I made a lucky shot, Miss Schmorgenborg. By the way, I don't watch television much, so I don't know who you are, but I'm sure you're good at what you do. If you want a real interview, talk to my friends Donna and Bill here. When it comes down to it, they won the thing for us."

Ellie, who was happy she decided not to paint her face with brown lipstick, stood in the background with Buzz with her arm around his shoulder while Wendy interviewed Donna and Bill together. She waved and mouthed, "Hi Bucky!"

A few hours later, fourteen whole seconds of the five minute interview made it on the air, to the cheers of the party crowd at Mark Johnson's house.

It was Donna, who was quoted speaking with perfect aplomb. "I knew Buzz would make that shot. He practiced it five hundred times this morning. He wanted to win it so we could go to Fatima together with the prize money." Her quote had been preceded by a replay of Buzz's long bomb.

The sportscaster followed her sound bite with a smirk.

"Fatima? Isn't that in Saudi Arabia?"

Fake laughter from the ditsy anchor woman followed his quip. He cleared his throat.

"Proceeds from the Revco Ten Thousand go to the Rainbow Babies and Childrens Hospital…"

2

Sam walked up to Buzz and Ellie as they stood next to the Weber grill in Mark's backyard. Sam put an arm around Ellie's shoulder.

"Tell me something, Buzz," Sam inquired.

"Yeah?"

"What were you thinking when you took the big shot?"

"You know how it is. I had a split second to prepare before the ball came to me, and I didn't want to think about how big a shot it was, so, I made believe I was alone, practicing the shot with no pressure on me."

"Funny, I was thinking the same thing, Buzz. I was thinking about you practicing from that spot this morning."

"Really?" Ellie asked. After Mass, she had come to Buzz and Sam's second practice session. "I thought Dante was going to block it."

"I knew he was there," Buzz explained. "But I didn't want to think about him."

Sam glanced back to the house. Through the bay window, he saw Dante sitting on a chair next to Mark, who had a temporary cast on his knee. The surgery was already scheduled for a few days hence, after the swelling subsided.

Donna was with them, gesticulating enthusiastically.

"We might lose our secret weapon, Donna Beck, to the Infernos next year. Did you know she knew Dante back in Little Italy?" Buzz asked.

"Really? So that's how she knew how to outsmart him. Is that a coincidence, or does that count as a signal grace?" Sam asked in reply.

His speech was slightly slurred. He was working on his seventh Bud Light. He was a lightweight.

"I dunno," Buzz replied honestly.

"Because I prayed for it," Sam explained, wondering why he was bringing up the subject. "And it came true."

"What came true?" Ellie asked.

"Buzz's shot went in," Sam explained matter-of-factly.

Wow, Buzz thought.

"Now that's different, Sam," Buzz said, showing his surprise on his face. Ellie looked up at Sam.

"Yes," Sam continued. "I was sitting next to Ellie at Mass this morning, thinking about the game while everyone was going up to get Communion. Then I saw people coming back, kneeling down, praying. Everyone seemed to have something to pray about. Do you people say special prayers? I asked myself. I didn't know.

"So I figured I might as well pray for something. I bowed my head and closed my eyes. I was sitting, not kneeling."

Sam raised the bottle in his free hand and wiped away a mosquito on his forehead with the back of his hand. "And I tried to think of something nice to pray for. I thought about you, and how I was sitting in a church because of you, with this beautiful lady at my side, one week before my wedding…"

Sam trailed off. Completely out of character, he leaned over and gave Ellie a kiss on the lips.

"Sam!" she grimaced. "You smell like beer!"

"And?" Buzz prompted.

"Oh, yeah," Sam replied. "So I tried thinking about something nice for you. So I prayed, 'Dear God, if you're up there, or in there—" Sam was referring to the tabernacle "—please let Buzz hit the winning shot from his spot."

Sam ended by bringing his chin down to stifle a burp. He really was in his cups.

"So does that count as a signal grace?" he asked again, both eyebrows raised.

Buzz and Ellie were both speechless.

"What's a signal grace?" Ellie asked.

"According to Buzz, it's like a road sign from God, telling you you're on the right track," Sam said. "So, does it count?"

"I don't know. It sure is an answer to a prayer. I'm touched, Sam. I really am. I've never made a big shot like that in my whole life." There was real emotion in Buzz's voice.

"I've seen you sink game winners on the Rocky River courts," Ellie offered.

"Yeah!" Sam said loudly.

"That doesn't count," Buzz said modestly. "I like taking the big shot on the courts, but this game was different. It really mattered."

"I disagree, Buzz," Ellie said. "It all matters. You've been practicing game winners all summer. Mark has been a competitor his whole life. Bill White has been shooting well for weeks. The Man was his usual steady self. Sam played his role. I've been watching all of you. I don't know about God answering prayers, but I do know that you guys didn't get lucky today. You earned it. Donna scouted the other teams pretty thoroughly. I was with her. Otherwise, a bunch of priests could have beaten Dantes Infernos by saying a few Masses before they took the court."

Buzz and Sam were both jolted by Ellie's forcefulness in making her point.

After a moment, Buzz said: "You know, you two were really meant for each other." He leaned forward and engulfed them both in a gentle hug.

"All right, huddle up," he said, leaning his head onto Ellie's forehead. Sam hunkered down, and they shared shoulders with arms.

"Listen to me, you two," Buzz continued in a hushed tone. "I wouldn't trade you two for the world. Just seeing you together, happy and all; I would rather have missed that shot than not have you for friends."

Ellie's heart melted toward Buzz at that moment.

In the background, Bill White pressed a button on the CD player. The guitar strings from the Church's "The Milky Way Tonight" came streaming from a speaker placed next to a screened window.

"And you know something else, Buzz," Sam added.

"What?"

They began swaying to the haunting melody as if moved by a slow wind.

"When you made that shot, you know what I said to myself, Buzzboy?"

"What?"

"Thank God."

3

The phone rang in the Beck's kitchen. Mrs. Beck put down her tomato strainer, licked a runny thumb, and picked up the phone.

"Beck residence. May I help you?"

She listened for a few moments. "Okay, I'll get her."

She laid the handset down next to bowl of rising pizza dough.

"Donna!" she called into the living room, trying to hide the excitement in her voice. "Phone!"

Donna pulled herself up from in front of the television set. Her father was in his chair, cleaning up at *Jeopardy!* again.

"Yes?" Pause. "Oh hello!" Donna said excitedly, holding the phone with both hands.

"You've been accepted," the female voice on the other end of the line said evenly. "You can start in four weeks. We'll send you a list of things you'll need to do to prepare and bring with you."

Donna let her head fall back, closing her eyes, and raised her heart to heaven. Her mother clapped her hands together, and let out an elated cry as tears began to form in her eyes.

Thank God! Donna prayed.

The words burst through her soul like a ball through a hoop.

4

Bill White was cutting a felled tree into logs with a chainsaw in the sprawling backyard of Sam's new house in Shaker Heights, having a blast. His shirt was off even though the evening was bringing a slight drop in temperature. He had rushed over after work to help Sam and Buzz.

His back was aching.

In the front yard, on a patch of growth next to the front entrance, Buzz and Sam were digging a bush out from under its roots.

It was two days before the wedding.

"You know, Sam, if you can afford a house like this, you're supposed to be able to afford to hire some gardeners."

Sam laughed. "I can afford you. You're free. This is called keeping overhead down in the business world. Sweat equity in its purest form."

"You got the sweat part down, all right. We'll have to start calling Bill your coolie."

"What's a coolie?" Sam asked.

"Didn't you read your history books in school?"

Sam shrugged.

Buzz shook his head with mild disgust.

Buzz stepped back and leaned on his shovel. Next to him, the taller man lifted an ax into the air and gracefully brought it down on a root ten inches below the ground. The root sliced in two, surrounded by clumps of dirt. Sam had purchased the ax an hour earlier. It still had the price sticker on its head.

"Let's see if that does it," Sam said.

They had cut the bush down to a stump before digging around it. Buzz leaned over and grabbed two branches and yanked. It didn't budge.

Both men took a deep breath. Buzz picked up his shovel and began to dig again, searching for another root.

Sam looked at his house. It was a tudor, modest in size by Shaker Heights standards, with only three bedrooms and a small living room and dining room. A starter home in this old-money community.

The huge backyard, which was enclosed by fir trees planted in the 1930s, was one of the primary reasons why Ellie had insisted upon it—that, along with the hand-carved redwood woodwork inside. The kitchen had been remodelled just a few years ago, which Sam was thankful for, even though Ellie was planning to replace the cabinets. She didn't like the style.

"Too early-eighties," she had explained. She also had plans to remake the basement into a large home-office.

"Can I ask you something, Buzz?"

"Having cold feet about Ellie?"

"How did you know?" Sam was shocked.

"I'm a great guesser, remember? Besides, it's two days before the wedding, and you've been frowning every time you look at your new house. News flash: you're supposed to be thrilled, my friend, not depressed."

Sam frowned. "It shows?"

Buzz pulled his shovel out of the hole and jammed it into the grass. He pulled a pack of cigarettes from his pocket, fished out a Marlboro Light, and expertly popped his Zippo to light it.

Sam waited patiently as Buzz took a few puffs.

"Sam, it's my job as your best man to know these things. It's normal to have cold feet. Forget it."

"But I can't put my finger on it…" Sam trailed off.

He grabbed Buzz's shovel and began poking around in the hole.

"Then call off the wedding," Buzz advised sagely.

"What?"

"You heard me." Buzz raised his eyebrows.

"I can't do that—"

"Because why?" Buzz asked.

"Because we're in love!" Sam said angrily, jamming the shovel in. The blade hit a thick root. "Got one!"

"You see. You just said it. You love her. I'm only kidding about calling off the wedding; I was testing you. You passed. Besides, I hear the band is rockin' and I want to go dancing this weekend and drink free Pepsi.

"You love her. Marry her. Now relax. You're a nervous wreck, man. As your best man, I humbly advise you to take two aspirin, drink plenty of fluids, and call me in the morning. And give me a hand with this friggin' thing."

Sam threw the shovel down, picked up the ax, and hacked three times until he cut the root.

"Hey, Mister Green Thumb, you're gonna get blisters."

"Too late," Sam said, sucking a red blotch between his thumb and index finger. Buzz laughed.

"Okay. I'll play psychiatrist for you. Tell me, Sam, what exactly is giving you cold feet about Ellie? Does she have cold feet too?"

"Not that I can tell. She's as happy as a lark. It's me. Like I said, it's hard to put my finger on it. It's just something in the back of my mind, a nagging doubt. Something she said the other night."

"My lips are sealed. You know, if you were a Catholic, you could be talking to a priest who has counseled fifty gazillion engaged couples."

"Buzz, let's not get into the Catholic thing right now."

"Touchy touchy," Buzz joked, trying to keep the conversation on an even keel. *Sam sure is wired today.*

"So tell me what she said."

"She said she wasn't sure who she was. We were alone together, having a nice conversation, and she kind of broke down. It's like I saw a side of her that I never saw before."

Sam paused. "She said she didn't know who she was."

"Who does?" Buzz asked slowly, purposefully.

"Don't get cute, Buzz," Sam said.

"I'm serious. Look, cut her some slack. I mean, who are you? Who am I? It's the big cosmic question. Who *are* you?"

"I'm Sam Fisk," Sam said without thinking.

"Are you sure that Ellie wasn't, you know, going through her, you know—"

"No, I don't think it was that."

Buzz leaned down and gave a tug on the bush. There was some give, finally. He put his work boot heel on the largest part of the stump, and pushed hard. The stump gave some more. "Almost there. A little more digging. You do it."

Sam picked up the spade and began digging again. The sound of the chainsaw in the backyard came to a halt.

"I suppose Bill is done," Sam remarked, not looking up from his hole. "Boy, he's a bear for work. This is his third night in a row after work. Says his back is too sore to play pick-up, so he drives across town to haul dirt and cut down trees for me."

"He's quite a guy. I wonder why he never got married?" Buzz asked, looking up, as if he could see the backyard through the walls of the house.

"Why don't you ask him, Dr. Buzz?" Sam said a bit testily. Sam's shadow was making it hard to see into the hole.

"Man, would you cut it out. I can't wait until you're married and the good-old, super-dull, stick-in-the-mud Sam Fisk returns."

Sam stopped digging. "Sorry, Buzz. I guess I've got a case of the nerves." He rubbed his forehead with his forearm. "I've never gotten married before. I'm a wreck."

"Forget it. Take it out on me. I think I know what's bothering you about Ellie."

Sam didn't say anything. Buzz took his silence as a cue to continue. Sam resumed digging little clumps of dirt out of the hole.

"You see, when two people get together, they change each other. You and Ellie are changing each other. She's getting mixed up with all these westsiders, too. She's been calling Donna every night since the Revco Ten Thousand. She's reevaluating herself. It's normal. This is Buzz Woodward, amateur psychologist speaking now. You see, you've been *idealizing* her because she's so beautiful and you're so fugly and you can't believe she loves you. A few warts show up, like Ellie's recent, run-of-the-mill, totally understandable, garden-variety identity crisis, and you're flipping out."

"What does fugly mean?"

Buzz laughed. "You never heard of fugly? It's New Jersey slang for, uh, pretty darned ugly."

Sam frowned. "Those are some pretty fancy psychiatric terms you're using there, doc. Is this term fugly supposed to help or hinder my self-esteem?"

"The truth, as Freud said, is always good for one's self-esteem."

"No way Freud said that!"

"Okay. I just made it up. Freud said Oedipus'll wreck ya, or something like that. The point is—your lack of good looks notwithstanding—the point is that Ellie is going to change on you. Just wait until she has a baby, man. It's part of the whole 'for better or for worse' thing. Hell, you might wake up one day and decide to become a Bible-thumping televangelist. Is she supposed to dump you? People change. One day I was a fallen away Catholic, the next day I walk into a church, go to confession, and start reading Thomas Aquinas like I'm eating potato chips."

Sam thought about that. "I can see your point." He hesitated. "It's just that I've been having this horrible nightmare over and over again."

"You havin-zee nightmare?" Buzz twilled in his best terrible German accent. "Und vil shu tell zee Doctor Buzz about deze horri-bell drrrreams?"

Sam ignored the accent.

"I dream that I'm on the wrong side of the court, sinking hook shots into a basket. You, or the Man, or Bill is always telling me not to shoot, but by the time I realize it, it's too late, the ball goes in, and I've lost the game. Donna or Ellie is in the dream, always, sitting on the bench. I've had it four or five days in a row now. I wake up in a cold sweat. The images haunt me during the day. I can't concentrate at work."

Buzz rubbed his chin, then lit up another cigarette. Holding it between his teeth, he reached down to the stump again and gave it a huge heave.

"Rage! Rage, against the dying of the bush!" Buzz shouted theatrically.

The stump came out with a muted ripping sound, causing Buzz to fall onto his bum.

Nonplussed, he took a drag on his cigarette. "Got the sucker!"

"Cool!" Sam rejoiced.

"I think I know how to interpret your dream, Sam."

Sam sat down on the grass next to Buzz. He had an irrational urge to ask to take a puff on Buzz's cigarette.

Nerves.

"Your dream means one thing," Buzz continued, "and one thing only." He paused, watching for Sam to be perfectly still. *Don't smile,* Buzz thought. "It means you're an extremely dysfunctional basketball player!"

Buzz fell back laughing with vim *and* vigor.

Sam punched him lightly in the ribs. Buzz laughed harder.

"Stop it!" Buzz yelled. "You're killing me! A *dysfunctional* basketball player—hah!"

"Very funny, Doctor Buzz," Sam said, finally allowing himself a laugh, but only a short one.

Buzz caught his breath, and sat up, leaning back on one arm. "You know, Sam, Sirach says that any man who puts stock in dreams is a fool."

"Who or what is Sear Rack?" Sam asked.

"Sirach. Sirach was an Old Testament guy who was always giving out advice. You know the quote you read on the top of the Fact and Comment section in Forbes? You know, 'With all thy getting, get understanding?' That was old Doc Sirach. He's got a lot of cool quotes. My favorite is, 'Let no woman have power over you, lest she trample on your pride.'"

"You're kidding, aren't you?" Sam asked, unsure.

"I kid thee not. Anyway, I wouldn't worry about your dreams. It's in the Bible."

"Didn't Joseph have a dream telling him to take Mary to Egypt?"

Buzz squinted at Sam. "You've been paying attention during the readings at Mass, haven't you?"

"No. I just heard that somewhere. Well, does the Bible say to pay attention to dreams, or was Joseph not up on his Sirach?"

Buzz shrugged. "Ya got me. And I hate a Bible-thumper who doesn't even believe in the Bible. You would make a very annoying Protestant."

"Thank you," Sam said placidly. "Where are we going to put this stump?"

"Maybe we can leave it on the treelawn and some town guy will pick it up. It's your town. You never know, in Shaker you might have to recycle the freakin' thing."

"You sure have a mouth on you," Sam pointed out.

"Sorry. There's another quote in Sirach that says to never start using foul language, because if you do, you'll never be able to stop. I started when I was a kid, and therefore, according to Doc Sirach, I'm a hopeless case. After all, it's in the Bible."

Sam chuckled. "If you're trying to make me laugh to help me with my nerves, well, it's working."

"Good, tell you what—"

"—Hey guys, can I borrow that ax?" Bill White called as he came around the side of the house.

"Sure Bill," Sam said. "What for?"

"I want to split the logs. Do you have a splitting wedge?"

"I don't even know what a splitting wedge is," Sam said. "I'm not much of a Harry Homemaker."

"You're gonna hurt your back, Bill. Why don't you call it a night?" Buzz suggested.

"Gee, Mom, thanks for your concern."

Sam laughed. "Buzz is right. Let's head for the adult beverages. Buzz has a special video for tonight."

"What is it?" Bill asked.

"An absolute classic," Buzz explained. "Charles Grodin in The Heartbreak Kid."

"Never heard of it," Sam said. "What's it about?"

"It's about a guy who marries this girl and falls in love with a younger, beautiful woman on the honeymoon. It made Grodin a star. It's really weird, but funny."

"Hey, you just described yourself, Buzz!" Sam said.

"Thank you."

"Is that the kind of movie Sam should be watching two days before he gets married?" Bill asked seriously.

Sam and Buzz exchanged knowing looks.

"I think," Sam said with a smile and a nod, "that it will probably be the perfect movie to watch. I need a good laugh."

After a quick meal of cold Dominos pizza leftover from the night before, they retired to the living room to watch the video.

The only furniture in the room was Sam's couch and the television stand. Neither Sam nor Ellie had moved in yet. There were no rugs on the hardwood floors.

As the plot became more absurd and more hilarious, the laughter from the three men echoed throughout the house.

5

Donna, Ellie, and two of Ellie's classmates from Saint Marys spent that evening at Bucky's house. Sue McCormack, Ellie's roommate in college, was the maid of honor, while Jennifer Towey and Donna were bridesmaids. (Weeks earlier, Sam had asked Ellie to make Donna a bridesmaid so she could match up with Buzz during the wedding after all the formalities were covered, and Ellie had reluctantly agreed. Ellie now wondered why she had been reluctant.)

They had gotten their hair done by a professional stylist Ellie had hired for the evening. A manicurist had also been hired.

Donna didn't dare ask what the cost of all the primping and fussing was going to be, and wondered if she was expected to chip in. She had already been "forced" to spend one hundred and eighty-five dollars on the dress.

The hired help had departed.

Donna had barely uttered a word all night, intimidated by the "career talk" as she thought of it, between Ellie, Sue, and Jennifer. Sue was a lawyer, practicing in a huge firm in Chicago, and Jennifer was a financial something-or-other for General Motors in Pontiac, Michigan.

Sue and Jennifer had greeted Donna politely but did not make a great effort to include her in the conversations. *Maybe that's their way of being nice.*

She felt like a pet.

"Honey, we're going do something about your make-up," Ellie said maternally, as they both admired Donna's new hair-cut at the vanity in Ellen's huge bedroom. Her room was bigger than all the bedrooms in the Beck's house combined.

Donna was both thrilled and terrified by her haircut and style; she had trouble believing that she was looking at herself.

"My sister was going to help me with make-up for the wedding," Donna blurted. *Well, Cindy **will** help me if I ask her.*

"We'll hear nothing of the sort," Ellie insisted. "We'll all help each other tonight; that way we can be certain our make-up doesn't clash with our dresses."

Sue and Jennifer nodded as if Ellie had just said that the world is round and the grass is green. They were sitting on the bed, a mile away.

"Don't worry about them," Ellie leaned in close to Donna's ear so her two friends couldn't hear. "Sue is hopeless; she can't do make-up to save her life, but doesn't know it. I'm doing this for her. Just play along. Trust me, you'll look fab."

Donna could not be sure if Ellie was telling a white lie or not. She wanted so much to believe Ellie, who had been treating her so—and Donna still hated the word—wonderfully since the Revco Ten Thousand tournament. She decided to believe her, because if it was a white lie, it was designed to make her feel good about the whole thing.

Sue and Jennifer were up first.

An hour and a half later, Ellie stood behind Donna, looking into the mirror, and exclaimed with completely convincing candor: "Donna, we've brought out the real you! It's so exciting! Promise me, oh promise me you'll come over on Saturday and let me do it again, just like this, for the wedding! Oh Sue! Look at her!"

"You look fab!" Sue said in admiration. Jennifer nodded.

Donna blushed beneath her blush. She wasn't used to this girl-stuff. She held back tears. *If only they knew where I'll be in a few weeks!*

"Sue, could you help Jen bring us the champagne from Bucky's bar in the den?"

"Sure thing."

After they left, Ellie gently turned Donna around on the pearly white vanity bench.

"Hey, kiddo, we'll make Mr. Buzz Woodward stand up and take notice of Donna Beck, won't we?"

"Well, I suppose so…" Donna looked down.

"Donna?"

"Yeah?" She kept her eyes down, wondering how Ellie's legs stayed so perfectly, wonderfully slim.

"Thanks for being a part of our wedding. It means a lot to me and Sam. It means a lot to me."

Donna looked up. Tears welled in her eyes.

"I'm sorry, Ellie. You're treating me so nice and, and I've been so cold to you—"

"No you haven't. Don't say any such thing! You've always made me feel comfortable, like a friend."

"Maybe…well, maybe I was nice on the outside, Ellie. But in my heart, I was—"

Ellie put a finger up to Donna's lips. They both heard the sound of the other two women coming towards the room.

"Sssh. I understand—maybe more than you know," Ellie finished. "We both love him, don't we? Here, take this. Quick, face the mirror." Ellie handed Donna a handkerchief.

Ellie turned around and cleared her throat just as Sue and Jennifer entered the room. "Let's all toast!"

"Yes, let's toast. What should we toast to?" Sue asked.

"To Love?" Jennifer suggested.

Donna was recovering quickly. *What? We both love him?*

"Let's toast to Sam," Ellie said, sharing a quick, secret smile with Donna.

Donna nodded her head slightly as Sue handed her a glass of champagne.

"Yes, to Sam," Donna seconded with heavyhearted enthusiasm.

They all drank.

✝ ✝ ✝

"Why are they staying in a hotel? With Bucky out of town for the night, there are plenty of extra rooms here, aren't there?" Donna asked later, after Sue and Jennifer left.

They were sitting in the enormous kitchen, drinking tea on a table made from solid oak and finished with twelve coats of urethane.

"You don't want to know," Ellie said.

"No, tell me."

"You can't guess?" Ellie asked.

"Now I'm really curious."

Ellie smiled indulgently. "They said they were going to the Flats. They're both single. It's still early. Even after years of bad relationships, neither one has learned to raise her standards, and well, one or both could meet a man, and…"

After a moment of thought, Donna understood.

"Oh," she said weakly.

A moment of silence passed.

"You were never that way, were you, Ellie?"

Ellie laughed. "Me? No, I have self-respect." Then, after the laughter left her voice, she added, "Like you."

Donna let that sink in. *Should I tell her?*

"El, you know what you told me before, upstairs? About Sam?"

Ellie didn't respond.

"Can you keep a secret?" Donna continued.

"Of course."

"Well, I've been doing a lot of thinking, and a lot of praying, and I've come to a decision…"

Chapter Seventeen

1

The wedding rehearsal dinner was tonight. Summer was springing away, falling into autumn.

Buzz followed Donna out of his apartment to the parking lot behind his building. His car was near the door, next to a green dumpster.

Donna was not comfortable in her new dress. *Great, my dress is dumpster green.*

She felt like she was wearing a cardboard box in the swimming pool. She was self-conscious about her knees. The dress was too shiny. Too slick. Too plastic.

I shouldn't have let Cindy talk me into this dress! It's too short!

Donna had spent two days surfing the malls with her sister looking for this dress. The cost of this dress and the bridesmaid dress had cleaned out her bank account. She was forced to put the wedding gift—a pathetic wall clock she was certain Ellie would throw away—on her credit card. Buzz had chipped in with her for the clock.

She looked at Buzz, who looked happily comfortable in his classy gray suit. Perhaps he was comfortable because it fit so loosely. It was at least a size too large; he had purchased the suit at the Goodwill. His paunch was almost gone, and his face looked thinner. He still had a crewcut, though, and his eyelids were half-closed with that sleepy, almost sly, natural expression. In honor of the occasion, he had applied Dippity-Doo to his hair.

Despite being secondhand, it was a quality suit, a Ralph Lauren. Buzz could stretch a dollar across the Cuyahoga

River. His search for a nice suit had spanned ten thrift shops and five weeks before finding the Lauren. "I may be poor," he had explained to Donna, "but I have nice taste in suits and shoes."

His Johnston & Murphy wingtips, a relic from his prefab chimney days, had been re-soled and shined to perfection.

"You look dashing!" she told him, her head cocked in admiration. "Look at those shoes! I need sunglasses to look at them directly."

"I'm a fan of the whole concept of re-soling, both for shoes and men's souls. It reminds me of confession. And my dad might have been a drunk, but no matter how wasted, he always shined his shoes. I remember watching him in the morning, hacking and coughing, sitting on the bed wearing boxer shorts and a guinea-T, shining his shoes with his back to me. His father was a Marine. Now, I can't feel dressed up if my shoes aren't shined properly."

This brought a smile to her lips. He had just forced her to wait for ten minutes while he shined them. Now they were late.

They paused next to the damaged side of Buzz's Festiva. He didn't have the money to repair it after the accident on the way home from their trip with Sam down the shore. The long, wide scratches on the fenders and panels had started to rust.

They looked like two models placed into a car ad from the Twilight Zone.

Buzz reached to open the door for her, but stopped, taking a good look at her. He whistled softly.

"You look like a million! Truly marvelous, Dah-ling. Your hair especially. It brings out your enchanting smile."

She heard the sincerity, as well as the excitement, in his voice, underneath the gentle teasing. Buzz rarely commented on what she wore or how she looked.

"Go on, Buzz!"

The door creaked as he opened it. His manners made her feel ladylike. She looked at her hands after she sat down. The lovely manicure at Ellie's had helped her convince Cindy not to paint her fingernails green to match the dress. Donna insisted on a neutral, beige color. Her nails looked nice. *Nice and plastic.*

They headed across town toward Saint Ann Church in Cleveland Heights.

"You're kinda quiet, Buzz," Donna said finally, looking across him to Lake Erie as they came through the city.

Buzz smiled. "I've been rerunning this summer in my head. I don't want it to end."

"I do," Donna found herself saying.

"You do?"

She didn't answer him. *Just tell him!*

"Come on, Donna—you holding out on me?"

"No, not at all. I'm looking forward to tonight. I've never been to a place like the Garden Club. I want to enjoy this wedding."

"That's what I mean. I'm going to enjoy the wedding, too, but the whole thing is going to be like a period at the end of a long, really cool sentence."

"What do you mean?" she asked.

"Let's face it: once Sam moves to Shaker, we won't see him much…"

"But his offices are in Rocky River."

"For now," Buzz said darkly.

Boy, Donna thought, *he sure is moody tonight.*

"Buzz, are you okay?"

"You mean, are the blues back?"

She nodded.

"No, I'm fine," he lied perfectly. "We're gonna have fun!"

"That's the spirit," she encouraged him.

✝ ✝ ✝

After the practice run at Saint Anns, the wedding party repaired to the Garden Club in Beachwood. The club was honoring Edward Fisk's reciprocal membership in another country club in Michigan.

Buzz and Donna entered to the sound of a quartet playing Mozart. It was the Divertimento in D Major.

Neither had a clue about the name of the piece.

"Look at that," Buzz said, pointing to an elegant standing ashtray. The initials *GC* had been formed in the sand. Buzz took two cigarettes out of his pack, and plunged them into the sand, forming periods.

Donna sighed. "Oh Buzz! Behave!"

"Yes, of course, milady, I have no idea what came over me! Doubtless, the sad cause is a lack of breeding, to be sure."

Edward Fisk walked up to them.

"Welcome! Welcome Buzz, welcome Donna. My, you look lovely, young lady!"

He took Donna's hand into both of his. Edward's hands were warm, wrinkled, and soft. He was about as tall as Buzz, and had an upright bearing. He had a full head of white hair, and a way of looking a person in the eye without blinking. She wondered briefly if Sam's mother had also been tall.

Donna resisted the urge to respond, "Charmed," and managed to smile. She and Buzz had met Edward after attending an incomprehensible lecture months earlier in the summer.

At least Donna had found it incomprehensible; Buzz understood it perfectly, and told her later it was difficult to hold his tongue during the pleasant but formal dinner that followed. Sam had treated his father and his two friends to a fine meal at the Stouffer's Hotel.

"Was your drive down pleasant?" Buzz asked, attempting to be courteous, but feeling foolish.

"Quite so. Perhaps you and Donna wish to have a cocktail?" Edward motioned toward the bar with an open hand.

Bucky walked in behind them.

"Edward!" Bucky cried with a cigar between his teeth.

"I'll take her, sir," Buzz said quickly.

They scurried to the bar, leaving Edward and Bucky behind.

"Pepsi for you?" Donna suggested.

"Get me a Seven-Up. I'm driving."

She giggled. "I feel so wooden."

"Me too."

Sam came up to them as Ellie placed her purse on an immaculately set table. Donna felt a tinge of an old, worn out envy when she spied Ellie's dress. Silky and elegant, the dress had low cut shoulders. The hem, just above the knees, balanced on the thin line between classy and seductive.

Donna thought (as did just about every movie buff who ever saw Ellie) of Grace Kelly in *To Catch a Thief*. She briefly wondered if Ellie had any acting ability. *She'd take Hollywood by storm if she could act.*

"Donna, wow!" Sam burst out when he walked up. "You really... you really look wonderful!"

Donna blushed.

"And what about me?" Buzz said.

"You look sharp, too, Gwynne," Sam deadpanned, not taking his eyes off Donna. His gaze slowly rose and fell twice, his smile building after each ascent.

Donna felt a spark in his eyes as he stared. She had seen that look before—in her own eyes, as she looked in the mirror in Ellie's bedroom. The look of meeting someone anew. She was not used to being looked at this way by men.

"We have dancing tonight. Will you save a waltz for me?" he asked, breaking his gaze, looking down at his shoes.

"Of course, Sam. I love to dance!"

"Donna, you look stunning!" Ellie cried, hugging her debutante-style: quickly, barely touching, throwing a kiss that made a shortstop zipping across second base on a double play seem methodical by comparison.

Donna felt as if her ability to blush had passed its limit.

"Thanks to your hair stylist," she managed to say with her accustomed bluntness.

The cut of Sam's suit gave the illusion of filling him out. He looked impressive, almost imposing. And completely at ease, as if he had been born in it.

"Time to break up into little groups," Sam said finally, looking to the two small dinner tables.

The entire party had arrived and everyone sat down for the meal. White-gloved waiters served a Romaine salad with cashews and almonds. Buzz was seated with Bucky, Edward, Sue McCormack, Ellie and Sam.

Bucky had brought along his "rent-a-date," a widow from the club who played in his gin rummy circle. Ellie had assured Sam that the arrangement was one of convenience, not love. In return, Bucky attended many of her formal family functions. Her name was Mrs. Gloria "Bunny" Macpherson, wife of the late Mr. Oliver "Binky" Macpherson "of the Cleveland Alternator and Diesel Cam Macphersons," Ellie explained further. "She's an insufferable snob who hasn't worked a day in her life. But Daddy likes her."

Johnny Traverse was also a groomsman, along with a man named John Bambara, whom Buzz had met a few times at Edwards & Associates. They were seated at the other table, along with their wives, Donna, and Jennifer Towey.

Buzz and Donna both refrained from conversation, feeling more and more out of place as the dinner progressed. Finally, veal chops, rice pilaff, and asparagus tips were served.

Buzz cleaned his plate quickly, and was embarrassed to find that no one else at the table was yet halfway through a veal chop. He sat rigidly, his hands on his lap, resisting the urge to play with his fork, embarrassed that the only item left on his plate was a purple salad leaf.

Am I supposed to eat it?

He decided to wait and watch how the others handled the situation.

Then he wondered if it was *grown* purple, or if somebody had to *dye* it that color.

Is there a Garnish Dye Guy in the Garden Club kitchen?

He tried to become interested in Bucky's ramblings about interest rates and the stock market. Discussion moved to local bond issues, school levies, and the merits of the new baseball stadium and whether it would help the local economy.

When Edward brought up a commentary he had recently heard on National Public Radio about the homeless crisis and "the *current* administration's" failure to address the situation properly, Buzz excused himself to go to the men's room.

He was half-expecting to see a black man sitting at a table in the entrance to the entrance of the men's room.

There was a towel man.

He's probably called a Restroom Attendant nowadays.

He was white. *Welcome to the nineties, Buzz.*

After washing his face and re-shining his shiny shoes, he tipped the towel guy a dollar. Then he paced in a hallway filled with red, forest green, and brown carpets, walls, and ceilings. He power-smoked two cigarettes, guiltily stamping them out in another fancy ashtray.

I wonder if they call the guy who imprints the sand design the Ashtray Attendant?

Buzz spotted an electrical outlet next to the ashtray. There he was, the socket man, his old friend, calling out, *"Nooooo!"*

"Hey little guy," Buzz whispered under his breath. "They trapped you here, too, eh?"

Mercifully, the music started up again shortly after he returned to the table. Coffee and cheesecake appeared out of nowhere. Not knowing or caring if it was proper or breaking unspoken rules, he asked Ellie to dance. She graciously accepted. Bucky and Bunny followed them to the floor, along with Johnny and his wife, Eudora.

At the table, Sam watched Buzz walk off with Ellie and sighed. Sam knew that Buzz was not comfortable because Sam wasn't comfortable either.

I'm just better at hiding my discomfort, my friend.

Sam had rejected the country club lifestyle by default the day he quit his job at IBM years earlier in Chicago. He had a sudden, jolting, violent urge to rip off his tie, pull off his jacket, and storm out of the Garden Club. He reached up and pulled on his collar instead.

I'm gonna get neck zits, he thought, detesting the Monkey Suit and all it stood for.

He looked to the other table and saw Donna, her eyes on her hands, silent, managing to look completely alone. She looked up and found him looking at her. She was instantly delighted. It showed on her face. *Rescue me,* her eyes told him.

Sam didn't look down...

The quartet played the Voices of Spring waltz by Johann Strauss. It filled the room like a bouquet.

"I don't know how to waltz," Buzz apologized to Ellen, as he carefully placed his hand on her waist. He tried to ignore the sensation of the supple yet taut fabric of her clinging dress on his fingertips, but could not.

Her perfume was subtle, barely noticeable, enchanting. He was reminded of a documentary about Grace Kelly, Ellie's look-alike. *"She was a genetic perfection,"* one of her directors had said.

She looked into his eyes for a moment and smiled. "I'm sure you're quite good at improvising. Remember, I've seen you play basketball. You're a talented athlete."

And you're charming me, Buzz thought. *And I'm letting you.*

Ellie was in a magnanimous mood, that was obvious.

Wouldn't you be magnanimous on the eve of your wedding? Buzz asked himself.

He found his feet, and let them move on their own, and in his effort to not embarrass himself by looking down at them, looked directly at her.

You are a beautiful woman, he thought, feeling an ache in his heart, hoping she couldn't read his thoughts. *What am I saying!*

He heard Bunny Macpherson laugh with Bucky behind him. Buzz swayed with the music.

He's had to have taken lessons, Ellie thought mistakenly. He was a better dancer than Sam, who had taken lessons as a boy.

She tightened her grip on his hand, letting him whirl and sway more purposefully. She loved to dance. She loved to waltz. Here was an opportunity, she realized. *And on such a lovely night!*

"You see," Ellie said to him. "You're a marvelous dancer. The secret is not letting me lead. Use your natural strength. Waltz with your back and your shoulders, not your legs. Hold your elbow straight like this. See?"

He saw. He slipped his hand onto the small of her back, held his shoulders square—*Like shooting a basketball!* he thought, elated—and instantly felt the control he had over her. It was a rush.

With just a bit of pressure here and there, her whole body went where he willed it.

She was almost as tall as him. They were perfectly matched. She loved being moved so effortlessly. During a turn, she instinctively released a small breath of joy as she threw her head back and to the side ever so slightly, her eyes closed.

"Keep going, Buzz. You're a natural!"

Cool, Buzz thought wildly, his head beginning to spin with the music and the moment and the sound of her sweet words. Even her voice had a dulcet quality that complemented her beauty.

It's no wonder Sam's in love with you. You're—intoxicating.

Better take it easy, Buzz, his conscience piped in.

Not quite sure if he was ignoring or listening to it, he looked around the room until he noticed an outdoor balcony a few feet from the dance floor. *I bet those doors are unlocked.*

"Wouldn't it be cool to dance on that balcony?" he suggested with his own easy charm...

Sam rose to his feet, walked to Donna, then offered her his hand. She took it. He saw Ellie and Buzz walking toward the balcony. Buzz opened the door.

Great idea, Buzz! The weather is perfect!

Everyone was dancing now. Edward was waltzing with Jennifer Towey. Their technique was perfect.

Sam led Donna by the hand to the balcony, where Buzz and Ellie had resumed dancing.

"Hey big guy!" Buzz called over.

Ellie looked at Sam, smiling, and Buzz couldn't help but steal a closer look at her while she turned her head; he admired the perfect skin on her cheek, and the round curve of her jaw, the silky blond hair pulled back over her ears—

Cut it out! he told himself.

Sam smiled back, his big, toothiest grin.

"Do you know how to waltz?" Donna asked him.

"Yes."

"Good. My daddy taught me. He's a trained dancer."

Sam and Donna began to dance, the quartet's music easily drifting past them to the fairways, putting greens, and sculpted stands of trees below them. There was a carved, wooden overhang above the balcony.

While parents and college friends danced indoors, the two sets of friends danced wordlessly for several minutes.

The quartet began another piece, the Waltz of the Flowers by Tchaikovsky.

They did not switch partners. Ellie was relishing her waltz with Buzz too much to want it to end. She was aware that he was admiring her, and she was enjoying that too, taking a kind of innocent delight in her own beauty.

I'm getting married tomorrow, she thought over and over, *and the world is all right!*

Buzz truly was a naturally gifted dancer. She deplored being forced to dance with men who let her lead. Sam? He was okay. She loved him for other reasons. But this, this was different. This was a kind of living art. A rare pleasure that seemed to fit the singular nature of the occasion...

Just a step away, Sam found himself locking his eyes on Donna's. She was also very good at waltzing, and had always looked him directly in the eyes.

They held each other with their hands. They held each other with their eyes. The music held them both.

And Sam, not ready for what was about to happen to him, saw Donna's soul behind her eyes for the first time.

You love me, he finally understood perfectly.

The words fell into his mind in a dream-like fashion, forming as if one word.

You love me completely. There were many ways to formulate the one word. It was just *there,* a single rose blooming in a snow-covered field. *Donna loves Sam.*

There was a seductive rightness to this word. It begged for closure, for complementarity. Unrequited, it seemed half its own self.

It was a rose, a magnet, a love, a flame: a word.

This word, this freshly observed love, had its own vector, its own power of movement. It was a spinning ball heading inexorably toward an iron ring.

He could not deny its existence, its heat, its fragrance. Letting the word guide him, he pulled her closer, vainly trying to grasp the word, feeling for the first time an urge and a stirring that was both exciting and terrifying.

Not at all aware of what he was reading in her soul, Donna was trying to savor her first, and perhaps last, dance with Samuel Fisk. She was aware that she might never have another chance to look so intimately into his eyes.

It surprised her momentarily when he pulled her closer. But she was not used to the ways and whims of formal places like the Garden Club. She assumed his gesture was one of friendship. Besides, he had not held her since the night on the beach, when she had been spooked in the upstairs apartment.

He might never hold me again.

She was saying good-bye.

I used to love you, dear Sam, she told herself, resting her head on his chest, closing her eyes. *Before I found a greater love.*

Their dance had slowed to a simple sway.

Another word fought to take root in Sam's heart. He was keenly aware of this other word, in a far-away place inside, on the very edge of his consciousness. He could deny this other word. He could refuse to speak it. He had the power to delete it like a word on a computer screen.

Ellen, his morning bride, was dancing not five feet away from him, but she might as well have been on the other side of the earth.

A dark evil, concealed as subtly as a spider in the recesses of a rose, sprung to prompt him.

Say your own word, Sam, it whispered innocently. *Donna loves you! Speak your own word in reply. Be a man!*

He desired to speak this false word, to submit to its power, not realizing that the source of this word might be a mind that was not his own, a mind bent upon his destruction. He wondered what it would sound like on his lips, this other word, which *seemed* so lovely, and *appeared* so beautiful, and *sounded* so, perhaps, practical.

His curiosity fooled him. His practical nature ensnared him. The music lulled him. And an evil thing, not Donna, seduced him.

And I love you, too, Donna, he spoke the false word in his heart. Swish.

He closed his embrace into a tighter circle around her, his mouth resting near her ear.

Now say it out loud, a spidery voice, still musical and soothing, urged him.

2

Ellie looked away from Buzz, and saw Donna resting her head on Sam's chest. She looked back to Buzz, who saw a flash of concern in her eyes. She knew she had not been able to camouflage it quickly enough for him.

What's the matter? he thought instantly.

Buzz looked at Donna and Sam. There was something odd about the way Sam was holding her, just standing there, not even swaying to the music.

Buzz snapped to reality with a jolt.

"Ellie, I'm thirsty," he said coarsely, throwing her the first words he found.

"But the song has just begun," she protested as if following a script.

He knew he should make a scripted reply. *She needs to go, to leave.*

Buzz Woodward had just fallen in love with Ellen James, and like an awkward knight from another millennium, he was willing to die for her.

He stood still, looking directly into her eyes, trying to read her, no longer distracted by her outward beauty, desperately wondering how to respond to his newfound, altruistic love, overwhelmed with concern for the only thing that seemed to matter right now: her very soul.

She waited, a confused, horrible fear in her eyes.

He prayed beyond words, and grace answered him beyond time.

*Cut it down. Cut it down. Whatever it is that's got a hold on Sam: **Cut it down.***

But first things first.

He took his hand out of her hand, and removed his other hand from its place behind her back. There was a stillness.

The world kept moving around them.

"I know," he found his voice. "But I'm really thirsty. Let's get a drink."

"Okay," she replied with false casualness, refusing to let herself look at Sam again.

Buzz offered her his arm.

"We're getting a drink," Buzz called over to Sam, slicing into the disturbing reverie.

Sam looked up, and looked at Ellie. There was hurt in her eyes behind the false smile she gave him. He saw it clearly.

Everything was so clear now.

I don't even know you, Ellie, Sam thought. *Have I been walking around in a daze my whole life?*

Buzz and Ellie walked away, past the band, to the bar.

✝ ✝ ✝

Sam turned to Donna. She stepped back, feeling as if she had just woken up from a sound sleep.

"Sam, what is it? You look like you just saw a ghost?"

Sam opened and closed his mouth. He looked down at his shoes, and then up, over her shoulder.

"I think I'm marrying the wrong woman tomorrow."

Air left her lungs with one breath.

"What are you saying, Sam?"

"I said I think I'm marrying the wrong woman. I think— no, that's the wrong word, I know, that I love you. I should be marrying you instead."

His words sank in.

She took another step back, a look of horror on her face, her mouth open. He reached out. She pulled her hand away.

"Don't leave me," he heard himself saying.

Donna Beck, her jaw tight, stumbled backwards, then ran from him. She slowed as she walked by the quartet, then picked up her pace as she hurried by the bar.

Buzz watched her just as she went by; he noticed the distress on her face. He looked back to the balcony. Sam was standing there, uncertainty in his posture.

"Go talk to Donna," Buzz ordered Ellie.

"But—"

"Just go talk to her. Something's wrong."

Buzz left her at the bar, and walked purposefully to the balcony.

Please, God, don't let it be what I think it might be. Sam! I could kill you!

✙ ✙ ✙

Her high heels sunk to the soles in the thick, wet sod as Ellie walked to the gazebo on the grounds beyond the parking lot. A clump of trees formed a barrier between it and the road. She found Donna, weeping, leaning against a pillar. It was not as warm here as on the balcony. A fluorescent fixture filled the gazebo with a dull light, making the frilly white posts and railings seem bluish.

"Don't talk to me! Leave me alone," Donna told her, burying her head in her arm, ashamed of her tears.

"What is it? What happened! Why are you so upset?" Ellie said, putting an arm around Donna. "Come, sit down. Here."

Ellie handed her a napkin that she had mindlessly brought from the bar. It was crumpled and slightly damp from being in her sweaty palm.

They sat together on a white bench in the gazebo. The crickets were loud. Donna blew her nose.

Get a hold of yourself! Donna ordered. *Now!*

"What is it?" Ellie persisted. "Did Sam say something that hurt you?"

Donna realized that Ellie did not know what Sam had said. A nasty little voice whispered in Donna's ear: *You can crush Ellie. You can have Sam. This is your chance.*

No! Donna responded. She shook her head.

"Where's Buzz?" Donna asked.

"He's talking to Sam."

✝ ✝ ✝

"Buzz, you have to help me," Sam pleaded.

"Help you? What's going on? What did you say to Donna?"

Sam turned away and walked to the balcony's ledge. Buzz followed him, pulling a cigarette from his jacket pocket.

"I told Donna that I was in love with her," Sam said, looking out at the shadowy greens.

Buzz soaked in the meaning of Sam's words.

"It happened so suddenly," Sam explained. "It seemed so right. She was in my arms. It felt so right. I realized that I'm marrying the wrong woman tomorrow. Everything is so clear."

Buzz finally found his voice. "You don't know what you're saying."

Sam turned to Buzz. "Yes I do. This is my life we're talking about here. Marriage is a big deal. I love Donna. That's what my dreams meant. Marrying Ellie is like shooting into the wrong basket."

The certainty in Sam's voice slammed Buzz with a force equal to the meaning of his words.

"Wait," Buzz said. He dropped to the floor and began to do push-ups.

"Buzz!"

"Shut up!" Buzz ordered. He stopped at five push-ups, and jumped back up.

"Well?" Sam asked, looking back to the room. No one was watching them. Everyone was still dancing.

"That didn't help," Buzz said, as much to himself as to Sam.

They turned to face the grey trees and dark fields.

"Do you know what this will do to Ellie?" Buzz asked.

"I haven't thought that far ahead," Sam said.

Buzz grabbed Sam's arm and turned him. "I'm gonna pop you, Sam Fisk! You better *start* thinking that far ahead because a lot of hearts are hanging in the balance, my friend, including mine."

"What do you mean by that?" Sam asked.

"You can't call off the wedding, and that's that," Buzz said, ignoring the question. "You just can't."

"Why not? You would. You're not afraid of breaking conventions. It's crystal clear to me that I can't marry Ellie if I love Donna. And I know Donna loves me."

She sure does, Buzz thought. *Maybe that's what she's been holding out on me lately.*

"I can see by the look in your eyes that you know she loves me, too," Sam surmised aloud.

"Why did she just run out of here, then, in tears?" Buzz breathed desperately, grasping at straw.

"I don't know. It's the shock."

"What did she say?" Buzz pressed.

"Nothing."

"That's just great."

Buzz stamped his cigarette out on the fancy floor. "Tell me, Sam; what's really going on here? What's the truth?"

"The truth is: I love Donna. It all makes sense now. It's like you said, I've been idealizing Ellie from the start because she's so beautiful. I don't like this country-club lifestyle. I don't want an expensive house in Shaker Heights. I want to live on the West Side, near my friends. I want to work on computers, and I don't listen to NPR. Ellie's sucking me into a life I never wanted. She can't help it; it's the way she was raised. I need a practical woman, a woman like Donna. Donna doesn't give a crap about appearances."

Buzz was at a loss. He was losing hope.

What if I'm wrong? he thought. *What if Sam is meant for Donna? Who would know better than Sam?*

Then he prayed: *Saint Anthony help me find the words that save souls.*

"Listen to me, Sam, and listen carefully, because our friendship depends on it."

Sam turned from the shadows and looked Buzz in the eye.

"If you don't marry Ellie tomorrow, I'll never talk to you again—"

"That's absurd—"

"Just try me, Sam. I mean every word. The devil has you spinning in circles, man, with phony dreams and false loves. That's how the devil works. He always presents you with something good to take you away from something better."

"I don't believe in the devil," Sam said. "I believe in the truth. But keep talking. I'm listening."

He's listening to me to prove his point, Buzz thought, suddenly enlightened. *If I don't convince him now, I never will.*

"Sure, Donna's always been in love with you, but you were too stupid to see it. You had your chance, a year ago, but you blew it. Love isn't a feeling. It's a decision. It's not a deal you cut. You decided for Ellie a long time ago. You made Ellie fall in love with you."

"I don't know what you're talking about. I never made Ellie fall in love with me, she—she pursued me—"

"And you didn't ask me for advice about sending her flowers and when to call her? Give me a break."

The disgust in Buzz's voice was palpable.

"You wanted her, Sam, and you got her, just like you get everything you ever want. Things come to you. They always have. Your big contracts, your talents; it's the 'Sam Way,' all kindness and easygoing sweet nothings. Your problem isn't Donna or Ellie; it's that you don't even know why people love you."

"You're talking in riddles, Buzz…" Sam replied uncertainly.

"So what? I always talk in riddles. You know I'm onto something. *Love is a decision.*"

"So can't I decide to stop loving Ellie, and decide to love Donna instead? Isn't that what just happened out here? I'm not married yet. I was listening to my heart. You're always talking about how I should believe in things that I can't feel or touch to find God. Well I can't touch whatever it is in my heart, but it's there. It's there right now, as strong as when I first listened to it, ten minutes ago. And it says Donna, Donna, Donna."

Certainty, a concrete sureness, had returned to Sam's voice. It was his calmness that bothered Buzz the most. It all sounded so reasonable. There was no way to reason against it. How do you reason against the heart?

Buzz sighed. *Try again. Please, God, help me.*

"Sam, I know you. I know Ellie. While I was dancing with her just now, I found myself wishing I could have her, that she could be mine. Part of it was an animal desire, as strong as any narcotic. It scared the daylights out of me. She probably didn't even realize what was happening. Should I listen to my feelings and declare that I love her, too?

"That's the kind of thinking that leads to adultery, illegitimate children, and broken hearts. 'It feels right,' people tell themselves, leaving destruction in their wakes. I know what

I'm talking about. I've sailed that ship. I've been fighting these killer demons all my life. They'll destroy your soul.

"If you persist in this craziness, you'll wake up one day, maybe soon, maybe years from now, and realize that even if you decide to stop loving Ellie tonight, you'll have destroyed yourself. You'll have destroyed the one thing that makes you special: your unwillingness to hurt another human being.

"Ellie loves you, man. Can you break her heart? Can you? Can you! Can you break Ellen James's heart?"

"But Donna—"

"Forget Donna, you stupid sonufabitch! Think about Ellie! How can you do this to her? Didn't her mother leave her when she was kid? What did that do to her? If you leave her now, you'll leave a gaping wound in Ellie's heart that will never heal. And that's why I won't talk to you if you call off the wedding. I can't believe it's you saying this stuff. It's not the Sam I know."

Sam opened his mouth, then closed it. "I know what I feel inside, Buzz." His jaw was set.

Buzz closed his eyes and sighed. He felt exhausted. His round shoulders sagged.

"You're not listening to me so I'm done talking, Sam. Ten minutes ago, you were in love with Ellie. I'm going back in. Man, I wish I wasn't an alcoholic, because I could sure use a drink right now. I'll wait for you if you want to talk some more. You've got a decision to make. Only you can make it.

"But I meant what I said. If you abandon Ellie, I'll never talk to you again. You know, I didn't like Ellie at the start. But she's grown on me. I consider her a friend. She's a good girl. She hasn't done one thing to deserve this. She loves you."

Buzz left his friend alone.

Did you really mean it when you said you would never talk to Sam again? Buzz asked himself as he plopped down at his table.

It doesn't matter now. You have to keep your word.

3

Sam found himself alone. He closed his eyes. Buzz's words echoed in his mind: *Love is a decision.*

What's the rush? a little voice tempted him.

"Tomorrow's the rush," he said out loud.

Then I should decide right now, tonight. Donna or Ellie. I love Donna.

Forget Donna!

Do I love Ellie?

Love is a decision, a voice echoed.

Should I love Ellie?

Love is a decision.

I thought Buzz would understand. I thought he would see that Ellie's not right for me. He seems pretty sure about what I should do.

Has Buzz ever steered you wrong?

It's my decision, not Buzz's.

Love is a decision.

What about the dreams? The wrong hoop?

Only a fool pays attention to his dreams.

What about my feelings for Donna?

Feelings are like the wind. They come and they go.

Can you break Ellie's heart?

Can you?

Then, something Buzz said, which at the time seemed like just another Christian nostrum thrown into a jumble of arguments, resurfaced with perfect clarity.

That's how the devil works. He always offers you something that looks good to take you away from something better.

Good? Better? Ellie or Donna?

*No man, **looks** good!*

Buzz, how did you get in my head!?

I'm your friend. And I'm not shutting up. Ten minutes ago, you were in love with Ellie. Can you love her again? Can you hurt an innocent human being?

He looked out at the shadows and lights. Which was which? He closed his eyes, and came close to praying. He remembered looking into Ellie's eyes on the beach, the warm summer light behind her, seeing into *her* soul.

Who are you, Ellie?

The image of another man came to him. The eyes of the man in the painting. The El Greco. *Who are you?*

His father's words floated into his confusion: *The faint heart never captured the fair maiden. You promised yourself.*

Ellie?

Ellie is a fair maiden.

Everyone was mystery. Even himself.

"Who are you?" Buzz asked.

I'm Sam Fisk.

It's not like you, Sam.

It's not like you...

It's not like...

Sam decided.

"Sam? Sam? Are you okay?" Edward asked.

Sam opened his eyes, then turned from the railing.

"Uh, yeah. I mean, yes, father. I'm fine."

The music had stopped.

"It's time to go now," Edward said. "You've got a big day ahead of you tomorrow."

"Yes, father. I know."

✝ ✝ ✝

"You don't have to tell me what happened to you if you don't want to," Ellie said finally. "I'll just wait with you here until you feel better."

"You're so kind. But don't wait for me. Go back in. People are waiting," Donna said weakly. *You're making it easy to make up my mind.* "You'll miss your party."

"The party's over," Ellie whispered sullenly. There seemed to be more than one meaning to her statement.

"Ellie?"

Ellie looked up.

Please, God, Donna prayed. *Please let Buzz talk some sense into Sam before this gets worse!*

"Nothing happened in there." Donna tried to inject cheerfulness into her voice. "Nothing at all. I guess I just had a case of nerves. With the wedding, and my decision to go into the Poor Clares, I guess I just lost it. With the dancing and all. I've always had a special place in my heart for Sam, you know that. I suppose I finally realized that he's part of what I'm giving up. It got to me."

The delicate muscles on Ellie's face relaxed noticeably. A thoughtful crease appeared on her forehead. She sighed.

"Please forgive me," Donna continued, unable to read Ellie's silence. "The way we were dancing… it must have looked like something it wasn't…"

"Oh that?" Ellie waved a hand. "Forget it. You know how these dinners are. You know how men are. I was dancing up a storm with Buzz myself. He's something else. You know how men are."

No, I don't know how men are. Ellie was very convincing. *Maybe she **does** know how to act.*

"It's been a crazy summer for you, Donna. The Revco thing. This wedding. Your big decision. I admire how you're going into the convent. You've got a lot of guts. I told you that last night. But maybe the pressure's getting to you. I know I've been stressing lately too."

"You have? You always seem so, you know, in control."

Ellie laughed. "It's all a front. Divorced kids are great actors. Every shrink will tell you that. I'm a wreck inside."

"What about Sam?"

"What about him?" Ellie asked quickly. It was almost a snap.

Donna didn't reply. *She **is** acting.*

"As much as I love him," Ellie volunteered, "well, this is between you and me, girl-to-girl. Can you keep a secret?"

Donna nodded. There was a spark in Ellie's eye, a spark of anger mixed with disappointment, despite the easy breeziness in her shoulders and hands.

"You know how men are. Sam's no different. I know he's got a dark side. Divorced kids know that. Don't we all have a dark side?"

Has she guessed what Sam told me? Donna wondered.

"I guess we do," Donna said finally.

After a moment of silence, Ellie sat up straight, then said brightly, "Ready to go in, kiddo?"

Donna answered by standing up.

✝ ✝ ✝

The dancing had stopped. Uneaten desserts had been whisked away. The tables had been cleared. It was time to go.

Ellie and Donna came in from the suddenly chilly night. Buzz saw the redness in Donna's eyes. He took her by the arm.

"Are you okay?" he asked in a hushed tone.

"Yes, I'm fine," she said with a sniff.

Edward and Sam said their good-byes to the other guests. Buzz watched Sam carefully, looking for clues.

Sam and Ellie walked alone over to the balcony and came back a moment later.

There was no expression on her face: no happiness, no disappointment. After giving Sam a formal hug and kiss, she left with Bucky and Mrs. Macpherson.

Buzz said to Sam and Donna: "Let's go to the gazebo. One last conversation for the old gang."

A minute later, they were at the gazebo. Sam asked Buzz and Donna to sit on the lone bench. He stood before them, directly under the light, shadows on the sharp features of his face.

"Buzz, I want you to hear this," Sam said, looking at Donna.

"Just get it over with," Buzz said, overcome with pessimism.

Sam shook his head. "It's not what you think. I'll keep it short."

The tall man took a deep breath.

"Donna," he began earnestly, "I owe you an apology. Please forgive me for what I said on the balcony. Forget it, if you can—"

Donna opened her mouth to speak.

"—No Donna. Don't say anything. I was wrong. I had no right to say such a thing. If you can forgive me, I'll be forever grateful."

The words came out of his mouth like shells thrown into the ocean.

I love you! The alien word was still in Sam's heart. He ignored it.

Buzz listened in amazement.

"I forgive you," Donna said, not looking him in the eye.

"I can't make you do anything, but I would ask that you never mention this to Ellie. Have you told her anything?"

"I haven't told her," Donna said woodenly. "And I won't ever tell her. I'll chalk the whole thing up to you having the jitters."

Sam stopped himself from responding. *It wasn't the jitters!*

"Thank you, Donna," he said formally, nodding.

He turned to Buzz.

"Thank you. You're a true friend. I don't have anything else to say." His voice began to crack.

Sam turned and walked off the grounds to the parking lot before they could think of a response. They watched him get into his Honda and drive away.

✝ ✝ ✝

"What just happened? What did you tell him?" Donna asked.

"I told him that I would never speak to him again if he dumped Ellie," Buzz said, melancholy in his voice.

"Oh, Buzz," Donna said, her own sadness creeping up, surrounding her like the chill in the air. "Why does life have to suck all the time?"

She began to cry.

He put an arm around her shoulders. "It doesn't have to suck, Donna. We can find joy in sadness."

"That doesn't make sense," she said between sobs.

Buzz's eyes were dry.

"I don't know if it makes sense or not. I may have lost my best friend just now. But I know he did the right thing. There's always joy in that. I know you, Donna; you would never have had anything to do with Sam if he dumped Ellie the day before her wedding."

"Don't be so sure, Mr. Buzz," she said weakly.

"Oh?"

"Oh nothing. You're right. Something got into him. It's all my fault. We were looking at each other… he got confused, that's all."

"Don't blame yourself," Buzz told her. Her tears had subsided.

After a long while, she said, "Ironic, isn't it? He could have had me any time he wanted. Now he can't. Ever."

Buzz was silent. He sensed she wanted to tell him more.

"I'm going into the Poor Clares next month," she said with resolve, lifting her head and shoulders. "Sam didn't know. If he did, none of this would have ever happened. He was about to abandon Ellie over a ghost."

"Donna! The Poor Clares! Why didn't you tell me?" There was a small hurt in his voice.

"I tried to tell you. You were so happy about going to Fatima that I wanted to wait until after the wedding. You were so happy about the wedding, too! I didn't want to distract you.

"Oh, there were a million reasons that seemed so important an hour ago. Now they seem stupid. I didn't find out that they accepted me until a week ago. I was hedging my bets, thinking I could change my mind and only my parents would know that I chickened out. Boy, was my timing lousy."

"You can say that again," Buzz said automatically.

"My timing was lousy."

He laughed lightly.

"Donna?"

"Yeah," she said, looking up at him from her cradle in his arm.

"I love you, you know," he said sadly.

"Yes, I know. It's the latest fad."

A heavy silence ensued.

Donna spoke first. "I don't think Ellie will ever know how tempting it was to tell her what Sam said to me on the balcony."

"What stopped you?"

"I don't know. It wasn't one thing." She paused. "I gambled that you were trying to talk sense into Sam. The Poor Clares. God's grace. Mostly, though, it was Ellie. She's been so nice to me lately. She's a good girl. I was wrong to judge her so harshly when I first met her. Did you know that she went to confession with me this morning?"

"You're kidding! That's wonderful. What happened?"

"Last night, I told her I was going into the Poor Clares. She asked me if she could get me a gift or something. I asked her to go to confession and she agreed. She met me at Saint Chris this morning. I called ahead and arranged for Father to be in the confessional and everything. She hadn't gone since she was a freshman in high school. You know how it is nowadays."

"Amazing."

"Yeah."

"I mean, it truly is amazing," Buzz added. "There's probably a million girls like Ellie, good-hearted and broken like the rest of us, even though it doesn't show on the outside, who would go to confession if somebody just invited them."

"I disagree," she said kindly, slowly shaking her head. "You have to have friendship first. If I asked her last month, I'm certain Ellie would have politely declined my invitation.

"We just started warming up to each other. A lot of it has to do with my decision to be a Poor Clare. She must have felt it, or her guardian angel told her soul or something like that. Or at least that's what I thought. Sam was no longer between us."

Buzz contemplated her point.

"So you're saying the real problem is that there aren't enough good Catholics making friends with people like Ellie, who was never really given the fullness of the faith."

Donna nodded. Buzz had a sudden thought.

"Will they let me visit you when you go into the convent?"

Donna's heart sank.

"No. I'm giving you up. And everything I love in the world. For a greater love. After tonight, I'll never doubt my vocation again. But you'll be in my heart, you know that."

"I know that," he said, finding joy in sadness. "Let's get out of here. It's getting cold. And I hate country clubs."

"Me too."

4

Buzz was not familiar with the East Side, and decided to pick his way north through side streets to I-90. The Shaker Heights area was a maze of winding curves. It was dark. He became disoriented, then lost.

"Where are we?" Donna asked fifteen minutes later. "Oh, there's an exit for 271!"

"We've gone east!" Buzz exclaimed, exasperated.

Donna sighed. The emotions of the night, and the late hour had brought a bone-weariness to both of them. She rested her head and closed her eyes.

There was construction on 271. The highway was practically devoid of vehicles. Buzz watched the orange drums whisk by his little car. The effect was hypnotizing. He took mental snapshots of the idle construction vehicles parked randomly in the work zones to keep himself alert. Then, jutting out dangerously close to the driver's lane, he saw a large, oddly-shaped machine. He recognized it. It was a cement cutter, with a large, round saw blade…

He bolted wide awake. *Cut it down!*

The words electrified him.

"Donna? Donna! Wake up."

"Wha?" she asked drowsily.

"Wake up. This is important."

The urgency in his voice was like a slap.

"What it is? Are we in danger?" She sat up and rubbed her eyes.

"No. Not us."

"What are you talking about?"

"Sam. Tell me, what would you do if you were Sam, and you had an evening at the Garden Club like he just had?"

Donna was confused. "I don't know."

"Would you pray when you got home?" The pitch of voice rose almost maniacally.

"Yeah, I would pray…" It hit her. *I would pray.* "But Sam doesn't pray. He doesn't know how."

"You wanna know something, Donna? Tonight wasn't like Sam. Did you notice that? Sam wasn't Sam. It wasn't like him. There was an edge in his voice when I talked to him on the balcony that I've never heard before. I even said to him, 'You don't sound like Sam.' Something fishy was going on."

"What are you driving at?" Donna asked, following every word carefully.

"Maybe something evil got to him…"

"You're giving me the creeps, Buzz."

"Good. The poor guy. He's been spun around in circles. It must have taken a lot out of him to say what he said on the gazebo. You could tell his heart wasn't in it. I bet he's getting pounded from every direction right now. All alone."

"We've got to do something. The wedding is—the wedding's hours away! Oh Buzz," Donna's voice had a sudden tone of despair. Buzz noticed it.

"Relax," Buzz said, smiling in the dark.

"Huh?"

"Come on, little one. Get with the program. Where you goin' in a month?"

"The Poor Clares?" Donna guessed weakly. *Enough with the riddles!* Her heart leapt out for Sam, reaching into the darkness beyond the highway.

"And what do the Poor Clares do?"

"Pray!"

"They don't just pray, little one, they intercede. They *intercede.*"

He turned his eyes from the road and looked at her. She saw the joy in his eyes under a passing lamp from above.

Buzz felt like crying with joy!

"Stop with the riddles, Buzz! What's going on in that crazy, beautiful head of yours?"

They came out of the construction zone. A huge yellow arrow blinked in front of their car, directing them toward I-90.

"Don't you see it, Donna? Sam's not Sam? The night before his wedding. Us getting lost! We were supposed to get lost! Damn! I mean, Praise God!

"Strap on your seat belt, Little Poor Clare. We're going to Fatima after all! Only we're not going to Fatima. We're going to Lourdes instead! Right now!"

*Cut it **down!***

She felt the acceleration as Buzz unconsciously put pressure on the gas peddle in his excitement. He was out of breath. It gave Donna a chance to solve the riddle.

The Lourdes Shrine, clicked in her head. *It's the next exit!*

"There's a big-ass ugly old evil thing pinning *our friend* to the ground," Buzz continued, finally calming down. "Somebody's gotta cut that sucker down. The battle is not over."

Donna was now fully caught up in his enthusiasm. *Everything matters,* she thought.

"Everything matters," she said with a clear voice.

Buzz heard her calm battle cry and was instantly worked up again.

"That's it! Everything matters! The Lourdes Shrine! Stuff by the side of the road! The world! I love the world! I love the guy in the electrical socket! If only everybody could see what we see every day, my sweet, lovely, little one!"

His eyes were filled with tears. His voice was cracking with every word. She never loved him more than at this moment.

My crazy Buzz!

She fought back tears.

Somebody's got to stay sane if we're gonna pray.

"Buzz, you just get me there alive. I'll pray enough for the both of us."

✛ ✛ ✛

The wrong-hoop dream came back to Sam with a vengeance that night. In desperation, after waking up for the third time, he went to the kitchen and gulped down four aspirins and a beer.

He fell off into a fitful sleep. *I'm marrying the wrong girl. I'm marrying the wrong girl. I'm marrying the...*

In the dream, he was wearing nothing in a jungle garden. Snakes everywhere. He heard something moving in the bushes. The hair rose on his skin...

✛ ✛ ✛

Donna ran to the grotto.

She threw herself down on the kneeler, oblivious to the chill and the dewy moisture on the railing. Her dress felt more plastic than ever. She looked up at the plaster statue of the Immaculate Conception, and it disappeared from her view.

In its place, she saw Our Lady in her mind, as she always did, and asked, like a child asks: *Please, Mother, I have a friend. I've told you about him so many times. Take care of him tonight. His name is Sam. You know him. He doesn't know how to pray. I offer you these roses for him.*

She pulled the rosary beads from her pocket. She had worn them in over the summer, in preparation for her own wedding.

Next to her, Buzz prayed like this: *Jesus. Jesus. Jesus. Sam. Sam. Oh, I don't know what to say! Just cut that nasty, ugly thing out of Sam's life. Right now! And if you don't want to listen to me and I don't blame you because you know I'm just a broken-down drunk, then listen to this little one, Donna, right here next to me.*

"Let's start, Buzz," Donna said softly. Her voice was as peaceful as his had been manic minutes before.

"Sure, little one."

For the next forty-five minutes they prayed a full Rosary, in their own ways; he with blind faith, feeling nothing; she with visionary faith, feeling everything.

✝ ✝ ✝

God allowed Sam, who had no faith, to see the monster. It was a prehistoric dragon. The thing had red-black, coarse leathery skin. It hurtled like a lance through the giant, scaly green leaves.

Sam was paralyzed, like a deer in headlights. His feet sunk into the bubbling muck. He tried vainly to pull them out of the mire.

The evil thing came to him. Towered over him. Breathed on him.

From the bottom of Sam's diaphragm a primal cry of complete, unfettered fear rose through his body.

But from his lips there was no word.

The enormous jaws opened, gushing saliva and mucus, thick teeth-razors ready to rip him to shreds, preparing to pull his head from his torso as unbearable heat—dragon's breath—engulfed his silent scream...

The enthusiasm and concentration of Buzz and Donna's prayers faded as time, cold, fatigue, and repetition weighed down upon them. They both felt it.

Are we crazy? he questioned.

Are we being silly, chasing dragons that don't exist? she wondered.

It all mattered.

The jaws closed on Sam, and he was slain by his nightmare. Then he resurrected into another dream. His eyes were closed.

He smelled grass.

He inhaled slowly, deeply. The scent was—perfect. He lingered on the fragrance of roses and lilacs—balanced.

He opened his eyes and found himself sitting by a pond, his feet in cool water. He was wearing Levis and a perfectly clean white cotton T-shirt.

He looked around. As far as he could see was a harmonious natural beauty: verdant fields and rolling hills, roses and lilacs everywhere. Tall strong oak trees climbed the sky; they were ageless, as if no mere man could cut them down...

...then he heard the music. It was simple music, melodic and balanced—harmonious.

He knew the instrument's name. It was a lyre.

He heard a boy's voice drifting over the fields, singing. He could not make out the lyrics. Sam did not see the boy, but knew the boy could hear him.

"David, come closer," Sam said peacefully. "Sing for me."

Sam knew the boy was a king.

Who is the queen?

The boy, still unseen, began to sing, his voice embodying strength, wisdom, youth, and above all, balance, for in this place, all things mattered.

Sam heard this song:

The Lord is my shepherd, I shall not want.

He maketh me to lie down in green pastures, he leadeth me beside the still waters, he restoreth my soul.

He guideth me in paths of righteousness for his name's sake.

Yea, though I walk through the valley of the shadow of death, I shall fear no evil, for thou art with me, thy rod and thy staff, they comfort me.

Thou preparest a table before me in the presence of mine enemies. Thou anointest my head with oil, my cup overfloweth.

Surely goodness and mercy shall follow me all the days of my life, and I shall dwell in the house of Lord forever.

When the song ended, he sat peacefully by the water, waiting for the word of the Lord.

Lord, who is my queen?

The word came.

"She is in my heart!" he called out joyfully.

She had been there all along.

Ellie.

✝ ✝ ✝

She stood by the side door of her parents' house. The motor of Buzz's car was running. He had jumped out to open the creaky door of the Festiva for her.

"Do you think it worked?" Donna asked.

"What worked?"

"Don't be silly. The prayers."

He looked at the stars, and imagined a little piece of the True Cross way above their heads, circling the world.

It's there.

"Sure. It worked great. Get some sleep. We got a wedding to go to tomorrow."

She smiled, hugged him with a passion, letting him go with a shudder, then put her key into the door.

Chapter Eighteen

1

Buzz waited calmly in the sacristy, feeling clean and dapper in his rented tuxedo. Sam was late.

Finally, the tall man walked in. There were dark rings under his eyes. He smiled at Buzz; they shook hands.

"Well?" Buzz asked. The question had a hundred meanings. He glanced at the priest on the far side of the room. They were out of earshot.

"If you're worried about last night, quit worrying. I'm over it. I had some weird dreams last night. I don't quite remember any details."

"Now you're the one talking in riddles," Buzz said with a broad smile.

It's going to be all right.

He thought of the Lourdes Shrine, and the peaceful look on Donna's face as she prayed, her eyes closed.

"You're wrong about dreams, Buzz. There are two kinds. Sirach dreams and Joseph dreams," Sam continued cryptically. "But to get to the point, the only point that matters this morning: I'm marrying the right woman. I love Ellie. I don't love Donna. If love is a decision, then I never did."

A long, motionless silence held between them.

Sam cleared his throat. He opened his arms. The two men embraced.

"Thank you," Sam whispered.

"Forget it," Buzz croaked, hugging Sam tighter.

"I can't. You're the best. You're a true friend."

"Aw, hey. I'm just doing my job. I'm the best man."

Sam chuckled at the weak pun. They ended the embrace.

The priest finished donning his vestments and walked over. Two altar boys came out of a side room. Buzz handed them an envelope with four ten dollar bills in it—their tip.

"Ready, gentlemen?" Father asked.

Months later, during his darkest hours, the only image Buzz seemed to be able to recall from the wedding and the reception was that of Ellie's lovely face, her eyes closed, her head back, as dozens of people whirled past them as he danced with her.

"You're my knight in shining armor," she had whispered to him on the dance floor, making his heart soar and expand until he thought it would burst.

There are different kinds of love, he kept telling himself then. *Maybe friendship is the best kind.*

Sam and Ellie flew to Aspen for a week-long honeymoon. Neither knew how to ski. The glamorous town was not crowded in the off-season. Skiing was not a priority, anyhow.

They rented a chalet off the beaten path, and wandered into town each evening to enjoy the fine restaurants.

On the last night of the honeymoon, there were two unexpected developments.

Ellie became pregnant—by accident. Of course, neither became aware of this development until weeks afterward.

The second development occurred when Sam asked Ellie if she would agree to selling their new house in Shaker Heights before they even moved into it.

They were enjoying a cup of tea, sitting Indian-style on a bear-rug before a crackling fire. They were dressed in practically nothing; it was roughly twenty minutes after their child had been conceived. Three angels hovered above them now.

She raised an eyebrow when he made his halting request to sell the house. The strange stuff that had occurred during the rehearsal dinner had not been mentioned between them. Somehow, both knew that Sam's request was related to the events on the balcony.

"Sure thing, Sam," Ellie told him. "Under one condition."

She saw the surprise in his eyes. He had been expecting a heated debate or at least heavy resistance.

"What's the condition?"

She let him wait, sipping her tea.

I love that house, she thought sadly. *But I love you more.*

She knew this meant leaving Bucky in Beachwood and having to attend parties in small backyards in Rocky River. Somehow, these prospects didn't seem so distasteful anymore. She was even attracted to them.

And I can watch Buzz and Sam play basketball!

"The condition is non-negotiable. If we're going to live on the West Side, you'll have to buy me a house on the water. I'll pick out the house, too—don't worry about that. I want to look at the lake when I wake up in the morning."

Shaker Heights for a view of Lake Erie. Even Steven.

"That's all?" he asked, not breaking her gaze.

"You won't say 'that's all' when you find out what a house on the lake in Bay Village costs, honey," she replied sweetly.

Maybe I can get Bucky to move to the West Side?

She would always be a step ahead of her men. Divorced kids can be that way.

She leaned over her tea and gave him a long, loving kiss. She pulled her lips away slowly, and looked closely into his eyes. She thought of how his whole body had shaken with nervousness the first time she had kissed him in his car at the Garden Club.

The burning in her belly from that night was still there, a bit duller because of the events on the balcony, but the dark image of Sam holding Donna had been obliterated by many other, more passionate memories on this mountainside in Colorado.

The balcony image had also been overlaid and obscured by another, softer image: that of Donna kneeling in a pew at Saint Christophers, praying so earnestly as Ellie opened the door to the confessional the morning of the rehearsal dinner.

Ellie had put three men behind her in that confessional, men she had slept with but had never loved. She felt she owed Donna for that. Ellie felt that if Jesus could forgive her for sleeping around, then she could forgive Sam for an indiscretion with Donna that had led to nothing.

Everyone has a dark side, she thought now.

"I love you, Sam," she said confidently.

"I love you, too," he replied hoarsely.

It was a match made in heaven. And on earth.

2

Three months later, on a Sunday morning, Sam still didn't believe in God, or heaven, or the devil, or hell, or angels. But he was working on believing in saints, and if there was a heaven, he now knew what it sounded like.

It sounded like the Poor Clares singing behind the screen during Mass.

I wonder where Buzz is? he thought, disturbed, trying not to draw attention to himself while looking past Ellie in the small chapel of the monastery. It had been Buzz's idea for them to go to Sunday Mass here on a regular basis. *No sign of him.*

Sam was becoming more familiar with the parts of the Mass, and the priest assigned to celebrate here was a good homilist.

And my father would appreciate the music. It's a shame.

More and more, Sam was coming to appreciate the cultural aspects of Catholicism, despite his lack of belief.

There was a simplicity to the lessons Jesus taught in the Gospels. There was a practicality to having a professional scholar enlighten and flesh out those lessons. The ritual of the Eucharistic prayer, especially when done with the reverence shown by Father McBride here, was comforting, even beautiful. He even tried, vainly, to pray, as the others went up for Holy Communion. He was amazed that half the time, Ellie couldn't remember what the subject of the Gospel readings had been ten minutes after leaving Mass. Sam rarely forgot, and found the simple parables of Jesus or the points of the homily staying with him for several days...until the next Sunday rolled along.

It's a nice routine.

My father is foolish to scorn these rituals. This, too, is high culture; what harm is this to society? It's no wonder the museums he loves so much are full of art produced by Catholics. I wonder what he would think of Catholicism if he went to Mass every Sunday?

Sam had no illusions that he or his father would ever receive the gift of faith. The few signal graces from summertime had stopped completely.

Faith just isn't for me, he concluded. *Or it would have come by now.*

That's okay. Donna has enough faith to make up for all of us. She has sacrificed her whole life for her faith.

Somehow, even though Donna had not said so explicitly, Sam, Ellie, and Buzz all felt that she had sacrificed her life *for them* in particular. They knew she prayed for them every day in the hidden chapel not thirty feet away.

Sam's first reaction when Ellie told him during the wedding that Donna had decided to become a Poor Clare was: *What a waste. Who would want to spend the entire day praying?*

When he mentioned this to Ellie, she had responded: "Is it any more a waste than you spending the bulk of your day screwing around with computers? I respect her for following her dreams. She wants to pray. She says it makes her feel complete."

He squeezed Ellie's hand now. She looked at him and smiled. Ellie no longer skipped Mass on the odd Sunday.

I guess she likes it here, too. I wonder when the baby will start to show?

It was not unusual for Sam's thoughts to skip around like this during Mass. Outside this chapel, unlike Buzz, Sam was single-minded by nature and habit. Mass had become a time for Sam to relax his brain; it was a time to step away from the rush of modern life, the pressures of running a successful company, even the insulated existence of being married. He often let his mind wander from subject to subject during this hour of peaceful culture. Maybe the Catholics here were supposed to pay attention, but as a nonbeliever, he thought he was within his rights.

The chapel was shaped like a *T* and attached to a larger building that housed the nuns. In effect, there were three chapels in one. Thirty people could fit into the "public" chapel, which formed one end of the top of the *T.* Until the Poor Clares sang, it was easy for a newcomer to mistake the white wooden screen to the right of the altar for a wall. It was here, to the side, where the Poor Clares attended Mass in a tiny second chapel. They spent the majority of their days, however, adoring the Eucharist in a third chapel that was opposite the public chapel. There was a small opening in the wall between the public and private chapels in which a monstrance was placed so both laymen and cloistered could adore Jesus from their separated worlds.

Buzz had mentioned to Sam that Notre Dame's alumni magazine had featured an article interviewing Phil Donahue, a Notre Dame graduate who had grown up nearby. The television personality was now a vocal, practically daily critic of the Catholic Church.

Phil used to serve Mass here when he was a kid, Sam thought, trying to picture the scene in his mind. *Was his hair white when he was a kid? Weird.*

Sam admired the public chapel as a perfect marriage of beauty and simplicity. Beautiful statues represented the Poor

Clares' king. The simple architectural structure exemplified their vow of poverty. Spare, exquisite wood carvings portrayed the stations of the cross. Simulated-stone linoleum covered the floors to accommodate the often wet, slushy weather brought in on pilgrim's feet.

So this is where Donna works.

Outside, a tall brick wall surrounded the spacious grounds where the nuns recreated, worked, and prayed. Some of the Poor Clares here, Ellie told him, had not seen the world outside the walls for decades.

"Wow," Sam whispered under his breath.

It was Communion time now. Others climbed by him to go up for Communion. The singing began again. The feminine harmonies of the sisters were truly—well, angelic. Their singing reminded him of listening to a beautiful orchestra. It was hard to believe that Donna was behind the screen, playing her part. *Weird.*

He missed her. The morning of the wedding, he had woken up with his love for her intact, but his desire *to possess her* was completely gone. He did not remember the details of his dream in the green pastures, only that marrying Ellie was the right thing to do.

Ellie is my queen, was the word that popped into his head that morning. And that word had stayed with him to this day.

He watched his wife come back from Communion. She knelt down to pray.

I wonder what she's praying about? he thought.

Dear Lord, why did you let me get pregnant? she asked silently. *I don't want to be a mother yet! Help me!*

To Sam, she appeared completely serene. He envied her. He knew he was on the outside looking in.

All around him, nuns and laymen were pouring their hearts out to the Word Made Flesh.

His mind wandered to his financial affairs. When he came home from the honeymoon, he wasted no time hiring subcontractors to refinish the wood floors in the Shaker Heights house, then invested several thousand dollars into the landscaping, which was uncharacteristically shoddy for the high-brow town. Two weeks after he put it on the market, with his typical golden-touch, he sold it for a net ten-thousand dollar profit. This made up his loss on the original closing costs, and even covered some of the closing costs on their new home in Bay Village. Fortunately, Ellie had fallen in love with a small cape cod on the lake that was only modestly more expensive.

His golden touch had extended to Edwards & Associates. The new girl, Amy, had turned out to be a Johnny Traverse clone. She had just closed a multi-year deal to redesign, install, and maintain the network systems for one of the biggest banks in Cleveland. Over the course of the contract, the deal was worth several million dollars in fees (and initially, several months of long hours for Sam, who again needed to recruit and train more employees).

Amy had even managed to get the first six months payment up front. His cash flow was excellent, and along with heavy profits from several other "bank jobs," as Johnny had taken to calling them, Sam planned to share out a large portion of the year-end profit in the form of bonuses to his workers. He calculated that he would be able to give a seventy-seven thousand dollar bonus to himself. He didn't feel the least bit guilty about his bonus. Johnny would get a hundred thousand, and Amy almost fifty. It was good to reward hard work—

"Sam?" Ellie whispered, looking down. Everyone had stood up.

"The Mass is ended, go in peace," Father McBride intoned.

"Thanks be to God," Sam said, noting the irony of the response.

They walked out of the chapel. Ellie noticed a poorly designed flyer on a table in the exit hallway.

Maybe I could help them produce better-looking, more effective product literature? she thought, not realizing that she was responding to grace; grace speaking to her in her own language.

3

"I've been wondering what to do with my bonus after the year ends," Sam told his wife as they drove north on Rocky River Drive toward Hilliard.

He looked over at her; she was letting her ponytail down, and the willowy blond hairs were scattering in the cold wind. She liked to ride with her window half down, even on cold December days.

"The way I see it, we have two options. Invest the bonus or buy something with it," he continued, his eyes back on the road. "I was talking with Bill White, and he's investing in tax-free municipal bonds. Or we could splurge and buy a BMW or something. I just got a thing in the mail last week from them. It's uncanny how these marketing guys figure out who to send their stuff to. We could splurge.

"Or, we could go for remodeling the new place. You know, add a deck, new floors, new furniture: the whole nine yards. That's sort of like the best of both worlds because it raises the value of the house. Seventy grand sounds like a lot, but it isn't, because after taxes—"

He stopped talking. Something was wrong. She hadn't made a sound when he mentioned remodeling.

"Ellie darling, are you listening to me?"

He glanced over and saw that she was reading the flyer she picked up at the chapel.

"Sam. We have a third option. When was the last time you gave anything to charity?"

"Charity? Me? Well, you know, there's the annual shake-down from the United Way at work, but that's like taxes, really. Those guys never let up. Then there's our membership in the Szell Society for the Cleveland Orchestra."

He didn't mention the couple hundred bucks he slipped to Buzz every so often to help with child support.

"How much did you give out of—let's see, what did you make this year, bonus included—two-hundred and forty thousand dollars?"

"I don't know. Couple thou," he said, feeling slightly uncomfortable. "But after taxes, with the wedding costs, the new house, that's not as much as it seems. I know where this is headed. What's on the flyer?"

"I'll get to the flyer in a sec. Spare me the poor-mouth lecture, Sam. I have a degree in finance. I know what the taxes are. I hate it when you talk about money and sound like Bucky and his friends at the Garden Club. You know what I gave out of my salary of thirty-four thousand?" she asked, a hint of smile on her lips.

"I have no idea." The comparison to the Garden Clubbers hurt. *I bet she gave more to charity than I did.*

"Nothing," she said. "Not a red cent."

"Nothing?"

"Nothing," she confirmed. "And I feel like a cheapskate."

He felt the same way. He hadn't really paid much attention to charitable giving, despite his large income. Mostly, he thought about how to invest his money or hide it from the tax man. Even his gift to the United Way had been partially a way to beat Uncle Sam out of a few bucks; the government was insatiable. Giving to charity was for the future—sometime, but not now.

He thought now of Buzz on the beach in New Jersey, saying, "Sometime never came."

"Me too," he said softly.

She heard the smallness in his voice, and allowed him to digest it.

A few minutes later, they pulled into the long driveway of their new home, and drove around back to the garage. They got out and walked to the edge of the backyard. A cyclone fence shielded them from the danger of a fifty-foot cliff, filled with wild shrubs, trees, and even a few pieces of garbage.

They looked at the lake, which stretched as blue as an ocean as far as the eye could see. Unlike an ocean, there were no whitecaps or waves. Despite the cold temperature, it was not windy today. The cityscape of Cleveland was clearly viewable to their right, ten miles away. The view was spectacular.

He stood behind her, folding her in his arms, looking over her shoulder at the lovely scene. Without turning, she reached up with a leather-gloved hand and cradled his cheek.

"God has been good to us, Sam."

He didn't respond.

"Sorry," she said. "Sometimes I forget."

"Don't worry about it. What's on your mind? What was on that flyer? Does Donna's convent need a few thousand bucks for something?"

"More like a hundred grand," she said without breaking stride. "Their chapel is too small. They have more postulants than they can fit into it. Five more came in with Donna. They've raised almost two hundred thousand by cashing in a few bequests, but they're tapped out. They didn't even make up the flyer I was reading. One of the people who goes to Mass there every day did. It's signed Dan Peplin."

"I thought there was a problem with dwindling vocations?" he asked, remembering something Buzz had mentioned one time. *Or was it Mark Johnson?*

"Not for contemplative orders like Donna's. Many are growing according to the flyer. I want to help them, Sam. I want to help Donna."

"That chapel is kinda like their office, isn't it? They get their business done in there," he observed. "Fine. How much should we give, five, ten thousand?"

"Why not all seventy-seven?" Ellie asked.

It was her first "close," as she was taught in business school. Well trained, she waited in silence for his reply. She waited thirty seconds.

"How serious are you about this, El?"

"I won't take no for an answer."

"And you're willing to give up remodeling the house or a BMW?" he asked.

"Isn't that the whole idea? Donna gave up her whole life."

"I don't know, Ellie. That's a lot of money."

"Not for you," she said. *He doesn't want to do it.* "Besides, you can write it off."

"Things could go south at Edwards. Johnny could listen to those headhunters who call him every other day and jump ship—"

"Oh cut the crap, Sam. Are you going to give her the money or not?" Ellie was not feigning impatience.

"I'm not even a Catholic!"

"What does that have to do with it? Those nuns need more office space! They can't go out and earn the money themselves!"

Her exasperation was complete. She turned around to face him.

He smiled broadly.

She had won.

"Fabulous," she said with perfect blue-haired grace. Then she arched an eyebrow. "Now, I want you to call Bill White and shake him down for the other twenty-three thousand. He's loaded."

He laughed with admiration. "You're in the wrong business, sweetie. You should be a professional fund raiser."

She frowned when he said that. The expression didn't look natural on her face.

"We're not doing this for charity, Sam. We're doing this for a friend."

4

"I thought you would be jumping for joy about the Poor Clares getting a bigger chapel," Sam told Buzz the next day over the phone.

"I am," Buzz replied. "But I'm having a hard day at work. They put me on probation today."

"What for?"

"Being tardy. They're pretty strict at UPS about being on time."

"Buy a second alarm clock or something. The last thing you need is to lose your job," Sam tried to say with a tone of encouragement.

"It's not that. I wake up fine. Sometimes it's hard dragging myself out of bed. Or I start daydreaming in the shower, or lose myself fiddling with the spoon in my cereal bowl, and then I end up leaving five minutes late. I got a ticket on the way to work because I ran a red light today. That's why I was late."

"Oh Buzz."

"Yeah. Oh Buzz. Stupid, stupid, stupid. One more tardy, and I'm suspended. My union representative told me his hands are tied. They've got me in a corner. I'm scared I'll blow everything."

"You could always work for me..." Sam said.

"I could never do that. I'm no good at computers—"

"But you know how to sell, you could catch on," Sam offered. "Make some good money. I'm hiring now, too."

"I'd burn out. I don't think I could take the pressure of selling right now, and I don't think it would be right to work for a friend," Buzz said firmly.

Sam heard the note of desperation in his friend's voice.

"Buzz, what's really going on? Are you okay?"

"I'm fine," Buzz lied. "Look, I've got a bunch of pickups to make. I can't be late. I've been making mistakes on my routes, too. If my manager—look, I can't go into it. I'm okay. So long."

Buzz hung up the phone before Sam could say good-bye.

Something's wrong, Sam thought. *I'll invite him over for dinner.*

Sam hadn't seen Buzz in over two weeks. With outdoor pick-up basketball long over, the craziness of selling and buying the houses, the new big contracts at work—well, it seemed like Buzz had gotten lost between the cracks.

I'll call him, Sam promised himself, then turned to the stack of resumes on his desk. *How am I going to find six good technicians in less than a month?*

5

Buzz completed his appointed rounds the day of the phone call, and managed to go into work on time for the next several days.

It was two days before Sam got a chance to track Buzz down for dinner. He came to their house on the lakefront. They watched a video—*It Happened One Night* with Clark Gable and Claudette Colbert—and Buzz seemed perfectly normal, joking and pontificating as usual about all things under the sun.

Only Ellie noticed that he was pressing, and mentioned it to Sam at bedtime.

"We'll have to keep an eye on him," Sam said. "Did you notice how he didn't bring up Donna?"

"Yes. I noticed. He was silent when I told him Bill White is helping with the chapel. He's putting on weight, too."

She slipped on her nightgown, and crawled into bed next to him.

"Do you think he's started drinking again?" she asked.

"Buzz? No way. I've seen him around booze a hundred times, and he doesn't even pay attention to it. He's just going through a rough time. Basketball is done with until spring— I just don't have time to play at the Y in the mornings with him. Neither does he with his night owl habits. Donna is gone. Mark has his family. We've been preoccupied with a hundred things. He's lonely, that's all."

Buzz kept from mentioning Donna because the thought of her, as happy as he was that she was in the Poor Clares, made him feel blue. Her leaving opened a gaping hole in his daily routine. Buzz couldn't bring himself to resent her, but the temptation to do just that made him feel guilty.

He didn't mention that his ex-wife's parents had suddenly moved to Florida to be near their daughter and grandchild, and that Sandi was engaged to be married. He also didn't mention that he had cancelled his trip to Fatima altogether to pay off credit card debt and the moving violation fine. His tournament prize money was gone.

With just one more speeding ticket, UPS would have the grounds to fire him—even if he did manage to get to work on time during the probation period of one year.

Buzz also didn't mention that he had stopped going to his AA meetings at the Unitarian church hall in Rocky River, and had taken to watching an average of two videos a night most days of the week. When he didn't watch videos, he spent time in the Rini-Regos supermarket looking for pulp fiction to distract himself. He discovered Dean Koontz, and began to read everything by Stephen King he could get his hands on.

He read novels, watched videos, ate fast food (even though he couldn't afford it), and drank too much Pepsi at night, making it hard to fall asleep.

His daughter, Jennifer, was coming Christmas week, and he was out of vacation time. Her arrival was one week away. He didn't know what he was going to do with her while he was at work. Sandi's parents had always taken care of that. The last week before Christmas at UPS was sheer madness: every truck was overstuffed with holiday gifts, and no driver was allowed to return to the center without delivering every single one. Buzz didn't mind the taxing labor once he dragged himself to work. It kept his mind occupied. But he had already started to come home after eight and it was only going to get worse.

His bank account was empty, and he had come close to missing his last rent payment. His Festiva needed a new battery and a tune-up he simply couldn't afford. Thank God the trusty little thing started in the morning. If it failed him, he would lose his job.

6

Two days before Jennifer Woodward was scheduled to arrive to visit her father, Bill White opened his eyes and pressed the button on his alarm clock. It was five o'clock. Even the birds were still asleep. He sat up in bed, rubbed his eyes, and began praying his morning offering.

He took a shower, got dressed, and ate a simple breakfast. An hour and a half before he was due at the offices of his own advertising agency, he sat at the modest desk in his modest apartment not far from Buzz's apartment. He read from the Gospel of Luke for thirty minutes. He carefully read the enlightening commentaries supplied for each passage, underlining particular passages that struck him. He then copied a few notes in a handsome, leather-bound notebook.

There were seventeen full notebooks of the same type in the case next to the desk. Next to the notebooks were several dozen spiritual classics that he had read over the years, each one with pages underlined and notated in Bill's methodical hand.

Then he read for fifteen minutes from a well-worn copy of *In Conversation with God,* one volume of a set that contained spiritual commentaries for every day of the year. This particular series was all the rage in one of Bill's social circles.

Rising early, reading spiritual commentary, followed by mental prayer, followed by Mass: these were his norms. He never mentioned these norms to anyone besides his spiritual director, who was a priest in Opus Dei, a low-key religious association. Bill had become involved with Opus Dei during college. Within the Catholic Church, Opus Dei was technically known as a personal Prelature, which meant that its full members were primarily subject to a bishop appointed to Opus Dei.

He attended regular meetings on spiritual subjects led by numeraries—unmarried members of Opus Dei who answered a call to give up married life to serve the group, often while holding down full-time jobs outside of Opus Dei.

Bill was not a numerary, and didn't feel called to become one. He wished to get married. Despite serious relationships with several women over the years, he had not been fortunate enough to find the right woman. He was at peace with keeping the norms, working at his secular job, and letting his life be a silent beacon leading other souls to Christ.

He drove to Saint Christophers, where he attended morning Mass. He noticed that Buzz was not in attendance, something that was not unusual lately.

Perhaps he's found a midday Mass? I haven't met him for lunch in how long? Two months?

Taking his thoughts as a small prompting of the Holy Spirit, Bill offered his communion for Buzz. After Mass, cognizant that Christ remained fully present in the Sacred Host before digestion took place, he prayed his daily Rosary. He concentrated on speaking directly to the Savior within his body with every prayer.

After Donna's decision to become a Poor Clare, Buzz had approached Bill about the possibility of accompanying him to Fatima in her place.

"Not now," Bill had told him. "Maybe in the springtime. I can't get away from work this time of year."

Bill had noted the disappointment in Buzz's eyes, despite Buzz's "No big deal" reply.

I've got to call him, Bill told himself. He reached for his pocket calendar, and made a note on his to-do list for the day.

7

Donna dressed and showered in complete privacy, as all religious do if their congregations are serious about maintaining a high level of purity.

Religious life is not natural; it is not natural for women who are not related by blood to live in such close quarters. In fact, religious life is supernatural, and impossible without grace and a special charism given by the Holy Spirit to the world through their founders.

She was not tired. The schedule, tested over the centuries, allowed for plenty of rest for a healthy person, young or old. After a few weeks, she found herself growing accustomed to the rhythm of the schedule, and the ringing of the bells which punctuated the different activities of her day.

She took special pleasure in this part of preparation for the day. She knew that, barring illness requiring medical treatment or attention, that only her betrothed, Jesus, would look upon her body. She had not only given Jesus her time, her prayers, her desires for worldly things, but also her very body.

It didn't seem like much to give. Oh, she took pains not to abuse her strong, almost powerful, figure. The Poor Clares led a surprisingly active life. There was time in the schedule for exercise and work. She knew the Father had blessed her with health and strength.

But my spouse has given me His body. And His body was perfect, sinless, and glorified.

She would consume His Body at Mass before breakfast.

That's wild, she thought, pulling on the special garment of the postulant. She thought of Buzz, and his musings about the spectacular mystical wildness of the Catholic faith during their trip to New Jersey so long ago.

I wonder how he's doing? she thought sadly.

She was still not habituated to being out of touch. She had an urge to call him, but knew the urge would be unfulfilled. *I'll write to Ellie and ask her for an update.*

When her superior had come to her with the news that Sam and Ellie had contributed one thousand dollars to the chapel fund, Donna had been required by the rules to write a thank you reply because the check had come in a letter with Donna's name on it.

Donna had told Ellie and Buzz about the rule the day before she left the world, with a wink. "Just make sure you put five bucks in every letter you send me! I'll be under obedience to write back to you!" (There were also rules, centuries old, about when letters could be read and written by the nuns. For certain months of the year, associated with the Church calendar—Lent was such a time—the Poor Clares even gave up the pleasures of correspondence.)

Thus empowered, Donna wrote back to Ellie immediately, excitedly describing in great detail how the mother superior had been in tears while announcing to the community that an *additional* gift of ninety-nine thousand dollars had been earmarked for the expansion of the chapel. She further described how the larger donation had arrived from a bank through a designated third party, making it completely anonymous.

"Your one thousand dollar gift added to this surprise anonymous donation means we have exactly the right amount," Donna wrote. "It's a direct answer to all of our prayers. I'm so psyched! Please tell Buzz! I know he's been praying for us all."

Donna would never know that she was writing to the anonymous donors. The anonymity had been Bill White's idea.

She opened the door to her cubicle, filled with hope for her day.

Yes sir, I'll have plenty of time to pray for Buzz today. The world was all right.

8

It was a Saturday afternoon. She had muttered one sentence to him after she came down the ramp at the gate.

"Not here, Buzz," she said when he tried to give her a hug.

"When did you decide to stop calling me Daddy?" he asked his daughter.

She made a bored face, and didn't favor him with a reply.

Buzz and Jennifer walked up to his car in the parking lot of Hopkins Airport. She was seven years old, and already had her mother's world-weary eyes. She had Buzz's thick, brown hair. His heart sank when he saw the disappointed expression on her face. She was embarrassed by his beat-up Festiva.

She saw his disappointment and pounced. "Mommy's new husband drives a Cadillac."

"Is that so?" He feigned innocence.

He knew all her tricks. Even though he knew what she was doing to him, he still ached to be able to afford a nicer-looking car.

He resolved not to let it get him down.

"So what's new in school?" he asked her when they got onto the road.

"Nothin'."

Silence for three minutes. She was wearing a dreadful tie-dyed T-shirt that was too tight for her already too thin torso.

Is she being fed down there?

Her fingernails were painted black with grey polka dots, and she chewed a huge wad of gum with her mouth open.

The T-shirt made her look like a tramp.

"How's Mommy?"

Silence.

He cleared his throat. "Jen, sweetheart. I asked you how your mother was."

"'kay," she muttered, looking out the window.

We're off to our usual start, he thought.

Sometimes she warmed up toward the end of the week. But he only had today and tomorrow.

He thanked God that Bill had called and volunteered, with a little help from the Johnsons, to look after Jenny while he was at work. It had been a blow to Buzz's pride to ask Bill for help, but he had no other place to go. He had resolved not to burden Sam and Ellie. Bill, for his part, made the idea of taking the bulk of his days off the week before Christmas sound trifling.

Bill's a good actor. I'll never be able to repay him.

Ten minutes later, Buzz pulled into the parking lot of Saint Angela Merici Church. He left the motor running to keep the heat blowing.

"Let's go thank God for being together again," Buzz suggested brightly, acting the part, knowing what would come next. "Just a few prayers."

He expected hemming and hawing, or at least silence. He wasn't prepared for her answer.

"Is that a Catholic church?" she asked.

"You know it is, sweetie. We go here every time you visit."

"Mommy says that I can't go in there. That when you got a nullmint, that the Church made me into a bastard."

Buzz's jaw dropped. The man who was so glib and witty with his friends was speechless.

She looked away from him, chewing her gum loudly, both of them knowing that she knew the sound annoyed him.

Finally, he found his voice. "That's not true."

She spit two foul words at the window, making him the target of the sexually explicit epithet.

Now's she cursing! Did she learn that from Sandi's new husband? Is that what he's like?

He's probably a lot like you used to be, a little voice taunted him.

It took all his strength to ignore the voice and keep his usually deeply-buried temper in check. This was turning out to be worse than ever. And they were only in their first hour of the visit.

Buzz wearily shrugged off despair, as he had done a thousand times before over the years, which hugged him intimately, like a dead lover. Buzz shook his head, and rubbed his face with his hands.

He realized that he had forgotten to shave this morning.

"Look here, young lady!" He had conjured up his sternest fatherly voice, sickly aware that by using it so early in the visit he would have little effective recourse to it later. By forcing him into this mode, she was punching a screwdriver into the gas tank of his thinly armored authority.

She turned her head slowly, an utterly jaded look in her eyes. She rolled them in her head with a practiced *I've heard that a thousand times before* expression. She blew a bubble and popped her gum.

He opened and closed his mouth. He gave up.

"You can treat me like you hate me for the rest of the week, Jennifer. I know you love me somewhere inside that heart of yours. But I get the picture; I don't expect you to show it. But I will not stand for you treating me with open disrespect. I'm still your father. Do you understand me? I'm—I'm drowning in sorrow here."

He saw a small spark in her eyes. Was it love or resentment?

"Okay Buzz," she said disdainfully, then offered him a wan smile.

He took what she offered, as little as she offered, knowing that the pickings were going to remain slim.

"Now I'm going inside to pray. You can stay here or come in with me. I won't take long either way."

"I'll stay here," she said, turning back to stare out the window. "Can you leave the keys so I can listen to music?"

"No," he said quickly, and jumped out of the car into the cold winter air. At half past four, it was almost dark already because of the setting back of the clocks.

These few days before Christmas, in fact, were the darkest days of the year.

PART FOUR

The Ocean

When you are young and dying, when your heart was made for a
love stronger than death, but your body wasn't,
you get trouble in the soul. Buckets of trouble. Ages of grief.
Death comes like release.
*Michael O'Brien, **Strangers and Sojourners***

I layed down for a while, and I woke up on the ocean,
floating on my back, and staring at the rain,
it was completely still, 'cept the pounding of my heart.
School of Fish

I'm no good at being noble,
but it doesn't take much to see that the problems of three little
people don't amount to a hill of beans in this crazy world.
*Rick to Ilse in **Casablanca***

When principles that run against your deepest convictions
begin to win the day,
then battle is your calling, and peace has become sin.
Abraham Kuyper

But if I can't swim after forty days,
and my mind is crushed by the thrashing waves,
lift me up so high that I cannot fall.
Jars of Clay

Chapter Nineteen

1

Somehow, Buzz Woodward survived the horrible week with his daughter. Bill tried his best to entertain her by taking her to museums, playgrounds, and malls. She gave him the same silent treatment she had given her father. She warmed up a bit during afternoon visits to the Johnsons. She played fitfully with Sarah, who was a year older.

On the following Saturday, the day before Christmas, Buzz gave her his Christmas present (a Nintendo game for her player in Florida). He put it on his one credit card. He drove her in silence to the airport, and put her on the plane, getting a dirty look from the attendant at the gate, who had seen dozens of divorced kids walk alone down the ramp that week.

He spent Christmas Eve with Sam and Ellie. They gave him a woolen Red Sox jacket with leather sleeves which almost made him cry. He gave them a bottle of wine, the best he could afford. He spent Christmas at the Johnsons with Bill White. It took all his energy to appear energetic, all his wit to act humorous, all his stealth to hide his sorrow.

Two weeks later, on a freezing January night, Buzz arrived late for a gathering at Mark Johnson's house. It was late; the Johnson children were in bed. Bill, Ellie, Sam, Mark and Maggie were reclining in the living room, Leo Kotke guitar music playing softly in the background.

Buzz helped himself to a can of Pepsi from the fridge and plopped down on the floor between Bill's rocker and Sam and Ellie's love seat.

"What's the topic of conversation tonight?" he asked.

"Nothing much," Mark answered. "Maggie and I were telling Sam about being married, having kids."

A silence passed.

"Let's talk about grace," Buzz suggested out of the blues. They were accustomed to his quick tangents.

"Grace Kelly?" Sam said with a straight face. "I married her."

Everyone smiled or chuckled.

"What do you mean, Buzz?" Maggie asked.

"How it works. It's a catchall phrase for most of us. I mean, how come I don't get it when I ask for it? When I need it the most, it seems. I've prayed for my daughter to get it, but every time she visits, it's a disaster."

"God isn't like a vending machine," Mark said after a moment of pondering. "For weeks, I asked for help when Maggie kicked me out, but nothing came, even though I was plunking quarters into the machine. Maybe I wasn't ready for what happened to me at Steubenville until it happened."

One way or another, the group had become familiar with Mark and Maggie's story. During the New Year's party at Bill White's, Mark had held them all in rapt attention when he told them about his dream in the Port at Steubenville.

Maggie, who was sitting next to Mark on the couch, turned to look at him. "Maybe it was grace that prompted me to kick you out. It doesn't sound right—kicking your husband out— but I decided that I wouldn't deal with you until you treated me with respect. The decision took a lot out of me. I needed strength to cope without you. It felt like that strength came from outside of me. Maybe that's grace."

"I never know where the line between grace and my will ends," Bill threw out for the group. "If I get up early and read the Bible, is it a response to grace, or my will? My whole day is different depending on what I do when I get out of bed."

Buzz nodded, and took a sip of Pepsi. He noticed that Sam was following the conversation closely.

"The Church says grace comes through the sacraments," Bill continued. "I'm just plain different after I go to confession. It's easier to pray, easier to jump out of bed. Easier to go the extra mile for somebody. It's easier to be good knowing my sins have been cleansed away. That's grace."

"I get grace at work," Mark piped in. "I don't exactly feel it. It's like it works through my instincts. I don't have much concern for losing my life in the White Collar Unit, but I prayed all the time for my guardian angel to protect me when I was tracking down Mafia guys. Once or twice, it was like a little voice told me not to walk through a particular door. Sure enough, there would be a loaded gun behind that door. Other agents could tell you stories…"

"Even ones who don't believe in God?" Sam asked.

"You know the old saying, Sam. There are no atheists in foxholes. I've seen cold-blooded murderers pray when they were in danger."

Buzz looked at Ellie. *What do you think?* he asked silently. She felt emboldened by the ensuing lull in the conversation.

"I think," she started, pausing just for a second. "I think that I'm not sure what you're all talking about. I never gave much thought to grace before meeting—before meeting all of you. I've always felt that God was out there, watching over me, but not, you know, very active in my day-to-day life. I don't think of grace in terms of voices, or getting out of bed, or anything like that. I think of Donna, right now, praying for us. It's like she's joined with God in watching over us."

"I like that," Buzz said. "I think about Donna a lot lately. I miss her."

"I do too," Sam said.

Ellie gave her husband a look. Sam didn't mention Donna unless somebody else brought her up.

"I don't know much about grace," Sam added. "But I believe in love. What else explains why someone would marry another person? A voice inside says: this is right for you."

"I think, if Sam doesn't mind me bringing this up," Buzz offered, "that grace works with great power for people who don't believe in it. I've watched Sam build his company. Every decision he makes at work affects the lives of a lot of people. He provides jobs for families, and indirectly helps provide jobs for his client's workers. It really is uncanny how he makes his decisions involving tens of thousands of dollars based almost solely on his business intuition—what do you think, Sam? Do you feel an outside force guiding you at work? Or is it just intuition?"

Sam paused to ponder. "To tell you the truth, it's intuition. I don't feel anything outside of me. I just try my best. I know people depend on me to make good decisions, but even if they didn't, I would still try to make decisions according to…" he paused again, searching for the right words.

"According to right reason?" Bill prompted.

"Sort of," Sam answered. "If what you mean by right reason is logic and reality. I've noticed that my worst decisions usually come out of a false assumption; that is, I make a mistake because I base my decision on something that turns out to not be true, or not in tune with reality. I assume the market wants a certain kind of software, but in reality it doesn't, so we waste resources trying to sell customers on it. I usually don't find out what the reality of a situation is until afterwards, though. There's a lot of guesswork—a lot of guesswork. "

"So if it's guesswork, how come your decisions turn out so well most of the time?" Maggie asked. "And thanks for being so open, Sam."

They all knew she was referring to his unbelief.

Sam laughed softly. "After two years with Buzz, I'm used to being the token nonbeliever. But I don't feel like the odd man out here. You all let me be me. Uh, what was the question again?"

"How come your decisions come out right more than your competitors' decisions?" Maggie repeated. "Is it guesswork? Or could it be that you're guided by grace you don't believe in, for the sake of the people you employ?"

"I don't really know," he answered honestly. "Other competitors, men and women, have better educations, more financial backing, more experience—even better relationships to start with customers—but the combination of me and

Johnny Traverse outperforms them every time. Johnny doesn't pray or go to church, by the way, although he says he's a Methodist.

"Another thing. They're not strictly my decisions anymore. Half the time, I just trust the people who work for me. I'm a programmer at heart. I don't like to sell. People in the industry don't believe me when I tell them that I spend thirty percent of my time in the office reading about the industry, customers, trends. You'll all love hearing this: even the things I hear at Mass help me at work. I look for sound principles to base my decisions upon."

"For example?" Bill asked.

"You know what I mean, Bill. You run a company. Principles like 'if a customer has a problem with your product and you fix it, he becomes more loyal.' That's a big one at Edwards & Associates, because computer systems always have problems. The best 'fixers' win the long-term contracts. That's not too far off from 'If your brother asks for your shirt, give him your coat and your sandals as well.' Didn't Jesus say something like that? Our company provides that level of service."

Sam felt odd. The conversation had started on the subject of grace, and had turned into a business lecture featuring the agnostic.

"The advertising industry doesn't forgive mistakes," Bill began thoughtfully. "Too much money is involved that you can't get back if the campaign fails. There are absolutes in morality; I think there are almost absolute principles in business, too. Example: 'Poor cash flow kills your business.' I know several talented admen who failed in this town because they had negative cash flow."

"I'm not following you," Buzz addressed Bill. "I don't understand stuff like cash flow."

"You're not the only one," Ellie said. "I remember struggling with it in my courses at Saint Marys. Basically, it means that even if your company has a good product, unless you get paid in time for the products you have sold—with more money than it costs you to produce those products, yet with enough to spare to fill the new orders you're getting—you'll grind to a halt. Someone will order your product, but you won't have the money to produce it."

"I'm more confused than ever," Buzz said.

"That's what I like about you, Buzz," Mark interjected, smiling, leaning forward on the couch, placing his elbows on his knees. "You're never afraid to say when you don't understand something. I have no idea what cash flow is—"

"That's why I keep the family checkbook," Maggie chided gently, patting him on the back. "Buzz, it's not so complicated. Negative cash flow is not having enough money in the bank to pay your bills. If your income doesn't cover your expenses, the phone company turns off your phone. If you need that phone to make money, you go out of business."

"Well said," Sam agreed. "I knew the definition of cash flow before I started Edwards, but I didn't *understand* it for about a year. I took three contracts that didn't pay me enough in the first year, and lost all my savings before I caught on that I had to either charge more or deliver my services for less cost. Or both, as it turned out. I came this close to going under many times in that first year."

Sam looked through a tiny gap between his index finger and thumb.

"So what does any of this have to do with grace?" Ellie asked.

"Nothing," Buzz answered.

"I don't know about that," Maggie mused. "Maybe grace is like cash flow. If you choose to live according to right reason, as Bill calls it, or good principles, as Sam calls it, then you are opening yourself up to enough grace to overcome the negative things in your life, even if you don't believe in God. Maybe being a Catholic is a matter of having the best grace-flow, because we have the sacraments." She took a breath. "There's another thing we're all missing here."

"What's that, hun?" Mark asked.

"There's no grace without suffering. It sounds like Sam suffered to build Edwards & Associates. We suffered before we got back together, Mark. The joy of married life, raising children, is just plain day-to-day sacrifice."

That gave the group something to ponder.

"But what about—no forget it," Ellie said.

She felt lost in this conversation, except for the business talk. She loved to talk business.

"What is it, Ellie?" Maggie asked.

"Well, when I was a kid, I suffered when my mother left us. I suffered every time she had an argument with Bucky. I cried myself to sleep every night. I was so young. I thought I was somehow responsible. I didn't get any grace out of that."

She looked down at her hands, fumbling with her engagement ring, turning it over and over.

Sam reached for her hand. There was an old, old hurt in her voice. She never talked about her mother leaving, even in private. *What's gotten into her?*

Grace? a little voice asked him.

"I cried myself to sleep when I was a kid," Buzz said sadly, looking down at the carpet in the middle of the room. "I thought it was normal to be sad. I'm still that way. I know I was happy last summer, but that's like a dream. I might look happy on the outside, but inside, I'm crying. I'm doing it right now. That's why I asked about grace. I'm waiting and waiting and waiting…"

His words trailed off.

In his mind's eye, Mark saw again the flies crawling into the wounds in Christ's feet. *No one came for Him. While His mother wept, He waited.*

They all loved Buzz. They had suspected that he was down. It was one of the reasons why Mark had planned the gathering; Buzz had been avoiding their phone calls.

"Buzz, I admire you," Mark said with a strong voice. "I admire anybody who fights the battles you fight."

"Sorry I got maudlin," Ellie threw out quickly. "Sorry, Buzz."

Buzz looked up. His eyes were watery.

"Hey Mark!" he cried out suddenly. "This is better than AA! Let's do it again next week!"

They all laughed politely.

"Let's all pray for each other," Maggie said with a serious tone a moment later. Then she remembered Sam. She looked at him.

He smiled and gave her a quick shake of his chin. *Don't worry,* he told her with his eyes.

"Sure," Ellie said. She had prayed a few Rosaries in the last month after gentle promptings in Donna's letters.

Bill and Mark nodded. They had been praying daily for Buzz.

Bill, who was the most well-read theologically, thought: *I don't think any person on this earth really understands grace. Believe in grace? Sure. I can quote you chapter and verse. But understand?*

"Well!" Mark said, looking at his watch. "It's getting late."

After pleasantries, the gathering broke up quickly.

✜ ✜ ✜

Bill drove off. Mark and Maggie closed the door. Ellie, Buzz, and Sam stood next to their cars in the driveway.

"Before we go home, let's go for a walk," she suggested. "I love the cold air."

Neither man detected her white lie at the tail end.

"Sounds good to me," Buzz said through white puffs with feigned enthusiasm. *Anything to relieve this dark cloud!*

She stood between them and took their arms.

"My big guys," she said happily as they walked up the sidewalk on the side street in Rocky River. It was past eleven and there were no cars on the road.

The suburbs always sleep.

"Buzz," she began after a few minutes. "How bad is it?"

"Real bad," he told her. "I know you guys are trying to cheer me up. I love you for it. But nothing seems to work."

"Can't you see a doctor?" Sam asked.

"I tried that once. The drugs made me crazy. I suspect because I'm half crazy already. I get manic. I would lose my job, or worse, run over some kid. Driving a UPS truck is not a responsibility to take lightly.

"Plus there's the other thing," he finished, leading them.

"What?" Ellie asked.

"I'm an alcoholic. I have an addictive personality. I don't want to go near drugs. Just the thought of taking drugs makes my skin crawl. Caffeine and nicotine are about all I can handle."

"So where does that leave us?" Sam asked.

"Us?"

"Yes, us. We're in this together. I don't mean this to sound like a rebuke, but you haven't been answering your phone."

But it did sound like a rebuke to Buzz. He couldn't help it. *Sure, but you're married now,* a dark voice prompted Buzz.

"You guys can't solve my problems for me. I appreciate the concern, but even if I moved into your living room, I would still feel lousy."

"Have you been going to Mass? That always makes you feel better, doesn't it?" Sam asked.

Here's one for you: my husband the agnostic asking Buzz to go to Mass, Ellie thought.

Buzz laughed darkly. "I mean to go. I miss it in the morning, and then, well, I miss it after work if I get home late. My manager is really loading up my routes. It's official, now. He wants me out. He told me the other day after the morning meeting. He took me aside, and said, 'I don't care what the union does. You're not performing. I'll get you out one way or another.'"

He heard Ellie gasp a bit. "That's terrible! Can you report him or something?"

"Not really," Buzz said. "He's well-respected. Everyone loves him. He's got a point, too. I haven't been doing a good job lately."

They heard the self-castigation in his voice.

"He's riding you, Buzz. Come work for me."

"Sam, I can't. I like this job. Managers come and go. I'll outlast him. The union is behind me. My shop steward is on my side. And I'm not much good to you in this state of mind. I don't think I could take it if I washed out with you at Edwards, either. Look, I've got to ride this out on my own. I always do. This monkey's one stinking bad ass, though. I can't seem to shake it off my back. I almost didn't come tonight. I know Mark planned it for me."

That led to a long silence.

"Oh Buzz," Ellie said. "Isn't there something we can do?"

"You're doing it right now."

They turned the corner. They had gone around the block, and were back in front of the Johnson's house. Buzz felt the cold on his lips, which were beginning to feel pressed on like separate pieces.

Mr. Potato Head, Buzz thought disjointedly.

"Hang in there, Buddy," Sam said.

"I will. It's this friggin' endless Cleveland winter. That poem was wrong. April isn't the cruelest month. It's February. Come spring, I'll feel great. We'll play hoops."

"That's it!" Sam said. "I'll play hoops with you at the Y. They have that seven-to-eight morning thing in Lakewood. I'll bang on your door in the morning and get you up."

"Aw," Buzz said. "You don't have to do that." *Will you, man?* his eyes pleaded.

"Sure he will. He's getting fat," Ellie teased. "He's been working too hard lately on the new contract."

"Maybe we could get Bill to go?" Buzz thought out loud.

"I'll ask him. Mark too. We'll get the old gang together," Sam said, warming to the idea. "Do you know how to contact the Man? We'll get the Scaps going again."

"I have no idea where the Man is. He's like a summer ghost." Buzz said.

"I'll see you tomorrow at six forty-five then," Sam said.

"Sure," Buzz replied unenthusiastically. "Six forty-five."

Ellie stepped over and gave him a hug. She was surprised again by his powerful build. Hugging him was like hugging a piece of furniture. Then she remembered waltzing with him at her wedding—and the night before the wedding. *So much locked inside, waiting to get out,* she thought suddenly.

"Thanks," she told him.

"For what?" Buzz asked, confused. "I should be thanking you."

She pulled away and gave him a look that Sam couldn't see because he was standing behind her.

"For Sam," she mouthed silently.

Oh yeah, Buzz thought. *The wedding.*

He was bitten by an old, ardent longing for companionship, and willed himself not to be envious of Sam.

Everything seems to come to Sam, and run away from me, his depression told him.

After saying good-bye, he walked to his car, which was blocking the Fisk's. He lit a cigarette before driving away.

Sam and Ellie watched his red lights disappear around the corner.

"You've been driving yourself pretty hard at work," Ellie said with concern. "Are you sure you can get up that early?"

"I'll have to. You can help me, can't you?"

"No problem. I'll barf on you."

"That's looking at the bright side of morning sickness," he joked.

She hit him on the coat with decent force.

"Hey! Wanna play rough, do you?" He attempted to tickle her through her heavy wool coat. She whirled away with ease.

"You're slowing down, old man!"

2

Sam and Ellie made love that evening, quickly, like a couple who had been married for many years. When they were done, he propped himself up, and rested a hand on her belly.

"When will it show?" he asked innocently.

"It already is. Can't you tell? My pants don't fit anymore around the waist. I had to get my fat-pants out of the closet. I haven't worn those since college."

He heard the resentment in her voice.

"You don't want this baby," he said.

"It's not that. I want the baby. Maybe the timing is terrible. What will I do with my company?" she asked.

"What do you want to do?"

"We can afford day care," she muttered.

"You don't sound like you're thrilled with the idea."

She looked him in the eye. "Are you?"

He didn't answer her. She could guess what he thought of day care. She didn't have to ask what Maggie thought. She knew what Donna would think.

What do you think? she asked herself. *A year ago, it would have been an easy question to answer.*

She wondered if the baby was a boy or a girl.

Why did I let him talk me into moving to the West Side!

She hugged herself and felt him take his hand off her stomach.

Grace, a little voice answered her. The voice sounded masculine, but a bit lazy, a bit casual and high at the same time—a little like Buzz.

"I don't want to talk about the baby right now," she said with finality.

"We'll have to talk about it sometime."

"Not tonight."

"Is that why you were somewhere else tonight?"

"No."

He waited for her to explain. She didn't. Instead, she blew out the candle on the night stand. The smell of the vanilla in the wax, like other smells over the past few months, made her feel like blowing chunks.

"You just make sure you get up for your friend Buzz tomorrow, or else," she said after another long minute, and turned from him, taking the sheets over herself.

In her haste to turn from him, her Miraculous Medal, the same one she had been wearing on the night he first met her in Mama Santas, got caught in a tangle of her hair, and landed on her back.

He carefully reached for it, untangled it, and let it fall, unseen now, onto her breast.

"Thank you," she mumbled.

"I love you, Ellie."

"I love you too. Remember about Buzz."

Or else what? he asked himself, wondering if he was having or avoiding an argument.

✝ ✝ ✝

She fell asleep and dreamed of a white knight, lying in a ditch next to a dead horse. Tree-lined hills cut off a view of her surroundings. She saw only the gully below her. Dark clouds filled the sky, portending a deluge. The wind was loud up here, on the small hill.

Where am I? she asked herself.

Across the ocean, a sweet voice told her.

She looked at the knight, then ran down the hill to his side, standing above him. She turned her nose from the stench of the horse, clenching her eyes tight. She felt like throwing up. The ground here, next to a brook, was covered with white, wet sand.

She heard him moan. She forced herself to look at him. There was a broadsword sunk deeply into his chest, below his heart, thrust through gnarled, chained armor. The sword was so buried into him that she wondered if it was all the way through, pinning him to the sand. His head was raised on a pillow of black rock, and the rock was covered by clusters of barnacles. She heard wet, little ticking noises coming from the barnacles.

They're alive!

The sand was murky with his blood.

His nemesis has left him for dead.

"Get up!" she screamed, terrified. "You're not dead yet! Get up!"

His silver helmet covered his face. He moved his head in her direction, disoriented.

"Guinevere?" she heard his pained, confused voice ask. "I've waited for—I've been waiting forever."

His voiced reeked with despair.

"Get up Buzz!" she cried, falling to his side, her pink, flowing gown blowing in the chill wind, speckled with droplets of blood. Blood everywhere. Her blond hair flew in the wind, getting into her eyes, her mouth.

The flies are coming. And their lord with them, a witchly voice whispered in her ear, then laughed with false elation.

"I'm dying," he croaked.

The princess reached for his faceplate, despite her fear of the grim visage that would be beneath the two chevron slots, but she couldn't pull it open.

"I can't breathe. Too heavy. This armor is too heavy," he rasped.

She saw blood ooze from the slats, and she began to scream: "Sam! Where are you! Can't you see he's dying?"

She gave up on opening the faceplate. She reached for his metal-covered hand. Her bitter tears mixed with blood.

Like most dreams, she didn't remember this one clearly, as if the waking day air was a darkened lens.

3

Bill White declined the invitation to play morning hoops because of his norms. Mark Johnson promised three days a week. Sam managed to arrive at Buzz's apartment door at six forty-five for three straight weeks, right smack into February.

Buzz's spirits seemed to pick up. And Sam enjoyed the exercise.

Then Sam had to leave town for a week-long computer show in Long Beach, California. Mark showed up at the Y like clockwork, but Buzz missed one day, then two. Then Buzz sprained his ankle slightly in late February. Sam stopped going while Buzz recovered.

Buzz was afraid to skip work because of the injury, and the ankle re-sprained on the job.

4

Dear Postulant Regina:

It's so hard not thinking of you as Donna. I don't have much time to write.

Pray for Buzz. Oh, I know you do already, but I'm really worried about him. He doesn't answer his phone at night. He won't see a doctor. Sam tries to get through to him, but it doesn't always work. I'm praying a Rosary for him every day now. I can't seem to concentrate unless I say the Sorrowful Mysteries. The fifth sorrowful decade is so sad. Mary is so sad.

Much Love, Your Friend, Ellie.

5

UPS Centers are a maze of four colors: black conveyor belts, gray concrete floors, gunmetal ceilings, brown trucks, and dull yellow-painted cinder block walls.

Buzz ran from his car, stopping only to flash his ID card at the gate, then raced through the huge building to the time clock. He punched in with two clicks to spare.

Norman Porcine, his manager, stood next to the clock and smiled wanly.

"Screw you, Norm," Buzz said with smile, then turned away.

"You'll hit a couple red lights on your way in one of these days," Norman called to Buzz's back.

Buzz saw a new color when he walked into his section a few minutes later—after he shined his boots.

Into the grays, blacks, dull yellows, and browns, he saw red and silver.

Norman Porcine cleared his throat. "Gentlemen and Ladies, meet Maxine Corcoran. She's just transferred over from the Lakewood section to drive split."

In the equal opportunity world of American industry running at the speed of business, a female UPS driver was commonplace. A few old-timers had to stifle an urge to wolf whistle.

Not that Maxine was a fashion model. But she was built nicely, had cute blue eyes, and a freckled complexion that made up for relatively average features.

Her thick, straight, deep red hair took care of the rest.

Buzz immediately fell in love. The Miraculous Medal around her neck raised his sagging hopes.

The Medal. Corcoran. She's got to be Catholic! But what kind of name is Maxine?

Her truck happened to be parked next to his that day. They were both split drivers.

"Where do the guys hang out for lunch?" she called over as she adjusted her seat and completed her inspection.

"Uh, on your route, Georges on Lorain. Lousy food, lousy service, cheap prices," he called back.

She laughed. She had a deep voice for her size. A little like Donna's. Buzz watched her carefully. Like many female UPS drivers, she walked a bit like a man.

Maybe she's a lesbian.

She smiled at him, and his lonely heart melted.

"See you there?"

"Sure," he said as he started up the engine, and began to pull out carefully. There was less than six inches between the twenty-odd package cars lined up in two facing rows with conveyor belts behind them. The rounded cabs of the trucks allowed just enough room for a big man like Buzz to squeeze through. It was dark. It was always dark near the trucks.

UPS didn't believe in wasting valuable resources on superfluous lightbulbs.

✝ ✝ ✝

Georges Kitchen was out of Buzz's way that day, so he ran to every doorway to buy clicks (UPS measured time not in sixty minutes per hour, but in one hundred 'clicks' per hour—it was more efficient).

At the doorstep of the last house, he laughed after he read aloud the two words on the welcome mat: "Go Away."

He waited another thirty precious clicks for Maxine to show up at Georges.

For some reason, he was the only other driver there on this day. Usually there were three or four. Maxine slid across from him on a plastic-coated bench. There were fake green plants hanging on the walls of their booth.

Buzz splurged and ordered a hamburger, a bowl of soup, and the inevitable Pepsi with a lemon twist.

"Let me buy you lunch on your first day in Norman's section," he offered even though he couldn't afford it.

"I hear he's a real ball-buster," she said. She was direct.

Buzz snorted. "Don't let me get started on Norm. Did you know that Porcine means pig-like?"

She laughed heartily. "You're pulling my leg?"

He shook his head slowly. He hadn't felt this good in, well, a long time.

"You wear a Miraculous Medal," he said, pulling his own out from under his shirt.

She smiled. He noticed a gap between her front teeth for the first time. *Well, nobody's perfect.*

"Yeah, you too, eh? I got mine in Fatima."

"I've heard about that place. Is it for real?" *I've hit the jackpot!* Buzz thought wildly.

She told him all about it. She had been dragged there by her mother, who was very devout. She said she enjoyed the place and went to confession there for the first time in years and years.

Buzz soaked up every word; he thanked God it was a Monday. There was a good chance that they would both have the same routes for the rest of the week.

✝ ✝ ✝

As luck would have it, they did have the same routes. They met for lunch Tuesday, Wednesday, Thursday, and Friday. Buzz had little trouble showing up for work on time that week.

But what kind of luck was it?

It turned out that Maxine lived alone in Parma in a house her widowed grandfather willed to her upon his death a year before. She had a brother in the Navy. Her parents lived in Parma Heights.

She liked to talk, and Buzz found himself finding out all about her. He was disappointed that her Catholic faith did not appear too deeply entrenched. But she was going to Mass on Sunday now and said she prayed the Rosary on occasion since Fatima.

She had played softball for Parma High School; he liked that. She didn't play basketball.

On the rare instances when she asked him about his past, he hedged on details, but did tell her that he went to Notre Dame. She seemed to like that.

He convinced himself that she was on her way into the faith, not on the way out. He wondered if she was the one for him. He decided that his hateful February was over, and that he wanted to find out for certain. During the Friday lunch he summoned the courage to invite her to go to the movies with him that evening.

"You know that's against the rules," she told him. "We could both lose our jobs." UPS workers were not allowed to date each other.

"Others do it. Who's gonna find out?" he countered with an impish smile, a new sparkle beneath his half-closed eyelids.

She smiled.

He was growing to enjoy that smile, despite the gap.

✠ ✠ ✠

They saw a terrible Stallone movie. Afterwards, they ended up at her place. He immediately noticed that the place was still furnished with her dead grandparents' furniture. There were patches and holes in the screened porch off the kitchen.

She led him to the kitchen, where she showed him pictures of her brother and parents on the refrigerator before opening the door.

The place had a vague prune smell to it.

"Beer?" she asked.

"Naw," he said. *I'm an alcoholic. Tell her!*

But he didn't.

"Come on," she urged.

"Naw. I've got a bit of a headache from the movie," he lied uncharacteristically. Buzz normally hated white lies. After months of telling his friends he felt good when he didn't, they were becoming a habit.

"Suit yourself," she said.

He followed her into the tiny living room. There was a black and white television on a cheap cart, and a grey checkered blanket over the couch; it sagged when they sat down on it.

She took a gulp of her beer, and offered it to him again.

He shook his head. He was not tempted in the least.

"Well," she said with finality.

He felt like a high school kid. *What do we do next?*

"Tell me about Fatima again."

"It was great," she said, and leaned toward him. She snuggled her nose into his ear.

Buzz felt the dingy floral-patterned walls closing in on him. *She's going to kiss me...*

Do you want to kiss her?

She reached over and turned off the light. The faded yellow and gray shade had a black hole in it where a lightbulb had burned into it, leaving crusty brown flakes near the edges.

"Hey Buzz," she cooed. "You're kinda cute."

She reached her hand down. He looked at the electrical outlet on the opposite wall, where the television was plugged in. There was no grounding hole in the old, faded beige-plastic outlet. The little socket guy was a mute, with no mouth to cry out.

He looked back at her hair. In the darkened room, it was a greasy, brackish color.

"Bye!" he practically yelled, jumping up.

"What the—" she hissed, falling into the cushions. The guy moved like a cat. "Where you goin—"

"Gotta go!"

"Where?"

"I uh, have to, uh, return a video. Sorry."

He ran through the kitchen, out the door, and to his car. He fumbled for the keys. His hands shook as he jammed the key into the hole.

Please don't let her chase me out here. What a fool you are, Buzz Woodward! Please God, don't let her chase me out here!

God answered this small prayer.

How am I going to face her on Monday? he thought five minutes later, driving carefully up 150th Street at twenty-five miles per hour. Every UPS driver knew that 150th was crawling with Parma cops day and night.

Maxine! I knew that name sucked.

So it turned out that his luck was bad after all.

6

That evening, as Donna prayed almost exclusively for him during her shift before the Blessed Sacrament, Buzz won a thousand battles, and lost only one.

Images invaded his imagination from the dark recesses of his past.

The first image was Maxine's hand, reaching down.

He swatted it back into his memory bank.

The next image was from a girl he was with in a dark basement during high school. He shooed it away.

The next, women from dusky saloons during his drunken days. He waved at them.

Cascading down, then bilging upward, pictures from dirty personal postcards buzzed into his head, as if carried on a black-graced wind exhaled from a leviathan beneath a frozen ocean.

He tried to pray, a veteran of these wars. They were the reason he had been missing daily Mass. Buzz was not the type to receive Communion if he was not in a state of grace.

Not again, he despaired, wondering how long he could hold out.

The Maxines burst through the holes in the screen of his muttered Our Fathers; he sat up in bed; he looked at the clock.

Too late to rent a video.

Sometimes this distracted him. Sometimes, if he forgot to ask Saint Anthony to help him choose the right movie, it made things worse. Tomorrow was Saturday. He could stay up all night watching videos and not have to worry about Norman the Pig standing by the click-clock...

Then *she* came, humming her cabaret hymn. The one from Eddy Street in South Bend. The one from Notre Dame. The one with the snake.

Kelly Pauling, carrying a huge white photo album filled with color-coded memories of their many illicit waltzes.

He had not seen her in a long time.

Think of Donna! Think of Sandi! Think of the Blessed Mother.

Why do I have to wait for grace?

Good faces turned into bad, and nightgowns fell to the floor…and the snake hissed, slithering into his bed, escorted by a vanguard cloud of fat, black flies.

He didn't waste time. He fell, his soul pierced by many swords from his own past…

✝ ✝ ✝

He turned his head. He muttered an act of contrition, fearing death, yet longing for it, too, for he was alone now, the sirens long gone, the flies and raspy forked tongue leaving him alone in the pool of despair.

Alone.

His victory at Maxine's completely erased from his memory, a page now in the closed book of his many pasts.

Please God, help me find a priest tomorrow.

He had forgotten to pray his Rosary.

That's two days in a row. No wonder.

Feeling too soul-sick to leave his bed to get his beads on the dresser, he began the Rosary again and again, repeating *I believe in one God* over and over, unable to finish the first line, as if an enormous cold anvil had been placed on his being…or perhaps a giant broadsword had pinned him to the coil of wet, sandy earth.

Chapter Twenty

1

Buzz Woodward didn't remember falling asleep on the night of the flies…

…he dreamed he was floating on an ocean in a warm womb. His mother's womb. His thumb was in his mouth. When he pulled it out and looked at it, he noticed with amazement that he could see the veins in his fingers and hand, illuminated by an unseen light.

I'm unborn, he told himself, accepting the fact without question in that strange, awfully logical way of dreams.

I am in my mother. I'm alive. I'm small. I'm alive. I am in my mother.

He longed to see the world outside, despite his comfort, because he knew there were people waiting for him there.

Who is waiting?

The baptized, his Father spoke in his heart. *Come to the water.*

But I like this water. I don't remember my mother. Will I get to meet her among the baptized?

Come to the water, the Father answered, as if this phrase explained everything about his mother. *And I will give you a new mother.*

Why do I need a new mother? I like this mother.

The child felt the Father's disappointment.

Eve cannot be your mother. You must be born from the womb of the New Eve, the one who is conceived without sin. To be the brother of her son, you must suffer.

On the horizon of the ocean, a sliver of soft light appeared.

Why must I suffer? I'm afraid.

The Father did not answer.

Father? Are you there?

Buzz's fetal heart began to pound quickly.

All my sons must suffer. I have taken your hand and put it to the plow. Do not look back. You must suffer for another. When your labors are completed, my Son will be waiting for you at the well. The water He will give you is from a fountain that will never run dry...

The Father's voice faded.

Buzz heard his own adult voice from beyond the womb, praying: *Give me a plow to put my hand to...*

Colors that were not black or brown or gray came over the horizon to the east and Buzz fell into another dream...

2

He woke up past noon. He remembered the lost battle of the night before. He buried his head beneath his pillow, to keep the light streaming through his window away from his eyes; he tried to fall back to sleep.

He did.

He woke up after two. He did not shower or shave, and after a trip to the refrigerator, upon finding no orange juice, drank a glass of Pepsi using an unclean glass from the night before.

He avoided prayer and memories; he sat before the television. The NCAA games were on.

Later, the phone rang. He heard Sam leave a friendly message on the answering machine, but did not pick up the phone.

Bill White called during halftime of the second game of the doubleheader. Buzz did not pick up the phone.

He stared blankly at the screen, unable to concentrate on the game, the anvil still on his shoulders.

At seven, he realized that he had not changed out of his pajamas.

Mark Johnson called at eight; Buzz picked up the phone in the kitchen without thinking, out of old habit, regretting his lapse from disciplined sloth.

"Buzz, what are you doing tonight?"

"Nothing much. I'm watching March Madness." Buzz tried to inject normality into his tone.

"Don't follow that much. Hey, wanna come over and wrestle? You wanted lessons—"

"Uh, gee, thanks, Mark. Not tonight. I'm dog tired. I just jogged a few miles…"

"Oh. Great. It's good to exercise. Lifts the spirit, doesn't it?"

"Sure does! I feel great!" *I hope I'm not laying it on too thick.*

There was a pause on the other end. "Sure you don't wanna drop by? The girls would love to see ya. Or I could come over there if you like."

Mark wasn't buying Buzz's line.

You can't snow an FBI guy, Buzz thought glumly, feeling like trash for lying to Mark and getting caught in the lie.

"I really can't. Not today. I've got a few things to do around here." *Like watch television all night.*

"Sure?"

"Yeah. Thanks. Some other time. Thanks Mark. Say hi to Maggie for me."

"I will. Give me a call, Buzz. Anytime. Check that. I'm flying to Atlantic City tomorrow for a stupid conference. I'll be gone for a week. Call me after. Or get the number for me in Atlantic City from Maggie."

"Yeah, sure, thanks."

Buzz hung up the phone.

He stared at the ceiling.

I'm a liar, too.

The lying was like slipping into an old, well-worn pair of Levis that he had found in the back of a closet.

I'm back! Bigger and better than ever before!

An old thirst tickled his palette as it did a hundred times on every day.

And after years of struggle, years of fighting, years of vainly searching for a home, he gave up struggling, fighting, and searching.

He was giving up. The giving up came so fast, so quickly, that he almost missed it.

He looked around the room. He saw his green leather chair. The cut-out Thunderbird collage on the wall. The cast iron skillet. The books on the shelves. It was the same.

He was different. He chose it.

He turned his head quickly. The anvil was still there, as heavy as ever, but now at least, Buzz had a false hope that it would be lifted soon.

He noticed the socket-man, the one who lived in the wall next to his favorite green chair.

"Nooooo!" the little guy pleaded.

"Sorry, man," Buzz said out loud. "I'm tired of you, too. I'm tired of waiting for—things that never come. Now shut up and leave me alone. You're not a little man. You're a friggin' three-pronged electrical socket."

He found an empty glass on the counter, and whipped it across the room. It shattered on the socket, leaving shards of glass on the wooden floor.

Buzz walked over the glass to his bedroom, oblivious to the sliver that jammed into his heel.

Achilles heel, he thought disjointedly.

Say a prayer? a little voice suggested bleakly.

What for? he answered himself confidently. *I'm a drunk. I'm a liar. I'm a sinner. I'm tired.*

It all made perfect sense to a madman.

Come to the water, an evil voice proposed.

Maybe I will, Buzz answered, feeling stronger by the second.

He missed feeling strong. He was tired of weakness. He was tired of being tired when he woke up in the morning.

Maybe I will.

3

Buzz showered, then shaved carefully. He slipped on a pair of jeans, his Scaps T-shirt—this gave him a chuckle—his Stan Smiths, no socks, and grabbed his wallet, checking to make sure his one credit card was still tucked safely within.

Let's see; how about…yeah, that's the place.

Buzz jumbled down the steps of his apartment, walked purposefully to his car, and paused over the rust marks.

Looks like a shore car. All corroded by salty ocean air.

He filed that notion away in a special file in his head.

He drove to the establishment he had in mind. It was only a few minutes away. He smiled at the blinking red neon light in the window.

High Life.

That's the ticket.

He waited for a moment. Perhaps some angel would appear to ward him off. Or he would be struck with the sweats, a paralyzing fear. Maybe his hand would refuse to move toward the handle of the creaky door of the piece-of-crap car.

Surely, God would make this whole project a tad bit harder to pull off.

Nope. Nothing.

He opened the door of the Festiva, skipped to the entrance of the establishment, then pulled the brass handle with a whirl. He felt light on his feet.

Piece of cake.

Come to the water, the voice suggested, far away, another siren song.

Be just a minute, the madman replied.

He took a stool. It was sufficiently dark. The lacquer on the long counter was pleasantly thick.

He fished a cigarette out of his pocket, and popped his Zippo. There was no one else in the place except the man behind the counter. A new guy.

Buzz took a long drag on his smoke.

"What'll it be?" the bartender asked.

Buzz briefly thought of George Bailey in *It's a Wonderful Life,* in the famous bar scene. He rejected the idea of ordering Bailey's Irish Cream. *Too sweet.*

"Let's start with a shot of Jack."

He flipped his credit card on the counter.

"One Jack Daniels coming right up," the bartender confirmed, turning away.

The years between his last drink and his next drink seemed only an interlude to him now—a pause between scenes while watching a video. The bartender returned with the drink.

Well at least you were always a happy drunk, Buzz consoled himself. *You gotta give yourself that much.*

Happiness. The notion was intoxicating.

There was a March Madness game on the television suspended over the other end of the bar. The barkeep was drying a glass with a rag, watching.

On the juke, Bruce Springsteen sang an appropriate, tawdry, self-absorbed tune about the most important thing in the world to him—Bruce Springsteen—in the background.

That night we went down to the river, and into the river we dived...

Such familiar little sights and sounds.

The sounds of home.

Buzz raised his shot glass. Still waiting for the divine intervention that he knew, just knew, was not going to come.

If you down it, Buzz told himself, dipping a mental pen into ink, preparing to sign a treaty that would call off the dog-demons that haunted him, *you've got no one else to blame but yourself.*

Inside him, a little boy, the one conceived without sin, the one that Donna, Ellie, Sam, Bill, and Mark loved, struggled in a darkened womb.

Fair enough. And now, a toast.

"Cut it down. Cut it all down."

4

A few blocks away, Sam had stayed late at Edwards & Associates working on the new bank contract. Ellie had come by with Chinese takeout.

They ate at his desk.

"What's that?" Ellie pointed to the bookcase.

"What's what?" He looked up from his spreadsheet and noodles.

She put her box of chow mein down and walked across the room.

"Oh, it's a Miraculous Medal!" she exclaimed.

"Yes. Donna gave that to me, oh, it must have been a year ago." For the first time he remembered that Mark Johnson had noticed the same medal when they met. *Signal grace?* "Before we knew Mark."

"Really?"

He smiled. "Really. I have no idea what to do with it."

Ellie frowned.

"Sam Fisk?" Her voice dropped with exasperation.

He looked her in the eye. The medal dangled from the chain in her hand. It caught a gleam off the florescent light above.

"You don't want me to put it on, do you?" he asked.

"Come now, dear husband. Look, it even matches my gold one. It's lovely."

"Superstition."

She snorted.

"Jewelry."

She tossed it across the room. He raised his hand and caught it in his fingers.

Sam laughed lightly. "I bet Buzz would get a kick out of this. Jewelry, eh?"

He put it around his neck and tucked it under his polo.

She eyed him closely. He scooped up a forkful of noodles.

He looked up. "Quit staring at me. It means nothing."

"Are you afraid of a little piece of metal?"

"It's not that," he told her. "It's just that I feel like a hypocrite, not believing in it or anything."

"Well, maybe you'll get a miracle."

She came and jumped onto his lap. He almost spilled his noodles. She gave him a long, soy sauce-laced kiss.

"It would be a miracle if I got this spreadsheet done before midnight."

"My, aren't we being workaholics today," she teased, and kissed him again.

They both wondered what had gotten into her.

"Let's go home," she whispered into his ear. "And see what happens in front of that big bay window with a view of Lake Erie."

She gently bit his ear. "I miss you."

"You've been here half the day!"

She shook her head. She raised one eyebrow, holding his gaze. She knew what her beauty did to him.

He pulled her closer.

"Okay, El-darling. We'll watch a video," he joked. "I'll call Buzz again."

She slapped him on the arm.

"Sure, after the lake, dear. After the lake."

☩ ☩ ☩

"Was that *Buzz's* car in front of O'Donnell's Tap House?" she asked incredulously as they drove by on the way home.

Sam missed it. He looked in his rearview mirror. It was too dark outside.

"I can't see it."

"Should we turn around and check?" she asked urgently.

"Naw. It's a strip mall. He's probably at the Laundromat or the pizza joint."

Sam was too young in his marriage to learn to trust a woman's intuition.

"Guess you're right." So was Ellie.

Later, after their time together before the view of the lake, and after Buzz failed to answer his phone for the second time in one day, as Ellie watched *Roman Holiday,* she couldn't shake from her mind two notions about Buzz.

He's got a laundry in his apartment building.

He never eats out. He can't afford it.

That evening, she again dreamed of the dying knight in tarnished armor.

5

Postulant Regina felt an immense urge to leave the Poor Clares the next morning, Sunday. The urge was a giant cloak around her, suffocating her as she dressed, mumbled her morning prayers, and prepared for Mass.

Where is my vocation? she asked herself, alarmed.

She looked inside herself, and found nothing.

A voice kept taunting her: *Leave here, leave here, leave here! You're needed outside. Buzz needs you!*

Oh, what a clever lie.

The Mother Abbess Catherine had warned her and the other new girls about the clever lie of the evil one; a lie designed to destroy their vocations.

"The evil one will always offer you a good thing to seduce you into abandoning your mission!"

She fought the lie.

Buzz needs me in here.

She prayed the Saint Michael Prayer. But the cloak still engulfed her, blocking all the light, as she entered the tiny chapel.

Construction for the expansion was scheduled to begin in a matter of days. In the meantime, they were filling the aisles with makeshift benches, and this added to Donna's sudden sense of claustrophobia.

During the singing, she kept missing the notes, beginning when she knew she should end, singing low when she knew she needed to sing high.

Have I forgotten how to sing in just one day?

Her mind wandered again and again during the readings. She could not remember what she had heard moments earlier.

She suppressed a desire to bolt to the screen and call out to the laymen: "Let me out of here! I'm suffocating."

Maybe Sam and Ellie are out there? Maybe Buzz or Bill are out there. They could help me escape.

She stood, kneeled, and sat like a marionette.

During the Eucharistic prayer, she had oppressive, horrible doubts about the True Presence of Jesus in the Eucharist.

She lost her voice completely during the singing of the Our Father. She felt like a traitor, an interloper, a worthless pile of dung compared to these holy, faithful sisters.

I don't belong here. She was too ashamed for tears. *Nothing matters. I'm wasting my time. I'm wasting God's time.*

By the Lamb of God, she was mentally and emotionally beaten, and had given up the battle, content with taking blows until after Mass. She vowed to tell the Mother Abbess that she would be leaving the monastery soon.

I'm worthless, she believed with every ounce of her existence.

Then the priest raised the chalice and the wafer, intoning the sacred words: "This is the Lamb of God who takes away the sins of the world. Happy are those who are called to his supper."

Donna raised her eyes, preparing to echo the pagan centurion whom Jesus Christ said possessed the greatest faith in all of Israel. She knew that each word was utterly, undeniably true.

"Lord, I am not worthy to receive you, but only say the word, and I shall be healed."

The Lord spoke the word. The cloak of doubt was lifted from Donna's soul.

She approached the altar with fear and trembling, and received the Word onto her tongue, as tears of sublime joy broke like waves onto her cheeks.

Just another day at the office.

6

For the first time in years, Buzz missed Sunday Mass.

On Saturday night, he had stumbled back to his apartment, threw up in the toilet, then passed out.

Come to the water greeted his mind when the pounding in his temples and the bile in his stomach woke him more surely than any alarm clock the next morning.

Well that takes care of the problem with getting up in the morning, he quipped sardonically.

He knew all about mornings after. Time to drink lots of water to stave off alcohol dehydration headaches.

He sat up, braced for the pain, dealt with it squarely, found his feet, stumbled into the kitchen and drank two quarts of water directly from the faucet, wondering all the while where his next shot of booze would come from.

It's like riding a damn bike, he thought darkly, pleased to have traded the anvil of depression for the relatively sedate pain of his hangover.

It made perfect sense to a madman.

Last night was not a blur. He was surprised that he remembered it. He had been thrown out of the bar after last call, laughing at and wildly taunting the barkeep. He smiled as he remembered.

He stuck his head under the shower, toweled off his hair, dressed, packed a duffel bag, grabbed his box of audio tapes, checked his wallet for his credit card, and headed out the door for a brave new day in a cowardly old world.

He sat dumbly in his car, wondering where he should go next.

Here's your hat, what's your hurry, Mister? Are you running away? a little boy in his head asked him.

I'm insulted that you would ask, dear little boy. Of course I'm running away! I'm a drunk. Someday is right around the corner, and we mustn't let it catch up to us.

The stupid little boy persisted. *I've got a chainsaw here, Mister. We could cut down a few trees or Chevrolets...stay home. Stay home in Cleveland.*

Buzz felt like smacking the boy, if he could only see him.

Now my conscience shows up! He laughed out loud, exacerbating his pounding headache.

And it's a stupid little kid!

"A little late, ain't ya, God?" he taunted out loud.

It was a bright, cold day. A perfect day for a road trip.

Shut up, you dumb little piece of crap. This ain't my home. My home is...

He was struck stupid with blankness.

Come to the water, the evil one taunted, having fun. *It's so easy to talk to a madman. They're so reasonable, after a fashion, and open to any fad.*

New Jersey. Down the shore.

That was home.

That's the ticket.

He started the Festiva, finally relieved that he was no longer worried about having to get it fixed. When it broke down, he could just leave it somewhere, anywhere. But here.

He stocked up on supplies at the state liquor store in the strip mall on Center Ridge Road down from the Rini-Regos supermarket. Today's special friend: Old Grand Dad. An old family favorite. Plus the unusual family pet, Wild Turkey.

A big hit with dear old departed dad, if I do recall. The king is gone, but he's not forgotten.

A sentimental favorite for such a beautiful day.

He fumbled the top off and took a swig. The false heat stung his tongue and almost brought tears to his happy eyes.

*It won't be long now. Me and Mr. Visa Card are takin'
Grampa on a trip. The ocean is so lovely this time of year.*

Freezing, cold, and deadly.

7

He was a good drunk driver, from years of practice and because he had been given the gift of quick reflexes. He was a
professionally trained driver, too, of course.

Like most alcoholics, his tolerance level had dropped to a
point where just a few swallows gave him a nice, easy driving buzz.

He played the old drinking favorites during the ride across
the badlands of Pennsylvania: the Rolling Stones, the Who,
Mott the Hoople, and the king of the Buzzbands, the Kinks.

There was something about Ray Davies' voice that really
made him melancholy. But it was a good melancholy, not the
oppressive darkness that had hounded him during his sober
interlude.

He found a tape by the Bay City Rollers in his box on the
passenger's seat, and tossed it out the window, not three miles
from where he had crashed with Donna and Sam almost a
year ago. He inserted another tape.

Michael Stipe of R.E.M. started bragging about losing
his religion, and entertained Buzz for several miles with a
snappy little tune about the end of the world as we know it.

I feel fine.

There weren't many troopers on this truck route that passed
exactly zero major cities in Pennsylvania.

He stopped for a Whopper near Mile Run. The sign on
the road gave him a laugh, as it always did: *Mile Run: 2 Miles.*

Bet their cross country team sucks, he told himself the
same old joke. *They're still trying to break the eight minute
mile there.*

After all, he was a happy drunk.

He pulled into a rest stop near Clearfield.

It won't be long now, he told himself, setting back his seat. No need to waste precious Visa dollars on a motel when it was needed for family friends like Old Grand Dad.

What won't be long? the little boy asked politely.

Shut up, kid. Go talk to the socket man you love so much.

The little boy went away, crying for his mommy.

Serves him right, Buzz told himself. *Pain-in-the-ass kid. I'm not taking him down the shore. No way, no siree. He'll just spoil all the fun.*

He passed out in a stupor, feeling very adult.

8

It was late Sunday night when the phone rang in the Fisk home.

"Buzz is gone," Bill White told Sam over the phone.

"He is? Where?" Sam asked. The alarm in Bill's voice had transferred immediately to Sam's.

"What's the matter," Ellie asked, looking up from a cake she was baking. The child inside wanted chocolate cake, so Ellie was baking one. "It's about Buzz, isn't it?"

Sam nodded, but waved her off to hear Bill. He listened intently for several minutes.

"Right. Mark's where? Atlantic City? Oh. Okay. Did you check the Y?" Sam frowned when he heard the answer.

He hung up the phone.

"What's the matter, honey? It is Buzz. Is he okay?"

"Bill's been all over town searching for him." Sam spoke clearly and deliberately. "He wouldn't answer any phone calls yesterday or today. Mark got through to him and told Bill that Buzz sounded kinda crazy."

He saw the alarm spread to Ellie's eyes. A crease of worry set up shop on her forehead.

"Mark had to go to the East Coast for some FBI thing, so he's not available. He flew to Newark this morning. He told Bill they have to wait seventy-two hours to file a missing persons report."

"Could he just be on a day trip? Maybe he took a ride somewhere—"

"There's more," Sam cut her off. "Bill went to Buzz's apartment building this morning, hoping to go to Mass with him, and when there was no answer on the buzzer, he got the landlord to let him into Buzz's apartment…"

Ellie closed her eyes, bracing herself.

"…and there was vomit in the bathroom. The place reeked of alcohol. His clothes, his bag—gone. Nothing."

She came to him. He took her into his arms.

"We saw his car last night—at the bar," she said weakly.

"Honey, don't. Don't do that to yourself. Last night is gone. We'll help Bill look around town. Check the churches, the bars. We'll find him, get him into a rehab center."

She began to weep, softly. She remembered her dreams clearly.

"But first we have to let Donna know, somehow," he finished. "Because she can pray," he heard himself adding with a perfect kind of agnostic faith.

9

Buzz woke up with a hangover and promptly threw up on the audio tapes on the passenger seat.

"Riding a bike, my ass," he commented, sticky saliva dripping off his lips. He wiped his hands and mouth on his shirt.

Back in the old days, you woulda barfed out the window like a proper drunk.

He followed with a string of foul words that would have made a New Jersey schoolboy proud on a playground— Catholic or public.

He started the car, and before pulling out, reached franti-cally for the two bottles of Wild Turkey he had stashed in the back seat.

One was left. Enough for the last leg to the beach, down the shore, on the ocean. His sudden anxiety subsided.

He checked his watch. Ten o'clock. *Old Pig Norm is probably filling out my pink slip just about now.*

This made him feel exuberant, despite his physical state. He lurched out of the car.

The car still running, he ignored his headache and drank deeply from the water fountain supplied to the rest area by the good citizens of the Commonwealth of Pennsylvania. That helped knock down the pounding in his head, but didn't slake his thirst.

He imagined the sound of breakers, and it brought an ugly smile to his face. He wiped his sweaty head with his hands, then drove off.

He stopped at a diner off the next exit and filled up on flapjacks and bacon. It settled his stomach. At the register, he caught himself thanking God that the diner took credit cards, then laughed hideously, giving the waitress a chill.

One more leg.

The badlands were behind him. Thunderclouds appeared on the horizon. He turned on the radio and flipped through channels until he heard a weather report. A big storm was going to slam the East Coast for the next three days.

He found another station, and the Talking Head's "Take Me to the River" flowed into the little car, filling his head with painful sound.

Good, he thought serenely. *Perfect weather for swimming.*

That made sense to a madman.

10

The extern of the Poor Clare Monastery opened the large wooden door and saw a tall man and his striking young wife. His arm was around her waist, and he had an open umbrella lowered now that they stood beneath the eave. She quickly observed that Ellen Fisk was pregnant.

Lines of concern were etched on their faces.

"May I help you?" Sister Elizabeth asked politely.

"We need to see Postulant Regina right away," Ellie blurted.

They saw surprise cover the peaceful gleam in the nun's eyes, quickly followed by a certain kind of knowing. She recognized Sam and Ellie from their attendance at Mass. (Externs are the sisters assigned to deal with the outside world for practical matters.)

"I'm sorry, but I'm afraid that is not possible."

"Surely there's some kind of exception for emergencies?" Ellen pressed, her tone rising.

"What is the nature of the emergency?" Sister's poise was unnerving.

"Her best friend is in trouble," Sam explained calmly. "He's missing, and we think he's on a drinking binge. He was a reformed alcoholic. His name is Buzz Woodward."

Empathy dawned on Sister Elizabeth's face. How many thousands of people had brought their worst fears and woes to these steps by voice, letter, or phone call since the monastery had been built?

She was a veteran of these kinds of wars.

"It's not within my authority to grant you permission—"

"—then can we speak to someone who is in authority!" Ellie cried out. "I have to see Donna! We helped build your chapel!"

Ellie broke down into horrible sobs. Sam became concerned for the child she was carrying.

"Please, sweetheart, please, please, please," Sam consoled her, kissing her on the cheek. He turned to the nun. "My wife is upset. She loves Buzz. He came here all the time. He introduced us to this place.

"I understand you have rules. That's what makes this place special—your special rules. We understand. We don't have to see Donna. I don't think we came here to see her anyway. Well, Ellie did. I came here to speak to your, uh, to your God.

"We don't even have to speak to him. Tell Donna to speak to him for us. Tell Donna to tell him to find Buzz and help him. He's our friend."

Sam's eyes were full of tears. He turned Ellie around in his arms, and led her down the steps to the pathway to the parking lot, holding the umbrella over her, keeping the water away.

11

Bill White left a message for Mark at his hotel in Brigantine, New Jersey, which was just north of Atlantic City, then pressed the end button on his cellular phone.

Wish you were here, friend, he told the rain, looking up at the starless sky. *We could sure use your help.*

He walked back to his car. He had checked two dozen parishes on a hunch that Buzz would find his way to the Eucharist.

He had called every police station in town, and charmed the station officers as best he could to put out the word to keep an eye out for Buzz in the bars and hotels in the area. There were hundreds of bars on the West Side alone. Too many to search. He had checked over twenty near Buzz's apartment after confirming that Buzz had gotten blitzed at O'Donnell's.

There had been no sign of him since.

Bill tempered his worry with a faith-filled certainty: it was time to pray. He started his car and drove to Our Lady of the Angels.

There was a perpetual adoration chapel there.

It worked for Mark. It'll work for Buzz, he steeled himself. Bill knew his prayer would be dry, perhaps even tedious. It almost always was so. That didn't matter to him.

He had trained for this war. That did matter.

Chapter Twenty-One

1

Thunderclaps woke Buzz to the persistent pelting of heavy raindrops on the thin roof of his car.

He looked around. It was not yet dark. The clouds merely gave an illusion of nighttime. He wondered if there was a way to drink the rain to slam his headache back a bit.

H-two-O.

"Aiche-two-oh," he whispered coarsely.

Doesn't matter anymore, a voice soothed him. *We're almost finished. Time to take the long walk, Buzz. Plenty of water at the end of the walk. Then we'll swim.*

He was parked in the driveway of his uncle's duplex. At the ocean, down the shore.

To the beach.

There was an empty bottle next to him on the seat. The last leg of the trip was lost in a puddle of blackout. The stench from his vomit was sickening.

He opened the window of the car, inhaled the wet, salty air, and began to dry heave.

This lasted for several grating minutes.

Musta passed out when I parked, he deduced, falling back into his seat. He was feeling a bit sober.

Maybe I ran out of the stuff for the last hundred miles.

This alarmed him. Where to get more booze?

He reached for the key and despaired. It was in the *on* position. He had left the car running; the gas tank was empty, the battery dead.

Dead.

In the house, you moron, the voice prompted.

His spirits rose.

You gonna kill yourself, Mister?

That damned boy was back, all filled with ageless concern.

*I'm leaving you in the car with the stink. And no, I'm **not** going to kill myself. I'm going for a walk. Good-bye.*

But Mister—

He grabbed his wallet and opened the door, collapsing out of the car, his face and crewcut pressing into the coarse, pebbled concrete.

He began to bleed.

Close the door, you idiot, the adult voice reprimanded. *Before that freakin' kid gets out.*

Buzz was too disoriented to comprehend. His temples pounded. He tasted blood. He touched his cheeks.

It tasted good. Salty, like the raging ocean forty yards east.

Lightning lit up the ghoulish smile on his face.

Yeah, the long walk. Then a swim.

He crawled for a few yards, then collapsed when the muscle in his calf spasmed, sending a hot spiked message of pain up his spinal cord, crashing through the competing pains standing sentry there. The big man's shrieks punctuated the thunder. Or was that the pounding in his head?

It doesn't matter.

Nothing mattered

Except the hooch in dear uncle's cabinets.

Sitting on his rear, he rubbed out the cramp, then found his feet. Feeling his strength return like a slow tide, he began a hunched march to the front deck of the duplex.

The front door was locked. He checked around for nosy neighbors. There wasn't a light on in any house he could see.

Alone.

He grabbed a heavy pine picnic bench, and cast it through the front window next to the door, timing his blow with a crack of thunder.

He cut the palm of his hand climbing through the window. That was not enough pain to get his attention.

The next drink was near at hand, and that felt good. That felt real good. He found the light switch, shuffled to the cabinet next to the sink, and hungrily snatched the first bottle of hard liquor within reach.

Gordon's Gin.

Hi Gordy.

A cousin to Jack and Grampa.

You'll do.

He poured it down his throat, gagging at the third gulp, scorning the air for the alcohol.

He slid down the cabinet, oblivious to the long gash the square edge of the oven handle opened in his back.

He was delirious now. He closed his eyes, and saw a dragon, breathing fire. He opened his eyes again, with a quiver.

That friggin' boy was back, standing in the corner in front of the fridge. He had a crewcut. He was wearing brown shorts and a black and yellow Charlie Brown shirt. His legs featured thick, bony knees with scratches on them.

He was holding a big green chainsaw in his right hand; a spinning basketball hovered an inch above the linoleum at his feet. He was watching Buzz intently.

You again! Buzz shouted in his head. *How did you get out of the car! Why don't you get the f—"*

But the boy cut him off with the raising of his right hand, bent at his elbow, making a curious-looking peace sign.

Donna's coming, he said placidly. *And she's bringing my friend.*

Buzz tried to curse, but thunder rolled in, lightning flashed like a giant bulb, and the boy was gone. Buzz found himself staring at the Hotpoint refrigerator.

Buzz's eyes closed, more from fatigue than tiredness.

Wake up!

He bolted upright.

Come to the water, Buzz. Forget the boy.

He pulled himself up to his feet. He wasn't really tired. Just worn out. Plenty of energy to finish the job. To take the long walk. A little dip.

He methodically took off his pants and shirt, and stood in his boxer shorts. Waiting. He looked at his watch. It was three o'clock.

I'm always waiting.

2

Donna knelt before the Blessed Sacrament. There were two other sisters in the chapel. It was three o'clock.

She spoke directly to Jesus, not with words, but with a word. Like a lamb, she gently placed a word on the altar.

His name is Buzz, she said.

I am the Good Shepherd, the Word replied. *I know my sheep.*

Her prayer was ordinary. She was confident. She was in the world, but not of it.

3

On Sunday night, not knowing where else to go, or what else to do, Sam and Ellie returned to their empty home and fell asleep on the couch in each other's arms, waiting by the phone. They slept until eight, awakened by the sound of rain spitting on the window with the view of the lake.

Sam took Monday off. It was a bitter cold, blustery day.

They went through the motions of preparing for the day, waiting for eleven o'clock Mass at Saint Chris, unable to eat their cold cereal.

They went to Mass and returned to wait by the phone. Bill had given their number to the authorities.

At two forty-five, they left to drive to Saint Christophers in Rocky River to pray the Divine Mercy Chaplet.

Sam mouthed the words to placate his sullen wife, certain that he was giving voice to meaningless sounds that no one heard but her.

4

One last lie for Donna's sake, the poor girl, Buzz rationalized. *Maybe it will keep that damned boy away, too.*

Like a good drunk, he had an angle.

He was sure she wasn't coming. She was locked away in her own world, with her own family, no longer a part of his, a million miles away.

I won't tell them where I am.

Wind keened through the broken window. He took a gulp of gin straight from the bottle, exhaled, then picked up the phone on the kitchen counter.

If he's home, hang up.

He dialed Sam's number.

He was lighthearted when he heard the answering machine click on. The message startled him.

It was Ellie's voice on the recording: "Buzz, if it's you, tell us where you are. We'll come get you. We'll help you. We love you." *Beep.*

He was suddenly aware that he had not prepared his farewell speech.

Farewell speech?

The machine clicked off. He hung up the phone.

He took another snort, and looked through the wind for the first time at the jetty.

The huge rocky leviathan lay motionless in a fury of foamy waves, which crashed impotently against its spine, causing soaring arms of water to reach for darkened clouds.

Yeah. I'm just going for a swim. The weather is perfect, he reassured himself, biting his lower lip with a nod.

He dialed again. He shut his ears to Ellie's voice, which was dripping with expectation. He flushed the image of waltzing with her out of his mind.

No time to get sentimental.

He got the message down this time, cold.

5

When Sam and Ellie arrived home, it was Ellie who reached the answering machine first.

Click. *Beep.* Nothing. The sound of thunder.

Click. "This is Buzz Woodward. I'm going for a long walk." There was a sound of a short, coarse laugh. An insane laugh. "Tell Donna that she had nothing to do with this. Tell Ellie that I'll be back for another waltz." There was another sound, indecipherable. "And Sam, you were right all along. Thanks, man." *Beep.* Click.

Ellie looked up in confusion. "What does it mean?"

Sam fell to his knees. He tore open his oxford, the buttons scattering on the wooden floor. He flooded the room with an agonized, inarticulate cry of sorrow.

"Sam!?"

She went to him.

"What did he mean?!" She barely kept her voice below a scream.

You never could lie, you poor bastard, he thought despondently. *Three lies.*

"It's a suicide note."

He fell to the floor. His right hand clasping his Miraculous Medal.

"Sam. You're scaring me. How can you be sure?"

He ignored her, and between sobs that expanded his chest in great heaves, he whimpered, "No, Buzz. No Buzz. No Buzz."

"No Buzz *what?*" Ellie demanded hysterically.

"I'm not right. I'm not right, Buzz."

He looked up to her.

"I'm not right, Ellie. Buzz is right."

"Sam," Ellie said hoarsely, ordering him to look at her with her tone. "Get a hold of yourself. What do we do next? Maybe he's nearby. Maybe we can find him before—before it's too late."

He was still on the floor, leaning forward on his gangly knees and elbows, his hands raking his thinning hair.

"Get up," she commanded. "Find Buzz."

She punched him in the ribs with all her might, and cut him with her ring.

This worked. He raised himself to his knees, then to his feet. He was a flexible tower again, unbroken by the gale that had just bent him over. He took a deep breath.

"Where is he, Sam?" Ellie asked calmly, hiding her darkest fear.

Far away, grace told her. *Far away.*

"Is he far?" she questioned him, knowing that things always came to Sam, just as she had come to Sam herself. It would come to him.

"Play the message again," he told her.

6

Buzz stood on the dunes ten yards beyond the deck of his uncle's house. The bottle was in his hand, a half liter remaining, lapping in tiny waves inside the glass walls. He looked up at the sky. The clouds were darker now.

Come to the water.

He took a burning sip. He didn't want to pass out before reaching the jetty. He looked at the sky again, looking for the cross, which was just a piece of wood now to him.

It's probably over China right now, anyway. Stupid, made-up story. Only kids believe in stories. Sam was right.

He flicked the last cigarette he would ever smoke into the wind.

7

Donna wanted to continue praying, but the bell rang. It was time for dinner. She had already been given permission to pray longer than usual.

She rose calmly, being careful not to linger even slightly. She would obey the bell, freely, with confidence. This was the only way, Mother Abbess had assured the postulants.

Obedience mattered.

For in obedience, there was grace in abundance.

I'll eat dinner for Buzz, she thought cheerfully. *Then I'll sing for Buzz. Then I'll sleep for Buzz.*

And Sam, grace told her. *Sam, too. For all your friends.*

8

The phone began ringing as he inserted his key into his hotel room door.

"Mark, this is Sam."

"Hi Sam, I got Bill's message. What can I do to help?"

Mark had forgotten his wallet, and returned to his room from the meeting to get it on an impulse.

"Buzz is on Long Beach Island. 121 Muriel Avenue. We think he's going to kill himself, or do something crazy. How far is that from you?"

"How far do you need it to be?" Mark asked without a trace of irony.

"Right now, Mark. You've got to get there right now."

"I'm on it. Is there anything else?"

"There's an Acme on the boulevard on the opposite side of Muriel—"

Mark didn't even say good-bye or hang up the phone. Ellie, who was listening on the second line in the kitchen, heard the sound of a door slamming shut.

9

Less than two minutes earlier, Bill White had taken a call from Sam on his cellular phone, right inside the Eucharistic Chapel at Our Lady of the Angels.

He was reading *The Way* when it rang.

"We found Buzz," Sam said calmly. "Give me the number at Mark's hotel."

"Where? Why?"

"No time. Just give me that number fast."

Bill fumbled open his pocket calendar. He nervously relayed the phone number and the room number to Sam.

He heard Ellie say thank you on the line, and a click.

"Sam, you still there? Ellie?"

"It's me, Bill. Ellie."

"Don't you need to call Mark?"

"Sam's dialing on the second line right now."

"How did you find him? Where is he? What's going on?"

"He left a phone message. He's down the shore. In New Jersey. Sam thinks he's going to kill himself."

She heard a long, static silence.

"Sam figured it out," she explained to fill the void. "Buzz didn't say where he was. Sam listened to the tape seven times. Then he heard the seagull."

"Huh?"

"Don't worry about it. It won't matter if we don't get to him in time. Mark's fifty minutes away. Bill, if you ever prayed in your life, now's the time."

"What are you going to do?"

"We haven't thought that far ahead," Ellie explained. "At least I haven't. Sam? Sam—"

Bill was confused. Ellie was no longer speaking to him.

"Sam? Uh, Bill. Gotta go. Love you." Ellie hung up.

She heard the sound of screeching tires in the driveway. She sprinted across the house to the dining room window, and saw the red tail lights of the Honda as it pulled away on Lake Road, picking up speed.

Sam was gone.

✝ ✝ ✝

In the Eucharistic chapel a town over, Bill looked down at *The Way.* His thumb was next to a passage.

Conversion is a matter of a moment. Sanctification is a work of a lifetime.

10

The tide was high. The storm, in a maelstrom waltz, increased in intensity.

The Miraculous Medal and chain dropped from Buzz's hand onto the wet sand and became tangled in the high dune grass.

Come to the water, demons sang sweetly.

He took a step toward his jetty. The long walk had begun. In the footprint he left behind, the sand was stained with blood.

Buzz was no longer a cheerful lush.

Don't screw this up. Be a man. There's nothing I hate worse than an incompetent drunk…

The wind was so loud, he realized that he could barely hear his own thoughts.

That's a relief.

11

After ripping the keys out of the hand of the mystified police chief of Brigantine in the meeting room of the hotel, Mark worked his way up to one-hundred miles an hour in less than three minutes, sirens wailing and lights flashing.

He did the math in his head.

Forty-five minutes at sixty miles per hour. Twenty-two minutes at one-hundred and twenty miles per hour.

Twenty-two minutes.

Not enough time to reach Buzz.

But enough time for a Rosary and a Divine Mercy Chaplet.

The FBI agent prayed for two intentions.

That he not hurt any drivers, pedestrians, or himself.

That the big strong bull, Buzz Woodward, would pass out before twenty-two minutes was up.

12

The Honda screeched to a halt. The driver jumped out and ran to the entrance of the building. Sam walked purposefully up the main aisle of Saint Raphaels Church in Bay Village. He had not been in this church before, but it was the one closest to his home.

It was empty. The lights were off, except for a spotlight on the altar. Even in the dim evening light, he could tell that this was one of the ugliest Catholic churches he had ever seen, with sixties-style colors and odd designs on the walls.

That didn't matter.

He was momentarily dismayed when he didn't spot the red candle.

There's always a red candle. Buzz told me himself.

He walked to the altar and scanned desperately.

It was usually behind the altar!

Is this really a Catholic church?

He wasn't certain. He was losing priceless time.

There it was, flickering, alone, throwing red shadows on the wall to the side.

Waiting for him. Waiting, for a long, long time.

13

There's that damned kid again! What's he doing out here in weather like this!

He spit and cursed. Buzz was only ten yards from the jetty and the wind almost blew him over when he stopped.

The boy and his creations stood athwart his goal.

The child was standing before a tall sandcastle. It looked as if it had been crafted in a medieval guildhouse. It was as tall as the boy.

Next to the sandcastle, there was a sculpture of a huge sanddragon, its teeth large, not the least decayed by the ravages of the wind. It hovered over the boy.

The boy was holding a wooden sword, facing the sanddragon. A child's toy. He was oblivious to the gusting wind, which was buffeting Buzz in angry waves.

Hey kid, what are you doing out here?

He turned and looked up at the adult Buzz.

I could ask you the same thing, Mister.

The boy smiled with his sleepy eyes, then skipped around the dragon, laughing effortlessly, brandishing his sword with glee.

"Get out of my way," Buzz ordered.

The boy ignored him. He sliced the head off the dragon. Buzz's head was hammered with pain.

"Cut that out!" Buzz screamed. *He can't hear me in the wind.* "I'm just going for a swim!"

Liar, liar. Pants on fire!

Still looking away from Buzz, the child thrust his sword into the heart of the dragon. Buzz heard an unearthly wail, far way, beyond the ocean.

The boy stopped. He turned and addressed Buzz with absolute seriousness.

Let me out. Let me in.

"You're crazy!" Buzz screamed, swaying, clamping his hands over his ears.

The king saw the queen's name in the pines, Mister, and He remembers, he heard the boy say earnestly.

Pines? What pines? What king? Buzz thought, confused.

The pines we cut up that day. Remember? Buzz! Buzz! Buzz! He lifted his pathetic sword.

I don't remember that, Buzz lied. His eyes unleashed tears despite himself. He stifled a sob. Only little boys cry.

Come to the water, a confident voice called from the jetty, beyond the boy. *Kill the boy. Kill the mirage.*

Buzz nodded sagely. It made sense to a madman.

"You're a mirage," Buzz told the boy, having wisened up. "I'll walk right through you. This is not a game. I'm taking the long walk today."

He saw the boy's face show fear. A huge wave came in from the surf, and whispered violently through the boy's legs and the sandcastle. They were untouched, ghosts. The boy looked down to his feet. He looked up, opened his mouth, but no words came out.

"Gotcha, you little weasel."

Buzz took another bloody step forward, leaning into the salty, wet wind. *Little brat.*

Buzz sliced through his ghosts, ignoring the sobs of a little boy.

14

Sam stood before the tabernacle, his feet spread shoulder length, his hands together, composing himself before the King.

He reached up and grasped the Miraculous Medal around his neck.

"Jesus, my friend Buzz is sick and is going to die. He needs your help. I can't go where he is. I know I don't have to be there.

"As you know, I run a business. I have employees who work for me. I tell them what to do, and they do it. I know you have workers everywhere now.

"I ignored you for so long. Now I feel your heart in Donna. I behold the beauty of your creation in Ellie. I watch your steadfastness in Bill. I marvel at your strength in Mark.

"I don't deserve these friends. I am not worthy for them to even come into my home. I know you will heal Buzz with your word. Thank you.

"I never knew my mother. I'm looking forward to meeting yours. I'm going back to my wife now."

He turned and walked out of the Church of Saint Raphael the Divine Physician.

✝ ✝ ✝

Buzz scaled the rocks quickly, falling only once when a large wave crashed over him.

He scraped his forearm on the barnacles. More blood.

He picked his way among the craggy boulders, carefully placing his feet, taking advantage of his low center of gravity, avoiding the green, slippery seaweeds adhering to the surface of the rocks closer to the water.

Don't look back. The suffering is almost complete.

With the boy behind him, he was feeling better, stronger, more in alignment with the vast forces buffeting him.

He was well beyond the waterline now. He stood up fitfully, carefully, on the precipice of a high, jutting boulder, the roiling water on three sides, a body-length away. The wind gusted, and he almost lost his balance, barely avoiding falling in.

Just fall in. Stretch your hands wide and fall in. Even if you try to swim, you'll never get to the shore. If the rocks and waves don't get you, the booze and freezing water will.

His final instructions understood, he paused to relish the beauty of the torrential scene. He stretched out his arms, and brought his feet together, opening his eyes wide, perhaps for the first time. Rain fell on him. He opened his mouth, drinking it in for one last time. He allowed himself the luxury of one final wonderment.

Nature's Cathedral, Sam and Donna called it.

Lightning cracked, illuminating the beauty and grandeur of God's fury. Bill White had guessed correctly, for Buzz had gone to church after all.

My life hasn't mattered.

Then Buzz heard a voice, and began to turn to look through squinting eyes back toward the sand.

That pesky kid is back for certain, determined to spoil everything!

"Gwynny."

It was a strong, clear voice, the voice of a man, and Buzz heard it as if there were no wind, waves, rocks, or thunder.

The man stood on the boulder a yard away, perfectly, beautifully balanced. He was dressed in shining silver armor, the mail immaculately wrought, a gleaming broadsword in his right hand. He had no helmet. His curly red hair was cropped to his shoulders.

"Who are you?" Buzz shouted. "Are you a ghost? Where's the boy?"

The knight smiled mysteriously.

"Do not lay a hand on the boy. Do not do anything to him. You have come to the water, and the others have been spared by your suffering. Our king saw the name of the queen in the pines."

Buzz blinked in confusion. He felt weak. He was cold. His heart pounded violently, competing with the hammer blows in his skull. He heard a siren.

He collapsed onto the rock at ocean's edge.

A huge gush of water rushed over the jetty, carrying away many things, but not the body of Buzz Woodward. Red and blue lights formed a second wave.

Mark Johnson rammed his cruiser into a drift, threw open the door, and bolted down the shore to the jetty.

He scrambled across the rocks to his friend, knelt on one knee and felt for a pulse on Buzz's neck. After a moment, he smiled at the thunder.

"Thank God."

Mark spied another huge wave, building in power and ferocity, speeding toward the jetty.

Tough sonufabitch, aincha?

He lifted him with mighty arms, picked his way back over the rocks, jumping gingerly onto the sand, crushing a mound that resembled a sandcastle. Buzz's arms swung in the wind.

As Mark walked by, he did not notice the wooden toy sword jammed into another pile of sand that had once been shaped like a dragon.

Chapter Twenty-Two

1

Not long afterwards, there was a video on the seat of Buzz's empty car. *Song of Bernadette*. They would all watch it later, after the party.

Inside, Sam listened to Donna sing. Friends were with him. Bill. Mark and Maggie with their new son. Even Edward, still the atheist, was here, in God's cathedral.

Sam stood up. He reached for Ellie's hand. She squeezed tight, holding on. She would never let go. He looked at Buzz, who nodded.

The homily and baptism were over.

It was time. Sam Fisk began to pray with his friends:

"We believe in one God, the Father, the Almighty, maker of heaven and earth, and of all things seen and unseen..."

2

A summer evening. Low tide. A breeze came off the ocean. Ellie stood on the jetty, holding the hand of a child. Her blond hair glistened in the setting rays. The two men kept an eye on the mother and son from the deck.

"You know, Sam, throughout those horrible days, I never lost my faith in God. I deserved to die on that night you and Mark saved my life. You see, my sin wasn't taking that drink in O'Donnells. My sin was choosing madness over the sanity of the cross. When I went to confession, that's what I told the priest—that I cut down the cross. There's a difference between losing your faith and despair."

Buzz sighed, then took a sip of water.

"I sure wish Donna was here. I wish I could find that Miraculous Medal I dropped in the sand. I wish that Jenny would love me. I wish for a lot things.

"I don't drink anymore, but my heart is still heavy. I suspect there's no cure for the kind of soul I've got. Maybe there is. Now when I read Sirach, I take him seriously. When I pray the Rosary, I can picture Mary in my head, and the snake is gone. That's a good thing. I'm willing to wait for heaven. Besides, I'll always have the man in the electrical socket."

Buzz laughed.

Sam nodded knowingly.

He had waited too, before faith came. Things always did.

"I'm gonna be okay, Sam. When I look at you and Ellie and little Christopher, and think about Donna, and see how happy you are—well, that's enough for me. That's got to be enough. Friendship is the best kind of love. I know that now. Thanks for giving me a second chance. I guess you got one, too.

"I know why I'm here. I'm here to cut things down. I read once about Saint Boniface cutting down this big oak tree the barbarians worshiped. There was a big crowd. He hacked it down. He turned to them and said, 'Where's your god now?' Man, I loved that. I'm sure me and Bonnie would have gotten along just fine. Just fine.

"But there's always a choice. You gotta watch where you swing that ax. I just hope I never try to cut down the cross again."

The beautiful woman came off the jetty, carrying her child. She called out. Buzz and Sam stepped off the deck onto the warm sand. They walked toward the water to meet her.

Epilogue

Jesus entered Capernaum. There was a centurion who had a servant whom he valued highly. This servant was sick and about to die.

The centurion heard of Jesus and sent some elders of the Jews to him, asking him to come and heal his servant.

When they came to Jesus, they pleaded earnestly, "This man deserves to have you do this because he loves our nation and has built our synagogue."

So Jesus went with them.

He was not far from the house when the centurion sent friends to say to him, "Lord, don't trouble yourself, for I do not deserve to have you come under my roof. That is why I did not even consider myself worthy to come to you.

"But say the word, and my servant will be healed. For I myself am a man under authority, with soldiers under me.

"I tell this one, 'Go,' and he goes; and that one, 'Come,' and he comes. I say to my servant, 'Do this,' and he does it."

When Jesus heard this, he was amazed at the centurion, and said, turning to the following crowd:

"I tell you, I have not seen greater faith in all of Israel."

Then the men who had been sent returned to the house and found the servant well.

Did You Enjoy Reading
Conceived Without Sin?

Would you like to introduce Sam, Donna, Mark, Ellie, and
Buzz to your…

Parents

Brothers and Sisters

Friends

Relatives

Prayer Group

Church or Parish

Business Associates

Local Bookstore Owner

Neighbors

Local School

Local Library

Pastor or Priest?

Saint Jude Media would like to help you.
We're ready to send you as many copies as you want for a
nominal donation. Use the convenient Request Form on the
next page and write to us today. Available at Catholic
retailers everywhere. May also be ordered through most
bookstores.

If you would like to begin reading
Bud Macfarlane Jr.'s first novel,
Pierced by a Sword
turn to the page after the last request form.

Conceived Without Sin
REQUEST FORM # 1

Dear Saint Jude Media:
Please send me a copy (or copies) of **Conceived Without Sin**. I understand that the first copy is free and that a donation is **not required** for one copy. I am not asking you to send a book or books to anyone other than myself.

Signed: _____

(Please Print)

Name: _____

Address: _____

Town: _____

State: _____ Zip: _____

Suggested **Optional** Donation for one book: **$1 to $10**
Donation for **more than one** book, any quantity: **$2 - $5 each**
(For more details about Saint Jude Media, see next page.)

Quantity Desired	**X**	**Donation Per Book**		**Subtotal:**

_____ X _____ = _____

Optional extra gift for shipping = _____

Optional gift for Saint Jude Media = _____

TOTAL DONATION* = $ _____

*Your contribution to Saint Jude Media is tax deductible. Any questions? Call (216) 333-4723. Sorry, no phone requests for books accepted. We'll ship your book the day we receive your letter.

CWS1

Please make checks payable to "Saint Jude Media" & send to:
Saint Jude Media
Box 26120 • Fairview Park, OH 44126

How Saint Jude Media Works

- If you do not have a request form, writing a simple letter to receive books is okay. Request forms are also available at www.catholicity.com on the Saint Jude Media homepage.

- Personal correspondence is encouraged. Tell us what you think of this book. We also welcome typographical, grammatical, and fact-checking suggestions for future printings (please include page and line number). Email us at saint.jude.media@catholicity.com

- We will send one free book to each person who writes to us directly. A donation for one book is not required, but you may send a donation if you wish.

- Using the honor system, we ask that you please refrain from sending us the addresses of people other than yourself. Please ask others to write to us directly. We will only send materials to those who personally ask for them, whether a donation is enclosed or not.

- At the present time, we only accept requests for materials by mail. Sorry, no phone requests. Only requests from the United States and Canada will be honored unless a sufficient donation to cover shipping is enclosed.

- Saint Jude Media will gladly absorb shipping charges on all requests, but feel free to add extra for shipping if you wish.

- Fast Delivery—All requests will be shipped on the day we open your envelope!

- Under normal circumstances, we are not able to "advance" quantities of books before receiving a donation.

- We will periodically write to let you know about new books and developments, but you will never receive a "fund raising letter" from us. We will not sell or lend your name to other groups—ever.

- These details apply to individuals as well as organizations such as bookstores, etc. Individuals, bookstores, gift shops, schools, and other organizations may accept donations for this book no greater than $5. A promotional retail display is available upon request.

Conceived Without Sin
REQUEST FORM # 2

Dear Saint Jude Media:

Please send me a copy (or copies) of **Conceived Without Sin**. I understand that the first copy is free and that a donation is **not required** for one copy. I am not asking you to send a book or books to anyone other than myself.

Signed: _____

(Please Print)

Name: _____

Address: _____

Town: _____

State: _____ Zip: _____

Suggested **Optional** Donation for one book: **$1 to $10**
Donation for **more than one** book, any quantity: **$2 - $5 each**
(For more details about Saint Jude Media, see next page.)

Quantity Desired	X	Donation Per Book		Subtotal:
_____	X	_____	=	_____

Optional extra gift for shipping   =   _____

Optional gift for Saint Jude Media   =   _____

TOTAL DONATION*   = $ _____

*Your contribution to Saint Jude Media is tax deductible. Any questions? Call (216) 333-4723. Sorry, no phone requests for books accepted. We'll ship your book the day we receive your letter.

CWS1

Please make checks payable to "Saint Jude Media" & send to:
Saint Jude Media
Box 26120 • Fairview Park, OH 44126

How Saint Jude Media Works

- If you do not have a request form, writing a simple letter to receive books is okay. Request forms are also available at www.catholicity.com on the Saint Jude Media homepage.

- Personal correspondence is encouraged. Tell us what you think of this book. We also welcome typographical, grammatical, and fact-checking suggestions for future printings (please include page and line number). Email us at saint.jude.media@catholicity.com

- We will send one free book to each person who writes to us directly. A donation for one book is not required, but you may send a donation if you wish.

- Using the honor system, we ask that you please refrain from sending us the addresses of people other than yourself. Please ask others to write to us directly. We will only send materials to those who personally ask for them, whether a donation is enclosed or not.

- At the present time, we only accept requests for materials by mail. Sorry, no phone requests. Only requests from the United States and Canada will be honored unless a sufficient donation to cover shipping is enclosed.

- Saint Jude Media will gladly absorb shipping charges on all requests, but feel free to add extra for shipping if you wish.

- Fast Delivery—All requests will be shipped on the day we open your envelope!

- Under normal circumstances, we are not able to "advance" quantities of books before receiving a donation.

- We will periodically write to let you know about new books and developments, but you will never receive a "fund raising letter" from us. We will not sell or lend your name to other groups—ever.

- These details apply to individuals as well as organizations such as bookstores, etc. Individuals, bookstores, gift shops, schools, and other organizations may accept donations for this book no greater than $5. A promotional retail display is available upon request.

Conceived Without Sin
REQUEST FORM # 3

Dear Saint Jude Media:
Please send me a copy (or copies) of **Conceived Without Sin**. I understand that the first copy is free and that a donation is **not required** for one copy. I am not asking you to send a book or books to anyone other than myself.

Signed: _____
(Please Print)

Name: _____

Address: _____

Town: _____

State: _____ Zip: _____

Suggested **Optional** Donation for one book: **$1 to $10**
Donation for **more than one** book, any quantity: **$2 - $5 each**
(For more details about Saint Jude Media, see next page.)

Quantity Desired   X   Donation Per Book   Subtotal:
_____

_____   X   _____   =   _____

Optional extra gift for shipping   =   _____

Optional gift for Saint Jude Media   =   _____

TOTAL DONATION*   = $ _____

*Your contribution to Saint Jude Media is tax deductible. Any questions? Call (216) 333-4723. Sorry, no phone requests for books accepted. We'll ship your book the day we receive your letter.

CWS1

Please make checks payable to "Saint Jude Media" & send to:
Saint Jude Media
Box 26120 • Fairview Park, OH 44126

How Saint Jude Media Works

- If you do not have a request form, writing a simple letter to receive books is okay. Request forms are also available at www.catholicity.com on the Saint Jude Media homepage.

- Personal correspondence is encouraged. Tell us what you think of this book. We also welcome typographical, grammatical, and fact-checking suggestions for future printings (please include page and line number). Email us at saint.jude.media@catholicity.com

- We will send one free book to each person who writes to us directly. A donation for one book is not required, but you may send a donation if you wish.

- Using the honor system, we ask that you please refrain from sending us the addresses of people other than yourself. Please ask others to write to us directly. We will only send materials to those who personally ask for them, whether a donation is enclosed or not.

- At the present time, we only accept requests for materials by mail. Sorry, no phone requests. Only requests from the United States and Canada will be honored unless a sufficient donation to cover shipping is enclosed.

- Saint Jude Media will gladly absorb shipping charges on all requests, but feel free to add extra for shipping if you wish.

- Fast Delivery—All requests will be shipped on the day we open your envelope!

- Under normal circumstances, we are not able to "advance" quantities of books before receiving a donation.

- We will periodically write to let you know about new books and developments, but you will never receive a "fund raising letter" from us. We will not sell or lend your name to other groups—ever.

- These details apply to individuals as well as organizations such as bookstores, etc. Individuals, bookstores, gift shops, schools, and other organizations may accept donations for this book no greater than $5. A promotional retail display is available upon request.

PIERCED

BY A SWORD

BUD MACFARLANE JR.

Foreword by Michael O'Brien — Best-Selling Author of Father Elijah

Characters so real you'll swear you know them. A plot that twists and turns so fast you'll lose sleep to find out what happens next. A riveting story that whisks you from Salt Lake City to Chicago to Rome to Notre Dame. A supernatural thriller that will rock your world.

PIERCED BY A SWORD

A savvy drug dealer from the meanest streets of Cleveland…

A no-nonsense Irish Pope who drives his own car and travels in disguise…

A beautiful, unmarried pregnant woman with a quick wit and quicker temper…

A relentless, aging tycoon from Utah…

A mysterious Dark Man who sees the future before it happens…

A handsome, hard-drinking, hard-living securities broker…

A soft-spoken, shy, gigantic former NFL football star from Louisiana…

A fast-talking young priest from New Jersey with a penchant for causing trouble…

…And the Mother of God.

PIERCED BY A SWORD

BUD MACFARLANE JR.

SAINT JUDE MEDIA
CLEVELAND, OHIO

Foreword

Long after our century is over, long after the fifty thousand titles that are published in English each year are forgotten, you and others will turn to tattered copies of *Pierced by a Sword* and smile, and puzzle over it, and wonder how it was written, and thank God for it. You will remember the darkness of our times and realize that God prepares, that He always sends us his messengers the prophets, his truth-sayers, his servants.

You may be cracking open this book just to please a friend or neighbor or aunt or son or mother or father or pastor who gave it to you. You may be asking yourself whether it's worth the effort to invest time to begin reading it.

You should.

The supermarket tabloids are flooded with "end times" prophecies these days, predicting disasters of all kinds, promising saviors of all kinds, and stirring into the mix a distorted version of what Catholic prophets and mystics have been warning us about for centuries. Although *Pierced by a Sword* plunges us into an exciting roller coaster ride through the coming years, it is not that kind of prophecy. It does not attempt to predict what the future will be—rather, it is a superb story of what the future might look like, feel like, and how each of us might fit into the drama. In this book, you will not find **the** future, but you will find **a** future.

Pierced by a Sword is the story of a group of ordinary men and women who change the world, and do so at a time in history when the powers of darkness appear to have fatally undermined the political, economic, and cultural landscape. The characters in this book are more than just fascinating and believable. They are real. You will meet poor men and yuppies, investment brokers and drug dealers, parish priests, housewives, native Americans and Irish nuns, bad Catholics and good Protestants—and vice versa, atheists and agnostics, college professors, saints, popes, an antipope, a Russian general, U.S. Marines, a New Age guru, jaded street-kids, suburbanites, corporate magnates, a hot-shot pilot, a pro football star, a grade school teacher, authentic visionaries, hit men, and both shades of angels. And many, many more. This is our world. This is your world.

Let me tell you a little about the storyteller, the author of *Pierced by a Sword*. Like so many readers of this novel, I first heard of it when it was sent to me by a friend. She thought that since I had written a novel about a fictional apocalypse, I would enjoy reading something by another "end times novelist." My curiosity was aroused, but I was simply too busy to spend precious time on a paperback that was two inches thick and looked like it came from the pulp fiction rack at the local corner store. Who has the time to read nowadays? Besides, I didn't need another book chock-full of bad news. (I was especially wrong about the last item.)

Eventually, unable to sleep one night, I picked it up and thought I would just skim through it, in order to be able to tell my friend that I had read it. After the first few pages I was no longer skimming. Despite myself, I was reading it. A few more pages after that and I was hooked. After a chapter or so, I was completely *inside* the story, living its startling events as if I were there. The story was tremendously satisfying! It was wild and humorous and moving, and full of powerful insights. The characters breathed. The author's imagination was buzzing with life. The writing was fresh and captivating, even though it was a first novel written by a young man. I realized that this was no cheap potboiler. It was something more. Much more.

I took the publisher's invitation to write in with my reaction, and even included a few pointers for the young author. I tried to be as diplomatic as possible, for I too have made mistakes over many years of writing fiction. To my surprise, Bud Macfarlane Jr. phoned me after the letter was passed along to him. (My novel *Father Elijah* had not been published at the time. As the editor of a small, Catholic family journal in Canada, I was virtually unknown in America.) We chatted briefly, compared notes on the state of the world, writing, and the difficulties of apostolic work. From the start it was obvious that Bud Jr. was a very funny guy, a man with a fabulous sense of humor. And that struck me as odd, considering he had written a book about a very serious topic. I went back to his novel and reread it, and found many examples of his wit, and many more examples of his deeply reflective nature. What reconciled these two traits, what made them work together, was Bud's great gift of hope. His novel seemed to be saying that, yes, modern people are in pretty rough shape, and yes, there is darkness growing in the world, but the darkness cannot overcome the light. Especially when we are laughing.

A few months later, I was invited to speak at a conference in Chicago. I phoned Bud, who was going to be in the area that weekend, and we agreed to meet. The day before my flight, it began to storm. A freak blizzard appeared out of nowhere in late spring and dropped two feet of thick snow on us within twenty-four hours—a very unusual occurrence in my part of Canada. As I shovelled off the steps, I recalled one of Bud's last comments about the "coming tribulations," as he called it. He had mentioned that in all probability the next stage in unfolding world events would be an increase in the frequency and intensity of natural disasters. I argued with myself that weather in Canada is unpredictable, and one shouldn't read too much into the snow I was shovelling. As I was lifting one last heavy shovelful, there came a tearing pain in my lower back and I collapsed to the ground. I had suffered from a sore back a few times over the years, but nothing like this. I was in agony, paralyzed, unable to move.

I desperately wanted to phone Chicago and cancel my speaking engagement, but knew I had given my word that I would be there. I assured myself that I would probably be able to walk a little after I reached the airport, which was a two hour drive away. I crawled on hands and knees to the car, somehow managed to drag myself into the seat, and backed the vehicle out of the partly cleared drifts onto the treacherous highway. The drive to the airport was one unending torture session, during which I remembered what I had so often forgotten during my twenty years of lay apostolic work: every time I was to give a talk or do a significant work in the service of God, I was struck by severe sickness, car troubles, or any number of similar problems which arrived in waves with uncannily bad timing. I had always chalked it up to coincidence, but now I could no longer ignore the pattern, and it was a perfectly *consistent* pattern. If you do a work for Our Lord, you're going to take some flak; you're going to be hassled. Stop doing the work, and your troubles will just melt away like a late spring snowfall under a hot sun.

That stiffened my resolve, and it seemed a miracle when I managed to board my flight and arrive safely in O'Hare Airport in Chicago. As I hobbled out of the arrival gate, I was met by a huge, grinning bear of a man, who introduced himself as Bud Macfarlane Jr. I was almost doubled over and having trouble walking. I told him my tale of woe. He smiled again and explained that only a few hours earlier he had been released from jail. Driving to the city the previous evening, he had been caught in a speed trap by the local police. The officer had checked Bud's license on the computer and found that it had been suspended. The car was impounded and Bud was put in jail for the night. He was totally perplexed by this surprise turn of events because he knew that there was nothing out of order with his license. There would be fines and a trial and no end of inconvenience getting it all straightened out. Weeks later the police bureaucracy discovered that the computer had made an error, and that Bud was completely innocent. But in Chicago that weekend, the hassles were mounting.

"Looks like Ol' Sparky's giving us some trouble," Bud said. "It's a good sign! Nah—it's a really great sign!"

A great sign?! I was not convinced.

We spent the remainder of that day driving around Chicago and going to the University of Notre Dame, a couple of hours away. We saw first hand the places where many of the events of *Pierced by a Sword* take place. We sat in Bruno's, the Italian restaurant in the novel, eating pizza (which is a staple of Bud's diet), and discussing books. Gradually our excitement grew as we compared notes about the craft of writing and spiritual truths. So many of our experiences, especially ones regarding the faith, were identical. We were citizens of two different nations, had come from different backgrounds and cultures (he from suburban New Jersey and me from the Great White North). I was fifteen years older than he. Yet we shared the same vision of supernatural realities and had come to the same conclusions about what is happening in the world. Later, we drove back to the conference center in Chicago, carefully parked in the lot, and called it a night. The next morning Bud awoke to find that the car had been towed away. He was *laughing* when he showed me the empty spot. We decided to walk together (despite my back!) the few miles to the towing garage, and hours later and a hundred dollars lighter, he was restored to his car. This time I laughed, too, reinforced by a new understanding of the nature of the battlefield we all fight upon.

"This is a good sign," I said to him. "In fact, it's a really great sign!"

He smiled at me, nodding.

So began a friendship that should last forever.

Bud Macfarlane is thirty-four and in love with his wife and two sons. He took a degree in History from Notre Dame, taught high school, drove a UPS truck, travelled the nation as a successful executive in two different industries, played all your American sports, cooked in restaurants, and is now the founder of the Mary Foundation, which is the world's largest producer of Catholic audio tapes. Millions of people have heard these tapes, and millions more will hear them as the work of the foundation continues to grow at an astounding rate. Yet, for all that, Bud remains a humble man, is quite "normal," and is more dedicated to his family than to his work, only a part of which is writing novels. He has devoted his life to conveying heaven's messages to the world. He doesn't bowl anybody over: he trusts that most of us are open-minded, and will respond to the truth if presented in a respectful and straightforward manner.

These messages are of the greatest importance, and we ignore them at our own risk. In *Pierced by a Sword,* the author has blended them into a fascinating, compelling story. This third printing of the book boasts a beautiful new cover, and the text has been fine-tuned by careful editing. The story is largely unchanged, although some sections have been expanded in order to enrich the tale and to clarify certain points that might have been misunderstood in the first version.

A novel which attempts to imaginatively express the spiritual drama of our times may take many forms. It can be populated by saints or sinners, or both. It can be situated in times of war or peace, or both. It may be well-written or not so well-written. It can show how low man is capable of sinking and how much in need of redemption he is, or it can restrict itself to pious platitudes and cardboard figures trotted through simplistic morality plays. It can err in the direction of being too explicit in describing sin, thus glamourizing it; or fail to show us the urgency of the struggle over every human soul. It can make the mistake of overestimating the power of darkness or underestimating it. The underlying theology of a work can all too easily veer slightly off track and cause damage to an unknown reader; alternatively, it can pull back so far from realism that it loses credibility and ceases to touch the heart. When writing about the things of God and the things of man and the things in between them, the dangers are great. The author faces a minefield of choices.

Even though I have been through every line of this book with Bud during the rewrite, I'm still not certain how he managed to avoid all the dangers listed above. I believe this is the gift of inspired storytelling. Many have used this gift for good or for bad, or for personal gain, or for fame, or even let the gift atrophy while pursuing other things. The author has given Catholic readers much that is familiar and much that is new. Our Protestant brothers will be pleasantly surprised to find farseeing insight into spiritual warfare and the Bible. Those who think the End Times are hogwash can read it for fun (you'll find that it offers more page-turning pleasure than Stephen King or Tom Clancy!). And I would challenge the reader who is skeptical about the things of God, but is sincerely questioning, to jump in and try to find your own story in one of the characters.

The universe is big—much bigger than we suppose. Don't be afraid. This book is not a trite put-down of sinners. In fact, sinners are the protagonists of this novel. Perhaps this is because the author knows that we all struggle with darkness. It is obvious from the opening lines that Bud is in love with his characters. Maybe that is what makes them so real. They are *us*. They stumble through the confusing temptations and stagger toward the enticing mirages that dominate our culture; they are imperfect, they fall, they are in pain, and they long for something better but don't know where to turn for help. Sound familiar?

And as the author reveals to us the destruction we bring upon ourselves in so many ways—carnal, ideological, spiritual—he steers carefully away from obsessively focusing on our sinfulness. At every turn he demonstrates that grace is more powerful than evil, divine providence is always going ahead of us preparing the way for moments of choice, moments of conversion, moments of light.

"Private revelation" is a tricky thing, controversial to say the least. Wisely, the author entrusts the final decisions on these matters to the discernment of the Church. Those who have met him know he is quick to point out that this novel is a piece of fiction. The purpose of prophecy is not to give an inside track on the future: that would merely be a kind of "baptized" fortune-telling. Genuine prophecy, by contrast, is concerned with the timeless truths as they apply to the current situation. One hundred years from now, virtually every person alive today on this earth will be dead. In this sense, we are always in the End Times.

Pierced by a Sword is an imaginative apocalypse. It is more concerned with raising the question:

What if?

What if it turns out this way? What would I, the reader, do in such a crisis? Where would I place myself in this vast landscape of chaos? How would I personally resolve the dilemmas faced by the men and women in this novel? What choices would I make if I were in their place? And most importantly, will I be ready?

As you read this book, you will gradually come to understand the principles at stake whenever good and evil confront each other. I will not spoil the story by giving away even the smallest part of the plot. Plunge in! Discover it for yourself. Get ready for a journey of epic proportions—rather, *cosmic* proportions. You hold in your hands a little treasure, a marvel. This is an adventure, a comedy, a tragedy, a turbulent odyssey and a peaceful stroll. Most of all, this is a love story like no other I have ever read. A new kind of love story. I'll see you inside...

MICHAEL D. O'BRIEN
12 DECEMBER 1996

Preface

I believe that most novels get read because readers find
them entertaining. Hopefully, you won't be able to put this
book down once you get a few chapters into it because you
are enjoying yourself and are pulling for the characters.
And you'll feel disappointed when the story is over because
you'll want more. *And* you'll like it so much you'll recommend it to a friend. That's the greatest compliment you can
give me as an author. No amount of marketing can replace
a good story.

My friends and relatives may notice fictionalized scenes
from their lives in this book. Some of the characters are
very loose composites based on people I know. Thanks for
the material. I'm sure most readers would be surprised to
find out that many of the more outrageous and improbable
events in this book are "based on true stories." It's still
fiction, though—remember that. I'm not a prophet.

Strap on your seat belts and enjoy the ride. Trust me—
I may drive fast but I know where we're going. Nathan
Payne, Becky Macadam, Father Chet, and other friends are
waiting for you. *Oremus*.

BUD MACFARLANE JR.
13 MAY 1995

And Simeon blessed them, and said to Mary…"Behold, this child is set for the ruin, and for the resurrection of many in Israel, and for a sign which shall be contradicted. And thy own soul a sword shall pierce, that out of many hearts thoughts may be revealed."

Luke 2: 34-35

Prologue

24 R.E. (Reign of the Eucharist)
Marytown, Indiana

The lone bell of Immaculate Conception Church rang in the distance as Denny Wheat sighed, then leaned forward and cut the motor of his battered John Deere. Noon.

Time to whisper into the ear of my Lord.

He bowed his head. Denny's son Zack, silhouetted in the October sun, stopped working on a Cessna 172 fifty yards to the west and also bowed his head. The entire population of Marytown was praying the Angelus.

Denny finished his prayers and turned the old tractor back on. *We're not much different than simple farmers hundreds of years ago in Christian Europe,* Denny thought. *Except now, every person in Marytown feels like they are whispering into the very ear of Jesus. The Eucharistic Reign of Christ, we used to call it in the Dark Years, not knowing what it meant. It turned out to be so simple! What took years of discipline for the great mystics like Saint John of the Cross is like breathing for the residents of Marytown.*

Denny looked at his son Zack, who was twenty-two.

The 1990s, the Dark Years, are to Zack like that movie **Star Wars** *was for me in my youth—sheer fantasy. A time so evil that it can barely be imagined by those who were born in the Eucharistic Reign.*

Denny was reminded of the role he played during the Dark Years. He remembered the heroes and heroines he knew during that horrible and strangely exciting time of suffering and redemption—Nathan, Becky, Father Chet, others.

And Lee Washington! I knew them—I lived through it. I lived to tell...

PART ONE

The Remnant

There is nothing that does not participate in beauty and
goodness, because each thing is beautiful and good
according to its proper form.
Saint Thomas Aquinas

Called up my preacher; I said, Give me strength for my
fight. He said, You don't need no strength,
you need to grow up, son.
John Cougar Mellencamp

Each man has his own vocation. The talent is the call.
Ralph Waldo Emerson

Well I'm goin' out, I'm goin' out lookin' for a cynical girl,
who's got no use for the real world.
I'm looking for a cynical girl.
Marshall Crenshaw

But then, O Immaculata, who are *you*?
Saint Maximilian Kolbe

Chapter One

1

Mid 1920s, Summer
Woodland Section
Cleveland, Ohio

Father Greg walked through the courtyard of Saint Nicholas Church with Sister Susan, the principal of the parish grammar school. They were saying their daily Rosary together for the parishioners. Father Greg was meditating deeply on the fourth Sorrowful Mystery—Jesus Carries the Cross—so he didn't notice when his Miraculous Medal slipped out of the hole in his pocket down to the ground. The medal had been a gift from his mother on the first anniversary of his ordination twenty years earlier. He carried it in his pocket because he didn't like wearing medals around his neck.

After weeks of searching, Father Greg gave up looking for the medal, praying: *Dear Mary, let someone who needs it find it. I had it for twenty years—that's enough for me. I'll make you a deal! I'll trade you the medal for a bigger church and a new school for Sister Susan.*

In the 1920s the Woodland Section was still a vibrant community, and many new parishioners were joining Saint Nicholas. The steel mills and car factories of Cleveland were running at full steam. It was a safe and wonderful place to raise a family.

2

Early 1980s, Summer
Woodland Section
Cleveland, Ohio

The heavyset kid swung mightily and whacked the tennis ball.

Lee Washington turned and ran as fast as he could, looking over his shoulder. The black youngster was straining to catch the tennis ball off the broomstick of LaPhonso Mack. LaPhonso was already a legendary power hitter in the rough and tumble annals of Woodland stickball. Part of a three-man team, Lee Washington was the lone outfielder. He was an expert at dodging the abandoned cars, wild dogs, and old tires that filled the back of the empty lot which served as an illegal dump in the ghetto neighborhood. Lee strained his eyes against the setting sun while his teammates cheered him on. He prepared to dive headfirst for the dirty green ball.

I'm gonna catch it!

Lee tripped on a rusty bumper from a 1965 Chevy pickup and missed the ball. Dirt filled his mouth. Game over. His teammates cursed in a good-natured way as the laughing LaPhonso rumbled around the makeshift bases.

Lee, who was not a particularly good or bad player, was not disappointed. The shy, fatherless boy had given chase with supreme effort—as usual. Despite their perfunctory curses, he knew his teammates appreciated the hustle. No one else but Lee would have been crazy enough to dive for a ball in the debris. Summer was only half over and stickball would resume tomorrow.

He spit the dirt out of his mouth. Then he waved to his friends, hollering brightly, "I'm okay! See you tomorrow!" He put his hands on his hips and surveyed the dump.

His friends called back their good-byes and turned to go home. He continued to dust the dirt and grime off his pants and suppressed an urge to kick the truck bumper. He looked again at the twisted, rust-covered hunk of metal.

Must be a new piece of junk, he mused. *What's that gleaming there? A quarter?*

Lee Washington took a step and bent over to pick up the quarter. But it wasn't a quarter. He didn't know what it was. He had never seen a Miraculous Medal before. It was mostly caked with dirt.

It was made of silver, like a quarter, and Lee thought it might be worth some money. *Maybe I could sell it? Get some candy for it. Yeah, I'll get a couple Marathon bars.*

Lee, despite being soft-spoken and shy, was known by his schoolmates as a deal maker. The little entrepreneur loved to buy and sell. He also had a reputation for fairness. Fairness was good for business. *I'm gonna be a mill-yanair someday.*

The dirty Miraculous Medal was large—almost as big as a quarter, but oval shaped and thicker. He spit carefully on the medal and wiped it off with the flap of his shirt. His brow furrowed with curiosity as he studied the sculpted images on both sides. He liked the picture of a woman stepping on a snake on the one side and the two hearts on the other. One heart had a crown of thorns upon it, and the other heart had a sword going through it.

Cool! Wonder what the round thing with the points on it is? He didn't know it was a crown of thorns.

He tentatively sounded out the words on the front side, "O Mary, conceived without sin, pray for us who have recourse to thee." When he pronounced *conceived* he said: Consee-ive-ed. *So it's a religious thing. Cool.*

Lee had been abandoned by his father before he was born. He had no religious training from his mother, Shawna Washington. He figured that "Mary" must mean the mother of Jesus. He had seen the Christmas crèche in front of the local Baptist church during Christmas time. Lee was an intelligent boy, and correctly deduced the words to be a prayer.

What the hell. Might as well say it. He took a deep breath. "O Mary con-see-ive-ed without sin, pray for us who have recourse to thee." *Cool.*

When Lee got home to the tenement, he found a sturdy steel chain in his mother's huge costume jewelry collection, and attached the medal. He hung the large silver medal around his neck, looking at himself in the mirror. None of the other boys had medals. He liked it. He decided not to sell it after all.

Over the years the Miraculous Medal became his good luck charm. He did not attach any religious significance to it beyond the one prayer he said in the sandlot the day he found it. That prayer was the first prayer of his life. His second prayer would come years later.

Lee never discovered, however, that the sandlot where he had found the medal was on the former grounds of Saint Nicholas Church, which had been demolished right before the Great Depression. Old Father Greg had done well as a pastor and he eventually decided to sell the lot and the church to build a bigger, better church several blocks away. The original building was deconsecrated and demolished with the blessing of the bishop. Sister Susan was thrilled to get a bigger, brand new school in the mix. And Lee eventually got a Miraculous Medal. A good deal all around.

3

The Late 1990s
Saturday Afternoon
7 October
Chicago, Illinois

Cities are full of beautiful women. Becky Macadam was more than beautiful. She was *achingly* beautiful. She was blond, twenty-six, and in trouble.

"My Grace Kelly with dark brown eyes," as Daddy used to say, Becky thought rather miserably. Bad news on the horizon. The little red plus sign she was looking at said so.

She was quite stunning—despite the sweat suit hiding her athletic limbs as she knelt on the living room floor. Her simple but elegant short haircut was all in a mess. Had she been a bit taller and thinner, Becky might have been an extremely successful model. As it happened, she was a mildly successful advertising executive.

Her eyes focused again on the square piece of plastic on the expensive throw rug on the wood floor. She read the result of the home diagnostic test and knew for certain what she had already guessed by feeling. *I'm pregnant. I can't believe it. A muffin in the oven,* she thought with a mixture of sadness and distant jubilation.

Condoms! They don't really work, now do they?

Becky suddenly thought of her father. Walt Macadam had died of lung cancer when she was in grade school. An only child, Becky had been devastated. *Why do you keep popping into my head at a time like this, Daddy?*

Anger and frustration flashed inside her. She stared at the red plus sign on the little plastic square. She threw it across the room. Becky had a strong arm and it glanced off Sam's picture. *There, now I feel better.*

She thought of Sam, who had been her domestic partner for over a year.

*That's the sixty-four thousand dollar question, isn't it? Will Sam want me to keep it? It? Try **him** or **her**.*

She got up, went to the kitchen, tiny as all kitchens are in the apartment world of Chicago, and poured herself a giant plastic cup of wine. The logo of the Chicago Cubs was on the cup. It was not expensive wine.

Cubs. I'm going to have a cub of my own. She lit a cigarette. *I'll be okay. I'll be just fine. I'm a big girl.*

Outside she heard a random car horn. A fly buzzed around the apartment ceiling and followed her into the living room where she collapsed on the couch. Becky inhaled deeply on her cigarette and exhaled a long slow mist of smoke.

Hi little Cub! I'm your mom. What's it like in there?

Then, the most beautiful woman in the whole city began to cry like a little girl in soft, reluctant sobs. Her domestic partner was due home from shopping in less than an hour. Both were then supposed to get ready for a party at Nathan Payne's later that night.

4

Sunday Morning
8 October
Indiana Tollway, Indiana

The black convertible Mustang sliced through the air, top down, at eighty-five. Nathan Payne scanned the horizon for state troopers. The rock music on the CD screamed "Three Strange Days" by a group called School of Fish. In the passenger seat a young lady with wavy, shoulder length auburn hair and a snow white complexion was sleeping deeply. She had been out like a light since way before the Skyway.

God, she's different, he thought wistfully, gripping the steering wheel more tightly, keeping one eye on the road. *Inside and out different.* Her name was Joanie Wheat.

As if she could read his thoughts in her dream, she gave a low moan, adjusted her position on the gray leather seat, but didn't wake up. She was wearing baggy jeans and an oversized gray sweater which hid her thin figure.

I wish she would open her eyes. She had the clearest blue eyes Nathan had ever seen—and he had looked closely into many a woman's eyes. Joanie Wheat was not the most beautiful woman Nathan had ever been with, but she did have the most enchanting eyes.

He decided against waking her up and turned his complete attention back to the highway, which was whizzing by in a blur. Chicago was now seventy miles to the west. The rolling hills of western Indiana were starting to level out into good old Hoosier flatlands.

Nathan was a slender, handsome man with inscrutable green eyes that made him seem older than his thirty-one years. He glanced at the young lady again before taking another sip of the Jolt which was keeping him awake after the big party last night in Chicago.

I've got to call my voicemail and let Chet know where I'm going.

Nathan had given Chet the number.

Chet was Father Chet Sullivan, Nathan's boyhood friend visiting on vacation for a week in Chicago. Chet was a parish priest from New Jersey. He was the same age as Nathan. Despite Chet's protests, Nathan had thrown a big party on Chet's second night in town. Forty people had been crammed into Nathan's large high-rise apartment, which was located on the lakefront—Chicago's chic Gold Coast.

Nathan had met the girl in his passenger seat for the first time at the party. Coincidentally, Joanie had been an acquaintance of Chet's ten years earlier during his undergraduate days at the University of Notre Dame. Chet had been pleasantly surprised to see Joanie there.

She was a friend of a friend of a friend who heard about the party. I was pretty wasted before she even showed up. What number would she have been, forty-eight? Nathan was suddenly aware of a strange emotion. It was far away, like the sound of a ship's foghorn.

*What is that? **Guilt?** That's not like you, Fat Boy. Not like you at all. The Fat Boy does not feel guilt! She was a consenting adult, even if she was a somewhat drunken one. You didn't even go all the way with her, though you got pretty close.*

Nathan's tongue-in-cheek nickname for himself was Fat Boy. He had called himself that since high school. At the time, Nathan had been overweight by forty pounds. He had been overweight for practically his entire life up until the summer before his senior year at Fenwick High School. Fenwick was a Catholic school run by dedicated Dominican friars.

The guilt over last night was still there.

A dry little voice spoke to him: *What have you become that you're trying to seduce drunk girls, especially nice girls like Joanie? She cried so sadly before passing out last night. For heaven's sake, she knew Chetmeister! If Father Chet had seen you sneak away with her, he would've barged in to break it up, claiming to be looking for his keys or something.*

Chet had been out on the open air deck trying valiantly to bring Christianity to Nathan's many heathen friends while making them laugh at the same time. *Good old Father Chet. Mr. Missionary. My friend through thick and thin. Why does he still waste a week on me every year?* Chet was the only person from New Jersey who Nathan still kept in touch with since moving to Chicago.

Probably going to get one or two to church today, if I know the cagey Irishman. Nathan's thought was not very far from the truth. In fact, it was right on the money.

Forty-seven. Nathan had been keeping track of how many women he had slept with since the first, a girl he would forever remember as Sally the Waitress. In a way, he couldn't help but number them because he had a special gift for numbers. During his freshman year of college, Sally the Waitress had been serving him drinks at a bar near his apartment at the University of Illinois. Sally had told Nathan that she wanted to see his room, and one thing had led to another. *How long ago was that, twelve years? I've been sleeping around for over a decade?*

Almost against his will Nathan divided forty-seven women by twelve years and instantly came up with 3.916666—on to infinity. Two numbers had presented themselves and his mind automatically called forth their mathematical relationship.

His ample mathematical skills gave Nathan the edge— along with his voracious appetite for competition—that made him the top trader in the smallish but respected brokerage firm for which he worked. Over the last two years he had earned well over three hundred thousand dollars per year. Nathan invested most of his money right back into his own daring trades.

Let's round it off to four women per year. That's not that many, really. Nathan wondered why it seemed that somewhere around number seventeen his sexual activities started to feel more like running on a treadmill than a day at the amusement park. *The word you're lookin' for is empty, Fat Boy. Sex gets old, like playing Pac Man over and over again.*

Nathan did not consider himself promiscuous. He was relatively inactive compared to some of the other men in his circle. *Only four a year, and not as many in the last few years,* he told himself, trying to assuage his guilt. *Old Charlie goes through that many every month, easy.*

Charles "Charlie" VanDuren was the owner of Nathan's firm, VanDuren, VanDuren, and Brooks—known as VV&B on the exchange. VanDuren had inherited the firm from his father and relied heavily on Nathan's abilities, even though Nathan was not a partner. Charlie had promised Nathan a stake in VV&B two years earlier when he lured Nathan from another trading house. Nathan was somewhat bitter, but not surprised that VanDuren had strung him along about becoming a partner. He didn't trust VanDuren. He trusted very few people in this world except for Father Chet Sullivan—and he didn't even trust Chet on morality. He took pride in finding his own way through life. He even held the VanDurens of the world in disdain for needing to conquer women to puff themselves up.

Don't need no woman, he thought. *I'm the captain of my own ship. A veritable master of my own destiny, an island—a rock. A rock! And a roll. A donut, really. A jelly donut. With sprinkles.* **Chocolate** *sprinkles—jimmies.*

Nathan took another sip of Jolt as he chuckled numbly at the strange stream of humorous flim flam that sputtered from his mind like stock numbers slipping silently across the big board. Only he could read the numbers.

For Nathan, sleeping with women was more a form of relaxation than anything else. He never got emotionally involved with the women he slept with, and was always perfectly clear about his intentions towards them beforehand. At least he thought he was.

A modern version of a gentleman.

Did this nice girl really want to sleep with you? The voice was back, asking questions Nathan didn't want to answer. *Shut up!* He ordered. *I'm a rock, remember? With jimmies.*

By his own lights he was a moral person. He didn't lie, he didn't cheat on his taxes, and he didn't mess with people's heads like Charles VanDuren often did. He knew for a fact that VanDuren had a knack for juggling several women at once. An image of Charlie juggling buxom starlets on the Ed Sullivan Show—replete with circus music—popped into Nathan's head. He let up on the gas a little and looked queerly at the can of Jolt. *What are they putting into this stuff?*

A moment passed. *And I don't sleep with married women like Charlie does.*

For Nathan this somehow made sleeping around okay. He had told Father Chet just that several times over the years during their infrequent discussions on sexual morality. Nathan didn't like to talk about those kinds of things with Chet. Moral conversations made Nathan uncomfortable. *Old Chetmeister made a lot of sense, even if he was wrong.*

How can Chet make sense and still be wrong, Fat Boy? His little voice mocked him.

Don't go using logic with me, he shot back. *I'm a numbers man.*

Nathan was also living his life under a burden which the vast majority of men never carry. Women were *extremely* attracted to him. It was not uncommon for him to enter a nightclub and within an hour have three or four women make it clear to him that they wanted to sleep with him.

It's like they smell something on me, he often thought as they lined up before him at the bars and pool tables in loud smoky dance clubs. *They don't even know me. It's like they think they can sign up for me like signing up for Little League.*

His ability to attract women was legendary among his party friends. Even Charles VanDuren held him in a kind of awe. VanDuren tried much harder than Nathan to add women to his own list, which ran into the hundreds. Most of Nathan's friends assumed he seduced many more women than he actually did.

He was also much less promiscuous than his own father, who had been more like Charles VanDuren. Harry Payne had given Nathan the distinct impression that being a man meant sleeping with a lot of women. His father had also been cruel, distant, and lacking in all affection. Nathan hadn't talked to him in years. He couldn't—Harry Payne had been murdered in jail.

Okay, when this chick wakes up, just ask her. If she didn't want to get started with you, she'll tell you. If she did want to, fine. If not, say you're sorry. End of story. Now shut up, Fat Boy!

Fat Boy, Nathan thought, and remembered George the Animal. George Moore had given Nathan the nickname Fat Boy at Fenwick High School in Oak Park, Illinois, during Nathan's freshman year. Although Nathan wasn't thrilled with the nickname, he was very shy and not many students at Fenwick had noticed him enough to tease him, much less call him Fat Boy to his face.

Nathan tried to avoid the Animal. George Moore was not a mental giant. He also had the annoying habit of teasing all the students who were smarter than he was—which is to say, practically the entire student body. Students were terrified of the Animal. George Moore was over six feet tall and weighed a muscular two hundred and fifty pounds. Everyone expected him to get a football scholarship to some Big Ten school. Even teachers looked forward to the day of his graduation.

During Nathan's junior year, George saw Nathan chatting with Betty Gabelli at a football game. Even as a somewhat pudgy teenager, women were attracted to the painfully shy Nathan. She had struck up a conversation with Nathan, who happened to be standing next to her so he could get a better look at the field. Like George, Betty was no rocket scientist. Betty was not even a rocket scientist's *assistant*. Nathan was quite uncomfortable. He failed to see George glaring at him from the huddle on the field. He didn't even realize that the Animal had taken offense until a couple of days later, before gym class.

Two days after seeing Nathan talking with Betty Gabelli on the sidelines, George lingered in the locker room and asked Nathan to stay behind and help him "with something." He naïvely waited next to George as the room cleared out, figuring the Animal was going to ask for tutoring help in math.

George stood, pushed Nathan into the locker and punched him in the stomach. Nathan doubled over. Then the Animal kneed Nathan in the forehead, barely missing his nose. Nathan, dazed, collapsed on the cold concrete floor of the locker room. He could still remember seeing George's shoelaces from his prone position.

George leaned over and spoke menacingly, "Stay away from Betty, Fat Boy."

Then George spit on the floor next to Nathan and walked out. It took Nathan a few minutes to regain his wind, and a few more to figure out what George was talking about.

Betty who? Betty Gabelli? He suddenly remembered talking with the airhead cheerleader during the game. He hadn't even known that Betty was George's girlfriend!

Three minutes after he figured out the reason for George's violent warning, Nathan formulated a plan to get revenge. He made up his mind to follow through with it. It would take about ten months to accomplish, he figured, and it would do the entire school a favor. Nathan mentally dubbed his plan Nathan Payne's Personal Bequest to Fenwick High School. Someone had to tame the Animal before he killed somebody.

The next day Nathan went for a jog. He also signed up for Judo classes at a dojo in Elmwood Park. He took a job after school at McDonalds to pay for the Judo classes. Within four weeks he was running five miles a day and lifting weights in his basement for two hours a day, three days a week. He often played the theme to the movie *Rocky* when he lifted weights— not for inspiration, but because it struck him as funny. *Yo Adrian! You don't understand! I gotta fight dis guy! Gotta fight da Animal!*

Nathan decided the Fat Boy wasn't going to be fat ever again. He didn't have any close friends so there was no one to miss him after school. His only extracurricular activity was the Math Club, which met twice a month.

Nathan took up cigarettes despite his running because he associated smoking with mental toughness—and his father. His chain-smoking father was doing ten to fifteen for grand larceny at Rahway State Prison in New Jersey at the time of Nathan's little high school project.

He surfaced from his reverie about George Moore. His Mustang had rapidly caught up to a truck laboring up a long, low hill. Considering the speed at which he was traveling, Nathan guided the Mustang around the truck with a deftness that belied the difficulty of the maneuver. He pulled a cigarette out of the pack with his lips, expertly popped his Zippo in the wind despite the top being down, and stepped on the gas pedal. The needle shuddered up to ninety. The edges of a green sign glimmered as the sun rose beyond it: Notre Dame 7 Miles. *Notre Dame. Knute Rockne. Rudy. Fighting Irish— the whole nine yards. Chet says it's the most beautiful campus in the country and Joanie here is from South Bend. Maybe I'll drop in, see the place. Need gas.*

Nathan's high school memory persisted. George the Football Animal. Ten months after taking up his bequest, Nathan patiently waited for the big football player near the back of the school building.

"Hey Fat Boy!" George sneered when he spotted Nathan, who was smoking a Kent. "See you ain't so fat no more." George laughed at what passed for a joke in George's book.

Nathan casually flicked the butt down and ground it under the heel of one of his Converse All Stars. *You can do it, Rocky!* Burgess Meredith's gravelly voice rang in his head.

The two loners were alone together in an alley of sorts, with a cyclone fence on one side and the red brick wall of the gym on the other. Nathan stood in the middle of the path. Some brown leaves from the previous autumn scattered the dirt path that was a favorite shortcut through the woods for some students. Senior year had started a month before. Nathan had been studying George's habits for weeks. Every day the Animal walked alone down this path after football practice. Nathan felt a mixture of fear and anticipation.

He had imagined walking up to George and insulting him, picking the fight, beating on him for several minutes, and then calmly telling him something like, "Watch who you decide to beat up for the rest of the year, you animal." Now that the moment of revenge was upon him, Nathan waited until George was a stride away before speaking to the massive football player.

"Stop," Nathan stated calmly but firmly.

George stopped, looked at what he thought was a now pitifully thin Nathan, and came up with this brilliant retort, "What's your problem, Fat Boy?"

George was in a hurry. He wanted to get home and watch his new pro wrestling video.

With one economical but powerful motion, Nathan cracked the fingers of his left hand crisply onto the small but sensitive area just below George's nose and above his upper lip. George collapsed in pain, completely surprised by Nathan's blow.

The Animal goes down! Just like they taught me in the dojo, Nathan thought absently. *Wax on, wax off.*

Nathan stood over George's body. No insults. No kicks. Still writhing in pain on his back, George comically tried to kick Nathan, who easily grabbed his ankle and twisted it just so, knowing George could feel pressure at the knee. George screamed again, more out of fear than actual pain. A scream echoed off the brick wall of the school.

"Don't hurt me, Fat Boy!" George begged in a whiny voice.

What a moron! The dumb bastard is still calling me Fat Boy!

For months Nathan had imagined he would be elated at this moment, and now, almost like a surgeon observing a new procedure, he felt nothing but cold surprise. And then boredom. He dropped George's leg, which made a small thud on the dirt path.

Nathan leaned over and put his mouth next to George's ear. George had his eyes squeezed tightly closed, and was whimpering.

"Stop," Nathan repeated, softly, coldly. He turned and retrieved his books, which he had stored next to the brick wall.

Let him figure it out for himself, Nathan thought. Then he walked away. It had been the last time he struck anyone in violence.

Neither George nor Nathan ever mentioned the incident to anyone at Fenwick. Keeping it a secret gave Nathan a certain satisfaction. George had his own obvious reason for keeping silent. He had been humiliated by a nerd and the fewer people who knew about it the better.

Happily, the Animal seemed to have figured out Nathan's cryptic command and immediately ceased teasing and bullying other students. Nathan avoided the Animal but gave him a look across the lunchroom the next day.

Stop being a bully or I'll really hurt your knee next time. No knee. No scholarship. No football career. I can destroy you, George Moore. It's our little secret. Down boy!

To the surprise of both Nathan and George, a kinder and gentler Animal made a few friends as other students realized that George had somehow changed. Nathan's outlook on life also changed. Feeling good about himself and his bequest to Fenwick, he became slightly more outgoing in the Math Club, and struck up friendships with some of the other shy students. It was the beginning of his new social personality, which he quickly built upon at the University of Illinois the following fall.

In his Mustang over a decade later, Nathan was pleasantly surprised to find that he held George's memory with nostalgia, not rancor. *Before the fight, nobody knew either one of us, really. Maybe we had that in common. I wonder if George's dad was a first class jerk like mine was? We changed each other.*

After Fenwick, George Moore got a full ride to the University of Iowa, but ironically, hurt his knee during a practice in his junior year and never amounted to much of a player. Nathan lost track of him after that. *Wonder what the Animal's up to nowadays? He'd probably laugh if he knew they call me Feel the Pain Payne on the trading floor.*

The Notre Dame exit approached.

Notre Dame it is. Why did I decide to drive Joanie home anyway? She came on the train. I could have put her on the South Shore Railway.

He looked at Joanie for a long time and almost missed the exit.

5

Three Months Earlier
Woodland Section
Cleveland, Ohio

Lee Washington was slightly buzzed on three Colt 45s. His most distinguishing characteristic was his brown skin. Lee was neither tall nor short, thin nor heavy, handsome nor ugly—but he was surprisingly strong. He had a loaded pistol tucked under his thigh as he drove his aging Oldsmobile Cutlass down a dark side street in one of what the white folks in the suburbs would call "a bad neighborhood."

Where is that boy? Yeah, there he is. He better have his money, Lee thought coldly.

He pulled the Cutlass up to the curb. A black man in a tan and white t-shirt ambled up to the car after a furtive glance to check for the police. Lee powered the window down and quickly exchanged the vial with the white crystals for the right amount of rolled up cash.

Easy does it.

Slowly, Lee pulled the car away. He was only twenty-five years old, and a small-time pusher. Lee made his money on the margins—not unlike Nathan Payne—only in a different market. A dangerous market.

Careful. Don't wanna get the big boys ticked at a small-timer like me. Get this stuff in Toledo and drive all the way back here to make a lousy fifty per gram. Better lay off for a few days. Why blow my big deal on the odd chance of getting busted? Now, should I go see Tawana or Kristianne?

Lee couldn't keep his mind on either girl, as luscious and willing as they tended to be toward him. He was more interested in real estate. Five months earlier, half serious and half high on Colt 45s, he had called the 800 number after watching one of those late night infomercials. He bought the whole "Make Millions Through Real Estate" home study course for a hundred bucks using a stolen credit card number. Lee had the package sent to an abandoned house in his neighborhood. He tipped the UPS driver to keep his mouth shut—the driver knew the house was abandoned.

It took him a month to listen to the tapes. He found he could understand the books if he took his time and skipped over the bigger words. Lee quickly grasped the concepts—after all, he had been in business for himself since he was in grade school. From personal experience, he understood the concepts of cash flow, strategic planning, and how to get the most out of people. He had a knack for making deals. The young entrepreneur probably knew more about corporate espionage than a typical Fortune 500 CEO.

Starting with five grand he had saved from his drug trade, Lee began to buy up distressed properties. By the end of his third month as a big time real estate dealer, as he now thought of himself, he had quietly bought and sold several properties just outside of his immediate neighborhood—some at tax delinquency auctions downtown, most with little or no money down.

He avoided buying properties owned by the big drug dealers. Despite his efforts to hide his activities, a few of his friends reported that his name was circulating in what Lee considered the wrong circles. One of the meanest crack dealers, Elmer "Fudd" Matthews, had been asking around about him. That wasn't a good sign.

But Lee had just executed a plan that would make the downtown real estate specialists jealous. Without a doubt, his deal would baffle the neighborhood drug dealers, who were more interested in whores and cars than houses and contracts. Tawana, who liked the milder drugs Lee supplied her, and who worked in the mayor's office downtown, had heard rumors that the Cleveland Clinic was planning a major expansion. The Clinic was a huge medical complex located in the center of the most dilapidated part of Cleveland.

Apparently, a lot of the money was coming to the Clinic Foundation from HUD, HHS, and Federal AIDS Research Grants. The Clinic was planning to expand south toward the Woodland and Cedar sections. The deal was still in the planning stages—and not a done deal by any stretch. It was months away from any public announcement, but timed nicely to coincide with the mayor's re-election campaign.

Most of Lee's properties were right smack in the middle of the expansion. Lee had already been offered $150,000 for all of his properties by a major development company, which had sent a slick, pony-tailed lawyer in a fancy suit to his mom's tenement. He didn't even shake hands with Lee. The lawyer smiled furtively at Shawna Washington, who was watching

Wheel of Fortune on television. She seemed oblivious to Lee's deal.

During the brief meeting, the lawyer had mistaken Lee's lack of social graces and ghetto vocabulary for stupidity. After a minute or two the lawyer made a lowball offer.

It's worth three times that, you ugly freak! Lee had wanted to scream. Instead, he quietly told the lawyer that he wanted $345,000 in cash plus lawyer's fees (just like Lee's real estate books suggested) or he would go to MBM Management, a major competitor which probably didn't even know about the Clinic Foundation's plans.

Just like a dealer, man, Lee thought, steadying himself. *The richest—and oldest—dealers always stay cool, man. Scream inside, whisper out. Then I can take me and Mama and get out of this dump.*

The Ponytail Man called up the next day with a final offer of $335,000 and half the lawyer's fees. Lee was going to roll the legal fees into the deal anyway, so it didn't matter.

After putting the phone down he took a few minutes to add and subtract the numbers. *After paying off the paper I'm holding on these properties, I'm goin' to clear over $112,000! Later, Woodland!*

Elated, he tried his best to fake indifference when he called back the next day and took the offer. Lee had gone big time.

That had all occurred three weeks ago, and now he made his drug runs more out of habit and for cash flow. The papers were signed but the lawyers were still hashing out final transfer details, tying up Lee's cash. Lee did not trust the lawyers, or anyone else for that matter. No one in the neighborhood knew about his fledgling real estate empire. If everything went right, no one would.

Lee and his mom were planning on flying to Los Angeles in four days. Then they would spend a couple of weeks in a posh hotel while Lee bought them a nice house—with little or no money down, of course. Then he would start a new empire. The general idea was to try to forget he ever set foot in the Woodland Section of cold, stinking Cleveland, much less grew up there his whole damn life. The legal eagles, following Lee's explicit instructions, were going to transfer all the money into a Los Angeles bank.

Screw this drug dealing from now on. It's too dangerous. Be dead before I'm thirty. Who would take care of Mama?

He pulled into the parking lot of his mom's tenement. He sighed as he got out of his car and shuffled to the back door. *I hope Mama bought the plane tickets just like I told her,* he thought as he climbed the ratty steps of a stairway that smelled faintly of urine and marijuana.

6

Saturday Morning
7 October
Walcott, Wyoming

Manuel knew he had no business in Karl Slinger's garage. The little Mexican groundskeeper said a quick Hail Mary under his breath as he tried the door to the limo. It was open. He quickly pulled the audio tape on Marian apparitions out of his coat pocket and placed it on the center of the plush passenger seat. He closed the limo door and silently padded out the back door of the big garage.

Manuel glanced over his shoulder at the huge summer residence of Karl A. Slinger, Chairman of the Board and CEO of SLG Industries, one of the two or three largest agricultural corporations in the United States.

Señor Slinger is a nice man. He always says hello and calls me by my first name. He's even a Catholic, although he never leaves to go to church on Sundays. He'll probably just throw the tape away. I'm a fool. Will Señor Slinger guess it was me and have me fired? Who knows?

Manuel thought of Diego Baerga, who also worked on the grounds of the Slinger Ranch. *Diego didn't go to church on Sundays before hearing the tape by Professor Wheat of Notre Dame. Now Diego goes every day—and says a daily Rosary.* It had been Diego's idea to plant the tape in Slinger's limo.

"Hey, *hermano,*" Diego had reasoned, "just because Señor Slinger is rich doesn't mean he don't need to hear this stuff. Think of his soul, *'mano.*"

Aw, he'll probably just throw the tape away, thought Manuel as he walked to the tool shed. *Then again, maybe he won't.*

Chapter Two

1

Saturday Morning
7 October
Walcott, Wyoming

"Nice game, Lenny," Karl Aquinas Slinger told his tennis partner and attorney, Leonard Gold. Lenny grunted. Slinger continued, "You taking the later flight back to Salt Lake City? I'm taking the limo to the airport myself in thirty minutes."

Karl wiped what was left of the hair on his balding scalp with a towel in the opulent shower room in the bath house near the tennis court on the Slinger Ranch.

Lenny Gold picked up his racket and waved it regally. "I'm going to sit around on my duff and relax after letting the boss beat me again at tennis. I'll take the rental car to the local airport, Karl. I have to take the corporate jet to Portland to check that new deal in Oregon you've got me working on for Monday, and I want to go over the numbers again before I leave this hovel. You'll have to drive to the real airport in Cheyenne and fly commercial."

Lenny Gold had been Karl's lawyer for over thirty years. Lenny got a kick out of calling Karl's multimillion dollar ranch a hovel.

"Fine with me, Lenny," Karl replied cheerfully. "And what do you mean, 'letting the boss beat me'?" Karl gave Lenny his best poker face before continuing, "I can kick your skinny little lawyer butt whenever I want. I've got an all around game."

It was a true statement.

"Come on, Karl, I was only kidding," Lenny protested mildly. "I've never met a man more focused on winning than you in my whole life. My brains and your guts. You've got to admit, it's gotten us far, hasn't it?"

Karl nodded, then smiled at his friend, "And we're just getting started, Lenny!" Karl echoed his favorite phrase. He had said that hundreds of times to Lenny following all their deals. Most of the deals had worked out pretty well. Karl was worth hundreds of millions of dollars, not including his SLG stock and options. Lenny was worth millions.

"Indeed we are. This skinny lawyer will see you back in Salt Lake City on Tuesday." Lenny finished dressing and picked up his bag. He headed out the door toward the guest house, which was quite spectacular, although small compared to the main ranch house. Beautiful Elk Mountain outlined the diminutive lawyer in the distance.

A few minutes later, Karl finished dressing and then walked to the garage where the limo driver already had the car warmed up. The driver jumped to open the door for him. Karl climbed in and almost sat on the audio tape on the seat.

"What's this all about?" Karl asked his driver, holding up the tape.

"I have no idea, sir," the driver said, a hint of nervousness creeping into his voice. Mr. Slinger was known for his volcanic temper, although he seldom vented it on the help.

"Hmmn. 'Marian Apparitions.' I wonder what that means?" Karl asked, holding up the tape. He hesitated, as if he was about to hand it to the driver and tell him to throw it away.

"Are we going to the local airport or do we have to go to Cheyenne?" Karl inquired.

"Cheyenne. A little over two hours, sir," the driver responded, a slight note of relief in his voice.

"Very well. Let's go then."

Karl's tone dismissed the driver, who quickly pulled out, heading away from the mountains toward Interstate 80.

Karl looked at the tape and thought of his mother with not a little bit of guilt. The last time he had given religion a thought was at her funeral. Karl had been devout as a boy, even entertaining thoughts about being a priest in eighth grade.

I don't know why. Our parish priest, Father Wyznieski, was a mean old coot. Why did I ever want to be like him?

Karl had stopped attending Mass during college. That had deeply disappointed his mother. He could still remember her chiding him in her thick Polish accent from time to time, until her death ten years ago: *"I don't care how much money you make, Karl Slinkowicz, or how many houses you buy me! You are a poor man if you have no faith in Holy Mother Church. What will become of you, Karl? Look at your mama when I talk to you! What will become of you?"*

All he could ever reply was, *"It's Karl **Slinger** now, Mama, not Slinkowicz!"*

It wasn't that Slinger hated the Church or the faith. He was just too damn busy. *Let Dottie go to Mass. If I don't believe, why should I go? Is it as simple as that? I don't believe in God? Well, now that I think about it…I guess not. So what?*

Karl was suddenly overwhelmed with a strong urge to toss the tape out the window. But he didn't. He hated long car rides (in fact, he hated to be silent, still, or alone) and he was big on listening to business book tape summaries during his numerous trips in cars and planes. But he didn't keep the tapes in *this* limo (SLG Industries had several limos located around the country). And there was no one to call on business on a Saturday.

Oh, what the hell, he thought, *maybe it will pass the time. Marian Apparitions, eh? Maybe it'll make me laugh like those money-grubbing televangelists on late night TV!*

Slinger tapped the window separating him from the driver and handed the tape through.

"Play it," Slinger ordered tonelessly.

Without saying a word, the driver reached back, took the tape, and inserted it into the tape deck, adjusting the controls to send the sound into the passenger compartment. The driver made sure he could not hear the tape. Mr. Slinger, who didn't even have a laptop computer, hadn't considered learning how to use the sound system installed in the back of his limousine. Slinger preferred to delegate such trivial matters to his driver. Karl barely knew how to use his car phone, which was ironic because SLG Industries was one of the most technologically advanced companies in the world.

As the first ten seconds of the tape crackled, Karl saw in his mind's eye an image of his mother in her casket. That serene look on her face had seemed just a little bit too serene to have been arranged by the body baggers at the funeral home. Mrs. Slinkowicz had her rosary beads in her hands. He looked at her face in the image and half-expected to see Mama's eyes open.

They didn't. But the corners of her mouth seemed turned up in a little smile. Little did Karl know that in the next hour and ten minutes the eyes that would be opening were going to be his own.

2

Early Friday Morning
6 October
Amsterdam, The Netherlands

His eyes were coal black. They opened.

New York. Yes, it will be New York first.

He closed his eyes again, and smiled while he slept. His room was exquisitely appointed. The beautiful blond woman who had slept with him had left earlier. She was the finest money could buy. No matter how much they cost, no woman could bear to sleep next to him in his cold bed. He was a prime agent of the Prince of this World. In his cobblestone drive sat a Jaguar. In the garage, a Ferrari. In the morning, he would arise and don the most finely tailored suit of clothes that good European taste could select. He would comb his perfectly coifed hair with oil that cost over fifty dollars a bottle.

He called Amsterdam his home, but he had lived in many cities during the past five decades. He was a highly placed official in a powerful international banking institution. Although completely anonymous in a public sense, his name was well known in certain elite, secret circles—circles of men who sat at the green, felt-topped tables of power in the purple-marbled halls of international affairs, beyond the influence of any democracy.

The dark man was handsome. He photographed extremely well. He dressed and acted European, but his sharp features and lightly tanned skin suggested a hint of his Semitic forefathers, who had migrated to the continent before most histories were written. It was rumored that his lineage was traced to one of the finest noble families of Russia—bankers who wielded influence even before the days of Ivan the Terrible. But no one in the elite circles he now navigated seemed to be directly related to him. It was also whispered that both his parents died while he was young. His *real* parents were the headmasters of the finest boarding schools of Europe; it was further rumored that he descended from the Czars themselves, not their bankers.

This was not true.

Actually, he was of royal lineage of a sort, from a kingdom that no longer existed except in the dry, dusty tomes of libraries. If one could—and one certainly could not, for records of this particular man's lineage were not kept, or were destroyed, or simply didn't exist—one would trace his blood to the Kingdom of Babylon. In fact, his mother had been a whore, and he had been born in Egypt.

The dark man opened his eyes again. The room was perfectly opaque. The plush, thick curtains were drawn to seal off even a tiny beam of moonlight penetrating the murky sky of the Netherlands. His eyes were like black creatures merging with the darkness.

New York. Gone. Just like the others—only much worse.

He had been told about Hurricane Andrew the same way in 1993. Bosnia and Rwanda in 1994. Kobe, Japan, in 1995. The explosion of TWA Flight 800 in 1996.

His eyes closed and the smile returned. He needed to rest because he was scheduled to fly to Rome in the morning.

Over one thousand miles away, a fault that lay dormant since before science recorded such things trembled slightly. The tremor was not strong enough to be noted by the technicians who monitored the seismic instruments.

The microquake did nothing more than cause ripples in the several small, man-made lakes that surrounded the outskirts of a certain city in the Middle East. Ripples in the lakes—as if a huge, rough beast approached their banks. And Jerusalem slept.

3

Saturday Morning
7 October
Interstate 80, Wyoming

The tape finished and Karl Slinger was perfectly still. The limo driver, worried when he saw the blank stare in Karl's eyes, lowered the compartment window and inquired, "Is there anything the matter, Mr. Slinger?"

Life came back into Karl's eyes so quickly the driver was reminded of the water turning hot during his morning shower when his wife turned on the cold water in the sink.

"I'm quite all right, thank you," Karl replied distantly, then somewhat forcefully, "Rewind and play that again. I bet I can get most of it in again before we reach the airport."

Wow, the driver thought, *the old man never listens to a tape twice. Marian Apparitions? Must be pretty hilarious.*

Then again, I don't recall Mr. Slinger laughing very much. He looked like he was having a heart attack back there.

"Pretty funny tape, Mr. Slinger?"

"What? Funny you say?" Karl sounded distant again. "No, not at all. Quite the opposite. Is it still rewinding?"

The driver nodded. "Yes sir."

"Good. Listen, when we get to the airport, see if you can buy me one of those portable tape players, you know, the ones that kids are always glued to—"

"—a Walkman, sir?"

"Yes. A Walkman. That way I can listen again on the plane back to Salt Lake City."

The tape stopped rewinding. Within a few seconds, the deep-timbred tones of Professor Tom Wheat filled the passenger compartment of the limo for the second time. The driver debated turning the sound up in his own compartment. That was against the rules. One didn't become Karl Slinger's personal driver without a certain amount of discretion.

That's right, he didn't even know where the tape came from before he got into his car. First thing I do when I get back is ask around. Maybe the old man would like to know who planted that tape on his seat.

4

Sunday Morning
8 October
Chicago, Illinois

Becky Macadam had a hard time sleeping after last night's party at Nathan Payne's apartment. She tossed and turned all night. Finally giving in to insomnia, she left her bed and tried to read a Clancy novel until after the sun came up. She fell asleep on the couch at eight.

The phone rang, waking her up. She walked to the kitchen to pick up the portable phone. She wasn't in a good mood. Her eyes were bloodshot. It hadn't gone well when Sam came home last night before the party.

It's probably Sam. Calling to apologize for being such a coldhearted jerk.

She decided to answer the phone.

"Hello, is this Becky Macadam's residence?" the friendly male voice on the other end asked.

"Yes it is," Becky replied warily. "Who are you?"

"Chet Sullivan. *Father* Chet. We met last night at Nathan Payne's party. Remember me, the priest from New Jersey?"

An image of Father Chet Sullivan surfaced from her memory. *The priest at the party!* She also remembered her vague promise to show him the Art Institute. She had been more than a bit surprised to see a Roman collar on such a young-looking man, much less at one of Nathan Payne's parties. The young padre had been drinking liberally, although he was obviously able to control his liquor. Like many people who don't know priests personally, Becky was somewhat shocked to see a priest act like a normal person. Chet was charming and friendly. Funny, too.

"Oh, yes Father, you must be calling to take me up on my promise to show you the Art Institute." *Oh no! Why did I ever promise such a thing?* she asked herself. *Because he was so decent, despite that New Jersey accent.*

"Father, listen, I never meant—"

"Look, if it's not convenient, I'll understand. You mentioned that you knew it well, and I've never been to the Art Institute in all these years. I just thought, well—"

"No, no, it's not that, it's just that it's not a good time for me right now…" she stopped herself short of sharing details of her problem with Sam. *Don't tell him anything—don't even hint at it.* "…but I found out some very, ah, disturbing news last night before the party." *Now why did I say that?*

Chet's voice changed noticeably. It became lower, almost professional. "Look, I'm on my vacation but I'm always a priest. Actually, what I'm trying to say is, if you need to talk about something, well, I *am* a priest, and sometimes it helps to talk with someone you don't know very well. Please, if my offer isn't welcome, just say so. No big deal."

"Oh…no, Father, I'm glad you offered. It's sweet of you." *I'm recovering nicely,* she thought. *No way I'm going to talk to this, this—stranger. Blow him off.*

"Maybe we could just get a cup of coffee and skip the museum. Are you with anyone, Father?" she heard herself say despite her resolution. Something inside told her to trust the man.

"As a matter of fact, I was planning on inviting Nathan Payne along," Chet answered, "but the man was last seen headed east toward South Bend with a lovely girl named Joanie Wheat. I'm staying at his apartment." The young priest paused. "Just coffee?"

Father Chet now sounded relaxed and confident, as he had sounded at the party. In reality, he was quite nervous and silently began to pray another Hail Mary for Becky, prepared to wait a long time for her reply.

Indeed, Becky paused for a long time.

"There's a coffee shop just down the block from you near the lake, on Sheridan, next to a pizza place named Leona's," she suggested finally, but nervously.

"Got it. I'm walking now. Ten minutes?" he confirmed.

"More like twenty. I have to do my makeup." She hung up by pressing a button.

My makeup! I sound like a ditz. I'll just go have coffee with him and catch up on Nathan's secret past with his boyhood priest buddy and find out all about that lovely girl he spent so much time with at the party last night.

Becky went to the bathroom to get ready. *I don't really wear much makeup, do I? Dad's right. He always used to say that wearing makeup is like putting chrome around the Mona Lisa. "And the frame God gave you ain't so bad either, like your mother's."* She could still hear her father's easygoing laugh.

Maybe if you didn't have such beautiful brown eyes, Sam wouldn't have bothered to fall in love with you. Love you? He doesn't even know you.

Suddenly, the emotions of last night's fight came back to her, followed quickly by the memory of Sam's cold words, couched as they were in such warm tones:

"Oh honey," he had said, "it's going to be all right—I'll even help pay for the doctor."

Her heart had jumped. *He wants the baby!*

Then he had gone on with the phoniest tone of compassion Becky had ever heard from him. It was almost a whine and had reminded her of a whimpering dog. "I know a guy at work whose girlfriend went to a clinic where they have counseling and everything before they, you know, take care of the problem. He drove her and stood by her the whole time. You know I'll do the same. I'm here for you, honey."

At that precise moment Becky Macadam had ceased to be pro-abortion and became prolife. *Abortion isn't for women,* she had decided, *it's for the stinking convenience of men!*

She had replied slowly, seething, "You can be so cold, Sam. This is your baby, too."

"Baby?" Sam had laughed nervously. "What baby? It's a blob of tissue. Look, when did you become such a prolifer?" He visibly caught himself, knowing that he had crossed some kind of line with her.

"Oh honey," he said with false sincerity, "it's your choice. I know that. I'll stand behind your choice either way." The way he said "choice" sounded like he was describing dirty linen.

"Even if I decide to keep little Sam or Samantha?" she rejoined, looking at him, her brown eyes narrowed to angry semicircles. *Daddy always said I made snap judgments,* she thought now. *Later on he told me that I was a "choleric." Some kind of medieval psychology thing. Why am I thinking about Daddy again at a time like this?*

Somehow she had known what Sam's reply would be. A lie. She put her hands on her hips, waiting.

"Sure," he had said, flatly. Sam was staring over her head, beyond the couch, to the window. "Sure," he repeated, "whatever you decide. I'll stand by you."

Thoughts rushed into her head like the broken remains of a ship crashing in on a huge wave during a storm.

You're lying, Sam! My God, you're already wondering where your next apartment is going to be! You sound like the Robot on Lost in Space. What did I ever see in you, Mr. Robot? Why, I oughtta smack you back into last Tuesday.

She still had her hands on her hips.

Who sounds like that? God, now I even think like Daddy!

Somehow that thought had made her even angrier. Then she did slap him. Hard. *Just like in the movies, Rhett Baby*, she thought wildly.

"Get out. Now," she hissed softly.

When he hesitated, Becky began to throw things. Sudden Sam scurried out the door like a scared cockroach. After he left she started breaking things. His things. First in the living room. Then she went into the bedroom and pulled all the drawers out of his dresser, whipping the clothes all over the room. She had worked her way to the bathroom by the time the landlord came by to find out what the racket was.

It had still been early and even though she didn't feel like going to Nathan's party, she felt like hanging around her apartment even less.

When Becky got to Nathan's party, she didn't talk much except to the nice young priest. And she didn't breathe a word to anyone about her brave new life as an unmarried, pregnant woman.

✝ ✝ ✝

The smell of cologne brought Becky out of her funk. She looked at herself in the mirror, seeing no beauty, only sadness.

A fly landed on the mirror, distracting her from the memory of the big fight with Sudden Sam. Surprising herself, she smacked the fly dead so fast and so violently that she cracked the mirror. Disgusted, she quickly washed her hands in a sink filled with broken bottles of Sam's cologne.

It stinks in here. Oh, Daddy, why did you have to die?

She threw on some black nylon tights and a big rumpled, white sweater. After donning her Keds she grabbed the keys.

Hi Father Chet! I'm Rebecca Macadam. You know, Macadam like in asphalt? By the way, I'm pregnant. You Father. Me Mother. Ha ha ha. Jeeze. Get a grip—you're just going to get some coffee.

She closed the door behind her and started down the stairs, headed for the coffee shop and Father Chet, a Catholic priest.

5

Sunday Morning
8 October
Notre Dame, Indiana

Nathan Payne took a left off Angela Boulevard and turned onto Notre Dame Avenue, which was lined by enormous oak trees on either side. He saw the famous Golden Dome at the end of the street, topped with a statue of Mary. She was crushing the head of a snake with her heel. The statue itself was over two stories tall. Nathan was so distracted by the dome that he almost drove directly onto the campus lawn where the South Quad intersects with Notre Dame Avenue.

So that's why Chet always goes on and on about this place. She is impressive.

The Notre Dame campus is unique. It has no streets except an access road that circles its campus proper. Nathan was forced to park the Mustang in the lot of the Morris Inn.

Time to wake this girl up and find out where she needs to go next.

He looked at her. *She looks like that actress, Bridget Fonda, only with wavy, auburn hair.* Nathan was still troubled by his newly assertive conscience. *She definitely didn't have much experience doing what we did together, and she was more drunk than I was. Probably has a heck of a hangover coming.*

He looked at her for a full two minutes and decided not to wake her. He grabbed a Kent and lit up. As he looked at the pack of Kents, the cigarette triggered a memory of his dad.

Still smoking that bastard's brand.

✝ ✝ ✝

Suddenly, Nathan was four years old again, sitting on the floor in the hallway next to the kitchen, with salty tears in his eyes, trying not to cry. It was Bloomfield, New Jersey. His dad had just snapped at little Nathan to get back to bed *or else.*

The men in the kitchen didn't know that the little boy could hear them. Nathan could smell the cigarettes and cheap cigar smoke. His dad's friends were enjoying their weekly poker game. Mostly they talked about sports or work. Sometimes, politics. There was a lot of foul language and some drunken laughter.

Nathan's dad was a postman, and this particular time, the old man was relating one of his many stories about seducing or being seduced by one of his several "regular" women on the route. Two of the other men were also postmen and shared their own crude stories.

Nathan only vaguely understood what they were talking about, but he knew it was about women, and Nathan knew his mom was dead, and that he didn't have a woman like those men had women.

His mom had died when Nathan was three. He didn't know why. Some kind of cancer. His dad didn't beat him as often after Sarah Payne died. Not getting smacked around made him feel happy his mother was gone. His father had beaten Mom, too.

Then, feeling happy about his mother being gone made Nathan feel terrible, worse than ever.

He gave up crying a few months after his mother died because it didn't make him feel better. More often than not, his tears earned him a slap from the old man.

Life was a dark, silent hell until Nathan went to school a couple of years later. His only consolation before school started was his Babsie, his Polish grandmother on his mother's side. Babsie lived in Nutley. She came over once or twice a week to look after him. She also took Nathan to Mass every Sunday.

The tender old woman taught little Nathan how to pray and told him stories he could only vaguely remember now. One story was about a painting of Mary where some soldier died when he struck it with a sword. The other was about a priest-dude named Max who died in a Nazi concentration camp. (Nathan mistakenly thought concentration camps were places where there was no food except bread and everyone had to try to concentrate on math problems or else bad guys would kill you. This lasted until Nathan was in fourth grade and learned about real Nazis in social studies class.)

Babsie often told Nathan that he descended from noble blood, insisting that he was from a line of kings. At the time, Nathan thought noble blood was blood that did not come from bulls.

God, talk about the fairy tales a grandmother makes up to console a pathetic little kid, Nathan thought as he took another drag on his cigarette.

Babsie died the day the boy went to school for the first time. No one bothered to tell Nathan about Babsie's death. When he asked his father where she was, his dad said Babsie went away, and told the boy to shut up.

Nowadays I would've ended up in some special class for the emotionally disturbed.

Young Nathan started to eat too much (his dad's favorite meal was boiled hot dogs and lots of potato chips) and by second grade he was considered chubby by teachers and classmates. Nathan wasn't quite fat.

I probably didn't eat one vegetable outside of school until I was fourteen years old. By the way, what's going on here, This Is Your Life, Nathan Payne? Must be the booze from last night. God, how depressing! Weren't you ever happy as a kid?

The answer was yes. On the first day of school, an Irish kid sat behind him and immediately started whispering in Nathan's ear about the teacher, Sister Leonardo Mary. The Irish kid kept calling her Sister "Lardo" and would puff out his cheeks like a bullfrog—intimating that the good sister was less than svelte. Indeed, she weighed well over two hundred pounds. Nathan giggled.

By the third day of school, Nathan surprised himself by trying to come up with his own jokes to whisper to the Irish boy. Although he was never quite as funny as the skinny Irish kid with the gleam in his eye, Nathan got off a few good ones. They sat next to each other at lunch, then began to hang out on the playground.

The Irish kid's name was William "Chet" Sullivan. The nuns called Chet "William," but all the kids called him Chet, which wasn't a common nickname in Catholic schools. In third grade Chet told Nathan that Chester was his mother's maiden name.

Presently, Nathan wondered if he would ever have had any friends if a funny Irish kid named Chet hadn't sat behind him on that first day of school. With a capacity only children seem to have, Chet decided instantly that the shy, portly kid with the green eyes was his best friend in all the world, and that was that.

Chet was Nathan's ticket to a normal life. Chet had three older brothers who protected both their youngest brother and Nathan from bullies. The Sullivan boys all played together after school. Chet and Nathan shared a somewhat sarcastic, wry sense of humor. Chet was cool. Therefore Nathan was cool.

Even though Nathan was not the biggest or fastest kid on the playground, he was deceptively quick and coordinated. Most kids wanted him on their team for boxball, stickball, team tag, and all the other games kids played on the asphalt playground.

It's amazing how important playing games was in grammar school.

Nathan was an exceptionally adept game player. He was usually chosen captain of the team because he had a knack for picking players. He knew which ones would mesh into a winning team.

Nathan also had the uncanny ability to see everything and everyone in the field of play and could guess what was going to happen next. He was almost prescient. On the playgrounds of grammar schools, these were highly valued traits, and seemed to make up for Nathan's quiet demeanor in the eyes of his classmates.

Why did I forget all this? Nathan asked himself now, exhaling a plume of smoke in the direction of the dome. *Those were great days. I never even think of them anymore. Why did I stop playing sports?*

He didn't know. Then he remembered.

Oh yeah, my dad the felon, he thought sarcastically. *Harry Payne, number 12345-whatever at Rahway State Correctional University.*

When Nathan was in seventh grade, his dad was sent to prison for trying to steal something expensive from the post office. *Was it the safe?* Nathan wasn't sure of the details. Within days of his father's conviction, Nathan had been put on a bus to Chicago. He didn't like his new "family." They were distant cousins on his mother's side. A social worker had recruited them to take him in.

*Or was it I didn't **let** myself like them? The Wojtals. Jeeze, I can't remember doing anything with them but eat dinner.*

They both worked all the time. No kids. Back to the depressing part of The Life of Nathan Feel the Pain Payne.

He never really found friends in the public grade school he attended in the Chicago suburbs. *I was the invisible kid.*

Before moving to Chicago, he had practically lived at the Sullivan home, eating dinner there a couple of times a week and generally getting into harmless trouble playing pranks with Chet. His grades didn't reflect it, but the teachers knew Nathan was smart and treated him kindly. Especially the nuns.

Although he considered himself an agnostic and carefully avoided setting foot in church after his Babsie died (except for required Masses at Our Lady of Lourdes Grammar School), it always bothered Nathan when comedians made jokes about cruel, heartless nuns.

Old Sister Lardo used to look at me with such gentleness, and seemed to sense I was troubled. She never pushed me, but always told me how intelligent I was. Most of the other nuns were the same way. Next to Chet's family, nuns were the nicest people I ever knew.

One day in fifth grade, Sister Leonardo held Nathan after school. She was now the principal of Our Lady of Lourdes. She threw him for a loop that day: *"You know, Nathan, you've always been my favorite student. Don't look so surprised young man! I know you and the Sullivan boy called me Sister Lardo in first grade. The elephant never forgets."* The big woman laughed cheerfully, letting him know that the joke was okay in a strangely adult way. He was particularly confused after the elephant crack.

Sister Lardo had continued: *"Nevertheless, I'm entering you in the diocesan math contest. I know you can do better at math, much better. We have tests."*

God! She must have been referring to IQ tests! Nathan now realized.

"I have a feeling that you'll do quite well if you consider math a game. I'm going to help you after school. Don't look so long-faced, young man. Just fifteen minutes a day. Then

you can run along to the Sullivans' house and play. The elephant has spoken, young man, and you shall obey."

The gigantic nun did tutor him—every day for two years. And Nathan won every math contest he ever entered. Nathan was doing college level calculus by the end of eighth grade. In Chicago, his math skills earned him a full scholarship to Fenwick High School. The scholarship was sponsored by a math-whiz alumnus who had made millions manufacturing drinking straws. It was called the Straw Man Scholarship by Fenwick students. Nathan aced his SATs (in both Math and Verbal) and won a full ride to the University of Illinois.

Chet got into Notre Dame, and the two friends made a ritual of meeting in Chicago on weekends a few times a semester. Chet had been a faithful pen pal since the move. Only now did Nathan consider that Chet might have been deeply saddened when he moved away. *I was so selfish that I shut everybody out—and I almost shut out Chetmeister. Chet used to write to me four times before I ever wrote him back.* By the time they got into college, both young men were more interested in partying than anything else.

We were a killer team until old Chetmeister got religion. Ten years ago. Funny, I never came to visit Chet here at Notre Dame. Not even once. Was I avoiding this place?

If a stranger could see Nathan sitting in the Mustang with the sleeping woman next to him, it would seem like he was having a telepathic discussion with the statue of Mary on the dome.

Yeah, I used to love you, Mary. Babsie said you knew Mom and I would get to see you both together someday. Babsie would never tell me when someday would come. Well, there you are. Where's Mom?

He tasted salt.

Have I been crying?

He looked over at Joanie. She was wide awake. For a brief moment Nathan saw empathy in her eyes. It disappeared quickly.

"Hi Joanie," he said softly, awkwardly. He looked down at his lap, embarrassed by his tears. He closed his eyes for a heartbeat, and looked back to the pretty, silent woman next to him. This was his first sober look into her eyes.

Nathan Payne fell in love. Just like that—much in the same way Chet had decided to be Nathan's best friend on the first day of school so many years before.

"I want to get as far away from you as I can as soon as I can!" Joanie Wheat came down on each word slowly and distinctly, as if she had practiced them. "And I'm going to start right now. Thanks for the ride, Mister."

She didn't even open the door. She hopped over it instead and stormed away, toward a brown statue of a guy who was wearing a funny hat.

6

Sunday Morning
8 October
Notre Dame, Indiana

Professor Thomas Wheat finished collecting his lecture notes and left his office in O'Shaughnessy Hall—known as O'Shag to students and teachers. He had come in on Sunday to gather the notes so he could review them for his class the next day. He had a crew cut, was average height, with rough good looks. He looked more like an NFL quarterback than a History professor, except for his typical professorial uniform of khaki pants, oxford shirt, and herringbone jacket. One month past his sixty-first birthday, coeds still seemed to get infatuated with him. Their crushes barely registered on Tom—he was a happily married man and a father of seven.

He had eight grandchildren already. His wife Anne got a kick out of his tradition of making grandchild projections at the family Christmas gatherings. Last Christmas, he had predicted two more grandkids—and was thrilled when three were born. Tom and Anne lived in a modestly large farmhouse in Mishawaka, ten miles from campus.

Unlike his politically correct and research-oriented peers, Wheat taught for the sheer love of it. He was deeply satisfied when his students finally grasped that history was more than a recitation of facts. Most of his peers considered him a relic for the simple reason that he believed one could discover objective truth in history. Surely he would never have gotten tenure in this day and age of Political Correctness. As for his students, they loved the way Wheat told stories.

He had an avocation outside of academia. Fourteen years earlier, he had become entranced by William Thomas Walsh's book, *Our Lady of Fatima*. He had dedicated his spare time and research to finding out all he could about the alleged apparitions of Mary, the Mother of God. These apparitions had multiplied around the world in recent decades. Soon he was giving talks on the subject at local parishes. His natural storytelling ability and his flair for the dramatic had made him famous in a small subspecies of the huge body of Catholics in the United States: Catholics who actually believed that Jesus had the power to send His Mother to the world as a prophetess—just as Yahweh had sent Noah to warn the world before the Great Flood.

Joe Jackson, an enterprising member of the local Knights of Immaculata group recorded one of Wheat's talks and—against Tom's mild protests—started distributing the audio tapes freely to anyone who asked for them. Jackson never charged for the tapes, but free will donations seemed to cover the costs.

That had been almost five years ago. Millions of audio tapes had been distributed by Jackson's Kolbe Foundation in the meantime. Now Wheat was considered the foremost English-speaking expert on Marian apparitions—but only by those few Catholics who were predisposed to listen to him. There were almost sixty million Catholics in the United States.

Relatively few—perhaps several million—knew of the reported messages from the Mother of God in any detail.

His colleagues, had they known about his secret career,
would have laughed. "There goes that old dinosaur Wheat—
on and on about superstitious and deluded children seeing
the Mother of God!" Wheat wouldn't have bothered to point
out to his learned colleagues that Mary had predicted at
Fatima the rise of Communist Russia before the Revolution
in 1917. She had also predicted when World War II would
start—thirty years before it began.

*Not to mention her predictions to children in Rwanda of
the wholesale decapitations in 1994—ten years before they
occurred,* Tom mused darkly.

Professors at Catholic colleges like Notre Dame had
dropped Marian devotion decades ago. Wheat's colleagues
were a microcosm of Catholics in general. Wheat knew the
statistics well. Less than forty percent of Catholics attended
Sunday Mass. Of those who did attend, less than twenty percent actually believed the teachings of their own Church. This
meant only seven percent or so of the entire Catholic population were like Wheat—true believers. It was not uncommon
for the remaining seven percent of orthodox Catholics to fight
with each other over the authenticity of particular Marian
apparitions. Some of the more traditional Catholics, who were
understandably embittered by the *de facto* prohibition of the
beautiful Tridentine Mass, considered adherents to Marian
apparitions to be End Times fanatics. Of course Tom Wheat
didn't consider himself a fanatic. He considered himself a
sober reporter. If the Mother of God and her Son were saying that the world was about to undergo a period of unprece-
dented tribulations, who was he to ignore their words?

The whole situation is one giant mess, Wheat thought
dejectedly. *It was my generation that dropped the ball. Twenty
centuries of faith stopped cold by one generation of baby
boomers. Martyrs spilled their blood so my generation could
skip Sunday Mass to watch pro football. Communion of Saints
exchanged for the New Orleans Saints.*

The majority of Wheat's students were so poorly educated in matters of the faith that they would have had trouble reciting the Ten Commandments.

Ninety-three percent of baptized Catholics rejected part or all of the ageless teachings of Catholicism. This vast majority got divorced, contracepted, aborted, and generally acted like everyone else in nominally Christian America. To Wheat's liberal Catholic friends, these same statistics meant seven percent were still following the "superstitions of Rome."

Liberal Catholics didn't disturb Wheat's equilibrium. He avoided arguing with them—their minds were pretty much closed to the facts. Wheat was secure in his love for the Catholic Church, which he loved more than teaching and more than his wonderful wife, Anne. The Catholic Church was the Mystical Body of Christ. To love the Church was to love Jesus. It wasn't complicated.

Wheat also believed for a logical reason: the Catholic Church was unique in all of history. It was the very measuring stick of history. He could not deny any of its teachings, which he knew with the precision of a dedicated scholar, nor the beauty these truths brought into his life.

More than that, Tom Wheat believed because his prayers were answered, which had been the case since he was a boy. He had experienced first hand what the famous French convert Pascal was driving at when he challenged atheists and agnostics with his famous Wager. Blaise Pascal believed that if a person sincerely acts *as if* he had faith with devotion for a period of one year, the gift of faith will be given to him. After all, if God doesn't exist, you've lost little. If He does exist, then you've gained an eternity filled with infinite reward by making a finite wager of a part of your life. Tom Wheat was well aware of the fact that thousands had converted to the faith after taking up Pascal's Wager. By this stage in his life, he was a lot more worried about his family and friends choosing to forego those rewards than missing them himself.

As Tom studied the apparitions of Mary, he started to respond to what Mary was saying. *My colleagues would say I've internalized it,* he thought with a grin.

He took the Queen of Heaven's advice and began to fast on bread and water twice a week. He made a concerted effort to love his wife and children in the little things. Wheat offered up the small inconveniences in his life for the conversion of sinners. He enlisted in Mary's humble army by joining the Knights of Immaculata. In short, Tom was becoming a saint. He was a preacher who practiced what he preached—a rarity.

Wheat looked at his Longines wristwatch. *Time for Mass*.

For some reason, as he left O'Shag, Tom decided to walk down the South Quad toward Sacred Heart Basilica instead of his usual path by Zahm Hall via the North Quad. Such is the prompting of chance—or grace. For this little detour would bring him into contact with Nathan Payne—and would change the fates of countless people.

Chapter Three

1

One Month Earlier
Hilton Hotel
Los Angeles, California

Lee's mother was really starting to get on his nerves.

Doesn't Mama know I'm doing this for her? God, I'm going to have to cut her off like I used to cut off my junkies when they couldn't pay. She's addicted to clothes, furniture, and lottery tickets! Amazing.

He snorted up another line of coke off the small mirror he had placed on the expansive desk.

What about you? Gonna cut yourself off, boy?

He ignored himself.

A beautiful black woman, a relatively famous rap singer named Raja X, lay sleeping in the bed. It was a king-size bed with fine mahogany posts.

Time to call the office.

The irony, of course, was that Lee would never have done coke while selling it in the Woodland Section of Cleveland. That would have been bad for business. Back then, he held addicts in contempt. He preferred alcohol as his drug of choice. But Cleveland was in another universe altogether.

Lee was now in what he considered a much more desirable universe. In less than three months he had parlayed his minor fortune from the Cleveland Clinic Foundation deal into much, much more. After moving to Los Angeles with his mom, he quickly began to study the landscape for deals

similar to the one he pulled off in Cleveland. For a home, he
bought a modest two-bedroom split-level in El Segundo—as
close to the airport runways as he could find—to take advantage of the lower property values. He quickly moved in with
his mother and their few meager belongings. He gave her
four thousand dollars and told her to buy some clothes and
furniture. It took her less than one day to spend it. Lee leased
a new Chrysler Concorde—with practically no money down,
of course.

Lee was so impressed with the results from the real estate
course that he spent days at the local library studying everything he could find on the subject. He also bought a book on
dressing for success (to Lee this meant dressing white).

A clerk at a bookstore recommended a few titles in the
Human Potential Movement section. Lee bought a few of
those books on a whim and really dug them. Soon he was
regularly purchasing audio tapes at the Scientology bookstore after reading in *People* magazine that John Travolta was
a big-time member.

He watched CNI and practiced pronouncing words like
the white folks. His mother laughed at him but Lee paid little
attention. After a few weeks he had to buy Shawna her own
separate television set for her game shows and Oprah.

Lee knew instinctively that it was a white world and that
he owed his Clinic deal to no small measure of luck.

He spent another five grand on a new wardrobe, relying
on the advice of a homosexual clothier named Fabian who
got a kick out of Lee's request to help him dress "like a honky
lawyer."

Lee doubted Fabian was the homosexual's real name. He
suggested in a slightly lisping voice that Lee should visit a
certain hair dresser who could supply Lee with a honky hair-
cut. A friendship began. Fabian invited him to a party a few
days later and Lee did not decline.

He kept his mouth shut at the party out of fear of embarrassing himself with his ghetto speech, and partly to observe

carefully the new world of upper and middle class whites, blacks, and gays of both colors.

So this is where all the money is, he thought.

He was struck by two things. First, (and this was hard for him to admit to himself) he was as smart or smarter than most of the people he met. This was especially true despite his lack of reading and writing skills. He had been sizing people up his whole life, as a survival instinct, and he knew that he could out-think most of the people in the room except, curiously, the gay haberdasher Fabian.

The second thing Lee noticed was a complete revelation. For the first time in his life, he could not smell fear on the skin of whites when they looked at him.

Standing in the corner of Fabian's apartment, Lee put down his glass of watery light beer and looked at himself in the mirror that covered the entire wall of the smoky living room.

I look more like Bernard Shaw on CNI than any of the homeboys back in the Woodland Section. I didn't have to move to LA to get away from Woodland. All I had to do was shop at Tower City! Tower City was an upscale mall in the center of the business district of downtown Cleveland.

These two revelations, namely, that he could disguise his poor background with clothing, money, and manners; and that he was more intelligent than most other people—even white people—added up in Lee's mind more quickly than he added profit margins during his deals: *I'm going to be rich!*

All his Personal Power tapes assured him basically the same thing.

Lee turned down two offers for cocaine that evening, excused himself early, and made sure he got Fabian's phone number before leaving. He drove his Concorde back to El Segundo. Instead of going to bed, Lee stayed up until two in the morning studying.

One week later, he convinced Fabian and two of his gay friends to take options on land in Oxnard near a hospital that was slated to receive huge federal grants for AIDS research.

Then Fabian introduced Lee to a gay soap opera actor. The actor happened to be black and was originally from Akron, Ohio. The two transplants hit it off. Lee discovered the actor was in the market for a condominium in Inglewood. Four days later, Lee passed the California real estate exam by one point and sold the actor a condominium the next day.

Three days after that, he rented a prime piece of office space in downtown Los Angeles across from the Hilton. Lee considered the office in the same category as his wardrobe—a disguise to fool whites and middle class blacks. He also hired a white secretary from a temp firm, and Fabian's accountant to do his books. Then he hired another one of Fabian's friends to resell the smaller properties in El Segundo that Lee had begun to buy. He called his company Washington Properties. Washington Properties broke even or made a few thousand on most of the smaller deals. Lee was so engrossed with his work that he barely noticed he was working eighteen hours a day. Shawna Washington began to complain that her son was too busy and started nagging him for more money.

Lee was investing almost all his Clinic Deal fortune, consciously betting on his own ability, bolstered by the human potential tapes and books he was reading. Financially, he seemed to be a good horse to bet on. When he made Fabian and his friends fifty grand each (and pocketed as much for himself, plus a cut) on the Oxnard properties, word quickly spread about the Boy Wonder from Cleveland.

In the hip and hyped world of Los Angeles, Lee gave halting, low-key presentations, delivered with his calm, quiet voice. His presentations were always augmented by impressive research neatly inscribed on yellow pads in his tiny, childlike handwriting. He was tough, fair, and even generous. Little did his investors realize that this was his practical and relentless way of investing in them. They were more valuable to him than any property.

Lee secretly relished the fact that he had maneuvered himself into a glorious position for any businessman: *Now I'm risking and investing other people's money, just like it says in all the books.*

He began to chant to himself over and over: *I will have a million dollars before the end of the year. And after two years I'll have ten million dollars. By the end of ten years I'll own the Lakers!*

He put the team photo of the Lakers on his desk, just as the tapes advised him, so he could visualize owning the sports franchise.

Fabian had made a pass at Lee several weeks earlier, and he didn't seem insulted when Lee turned him down. Lee decided that if he didn't want to collapse from exhaustion, he had better take a few hours off to relax with a woman. He was pleasantly surprised when the white women he met at the parties were willing to sleep with him. They were even willing to be seen with him at restaurants and nightclubs.

When Raja X took him to the bathroom at one of Fabian's endless parties and offered him a line of white powder, Lee decided one snort might help keep him awake.

One line was all Lee took at that party. After all, he was in control of himself and in total control of his own destiny. He was *creating* himself. He could handle one line. Besides, if all these rich folks could handle it—and afford it—couldn't he?

Just one line.

Raja was far more beautiful and insatiable than old Tawana. Lee had to admit that Tawana was a little fat in the thighs and not as, well, *cosmopolitan,* as Raja.

Unlike Tawana, Raja came from a middle class family and was well spoken. The rap singer had gone to a local community college before striking out into the music world. Raja worked out to stay in shape. She affected ghetto slang as part of her stage persona. Lee had a good laugh when she told him that.

Raja X laughed harder when he confided to her that he affected his honky pronunciation by watching CNI. They shared ambition and belief in creating themselves and more recently, their drug bills. Raja's real name was Ellen Snow.

A year ago I didn't even know the word cosmopolitan, much less understand it.

Lee eventually began to get high before sleeping with Raja. To relax. One night he bought ten thousand dollars worth of coke.

Ten grand? That's a few hours of work on my deal in Oxnard. That's like ten bucks back in Woodland. No sweat. I'll have a million before the end of the year...

Lee shook himself from his thoughts and focused his eyes on the phone again. He decided to put off the call to the office until morning. The drug was quickly taking effect. He climbed off the chair and onto the bed, kissing Raja on the cheek. She opened her eyes and looked at him, smiling warmly. Then she noticed his Miraculous Medal. She remembered a question which she had always wanted to ask him.

"Why do you wear that around your neck?" she nodded at his Miraculous Medal. "What's it called?"

"Oh this?" A puzzled look came to his face as he held the medal in his hand. "I don't know what it's called. Found it in a dump when I was a kid. It's my lucky charm. It helped me find you." Still looking down, Lee smiled awkwardly at his corny, romantic innocence.

He looked up and saw that Raja had raised her eyebrows, showing him her "I'm gonna have an Ambiance night" look. Curiosity about his medal had left her mind as quickly as it came. Lee forgot about his good luck charm.

"Come here, City Boy," she purred.

2

Sunday Morning
8 October
Notre Dame, Indiana

Nathan watched Joanie Wheat storm away toward the statue
of the guy with the funny hat. During his short adult life he
had always been the one to walk away, usually sneaking out
of bedrooms after one night stands. He *never* allowed himself to get emotionally involved with women—even those he
slept with more than once. When they realized this, they left
him soon enough.

Now Nathan felt pulled in two directions. He had always
prided himself on his detachment. He had little use for feelings and despised men who let women trap them emotionally. All his experience since losing his mother had taught
him to feel relieved when women deserted him, or vice versa.

Yet Joanie was somehow different. As she walked briskly
away, not looking back, he felt that she was taking something
with her that was *his*. He felt, no, he knew, that this was a
moment of great importance. It was like the microsecond
before he took a gamble on buying or selling a stock.

It was the time for a decision. Nathan decided.

What do I care? She's not even number forty-eight.

He took his eyes off the auburn-haired girl and put his
fingers on the key in the ignition.

The hell with her.

☩ ☩ ☩

At precisely the same moment in Chicago, the Reverend
William Chester "Chet" Sullivan was patiently waiting for
Becky Macadam to show up at a coffee shop. Thinking of
her brought his friend Nathan to mind.

After all, it was at Nathan's party where Chet met Becky. Chet—out of long habit—decided to say a prayer for Nathan, as he had a thousand times before in spare moments over the years. Just a simple, short prayer.

Dear Jesus, help Nathan find his way to your mother's Immaculate Heart, like you helped me. He's my friend.

Father Chet quickly forgot his little prayer when he saw the stunningly beautiful Becky Macadam walking up the sidewalk toward the cafe.

A song from a New Jersey group called the Smithereens popped into the priest's mind: *"Beauty and Sadness."*

Then, a line from the Gospel of Luke: *"A sign of contradiction"—like the Pieta in Saint Peter's in Rome. What's more beautiful and sad than the Mother of God cradling her dead Son?*

✠ ✠ ✠

As Nathan began turning the key to start the Mustang, he heard a woman's voice inside his head: *"Beauty and sadness, young man. Joanie is a sign of contradiction and so are you."*

"Is that you, Sister Lardo?" Nathan asked aloud, confused.

He looked to the back seat, half-expecting to see his first grade teacher sitting there as if transported through some kind of surreal time warp. The convertible's back seat was empty. He spun quickly to look out the windshield.

Then the voice came again. One word: *"Go."*

Even though he was wide awake, Nathan suddenly felt as if he had woken up from a dream.

One word echoed in his mind. *Go.*

Go, Nathan thought, rather disoriented. *Go where? Leave Notre Dame? Go after her, you stupid moron. Run!*

Nathan turned the car off and jumped out without opening the door. He sprinted toward Joanie.

What are you going to say to her, track star?

He caught up with her at precisely the moment she reached the strange statue.

"Joanie," Nathan called softly, out of breath.

She turned to look at him. Her blue eyes iced over with anger. His stomach pitched like a boat on a wave when he looked at her. He was breathing hard.

Say something, she's waiting!

"Well?" she asked impatiently.

"Uh, Joanie," he repeated desperately, "what's with the chef?" He gestured directly at the statue of Father Sorin above them. Sorin wore a boxed cap common to priests of the early 1800s. It was not unlike a chef's hat. Father Sorin had a long beard, too, which oddly added to the effect.

"What?" she asked as she looked up at the statue of Father Sorin. "Oh, that."

For a moment she forgot how angry she was.

"That's Father Sorin. He's the French priest who founded this place. Sorin came with some Indians when this was all wilderness and looked out and said, 'Someday, a great university will be here,' or something like that. That's his hat. There's a Latin word for it, but I don't know it. Hey!"

Her anger came back like a boomerang. He had humiliated her last night. Joanie Wheat was not *that* kind of girl.

"Listen, Mister. I already told you I don't want anything to do with you." Now her voice was cold.

"Joanie," he pleaded, still lost for words. *God! You idiot!* he chastened himself.

She remained silent, almost enjoying watching him squirm. *How can you look directly into my eyes like that?* she thought. *Aren't you ashamed?*

"What if I said there's been a mistake?" he suggested desperately. Nathan hesitated. Then he heard himself saying, "I'm so ashamed of myself." He noticed her expression soften just a bit. *Such beautiful eyes,* he thought distractedly. He continued to feel for the right words.

"I am..." he stuttered, then more firmly, "...so terribly sorry. You don't even know me and I've hurt you. I'm sorry."

The anger was draining from her eyes now. Then she squinted, appraising him.

Oh really? she thought. *Sure you're sorry. Sound pretty sincere, too. You must practice that line. Off you go, Mister!*

She prepared to drop the hammer on him, but she was stunned to hear her own voice mutter, almost compassionately, "I forgive you."

I can't believe I just said that, she told herself. Then she knew. *You said it because you meant it. You forgive him.*

They looked at each other, silently, for a long moment.

Nathan smiled. Now it was her turn to feel her stomach flutter.

Oh no, she thought.

Behind her, Nathan saw a man walk up. He was pretty rugged-looking. Then Nathan heard the older man clear his throat.

Joanie turned to see her father standing there.

"My daughter, I presume?" Professor Wheat winked at Joanie. Tom Wheat gave Nathan an appraising look before continuing, "And who is this fine young gentleman? A student?"

Professor Wheat was surprised to see his blue-eyed daughter's porcelain cheeks flush red. *Red, white, and blue,* Joanie's father thought absently.

Joanie tried to regain her composure.

"Oh, no Daddy! I mean, hi Daddy!"

She's flustered, Wheat thought as Joanie gave him a hug.

After the embrace, she continued nervously, looking back to Nathan as she spoke, "This is a friend of Chet's. I met him in Chicago last night. His name is Nathan…"

Joanie wracked her memory for Nathan's last name. *I get drunk, I spend the night with this guy. **Then** I forgive him. **And now** I'm pretty sure I just fell in love with him—and I can't even remember his name!*

"Nathan Payne, sir," Nathan said as he offered his hand to Tom Wheat. "Do you really know Chet Sullivan?"

Wheat noticed Nathan's unusually strong grip and liked it.

"Not very well, I regret to say. He was a student here a while back. He was an acquaintance of my son Greg. How do you know him? And isn't it *Father* Chet now?"

"It sure is, sir. I mean, it sure is Father Chet, and we grew up in New Jersey." *Why do I keep calling him sir?* "I guess you could say we're best friends."

This news seemed to please Joanie's dad.

Probably thinks I'm okay if I'm friends with a priest. If only he knew the hell Chet and I used to raise back before Chet got religion. If he only knew what I did with his daughter last night!

Nathan felt the blush coming to his cheeks. He looked at Wheat and suddenly realized that perhaps this old guy was well aware of Chet's not-so-priestly habits during Chet's undergraduate days. It was hard for Nathan to decipher Tom Wheat's gaze. He suddenly felt ashamed.

Wheat looked at his watch, then at Joanie. "Look, sweetheart, I'm headed over to Mass at the Crypt." The Crypt was a chapel in the basement of Sacred Heart Basilica, the main church on the campus. "Would you like to join me, Nathan? You're both welcome to have lunch with me afterward. That is, of course, if you're free."

Nathaniel Payne, who hadn't set foot in a Catholic church since seventh grade, looked at Joanie Wheat and quickly decided she still had some of *him* in her possession. He could even endure a Catholic Mass to be next to her for a little while longer. Deciding quickly, Nathan flashed his most winning smile at Professor Wheat.

"I'd love to go! That is, if you don't mind, sir. I'm free all day."

Wheat looked at his daughter, silently asking, "*Do you mind?*"

Men, Joanie thought, *they always dominate conversation.*

Then she looked at Nathan. *I'll give you one Mass and one lunch, Mister.*

"Then let's go," she said somewhat unenthusiastically.

Nathan and the Wheats left the watchful eye of Father Sorin and walked across the South Quad toward Sacred Heart Basilica.

3

Sunday Morning
8 October
Chicago, Illinois

A thin, bushy-haired Irishman wearing a Roman collar and a black cotton London Fog windbreaker walked into the coffee-house next to Leona's Pizza on Sheridan.

Father Chet found an empty table next to the window. It was another cloudy, windy day in Chicago, but not as cold as it looked. Nevertheless, it was good to get out of the wind. He remembered how beautiful Becky was and how she brushed off his attempts at small talk. Chet was a good priest—and he was a chaste man after long, hard years of practicing the virtue of chastity upon entering the seminary at Seton Hall University. But he was still human. Chet said a quick prayer asking Mary to help him remain chaste in mind and action during his meeting with Rebecca Macadam.

Praying about her reminded him of Nathan, who had been more than a little drunk while hanging all over Professor Wheat's daughter, Joanie. Chet hadn't seen Joanie Wheat in years, and hadn't known her well during his undergraduate days at Notre Dame. He had been surprised to see her at Nathan's party. She had not struck him as the wild kind of girl when he was at Notre Dame. He had partied pretty hard with her older brother, Greg Wheat, who was now a happily married lawyer in North Caldwell, New Jersey, not far from Chet's current parish.

Out of long habit, Father Chet added a short prayer for Nathan, too. Chet didn't know it, but at this very moment,

Nathan was sitting in his Mustang at Notre Dame, deciding whether or not to go after Joanie Wheat.

During his college years, and before he rediscovered his faith, Chet had not been an angel with the ladies by any stretch of the imagination, although he had never been as wild as Nathan. Chet was somewhat uncomfortable meeting alone with a woman as pretty as Becky.

Pretty is not the right word for her. Her beauty transcends mere prettiness. In fact, at the party her beauty had reminded him of her Maker. *If she's made in the image and likeness of God, then I can hardly wait to meet God.*

The priest reminded himself how forlorn she had seemed at the party last night and on the phone this morning.

He was only thirty-one but he had been a priest for over four years and had come to trust his instincts about people. He could intuit when a person needed a word of encouragement or a shoulder to cry on. At the party Chet knew in his bones that Becky was hurting. Chet believed in the gifts of the Holy Spirit, one of which was called the gift of counsel—the ability to give the right advice to those in need. He was prepared to exercise that gift now.

He spotted Becky walking down the sidewalk toward the door. Her unique beauty and stark sadness reminded him of a song, and then, the Pieta. He said another quick prayer, this time to Saint Anthony of Padua.

Help me find the patience to listen. Help me find the right words to say.

Father Chet stood up as she approached his table. She had a strong, athletic gait. He pulled a chair out for her.

Becky smiled wanly. "My, my, aren't you a gentleman!"

He laughed good-naturedly. "Sorry. It's the way my parents raised me and my three older brothers. My mom was afraid that four Irish boys growing up together would turn out to be oafs, so she emphasized common courtesy."

"Don't get me wrong. I like it," Becky protested.

There was a long pause. A waiter came and took their orders. Both preferred regular coffee, black.

"So how do you know Nathan Payne?" Father Chet asked.

"A girl who works at my advertising agency who used to work at Nathan's brokerage firm introduced us. I don't know him very well, really. I gather he's quite a lady killer. Tell me, Father," she emphasized the last word, arching an eyebrow, "how do *you* come to know the infamous Nathan Payne?"

This brought a smile to Father Chet's face.

"We go back to first grade, first day of school. He moved to Chicago in seventh grade. We were best friends in New Jersey. Nathan was like an extra brother in my family." Chet thought of Nathan's dad, Harrison "Harry" Payne, and the elder Payne's criminal conviction and subsequent death.

"We raised hell together in college. I went to Notre Dame and he went to Illinois. I spend a vacation week with him every year. I don't seem to have much effect on his, shall we say, bad habits."

I'm talking too much. Ask a question, Sigmund.

But no question came to him.

They both sipped coffee during a long silence. Becky was obviously uncomfortable now that their only common thread, Nathan Payne, was out of the way. Chet believed in quick prayers and prayed one. Two words. *Saint Anthony!*

"Look," he said, "sometimes it helps to just start."

Rebecca Macadam's pleasant smile died. Tears welled up in her eyes. She dropped her gaze, hugged herself with her arms, and let out a small, low sob. Her shoulders shook. Chet was now being guided by the Holy Spirit but he was too concerned for Becky to notice. He quickly made up his mind.

"This isn't the place," he whispered. "Let's get out of here. Get some fresh air."

He threw a five dollar bill on the table and helped her out of her seat, gently but firmly holding her shoulders as he led her out the door.

They walked toward the beach on the lake, a block away, and then right up to the water's edge. He stood back from her and turned toward the majestic Chicago skyline to the south, trying not to hear her gulping sobs over the brisk wind. True to his nature, he kept praying.

Would You Like to Finish Reading
Pierced by a Sword?

We will be happy to send you a free copy or copies for a nominal donation. Use the convenient Request Form on the next page and write to us today. Also available at Catholic retailers everywhere.

Pierced by a Sword
REQUEST FORM # 1

Dear Saint Jude Media:
Please send me a copy (or copies) of **Pierced by a Sword**. I understand that the first copy is free and that a donation is **not required** for one copy. I am not asking you to send a book or books to anyone other than myself.

Signed: _____

(Please Print)

Name: _____

Address: _____

Town: _____

State: _____ Zip: _____

Suggested **Optional** Donation for one book: **$1 to $10**
Donation for **more than one** book, any quantity: **$2 - $5 each**
(For more details about Saint Jude Media, see next page.)

Quantity Desired	X	Donation Per Book		Subtotal:
_____	X	_____	=	_____
Optional extra gift for shipping			=	_____
Optional gift for Saint Jude Media			=	_____

TOTAL DONATION* = $ _____

*Your contribution to Saint Jude Media is tax deductible. Any questions? Call (216) 333-4723. Sorry, no phone requests for books accepted. We'll ship your book the day we receive your letter.

CWS1

Please make checks payable to "Saint Jude Media" & send to:
Saint Jude Media
Box 26120 • Fairview Park, OH 44126

How Saint Jude Media Works

- If you do not have a request form, writing a simple letter to receive books is okay. Request forms are also available at www.catholicity.com on the Saint Jude Media homepage.

- Personal correspondence is encouraged. Tell us what you think of this book. We also welcome typographical, grammatical, and fact-checking suggestions for future printings (please include page and line number). Email us at saint.jude.media@catholicity.com

- We will send one free book to each person who writes to us directly. A donation for one book is not required, but you may send a donation if you wish.

- Using the honor system, we ask that you please refrain from sending us the addresses of people other than yourself. Please ask others to write to us directly. We will only send materials to those who personally ask for them, whether a donation is enclosed or not.

- At the present time, we only accept requests for materials by mail. Sorry, no phone requests. Only requests from the United States and Canada will be honored unless a sufficient donation to cover shipping is enclosed.

- Saint Jude Media will gladly absorb shipping charges on all requests, but feel free to add extra for shipping if you wish.

- Fast Delivery—All requests will be shipped on the day we open your envelope!

- Under normal circumstances, we are not able to "advance" quantities of books before receiving a donation.

- We will periodically write to let you know about new books and developments, but you will never receive a "fund raising letter" from us. We will not sell or lend your name to other groups—ever.

- These details apply to individuals as well as organizations such as bookstores, etc. Individuals, bookstores, gift shops, schools, and other organizations may accept donations for this book no greater than $5. A promotional retail display is available upon request.

Pierced by a Sword
REQUEST FORM # 2

Dear Saint Jude Media:
Please send me a copy (or copies) of **Pierced by a Sword**. I understand that the first copy is free and that a donation is **not required** for one copy. I am not asking you to send a book or books to anyone other than myself.

Signed: _____

(Please Print)

Name: _____

Address: _____

Town: _____

State: _____ Zip: _____

Suggested **Optional** Donation for one book: **$1 to $10**
Donation for **more than one** book, any quantity: **$2 - $5 each**
(For more details about Saint Jude Media, see next page.)

Quantity Desired	**X**	**Donation Per Book**	**Subtotal:**
_____	X	_____	= _____

Optional extra gift for shipping = _____

Optional gift for Saint Jude Media = _____

TOTAL DONATION* = $ _____

*Your contribution to Saint Jude Media is tax deductible. Any questions? Call (216) 333-4723. Sorry, no phone requests for books accepted. We'll ship your book the day we receive your letter.

CWS1

Please make checks payable to "Saint Jude Media" & send to:
Saint Jude Media
Box 26120 • Fairview Park, OH 44126

How Saint Jude Media Works

- If you do not have a request form, writing a simple letter to receive books is okay. Request forms are also available at www.catholicity.com on the Saint Jude Media homepage.

- Personal correspondence is encouraged. Tell us what you think of this book. We also welcome typographical, grammatical, and fact-checking suggestions for future printings (please include page and line number). Email us at saint.jude.media@catholicity.com

- We will send one free book to each person who writes to us directly. A donation for one book is not required, but you may send a donation if you wish.

- Using the honor system, we ask that you please refrain from sending us the addresses of people other than yourself. Please ask others to write to us directly. We will only send materials to those who personally ask for them, whether a donation is enclosed or not.

- At the present time, we only accept requests for materials by mail. Sorry, no phone requests. Only requests from the United States and Canada will be honored unless a sufficient donation to cover shipping is enclosed.

- Saint Jude Media will gladly absorb shipping charges on all requests, but feel free to add extra for shipping if you wish.

- Fast Delivery—All requests will be shipped on the day we open your envelope!

- Under normal circumstances, we are not able to "advance" quantities of books before receiving a donation.

- We will periodically write to let you know about new books and developments, but you will never receive a "fund raising letter" from us. We will not sell or lend your name to other groups—ever.

- These details apply to individuals as well as organizations such as bookstores, etc. Individuals, bookstores, gift shops, schools, and other organizations may accept donations for this book no greater than $5. A promotional retail display is available upon request.

Pierced by a Sword
REQUEST FORM # 3

Dear Saint Jude Media:
Please send me a copy (or copies) of **Pierced by a Sword**. I understand that the first copy is free and that a donation is **not required** for one copy. I am not asking you to send a book or books to anyone other than myself.

Signed: _____

(Please Print)
Name: _____

Address: _____

Town: _____

State: _____ Zip: _____

Suggested **Optional** Donation for one book: **$1 to $10**
Donation for **more than one** book, any quantity: **$2 - $5 each**
(For more details about Saint Jude Media, see next page.)

Quantity Desired	X	Donation Per Book		Subtotal:
_____	X	_____	=	_____

Optional extra gift for shipping   =   _____

Optional gift for Saint Jude Media   =   _____

TOTAL DONATION*   = $ _____

*Your contribution to Saint Jude Media is tax deductible. Any questions? Call (216) 333-4723. Sorry, no phone requests for books accepted. We'll ship your book the day we receive your letter.

CWS1

Please make checks payable to "Saint Jude Media" & send to:
Saint Jude Media
Box 26120 • Fairview Park, OH 44126

How Saint Jude Media Works

- If you do not have a request form, writing a simple letter to receive books is okay. Request forms are also available at www.catholicity.com on the Saint Jude Media homepage.

- Personal correspondence is encouraged. Tell us what you think of this book. We also welcome typographical, grammatical, and fact-checking suggestions for future printings (please include page and line number). Email us at saint.jude.media@catholicity.com

- We will send one free book to each person who writes to us directly. A donation for one book is not required, but you may send a donation if you wish.

- Using the honor system, we ask that you please refrain from sending us the addresses of people other than yourself. Please ask others to write to us directly. We will only send materials to those who personally ask for them, whether a donation is enclosed or not.

- At the present time, we only accept requests for materials by mail. Sorry, no phone requests. Only requests from the United States and Canada will be honored unless a sufficient donation to cover shipping is enclosed.

- Saint Jude Media will gladly absorb shipping charges on all requests, but feel free to add extra for shipping if you wish.

- Fast Delivery—All requests will be shipped on the day we open your envelope!

- Under normal circumstances, we are not able to "advance" quantities of books before receiving a donation.

- We will periodically write to let you know about new books and developments, but you will never receive a "fund raising letter" from us. We will not sell or lend your name to other groups—ever.

- These details apply to individuals as well as organizations such as bookstores, etc. Individuals, bookstores, gift shops, schools, and other organizations may accept donations for this book no greater than $5. A promotional retail display is available upon request.

For more on the Blessed Virgin Mary:

Audio Tape: **Marian Apparitions Explained.** And other free Catholic audio tapes. Optional donation accepted. Contact: Mary Foundation, Box 26101, Fairview Park, OH 44126. www.catholicity.com

Internet: **CatholiCity.** Contains homepages for numerous Marian organizations, national prayer movements, libraries, books, audios, chat rooms, links to other Marian sites. Contact: Box 26101, Fairview Park, OH 44126. www.catholicity.com

Book: **The Thunder of Justice** by Ted and Maureen Flynn. Summary of Marian apparitions and the End Times. Contact: MaxKol Communications, 109 Executive Drive, Suite D, Sterling, VA 20166. (703) 709-0200.

Newspapers: **3 Special Editions** available. Summary of Marian apparitions. Contact: Pittsburgh Center for Peace, 6111 Steubenville Pike, McKee's Rocks, PA 15136. (412) 787-9791.

Book: **The Final Hour** by Michael Brown. Historical summary of Marian apparitions. Contact: The Riehle Foundation, Box 7, Milford, OH 45150. (513) 576-0032. www.catholicity.com

Medal: Handmade **Miraculous Medals** in silver, gold, and brass. Contact: Saint Catherine's Metalworks, 4289 Wooster Road, Fairview Park, OH 44126. (216) 331-1975. www.catholicity.com

Video: **Marian Apparitions of the 20th Century.** Contact: Marian Communications, Box 300, Lincoln University, PA 19352. (800) 448-1192.

Book: **To the Priests, Our Lady's Beloved Sons.** Contact: Marian Movement of Priests, Box 8, Saint Francis, ME 04774-0008.

Information: **The Knights of Immaculata.** World lay association of consecrated souls founded by Saint Maximilian Kolbe. Contact: Militia Immaculatæ National Center, 1600 West Park Avenue, Libertyville, IL 60048. (847) 367-7800. www.marytown.org

Booklet: **15 Decade Meditations on the Rosary,** with full-color iconography by Michael O'Brien. $2 (U.S.) each in any quantity plus $3 shipping. Contact: White Horse Press, Box 2000, Killaloe, Ontario K0J 2A0, Canada.

For more on the Catholic Faith:

Bethlehem Books: Catholic children's fiction. Box 2238, Fort Collins, CO 80522. (800) 757-6831, Fax (701) 248-3940. www.catholicity.com

CatholiCity: Internet site with chat rooms, dozens of Catholic organizations, free books and tapes, news, comprehensive links, more. www.catholicity.com

Catholic Answers: Apologetics books, *This Rock* magazine. Box 17490, San Diego, CA 92177. (619) 541-1131, Fax (619) 541-1154. www.catholic.com/~answers

Catholic Marketing Network: Professional association of Catholic suppliers, apostolates, and retailers. 6000 Campus Circle Drive, Suite 110, Irving, TX 75063. (800) 506-6333, Fax (214) 751-1124.

Envoy Magazine: Apologetics and evangelization. Box 85152, San Diego, CA 92186. (800) 764-8444, Fax (619) 698-3469. www.envoymagazine.com

Ignatius Press: Theology, fiction. **Father Elijah** by Michael O'Brien. Box 1339, Fort Collins, CO 80522. (800) 537-0390, Fax (970) 221-3964. www.ignatius.com

The Mary Foundation: Free Guide to 100 Catholic Resources, donation optional. Box 26101, Fairview Park, OH 44126. www.catholicity.com

Saint Joseph Communications: Audio tapes by Scott Hahn, others. Box 720, West Covina, CA 91793. (800) 526-2151, Fax (818) 858-9331.

Saint Raphael's Bookstore: Short wave radios, starting at $60, order by phone. (800) 548-8270, Fax (216) 497-8648.

Tan Books: Hundreds of titles, pamphlets, children's books. Catalog. Box 424, Rockford, IL 61105. (800) 437-5876, Fax (815) 226-7770. www.catholicity.com

WEWN 7.425: Catholic short wave radio, 24 hours/day. Order program guide. 1500 High Road, Vandiver, AL 35176. (800) 585-9396, Fax (205) 672-9988. www.ewtn.com

Moonie Buddhist Catholic: An autobiography by Thomas W. Case, detailing his fascinating journey into the heart of the Moonies. $16 (includes shipping and handling). 6723 Betts Avenue, Cincinnati, OH 45239. www.catholicity.com

For more on Catholic Family Issues:

<u>American Association of Prolife Ob-Gyns</u>: Provide referrals to prolife doctors nationwide. 4701 North Federal Highway, Building B-4, Fort Lauderdale, FL 33308. (954) 771-9242, Fax (954) 771-4166.

<u>Couple to Couple League</u>: Natural family planning, chastity education program. Box 111184, Cincinnati, OH 45211. (513) 471-2000, Fax (513) 557-2449.

<u>Financial Foundations for the Family</u>: Responsible use of money, tithing, family budgeting. Box 890998, Temecula, CA 92589. (909) 699-7066, Fax (909) 308-4539. www.catholicity.com

<u>Human Life International</u>: Books, newsletters, audios on prolife issues worldwide. 4 Family Life, Front Royal, VA 22630. (540) 635-7884, Fax (540) 636-7363. www.hli.org

<u>La Leche League</u>: Natural child-spacing through breast feeding. 1400 North Meacham Road, Schaumburg, IL 60173. (847) 519-7730, Hotline (800) 525-3243, Fax (847) 519-0035.

<u>National Association of Catholic Home Educators</u>: (NACHE) Network of homeschoolers, annual convention. 6102 Saints Hill Lane, Broad Run, VA 22014. (540) 349-4314, Support groups (619) 538-8399, Fax (540) 347-7345. www.catholicity.com

<u>Saint Joseph Covenant Keepers</u>: Resources for Catholic fatherhood. 3872-C Tamiami Trail, Port Charlotte, FL 33952. (941) 764-8565, Fax (941) 743-5352. www.catholicity.com

How Saint Jude Media Works

- If you do not have a request form, writing a simple letter to receive books is okay. Request forms are also available at www.catholicity.com on the Saint Jude Media homepage.

- Personal correspondence is encouraged. Tell us what you think of this book. We also welcome typographical, grammatical, and fact-checking suggestions for future printings (please include page and line number). Email us at saint.jude.media@catholicity.com

- We will send one free book to each person who writes to us directly. A donation for one book is not required, but you may send a donation if you wish.

- Using the honor system, we ask that you please refrain from sending us the addresses of people other than yourself. Please ask others to write to us directly. We will only send materials to those who personally ask for them, whether a donation is enclosed or not.

- At the present time, we only accept requests for materials by mail. Sorry, no phone requests. Only requests from the United States and Canada will be honored unless a sufficient donation to cover shipping is enclosed.

- Saint Jude Media will gladly absorb shipping charges on all requests, but feel free to add extra for shipping if you wish.

- Fast Delivery—All requests will be shipped on the day we open your envelope!

- Under normal circumstances, we are not able to "advance" quantities of books before receiving a donation.

- We will periodically write to let you know about new books and developments, but you will never receive a "fund raising letter" from us. We will not sell or lend your name to other groups—ever.

- These details apply to individuals as well as organizations such as bookstores, etc. Individuals, bookstores, gift shops, schools, and other organizations may accept donations for this book no greater than $5. A promotional retail display is available upon request.

Conceived Without Sin
REQUEST FORM

Dear Saint Jude Media:
Please send me a copy (or copies) of **Conceived Without Sin**. I understand that the first copy is free and that a donation is **not required** for one copy. I am not asking you to send a book or books to anyone other than myself.

Signed: _____
(Please Print)

Name: _____

Address: _____

Town: _____

State: _____ Zip: _____

Suggested **Optional** Donation for one book: **$1 to $10**
Donation for **more than one** book, any quantity: **$2 - $5 each**
(For more details about Saint Jude Media, see next page.)

Quantity Desired	X	Donation Per Book		Subtotal:
_____	X	_____	=	_____

Optional extra gift for shipping   =   _____

Optional gift for Saint Jude Media   =   _____

TOTAL DONATION*   = $ _____

*Your contribution to Saint Jude Media is tax deductible. Any questions? Call (216) 333-4723. Sorry, no phone requests for books accepted. We'll ship your book the day we receive your letter.

CWS1

Please make checks payable to "Saint Jude Media" & send to:
Saint Jude Media
Box 26120 • Fairview Park, OH 44126